PRAISE FOR *THE STRAITS*

"Reading Bradley P. Beaulieu's The Lays of An̶_____ ̶ike traveling through grand undiscovered country, being in a p̶__̶e that is familiar enough to understand and different enough to amaze. [...] *The Straits of Galahesh* continues the breakneck pace of a fight for an entire world, touched by passion, love, and loyalty. As a reader, almost every chapter added to my sense of wonder and realization. I can't recommend this fabulous fantasy series highly enough. Read it."

—Brenda Cooper, author of *Wings of Creation* and *Mayan December*

"With *The Straits of Galahesh*, Beaulieu returns to the vibrant fantasy he introduced in *The Winds of Khalakovo*. A gritty book packed with big ideas and Byzantine politics, and inhabited by compellingly flawed heroes, *Straits* is the sort of fully realized epic one can sink into for days. It sings with action, magic, and heart—the perfect second act in a brilliant series."

—Rob Ziegler, author of *Seed*

"The right combination of complex worldbuilding, compelling characters and supremely confident storytelling combine to produce this superb sequel to *The Winds of Khalakovo*...an exceptional series. Whether you're a novice or a grizzled veteran of epic fantasy, you're in for a wild, exhilarating ride."

—Gregory A. Wilson, author of *The Third Sign*

PRAISE FOR *THE WINDS OF KHALAKOVO*

"Sailing ships of the sky! Bradley P. Beaulieu's *The Winds of Khalakovo* is an energetic, swashbuckling novel with a distinctive flavor, a lush setting, and a plot filled with adventure, interesting characters, and intrigue. Exactly the kind of fantasy I like to read."

—Kevin J. Anderson, *New York Times* bestselling author of *The Saga of Seven Suns*

PRAISE FOR *THE WINDS OF KHALAKOVO*
(CONTINUED)

"Overlaid with the rich feel of Cyrillic culture, Beaulieu's debut introduces a fascinating world of archipelagic realms and shamanic magic worked primarily by women. Verdict: Strong characters and a plot filled with tension and difficult choices make this a good option for fantasy fans."

—*Library Journal*

"Elegantly crafted, refreshingly creative, *TWOK* offers a compelling tale of men and women fighting to protect their world. Politics, faith, betrayal, sacrifice, and of course supernatural mystery—it's all there, seamlessly combined in a tale driven by intelligent and passionate characters whose relationships and goals a reader can really care about. A great read!"

—C. S. Friedman, bestselling author of the
Coldfire and Magister trilogies

"...a page-turner with twists, turns and palpable danger..."

—Paul Genesse, author of *The Golden Cord*

"In *The Winds of Khalakovo* Beaulieu navigates through a web of complex characters... dukes, duchesses, lovers, and more, while building a rich and intricate world thick with intrigue. He plots the course of Nikandr Iaroslov Khalakovo, a prince laden with disease and courtly responsibilities, and deftly brings the tale to a satisfying end that leaves the reader hungry for the next installment. Beaulieu is a writer that bears watching. I look forward to his next novel."

—Jean Rabe, *USA Today* bestselling fantasy author

"Bradley P. Beaulieu is a welcome addition to the roster of new fantasy novelists. *The Winds of Khalakovo* is a sharp and original fantasy full of action, intrigue, romance, politics, mystery and magick, tons of magick. The boldly imagined new world and sharply drawn characters will pull you into *The Winds of Khalakovo* and won't let you go until the last page."

—Michael A. Stackpole, author of *I, Jedi*
and *At the Queen's Command*

THE STRAITS OF

GALAHESH

THE STRAITS OF GALAHESH

BOOK TWO OF THE LAYS OF ANUSKAYA

BRADLEY P. BEAULIEU

NIGHT SHADE BOOKS
SAN FRANCISCO

The Straits of Galahesh © 2012 by Bradley P. Beaulieu
This edition of *The Straits of Galahesh*
© 2012 by Night Shade Books

Cover art by Todd Lockwood
Cover design by Claudia Noble
Interior layout and design by Amy Popovich
Maps by William McAusland
Author photo by Joanne M. Beaulieu

Edited by Ross E. Lockhart

All rights reserved

First Edition

ISBN: 978-1-59780-349-6

Night Shade Books
Please visit us on the web at
http://www.nightshadebooks.com

This one is for Relaneve, my star, my bright and beautiful child.
May you one day know the kind of love I hold for you.

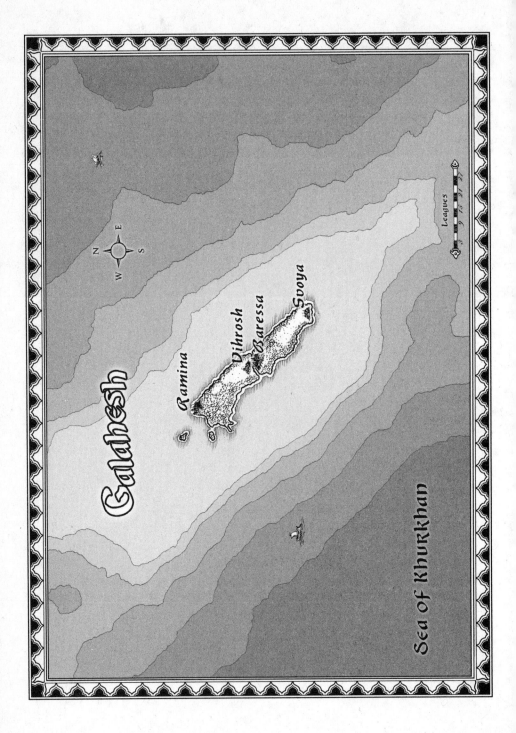

Galahesh

Ramina

Vihrosh

Baressa

Svoya

N
W   E
S

Leagues

Sea of Khurkhan

A SUMMARY OF *THE WINDS OF KHALAKOVO,*
BOOK ONE OF THE LAYS OF ANUSKAYA

As the story opens, the islands of the Grand Duchy are under siege from a blight to their crops and a deadly wasting disease that strikes royalty and peasants alike. A prince of the islands, Nikandr Khalakovo, is set to be married to Atiana Vostroma, a princess from a neighboring Duchy. A pall is cast against the nuptials, however, when a fire spirit attacks and murders the Grand Duke.

The gathered royalty demand justice, and Nikandr is sent to investigate. All signs point to a young autistic savant named Nasim, and it is this boy's mysterious past that Nikandr becomes entangled with. Nikandr believes Nasim is not to blame for the attack. He believes instead that he was used as a tool by the Maharraht, a ruthless sect of the peace-loving Aramahn that want nothing less than the destruction of the Grand Duchy. As escalations rise over the murder of the Grand Duke, Nikandr and Nasim escape to the island of Ghayavand, a place that holds many secrets from Nasim's past.

Meanwhile, Atiana is pressed into service as a Matra, a woman who submerges herself in ice-cold water and enters the astral realm of the aether, where she can project herself to tend to the defense of the Grand Duchy and to communicate with other Matri. While doing so, Atiana comes face to face with Rehada, Nikandr's Aramahn lover. Atiana later learns that Rehada has only been posing as Nikandr's lover, and that in reality she is a spy for the Maharraht. Not only has she been feeding the Maharraht information about the Grand Duchy for years, she's been in league with Soroush, a sworn enemy of the Grand Duchy who hopes to open a rift that hangs over Khalakovo. Tearing open the rift would cause untold destruction to Khalakovo and the other islands of the Grand Duchy, but Soroush cannot do this alone. He must use Nasim and his unique abilities to tear the rift open. Rehada's loyalties, however, are not so resolute as they seem at first. She has come to doubt the path of violence that Soroush and the Maharraht are following, and it is through this doubt that she begins to question her place in the Maharraht.

Nikandr learns more of Nasim's past and returns with him to Khalakovo, hoping to heal the rift, but before he can do so, Soroush steals Nasim away. Nikandr is forced to return home to Khalakovo without him, and he finds that tensions among the nine dukes of the Grand Duchy have reached the boiling point.

A battle between the duchies ensues, providing the perfect cover for Soroush, who takes Nasim to a small keep on the nearby island of Duzol. There he begins the ritual he's been planning for years. Using Nasim as a conduit, he will summon five elder spirits, and when all five have been summoned, the rift will be torn wide.

Soroush doesn't count on Rehada, however, who turns away from the path of violence. She warns Nikandr of what Soroush is planning, and together, Nikandr, Atiana, and Rehada move against Soroush and the Maharraht. Soroush completes his ritual, but Nikandr has come to understand his bond with Nasim intimately. He and Atiana use this knowledge to draw Nasim fully into the material world, an act that heals not only the blight, but Nasim as well. Nasim is now as whole as he has ever been in his life, and he may finally find it possible to learn and grow. The cost, however, is heavy. Nikandr's father is captured by the traitor dukes.

As the story closes, the Khalakovo family cedes control of their Duchy to the new Grand Duke, and Nasim is taken away by his people for his own safety. Nikandr, however, knows that the rifts are not permanently closed, and he vows to find Nasim and complete what they have begun.

PROLOGUE

In the southern gallery of the capital's sprawling kasir, Hakan ül Ayeşe, the Kamarisi of Yrstanla, stood at a marble balcony. The day was warm. Gardeners below tended to the rows of trees—lemon and fig and plum—that filled the southern acres. Far to the south, beyond the gardens, was a tall stone wall that had never been touched in battle. The wall was exactly three leagues long, and it separated Kasir Irabahce from the vastness of Alekeşir.

From beyond the wall, if the winds were calm and the noise from the palace was low, Hakan could hear the calls of hawking and barter that came from the spice market to the east, or the bazaar to the south. Today, however, was not such a day. Today, he heard the sounds of industry. Beyond the walking paths and the ordered rows of the vineyard, a dozen masons were spending their sweat on a gazebo that would house a bronze statue being made in his honor. He would not have wished it, but the city they'd taken in the ceaseless war with the Haelish barbarians to the west demanded celebration, even if the victory had been hollow. In weeks, perhaps months, the Haelish would have it back, for the Empire's resources there were too thin, spread too far along their border with the lands of the Haelish kings.

Behind him, the doors to the gallery opened. He kept his eyes on the rows of red grapes, nearly ready for harvest. Mingled with the sound of approaching footsteps—hard leather scraping lightly over the white marble floor—was the faint patter of bare feet and the jingle of tiny bells.

The sounds stopped a respectful distance behind him. The leather uniforms of his guardsmen creaked.

"Leave her," Hakan said.

More creaking, the guards bowing to their Lord, and the footsteps resumed, this time fading away until the door closed with a click that pierced the room.

Hakan turned and found the woman he'd summoned from the tower of the wives. She had joined his harem some three months ago. She was tall, nearly as tall as he, and beautiful beyond measure. She was graced with golden hair and striking blue eyes, so rare among the women of the Empire. Only far to the north, among the mountain tribes, were such women to be found, but they were too often coarse and unlearned. Arvaneh was refined, with a soft touch and a softer tongue—in both senses of the word.

The supple cloth of her white dress fell along her frame like a waterfall. From her ankles and hands hung chains with golden bells and ruby gems. On her head was an intricate gold headdress. Somehow it had never suited her.

"Remove the headdress," he said.

She bowed and complied, setting the headdress on a nearby table. When she regarded him again, it seemed to him that her smile was too satisfied, as if removing the finery had been her idea all along.

He moved to the table and from a small glass pitcher poured raki into two golden chalices. He handed one to Arvaneh and kept the other for himself, motioning for her to follow him to the balcony. She complied, calm and confident, as she had always been.

At the balcony, he brought the raki to his nose, smelled the anise and clove that infused it, then took a healthy swallow. He saw Arvaneh do the same, and the tension inside him eased.

"Tell me, Arvaneh, from what part of the empire do you hail?"

"From a village near the western border of the Gaji." She waved, as if it were nothing. "It is named Kohor, though you've probably never heard of it."

"Is it not in the Empire?"

"It is, Kamarisi."

He smiled. "I know of Kohor. What I don't know is how you came to Alekeşir."

She tilted her head, staring out over the garden as he'd been doing only moments before, except in her there was a clear hunger, a lust for life and the world that stood before her, whereas he had grown ... perhaps not weary, but certainly dissatisfied with life in the palace, in the city.

There was more as well. He couldn't quite define it, but she seemed to be looking beyond the horizon. She seemed, in fact, to be looking beyond her years toward distant ages past. But then the look was gone, and she turned to him with a steely glint in her eyes. "There was nothing for me in the desert. I wished to see the world."

"And yet you told me that you've remained here in the capital since your arrival six months ago."

"That's true"—she beckoned him with a smile—"but when one finds herself in the very center of the world, is there anything that might compel her to leave?" Upon saying these words, she studied him—she weighed him—deciding whether or not she should approach. She seemed to decide against it, perhaps sensing his mood, and he realized he had best be careful how much he revealed. Arvaneh was no one to fool with, not if what his seneschal had told him was true.

He watched as she took another drink. He mirrored her, if only to keep pretenses up.

She turned back to the garden, jaw set, apparently giving his question more serious thought. "Alekeşir is calm. Peaceful. Her roots dig deep into the earth. Why would I want to leave?"

"Perhaps there are places you don't wish to return. Did you leave someone there? In Kohor?"

Her head snapped toward him, her blue eyes cold and judgmental. But then they softened. "The people of Kohor have long since forgotten me."

"That I doubt." He finished his drink. "I doubt it very much."

As she stared, her eyes lost focus, and she shook her head to clear it.

"Do you feel very well?" he asked, taking her nearly empty chalice from her quivering hands. "Would you care to sit?"

She nodded. The bells on her wrists jingled. Her whole body began to shake. She didn't go three steps before she collapsed to the ground, golden hair splaying across the floor.

Hakan crouched on the balls of his feet, staring into her eyes, which had gone soft, unable to focus. "Now, would you like to tell me who you really are?"

She blinked. Her body shivered.

"You can speak if you want to. It simply takes more effort. Devrim has been watching you, as have the other women. They know that you leave the tower at night. That you spy upon my room from the gardens. Why? Why do you do this?"

"I..." A horrible shiver ran down her frame, preventing her from speaking. She closed her eyes tightly and opened them again, somehow managing to fix them on him once more. "I only wished to know you."

"For what purpose?"

She took a deep breath and released it in slow, halting increments. Blood trickled from beneath her left temple from where it had struck the floor. It trailed along the tile until it found a crease, and then it spread along the seam between the stones. "I wanted to know the sort of man you were."

"Who sent you?"

"I came of my own free will."

"Don't lie. You may yet live. There is a counter to the poison, but I cannot use it if I think you've spoken even one more lie to me."

She blinked, a slow and measured movement. Her breath was shallower than it'd been only moments ago. "I wouldn't lie." The words were soft, like the dying breeze of dusk.

Hakan cleared his throat, which felt suddenly constricted. He cleared it again. "There is more to the story. I would know, Arvaneh."

"My name ... is Sariya..."

He was surprised to hear fire in her words. He had underestimated her reserves of strength. "Sariya. I would know before you pass. Are you an assassin? Were you sent by the Haelish kings? Or the crones who live in the desert?"

"I am ... my own woman. And I ... know much ... of you."

"You know much..." Hakan wanted to smile, but something in her seemed primitive and ancient, and his heart withered at the notion of taunting her. "What could you know of me?"

"I know ... where you go. I know that with victory in the west, as shallow as it may be, you've set your heart upon the east."

Despite himself, he shivered. He had spoken of this to no one. The Haelish uprising, which had begun shortly before Hakan had been born, was a conflict that had plagued him for all of his years, and though it was not over, it was at a stalemate, and he had vowed to himself long ago that as soon as he was able, he would dedicate himself to reuniting the Old Empire. And that meant turning his sights toward the islands. Toward Galahesh and Anuskaya beyond it.

"How could you know?" he whispered.

"Do not fear, Kamarisi. I've told no one."

Somehow, the effects of the poison were no longer spreading. Her voice had regained its verve. Her cheeks had regained their color, and her eyes were once again sharp.

Hakan swallowed again. The tightness in his throat remained. His mind felt muddled, as if he should be more angry at what she had told him. He shook his head to clear it, but as he did, a wave of dizziness swept over him. He pinched his eyes, hoping to clear himself of the malady, but it refused to ebb.

When he opened his eyes again, he was pressed against the cool marble tiles. Ahead lay the balcony at which he'd been standing only moments ago, but instead of finding Sariya lying there, she was now standing, staring down at him with eyes both calm and collected.

His breath released from his lungs, long and slow. Drawing the next breath was difficult, as if the air itself had turned to wine.

"What ... have you done?"

"I have done nothing, Kamarisi. This has all been your doing." She smiled, her blue eyes glinting in the sunlight. She held in her hand the chalice from which she'd been drinking. "You wish to know who I am? Surely you've heard of the tales of Khalakovo? In the autumn of last year, a boy was brought to the islands by the Maharraht. They hoped to tear open the rifts that ran through the islands."

"The rifts ... are a myth."

Sariya smiled, a gesture that revealed perfect ivory teeth. "They are all too real, Kamarisi, and they are spreading. The boy, Nasim, was reborn of a man named Khamal. He was one of the Al-Aqim, one of those who broke the world. And I am another. My name is Sariya Quljan al Vehayeh."

Hakan blinked. His eyes were slow to open. His breath was shallower than it had been only moments ago.

"Fear not," Sariya said. "The end has not yet come. There is more yet to do."

He didn't understand what she meant, but at the moment he didn't care. All he could think about was his life being snuffed out here on the cold tiles of the kasir, the place he'd thought safest for him in all the world. "The antidote," he said.

"Ah, this?" She opened her other hand. In her palm rested a glass phial. She made no move to render it to him. Instead, she kneeled on the balls of her feet, as he had done—or thought he had done. "You will have it, Kamarisi, though it bears a price."

"What..." His fingers were numb. It was all he could do to force his lungs to draw breath. "What is it?"

"Something you will gladly pay... I wish to help. I wish to guide you eastward."

"Why?"

She smiled, and when she did, she became more beautiful a woman than he'd ever seen. "My reasons are my own. Suffice it to say there is a jewel in the crown of Anuskaya I would have back."

He could no longer feel his lips, nor his fingers nor his toes. He tried to take a deep breath, but could not. His lungs refused him. He tried to speak, but all that came out was a weak groan. His mind was alive with fear—he was too young to die; there was so much yet to do—but his body cared not at all. It seemed content to take its final rest.

He fought against the will of his body.

And nothing happened.

Sariya waited, staring down at him with a cruel smile. He knew that she could have forced him to drink it, but she wanted him to ask.

He fought harder, pouring himself into one small movement, something he hoped she would understand as assent. With one last push, he felt his head move up and down—a nod, though terribly weak; he wasn't even sure she would recognize it as such.

Apparently she had, for she kneeled next to him and rolled him onto his back. Lying there, looking up at her as she pulled the glass stopper from the phial, she looked like a mother caring for her sick child. He thought he should hate her for what she had done, but he didn't. To him, she was a guiding star.

She would give to Yrstanla her children lost in the War of Seven Seas. He was certain of it, and for this he was undyingly grateful.

As the liquid poured down his throat, he felt relief like he never had before. It was like being reborn.

When it was all down, Sariya kissed his forehead and tenderly stroked his hair. "Together, Hakan ül Ayeşe, we will do well. Together, we will build a bridge the likes of which the world has never seen."

The Kamarisi, blinded by his love, could only smile at the wonder in her eyes.

PART I

CHAPTER ONE

Nasim strode down a dirt road. It was bordered on its left by a steep hillside and on its right by a series of hovels with earthen roofs that looked as though they would fall to the next stiff wind. Only far ahead where the road curved to follow the hill were there buildings of any note—a compound of three taller buildings surrounded by a high stone wall with an archway built into it.

The iron gates set into the wall were swung wide, and when Nasim finally reached them, he found a woman waiting for him just inside. He stepped into the yard, and she shut the gates behind him. In one hand she held an iron ring with dozens of keys on it, but she did not lock the gate.

For this Nasim was glad.

"You're late," she said in Yrstanlan. Her dialect was heavy and rolling, something Nasim was not yet used to, new as he was to the northern edges of the Empire. She wore a drab gray dress and a threadbare dolman mantle with voluminous sleeves. Her face was severe. Worry lines made her appear old—older than Nasim guessed she actually was.

"You said to be sure I wasn't followed. That takes time." He glanced meaningfully at the orphanage behind her. "Take me to them."

She weighed Nasim with her eyes. Her lips were tight and furrowed, a gesture that seemed natural for her. He was as tall as she, but she managed to look down on him just the same. Nasim was only sixteen, whereas she had seen at least forty years. There was something about age that lent weight and authority, even if it wasn't deserved.

The matron glanced toward the mountains over Nasim's shoulder, apparently trying to determine whether the payment Nasim had promised was still worth it, but then she stiffened her lip and turned and led him to the porch of the largest of the three buildings. She stepped up to the heavy wooden door. "They're eating," she said while unlocking it and pulling it open. "Don't say a word. Just nod to the one and I'll pull him out."

He stepped in after her and this time she used her keys to lock the door. This made him nervous, but there was nothing to do about it now. She led him down a drab hallway of brick and plaster and into a room that was filled with children and the soft clink of cutlery and plates. The smell of cabbage and onion and cumin filled the air. Four dozen children were spaced on benches, bellied up against two long trestle tables, all of them eating, none of them saying a word, even when they'd realized someone new was in the room.

Hanging on the wall like decorations were two dousing rods—little more than wrought-iron circles with a rod through the center used to hold them. They were much more than decoration, Nasim knew. They would be used to quell any of the abilities of these children, should any find within themselves the talent and the will to use it, but they could be used against Nasim as well.

Two other women sat at the heads of the tables. They stared at Nasim, but neither was surprised by his presence. Their reaction made it clear that this was nothing out of the ordinary, and it enraged him.

Pulling his dark brown bangs from his eyes, he paced along one wall, staring carefully at each of the children. They were not dirty—it was clear they had been bathed—but there was evidence of their hours in the nearby iron mines: black around their ears, in the corners of their eyes, under their fingernails, even at the corners of their mouths. The children did not stare back at him, which was a relief. They seemed to know that he was after one of them, and he could feel their desire to be taken away from this place, if only for a day or two.

But he could only take one—the one he'd heard rumor of nearly two years ago in the capital of the Empire. He'd come to Trevitze in search, and he'd nearly given up hope of finding the child who'd stirred such feelings of power within him, but then, as the children had been riding back to the orphanage on wagons, Nasim had felt a hollowness in his gut. It had yawned open as they came closer and subsided as they traveled uphill toward the orphanage.

He'd experienced this before, many times in fact, though rarely so strong. Only on one other occasion had it been as such, and when it had, he had found Rabiah and convinced her to join him.

He'd talked with Rabiah for days before she'd finally agreed to join him. This time, he thought, little convincing would be needed.

The yawning feeling returned, though for some reason it was muted. He traveled up the length of the table, concentrating carefully on the children sitting on the opposite side. When he rounded the end of the room and came back along the other, he stopped halfway down. Sitting across from him, staring down into his mealy stew, a half-eaten crust of bread in one hand, was a boy, fifteen years old, maybe sixteen. He was not Yrstanlan. Nasim would know even without the void in his gut.

It was not rare for the Aramahn to be taken against their will—war, plague, criminal executions all played their part—but for some reason this boy having been taken and forced to work below ground, all day, for nothing, set Nasim's blood to burning.

"What is your name?" Nasim said in Mahndi.

The boy's head snapped up, but he immediately pulled his gaze back down to his bowl.

A whisper spread among the children until the snap of a narrow length of wood against the head of the table brought them back to silence.

The matron stalked between the two tables to the center of the room and stared at Nasim. "You will be silent."

"What is your name?" Nasim said again, ignoring her.

"You will be *silent*!"

Nasim regarded her. Outside the orphanage she had seemed muted, somehow, perhaps small under the stare of the sky and the mountain peaks, but here, inside her domain, she seemed arch and menacing, like a black widow at the borders of her web.

Taking the small pouch of coins he had prepared for her, Nasim threw it over the heads of the children. It landed with a dull clink near her feet. "Take your money, but order me no more." He set his sights on the boy. "Give me your name," he said for a third time, "unless you wish to remain here with them. If that is your choice, I will honor it."

The boy glanced to one side, mindful of the matron behind him. After a moment filled with consequence, he swallowed, placed his hands on the table, and pushed himself up from his bench. He glanced at Nasim, but was unable to hold his gaze long. "My name is Sukharam," he said in imperfect Mahndi. "Sukharam Hadir al Dahanan."

The matron grabbed his shoulders—"Do you think he is for *sale*?"—and shoved him back down. "Do you think this a house of slaves where children can be bought for the pittance you tossed at my feet?" Her face was grim. She could still be bought—it was the kind of woman she was—but Nasim's insults had raised the price.

Nasim walked to the end of the room and approached the space between the two tables. The matron dug her hands into Sukharam's shoulders, who winced in pain but made no sound.

"Release him," Nasim said.

She dug her fingers in further. A whimper escaped Sukharam's lips, which were drawn into a grim line.

The barest of drafts ran through the room. Nasim drew in a long breath, staring at the woman with a calmness he hadn't felt in ages. He wore no stones. Ever since the ritual on Oshtoyets, the small keep on the island of Duzol, he had been unable to use such things or commune with hezhan on his own, but through Sukharam he could feel a hezhan. Slowly his awareness grew. As a blind man hears the wind through the trees, as he feels the current of the water running over and around his feet, as he feels the weight of the very earth below him, Nasim felt the havahezhan, and he beckoned it.

It came, pulling at the air like the drawing of breath. It was easy now to discern the currents in the room. The air was chill, and already getting chillier. He could see the women stare into the corners, into the hearth along the right side of the room.

The expression on Sukharam's face was one of confusion and growing discomfort. Soon he would reach for his gut, as Nasim had done so often in his childhood. Nasim had never felt right doing this—using someone without permission—but were he to ask Sukharam now, he would not understand; he would be *unable* to answer, so for the time being Nasim would have to assume his answer would be *yeh* and give apologies later if he'd been wrong.

"Release him," Nasim repeated.

The matron looked back to the women, who seemed too petrified to move. "Get the rods!"

They stood and grabbed the wrought-iron dousing rods from the wall. One came up behind the matron, protecting her. The other sidled along the wall, keeping a close eye on Nasim as she went. The children began to rise until the matron shouted, "Sit!"

Time was running out.

Calling upon the havahezhan, Nasim summoned the wind. This was only a distraction, however. He called upon a dhoshahezhan as well, using it to touch the life that remained in the wood of the tables and benches. He pushed, drawing upon it more than he should, and a moment later he heard a ticking sound that steadily grew.

With increasing ferocity, the benches and tables cracked and snapped. Splinters flew, causing the children to stand and cringe and scatter from the benches. The planking along the floor buckled as the children stepped upon it, causing them to fall between the joists that supported the tongue-and-groove flooring.

The effect stopped as it neared the dousing rods, however. If the matrons were able to surround him with the rods, his ability to commune with the spirits would dissipate like smoke, but they were hampered now by the crumbling flooring and screaming children.

Nasim allowed the effect to continue up through the walls, to the ceiling. The plaster popped. Cracks ran through the entire room. And yet it was only when the structure itself groaned that the matron yelled, "Enough!"

Nasim willed the effect to fade, though not completely. A slow sifting of dust continued to fall from the ceiling. A piece of plaster fell and crashed to the floor between them.

The matron flung the boy away from her while staring upward, wondering if the floor above was ready to come crashing down. "Enough!"

Finally, though the hezhan was reluctant to allow it, Nasim brought everything to a standstill. He looked around the room, at the children who watched him in abject fear, at the damage he'd caused in mere moments.

It had gone too far. So much had been this way since he'd awoken after the ritual in Oshtoyets five years ago. He had struggled to find a way to touch Adhiya, finding that only through others could he do so, and then imperfectly. Too often it was more than he wished, or too little.

Still, he wished he hadn't needed to resort to communing with hezhan. He wished he were able to speak more convincingly—as Ashan had always seemed able to do, or Nikandr—but he could not. He knew his limitations, and there was more at stake than the damage to an orphanage in one small corner of the Empire.

"Are you ready, son of Dahanan?" Nasim asked Sukharam, who cowered at his feet.

Sukharam looked up and stared into Nasim's eyes. A bit of courage seemed to spark within him at those words. "I am."

"Then come"—he offered Sukharam his hand—"for there is much to do."

After the barest moment's hesitation, Sukharam stood and took it.

With Sukharam at his side, Nasim walked the cold streets of Trevitze, heading toward the city square and the hovel he'd rented beyond it. As he neared the rise that would give him a clear view of the square below, he saw a girl waving from the shadows of an alley.

"Quickly," Rabiah said.

Nasim could hear people talking on the street. They were still hidden behind the rise, but they were coming closer. He moved quickly and quietly, pulling Sukharam by the wrist. Sukharam, thankfully, heard the urgency in Rabiah's voice and remained silent.

They made it to the alley and hunkered down, using a fat rain barrel to hide behind. Dusk had fallen on Trevitze, but there was still enough light to see down the alley if one's eyes were sharp.

The voices approached, and soon several men and a robed woman walked by. One of the men wore a white turban of the style that many of Yrstanla's ruling class wore; it was large and curved, like an olive on a thumb.

It was not he that made Nasim's heart jump. It was the woman. Her name was Ushai Kissath al Shahda, and she had been following Nasim for months. He remembered hearing her name during his short time in Iramanshah. He had heard it again several times during his stay in the floating village of Mirashadal, so when he heard it once more in the slums of Alekeşir, he had known that Fahroz had sent others to find him, to return him to her care. Nasim and Rabiah had fled the capital the very same day, and from then on, from village to village and city to city, every time Nasim thought he had lost her, Ushai would turn up again, though thankfully he or Rabiah—who had become very adept at sensing the signs of pursuit—found her, and they had fled once more.

Ushai stopped suddenly. She continued speaking with the portly man, who was very likely the khedive of the city, but she cocked her head to one side as she did, turning ever so slightly toward the alley until Nasim could see the softly glowing stone of alabaster in the circlet upon her brow. The wind was low this evening, but it kicked up, tossing Ushai's long, dark hair around her shoulders.

Nasim's fingers went cold. Through Rabiah, he touched Adhiya for a bare moment, but then stopped and cursed himself for a fool. Fahroz had not been unkind to him, but he knew that he could not allow her to keep him from his path. He would do what must be done, but still, he could not harm Ushai—the Aramahn did not do such things. If the fates saw fit for her to find him, he would embrace it and find another way to continue his journey.

The moment passed. Ushai and the man moved on. Their voices faded, and soon, there was little sound but the baying of a pack of dogs somewhere in the hills to the west of Trevitze.

Nasim looked to Rabiah and Sukharam. Both of them looked as nervous as he felt. They left without speaking another word.

CHAPTER TWO

Khamal walks along the edge of the water as the surf rolls up against his feet. The frothing water is cold against his feet and ankles. The sound of breaking waves is all that he hears.

Ahead of him, two creatures walk. They hunch as they shuffle along the sand. The skin of their eyes has grown over. The features of their faces have shriveled, but their mouths are wide and hinged strangely, making them look like ashen things of clay, not creatures of flesh and blood. The two of them walk side by side, but they do not acknowledge one another. For all Khamal knows, they don't even know the other is there.

They are akhoz, creatures forged on this very island centuries ago to stop the spread of the rifts. The girl—the taller of the two—releases a call that sounds like the bleating of a goat. It is insistent and desperate.

And familiar.

Which saddens Khamal to his very core.

To Khamal's right lies a massive rock, dark gray against the white beach and the blue-green waters of the bay. The two akhoz stop near it, waiting obediently as Khamal approaches.

"Go," Khamal says to one of them, the girl.

She turns, her eyeless face looking up at him, her mouth pulled back in a feral grin.

"Go!"

She scuffles along the beach away from him. A wave surges up and sizzles as it rolls across her feet. She bounds away from the water, looks back one last time, and then gallops toward Alayazhar.

Khamal turns to the other akhoz—a boy whose limbs are so frail his joints look diseased—and motions him toward the rock.

As the boy begins to climb toward the flattened top of it, Khamal touches the handle of the khanjar at his belt, as if to assure himself that it is still there.

"Nasim, *wake*."

Nasim opened his eyes to find Rabiah kneeling over him. His clothes were drenched, and his breath came rapidly.

He swallowed, trying to clear away the feeling of cotton in his mouth, but Rabiah already had a clay mug in one hand. She held it out for him. He accepted it, feeling—as he always did upon waking from one of these episodes—like the Nasim of old, the Nasim who could control nothing, who could not differentiate the material world of Erahm from the spirit world of Adhiya. He was better now—Fahroz and the mahtar had seen to that—but he had never found a way to free himself from the shadow of Khamal. These were not dreams. They were memories. Khamal's memories, playing as if they were his own. Some were simple, benign, but many were filled with pain and yearning and shame and a thousand other emotions that Nasim felt but did not understand. Not without more of Khamal's memories to work with.

He knew that these were the legacy of Khamal. He had no doubt thought to pass them to Nasim, to give him the clues he would need to return to Ghayavand to heal the rifts there, but Muqallad and Sariya had ruined his plans and cursed Nasim in the same moment, just as Khamal had been passing beyond his life and toward the next.

Nasim drank from the mug, felt the cool water fill his mouth and slip down his throat to his stomach. It felt good, and he was grateful for Rabiah's help, but he could not help but feel weak at times like this. He could not help but feel broken.

"He and I need to speak," he said, handing the mug back to Rabiah.

By the light of the crescent moon coming in through their lone window, he saw Rabiah nod, but he also saw the look of hurt in her eyes.

"We'll be back as soon as we're able," was all he could think to say.

He tapped Sukharam on the shoulder. The boy jerked his head up and looked around the room wildly. He focused on Nasim, and then looked away. This was a boy that had trouble facing his fears. It was a habit Nasim was going to have to break him of.

Assuming he came.

"Come," Nasim said. "We have things to discuss."

Sukharam stood without a word. He looked at Rabiah, who watched this exchange before lying down on her pallet and turning her back to them.

If Sukharam was confused by this, he said nothing of it. He followed Nasim out from their hovel, a room in the slums of Trevitze for which they had promised thrice the price for a bit of discretion. The air was chill. Their footsteps crunched softly over the frost-rimed grass. Around them were ramshackle homes, all of them dark, leaving Nasim feeling alone in the world with only

Sukharam as his companion. In many ways, this was very much the way of things.

"You should know that you are free to leave. You owe me nothing."

When Sukharam responded, his voice was tentative. Weak. "I owe you my life."

"Your life is your own, to do with as you will."

Sukharam did not respond, so Nasim gave him time to consider this. They turned to the east and took a narrow alley that led to a wider road. As they took this toward a bare, rocky hill, the bulk of Trevitze fell behind them, and as they rose higher along the hill, they could see more and more of the city described by the moonlight and the occasional lantern lit within a distant window.

"Do you know of the blight?" Nasim asked.

"I know of the blight, and I know of you."

"I was not aware the news had traveled so far."

Sukharam shrugged. "Even at the orphanage the word of the Aramahn comes."

"Then perhaps you've heard what I go to do."

"*Neh*"—he sounded ashamed—"I have not."

"I wish to heal the wound that festers in our world. Those who go to Ghayavand will be three. I am the first, Rabiah the second, and you, I hope, will be the third."

"And yet you said I owe you nothing."

"That is true, Sukharam. I would not press this upon you. If I did, we would be doomed before we ever left for the island." The road became more steep, their breathing more labored. "I will tell you more, Sukharam, son of Dahanan, and then you will have a choice—to stay or to go—but I hope that whatever you decide that you will keep this between only us. Much depends on it."

"I will," Sukharam said quickly. "Of course I will."

"Do not make this promise lightly."

This time, Sukharam took longer before responding. "I do not."

They reached the top of the hill, and Nasim paused, waving one hand to indicate their surroundings. To the west lay Trevitze, calm and quiet, and beyond it the dark and imposing peaks of the Sitalyas. To the east was the Sea of Tabriz, her waters distinguishable only by the blackness that lay beneath the subtle blanket of stars.

"If you have heard of me, then you have heard about the conflict on Khalakovo, but I wonder if you've heard anything close to the truth. Perhaps you've heard that I started the war by killing Stasa Bolgravya. Perhaps you've heard that I ended the war by killing Soroush Wahad al Gatha. Perhaps you've heard that I killed hundreds, or that I saved all."

"I've heard those, and others."

"As have I, but now you will hear the truth, or enough of it to make your decision." Nasim paused. He had told his story only to one other, Rabiah, and it had been one of the most difficult things he'd ever done—it felt as though sharing this was giving away too much of himself—but if he were to ask so much of Sukharam, he would first grant him the truth. "Three hundred years ago there were three arqesh, as powerful and as learned as there ever were. They were known as the Al-Aqim. Do you know of them?"

"I do not."

"The first was Khamal Cyphar al Maladhin. The others were Sariya Quljan al Vehayeh and Muqallad Bakshazhd al Dananir. The three of them had hoped to bring Erahm to indaraqiram. Do you know of this, Sukharam?"

His shoulders slumped and his gaze fell away as he answered. "I remember my mother speaking that word, but I know not what it means."

"Surely you know of vashaqiram…"

He stood straighter at this. "It is the perfect mind. The perfect soul."

Nasim, surprisingly, felt a flash of pride. "What vashaqiram is to our selves, indaraqiram is to the worlds, both Erahm and Adhiya. It is what every Aramahn hopes to bring about, a state of perfection not just in ourselves, but the two worlds that were split by the fates so many eons ago. The Al-Aqim tried to bring indaraqiram about using the Atalayina, a stone of immense power and insight, but the world was not ready, and they did little more than tear a rift between this world and the next. After the ritual, they became trapped on the island."

"How? And by whom?"

In the darkness, Nasim smiled, pleased that even after his life in the orphanage there still laid within Sukharam the soul of one who questioned, who challenged. "That isn't known, but they were left alone on the island, just the three of them, to heal what they had torn. They failed in this, but they had great hope in the beginning. They had used a stone, the Atalayina. Do you know of it?"

"I know that it was made from the tears of the Fates."

"So some say. Others say it was used to craft Erahm from the stuff of Adhiya. Others still say it is the fourth fate, cast down by the other three as punishment for creating the world. Whatever its origins, the Al-Aqim tried to bend the Atalayina to their will. It would not, however, be used thus, and it shattered into three pieces."

He gave Sukharam a moment to think about this. The sounds of the waves breaking on the rocks to the east was the only sound.

"We go, Sukharam, the three of us—you, me, and Rabiah—to find the pieces of the Atalayina and to make it whole."

"Can it be *made* whole? The Al-Aqim must have tried."

"They did not. They felt as though the fates were punishing them. They felt as though a riddle had been posed with the three pieces of this stone as the clues. They felt that they had to find a way, through searching themselves, through meditation, to close the rift with the broken pieces of the Atalayina the fates had seen fit to grant them."

Sukharam thought on this for a moment, but then he turned to Nasim. He seemed severe under the pale light of the moon. "How can you know these things?"

"Because I remember them. I was Khamal, and he granted me memories of his life. He, like the others, was trapped, and he came to believe that the only way to truly be free, to escape the shackles that had been placed on them and to try again, was to leave. To retain what he had learned in his next life—*my* life—and return to Ghayavand."

"He killed himself?"

"He was killed, by the others."

"But why? If he wanted to return, if he had planned to do so, would he not simply kill himself?"

It was a taboo thing they spoke of. The Aramahn did not take lives, others or their own, and it was a credit to Sukharam that he could speak of it at all. Sadly, though, it was probably a result of the distance he'd had from his own culture since finding himself at the orphanage.

"Do you remember things from your past lives?" Nasim asked him.

"I... Of course not. Not directly. That isn't—"

"But it might be, mightn't it? Do we not one day hope to remember more and more, so that we can reach vashaqiram?"

"Of course, but—"

"Khamal did so. He found a way, and his fate was so entwined with the others that he needed them to send him off. He could not do it on his own."

"So the others agreed to it?"

"They did not."

A rustle in the grass drew Sukharam's attention—a vole, perhaps. "I don't understand."

"Neither do I," Nasim replied. "I remember some, but much is still closed to me. The ritual Khamal had hoped to complete did not go as he planned. Muqallad and Sariya, at the end, tried to stop him, and to a degree they succeeded. I was reborn halfway between Erahm and Adhiya. I could... I could see both worlds..."

Nasim stopped. Even years after the ritual on Oshtoyets, even years after Fahroz had helped him to regain himself, images of that time returned to him. The lights of Adhiya, the sounds of Erahm, the touch of a human hand and the caress of a hezhan.

"Are you well, kuadim?"

Nasim focused on that which lay around him, the wind and the high clouds, barely visible against the star-filled sky. These things grounded him, but the title Sukharam had granted him helped as well. *Kuadim*, Sukharam had said—teacher, mentor, father, and many more things wrapped up into one.

"I am well." Nasim breathed deeply of the chill night air. "There are times still when I become lost. But I have long since returned to myself, and the memories of Khamal come to me, more and more."

"What of the others, Muqallad and Sariya? Will they not be lying in wait?"

"They woke when I was brought to Ghayavand five years ago, but it is my hope that they fell back under Khamal's spell, and that we will be able to do what we need before they awaken fully."

"But you know not?"

"*Neh*, I do not," Nasim replied.

Sukharam was silent for a time, perhaps considering the weight of Nasim's request. "What did you do to me, in the orphanage?" He said the words quickly, as if he were afraid to speak them, but once he had, he pulled himself taller. He was scared. Nasim could see it in the stiff way he stood, in the way the whites of his eyes reflected the light of the moon.

"As I said before, I was lost, but there was one who saved me. His name is Nikandr Iaroslov Khalakovo, a prince of the Grand Duchy. Five years ago he healed me on Khalakovo, but it was not complete." Nasim reached up and placed his palm over his heart. "I can feel him still. I owe him much, but it was the way in which I was saved that keeps me grounded to this world. In fact, it grounds me so fully I cannot touch Adhiya on my own. I can see it, I can feel it, but I can't touch it, not without the help of another qiram."

"You cannot commune with hezhan on your own?"

"I cannot."

"Then we are lost before we've begun."

"*Neh*," Nasim said. "With the Atalayina, I will find a way. Of this I am sure."

"Perhaps we can wait, find a way to heal you before we leave."

"I *would* wait, Sukharam, but the rifts have grown worse. The islands have felt it the worst, but surely you have felt it even here, and soon it will encompass the world. And so we must go. We must go to the island of Ghayavand to heal the rift that was forged on her shores. Too long has it infected Erahm, and it is time it was closed."

Sukharam was silent and pensive for a time. "Will we return?"

Nasim shook his head sadly. "We will not. When you make your decision to come, it will be knowing that you give your life to our cause."

"There were others, weren't there?" Sukharam asked. "There must have been if you've been looking for years."

"There have been others. I found three besides Rabiah that I thought worthy to the task."

"And they all declined."

"One declined," Nasim said. "The others agreed for the wrong reasons, so I sent them away."

This was the moment they'd been working toward. Sukharam had enough to make his decision, and there was nothing left but for Sukharam to weigh his choices. Nasim would not press. He would not manipulate. Those who would follow him would come willingly or he would have no one at all.

The wind rustled the thin bushes along the sides of the hill. Sukharam pulled his arms around his waist. He looked small and lost, and Nasim began to doubt whether Sukharam were made of stern enough stuff to come.

"Take your time, Sukharam, son of Hadir and Dahanan. Make your decision before the sun rises. Return to us if you will. If not, fare you well."

Nasim stepped down the hill, wending his way along the path, his feet crunching against the flaked stone, but before he had gone ten paces, Sukharam called out to him. "I would come, Nasim. I would join you."

"Even knowing what you know?"

"Especially knowing what I know."

"Tell me why."

"My parents were taken from me when I was young. My mother died from the wasting. My father was hung by the courts of Alekeşir for refusing a summons. I was taken and sold to the orphanage two days later. I do not remember my father well, my mother even less, but I remember this. We are ephemeral, here in Erahm and in Adhiya, both. There is so little time for us to do something great. Sometimes there is no time at all." Sukharam paused. "If there is something I can do to help us—to help all of us—then I would do it, or die in the trying. This is what my parents left me—the notion that in giving, we receive—and I cherish it."

Nasim smiled, for his words rang true. "Then come."

They left before dawn the next morning.

CHAPTER THREE

T he sun hung low over the western end of Ivosladna in the Duchy
of Mirkotsk. Long shadows stretched over the capital square that
sprawled near the old stone wall of the posadnik's mansion. The
weather had already turned cold in the northern islands, but the last few days
had brought with it a small reprieve from the bitter winds and early snows.

Still, Nikandr Iaroslov Khalakovo pulled the collar of his cherkesska up.
Two young streltsi wearing the gold-and-red tassels of Mirkotsk walked along
the stone cobbles of the square, the echoes of their boot heels clicking among
the monstrous buildings surrounding it. They glanced at Nikandr, but he
stumbled and caught himself, as a man too deep into his cups might do, and
they laughed and kept on moving.

He waited as a pair of ponies clopped past the street in front of him and then
ducked into a narrow lane that led down a steep slope toward the river. When
he came to the first intersection, he waited, but not for long. To his right, from
a doorway not far down the alleyway, a bearded man with a wine-colored
kaftan waved to him. It was Anatoliy, the nephew of Duke Yevgeny Mirkotsk.

Nikandr made his way into his home. Only after the door was closed did
Nikandr step in to hug him. They kissed cheeks and held one another by the
shoulders, slapping each other several times.

"You look well, Nischka." Anatoliy's long black beard waggled as he spoke.
He was thin—practically emaciated—and despite his warm greeting, his eyes
were sunken and dark and filled with worry.

"And *you* look miserable, Toliy."

Anatoliy smiled, ignoring the gibe. "I'm grateful you could come." He motioned to the next room, and the two of them stepped into his sitting room,
where a small fire lay dying in the fireplace. Nikandr unwrapped his scarf and
took off his coat. After setting it onto the back of one of the two chairs, he sat
while Anatoliy poured two healthy servings of vodka into wide pewter mazers.

He handed one to Nikandr before lowering himself carefully into the other chair, as if his body had only enough energy left to perform this one final act.

"Where is Kseniya?" Nikandr asked carefully.

"She could not bear to be here."

Nikandr thought that statement through. "Does she not approve?"

Before Nikandr had finished speaking, Anatoliy was already shaking his head. "She stands with me in this, but she cannot be here when you... When you try."

"And Mirketta? How is she?"

Anatoliy glanced up toward the second floor, where his daughter would be resting. "Not well."

"You gave her the elixir?"

"*Da.*"

"When?"

"An hour ago, as you instructed."

Nikandr looked through the wavy glass of the nearby window. He could see little more than the building across the street, lit by the pale light of the dying sun. "We'll give her some time yet."

Anatoliy released a deep breath, and with it some of the tension he was clearly harboring was released. "Thank you for coming. I wouldn't blame you if you'd decided not to."

"I wouldn't think of it," Nikandr said. "But what of Yevgeny?"

Anatoliy's smile in the darkness of the room was grim. "My uncle, the duke, would not wish to hear of your presence in this house, but he will not ask me of it, nor protest if he learns of Ketta's sudden return to health."

Nikandr shook his head. "I fear the same cannot be said of Borund. He *will* protest when he hears of it. And loudly."

"Borund can go fuck a goat."

Nikandr laughed, raising his glass and taking a healthy swallow of vodka. "*Da.* He can do that, and sooner rather than later."

Anatoliy laughed ruefully, sitting deeper in his chair. He looked defeated as he stared into the fire. "It is unfortunate what has become of us," he said, though he seemed to be saying it more to the darkness of the room than he was to Nikandr. "But what are we to do? The empire looms to the west, and here we are five years after the conflict, weaker than we were before."

The conflict was how most referred to the Battle of Uyadensk and the blockade that preceded it. Most had never heard of Nasim or what he'd done, or if they had they didn't believe that he'd saved Khalakovo from ruin. All they knew was that they were worse off. Hungrier. Less safe.

Nikandr swirled his vodka and clacked the mazer down on the arm of his chair. "It would not be so if Zhabyn did not tax our coffers bare and demand every stone we mined."

"You sit in a different seat than I"—Anatoliy bowed his head respectfully—"of this there can be no doubt, but from what My Lord Duke tells me, there is little choice in the matter. The tributes have become more dear."

"The Kamarisi has become greedy."

"Perhaps, but Yevgeny tells me they are in little position to make unreasonable demands. It is their war with the Haelish, not greed, that forces their hand. The war is twenty years old if it is a day, and now news has come that late this summer much of the bountiful land to the west was raided or burned. They are not desperate, but they must be careful, now more than ever, with the food they grant. So if the Grand Duchy comes to them yet again, our hands folded, asking to be fed, it will cost us, and dearly."

"I suppose I should not be surprised, but you would think the Kamarisi would have long ago settled a dispute that is nearly as old as he is."

"It is not a simple matter of pride. If they lose the land to the Haelish, the Wredes will become emboldened."

"If they would merely ask for our help…"

Anatoliy's smile was suddenly fierce. "Such a thing the Kamarisi will never do. Within a fortnight he would find a knife in his back and a cousin upon his throne."

Nikandr raised his mazer in salute. "We learned much from them, did we not?"

"Traditions handed down are difficult to set aside."

Nikandr finished his vodka and stood. "Come. The elixir will have done its work by now."

Anatoliy, for the first time since Nikandr had entered his home, showed vigor as he stood and lit a small lamp. He led Nikandr up the creaking stairs to a small bedroom with a single bed. Lying there was a girl of fourteen, bedcovers kicked away, her blonde hair and shift damp with sweat. She was calm, however—the primary effect of the elixir he'd had delivered to Anatoliy earlier in the day.

"I've said it in letters, Anatoliy, but I say it again. This may kill her."

Anatoliy's eyes searched about the room, looking for courage, or insight. Like so many others Nikandr had seen, he was making a decision for his daughter knowing it was risky, but knowing as well that doing nothing was just as dangerous. Those taken by the wasting did not heal of themselves. At least, not often. Nikandr could see in him the same sense of desperation that Nikandr himself had felt years ago, first when he'd been searching for a cure for Victania, and then again as he'd searched for himself. It was strange to Nikandr, the feeling that he himself had now become a potential cure, another of the long list of things that Anatoliy had no doubt tried. It was a measure of Anatoliy's desperation—in some ways no different than the grub Nikandr had eaten, and in other ways much worse—that he had contacted Nikandr in the first place.

"She will die if I do nothing, Nischka." He motioned to Mirketta, a simple but tender gesture. "Do what you can for her."

"I will," he said, gripping Anatoliy's shoulder. "Now, please, leave us. I must have peace and quiet."

"I would stay, Nischka."

"*Nyet*," Nikandr said. "If I do this, I do it alone."

Anatoliy seemed unsure of himself, but when Nikandr did not waver, he nodded and set the lamp on the chest near the bed and closed the door behind him.

As his creaking steps made their way down the stairs, Nikandr turned to Mirketta. He brushed her hair away from her face, feeling the burn of her skin.

And then he pulled his soulstone from inside his shirt. He stared at the unmarred surface of the milky chalcedony. In the dimness of the room it glowed ever so softly.

The stone was young, only five years old. He'd taken another after giving his first—the one he'd had since the day he'd been born—to Nasim. He didn't regret what he'd done—far from it—but this stone was a constant reminder of what he'd given up. He would now leave only half his legacy to the crypts of Khalakovo when he died. But in a way it was fitting. The time of his youth felt distant to him—like a different life, so changed had the world become. And, he told himself while shifting to kneel over Mirketta, there was still much he could do. There was still much he could leave behind for the sons and daughters of Khalakovo.

Not the least of which was this.

He pulled the necklace over his head. After a brief word of prayer to the ancients, he lifted her shift and placed the stone against her bare chest, over her heart. Mirketta's face had been still if not calm, but it grew worried as the stone rested there. This was not something he would have considered years ago—royalty did not give up their stones, to anyone—but he had found that it helped, and if he inherited some small amount of pain or discomfort from those he tried to heal, he would gladly accept that burden.

After placing his other hand over the stone so that he could feel both it and her heartbeat, he closed his eyes and opened himself to the spirit that had been with him since it had been summoned by the Maharraht on the cliffs below Radiskoye.

He had spoken not only to Jahalan about this, but many havaqiram. None of them had a clear explanation, some even doubted his claims, but the spirit was always there, waiting. He treated the hezhan with respect, as it seemed he should, for he considered this both gift and fortune, some small compensation from the ancients for what the Maharraht had done.

He felt his breath release as he reached across the aether's veil and touched the world beyond. His awareness expanded. He felt the draft in the room coming from the small window to his left, felt the wind as it ran across the rooftops and the streets of Ivosladna. He felt the clouds over the city and the larger currents of air as they drifted beyond the city and out to sea. It was at these times, when he had a foot placed firmly in both worlds, that he could touch those stricken by the wasting.

He stared down at Mirketta, her face flush, her breathing shallow. Her eyes were sunken, and the rank smell of her breath told him that she had little time remaining—a few weeks, a month at the most.

He could also feel something else near her—a spirit, in this case a vanahezhan. It drew upon her, slowly but surely, weighing her down and sapping her strength. He waited until he understood her well enough to approach, and then he drew upon her soul as his havahezhan led the other spirit away. Together, they began to separate the two. It was not easy, but neither was it dangerous for him. He'd done it dozens of times already, though he knew it was easier because most of the rifts had closed and those few that remained were narrow gaps—barely rifts at all.

He and Atiana had been searching for more of them ever since the ritual over Duzol. He did not wish more of them upon the islands, but he knew there would come a day when they would return, and they needed to be prepared.

He continued to draw the spirit away from Mirketta, but after a time, the vanahezhan began to resist. Mirketta's breath came faster. She thrashed in her bed, and for the first time Nikandr began to worry that he would lose her.

The first few times he had done this, he would settle his mind and anchor himself more fully for an extended fight, but he had come to realize that this was foolish, especially for a spirit like the vanahezhan. That was merely playing to the strengths of a spirit of stone and earth, and so he allowed himself, and Mirketta, to soar, to drift upon the winds that surrounded them. It had little effect at first, but soon, and with growing effect, she and the spirit began to part.

Mirketta's hold upon her physical form was weak, however, and he soon felt her slipping away from her mortal coil. He tried to pull back, but this allowed the vanahezhan a stronger hold, and now that it had been awoken it fought him fiercely.

Mirketta! he called to her. *Mirketta, hear me!*

She continued to drift. He became desperate, but this made him careless. He calmed himself, focused on the winds once more. He tried for minutes, for hours, hoping to coax the hezhan away. He even felt, near the very end, Mirketta awaken and fight as well. For a time it worked, but she was too weak and she had already expended what little energy she had.

Then, at last, there was no question as to the outcome.

Adhiya opened its arms and embraced her. Her presence faded.

And then all was still.

CHAPTER FOUR

Nikandr was deathly afraid to open his eyes. Yet he already knew what he would see.

When he did open them, he saw Mirketta lying there. Still.

Her breath no longer came. Her blood no longer coursed. Her flame no longer burned.

He held her hand for long moments, tears slipping down his cheeks as he stared at Mirketta's delicate features. He'd tried this ritual many times. He'd managed to save twelve souls, but he'd failed seven of them. Now eight. Eight deaths, and the same questions always haunted him.

Who might they have become?

He'd last seen Mirketta when she was three, but by all accounts she had grown into a fine young dancer. Could she have found herself in the ballet houses of Ivosladna or Volgorod or Evochka? Might she have mothered fine children, as her mother had? What friendships had just been lost? What joys she might have experienced? What pain?

He was shaken from these thoughts by a tapping at the nearby window. He wiped the tears from his eyes with his sleeve. The sun had set. He could see nothing but darkness. But he knew who was there.

After retrieving his stone and kissing Mirketta's forehead, he whispered to her, "Go well, dear child," and then made his way over to the window.

From the golden light of the lamp he could see the flapping wings of a rook, and then the outline of a head, and finally the intermittent glint of an eye blinking in the dark. Now that he wore his stone once more he could feel Atiana's presence. It felt strange to have her here after what had just happened—especially so soon after—but it was good that she was near, even if it was only in the form of a rook.

He wondered why she'd come, though. And why now? He left Mirketta's room and took the stairs down. Anatoliy met him at the bottom of the stairs, but he knew already what had happened.

Nikandr had difficulty finding the words. He'd been so confident when he came—perhaps *too* confident—and he'd allowed Anatoliy to feel some of it. He could see now this had been a grave mistake.

"I'm sorry, Anatoliy."

Anatoliy had seemed fragile before, and in many ways that was true, but a subtle change had overcome him. Now that the outcome was sure, he was stronger, perhaps in anticipation of finding his wife and breaking the news. Surely in the small hours of the night this would change, but Nikandr hoped for Anatoliy's sake, and for his wife's, that his courage would hold for a while longer.

"There was fight in her, but she was too weak," Nikandr continued. "When she went, she went quickly, and painlessly." He didn't know whether the last was true, but he saw no point in adding to Anatoliy's grief.

Anatoliy took one deep, quavering breath, and pulled Nikandr into a deep embrace. He did not kiss Nikandr's cheeks, but when he pulled away, Nikandr could see the pain and gratitude warring within him. "Thank you for trying, for coming here when my uncle, the duke, frowned upon it. But thank you most of all for caring for her."

"Please, go to Kseniya," Nikandr said, pulling him into a deep embrace. "You should be with your family."

The two of them kissed cheeks, and then they parted. Anatoliy nodded. "I will."

Nikandr took up his cherkesska and pulled it on in one smooth motion. From the floor above, the tapping sound came again, louder.

Anatoliy glanced up the stairs and smiled grimly. "Our duties follow us, do they not?"

"They do."

After one last hug, Nikandr opened the door and stepped outside, pulling the collar up around his neck, more for the warmth than to hide his appearance. Soon he was back among the streets, walking toward the northern end of the city, where he'd taken a room. As he walked, a flapping sound came from behind him, and a rook landed on his shoulder. It dug in its talons to remain in place, though it seemed tighter than it needed to be.

The rook nipped his ear, a gesture Atiana had taken to. "I'm sorry, Nischka. She was young and strong once, but the wasting had taken too much from her."

"I know." He walked, the sound of his boots rising above the sounds of revelry coming from the building on his right. Through the window, Nikandr could see a group of men laughing, two of them striking massive steins against one another, throwing beer into the air.

Atiana was silent for a time, but Nikandr knew she was merely giving him time to deal with Mirketta's death. "I'm tired, Atiana. Say what you've come to say."

"You were to tell me if you agreed to heal another."

"It's difficult to get word to you. You know this. And I didn't wish to make Anatoliy wait."

"I know you too well," the rook replied. "You came to help Anatoliy, but you wished to study the rifts over Petrochka as well."

Nikandr shrugged. "If there are clues on this island, I would study them."

"I told you the rift was not wide."

"It doesn't matter. We need to know more. And soon. I can feel it, Atiana. The world has been taking a deep breath these last many years, and soon that breath will be released. I would not be unprepared when it does."

"Neither would I, but there are realities to deal with as well."

Nikandr had nearly reached the far side of the capital square when a tavern door creaked open. Several men filed out, one of them wearing the uniform of a polkovnik, the second highest rank in the military of the Grand Duchy, beneath only the duke himself. The rook immediately flapped up and away as the men headed across the square. The polkovnik glanced at Nikandr, his brows furrowing momentarily, but then one of the men started a drinking song, and the others picked it up. Soon they were past him and Nikandr was up and into the higher reaches of the city.

On a wide street with tall iron fences on either side, the rook flapped down and landed on his shoulder again.

"What realities?" Nikandr said.

"My father, for one. He wants you where you shine the most—at the helm of a ship, commanding other ships."

"He doesn't think I *shine*. And he doesn't command me, Atiana."

"He is the Grand Duke."

"I know this well."

The rook flapped to keep its balance as he took a short set of stairs between two tall stone houses. "Your father agrees with him. He wants you home."

"A home that is threatened."

The rook paused as the wind blew through the narrow walkway. "There's no need to be cold, Nikandr. You know I agree."

"Then *help* me."

"I do."

"I need more."

"That's why I've come." The rook paused, and then took wing. It flew north, away from the inn where Nikandr had taken a room.

The way she'd said those words… *That's why I've come*… Almost as if she were standing right beside him.

He walked down the street. The buildings became homes with proper lawns, and then they became manors. When Nikandr reached the final bend in the road, he looked up and saw that the road led to a keep that had been converted into a boarding house. He knew this place. It was old, one of the few places outside the palotzas and the proper keeps of Mirkotsk that held a drowning chamber beneath the structure's lone turret.

As he climbed the hill, he could see a room on the third floor. A lamp was lit within, and he could see a silhouette standing at the window. It was a silhouette he hadn't seen for months, but as he looked upon it, a sudden sense of relief and anticipation swept over him.

When he reached the keep, the heavy service door set into the old wooden gate creaked open before he could knock. A squinting woman with a bullseye lantern leaned outside and eyed Nikandr while shining the lamp up and down his frame. After a grunt and a look of disapproval, she waved him inside and led him up to the keep's third floor.

Atiana, wearing a lush red robe, was still toweling her hair when he entered the room. The old woman remained, awkwardly watching this exchange. Atiana shooed her away and shut the door, nearly catching the lantern in it. After a *humph*, the woman's shuffling footsteps picked up and faded away, leaving Nikandr alone with Atiana at last.

Atiana stepped in and gave him a tender hug. She didn't exactly approve of what he'd been doing with his newfound abilities—finding those afflicted with the wasting and healing them—but she was setting that aside for him.

For his part, he was drained emotionally. He hardly knew *what* to feel. All he knew was that holding her now was like basking in the summer sun. He pulled her close, feeling her skin, which was chilled to the bone. He could smell the earthy smell of the rendered goat fat that would have protected her skin while she was submerged beneath the water. He could also smell the jasmine perfume she liked to wear.

The emotions that had been roiling through him since leaving Mirketta had been with him until now, but the truth was that he was so glad she was here that he felt nothing but relief and the deep connection he and Atiana shared. Their love had started on Uyadensk, when they were to be married, but it had grown since they'd parted after the ritual on Oshtoyets. They'd seen one another several times a year since then, and each time, he found that his feelings for her had grown since the last time they'd held one another in their arms, since they'd last kissed, since they'd last made love.

"Why have you come so far?" he asked.

She stepped back, staring into his eyes, perhaps to judge his sincerity. "If you think I would let a year pass without seeing you, Nikandr Iaroslov"—she stood on tiptoes to kiss him on the neck—"you are sadly mistaken."

He looked down at her, her porcelain skin and her bright eyes. Her hair fell down her shoulders and back, making her look more primal than he had ever seen her. She looked nothing like a princess.

She took a step back with a beckoning look.

He reached for her and she stepped away.

He didn't want to smile, and yet he did. He stepped forward, and she slid back, never taking her eyes from him.

She moved one hand down to the sash that kept her robe in place.

He pulled at his cherkesska, allowing it to fall from his shoulders as her robe slipped from hers.

He stepped toward her, and when she tried to dance away, he grabbed her wrist. She fought him, tugging, trying to make him lose his grip. She twisted her arm, crouched down, until he pulled her hard and brought her body up against his.

She embraced him then, her lips locking on his. Her skin was freezing to the touch, but she moved as though she were on fire, kissing his neck and chest, biting his ears and lips.

She pulled the clothes from him, never allowing his skin to go without her lips, her tongue, her teeth.

They fell upon the bed, the frame creaking.

She threw him back, pulling the last of his clothes from him and straddling his waist as she leaned forward, chest to chest.

She felt warmer now, and he could feel her heartbeat rising with his.

She slipped one hand between his legs and massaged him as he ran his hands over her shoulders, her back, her breasts.

And then he was inside her. She rode him, slowly at first but all too quickly—the two of them heaving breath in time with the other, bed moaning, headboard thumping against the wall—they fell into one another's arms as they rode the wave with one another. He shuddered and felt her constrict around him, over and over again.

They stayed in one another's arms for long hours after that. Both of them knew that there were things that needed to be discussed, but neither wanted to discuss them. Not in the dark of the night.

The morning, Nikandr thought.

Morning is the time for sharing secrets.

"I've found Soroush."

Nikandr opened his eyes, unsure who had spoken those words. He looked down to the floor, to the robe and his cherkesska lying there.

"You what?" He rolled over to find her sitting up against the headboard.

"I've found him," she said again, her face serious.

He sat up carefully.

"You didn't want me to go after him."

"I didn't," she said. "I don't."

"Then why—"

"Because you think it's important."

Nikandr could think of nothing in that moment except Mirketta, how he had failed to save her. His worst fear since he'd learned of the rifts was that he'd be powerless to prevent them from spreading and affecting the entire Grand Duchy, and now he had a chance to do something about it, to prevent things from becoming worse, assuming he could learn more.

And that was the crux of it. He'd learned—from Atiana and others—that a rift had formed over Rafsuhan. And it was deep. If he was ever going to learn about the rifts, he needed something like that, except Rafsuhan was distant and difficult to reach, but worse, it was an island of the Maharraht. Nikandr would never be allowed access to it.

Not unless he had someone like Soroush to speak for him.

"Where is he?"

"Mirashadal." She paused, waiting for the name to sink in. It was the fabled floating village of the Aramahn. It was also the place Nikandr thought the most likely destination for Nasim and Soroush and the others that had been taken from Oshtoyets after the ritual.

"It's real," Atiana continued. "Even now it floats above the northern seas, less than a thousand leagues from where we sit."

"It's true, then..."

"*Da*. I've seen it, and I'll lead you to it if you wish, but I'm still not certain any of this is wise."

She was speaking not of Soroush, but what Nikandr planned to do with him. "The rift over Rafsuhan is the only one we've found of any size, Atiana."

"Soroush will kill you given the chance. He'd kill all of us."

Nikandr shook his head. "You misjudge him. There's only one thing Soroush cares about more than our destruction, and that's his people."

"So you've said, but he may merely look at it as another reason the Grand Duchy must fall."

"He may, but in the meantime he'll be given the chance to help them. It's something he won't be able to ignore. Take me to the village, Atiana. Take me to Mirashadal."

Atiana pulled her legs up to her chest and stared at him over her knees. "I will take you, if that is your wish."

She wanted him to return to Khalakovo, or better yet, to join her on Kiravashya. Nikandr's father was there. He was now a trusted and valued member of Zhabyn's council. Nikandr could go there. He might not be able to marry Atiana, but at least they would be near one another. And in time, who knew?

But he could not abandon this cause; as much as he wanted to be with Atiana, now and forever, there were greater things to consider.

"It is my wish," he said.

She paused. There was sadness in her eyes, but no surprise.

"Then I will go." She breathed deeply and released it slowly, her eyes searching him for something, though he knew not what.

"Say it, Atiana."

"I have—" She swallowed and tried again. "I have news." As she spoke these words, she raised her chin so that they could see one another eye-to-eye. It was premeditated, something done to give her the confidence she lacked to broach this new subject—or so it seemed to him—and yet she still found herself unable to begin.

He reached out to touch her, but she shied away.

"I'm to be married," she blurted out.

The words struck him. They echoed in his mind. But the worst part was not their implication, but the way in which Atiana was staring at him, as if the words were a cudgel she'd very well meant to strike him with.

"Married to whom?" Nikandr asked.

"Bahett ül Kirdhash."

"The Lord of Galahesh? The Kaymakam?"

"The same."

He wanted to leave the bed. He wanted to leave the room. "Your mother arranged for it?"

"*Nyet.*"

"Your father?"

"*Nyet*, Nikandr. *I* arranged for it."

Nikandr shook his head, confused. "*You* arranged for it?"

"The Grand Duchy is dying, Nikandr. By slow increments every day, she is dying. We need grain. We need livestock. Yrstanla has become more hesitant to deliver. But were we to strengthen the bonds between Kiravashya and Alekeşir, they would begin to flow again, at least long enough for us to recover."

"Bahett is not the Kamarisi."

"Nor would the Kamarisi take me as his wife. Bahett is the key."

"He keeps a *harem*, Atiana."

"And I will become his ilkadin. The first wife. Do you know what kind of power they wield?"

"Their wives, even the ilkadin, are little to the power *Bahett* can wield."

"He will listen to me." She said those words with such passion that it made Nikandr realize just how serious she was. This was no discussion. She'd already made up her mind. She only wished to tell him of it in person from some sense of personal honor.

"We'll not be allowed to see one another," Nikandr said.

"We can see one another…"

"*Nyet.*" Nikandr waved to the bed. "Not like this."

He saw her swallow, but she did not otherwise answer. She knew, as he did, that they could perhaps see one another at functions, perhaps at a personal meal with Bahett in attendance, but were they caught with one another in carnal lust—especially on Galaheshi soil—both of their lives would be forfeit.

Nikandr stood, away from the bed, and stared at her. "You cannot do this, Atiana!"

"Our first duty is to our families, Nikandr, then the Grand Duchy."

He found his jaw tightened to the point of pain. "And I am not family. Is that it?"

"You are my love, but I will see the Grand Duchy healed. As you would."

"Is that why you told me of Soroush first? To test me?"

"You've made your position clear for years, Nikandr."

"Do you think I wouldn't marry you in a moment given the chance?"

"I know that you would, but we are not in that position, are we? We must do what we must do."

"And you must go whoring off to Galahesh?"

Atiana stood from the bed and slapped him across the face.

His head wrenched to one side. The entire left side of his face stung, and it did not subside as he turned back to look at her. She stared at him with a look he'd never seen, not since they were children, and then it had only been the petulance of youth. This was a look of deep-seated pain, and resentment that might never be wiped clean.

She began pulling on her clothes as he seethed. He wanted to apologize, but he couldn't find the words. Only as she was leaving the room did he reach out to her.

"Atiana!"

But then she was gone.

CHAPTER FIVE

Atiana climbed up the stair from her cabin to the deck of the *Zveazda*. The wind was brisk, and it was pushing the ship about, but Hathenn, the ship's havahezhan, was strong, and she guided them in with little trouble.

As landsmen began lashing the ship and the windsmen began securing the last of her sails, Atiana stepped down and onto the ship's perch, glad to be on solid land once more. As she walked toward the palotza, she silently thanked the ancients that her sisters had not come, nor Father or Mother. She needed to be alone, so she walked to the vast yard to the south of the massive palotza to the spire.

She stared up, marveling at it, wondering why she had ever left. The trip to Mirkotsk had been foolish, or if not foolish then at least ill-advised. How had she expected Nikandr to react? Exactly as he had, she thought. She didn't deserve the words he'd spit at her, but neither had he deserved to learn of her decision in such an abrupt manner. She'd meant to tell him the moment she saw him, but she had missed him so much. She had only wanted one more night together—as their life *might* have been—before telling him of her decision to marry Bahett.

She stepped forward and touched the smooth surface of the obsidian, stared into its mottled black depths. She could not feel the same sense of power that she could while taking the dark, but she liked to think that there were echoes of it at the very least, some small trace of the power that emanated from it in the aether. She had been out for nearly two weeks now. She would enter again—tonight, perhaps tomorrow—and guide Nikandr to Mirashadal, and when she did, she knew it would feel like saying goodbye, much more so than the way they'd left one another in Ivosladna.

"You've not seen the spire before?"

Atiana turned and found Mileva standing near the old stone fence surrounding the spire. Behind her stood the rookery and beyond that the bulk of Galostina. The wind tugged at the hem of Mileva's heavy woolen dress, blew the ermine collar against her neck momentarily. Mileva's cheeks were already pink from the cold winter winds.

"You're fortunate to have arrived when you did," Mileva said. She nodded pointedly over Atiana's shoulder.

Atiana turned and saw in the distance, gliding serenely beneath gray skies, no less than four twelve-masted barques accompanied a smaller, eight-masted brigantine, the one that surely carried the Kaymakam of Galahesh and the Kamarisi's personal envoy. It would seem that Yrstanla had changed little—an opportunity to show strength should never be passed by.

"Did you see him?" Mileva asked.

She meant Nikandr, of course. Atiana had not admitted to her mother the true purpose of her trip. Surely she suspected, but she hadn't raised objections because Atiana had been the one to offer her hand to the Kaymakam of Galahesh. She *had* confessed everything to Mileva and Ishkyna, however. They had chided her, but she could tell that behind their remarks they were sad over it.

"I saw him," Atiana replied.

"And?"

"You'll be pleased, Mileva. It was exactly the sort of farewell you said it would be."

Mileva glanced up to the approaching ships, her face serious and thoughtful, but not sad. "I'm not pleased, Tiana. I'm sorry. I had hoped that at least one of us would manage to find love."

"Well that isn't likely any more, is it?"

"Don't be so sure." Mileva smiled, but it was unconvincing to say the least. "I hear Bahett is an easy man to look upon."

After running her hands one last time over the cold obsidian, Atiana strode toward the palotza. "Don't make light of my love for Nikandr."

Mileva looked like she was about to respond with a biting reply, but then she pursed her lips and took Atiana's hand. Squeezing it gently, she said, "Come. There is much to attend to."

That entire day the palotza was aflutter with the arrival of the Kaymakam of Galahesh, and that night, they prepared for their welcoming celebration. Atiana stood at the open doors of the grand ballroom. Mileva was already seated next to her husband, Viktor. Ishkyna's husband would not be present, which was apparently fine with Ishkyna, who was standing next to a man from the envoy's retinue, a tall courtier with a closely cropped beard and a red silk turban. A ruby medallion with feathers of white decorated the center of the turban, just above his brow. Like many of the courtiers, he wore voluminous pants and a wide cloth belt. The sword hanging at his side seemed similar to those of the streltsi, but it curved more, and the hilt was carved like the head of a falcon, making it appear as if it would be clumsy and unwieldy in battle.

More people filed into the room, mostly relatives, both close and distant, of Atiana's, but there were others as well: diplomats, officers of the staaya, men and women of business and industry. Father had gone to great lengths, hoping to impress upon the Empire that Anuskaya was no plum ripe for the plucking. But still, he could not be too ostentatious. The day's events had to be reserved enough to give some sense of how seriously the islands needed the Empire's assistance.

Atiana hesitated to enter. The memories of Nikandr were still fresh, and over the past few years she had found herself becoming ever more hopeful of some sort of reconciliation between her family and the Khalakovos. When she appeared at functions such as these she often found herself wanting him at her side, escorting her to this grand function. It should have been, she thought. It should have been so long ago.

"The Kamarisi would be pleased."

Atiana turned to find an Yrstanlan, perhaps thirty years old, standing in the doorway. Unlike so many of the visiting courtiers, he was clean-shaven, and he wore a turban with no feathers—only a simple medallion with an emerald of the deepest, purest green.

"Forgive me," Atiana said, "but why?"

"In the capital they say Galostina offers little in the way of beauty"—he stared into her eyes, clearly enough to make his point but with a wry smile, as if waiting for some sharp rejoinder—"but it is clear to me now that they were wrong."

Despite herself, despite thoughts of Nikandr still fading from her mind, she immediately liked him. "I thank you." She bowed her head and touched her forehead with one hand in the manner of the Empire. "Though I doubt they've ever found their way as far as Kiravashya."

He stepped back and nodded, conceding the point. "Few now ever leave Alekeşir. A pity for them; more the pleasure for me."

"And the Kamarisi, does he ever deign to leave his enclave?"

"He does, but he has many places he must visit." He tilted his head and shrugged. "Perhaps after this I can convince him to come here."

"And how would you do that?"

He bowed his head with that same wry smile. "The Kamarisi's mind is his own, but he listens to the advice of those whom he trusts."

The man, this elegant aristocrat, became distracted as a group of women in gowns and beaded headdresses filed into the room. As he watched them weave toward their table, Atiana took him in anew. The clothes of all the visiting dignitaries were fine, but his, even if they were a bit understated, were especially so. He wore a silk jacket the color of ivory that perfectly matched his citrine pants and goldenrod belt. The emerald in the brooch pinned to his turban was of a color and clarity that marked it as an imperial stone, one that would be given only to the Kamarisi's most trusted advisors.

"Were Bahett ül Kirdhash to whisper in *my* ear, I would listen as well."

Bahett bowed his head, but did not break eye contact. "To a woman like Atiana Radieva Vostroma, I would do more than whisper."

"Be careful, My Lord. I am not yet your wife."

"Your words may be true"—he took her hand and kissed it quickly—"but so were mine." With that he walked away, leaving behind the scent of amber and sandalwood.

Across the room, Ishkyna was no longer speaking with the courtier, but with the Kamarisi's envoy himself, Sihaş ül Mehmed. He was a tall man, handsome, with a thin scar that ran through his eyebrow and down to his cheek. The scar somehow made him look *more* attractive, not less. He was young, only twenty-four, a year younger than the Kamarisi himself, and if word from Irabahce were to be believed, he was well trusted, the cousin to one of the Kamarisi's wives. It was anyone's guess why he had been sent along with Bahett, but Atiana reasoned it was because he was brash, an effective counter to Bahett's easy style.

Ishkyna spoke with him, a glass of white wine in her hand. She reached out, glancing occasionally toward Bahett. The envoy would not know, but Ishkyna was jealous; Atiana could tell in the way she stood, the set of her jaw. She was jealous of Atiana, first of her love for Nikandr and now of Bahett. She was nearly ready to go and speak with her, but just then father arrived with Aunt Katerina, and together they began speaking with Sihaş.

Father wore an impressive kaftan of gold and red. He wore the wide golden necklace of the Grand Duke, and he held himself proudly, but there was something in his bearing—a weight that had only seemed to grow heavier these past few years, and especially as this summit with Yrstanla approached. As Aunt Katerina listened to some story from Sihaş, Father's eyes studied the room. Anuskayan mingled with Yrstanlan. It was cordial, but Father was tense. She could tell by the way he breathed and the way his half-lidded eyes scanned the crowd, never lingering.

Atiana felt a hand at her back. She turned to find Mother standing next to her. Like Father, she was studying the gathering crowd, but *unlike* him, she did so with a certain amount of disinterest. And then Atiana realized that she was not merely studying the crowd, she was pointedly *not* looking at Atiana.

"What is it, Mother?" she asked.

Mother glanced down at her once, quickly. "Bahett is charming, is he not?"

"All the charm in the world, which should give us pause."

"It does, Tiana, but there are times when there is little room in which to negotiate."

Atiana looked up at her. "There's always room to negotiate."

"True words, daughter." She met her gaze and smiled. "It was not an easy thing you did."

"Agreeing to marry Bahett or telling Nikandr?"

"Both, but know this… It was the right thing to do." She turned back to look over the contingent from Galahesh. "And don't look so glum. Their customs are not our own, but their women are treated with respect. More, I suspect, than some of our own give the women of the Grand Duchy." She stared meaningfully at Ishkyna, who had never been treated well by her husband.

"I know it's needed, Mother, but…"

Mother glanced over, a suffering look on her face. "More Matri will be found, Tiana. More will be taught. Bahett is in a unique position to help all of us. Even the Khalakovos." Mother stepped closer to her until their shoulders were nearly touching. It was the closest thing to open affection she'd ever known from her mother. "And perhaps in time Bahett will allow you to return."

And that, Atiana thought, was as close to an admission that Mother *wanted* Atiana to return as she was going to get. But it was also a lie. No such thing would happen. First wife or not, a princess of the islands or not, once she was given to Bahett she would be an Yrstanlan wife, meaning she would remain in Baressa until the end of her days.

"I would like that," Atiana said while fighting back tears.

CHAPTER SIX

Atiana, skin already prickling, breath releasing in a thin white fog, stepped into the drowning basin. The ice-cold water came up to her calves. The muscles of her legs tightened like cords drying in the summer sun. The muscles along the bottoms of her feet cramped until she was able to calm herself at last. She was thinking too much about Bahett and Nikandr and not about the task at hand. She forced her muscles to relax and she took in one long breath before accepting the breathing tube offered by her young handmaid, Yalessa. When she sat in the water, she was in control, and the drowning chamber once more felt like an old friend.

"Tea?" Yalessa asked. Her hair was plaited in a circle around her head, making it look like a crown of auburn hair and bright yellow ribbon. As a handmaid, Yalessa was attentive, but she was too free with her thoughts, a habit Atiana had been trying to rid her of.

"Rosehip, I think."

Yalessa smiled, shivering in the cold of the stone room far below the lowest levels of Palotza Galostina. "Ovolla is making her squash biscuits. Would you like some?"

Atiana smiled, shivering and lowering herself further into the water. How she used to love those biscuits. "The tea will do."

Yalessa was a good girl, and she thought she was helping, offering Atiana something to comfort her when she returned to the world, but in reality it was dispiriting. Atiana had avoided the dark when she was young, thinking she would never come to love it, but in the years since she'd become a Matra, in name and spirit both. She had come to love the aether, and the tea upon awakening, however grounding it might be, was also a reminder of how long she would be away from the aether once more.

She lowered herself completely, allowing the water to rush over her. She did not enjoy this transition—her body still stiffened to the point of pain—but she had long since grown accustomed to it, and she had learned how to relax herself once completely submerged.

She exhaled through the tube, releasing all the breath she could manage before drawing air with a slow, measured pace. After her lungs were full near to bursting, she exhaled again and drew breath with a pace that was slower still. She repeated this several times, breathing in and out, in and out, and soon... Soon...

She drifts. Drifts from her body in the basin. Allows the currents of the aether to take her. She watches Yalessa as she frets about the room, but the souls of those scattered around the palotza, especially those she touched stones with recently, draw her upward, outward, until the entirety of the palotza—even nearby structures—fills her mind. They dance blue in the black of the aether.

The currents shift. It feels distant, however, and ancient, as if the bones of the earth are calling her from some hidden, faraway vale.

Like a spider along its web, she shifts her perception, moves subtly and swiftly toward the disturbance. Soon she finds Sayyesh, her father's most trusted qiram, adjusting the winds to drive a skiff toward the palotza's small, northern eyrie.

As she looks upon him, his drawing of the winds causes tufts of white smoke to drift against the deep, dark blue of the aether. The color is a telltale sign of a havaqiram. The disturbance she felt must have been him, but it didn't feel that way.

But she can no longer sense it. Only Sayyesh.

It must have been him, she thinks.

She pulls herself away, expanding her mind and drawing upon the currents that run toward and away from the spire. She aligns herself with the spire's tone, its pitch. Like pulling a rope taut she strengthens it, aligns the currents with the other islands in the archipelago and even beyond, to Nodhvyansk, to Dhalingrad, to Khalakovo. And to the spire at the southern end of Galahesh.

Her tasks take hours, and when she is done, she is tired, but there is time now to wander, to watch. She pulls her consciousness home, dragging herself away from the immensity of the islands. It is discomforting—such is the lure of the aether—but the aether is no child to be trifled with. She cannot linger when her mind is spread so wide. If she does she risks becoming lost, no matter how many years of experience she has in the drowning basin.

As the bulk of Galostina looms before her, she cannot help but think of Lord Bahett and his mission and the pending marriage that lies between them like a gauntlet. There are parallels with her journey to Khalakovo five years ago, but that was a marriage within the Grand Duchy—she knew from an early age to expect such things. Her pending marriage to Bahett is a thing of her own making, and yet she feels foolish, as if she is making a grave mistake, despite the benefits the marriage would bring.

She wanders to the wing the men from Yrstanla have been given. Mother declared them off-limits—they have ways of telling if they're being spied upon, she said—but she doesn't care. Whether it was her decision or not, she would see what sort of man he is.

As she draws closer to his room—the walls only subtly visible in the darkness of the aether—she finds him awake. He sits at a desk, a quill in his hand, but he isn't writing, at least not at the moment. He merely taps the quill against the paper, over and over again, in a distinct rhythm, as if a concerto is playing absently in his mind.

She comes closer and reads not the flowing script of Yrstanla, but of Anuskaya. As the words register, she becomes cold—more chill than the drowning basin could ever make her.

How many nights must I wait? the words on the paper said. *Come, Atiana. We must speak.*

Before the words can sink in, Atiana senses another Matra nearby. She recognizes the presence immediately as Saphia. Atiana isn't sure how long Saphia has been here, but there can be no doubt she's read the note as well.

Atiana reaches out, strengthens their bond. Saphia could stop it at any time, but she allows it. As much as Atiana has grown over these years, Saphia has grown stronger. She was the strongest of the Matri already, but her time in the lake deep in the village of Iramanshah has somehow tempered her even further. At times, her powers seem to dwarf Atiana's. And yet, as strong as her mind is, her body has grown frail. Just as Atiana can faintly feel her own body in the drowning chamber of Galostina, she can feel Saphia's in the lake of Iramanshah. She is thin, weak, barely able to remain awake when she allows herself to leave the cold depths of the water.

A beautiful man, is Bahett, Saphia says.

You should not have come, Atiana replies. *The others may sense you.*

So you always say, but they have not once sensed me, not when I've meant them to look past. They are ham-fisted children, Atiana, and it's best you come to realize that. Now come. There is something else you must see.

Atiana feels a pull on her soul. She is drawn away from Galostina, away from Kiravashya, away from Vostroma. She is pulled northward toward Galahesh. She had seen the city from the aether only once before, years ago, and only at the behest of her mother. She did not stay long because it was difficult then, but now, she is at relative ease.

There is danger, however. The aether swirls here, and the closer she comes to the straits that run through the center of the island, the more difficult it becomes, until at last she can go no further.

Yet still Saphia pulls, draws her closer. The hidden currents draw her thin, like smoke upon a growing breeze. She feels more and more of the Sea of Tabriz to the east, and the Sea of Khurkhan to the west. They are vast and deep and full of life. She knows that she's being drawn too far, but there's little she can do to prevent it. The aether and the storm that centers upon Galahesh have taken her.

Saphia!

She hears nothing. She feels instead the currents of the waters, the leagues that lie below. Feels the crust of the earth where it meets the impossibly dark depths. Feels the confluence as it struggles against Galahesh and the walls that stand high above the straits.

Saphia!

Slowly she feels herself drawn away from the edge. She is pulled inward, and it feels as though she is giving up a part of what she might be by doing this. The call of the aether is strong, especially when one has been drawn so wide and far.

Control yourself, child.

The borders of Galahesh enter her consciousness. She holds onto this like a piece of flotsam in the sea, and finally, at last, she is able to focus herself without the supporting hand of Saphia.

Thankfully, Atiana recovers faster than she would have guessed. *I am no child.*

There comes a laugh, an echo of the Saphia she once knew. *Perhaps you are not.* Saphia guides her attention toward Baressa, the massive city that sits along the southern edge of the straits at the center of the long island. *It is much stronger than it has ever been. The whorls and eddies prevent me from approaching the city for more than a few minutes at a time, and even then it is difficult.*

They have always been treacherous.

They have, but it has changed. It has become more dangerous. The cycle of the aether's tides have become erratic and unpredictable.

Why are you telling me this?

That laugh came again. *Your marriage to Bahett was surely arranged by the ancients.*

What do you mean?

We must understand what is happening in the dark. Arrangements have been made with Bahett for a drowning chamber in the city, though he refuses to tell us why. It is the reason, I suspect, he has written you his note. Go to him when you wake. See what it is he wishes, but by no means are you to deny him. You must reach the island, Atiana, and you must find out more.

Many times in the past several years, Atiana had felt the weight of the islands bearing down on her, but never as much as it does now. Word has come that Yrstanla, for whatever reason, has rekindled its interest in the east. It is surely why his envoy, Sihaş, has been sent when normally the Kaymakam of Galahesh alone would treat with the Grand Duchy. There is also the blight, which has lessened on Khalakovo and Rhavanki, but has grown worse on Vostroma and Nodhvyansk and Bolgravya. Atiana's father spreads the wealth of the duchies as well as he can, and he treats with the Empire to make up the rest, but it is always too little. The widespread hunger sparked riots all across the islands at different times of the year, and rumors of revolution are heard more and more among the streets of every city in the Grand Duchy. Some of the more fortunate islands, like Mirkotsk and Lhudansk, have even spoken of ceding from the Anuskaya, acts that would spell complete ruin whether they succeeded in their attempts or not.

And now there is this. The disturbances of the aether.

Would it spread? Would it move through the islands, preventing them from communicating with one another? Such a thing might lead to a slower death, but it would be every bit as disastrous as revolution.

There is no choice in whether she will go to Galahesh or not, nor is there a choice in following through on her marriage with Bahett. There never was. They were simply too desperate to demand anything of Galahesh, or her mother, Yrstanla.

I will go to him, she tells Saphia, *and I will go to Galahesh. We will discover what is happening, and we will survive, as we always have.*

I hope you're right, child. I hope you're right.

This time, Atiana doesn't complain about being called a child.

CHAPTER SEVEN

Nasim trudged along a mountain plateau. The sky was blue, the wind bitter, and the snow deep beneath his feet. To his right, behind him, stood the towering bulk of Nolokosta, the highest peak in the entire Sitalyan range.

He had wrapped his scarf around his head in such a way that he could see only through a narrow gap. It was necessary with the sun glaring down so strongly against the white snow. Had he decided on a shorter hike, he wouldn't have bothered, but he'd been gone for nearly a day, hiking to the top of Nolokosta the night before and watching the sunrise this morning. Without the scarf, he'd already be blinded by the snow.

He'd brought Rabiah and Sukharam here first and foremost to escape the attentions of Ushai, but he'd also come because this was a place they could rest. He needed to prepare Sukharam. He needed to prepare himself. He needed to *breathe* before beginning their journey toward Ghayavand and all that entailed.

His trek took him through a shallow vale and toward a ridge that would bring him to the place where he'd left the others, a saddle between two long valleys. He was weary, not because the climb was difficult, but because the snow was fresh and soft as twice-ground flour. He wore the wide, wicker-laced snowshoes he'd bought in Trevitze before leaving. Even though it was slow going, the simple exertion and the connection to his body felt wonderful. He'd been fixated for so long on finding first Rabiah and then Sukharam that he'd hardly rested more than a handful of days since leaving Mirashadal three years ago.

At last he crested the ridge and began hiking down toward their camp, such as it was. Their skiff was still nestled in a gentle fold of land where they'd set it down a week before. The white snow and black granite made it look like the windship was being cradled by a white-robed woman in repose. It was Rabiah who'd noticed it on their approach, and Nasim had thought it a fortuitous sign—the land itself was seeking to protect them—and so, after a quick flight to ensure no village or outpost was near, they'd landed and begun their preparations for Ghayavand.

Rabiah was sitting cross-legged on a snow bank beyond the skiff. Her hands were on her knees, and though she was facing away from him—toward the stunning green slopes of the eastern valley—he was sure her eyes were closed and her breathing was measured. Nasim admired her ability to do this. Taking breath. It was what he'd tried to do on top of the mountain, but as always, he'd found himself unable to calm his mind, unable to find the peace that so many Aramahn managed to find in such places. It had been so ever since he'd come to himself in Oshtoyets. Even in the idyllic meditation spaces of Mirashadal, Nasim had been unable to find peace. Perhaps it had something to do with the stone he'd swallowed—Nikandr's soulstone—but he could feel no other effects, nor could he sense the stone itself, so he wrote it off as another ill effect of the fractured nature of his life—of his *self*—since being reborn.

Sukharam stood on an outcropping of black stone far from the skiff. His arms were wide. His face was turned up toward the sky. It was a pose Nasim had taught him before leaving, and Sukharam had excelled not only at this simple pose, but in the bonding of spirits. It was amazing how quickly he was able to reach them, to draw them near.

When Nasim had asked him about it, Sukharam had said that the last time he'd attempted to do so was when he was eight, when he was still traveling with his father, but he'd admitted to having little success then. Here on the mountain, he'd taken to it so quickly, not just with spirits of the wind but with all the hezhan, that Nasim wondered if he'd been lying—perhaps he'd stolen chances to touch the spirits during his time under the yoke of the orphanage. But Nasim soon thought better of his mistrust, attributing Sukharam's abilities instead to the incredible potential within him that had surely blossomed as he'd grown older.

After they'd landed, he'd taught Sukharam for five days, and then, judging it enough for Sukharam to learn on his own, to simply *absorb* for a time, Nasim had left him with Rabiah.

Nasim slowed his pace while watching carefully. A fine dusting of snow lifted and funneled around Sukharam. A surge of pride welled up inside Nasim. Sukharam did not wave his hands to guide the snow, as some Aramahn did. Instead, he *urged*, and allowed the hezhan to do the rest, as was proper.

The closer Nasim came, the more he was able to feel Sukharam's connection to Adhiya, and he was surprised to find that it wasn't a spirit of wind Sukharam was communing with, but a jalahezhan, a spirit of water.

By the fates, he learned quickly...

The jalahezhan were difficult spirits to control. They were fluid, mercurial, sometimes capricious spirits. But here stood Sukharam, coaxing one to lift the snow from the ground as if it were merely the wind, and he was doing it so deftly that Nasim could barely tell the difference.

When Sukharam noticed Nasim approaching, the swirling snow spun away and fell in a swath along the finger of black rock he stood upon. He glanced behind him at the scattered snow, and then turned back to Nasim as if he'd been caught stealing honey from the pot. He stared at the ground, refusing to meet Nasim's gaze.

Sukharam was embarrassed for some reason, but Nasim was more pleased than he could express. "Sukharam, look at me."

He did.

"Try again," Nasim said, "but this time, bind water *and* earth."

Sukharam took in the landscape anew. His eyebrows pinched in concern. "Communing with only one spirit is difficult for me, kuadim."

"There's a time and place for humility, Sukharam, but it isn't now, and it isn't here." Nasim began unwrapping the scarf around his face. He squinted from the sudden brightness. "Earth and water are sympathetic. They won't *wish* to bond with one another, but you must act as the arbitrator. You must coax them."

"Coax?"

Nasim smiled. "Make them see reason."

"Forgive me, kuadim, but they aren't children."

Nasim opened his thick outer robe, allowing the chill mountain wind to cool the overheated skin of his chest. "I know, but they're self-centered just the same. They must be made aware of one another, which is difficult, but once they are they will cooperate."

Sukharam seemed doubtful. He flexed his hands while considering the granite beneath him. He licked his lips, and he tried.

No sooner had he closed his eyes than Nasim could feel the drawing of a jalahezhan, no doubt the same one he'd communed with moments ago. He tried to draw a vanahezhan as well, but the one nearest was rigid, uninterested.

Through Rabiah, Nasim had found that he could not only *control* spirits through others, he could draw them near as well, so that Rabiah, or now, Sukharam, could commune with them. He did this now, hoping only to draw the vanahezhan's eye so that Sukharam could do the rest.

Deep below the surface of the earth, he felt a rumbling. The earth shook. The stones near his feet skittered. Nearby, a snowbank, twenty feet high if it was one, collapsed, revealing a long swath of an escarpment that was striated with layers the color of bistre and coal. Rubble fell away, but the clumps of stone and rubble were caught by a sudden uplift of snow. Soon the rock and snow and ice were swirling, but unlike the funnel Sukharam had created moments ago, these swirled in a tight column.

The column pulled tighter and tighter, slowing, compressing, glinting beneath the sun, until at last it came to rest. It looked like a monolith of rock and crystal, but Nasim could tell that it was held by the two hezhan, which were now entwined so inextricably that he had difficulty telling them apart.

But then a crack rent the air.

The earth bulged at the base of the pillar.

Nasim could feel the vanahezhan, closer than he had felt any spirit since Oshtoyets, when five elders had been drawn by Soroush into the material world.

He tried to prevent the vanahezhan from approaching, but it shrugged him away.

Sukharam had overextended. He'd allowed the spirit too close, and now it had seized him.

Nasim began to run toward Sukharam. "Fight it!"

The vanahezhan was crossing.

"Sukharam," Nasim cried, "fight it!"

The pillar of rock and ice crumbled as the ground continued to rise. A low rumbling, like the opening of an ancient and massive door, emanated from the mound that was pulling itself upright. The hezhan unfurled its four arms, piercing sounds of snapping and cracking rending the calm of the snow-filled landscape.

The vanahezhan took one lumbering step forward. It was ungainly. It looked as though it would topple and fall and break apart, but it didn't. It took another step as Nasim reached Sukharam. As soon as Nasim had grabbed him by the elbow, however, Sukharam crumpled to the ground, unconscious, as the pounding of the vanahezhan's monolithic feet brought it nearer and nearer.

Nasim faced the hezhan, knowing he would never get Sukharam away in time. Sukharam was unconscious, which left Nasim unable to touch Adhiya. But the hezhan itself had a connection to the spirit world. He used this to push the hezhan away, push it back toward the rift that had allowed it to slip into Erahm. The vanahezhan would not be moved, however. It stood resolute, immovable.

Until Rabiah joined him. He couldn't see her—he could see nothing but the hulking beast standing before him—but her imprint was unmistakable. Together they pushed, harder and more desperate, as the hezhan took another ungainly step toward Nasim.

It spread its arms, groaning, its eyes twinkling in the dark depths of its head.

But its hold on the material world was not so sure as it had thought. Rabiah and Nasim drove it slowly but surely toward the rift.

Then, without warning, it fell to pieces in a rush of crumbling stone as if it had been rotting from within for eons and had just now succumbed to the pressures of time.

Rabiah closed the rift—at least as much as she was able—and soon, the only thing Nasim could hear on the mountainside was the huff of his own breathing. As he stared at the mound of stone, gouts of his exhaled breath were swept away by the mountain air. Rabiah was transfixed, both of them afraid for a moment to move.

Rabiah was the first to recover. "Nasim, we must go."

Nasim barely heard her. By the fates above, he had nearly killed Sukharam by pushing him to do something he wasn't ready for.

"Nasim, we must go!"

Nasim looked to Rabiah, then Sukharam. "He's in no condition—"

"There's a skiff approaching." She glanced over her right shoulder, southeast toward Trevitze. "It's Ushai. I sensed her while I was taking breath. She's leagues away still, but she's coming fast."

"How could she have found us?" Nasim asked.

Rabiah shrugged. "I don't know."

Nasim glanced in the same direction as Rabiah had, expecting to see Ushai sweeping in at any moment. Where would they go now? And how by the name of the fates would they throw Ushai off their scent? She was altogether too good at finding them. Desperation started to rise within him like the swelling sea, but then he came to a decision, one he probably should have made before now.

"Get the skiff ready," he said.

Rabiah nodded and ran.

Nasim kneeled next to Sukharam and levered him around his shoulders, picking him up and moving across the snow as quickly as he was able.

By the time he reached the skiff, his legs and chest burning from the exertion, Rabiah had the sail unfurled and the reins in her hands.

"Where will we go?" she asked.

Nasim set Sukharam in to the confines of the skiff as gently as he could. "We go to Ghayavand," he said as he slipped over the edge and collapsed between two of the thwarts.

The skiff lifted, and Rabiah summoned the wind to point them southward, away from Ushai's incoming path. "We're not ready."

"We have no choice."

"We're not *ready*," she repeated.

"We must *be* ready!" Nasim said. "Don't you see? The hezhan. The crossing. There's a rift, even here in the mountains of Yrstanla. The wasting has covered whole swaths of the continent to the south. It won't be long before the same happens here. The rifts grow more frequent. They grow wider. Hezhan will start crossing soon, Rabiah. On their own, with no help from anyone. And when they do, they'll feed, on the Aramahn, on the Landed, on the Maharraht. On children and fathers and mothers. They won't care."

From her position at the sails, Rabiah looked down at him. She was strong, but she was scared as well. Months ago, Ghayavand had seemed like a fool's dream, but now it was real. It was there before both of them. She opened her mouth to speak, but Nasim talked over her.

"It's time," he said. "I've found the two of you at last. We are three, as were the Al-Aqim, as are the fates. As are the pieces of the Atalayina. We go to Ghayavand, daughter of Aahtel, and we go now."

The wind picked up, and Rabiah harnessed it well. She looked down at him again while guiding them with strong and steady hands. She licked her lips. But then she nodded. "We go to Ghayavand."

CHAPTER EIGHT

Khamal stands within a grand celestia. Its fluted pillars rise up to the massive dome high above the gathered assemblage. The firelight from the three large braziers reflects against the mosaics on the underside of the dome, making it glint like the heavens with golden stars in place of silver.

Not one of the dozens who stood watching is allowed onto the floor of the celestia. They stand one stair down, watching as Khamal approaches the girl lying at the center of the floor. Only when he kneels next to her do twelve men and women step forward. They are suuraqiram, the most gifted of those left on Ghayavand. They chant a song of Khamal's choosing.

From his robes Khamal retrieves a blue stone. It is heavier than it appears and it is beautiful to behold. It feels as old as the earth itself, as old as the mountains. It feels as old as the fates, who are surely watching down from their home in the firmament. He wonders, though, are they smiling? Or do they weep over what Khamal is about to do?

He allows the stone to drop to the palm of his hand, and then he closes his fist around it if only to remove it from his sight, but the feeling that he is making a grand mistake does not fade, nor does the sense that he can no longer turn back.

He calms himself. He smiles for the girl, but she is fearful of him. Fearful of the stone.

He does nothing to comfort her. This is as much a test for her as it is for him.

Beyond the world of man, beyond the world of sky and earth, he can feel a spirit of fire, a suurahezhan. He does not beckon it. It comes of its own accord, hungering for life through the girl that lies before him.

He takes the stone and sets it upon the girl's forehead.

Her body goes rigid.

And her screams echo through the night.

"Nasim, wake up."

Nasim opened his eyes, blinking in the early light of dawn. These dreams—dreams that had been with him since a year after he'd been healed—were not so easily shaken. He'd seen this one many times before, but he'd never once seen what followed her screams. Despite this—or perhaps because of it—the girl haunted his waking hours. Who was she? What had Khamal done to her?

He knew it was part of the riddle he had to solve once he reached Ghayavand. He wished he knew more, but he suspected that more would be revealed to him once he reached the island. It must be so. The dreams were clearly a way for Khamal to pass Nasim his memories, and his desire for Nasim to return and complete his plans. Surely, when he came to the place where Khamal had died, he would learn more.

"Nasim!" Rabiah stood over him, her hand on the gunwales to steady herself. "Ushai is still following us."

Nasim sat up, the dream fading only with reluctance. With Rabiah's help, he stood and grabbed onto the skiff's lone mast for support. Sukharam held the reins of the skiff's lone sail, guiding them eastward. In the distance, near the horizon where the dark sea met the slate blue sky, he saw the sail of a skiff, golden in the early morning light. It was still leagues away, but there was no doubt as to who was harnessing the winds in order to follow them.

They had left the mountains four days ago, passing well beyond the Empire's land and over the Sea of Tabriz. Rabiah and Sukharam watched him, waiting for his word, waiting for him to protect them.

Nasim motioned Sukharam toward the bedding and blanket he'd just vacated. "Get some rest. We'll need you again soon."

Nasim took the reins of the sail from him. Through Rabiah, he touched Adhiya. He felt the wind as it slipped over the smooth windwood hull of the skiff. He felt the gathering storm to the west. He felt the currents as they played over the dark blue sea. He called to a havahezhan, not the one that was nearest, but the strongest. It came to him, tentative as Nasim offered himself, offered a glimpse of Erahm. It seemed like such a simple thing at times, but this bond wore at him, as it did any qiram, as the hezhan drank from the world around him. As it did, it drained, sipping not only on the world, but Nasim as well.

But he was rested. He was ready, and he called upon the havahezhan to guide them eastward.

As the skiff bucked under the newfound wind, Nasim glanced down at Rabiah. She clutched her stomach. She swallowed and licked her lips. She always felt discomfort when he did this, but Nasim was more gifted than she once he'd managed to bond with a spirit. For the time being—at least until they lost Ushai in the storm to come—it was necessary.

"I'm sorry," he whispered to her.

"Do not be," she replied.

Throughout the morning, they added distance. Ushai's ship was little more than a speck hovering just above the horizon. They lost sight of Ushai well before the storm caught up with them, and then, shortly after midday, it swept over them like an avalanche. Rain lashed down as they pulled on oiled coats. Nasim was less worried about Ushai as he was staying on course. He guided them as well as he was able, knowing he could adjust once he found the stars again, but not wanting to waste precious time and energy if he could avoid it.

The storm continued through the night and into the next day, and Nasim was growing exhausted. At last, when he thought he could take no more, the storm finally broke, and he allowed himself a rest.

Nasim had hoped they had lost Ushai in the storm, but Rabiah said she could feel her coming, and near dusk, they saw signs of her once again, close and coming closer.

Nasim took the reins again, this time using Sukharam to bond with a hezhan, but he had not yet recovered. He pushed hard once more, and again they added distance, but he found himself flagging much sooner than he'd hoped. Sukharam took a turn, but still Ushai gained on them.

"How can she do this?" Rabiah asked.

Nasim, sweat dripping from his brow as he glanced over his shoulder, shook his head. He cursed himself for a fool. "It's the mule that wins the race up the mountain," he muttered to himself, "not the dancing pony."

Sukharam looked at him, confused, but Rabiah answered with a look on her face like a scolded child. "We've pushed too hard. Ushai is calling upon her hezhan steadily, while we burn through ours in too little time. It's easier on the hezhan, easier on her, and in the meantime we exhaust ourselves trying to break away."

They adjusted their approach after that, moving only enough to stay ahead of Ushai, but it was clear it wasn't going to work. They were already exhausted, and the simple act of staying ahead taxed them heavily.

On the morning of their sixth day on the winds, it became too much. The morning was bright, the sky clear. The winds were mild, a welcome thing after the way the skies had tossed them about the last few days. Nasim, exhausted, released his hezhan, allowing Ushai's skiff to approach.

Rabiah's eyes went wide. "Don't give up." She stood and held out her hands. "Let me take over. She'll fail soon. She must." She was young and headstrong and brave, but also unaware of her own limitations.

"*Neh*," Nasim said, more weary than he'd been in years. "I would speak with her."

As the skiff approached, Nasim watched it carefully. He thought there might be others, spelling Ushai from time to time, but there was no one else. When her skiff came even with theirs, Ushai dropped the reins, allowing the sail to billow and flap and the skiff to float freely on the wind. She was a handsome woman with arresting eyes and strong cheeks. The wind blew the sleeves of her dusty yellow robes, and Nasim saw the bracelets there—one with a stone of opal, the other of tourmaline.

For a moment, Ushai and Nasim could only stare at one another. Rabiah watched, her hands flexing. Sukharam looked on, his eyes darting between Nasim, Ushai, and Rabiah.

"You look well," Ushai said, breaking the silence at last.

There was an awkward pause that followed in which they would normally have traded full names, but Nasim did not know his parents. He had no proper name.

"You may call me Nasim an Ashan, daughter of Shahda." It was not something Nasim granted lightly; he had effectively named Ashan his father, but he reasoned that if anyone deserved such a title, it was Ashan.

Ushai nodded, bowing slightly, her face remaining serious. The wind played with her hair and her yellow, travel-worn robes. Her gaze moved over their large skiff. "Where are you going, son of Ashan?"

"I go where I will."

"That isn't what I asked."

"That's the only answer you'll receive. I'll not return to Mirashadal."

Her eyes narrowed. "Is that why you think I've come?"

Nasim paused. "Isn't it?"

She shook her head. "You are old enough now. You may go where the fates take you. Fahroz will not prevent it, but she hopes you will one day return."

"She never said that to me."

"You were young when you were in her care, Nasim. And there were days when you were violent. It was in your best interest to keep you confined to the village until you'd learned more. Had you stayed, she would have told you eventually."

"Had she told me, I might have stayed."

She smiled, though there was a note of melancholy that seemed reluctant to fade. "That is the way of things, isn't it? We learn too late."

"Have you come to invite me back then? All this way for one small missive?"

"*Neh*, son of Ashan. I have come to give you warning. The place you are headed is dangerous."

"And where am I headed?"

"To Ghayavand."

To have it stated so baldly embarrassed him. It made him feel like a child to have someone so sure of his plans. "I go where I will," he said again.

"So you've said, but beware. Ashan has gone before you."

She let the statement hang in the winds between them.

"Ashan?"

She nodded over his shoulder, to the northeast, toward Ghayavand. "We believe he is there still, and if he has not returned by now, there is something amiss."

"How would you know where he went?"

"After he left Duzol, he spoke with few Aramahn ever again. He was only seen five times that we know of, and each time in the most ancient of libraries in Alekeşir and the Towers of Tulandan. We believe he wanted to find the way to Ghayavand, to unlock her secrets or perhaps to prepare the way."

"For what?"

Ushai nodded and steadied herself as the wind bucked her skiff. "For you. He knew you would one day return."

Nasim felt a great urge to look into Rabiah's eyes, but he forced himself to keep his gaze upon Ushai. He had brought Rabiah and Sukharam out of necessity—he couldn't do it on his own, so he had found those most like him: those gifted with the ability to touch Adhiya without stones—but he had hoped to spare Ashan from the same fate. He could not help, and so there was no need to place him in danger.

"Thank you for telling me," Nasim said.

"There is one more gift I will grant you." Ushai pointed northward over Nasim's shoulder. "You'll not find it easy to make your way to Ghayavand. Do not think of crossing by summoning the wind. Take your time, determine the wind, and then, when you're sure you've judged it properly, allow the wind to take you. And if you miss the island, wait until you're well beyond it to try again."

"And if I don't?"

"The wards will rend you apart and throw you to the sea."

"How do you know?" Nasim asked.

"There are clues left from those who survived the tearing of the rift, things gleaned in the years since Oshtoyets."

"Did Fahroz ask you to tell me this?" This seemed like the last kind of information Fahroz would want Nasim to have.

"I am my own woman. I left Mirashadal to follow my own path." Ushai seemed to gather herself before speaking again. "And I would come, son of Ashan, if you would allow it."

"I cannot."

Ushai continued as if nothing had happened. She took in Rabiah and Sukharam again, her expression not condescending, but certainly judgmental. *You cannot make it on your own*, her expression said, *certainly not with the likes of these*. "You are gifted," she finally said. "You are ambitious. Hopefully you have a plan. But you have not lived the life that I have. I can offer you much, Nasim, if only you'll let me."

Rabiah stared at Nasim with something akin to loyalty, letting him know she would support whatever decision he made, but Sukharam looked to Nasim as if he dearly hoped Nasim would take Ushai up on her offer.

Nasim found himself considering it. This had been a difficult journey since leaving Mirashadal, and he'd not yet reached the island. How much more difficult would it become once they touched down on her shores?

But he knew, as he had known since he'd been healed, that he could not allow himself to be clouded by the goals of another. If he had refused Ashan, he would refuse Ushai. And, he told himself, there was something about her—an eagerness he could not quite put his finger on—that he didn't like.

"I cannot," he said simply. "The way is clear before us, and it is a path we will follow alone."

Ushai paused. She was clearly disappointed in his words, so much so that she began to flex her hands. She noticed it shortly after Nasim did, and she composed herself.

"Tell me where you'll be," Nasim said. "I will find you when I'm done. If I'm able."

Ushai's lips drew into a grim line. "I know not where I go. Perhaps I'll find *you*." She smiled, an insincere expression at best. "I've become quite good at it."

Nasim bowed his head. "As you say."

"Go well, Nasim an Ashan."

"Go well, Ushai Kissath al Shahda."

The sky was a cloudless blue, the sea below the bright shade of sapphires in the sun.

Nasim could not yet see Ghayavand, but he could feel it. His time here with Ashan and Nikandr had been one of the more lucid times of his childhood. He remembered much of it, and he remembered the feeling it gave him as well: a feeling of profound discomfort but also of familiarity. This is what he felt now as he manned the reins of the sail and guided their skiff steadily northeastward.

Near high noon, the wind began to play with the ship, causing it to buck. Soon after, Nasim felt a strain on the bond to his hezhan. It became more tenuous, more difficult to maintain. Even so, he managed it until the island came into view, and then it became like fighting a gale.

"It's begun," Nasim said.

Rabiah studied the horizon while holding her gut against the magic Nasim was working with the hezhan. She looked brave. She looked prepared for what lay ahead. Sukharam, on the other hand, was studying the sea ahead while the muscles along his jaw worked feverishly.

"All will be well," Nasim told him.

Sukharam glanced up to Nasim, and then turned his gaze away.

"Look at me, Sukharam."

Sukharam did, though it clearly took him effort to hold Nasim's gaze.

"All will be well," Nasim repeated.

He nodded, putting on a smile that was clearly only for Nasim's benefit, and then he returned to watching Ghayavand, an emerald in a field of sapphires.

Nasim let him be and focused on the path ahead. He was not entirely sure he trusted Ushai and her motives, but he believed in her warning. He told the others to release their hezhan and to refrain from communing with another until they reached the island itself.

He did not release his own, however. It was not yet time. He began to feel his vanahezhan spirit more clearly. It felt *closer*, as if but one small tug would pull it through the veil between worlds. He suppressed the spirit, however, held it at bay while calling it to position the skiff so that the prevailing winds—once he released the havahezhan—would carry them over the island.

It was difficult, though. The winds were unpredictable here. But he could only do the best he could. He released it when he felt the hezhan was too close.

As soon as he did, the ship was tossed about. The skiff dropped suddenly. They held tightly to the ropes that were tied around the interior of the skiff.

A sudden upsurge twisted the skiff, tipped it dangerously. Sukharam was tossed over the edge of the gunwales, but he held on, and Nasim and Rabiah pulled him back to safety.

And then the skiff began to fall once more, spinning about so quickly that Nasim lost his bearings. He was nearly ready to ignore Ushai's advice and call upon a hezhan to help them, but the winds softened and then died altogether.

This was when he began to feel it—a subtle discomfort in his chest that began to grow the closer they came to the island. He began to cough, and soon he was forced to drop to the floor of the skiff and hold onto the thwart as his breath slowly left him in one long exhalation.

"Nasim!" Rabiah cried.

She helped turn him over.

She called to him, but Nasim couldn't hear her. He could only stare up at the blue of the sky.

When Ashan had brought him here years ago, he had *felt* the island. He'd felt the mountain peaks, the forests, the grassy plains. He'd felt the shattered city, Alayazhar. He felt all these things now, but he also knew that he was tied to it like he hadn't been before. He was part of this island, as the Al-Aqim were. He was trapped. There would be no chance of leaving.

He wondered, as stars played in his vision and Rabiah continued to shout his name, why he hadn't felt the same thing the last time. Surely this was Muqallad's doing, or Sariya's, he thought. Surely he hadn't felt it before because the two of them had yet to reawaken from the trap Khamal had lain for them.

But he felt a certain familiarity to this. It was as if he had done it himself…

And then it struck him. The wards that had been in place, keeping Khamal and Sariya and Muqallad here. *That* was what he was feeling. Not a trap laid by the others. Why, then, hadn't it happened the last time he'd come? The answer was obvious, though. He hadn't been himself when he'd been here last. He'd been only half a boy. The other half had been lost in Adhiya. The wards had not sensed him, but he was healed now, and surely whatever had been done to keep Khamal here was now working against him.

He was trapped, well and good. He knew this, but it also brought a sense of peace. He'd come here not planning to leave, but believing it was possible. He knew now that it wasn't. He knew that he would never leave, not unless he healed the rift or he died. It was a notion that was more freeing than he ever would have guessed.

So much so that as the pressure in his chest eased, he started to laugh, and once it started, he couldn't stop.

Rabiah knelt over him, a look of shock on her face, like she wanted to slap him. He wouldn't blame her if she did. He almost wanted her to.

"What's happened?" she asked.

"The wards," he said, pulling himself up to lean against the skiff's hull.

"What about them?" Her eyes narrowed, and she looked at him closely, as if she wasn't sure he was completely himself.

"I'm trapped, Rabiah, as Khamal was. As Sariya and Muqallad are. We are together again, as we were for centuries."

"As *Khamal* was, not you."

"I'm not so sure."

"I don't understand."

"Neither do I." Nasim reached up and scratched his scalp vigorously. It did little to shake the feelings of confusion from his mind, but it brought him back to himself. He realized they were drifting beyond the island. "Summon the winds. Bring us in."

She glanced at the sail, clearly nervous.

"You won't have trouble now. Just be careful not to allow it too close to you."

She nodded. Rabiah. Beautiful Rabiah.

She took up the reins and summoned the wind to guide the ship. They landed on a grassy plain to the north of Alayazhar. Part of him wanted to view the city, but another, the part that was terrified of this place, was simply not ready for it.

As he swung over the gunwale of the skiff and onto solid land, Rabiah rubbed her hand along his back. "We'll find a way."

Rabiah always seemed to know his mind. He looked into her eyes and in them saw compassion and hope, both of which, Nasim thought, were wholly misplaced.

CHAPTER NINE

Nasim debated on building a shelter, but he was afraid to do so, at least until he knew more. The aether was too thin here—so thin that he dared not risk communing with a hezhan again until he and the others had become accustomed to it.

Sukharam left to find firewood, and when he returned with a thick bundle of branches, he told them of the keening he'd heard to the south. "It was haunting," Sukharam said, "like a lone wolf baying for its pack."

Nasim gathered a pile of brown needles from the wood and ran a steel across the flint he'd brought from Trevitze. Sparks flew. On the third strike, it took, and he began building the fire quickly. "It's most likely a dhoshahezhan crossed over from Adhiya."

"Will it be drawn here?" Sukharam asked.

Nasim shook his head as the fire built. "From what I remember, the hezhan are confused here. They'll give chase if you come too close, but they don't search for life as they do from beyond the veil. Here, they have it already, so in a way, they are content."

"In a way?" Rabiah asked as she squatted down on the far side of the fire.

Nasim shrugged, struggling to find words. "They're also conflicted. They want to return to Adhiya, even though they yearned to touch Erahm while there. I think they know this place is not natural. They know this is not the way of things. And they yearn for the freedoms they had while drifting in the currents of the world beyond."

They brought out the blankets from the oiled canvas sacks and laid them out around the fire.

"Where will we go?" Sukharam asked. He was sitting on his blanket, his arms around his knees. Although he had a look of cold discomfort about him, he was staring straight into Nasim's eyes. It was good to see. Perhaps when they'd reached the island, Sukharam had crossed some sort of threshold as well.

Rabiah, lying on her blanket, her head propped up by her hand, stared intently at Nasim as well.

"Tomorrow we go to Alayazhar. There is a celestia on a ridge near the bay. More than anyone's, the celestia was Khamal's. It was his demesne, his source of strength and the place he felt most comfortable. If there was any place he would have left me clues, it would be there."

Sukharam asked more about the island, the last time Nasim had been here, the memories he'd inherited from Khamal; and Nasim did the best he could to appease him, but what Sukharam was looking for wasn't something Nasim could grant. He wanted to know what they would do and how they would do it. These were perfectly reasonable questions. Nasim just didn't know how to answer them.

"We'll know more tomorrow," Nasim finally said. "Get some rest. It will be a long hike to the city and back."

Sukharam eventually fell asleep, but Rabiah stayed awake. The fire played against her dark skin, giving her a ruddy glow that only served to make her look more beautiful than she already was. The flicker of the fire lent depth to her eyes. It made her appear old, like one of the fates, and the way she looked at Nasim made him feel like she could stare right into his soul.

"Are they here?" Rabiah asked.

She meant Sariya and Muqallad, of course. "I can't feel them, if that's what you're asking."

"Did you feel them when you were here last?"

"I did, but I wasn't the same then. This place affected me differently."

"They may have traps set on the celestia."

Nasim nodded. "They very well might have."

"And what of Ashan?" she asked.

The fire between them snapped, sending a cloud of embers floating up and into the night sky. The embers mingled with the stars like gemstones—citrine and diamond against a field of obsidian dust.

"I'm worried that he's been taken," Nasim said, still staring at the sky. "I'm worried they'll use him against us."

Rabiah was silent for a time as she too stared up at the stars. Almadn stood brightly overhead, her amphora overflowing with wine. "You cannot allow it," she said at last. "You can allow nothing to distract you from what needs to be done."

"I know," Nasim lied.

Though he was not at all sure of the answer. Ashan had done much for Nasim. He had cared for Nasim, taken him from Soroush when Soroush was trying to use him. He'd brought him to Uyadensk, where he'd met Nikandr, and he'd guided him from harm when the Landed were out for his blood. He was a man he would do much for, a man he might even die for, if it came to it. So he was not at all sure he could just leave Ashan to the fates if that's where his path led him.

"Even if we're taken," Rabiah continued.

"I know," Nasim lied again. "Now get some sleep."

Rabiah turned away, her back to the fire. She was quiet for a long time. He thought she'd gone to sleep, but then, as he was starting to nod off himself, he heard her say, "I'm glad you found me, Nasim."

"I'm glad I found you, too."

When Nasim finally fell asleep, it was with a warm feeling, a feeling he hadn't felt in a long, long time.

When morning came, the three of them headed north toward Alayazhar. They spoke not at all until they approached the outskirts of the wasted city. They could not yet see the sea and the oldest sections of the city, but there was a complex of broken stone buildings divided only by the streets and avenues and the dark shadows that defined them in the early morning light. Behind them, Sihyaan, the tallest mountain on Ghayavand, stared down at them, ponderous and brooding as if it disapproved of their voyage into a place that had become little more than a grave.

"It cannot be so easy as to go to the celestia and find Khamal's stone," Rabiah said as they took to the first of the streets.

The three of them walked side by side, Rabiah on his left, Sukharam on his right. The sand-colored stones they walked upon were amazingly well preserved. The stones were cracked—making the road look more like a layer of aged skin than cobblestones—but beyond this, other than some moss and the occasional tuft of wiry grass, it looked as though the sundering had occurred a dozen years before, not three hundred.

"I didn't say it would be easy."

"Khamal's piece of the Atalayina will be hidden and trapped," Rabiah continued.

"I'm sure you're right."

"Then how will we retrieve it?"

Sukharam watched Nasim carefully for his answer.

"We will see what we will see," Nasim replied. "My hope is that Khamal prepared for this. He must have, or how could he have expected me to finish what he began?"

Rabiah pressed. "What if he didn't have time to complete it?"

"He must have."

"What if he didn't?"

"He did."

"You can't be sure."

"I know, Rabiah. I know. The best I can do is go and hope that Khamal has prepared the way."

Rabiah was not pleased with the answer. Neither was he, but it was the best he could do. Nasim could tell that Sukharam was uncomfortable with this exchange. He wanted more assurance that what they were doing was the right thing. Nasim wanted it as well, but the cold truth was they had no such thing. They would have to move forward and learn as they went, trusting to the fates to protect them.

They approached an arcing stone bridge that crossed a clear stream. Part of it had collapsed, forcing them to walk single file to cross over it. As they continued on, they reached a section of the city that was markedly older, where the buildings were more densely packed. They were also taller, more grand, and in general their state of decay was greater.

It reminded him of his walk with Ashan and Nikandr and Pietr as he guided them through the maze of akhoz toward Sariya's tower. He half expected Ashan to step out from behind one of the buildings, to call out to them on the road, but of course he did not. Ashan was here—he could feel it—but not close. He only hoped that something hadn't happened to him.

He could sense the akhoz. They were hidden among the broken buildings, wandering, stalking, living out their miserable lives in this forgotten place. The feeling was not nearly so strong as it had been. Perhaps it was another symptom of the effect Nikandr's soulstone had had on him, or perhaps it was because he was now more distanced from Adhiya; whatever the reason, he could not tell where they were, or how close, only that they were here.

Soon they crested a hill, and below them, spread like a grand quilt before the bright blue waters of the bay, was the old city, the original settlement that had been rebuilt to contain the grandest structures. Near the bay was the white tower, Sariya's tower, and though the magic of its presence had largely dissipated, the tower itself seemed whole. Pristine. This was the place Sariya had focused all of her energies over the final decades of her time here on Ghayavand. It was there that Nasim might find answers, but it was not a place he would go.

Not yet.

He looked further up the ridge that ran along the water's edge. There, on a hill overlooking the city, was the tall dome of the celestia, the place Khamal went most often to take breath. As he raised his arm to point toward the celestia, a long call like the baying of a mule only infinitely more disturbing came from one of the nearby streets.

Rabiah shot nervous glances between Nasim and the city. Sukharam looked as if he were ready to turn and run back over the hill, but to his credit, he pulled himself up and waited.

"The akhoz," Nasim said. "They are the lost, the forgotten, and they will try to prevent us from entering the city."

"What *are* they?" Sukharam asked.

"They've been here since the sundering. I saw them when I was here last, and in my dreams ever since. They are part of the riddle of this place. It may be that in the end we will have to find the answer to that question before we can leave. At the very least we need to know how to move past them, for if they find us they will surely attack."

"How did the arqesh move through the city?"

"I don't know, but I can tell you how *I* did it when I was here last. The best way I can put it is that I slipped deeper into Adhiya. Come, I'll teach you."

He strode forward, keeping a careful eye out for the akhoz, but when he turned back he saw that Rabiah hadn't moved. She was a brave girl—braver than she ought to be at times—but this was too much even for her.

"We'll be careful. We won't go far. Not today."

She nodded, though not before visibly gathering her courage.

Together, the three of them made their way deeper into the city. As they walked, Nasim felt for the veil, felt for the world beyond. It was easy to do here, as easy as sensing the direction of the sun by the warmth it left on the skin.

"Can you sense it?" Nasim asked Sukharam. "Adhiya?"

"*Neh.*"

Nasim touched his shoulder. He felt Sukharam jump, but then he calmed down, and his breathing slowed. "Don't try so hard. It's much easier than you expect, and most likely you're looking beyond it."

They walked in silence for a time, and as they did Nasim pulled Adhiya closer, used it to envelop them as he had done for Ashan and Nikandr and Pietr. He could feel the akhoz now. They, like he had been, were creatures of two worlds, but their senses were largely attuned to Erahm, the physical world. By drawing the three of them deeper into the world of the spirits, he was able to skirt their perceptions.

Or so he thought.

The one nearest, the one that had called not long ago, moved toward them. It was already close, and now it was running.

Nasim pointed to an open doorway. "Inside, quickly."

And then he felt the others. How many more, he couldn't tell, but they were going to be on them in moments.

As they ducked inside the ruined stone home, Nasim touched Adhiya through Rabiah, preparing to defend them against the akhoz. Rabiah stared, eyes wide, though she seemed to have found some hidden source of resolve. Sukharam, however, was petrified. He moved to the corner of the room and hid his head between his knees. He shivered there, and a sad whimper escaped him each time he released his breath.

Rabiah turned to go to him, but Nasim held her arm and shook his head.

Crouching down, the two of them watched over the stone lip of the windowsill. Several buildings away, a girl of ten or eleven ran out into the street. She was naked, her skin ashen. She dropped to all fours, chest heaving, head swinging back and forth. The skin of her eyes had grown over, making her look like some grotesque creature made from clay, not someone who once had been a normal girl—a daughter or a sister.

Then came another akhoz, further down the street, this one a boy, a few years older than the girl. He approached in a feral crouch, his lips pulled back, revealing blackened teeth. The area where his nose had been was now nearly flat, the nostrils more like a frog's than a boy's. There was an intelligence in his gait and in the way he studied the girl, as if he had returned, at least somewhat, to the thinking, reasoning boy he had once been.

The girl backed away, clearly exhausted. The boy stalked forward, as if he had paced himself carefully in order to have reserves while his prey spent herself.

Rabiah squeezed Nasim's arm. She nodded to an alleyway close to their hiding spot. Another boy stepped out from the shadows, padding silently along. His left arm was bleeding from a deep, blackened wound along his shoulder. His left hand hung limp, and he favored that side as he walked. In his other hand he held a curving, rusted khanjar.

He was close now, but the girl sensed him. She turned and screamed, releasing a blast of fire from her mouth as she did so.

Her attackers rushed forward. The one with the knife leapt onto her. They tousled on the ground like rabid dogs. The knife was held at bay momentarily, until the other attacker reached them. Together, they pinned the girl down, and then the knife was drawn across the girl's throat.

Black blood oozed from the wound. Slowly, the girl lost strength and fell slack against the stones and the yellow grass that grew between the cracks.

Nasim didn't understand why they would be fighting. The akhoz protected the city; they worked together, or at the very least didn't fight with one another. Why would they have attacked?

Before any sort of answer could come, the akhoz with the khanjar used it to hew at the chest of the girl. The boy seemed to be taking great care. Nasim had difficulty watching the gruesome act, but also found it impossible to look away.

When the cut was wide enough, the boy reached into the girl's chest and with one more series of sawing motions, pulled out her heart. Then he stood, arms akimbo and blackened with blood, while scanning the empty windows of the nearby homes.

He paused and turned toward Nasim.

Nasim froze, ducking further into the corner of the opening. The akhoz watched, head swiveling. Nasim thought surely he would run toward them, would attack, would use the knife to cut his heart from his chest and claim it as some bauble he would hide away with dozens of others he'd collected.

But then the misshapen boy turned and after the release of one last heavy grunt began jogging northward toward the center of the city. The other followed a moment later, leaving them alone and shaken.

When Nasim could feel them no more, he left the home and treaded toward the body of the girl. Her chest was still wide, revealing its blackened interior. She was smaller than he had guessed, but this close she was grotesque, not just her form, but the putrid smell and the sickening way the sun shone from her dull, gray skin.

Behind him, Rabiah approached. Sukharam was behind her, but he stopped when he came within ten paces. He looked about the city, to the blue waters of the bay, anywhere but at the akhoz that lay at Nasim's feet.

"What happened?" Rabiah asked.

Nasim shrugged, unable to do anything but stare downward at this miserable thing. Perhaps it was better for her now that she was dead. But then he looked to her chest. "Why her heart?" he asked, more to himself than to Rabiah.

"Perhaps with Sariya and Muqallad gone, they've devolved into savagery."

"That was not savage," Nasim said. "That was filled with intent."

CHAPTER TEN

Nikandr stood at the bow of the *Chaika*, watching the black shape on the horizon for any signs of movement.

The *Chaika* had two masts above deck, in the starward direction, and two below, in the seaward. One more ran windward and another landward, bringing her total to six. She carried only one gun to the fore. The keel—comprised of the obsidian cores that ran through the center of the mainmasts and guided her along the ley lines—was too delicate for more cannons to be mounted, but she was light and spry, perfect for what Nikandr had planned.

For now, though, while they waited for news from the other ship, her sails were tucked in.

Nearly an hour later, well beyond the time they had agreed upon, a black rook winged across the bow of the ship and landed with a beating of wings on the perch that stood near the ship's helm. It was Vikra, Atiana's favorite.

"The *Strovya* is ready," Vikra said in a ragged voice.

The *Strovya* was their second ship, a stout, six-masted cutter. It had been sent ahead in preparation for their pending mission.

"Set sail," Nikandr said to Jonis, the ship's boatswain.

The sun had recently set, but the western sky still lit the masts above. Three large sails were unfurled along each of the two starward masts, while more crewmen did the same with the seaward masts below the ship. The headsail, which curved gracefully down from the mainmast to the bowsprit, was unfurled next, and finally the sails along the lone masts to landward and windward were set, and soon the ship was picking up good speed, making headway against the ley lines caught by the keel, which slowed the ship in a way not dissimilar from the sea against the hull of a waterborne ship.

Jonis returned to the helm when this was complete, snapping his heels together and bowing his head to Nikandr.

Nikandr nodded to him. "Light the lanterns and ring the bell."

As a dozen lanterns were lit and hung from hooks about the fore of the ship, Nikandr watched Vikra flap her wings from the corner of his eye. He had thought of asking Atiana to send another of the Matri to stand in her place—perhaps Nikandr's own mother, Saphia, or Atiana's sister, Mileva—but in the end he'd decided against it. Atiana knew his purpose already, and he didn't wish to explain any more than was needed. To anyone. They would finish this together, and Atiana could go where she wished.

Part of him hoped she would speak—the same part that desperately wanted to apologize to her for what he'd said on Ivosladna—but another part of him thought it just as well that the two of them were silent. Somehow it felt proper, for really there was nothing else to say. They'd both made up their minds. She was doing what she thought was right for the Grand Duchy, as was he. They were simply going about it in completely different ways.

One of his windsmen began ringing the *Chaika's* brass bell over and over, alerting the Aramahn to their presence.

The dark shape ahead was the floating village of Mirashadal. He could only see its silhouette from this distance, but it looked like an overturned wine decanter, circular at the top with a long tower hanging down from its center. When they came within a league of it, two skiffs floated up and away from the dark shape and approached the *Chaika*. It took little time for them to reach the ship. When they did, one stayed well back while the other approached. An Aramahn woman stood at the bow holding a siraj stone that gave off a rose-tinted glow. The stone of alabaster upon her brow glowed dully. She stared at Nikandr with a look of disdain.

Not so different from the stares of the Maharraht, Nikandr thought.

"State your name and your business in Mirashadal."

"I am Nikandr Iaroslov Khalakovo, and I have come to speak with Fahroz Bashar al Lilliah."

"You have come to a place where you're not welcome, son of Iaros. She will not see you."

"I thought all were welcome among the villages."

"That may once have been true, but we find ourselves in difficult times."

"Tell her I've come. She'll wish to speak with me."

She studied Nikandr for a time, and Nikandr thought he'd misjudged her, that she would simply refuse his request, but then she nodded to her dhoshaqiram, a man who sat at the base of the skiff's mast. "Come no closer," she said, and then they were off.

The second skiff remained, watching from a good distance as Nikandr ordered the sails pulled in. Then they waited, the *Chaika*, the skiff, and the dark shape in the distance all drifting on the wind like clouds.

Nearly an hour later, the skiff returned. It was the same woman, and her expression was even more dour. "Come."

They followed, heading toward the village as it loomed larger and larger. Nikandr had heard stories—stories that told of how large Mirashadal was—but none of them had done it justice. The closer they came, the more it struck him how massive the village was. It was the largest windborne structure Nikandr had ever seen. Elegant, rounded shapes, each as large as a windship, were connected by walkways. It seemed frail in some ways, but that certainly wasn't the case—nothing this size could withstand the gales of the open sea without a supremely rigid structure.

No sooner had the thought arrived than a ripple ran through the village like the endless swell of the sea. The structure gave, but it was strong as well, not unlike the canopies of the windwood forests of Uyadensk. The bulk of the village was patterned like the delicate tendrils of a windborne seed. Indeed, below the massive structure was an inverted tower that hung down toward the sea—ballast, in effect, but to call it so was to make it crude, and this was anything but crude. It was beautiful.

Fanning outward from the edge of the village were dozens of windship berths. Some were quite small—made for skiffs and the like—but others were large, for ships like the *Chaika*. Standing at the end of the berth they were being led toward were a handful of Aramahn—many of the stones in their circlets glowing softly in the bare light—and at their head stood Fahroz.

As the ship's mooring ropes brought the *Chaika* snug against the berth, Nikandr leapt down from the gunwales to land on the deck. It didn't sound like cut and cured wood. Rather it felt as if the wood itself were living, as if the entire structure of the village had been *grown* instead of built.

Fahroz, lit by soft siraj lanterns held by the other Aramahn, stepped forward. She wore no stone, but instead a golden chain with a delicate medallion. It glinted in the pale light of the stones, and Nikandr wondered, as he had before, how she had come by it and who had crafted it.

"Welcome, son of Iaros," Fahroz said, bowing her head.

"And you, daughter of Lilliah, though I wonder how heartfelt your words of welcome are."

She motioned Nikandr to follow her, and they fell into step beside one another, their footsteps sounding dully against the living wood of the perch. None of the Aramahn who had stood with Fahroz accompanied them, and soon they were alone, like two old friends catching up on one another's lives.

"I will admit to a certain amount of alarm."

"Only a few of us know of the village. Trust in me that it will be kept secret."

"Trust in you..."

"Is there another option?"

She motioned him down a winding set of stairs. They descended into the village, and soon they were among so many boughs and branches that he felt as if he were walking on solid ground, not floating in the dark northern skies.

They came to a structure that looked more like the trunk of a massive cypress than it did something man-made. Inside was a cozy home, a bed with a wash basin to one side of the rounded interior, a bureau and mirror made from deeply grained wood on another. Three low chairs surrounded a stone-rimmed pit filled with several of the glowing siraj stones.

Fahroz motioned Nikandr to sit in one of the chairs. When he had seated himself she moved to a stout mantle cluttered with books and bric-a-brac and a few bottles of liquor. She took down a small shisha with two breathing tubes. After filling the bowl with a healthy pinch of tabbaq, she lit it and set it between her chair and Nikandr's. As Nikandr took a healthy pull from the mouthpiece, Fahroz sat and did the same. For a moment, the only sound was the soft bubbling of the water in the clear glass base of the shisha.

"Please," she said, blowing the smoke up toward the ceiling. "You must have been preparing your words for some time."

He smiled. "In truth, I still don't know where to begin."

"You've come for Nasim."

He nodded, taking one more breath from the sweet-tasting tabbaq before releasing it slowly. "In part, but there's much more for us to discuss."

She looked at him seriously then, as if the first of her guards had been lowered, however tentatively.

"I knew after the incident on Duzol that I would leave Khalakovo," Nikandr continued. "Two years after I last saw you, I took to the winds with my mother and brother's blessing."

Her eyes smoldered under the ruddy light of the stones. "The Duke of Khalakovo did not object?"

Nikandr was surprised to see how much the words stung. Borund still sat on the throne in Radiskoye, exactly as Mother had predicted. Vostroma had delayed, they had made excuses, had made demands, anything to keep Khalakovo beneath their heel, but the strangest part of it had been the knowledge that Father had accepted it. He had gone to Vostroma, in effect a thrall of Zhabyn, the Grand Duke. But Zhabyn, despite his initial reluctance to trust Father, had eventually come to value his advice, especially as the blight had continued to put pressure on Vostroma and the other southern duchies. And father had taken to his role, in effect supplanting Leonid Dhalingrad as Zhabyn's most trusted advisor. And every time Ranos or Nikandr had brought up the need to pressure Zhabyn to return the throne to the Khalakovos, Father had demurred, saying only that the time was not right.

"I go where I will," Nikandr said. "The son of Vostroma has no sway over me."

"And where have the winds taken you?"

"It isn't where I've gone, but what I've found while there. The rifts have continued to surface, though none with such strength as the one on Uyadensk and Duzol. I've studied them. I can *feel* them. I know when they wax and when they wane. I can even find the places where they might be closed, if only I had the means."

He left the words there, hanging between them.

"Nasim has been lost to you. To all of you. You have no right to him anymore."

"He is part of me, Fahroz, and I am part of him. There is no separating us."

She swallowed. Nikandr hoped it was a sign that her resolve was flagging, but her eyes were as hard as they had been in the courtyard of Oshtoyets when she'd taken Nasim away. "It is a bond I wish I could break, but believe me when I say it is one you will no longer be able to leverage. We have burned you from him as well as we can, and fates willing, you will never see him again."

Nikandr allowed some of his annoyance to show. "We don't work at cross-purposes, you and I."

"It isn't your purpose I question, but the means you'll use to achieve it."

"I only wish to heal."

"And in your blindness you'll burn in order to do it."

Nikandr sat forward in his chair, setting shisha tube into its holder. "It is not I who am blind. Nasim must be taught."

Fahroz stared into the siraj stones, pausing, as if she were asking herself why she was doing this, and then she set her tube aside as if it had offended her. "Nasim *has* been taught, and now that he has, his teachings will guide him." There was pride both in her words and in her eyes. "He will be great, an arqesh among arqesh."

"The arqesh are not infallible."

Fahroz stood, quickly but calmly, her hands clasped together. It was an insult, what he'd just said, a reference to the three arqesh—the Al-Aqim—that had ripped the world asunder on the island of Ghayavand: Muqallad, Sariya, and Khamal, the man that passed his memories on to Nasim. "I am sorry you have come so far to receive so little, but there is nothing I can do."

Nikandr remained seated. "In truth, I knew there was little chance you would speak to me of Nasim's whereabouts."

"And yet you still came."

"Because there is more," Nikandr continued. "I mentioned the rifts, how they have until now been of no great strength, but there is another forming.

On Rafsuhan."

Nikandr watched her closely. She masked her response well, but it was there: surprise, followed immediately by the realization of his true goal here. But she held her tongue. She didn't want Nikandr to know that Soroush was here within this very village, only a short distance below in one of the lowest rooms of the ballast tower.

Nikandr fought to hide secrets of his own, however. The *Chaika* was lashed to the village and would be receiving all the attention of Mirashadal, but by now the *Strovya* would have reached the tower, and Anahid, his best dhoshaqiram, would have begun warping the living wood that kept Soroush imprisoned. Atiana was to signal him when they were done, but so far he'd heard nothing. He needed to give them more time.

"I know he's here, Fahroz. Give him to me. If I am to study the rift, I will need him."

Fahroz looked at him as if he'd gone daft. "He will kill you the moment he lays eyes on you."

"It isn't just his land that's at stake now. It's his people."

"They care nothing for the land. They will take to the winds, as they always have."

"I don't think so. They're rooted to Rafsuhan and Muhraban like never before, and Soroush knows it. He will not wish to see his people die. You do not wish it, either. You can make a difference for them, Fahroz. Don't let Erahm swallow them whole."

"The fates will do as they will!" She practically shouted the words, but in the ensuing silence she stared into Nikandr's eyes, chest heaving with breath, perhaps considering his words.

And then a bell began to ring, over and over. It was not from the *Chaika*. Someone had discovered them.

Fahroz ran to the door. "Stay where you are," she said to Nikandr as he stood. She put herself in the doorway as he approached.

"I must leave, Fahroz."

Her eyes were filled with a rage that had been pent up for years, but there was something else: the realization that she had been betrayed. He had always liked Fahroz, even respected her despite her rigidness—or perhaps because of it—and it pained him that it had come to this, but he knew she would never have given up Nasim or Soroush.

"You would *steal* from this village? I thought you different from your fathers, Nikandr, or I never would have allowed you to step foot onto Mirashadal."

"Soroush is not yours to keep. He is Erahm's." Nikandr took a step closer. "Now let me pass."

"I will not."

He tried to push past her. She resisted, but she was not a strong woman. Nikandr was soon past her and onto the walkway, but it made him feel small, smaller than he had felt in years.

There was nothing to do about it now. He rushed through the village and up toward the perch where the *Chaika* waited for him. More bells rang throughout the village.

He moved as quickly as he could, especially when the wind began to gust. Despite the cold, the air was becoming oppressively humid.

He flew up the winding stairs to the *Chaika's* perch. The winds at the top of the stairs blew so fiercely that he was nearly swept off his feet.

The perch he'd left a short time ago stood before him. Frost rimed the end of it, where two qiram stood, both of them facing out toward the sea. Two other Aramahn men stood to the side of the perch where the ship had been moored, each holding a curved knife.

And the *Chaika*...

The *Chaika* was nowhere to be seen.

CHAPTER ELEVEN

Nikandr's heart pounded as he searched the skies for his ship.

The two Aramahn with the knives approached him, but as they did they slid the knives into sheaths at their belts. They would not harm Nikandr—the beliefs they held most dear prevented it—but they could easily prevent him from leaving, and they would hold him if they thought it important to do so.

They had cut the mooring lines so the havaqiram could summon the winds to push the *Chaika* away from the village, far enough that Nikandr couldn't reach it. The jalaqiram standing next to him had probably drenched the ship in water, particularly the cannons and muskets—the lanterns, as well, Nikandr realized, so that he stood no chance of seeing the ship—and with the wind roaring through the village, and the bells ringing, there was no way he could *hear* the ship, either.

Through his chalcedony stone, Nikandr could feel the wind master's bond to his hezhan. He could feel his own as well. It called to him, begged him to draw upon it so that it could experience Erahm through Nikandr. He did so now, combating the winds that were summoned by the Aramahn.

As the wind died down, one of the Aramahn turned and addressed him. "Your ship is gone, son of Iaros. It is best you come with us."

Nikandr didn't know what to do. He searched the skies behind them again, but the dark beyond the siraj stones lining the perch was complete.

Where had the other ship gone? Had it been taken already?

What about Atiana? He hadn't heard her, nor could he feel her through his stone.

The Aramahn came closer. His robes of green and gray whipped about his knees and calves. His face was both serious and sad. "Please. You've done enough this day."

"What I did was necessary."

"You wear cloth over your eyes, and yet you claim to see the stars."

Nikandr looked to the other perches. Few of them had siraj stones, but those that did were achingly empty. He should have come with more ships. He should have come bearing weapons.

Nyet, he told himself. He couldn't have done such a thing, not to people that bore him no ill will, who would refuse to harm him even if he killed one of their own.

He stepped forward, ready to give himself to them, to wait, perhaps, for a ransom. They would not keep him forever...

But then a flapping of wings came. At the edge of the light, far beyond the end of the perch, was a flurry of wings darker than the surrounding sea.

A harsh caw came from Vikra. "Below, Nischka! Below!"

The havaqiram turned and raised his arms. The winds responded with the howl of a gale, blowing the rook end over end and out to sea.

Nikandr ran toward the edge of the perch. The Aramahn moved to intercept him. Nikandr reached it first and stared downward, searching frantically for what Atiana had been referring to.

The Aramahn grabbed his arms, began pulling him back.

He fought desperately, trying to keep himself near the edge.

But they had him, and they dragged him away.

And then he saw it. A glimmer of light, far, far below.

He railed against the Aramahn. They were strong, and there were two of them, but they were hindered by their wish to do no harm, while he was not. After a violent surge in one direction, he sent them off balance. He rushed forward, placing his boot behind one man's leg. The man went down as Nikandr twisted his arm sharply. He punched the other man in the throat and twisted beneath the man's grasp, spilling him awkwardly.

Freed, he sprinted toward the end of the perch. Anything to give him extra distance from the bulk of the village below.

"Do not!" the havaqiram shouted, raising his arms.

Nikandr kept running.

And he leapt.

For a moment the blackness before him simply held, motionless.

And then he was plummeting downward, wind whipping past him, tugging at his hair and clothes. The sound of the wind gained until it was a roar.

He opened his bond to his hezhan, but nothing happened. He continued to plummet, and he wondered when he would meet the sea and his death.

But then the wind responded. It was already rushing past, but now it *pressed* upon him. He could feel himself slowing. He spread his arms wide, and like a gull on the cliffs below the eyrie, he rode the wind southward.

Drawing upon the hezhan to such a degree drained him, as if there were only so much the hezhan could allow before it drew upon *Nikandr* for sustenance. He looked up to orient himself and from the few lights and the simple black immensity of it found the bulk of Mirashadal. He searched for the *Chaika*, squinting against the terrible wind, but could not find it. He tried to gauge how far the ship might have been pushed by the qiram on the perch; he scanned the skies, hoping they had been able to light a lamp, but he saw nothing.

His reserves were beginning to dwindle, and though he gave as much of himself as he could to the hezhan, he soon found himself unable to ascend.

And then he began to fall, slowly at first, but with growing velocity.

He tried one last time to find the *Chaika*, but he knew it was no use. But then, far below him, he found the light he'd seen from the perch. The *Strovya*. The kapitan had been told to remain dark throughout the infiltration and escape, but there it was, a lantern swinging back and forth on the deck.

He used the wind to push himself toward it, allowing himself to fall faster to conserve his strength while guiding himself in the right trajectory. Then, when he came within a hundred paces of the ship, he called upon the hezhan, giving more of himself than he ever had before.

The hezhan responded, but it was too late. He was falling too quickly, and there was nothing he could do.

But then he saw the sails. They were bowed, full of the strong northern winds.

Nikandr pushed himself toward it with his last strength.

He fell into the canvas just below the head of the sail, sliding downward, scraping against the seams, until the sail's wide foot caught him like a butterfly in a net. The sail sprung back and threw him forward. His leg caught against the boom, sending him twisting through the air to land hard against the deck.

He felt something in his ribs give. Stars filled his vision for long moments. He stared upward at the sail that had saved his life and the blackness beyond, wondering at how close he had come to death.

A lantern approached, carried by the ship's young kapitan. He was followed quickly by several crewmen.

"Douse the light," a raucous voice called.

It was the rook, Vikra, giving Nikandr the answer to the question of who had ordered the lantern to be lit.

It came mere moments before he passed out.

Nikandr woke to Syemon, the ship's pilot, who also served as the physic, hovering over him with a cup of vodka, administering it to him slowly. Nikandr coughed and waved the man away, realizing they'd moved him to the kapitan's cabin.

He was beneath a blanket wearing only his small clothes. He tried pulling himself up, but thought better of it when the room started to spin.

"How long?" he asked.

"Only a few hours. You hit the deck hard, My Lord Prince, but not as hard as you might've."

Syemon had a wicked scar that ran across his right eye. The color in his eye had gone nearly white, and it unnerved Nikandr. It made him feel as though the old gull could see right into his soul.

Though the man hardly needed any special insight into Nikandr's abilities with the wind. The men whispered it in their bunks, and it had been passed through the ranks of Khalakovo, first as rumor and then as legend. No one spoke of it openly, and many of them secretly wanted to be with a kapitan that could control the wind; others were wary of it, claiming it wasn't right for a Landed man to touch the wind as the Motherless wizards do.

"Bring Vikra to me."

Syemon bowed his head. "Beg pardon, My Lord Prince, but the rook's gone quiet."

Nikandr nodded, pulling himself up in the bunk. The dizziness returned, but not so bad as before. "Then bring Soroush here."

"My Lord?"

"Go on," Nikandr said, nodding toward the cabin door.

Syemon left with a deep bow, and while Nikandr sat at the edge of the bunk, clearing his head, he heard the sounds of the men on deck, the kapitan calling to the men, the snap of canvas as a sail caught a whorl in the wind.

Outside the cabin door, the sounds of boots on the planking approached, and the door opened with a creak and a groan. Syemon stepped aside and allowed two of the streltsi assigned to the ship to half carry, half drag Soroush into the cabin before tossing him to the floor.

The heavy iron manacles on his arms and legs clinked as he pulled himself off the floor. He wore outer robes of white and inner robes of yellow. His beard was long and unkempt, but other than fresh abrasions along his cheek and jaw, he seemed to be in good health. His turban was gone, however, making him seem lost and alone and frail—qualities Nikandr would never have thought to associate with Soroush. It seemed as though the Aramahn had robbed him of much more than his freedom, but then he stared up at Nikandr, recognition flickered, and his eyes became as cold and piercing as they'd ever been.

"Remove his manacles," Nikandr said, pulling one of the two chairs out from the kapitan's desk and setting it next to Soroush. Syemon hesitated as Nikandr pulled out the other chair and sat in it heavily. "Then leave us."

Syemon bent down, though he appeared hesitant to comply until Soroush held out his hands. Syemon unlocked the manacles, then he bowed and ushered the streltsi out, closing the door behind him.

"Please," Nikandr said in Anuskayan, motioning to the empty chair.

Soroush pulled himself up off the floor slowly. He lowered himself to the seat of the chair, wincing as he went; then he leaned back and regarded Nikandr, nostrils flaring, eyes darting, his long hair and beard rolling down his chest.

For long moments Nikandr could do nothing but stare. He had never truly been alone with Soroush, and it was unnerving, no matter how much he might be in the advantage. This was a man who had orchestrated dozens of deadly attacks on the northern duchies and helped to supply many more in the south. Scores had died at his hands; hundreds had been wounded. And here Nikandr was, sitting in his company as if none of that had ever happened. Nikandr felt the weight of his father on him. He felt like a traitor, as if even *speaking* to Soroush, no matter the cause, was little more than high treason.

And yet they shared a very personal connection. Rehada. They had both loved her, and in her own way she had loved them as well, and if this were true, how could they not share a certain bond, tenuous though it may be?

Soroush must have felt it too, for he was studying Nikandr with something akin to contemplation. Or forbearance. Or mercy. *Mercy.* As if Nikandr might be spared from the judgment he'd long ago meted out to the Landed.

Nikandr took from the shelves above the kapitan's desk a bottle of araq, something he had specifically asked to be placed here for this conversation. He poured two small glasses of the golden red liquid and set one on the desk near Soroush. The other he took back to his seat. He drank a healthy swallow of the bright, sweet liquor, hints of fig and pomegranate washing down his throat. To drink before he'd even formally offered the liquor to the man sitting across from him was considered very rude among the Landless, but Nikandr wanted him to understand the terms under which they were speaking.

Nikandr held his glass high and nodded toward Soroush's. Soroush didn't move, so Nikandr downed the rest of his drink in one swallow, slapped the glass down on the desk, and asked Soroush, "Do you know where I was before you took Nasim from Bolgravya's ship?" He was referring to the time after Ghayavand, after Nasim had awoken. Grigory had hoped to bring Nasim back as a prize for Zhabyn Vostroma, but before he could the Maharraht had found his ship and whisked Nasim up from the deck.

"Have you come so far to ask me of Nasim?" His voice was scratchy, but it had the same liquid timbre he remembered.

"We had just come from Ghayavand. We had bonded—you know this—and together Nasim and I used our bond so that he might be healed, and in doing so heal the rift, just as you were trying to use him to rip it wide."

Soroush stared, his eyes hard.

"I've changed since then," Nikandr continued. "I was sick with the wasting, but then I was healed, and though Nasim was taken away, I still felt him"—he tapped his chest—"here. Ancients willing, I'll feel him again some day, but until then I've taken to the winds, using what Nasim gave me to study the rifts as you once did."

At this Soroush's eyes went wide—only for a moment, but it was there. He looked over Nikandr's shoulder, to the dark cabin windows, where the wind lightly whined. He looked as though he wanted to ask a question, but he kept his mouth closed, his jaw set.

"I know more about the rifts than anyone alive, except for perhaps you. Or Nasim or Ashan. I've found small ones. Large ones. There are webs of them—so many small threads interconnected that it boggles the mind. Did you know that? That they connect to one another?"

Soroush took the glass of araq and took a sip.

"Of course you did. It was why you attacked Duzol instead of Uyadensk. You hoped that by tearing one you would rip open the other, and the others beyond that. Perhaps the whole of the islands would be affected, *da*?"

"Tell me what you're after, son of Iaros, or you can send me back to the hold."

"I've searched for rifts everywhere. Khalakovo, Vostroma, Mirkotsk, Rhavanki." He paused. "Even Rafsuhan."

And here Soroush's eyes sharpened. They became deeply distrustful and he sat straighter in his chair, the legs creaking as he did so.

"*Da*," Nikandr said. "There is a rift on Rafsuhan. Already large, and still growing." He paused again, hoping Soroush's love for his people would overcome his hatred for Nikandr. "It will grow larger than the one on Uyadensk, Soroush. Much larger. I can feel it already."

His hands, still holding the glass in his lap, were shaking. "And you would have me *help* you?"

"The rift is already causing sickness among your people. If you take me there, provide for my protection, perhaps we can learn more of it. Perhaps we can close it."

"You care nothing about them."

Nikandr stared deeply into his eyes. "You will find it hard to believe, but I do, son of Gatha. But it isn't merely about the people of Ashdi en Ghat or Siafyan. The rifts are spreading everywhere. Everywhere. Even as far as the Empire. It will not stop on its own. I know this now. Whether you love the Grand Duchy or you hate it, you must realize that if something isn't done, all of Erahm will suffer."

"If the fates will it, then it will be so."

"It will not stop here. Adhiya will be next. Or perhaps first. Who knows how these things work?"

"If the fates will it…" He left the rest of the proverb unsaid.

"If you believed that, you would never have become Maharraht."

Soroush's jaw clenched. "My people will leave."

Nikandr shook his head. "Some may leave, but you have settled in your cities. Many will stay, and they will suffer. And not only that, it will lead to a burden in their next life. And the one after that. You cannot want this for our world."

Something in him seemed to break then. He breathed out. His jaw unclenched. His eyes softened. "You will not change them."

"Your words are true," he said in Mahndi, using the Landless phrasing.

Soroush sat there, looking at his glass, the araq within golden and inviting. But then the wind picked up again, and it drew his attention. He looked up at the ceiling, or perhaps *past* it to the deck above, and his mood seemed to change. "How were you saved?"

Nikandr shook his head. "What do you mean?"

"You fell to the ship. I heard the men talking. How could you have lived?"

Nikandr thought of lying. He thought of telling him that the havaqiram had harnessed the winds, used them to stop his descent and send him into the ship's sails. But such a thing felt wrong, and he would have to tell Soroush of his newfound abilities at some point.

He reached inside his shirt and pulled out his soulstone necklace. He held it up for Soroush to see. "Nasim left me with another gift as well."

Soroush stared at the chalcedony stone, shaking his head back and forth ever so slightly.

"I can touch Adhiya. I can bond with a hezhan." He twisted the necklace between his fingers, making the stone spin before allowing it to fall against his chest. "I can feel it even now."

"You?" He squinted, incredulous. "A qiram?"

"I do not know what to call it," Nikandr said, unwilling to place that mantle upon his shoulders.

He looked down to his araq, then back to the soulstone. Then he stood and whipped the glass down to the corner. The glass shattered, the liquor splattering against the whitewashed wood. "You think I would help *you*?"

Nikandr rose to meet him.

Soroush reached out to snatch Nikandr's soulstone, but Nikandr grabbed his wrist. Soroush tried again, but he was weak.

And then his other hand shot to Nikandr's neck.

Soroush squeezed as Nikandr fought to pull him away. He finally managed to do so, his fingers raking across Nikandr's throat, as the streltsi stormed in through the cabin door and grabbed Soroush by the arms.

"You think I would help *you*?" He spit on the floor between them. His eyes were crazed. He looked at Nikandr with such hatred, such venom, that if Soroush had been able he would surely have struck Nikandr dead.

Nikandr nodded to the streltsi. They left with Soroush, closing the door behind them, and as the sounds of their retreat diminished, Nikandr continued to stare at the door, his chest heaving with breath.

All as the wind outside howled.

CHAPTER TWELVE

Atiana pulls away from the currents of the north. She still feels Nikandr's stone, bright like a lantern in the fog. He is distant, though, and as she retreats toward Kiravashya, he fades and is lost altogether.

It was painful to witness his fall and near death, not only because she cares for him deeply, but because she feels going to Rafsuhan—with or without Soroush's help—is a fool's errand. But she also understands that Nikandr believes it is the only way to learn more. And, she admits, Nikandr has a way about him of convincing others to follow him, of making them believe he is in the right. If anyone can convince Soroush to help, it will be him.

Before returning home, she stops roughly halfway. To the east is Khalakovo. To the west, and due north of Vostroma, lies the island of Ghayavand. She's tried dozens of times to penetrate the shroud that surrounds it. At first it was nearly impossible to even sense. It felt as though there was simply open sea— no land at all to ground her—but eventually she came to sense its boundaries, and then she tried to move beyond them. Each and every time, however, she was rebuffed. There was something—something very strong—that kept her at bay, far from the shores of the island.

She'd felt something like it once before when the rift on Duzol had been at its widest and Soroush had begun his ritual with Nasim. It felt the same then, as if there were some yawning gash between the worlds that might swallow her whole if she came too close. And yet there was one important difference. Within the keep of Oshtoyets, she was drawn *toward* the rift. Had she wanted to, she surely could have entered it, and who knew what might have happened then? Ghayavand, on the other hand, prevents her from reaching it. There are seals, guards set to protect it from unwanted eyes. Nikandr thinks this is Nasim's doing, or at the very least Khamal's—the arqesh he had once been—but Atiana isn't so sure. She knows Nasim, knows his scent, and there is not a single trace of him in the wards that stand against her.

She tries again to enter Ghayavand. She tries harder than she has in the past. Perhaps if she can sense Nasim, she might be able to convince Nikandr to abandon his plans. But it is not to be. She is rebuffed, as she always is, and she retreats exhausted toward home.

Palotza Galostina is old, the oldest of all the palotzas. She was built and re-built over the course of centuries. The drowning chamber lies a hundred yards below the surface of the cold and bitter landscape. It is toward this chamber that she heads, shifting in the aether, watching the twinkling souls of those with whom she has touched stones. Her father. Mileva and Ishkyna. Aunt Katerina. They are all within the palotza's walls, safe from the elements. But there is something else that attracts her, a shifting of light near the spire, the obsidian tower that she uses to guide the aether as part of her daily regimen.

She wills herself closer.

Against a canvas of midnight blue, near the base of the spire, the aether ripples. Lightning strikes the spire's tip, and it flashes, blinding her momentarily. When her vision clears, she approaches the base. A woman stands there. She wears the dress of an Aramahn, with doeskin boots and long, straight hair.

Atiana cannot hear—the aether is deadly silent—but she can see the woman's mouth moving. She is whispering, mumbling, while staring up and down the length of the spire, as if accounting for its dimensions, its history, its power.

Atiana thinks to assume a rook, to warn the palotza guard, but this woman... There is something about her. Though she hardly seems older than Atiana, she has the look of someone ancient, of someone who long ago came to know the intricacies of the world. Fahroz Bashar al Lilliah possesses some of these same qualities, but even she pales in comparison to this woman.

The woman is arqesh. Atiana knows this. But for some reason there seems to be little peace within her.

The woman continues to stare as a storm rages over the island. Lightning strikes again, and she turns her head. She looks toward Atiana, not directly, but close enough that Atiana fears she has been discovered. The woman cannot harm her, and yet she fears for her life just the same.

Atiana moves quickly toward the closest of their rooks, Zoya. Assuming the rooks is second nature, especially at times like this when she's lost any sense of her own body. As she slips into the rook's form, Atiana extends Zoya's wings, she flexes her talons and inherits her sharp eyes.

Zoya fights. She caws. She stands upon a golden perch near the base of the palotza's curving grand stairwell and struggles to retain herself while pumping her wings and hopping along the length of the perch.

But Atiana soon wins. After two quick beats of her wings, Atiana launches herself from the perch, flapping and gliding toward the far end of the hall.

She lands at the feet of the two streltsi who guard the door.

"Open it," she says.

"At once, Matra."

Soon she is out in the driving rain. She flaps hard to gain altitude, to crest the ridge that runs near the palotza grounds, and then she's off, winging hard toward the spire.

She hears the rain now, and when lightning strikes, branching in the sky before her, she hears the thunder, feels it in her chest and talons and wings.

She searches for the woman, but cannot find her.

She caws, the rook momentarily regaining control as her emotions run high. She regains control and circles the spire. She caws again and again as she searches the grounds frantically.

In the end, however, she searches in vain.

The woman is gone.

The next day, after recovering from her turn in the drowning basin, Atiana took to the halls of Galostina, striding with purpose toward Bahett's apartments. She thought at first she would take to the palotza's hidden passages, to keep prying eyes from knowing her business, but the more she thought about it, the more the idea irked her. This was her home, and if she wished to speak with the man she had chosen to marry, she would walk in the open, head held high, and meet him face-to-face.

At the tall, arched entrance to the wing Bahett and his entire retinue had been given, two Yrstanlan janissaries wearing burgundy coats and tall white turbans bowed their heads. They said not a word, making Atiana wonder what they'd been told. Did they think her little more than his wife already? And if *they* knew, who else knew? Did Bahett think her some sort of servant? A woman to be beckoned when he willed it?

She stopped for a moment, and nearly turned around.

How dare he!

But she knew she couldn't turn away. The way in which he'd left the message made her think that perhaps the Kamarisi's position was not so strong as everyone seemed to think.

Gritting her teeth, she bowed to the janissaries and continued to his apartments. When she arrived, two more guardsmen bowed respectfully. They showed no hint of amusement on their faces, and one opened the door for her respectfully. She entered and found Bahett sitting at the same desk she'd spied him at two nights earlier.

Two women, wearing the loose, flowing clothes popular in the center of the Empire, stood as Atiana entered the room. They bowed and backed out to another room, closing the door behind them.

Bahett continued to write in his journal, completely ignoring her, as if she'd already become part of his harem.

"Do you wish me to leave, My Lord?"

He shivered as he turned toward her—perhaps confused at finding someone other than his servants standing in his room—but then he smiled. After setting aside his quill, he stood and bowed low to her. "Please, forgive me. I was lost in thought."

"So I take it."

He paused, unsure how to proceed for a moment, but then he motioned her to the place the two women had just vacated, a vast pile of pillows with palettes of amber and crimson and persimmon. Atiana found them still warm, which was like a nettle beneath her backside. Only when she'd sat did he turn to a cart filled with liquor and pour two glasses of what looked to be raki.

She took the heavy, leaded glass he offered and sipped from it while he poured his own. The taste was not so different from araq, the liquor the Aramahn favored so much, though it was stronger, more filled with smoke and the spices of anise and clove. "How did you know when I was taking the dark?"

He fell into the pillows across from her and took a healthy swallow of his own drink. "In truth I didn't, but your sisters are not so easy to miss—Ishkyna especially—and there are few other Matri to account for."

She stared down at him, lying there as if he was fully expecting to bed her once the drinks were done and the foreplay of conversation was over.

He caught her look, and then stared at the pillows.

And then he laughed.

"We can get chairs if you like, sit on opposite sides of the room..."

She felt her face burn. "We're not accustomed to such behavior."

"The islands are cold, Atiana, but the blood of the Landed runs hot. Do we have to pretend it does not?"

"Chambermaids may be lulled by your beauty, Bahett"—she set her glass on the travertine floor nearby—"but believe me when I say that I am not." She stood, but he reached out and grabbed her wrist, preventing her from rising.

"Please," he said, rising in one smooth motion to sit cross-legged on a pillow the color of coral. "There are important things to discuss."

Slowly, so as not to offend, she pried his hand from her wrist, but she remained where she was. His face was earnest. There was even a note of panic in his eyes. If there were even a chance it was important to Vostroma and the Grand Duchy, she would hear it.

"Thank you," he said, situating himself as if it pained him to sit upright.

She motioned for him to continue with a nod of her head. "Please."

"The Grand Duchy is headed for difficult times—even more difficult than she's had over these past many years." He paused for effect. "Her coffers are low. Her shoals offer fewer and fewer fish. Her fields are worse, and her people, let's face it, have begun to starve—"

Atiana found herself seething at these words. "Her people are strong and her ships mighty. Her will is indomitable."

"Conceded, daughter of Radia, but she cannot stand forever, not without the help of the Empire."

"Your point?"

"My point is to make you painfully aware of your position, because—trust in me—the Kamarisi is *very* aware."

Atiana paused, choosing her words carefully. "The Kamarisi has been our ally since he came to power, as had his father and his father's father before him. We aided Yrstanla when the hordes in the hills stood at the doorstep of Alekeşir herself. We traded her stones and windwood when we had no need to do so. Power rises and falls, Bahett. Better to weather the storm with an ally than to brave it alone."

"Your words are pure gold," he said, bowing his head, "but I fear the Kamarisi will never listen to them."

"Then your words smack of either betrayal or deception, both of which would lead to the gibbet were I to share this conversation with my father."

For the first time since the conversation began, fire lit within Bahett's eyes. "I do not lie, Atiana, and I am fiercely loyal to the Kamarisi."

"Then explain yourself."

"When I am done, you will be left with a choice, but whatever you decide, you cannot tell anyone. It would bring ruin on us all." His eyes bore into her, and he paused to let the words sink in. "On us *all*, Atiana. Do I have your word?"

"If it does not leave me betraying my own family, I will keep our words between us."

This seemed to appease him, for he nodded and continued. "A year ago a woman came into the Kamarisi's harem. She was beautiful, as are they all, but she was of the Aramahn."

Atiana could not help but think of Rehada, a woman she had loathed, but had somehow—through everything that had happened on Khalakovo—come to respect.

"There was power within her," Bahett continued. "Everyone could see it. I think it's why the Kamarisi agreed to keep her, even after she exhibited these qualities."

"He doesn't keep qiram?"

"He does not. In the past, it has led to … regrettable circumstances. But no matter. The Kamarisi kept her, and she rose in favor. She went to him often, and even began to accompany him on official functions. The Kamarisi made the decision to come to Galahesh this month, and the woman, Arvaneh, has joined him while the ilkadin remains in Alekeşir."

Atiana raised her brows. Traveling to a place where treaties of such import might be signed was the place of the ilkadin, the Kamarisi's first wife, who was by all accounts an exacting mistress. Word had reached even the islands of the ruthless ways in which she defended her authority. Women of the harem had been whipped and scarred; some had even been found floating in the muddy waters of the Vünkal, their bodies ravaged, all for overstepping their bounds. Influence, indeed, if Arvaneh had begun to supplant her in even the smallest of ways.

"He has spoken to me of his intent. He will discuss the treaties your father and I and Sihaş may draft in the coming days. He may even sign it. But then he will come, with all the power that can be spared, and he will take the islands back."

"He will not win."

Bahett was already shaking his head. "Remember how this conversation began, Atiana. He will win. Have no doubt about this."

"Then again, I ask you, why would you reveal this to me?"

"Because the Kamarisi is not himself. He has been taken by this woman. As has the ilkadin. As have his generals."

"And why not you?"

He raised his thin eyebrows. "Have you not noticed that the Kamarisi has sent his own man to the proceedings? He no longer trusts me. Or *she* doesn't. Either way, I will soon be left out in the wind while the lion's share of the negotiations are given to Sihaş."

"You still have considerable power, Bahett. You would not be here if you didn't."

He shrugged. "Perhaps I do. Perhaps I do not. What I do know is this: if the Kamarisi comes for the Grand Duchy, he will win, but in doing so we will give up his hold on the west. The Haelish have been massing again, and this time, with so much being diverted toward the taking of the islands, we will be overrun."

"Is the Empire so fragile?"

"I would not put it so bluntly. Our resources are considerable, but they have also been drained for decades. We cannot sustain two wars along with our other, tenuous borders. Not now."

"Then why would the Kamarisi do it?"

"Have you not been listening? It is Arvaneh. She has taken hold of him. His will, his mind. It is not *his* desires that drive him, but *hers*, and she has decided that she wants these islands—for what purpose I do not know. The point is that she does, and she doesn't care what happens to Yrstanla as long as she gets it. And I tell you this as well: it was Arvaneh, not the Kamarisi, who wanted the bridge built over the straits."

"The Spar?" Atiana asked. "Why would she care that a bridge is built over the Straits of Galahesh?"

"She takes no council with me, Atiana."

"Then what would you have of me?"

"Come to Galahesh. In Baressa you will be well watched, but there is a place... I have had a drowning chamber made there." He paused. "For you."

"You would have me *spy* on them for you?"

The hint of a smile came to his lips, quickly hidden. "Would you not have done so long ago had you had the power?"

He was speaking, of course, of her inability to tread close to, or beyond, the straits. She and all the Matri before her—for generations—had wished to watch over Galahesh, but it was simply not possible, not without risking one's life in doing so. But if she were there, in Baressa, the distance she would need to travel in the aether would be greatly reduced. It might work. At the very least, it was worth the attempt.

"What do you wish to know? Specifically."

"I wish to understand her nature."

"Before you have her killed?"

He did not answer, but his eyes—the color of a rich bay stallion—were deadly serious.

Atiana was already shaking her head. "There are a dozen others you could find who would be better suited."

"I wish it were so, Atiana, but it is not. The few who see things as I do are too afraid. The rest are either too loyal to the Kamarisi or they are powerless to oppose him."

Atiana stared into his eyes, trying to weigh the truth in his words. There was no doubt that in time the Kamarisi could crush the Grand Duchy if he so chose. What did it matter to her, or Father, if Yrstanla was in turn done in by his ambitions?

"Did you not tell me," Bahett continued, "that were Bahett ül Kirdhash to whisper in your ear, you would listen? Well, I'm whispering now, Atiana, none too softly."

She considered for only a moment longer. "I will go with you to Baressa, and we will see what this Arvaneh is about."

CHAPTER THIRTEEN

Ten days later, Atiana watched from the deck of her Father's windship as the city of Baressa came into view. She had been to the city a half-dozen times, but never from the air. She'd insisted over the kapitan's protestations that it was too dangerous.

"I will soon live here, Kapitan," she'd said. "I will see it from a ship before that happens."

The kapitan had grudgingly agreed, but had told her that they could not come too near the straits, and if any sort of wind picked up, he'd take the ship back to the eyrie at the southern end of the island straight away.

Baressa was massive, much larger than Evochka, which was the largest city in not just Vostroma but the entire Grand Duchy. It wasn't surprising. Baressa was three centuries older than Evochka. One could still see the mix of architecture that had developed over the years—squat stone manses near the Mount, the spiraling minarets of Kasir Yalidoz, the sprawl of the bazaar with her rows and rows of tents and ramshackle buildings. As large and as populous as the city was, there was still one section to the southwest that remained a gutted husk of what it once was—a reminder from the War of Seven Seas, the Grand Duchy's twenty-year war of secession with Yrstanla. Why the line of the Kamarisi had never replaced it was anyone's guess, though if Atiana had to guess she would say that it was an indicator of their penchant for draining their coffers for the wars they waged in the west.

Beyond the city—barely visible from this distance—was a jagged line that bisected the island. The line revealed the ivory cliffs of the straits. To Atiana it looked like the island had ripped, half of it striving to remain with the Empire, the other half reaching for the Grand Duchy. It was not so far from the truth. Many on Galahesh had family and interests on both the continent and the islands.

Behind her, the old kapitan approached. "This is as close as we dare, My

Lady Princess."

"It's close enough," Atiana replied.

They were still several leagues from the straits, but the kapitan was worried over the ley lines that twisted and kinked the closer one came to the straits. Were they to attempt to fly over the gap itself, or even around it, they would risk being caught in a whorl, and there was no telling what might happen then. In all likelihood the ship would never make it out. It would crash to the ground or into the sea, as so many ships had while attempting to pass through it. Of all the advancements the Grand Duchy, Yrstanla, and even Galahesh had made over the centuries, they still hadn't found a way to unravel the mysteries of the straits, which was why nearly all of the goods being shipped between Yrstanla and the Grand Duchy were brought to an eyrie on the northern end of the island, ferried over land by wagons, across the straits on special barges, and reloaded onto waiting ships in Svoya on the southern end of Galahesh.

"By our fathers, just look at it," the kapitan said, his voice full of wonder.

He was referring to the bridge. It hadn't even been completed yet and people had already started calling it the Spar. And Atiana could see why. The straits at its narrowest point was nearly a half-league, and the land on either side was four hundred feet above the sea. Nearly five years ago the foundations of the bridge had been laid, a thing that had never been considered in the hundreds of years the Empire had controlled this island. The distance was simply too far to span.

Or so it had been thought.

This Kamarisi, this young man, apparently thought it necessary, and he had poured vast amounts of resources into the effort. Twenty-six columns—one for each of the emperors in Hakan's line—supported the bridge from below, and the spans between were nearly complete. Only in the middle, at the center of the bridge, was the stone still being worked.

"It's impressive."

"Impressive... Unnatural is what I say. Men shouldn't build such things."

"It will help trade, Kapitan."

"It will bring Yrstanla one step closer to the Grand Duchy." He strode away to tend to the ship. "And mark my words, nothing good can come of that."

Indeed, Atiana thought. The straits was a natural barrier between the two powers, and even though Galahesh had been in the hands of Yrstanla ever since the Great War, it was a fact that gave both sides some comfort that it would be difficult, if not impossible, to catch the other off-guard.

It fouled the aether as well, making it doubly dangerous for her when she prepared to take the dark. There were dozens of stories from Mother and Aunt Katerina and every other Matra old enough to remember the ancient tales of those who had wandered too close to the straits and had become lost. Most recovered in time, but Atiana's great-grandmother Tatiana had never returned. She died seventeen days after trying to spy upon the Kamarisi of Yrstanla, who at that time had been threatening war with the Islands.

Atiana turned when she heard light footsteps making their way across the deck. It was Ishkyna, who had convinced Father that she might prove herself of use on this journey. It was an excuse for Ishkyna to leave her husband's side—a game Ishkyna never tired of—but Atiana also knew that Ishkyna had become smitten with Sihaş, the Kamarisi's envoy.

"It does look grand, doesn't it?" Ishkyna said, gripping the shroud and leaning over the gunwales to look out toward the city.

"It looks dangerous," Atiana said, her gaze drawn toward the shattered remains of the city's southwestern section.

"Sometimes they go hand in hand." Ishkyna swung back and struck Atiana with her hip. "What of your man, Bahett? You haven't spoken of him."

"There's little enough to tell, Shkyna. I'm beholden."

"You mean smitten. With another..."

Atiana considered the two pieces of the island, split from one another by the straits. It felt like her and Nikandr, close at times, but never quite able to touch.

"Come now," Ishkyna continued. "You know how such things work. A man like Bahett will not begrudge you a man like Nikandr coming discreetly to the city for a time. You'll be the ilkadin. You could go for days, even weeks at a time. Besides, after a few months, Bahett will hardly remember you."

It was Atiana's turn to hip her sister.

Ishkyna laughed—a genuine laugh, not the one she used when she was stalking men. It felt good to hear. "You know what I mean. As pretty as you are, the Kaymakam of Galahesh has duties, and many women who might divert him from it. If you wish to see Nikandr, accept the hand of Galahesh and everyone will look the other way. Besides, we must look beyond the halls of Baressa, mustn't we? The Kamarisi stares ever harder beyond the shores of Galahesh."

Atiana knew her sister's words were false. She could not even allow herself the fantasy of believing in them. Even if she were willing to break her marriage vows to Bahett, Nikandr would not. He knew, as Atiana did, that it was too risky. Both of them could, and probably would, be put to death if they were found together.

Instead, she changed the subject. "Is that why you've hounded the envoy every moment you've had?"

Ishkyna stared at Atiana flatly. "He's no joy between the sheets, Tiana, believe me. Were it not for his station, I would gladly have looked to his servants." Her stare turned into a wry smile. "In fact, I already have. They're much more … pliable."

"I don't know how you live with yourself."

"Don't wrinkle your nose at wine you haven't tasted. You'll know soon enough..."

The ship bucked in the wind, forcing Atiana to hold to the nearby shroud to steady herself.

"There's a surge coming," the kapitan said. "Best you wait in your cabins."

"Best you tend to *your* business," Ishkyna said, "and let us attend to ours."

The kapitan left with a sour look on his face. The winds continued to kick, though, and Ishkyna soon went to her cabin at the rear of the ship. Atiana remained. She wanted to study the straits from the air as long as she could. She wanted to fix them in her mind for the next time she took the dark. The straits were dangerous, as she had known even before her recent visit with Saphia.

The winds eventually died down, but only after they'd turned and headed east for several leagues. The rest of the trip went uneventfully. They landed in Svoya and were met at the eyrie by a host of Bahett's servants. They took her and Ishkyna and the rest of their retinue overland in a train of coaches. The land was dryer here than among the islands, and so the landscape seemed spare, almost desiccated.

When they finally reached Baressa, they received a completely different view from the ground. Galahesh was by and large a long plateau of land. Indeed, except for the Mount, the massive hill that housed Kasir Yalidoz and the wealthiest homes, the city was flat. It felt strange, as most of the cities in the Grand Duchy were built onto slopes or mountainsides. And the people. They choked the streets. The traffic became so bad near the Mount they came to a standstill. They were in a street that had market stalls on either side. Hundreds became thousands as people wearing all manner of bright clothing wandered along the street, considering the stalls of silk and wool and knives and fruit and wine and dates.

Ishkyna pulled the curtain aside and stared out at the crowd. Her eyes were wide and a soft smile was upon her lips, an expression Atiana hadn't seen in years, not since their childhood. "Wouldn't you love to live here?"

Atiana didn't answer; she merely watched. It seemed as close to innocence as Ishkyna had come for as long as Atiana could remember. It felt nice to sit with her sister of old, the one who used to speak with her of her plans for her future, the days before she had been promised to Iyagor.

Ishkyna let the curtain drop. "*What?*"

"Nothing."

She glanced back at the curtain and then sat back, feigning indifference. "I suppose you'll grow tired of it before long."

Some of the merchants began approaching the wagons, offering dates and fried sweetbread on brass platters until the driver and coachmen yelled at them in Yrstanlan to keep moving. That, however, only seemed to draw them like flies to sitting fruit.

The crack of a whip cut through the air, and for a moment the din of the market subsided. From the rear of the coach that was directly ahead of Atiana's, one of the janissaries hopped down and yelled at an old merchant who lay on the ground writhing, his sweetmeats spilled over the street. The guard pulled his whip back and lashed the man once more. The whip cut a line through his shirt, and blood welled beneath the bright yellow cloth. Only after the man had crawled away and the crowd backed up did the coaches resume their slow trek.

At last, after what felt like endless hours through the city, they reached Kasir Yalidoz, a massive and expansive palace that dwarfed Galostina, at least in terms of the land it covered. Atiana was led by a dozen servants to her apartments, a set of three rooms that looked eastward toward Vostroma. The servants offered her hot mint tea and candied lemons. They asked if she wished to be bathed, offered to help her dress, gave her a list of small plates she might enjoy before the masquerade that evening. She knew it was an insult, but Atiana declined all of their offers, preferring the help of her handmaid, Yalessa, over this cadre of servants. Finally they left, and Yalessa helped her to change into her dress.

"Will you see Bahett tonight?" Yalessa asked.

"I imagine so, though this is more to put the Kamarisi at ease than anything else."

After brushing Atiana's blonde hair and pulling it up into a bun, Yalessa opened a case and began to powder her hair. In the mirror, Atiana could see her staring into the corner, her mind clearly wandering. "Bahett is beautiful, is he not?"

"I suppose he is."

Yalessa snapped her head toward the mirror, meeting Atiana's gaze. "I'm sorry, My Lady Princess."

"Whatever for?"

"Nikandr..."

She didn't like speaking of Nikandr, and Yalessa knew it. Why she would bring him up now—particularly when Atiana was away from home and unsure when she'd get to speak with Nikandr again—Atiana didn't know, but it grated. "Don't fear that I'll be watching who enters your chambers," Atiana said.

"It isn't that."

"Then what?"

"It isn't my place to say."

Atiana stared into the mirror, meeting Yalessa's innocent face with a serious stare.

Yalessa broke her gaze, brushing the powder carefully from Atiana's neck and shoulders. "It's just that, the prince... You've waited for so long to be with Nikandr. Why throw that away?"

"I'm throwing nothing away. Bahett is a powerful man. He can do much for Vostroma. For the entire Grand Duchy. Why should I throw *that* away for a marriage that might never happen?"

Yalessa nodded. "Of course, My Lady. As you say, the Kaymakam is a fine man."

Atiana stood, unwilling to let Yalessa bother her any longer, but as she did a soft knock came at the door.

"Send them away," Atiana said. "There's nothing else I need."

In the mirror Atiana watched as Yalessa moved to the next room and opened the door.

From the hall outside came a soft voice, polite but firm. "The Lady of Alekeşir, Arvaneh üm Shalahihd, wishes to speak with the Princess of Vostroma."

Atiana felt her face flush. She found herself looking about, for what, she didn't know. But then she composed herself. She had known this time would come; she just hadn't expected it so soon.

Yalessa bowed and stepped back, sparing a quick glance in Atiana's direction.

Through the doorway strode a woman wearing an elaborate headdress of citrine stones that complemented her long, golden hair. Her richly embroidered takchita was a dress that had long since fallen out of favor in the Empire, but Arvaneh wore it not just with confidence but with a bearing that made it seem as though she were the first woman ever to wear one.

"Leave us," Arvaneh said, never taking her eyes from Atiana.

Atiana gave Yalessa a small nod, and she left.

Before the door was even closed, Atiana's heart began to pound. However prepared she might have been, she hadn't been ready to stand before such a beauty, a woman with clear power in her every move, her every motion.

Arvaneh faced Atiana, regarding her with beautiful blue eyes. Her ruddy skin made her look like one of the Aramahn, but she dressed more like one of the southern tribeswomen. "Your time on the wind was not uncomfortable, I hope."

"It was as pleasant as it could be."

Arvaneh smiled, an act that seemed to tax her. "That is the way of things on the islands, is it not? You cling to rocks and complain when the wind takes you away."

"I wouldn't describe it so," Atiana said.

Arvaneh walked along Atiana's bed, casting an uncaring eye over the dresses that had been laid out—some of Atiana's finest. "And how *would* you describe it?"

"We are proud of our *rocks*, as you call them. We stand upon them with pride, and if the winds blow, we do not complain. We shoulder it as we do everything else."

"You take pride in this? *Shouldering* the wind?"

"Like everything on the islands, it is something that must be dealt with."

"That is where you're wrong, you and all of Anuskaya. Were you to embrace the wind, you might never have faced the opposition you do now in the Maharraht."

"And if the Maharraht were true to their beliefs, they would not be scrabbling for a piece of our islands."

"*Your* islands…" Atiana had shown no signs of anger during this exchange, yet Arvaneh smiled as if she'd already won this short trade of blows. She strode to the window, stared out over the Mount with a melancholy expression. "You are royalty, so perhaps your conceit should be forgiven, but do you think that once Anuskaya is gone, once the people of Galahesh are forgotten, once Yrstanla is no more, that they will still be yours?"

Atiana paused, confused at such a statement, especially from someone who had the ear—and the bed—of the most powerful man in all of Erahm. "Doesn't the line of the Kamarisi believe that all lands are theirs?"

Arvaneh paused and turned back toward Atiana. She opened her mouth to speak, but just then a knock came at the door and in swept Ishkyna. Arvaneh looked between the two of them, confusion playing across her face. "I wasn't aware that the other Vostroma sisters would be coming."

"Only *one* other." Ishkyna pulled the skirt of her dress wide and bowed her head politely. It was not the full bow that was commonplace in Yrstanla, but neither were they in Yrstanla proper. Galahesh was something of a meeting ground between the two powers, not only geographically but culturally as well. "The other," she continued, "is sufficiently chained to her husband that she couldn't think of making the journey."

Atiana motioned to her sister. "Arvaneh üm Shalahihd, meet Ishkyna Radieva Vostroma, eldest of the sisters Vostroma."

"Eldest by a mere seven minutes. Had I not fought so hard in those opening moments of life, I might have been forced to the donjon to take the basin as Atiana does."

Atiana felt her face flush. As sensitive as her purpose was, she didn't want the subject of taking the dark touched on if she could avoid it.

The look on Arvaneh's face was one of light amusement, but to Atiana it seemed forced, as if she found it difficult to suffer Ishkyna's presence but didn't want to offend. "You are no Matra then?"

Ishkyna smiled. "Not if it can be avoided."

"And why is this?"

Ishkyna glanced at Atiana—Atiana could tell she wanted to fire back a scathing reply—but thankfully her thoughts, and her sharp words, lay hidden behind her lips. "It isn't common knowledge as far west as Alekeşir, but the basin requires water as cold as the northern seas, as cold as the bones of the earth. It's no joy taking those waters, I can assure you."

It seemed that Arvaneh could no longer hold her feelings back. The smile she wore was patronizing, which made it clear just how much contempt she harbored not just for Ishkyna, but for the entire Grand Duchy.

"Forgive me," she said. "You have just arrived, and I have taken enough of your time. I hear we will see you at the dinner tonight."

Atiana bowed her head.

As Arvaneh strode toward the door, Ishkyna widened her eyes at Atiana.

Atiana could only shrug.

A moment later, Arvaneh was gone, leaving in her wake a cold sense that everything they had tried to hide from her had just been laid bare.

CHAPTER FOURTEEN

When Nasim turned the last of the switchbacks on the path leading up to the top of the ridge, and the celestia came into full view at last, he stopped, humbled. Without speaking, Rabiah and Sukharam did the same. It was so large that it seemed to take on different dimensions the closer they came, but the true immensity of it did not strike him until he approached the concentric steps that led up to the marble floor.

Before he reached the first of the steps, he stopped and merely stared. This was a wonder he would not rush. It was high noon and the sun was bright, casting much of the floor in shadow, but from six arched openings built cunningly into the center of the dome above, crepuscular rays shone down, creating six bright ovals that forced Nasim to squint when he looked upon them. Several of the fluted stone columns were overgrown with vines. They crept up and up, reaching even the exterior of the dome far above.

The vines did not, however, grow against the underside of the dome. In fact, the beautiful mosaics there looked pristine, untouched since their construction over four hundred years before. Much of it was a beautiful shade of blue, the blue of the deepest, clearest water in the ocean, but against this backdrop were constellations that Nasim could only guess were made of mother of pearl, for the stars shone like the brightest stars on the darkest of nights. He could make out the constellations of the winter solstice easily—Iteh and Almadn and Qyleh and Osht and all the others—but there was so much more than this: the smaller, lesser constellations that rested above them or between them in the firmament; major comets that graced the sky as the fates allowed; glinting lines that tracked the path of the moon at summer and winter solstice. The patterns were not just brilliant, but alive.

It nearly brought him to his knees. Little wonder that Khamal had chosen this for his demesne. The wonder was that Sariya hadn't, choosing her tower in its place, or that Muqallad had chosen the Aramahn village built into the mountains east of Alayazhar. How they could lock themselves away from the beauty of the sky was beyond him.

Sukharam, the hem of his robes blowing in the wind, climbed the stairs and examined the dome. The fear he'd shown earlier had spiked as they reached the center of the city, and although they skirted the area that held Sariya's tower, he had watched it with terror-filled eyes. Only when they'd gained the top of the hill and he'd seen the celestia in all its grandeur did his head lift and his shoulders unbunch. And now, he was staring wide-eyed as he walked forward.

Nasim realized just how far into the celestia Sukharam was moving. "The border, Sukharam!"

Sukharam stared down at the floor, where black inlaid stone described a vast circle several paces from the perimeter. "How could it still be active? Khamal died sixteen years ago."

"We shouldn't take chances."

"I feel nothing."

"And what would you look for?" Nasim asked. "Do you think it would be so obvious?"

Sukharam looked to Nasim, then the floor again. He shrugged, a simple, dismissive motion. As he paced around the edge of the floor, Nasim wondered if Sukharam was embarrassed and this was some attempt at regaining face. He hoped not. He needed them to be honest with one another. He couldn't afford to have any of them hiding things for vanity's sake. He promised himself he'd talk to Sukharam later, when the two of them were alone.

Nasim stepped to the edge of the black border and squatted, resting on the balls of his feet. He remembered standing here when he—when *Khamal*—had placed the protections over this place, allowing only himself to enter and leave, but he couldn't recall the details. Khamal's memories—the few that held any clarity at all—were no better than half-remembered dreams. He knew that a ward existed and that it was both complex and powerfully dangerous, but little more than that.

He walked the circle the opposite direction of Sukharam, until the two of them stood at opposite extremes.

"Stop," he said.

Sukharam obeyed. He and Rabiah waited and watched as Nasim searched his memories.

"What is it?" Rabiah asked.

"I've seen this before," Nasim replied.

"Seen what?" Sukharam asked, stepping closer to the black stones.

"Stop!"

Sukharam did, but he seemed petulant now, almost angry. "Tell us what you remember."

"Someone was standing there, as you are now, facing Khamal, but it's confusing. It doesn't feel real."

"What, the dream?" Rabiah asked.

"They're not dreams, Rabiah. They're memories."

"The memory, then."

Nasim shook his head. "The image. The person standing across from Khamal. The other person is standing on the other side, in Adhiya."

"That can't be," Sukharam said.

Nasim crouched, squinting at the pattern of stones laid about the celestia's interior. There was no immediate rhyme or reason, just darker patterns of pewter against the sandstone dominating the floor.

"Constellations?" Rabiah asked, walking along the edge and considering several of the patterns.

"*Neh*," Nasim said.

They all studied them as a breeze blew among the tall, vine-choked columns.

"They're meaningless," Sukharam said.

"*Neh*," Nasim replied, standing, understanding coming like a flash of lightning. "They're ley lines." The moment he said the words, he knew it was true.

Rabiah came closer as Nasim studied the lines. He could see the pattern now, not the islands themselves, but the confluence of energy that formed around them. The islands of Khalakovo stood out first. Uyadensk and Duzol and Yrlanda. Then the islands of Mirkotsk and Vostroma. To the west, the mass of Yrstanla loomed, pressing the ley lines, guiding them along the edge of the Sea of Tabriz.

The lines ran through the sea, guided by the seabeds that drew close to, but did not quite reach, the surface. The Aramahn had known since the time of the first wanderers that ley lines guided the aether, and that through these lines one could control many things. It was this knowledge that had led them to create ships with keels so that they could use them to guide windships as the rounded keel of a waterborne ship does.

Nasim studied the map closely, moving around the celestia floor as he did so, but he stopped when he noticed to the southwest the confluence of ley lines that focused on the island of Galahesh. He didn't understand it, but the lines of power coming from the Sea of Tabriz ran not *around* Galahesh, but *through it* to the deeper well of the Sea of Khurkhan. It was the straits, Nasim realized. The straits had always been impossible for the Landed to cross with their windships, and it was because of this—the surge of power running along the straits disrupted the natural lines that ran along the land mass of Galahesh.

In the center of the map was the only representation of a land mass. Ghayavand. Where he now stood.

It made sense that the builders would have worked the sea and earth into the stone flooring. What he didn't understand was why they would have chosen to show the ley lines. Why not the islands themselves? Why not both?

But then he realized just how much time Khamal had had on this island—more than three hundred years. As much as the tower was Sariya's demesne, this had been Khamal's. He could easily have reconstructed the entire celestia in that time, so recreating the flooring would have been simple. He could not have known when and in what form he would return, so he might have recreated this as a clue of sorts, something for his new incarnation to find and to open like a lockbox. But he couldn't make it too easy—lockboxes, after all, did have locks. It would be needed to prevent others from finding its secrets.

"There's something in the middle," Rabiah said.

Nasim looked closer. At the center of the celestia's floor was a circular brass plate. The plate was old, the metal discolored, which had hidden the fact that there was a bracelet resting there, a qiram's bracelet of beaten gold that held an opal in its setting. It wasn't the stone that mattered. It was the fact that he recognized it. He'd seen it a thousand times before.

It was Ashan's.

Ashan was arqesh; he knew all the disciplines and had one of every stone. The one that was left here, however, was the one for the dhoshahezhan, the spirit of life and growth.

It was a message, and it wasn't difficult to figure out who had sent it.

"Muqallad has taken Ashan," Nasim said softly.

Rabiah looked between him and the brass plate, confused, but understanding came to her moments later. "It's a clue, isn't it?"

Nasim nodded and stepped forward over the black line. Rabiah was right, and the fact that Muqallad had been here and left the bracelet was a sign that some of the wards of this place had been removed.

As he crossed over the line, Nasim sensed a shift, a subtle change—in this world, or the next, or the one that lay between. He couldn't quite place it. He'd never felt the like before, not since that day on Oshtoyets when Nikandr had saved him, when he'd been drawn from Adhiya to lie wholly in the world of Erahm. This was similar, though to a much smaller degree.

"Nasim..."

It was Rabiah's voice, and it was full of wonder. And worry.

He felt the stones shift beneath his feet. The ley lines... They were *moving* like waves upon the water. He stepped toward the edge of the floor, feeling more calm than he'd felt in years. Sukharam and Rabiah practically ran, their eyes nervous and darting.

As the lines continued to alter, Nasim wondered if the previous view had been what the lines were like when Khamal had last been here, or perhaps how they'd been at the time of the sundering. Either way, his alarm began to grow the longer he watched.

The lines gathered tightly around Ghayavand. This was to be expected. The rifts had formed here. They had been contained by the Al-Aqim and the other qiram who had survived, but they had eventually begun to expand. When the ley lines were laid out like this, however, the rifts appeared as a confluence—a whorl or an aberration in the otherwise-orderly lines.

What was worrying was the fact that there were similar patterns being formed around the islands of Galahesh and Rafsuhan. Galahesh could perhaps be reasoned away. It was well known that the island—and the straits that divided it—acted as a channel that funneled aether from the Sea of Tabriz to the deep well in the Sea of Khurkhan. It acted as a crosswind to the aether that ran beneath the surface of the water—the shallows that ran from the Motherland, through Oramka and Galahesh and on to the islands of the Grand Duchy. But the whorls around Rafsuhan made no sense whatsoever.

It must be another rift. And a large one at that. So much was changing, he thought, and none of it for the better.

The lines finally stopped moving. The rift running through Rafsuhan was deep, but not so bad that it wouldn't eventually close. The tightness around Galahesh, however, could not be sustained. Sooner or later, something was going to give, and he couldn't escape the feeling that it was being done consciously, nor could he escape the fact that Sariya and Muqallad had recently found a way to break the chains that had kept them bound for so long.

"Come," Nasim said to the others. "There's nothing to fear any longer."

Nasim led them to the center of the floor, and there Nasim squatted down and picked up the bracelet. The gold was heavy. The opal reflected the brightness of the day. He put it on, feeling something akin to familiarity. He remembered thinking once what it would be like to wear Ashan's bracelets. He knew that he didn't need such things, but it still felt good. It felt like he was one step closer to finding him.

He kneeled down and felt the plate. He tried to lift it, to twist it, to no avail. He tried for long minutes to *feel* for it, to see if there was some sign Khamal had left him to give some clue as to how to open it. But if he had, Nasim couldn't sense it.

"Should we try to destroy it?" Rabiah asked.

Nasim shook his head, his eyes locked on the plate.

What? he asked himself. What might Khamal have meant him to do?

Sukharam cleared his throat, and when he spoke it sounded meek, as if he'd been afraid to break the silence. "He would have taken breath here, wouldn't he? Perhaps kneel to it."

When the words were spoken, Nasim knew it was so. It was so simple. This place, of all places, was special to Khamal. He would have taken breath here countless days. And when Nasim had returned to this place, it would be a gesture he might stumble upon if he didn't guess it outright.

"He wants me to open it," Nasim said.

"Who? Muqallad?"

Nasim nodded. "Can there be any doubt?"

"Why?"

"Because he can't do it himself. He wants the piece of the Atalayina hidden within, and he's offering Ashan in payment."

Rabiah stared down thoughtfully. Sukharam looked between the two of them, then down to the plate. "We should take it."

"*Neh*," Rabiah said. "If he wants it, we should leave it."

Nasim stared at the bracelet, felt its weight on his wrist. "Sukharam's right. We must have it."

Rabiah shook her head. "We can always come back for it. Let's leave. Consider this more carefully."

"Consider what?" Nasim asked. "This is what we came for. It is one of the three stones we need, and it's powerful, Rabiah. It can help us against Muqallad."

"You may be giving him exactly what he wants."

"It's a risk we need to take." Still kneeling, Nasim placed his hands on the plate so that his hands and thumbs created a triangle, and then he kneeled down, touching his forehead in the center of the triangle.

He heard no sound, but he felt the plate vibrate momentarily beneath his fingers.

He sat up and pulled at the plate. It came up freely, and below it was a circular compartment set deep into the floor. He reached down—nearly to his shoulder—and felt something. His fingers tingled as he wrapped his fingers around it and pulled it up.

It was a blue stone the size and shape of a generous apple wedge. There was no mistaking what this was. It was a piece of the Atalayina, the very stone Khamal, Sariya, and Muqallad used centuries ago in their attempt to bring the world to indaraqiram, the state of complete understanding and bliss and oneness. The stone was very heavy for its size, and it felt ancient—as ancient as the world and the firmament above.

He stood and brought it over to one of the shafts of light shining down from above. He held it under the sunlight and examined it. He found it difficult to take his eyes from it. The blue of the stone was rich and deep. Copper striations ran through it like the ley lines of the celestia's floor. Emanating from within was a feeling of immense power, as if the world itself depended on this stone, and it the world.

And yet...

That very same power felt distanced, as if it were too far for the likes of him to reach.

Sukharam stared at it with wonder in his eyes. "Do the other two feel the same as this?"

Nasim frowned.

"What is it?" Rabiah asked.

Nasim hesitated, embarrassed though he wasn't sure that he should be. "I feel nothing. Or very little," he amended, "which is more than passing strange since this had surely been Khamal's piece of the Atalayina."

Sukharam held out his hand. "May I hold it?"

Nasim did not feel possessive of it, but he also felt it too powerful for Sukharam to hold. And yet, here they were on this island where they hoped to unlock the secrets of these stones. He had chosen Rabiah and Sukharam for a reason.

He handed it to Sukharam. When their hands touched, Nasim felt for a split second a deepening of the world, but then it was gone as Sukharam took it and stared into its depths.

"Strange that so much has happened because of it," Rabiah said, her eyes every bit full of wonder as Sukharam's.

Not so strange at all, Nasim thought.

"Come," he said, standing up. "There is much to do, and much to think upon."

CHAPTER FIFTEEN

Khamal stands beneath the celestia's dome, facing southward. He spreads his arms wide, breathing deeply while staring up at the dome's interior. The constellations patterned into the mosaics twinkle in the light of the dying sun.

Dawn tomorrow brings the summer solstice. It is a time of strength, of heightened expectations. It is an important time for Ghayavand, at least as far as the Al-Aqim are concerned. The akhoz become emboldened at such times, and it is more important than ever that Khamal take care so as not to be caught unawares.

But the solstice is made of more than ill tidings. It benefits him and his fellow arqesh, should they choose to avail themselves of it. He will use the dawn to his advantage, unleashing the first of the steps that will one day—hopefully one day soon—free him from this island prison once and for all.

Footsteps approach from the north, scratching over the gritty marble steps that circle the celestia. He doesn't turn, but instead waits for Muqallad to approach.

"The cardinal points do not listen," Muqallad says. "You should know this better than I."

"They watch over the island, Muqallad."

"Perhaps," Muqallad says, stopping nearby, "but if they do they are little more than witnesses. Amused witnesses."

Khamal takes one last breath, and then turns to face him. Muqallad wears a simple robe the color of the setting sun. His black, curly beard hangs almost as far as the wide leather belt that wraps his waist.

They rarely see one another, each of them preferring to meditate alone on their imprisonment and on the rifts and on the island itself, all in hopes of breaking the curse that's trapped them all. They've seen each other even less since Muqallad returned from his exile. Khamal and Sariya had banished him for a time for his words and thoughts. He had wanted the Atalayina even then. He had wanted it so that he could finish what they'd begun. The sundering to him had merely been a mistake—in his eyes, the world could still be brought to indaraqiram.

For this, he had been punished, but on his return he had seemed contrite. He had seemed penitent. Khamal knew now that it had merely been to bide his time so that he could turn one of them to his side.

"I would speak with you," Muqallad says, motioning away from the celestia.

Khamal looks up to Sihyaan, the island's highest peak, where Sariya takes breath. Muqallad chose this time so that there was no chance they would be interrupted.

"Walk with me," Muqallad says.

Together, they stride between two massive pillars of the celestia and take a bricked walkway that leads down from the hill toward the oldest part of Alayazhar. From this vantage they can see the blue swath of the sea on their left, and ahead, the northern reaches of the city, nearly all of it in ruins. The dark, snowless peak of Sihyaan looks down over the city, brooding and angry.

"We've been here too long, I think," Muqallad says.

"And why do you say that?"

"We strive, all of us, for a way to heal the damage we've caused, but we do it in our own way. We've been searching for so long that I wonder if we've started to see one another as obstacles."

"Is that how *you* see it?" Khamal asks.

"I?" Muqallad shakes his head. "*Neh*. Not I."

"Me, then."

Muqallad does not answer.

The wind blows upward from the base of the hill, bringing with it the smell of sea and sage as their footsteps crunch along the path.

"Sariya knows you have her stone."

"It isn't *her* stone," Khamal replies. "Nor is it mine."

"Of course. But there has been a shift in power because of it. It grants you something you shouldn't possess."

Khamal stops, forcing Muqallad to do the same. "I cannot give her the stone back."

Muqallad squares himself to Khamal. His chin rises. His jaw juts ever so slightly. "None of us can be allowed to keep two pieces."

"You spoke to me of taking all three, Muqallad."

"I spoke not of *taking* them, but of working together."

"To widen the rift. To bring about indaraqiram."

Muqallad raises his hands, as if to forestall the argument. "I told you. I've thought better of such things."

"Forgive me if I doubt your words."

"I speak the truth, but I wouldn't ask you to trust *me*." He motions to Sihyaan with a look over his shoulder and a wave of his hand. "I ask you to trust Sariya."

"She's become too close to you."

"She hasn't," Muqallad said.

"She visits you often, and you visit her."

"She's been trying to dissuade me, Khamal. And she's succeeded. We will meditate, as we have. We will learn. We will heal what has been torn. It's time we began to work together again. It's time we trusted one another. And that begins with her stone."

Muqallad steps in and hugs Khamal. The gesture is surprising, but also tender. They haven't done so in years. Decades.

"Don't believe *me*," Muqallad says as he pulls away and grasps Khamal by his shoulders. "Believe her. Go to her when she returns and speak to her of it. It's time we voiced our fears and brought them into the light of day. Only then can we move forward."

Khamal doesn't know what to say, but he can't deny that he wishes to speak to Sariya as they used to. He also wants to believe that Muqallad speaks the truth, but he knows that these are lies spilling from his mouth. It's why Khamal stole Sariya's stone in the first place. She and Muqallad had already begun making plans against him. But they need that stone, and they don't know where it is. They cannot risk forcing the issue, not while there's a chance he'll give it up willingly.

Khamal had hoped that he would be able to find a way to get Muqallad's stone as well. But it's too late for that. He needs to find a place to hide the stone so that they won't find it, at least until his own plans bear fruit.

"I'll speak with her," Khamal says at last.

"Good," Muqallad says. "That is good."

Nasim woke, sweating.

The room was dark, and he could sense more than see Rabiah kneeling over him.

"It's all right," Rabiah said, stroking his hair.

It felt good, her tender touch, but it came so close on the heels of the bitter emotions he'd borne witness to that he pushed her hand away.

"It's all right..."

He could hear the hurt in her voice, but there was nothing he could do about it. Not now.

"I'm here," he said simply, giving her an indication that he was once more in command of his surroundings.

"Khamal?" she asked.

"Who else?"

"What did you see?"

He shook his head against the floor, feeling powerless. He pulled himself upright and shuffled along the floor until his back was against the wall of the small house the three of them shared. They'd found it on their long walk back from the celestia. It felt strange, sleeping in a home as ancient as this one, but they had needed something besides the skiff, so they'd taken it for their own.

He could make out Sukharam's outline, and could tell he wasn't breathing heavily, so he assumed he was awake. A part of him wished Sukharam wasn't here—he wished he was alone with Rabiah—but he knew that such thoughts were foolish, selfish. He needed help, and what's more, he needed to spread the knowledge that he gained to those he could trust. There was a strong likelihood that he wouldn't make it out of this alive, and he couldn't risk passing beyond the veil again without unlocking the riddles of the rift running through Ghayavand.

"Nasim?"

His gaze shot to Rabiah. He'd nearly forgotten she was there. He'd nearly forgotten where *he* was. Again. It was such an easy thing to do. Especially when he was afraid.

"Nasim, what did you *see*?" Rabiah asked, more forcefully this time.

"Khamal," he said, swallowing to clear his throat. "Muqallad came to him in the celestia and confronted him. He'd stolen Sariya's stone."

"The one we found?"

Nasim shrugged. "Perhaps. It might be why I'm not able to feel it and Sukharam is."

"Is that what has you upset?"

"*Neh.*" He paused, simply breathing, trying to put words to his thoughts. "It's their nature. At one time they were thought to be akin to the fates. But that's not how they were. They squabbled. They plotted. In the end, they murdered. What could have made them do such things?"

Rabiah took up the hem of her robe and picked at it. "I'm disappointed as well. If it could happen to them..."

"It can happen to anyone. Exactly. And if they could fall to such madness, because of the island, the Atalayina—"

"Then it could happen to us."

Nasim shrugged. "I guess that's how I feel. That, and I..."

"What?"

"I feel responsible."

"For what Khamal did?"

"For what he did... For what he didn't do..."

"He couldn't stop them by himself."

"I don't know, Rabiah, but maybe he didn't want to."

"What do you mean?"

"Ghayavand had become a prison for them. Every hour of every day they were faced with their grandest failure. It ate at Khamal, as I'm sure it did the others. As he was planning to escape, he felt eager."

"He wanted to return so he could heal the rift."

"Maybe, but there was also a sense that he would be free. Free of the shackles that bound him here. In his heart of hearts, he wanted to leave it all behind."

"Wouldn't you?"

Nasim stared at the floor. "I don't know."

"It was three hundred years, Nasim. Anyone would grow weary of this place in that amount of time. But you're not him. You're not Khamal. You didn't make those decisions. *He* did. Live up to your own promise, and your own promises."

From a pocket sewn into his inner robe he retrieved the piece of the Atalayina they'd liberated from the celestia two days before. He spun it between his thumb and index finger. He could feel its power, but it was distant, unreachable, as it had been since he'd found it. He'd taken breath while holding it in his hands. He'd stared into its depths. He'd sat with the others with the stone between them, hoping to unlock its secrets, to no avail.

Rabiah reached out and touched his arm. "We don't have to go to Shirvozeh today, Nasim. We can wait. We can prepare."

"It's time for us to go. Ashan is there. Somewhere."

"We can take breath. We can—"

"We will go!"

Sukharam shifted. For no good reason, it infuriated him, though he had no one to blame but himself.

"Come," he said, noting that the sky was beginning to lighten. "We'd best get ready."

"As you say." Rabiah nodded, holding the gesture in the manner of an Aramahn disciple. This, too, angered him, though he wasn't sure why.

He handed the Atalayina to Sukharam and began his preparations for their journey to Shirvozeh, the Aramahn village in the hills to the east of Alayazhar. As he and Rabiah were leaving, Sukharam stepped out from their home and called to him.

"I wish to go, kuadim," Sukharam said.

"We spoke of this," Nasim replied. "Stay. Take breath."

"I should be with you."

"I cannot allow it, Sukharam. This is too dangerous."

"I knew it was dangerous when I agreed to come."

"That may be true, but you do not yet know how to protect yourself, or us. Not against Muqallad."

"And you do?"

Sukharam's entire frame had tightened. He was embarrassed by this, but Nasim would not relent. He calmed himself and took two steps toward Sukharam until they were face-to-face. "Are you my disciple or are you not?"

"I'm not useless," Sukharam said.

"I know you're not."

"I'm no wilting flower."

"I know this as well. We go only to search for clues. If we find them, we will return. I promise you this." After a deep breath, Nasim took Sukharam's hand that held the Atalayina. "You are the only one of us who has a connection to it. Do as we agreed. Take breath with the stone. Learn from it."

As the wind tugged at his dark hair, Sukharam's eyes widened. He tightened his grip on the stone, and then he regarded Nasim with a look of calm purpose. "I will," he said, bowing his head. "I will try…"

CHAPTER SIXTEEN

The village of Shirvozeh lay east of Alayazhar. The road leading up to it was paved in stone, crafted by dozens of vanaqiram masons centuries ago. It was cracked and decayed, but much of it was still intact, including the designs, which were made to look like the flow of water over a riverbed. Well before reaching the bridge near the village's entrance, Nasim guided Rabiah off the path and headed through the swaying grass and copses of short, twisted acacias, steadily making their way toward a cliff. Soon they could no longer see Alayazhar; they could no longer see the road they'd taken, either, making Nasim feel as if they were alone on an island untouched by the hand of man.

As their footsteps shushed over the wiry grass, Rabiah stared at the hills ahead with a nervous expression. "We should have brought Sukharam."

Nasim motioned to their left, to the ridge that stood between them and Alayazhar. The celestia was barely visible in the distance. "You saw how he was at the celestia. He's too unsure of himself, Rabiah. Too tentative."

"He was only trying to prove himself to you."

"That may be, but where we go is dangerous. Too dangerous for him."

"We need his help," Rabiah said.

"We need him safe. This isn't why he was brought here."

"Things have changed, Nasim. We must change with them."

For a time, they walked in silence.

When Nasim had finally found it in himself to leave Mirashadal and the care of Fahroz, he'd been terribly lonely. He'd nearly gone to Khalakovo to find news of Nikandr, but he knew that such a thing would be foolish. No matter what Nikandr might think, the Landed had not changed their ways. This resolve, the resolve to choose his own path, had taught him something. Trust. Trust in himself—for that, in the end, was all he could do. He could not trust Nikandr. He could not trust Sukharam. He could not even place his full faith in Rabiah, whom he trusted most aside from Ashan.

Trust was a luxury he couldn't afford. It was simply too dangerous. He needed to be sure that their path was the right one, and the only way to do that was to choose it himself.

"Perhaps we do need to change," Nasim said to her. "But not now. Sukharam must learn more."

Rabiah stopped walking. "Nasim..."

He refused to slow. She was just being stubborn.

"Nasim!"

Her voice was so full of emotion that he stopped and turned. She stepped forward tentatively while staring into his eyes, perhaps trying to see into his soul. "You're so protective of him," she said. "Why not me?"

He couldn't speak for a moment. He looked around, at the dry, mountainous landscape, at the overcast sky and the blue gap in the clouds far to the north. "Because I need you."

She blinked. He saw her swallow, as if she were suddenly nervous, and when she spoke again, her voice was quiet. "You say it as if it's obvious."

"Isn't it?"

She opened her mouth to speak, but then seemed to think better of it. She smiled and squeezed his shoulders. "You *do* need me, Nasim. But you need Sukharam as well. We all need each other."

He wanted to tell her that there was more. He wanted to tell her that he didn't just *need* her—there was so much more trying to bubble up from deep inside him—but the words, like so many times before, refused to come. It wasn't the right time.

It was never the right time.

"Come," he finally said. "We're already here. If Ashan was taken, then Muqallad would have brought him to Shirvozeh. I need to know if it's so."

He could tell that she didn't want to drop the topic, but she nodded anyway, and they continued.

They hiked down slope until they came to the edge of a sheer cliff. From this vantage they could see to their left a bridge that spanned the chasm below. The bridge's sand-colored columns rose up from the base of the valley hundreds of feet, arching gracefully to meet the supports to either side. In a handful of places the stones along the bridge's roadway had given way—from this distance it looked as if it had been chewed away by rats. By and large, though, the bridge was sound.

Suddenly, Rabiah clutched his arm, pointing southward.

Nasim scanned the far side of the chasm. And then he caught movement. It was a good distance away—an eighth-league or more—but he could see the form of a vanahezhan plodding through the scrub pine. Every few steps, some of its leg would ablate. It would then pause, glance down, and the leg would reform, but then a few steps later it would happen again.

As it grabbed for an old, misshapen acacia, pulling itself upslope, it fell and shattered against the ground. Rocks slid downward, clacking and clattering, spraying the hillside in the pattern of a candle's flame.

"Did it return to Adhiya?" Rabiah asked.

"It must have. When I came here with Ashan, there were hezhan all over the island. They had seemed a part of this place. Permanent, somehow." Nasim waved to the site of the vanahezhan's crossing, where dust still rose. "It might have been weak, one more likely to be drawn back to Adhiya, but somehow I doubt it. Things have changed."

Rabiah touched her chest, over her heart. "It feels unstable. The hezhan can cross easily, but it feels like we could step into Adhiya as well."

Nasim felt a mixture of pride and melancholy swirling inside him. It was a sign of her ability that she could sense this. "You're becoming attuned to the island."

She looked to him, her eyes bright and hopeful. "Is that good or bad?"

"A bit of both, I'm afraid." He pointed to their right. "Come, the trail head isn't far."

They soon found it, a thin trail hidden among the growth. They began taking it downward, watching the bridge constantly, but when they approached the halfway mark and still saw nothing, their nerves began to calm.

Far below, the rush of water could be heard, and they soon came to an overlook—the top of a massive fist of rock lodged into the otherwise loose soil. They rested there, looking down at the frothing rush of water.

"Where is it?" Rabiah asked.

In truth Nasim didn't know. He studied the landscape, hoping he would recognize landmarks now that he was here.

And then he spotted it. Near a shallow inlet of crystal-clear water in a patina-colored bed was a curving wall of red rock with flowering vegetation clinging to its sheer face.

"Beneath the vines," he said, pointing to it.

"Where?"

"Hiding beneath the overhang."

Rabiah studied the wall closely, but Nasim's attention was drawn by movement on the bridge far above. Rabiah began to speak, but he grabbed her arm and squeezed, willing her to silence. Rabiah looked up immediately and drew in a sharp breath.

There, in a staggered line, were a dozen akhoz heading toward the village.

Nasim remained frozen, hoping they were too far from the akhoz for them to smell their scent on the wind, but then he realized that they weren't all akhoz.

A woman followed at the rear of the line. With the distance he might not have recognized her as such had she not been walking upright, her hair flowing in the wind. The longer he watched, though, the more he realized she might not be a woman after all. She seemed young—perhaps twelve or thirteen, certainly no older than he and Rabiah—and her gait was not one of confidence, but of self-consciousness. She was out of place here, and she felt it.

Then, as one, he and Rabiah were drawn by more movement much closer to them.

At the top of the trail, shuffling along the ground on all fours, was a single akhoz. It sniffed the ground, moved a few paces, then sniffed again. It stopped, its mouth open as if it were tasting the wind. It remained there motionless for so long that Nasim thought it might not have sensed them, that soon it would return to the others, but then it arched its neck, bared its blackened gums and teeth to the sky, and shuffled toward them.

"By the fates, it's found us," Nasim said, pulling her by her arm.

They sprinted down the trail.

As steep as the hill was it was difficult to control their pace. Rabiah nearly slid off a curve in the trail and down the steep slope toward the water below, but Nasim caught her wrist, and they skidded along the dry, rocky soil to slow themselves.

Above, the akhoz was gaining ground. They could hear its breathing, snuffing and huffing, which sounded more like a wounded boar than a child. It hunkered down near a tree that hugged the side of the trail and sniffed, then it reared its head back and released a howl that made Nasim's stomach churn.

It continued, on and on it went until Nasim was forced to stop, to lean over and take deep breaths to keep himself from vomiting. A line of drool slipped from his mouth and fell upon the dry red soil

Rabiah was no better. Her face was white, and her lip quivered as she stared into Nasim's eyes. The veins along her forehead stood out, her pulse galloping.

"Draw upon a dhoshahezhan," he said. "Use it to shield us."

After coughing and pulling herself upright, she did. The walls of Adhiya were thin here. He could feel the hunger of the hezhan—dozens of them—to enter this world. Rabiah was forced to slow the amount of energy she was drawing in order to prevent its crossing.

But already her face was turning red. Spittle leaked from her mouth to fall upon the front of her red robes, and she tightened her fists so hard that the whites of her knuckles and the tendons of her hands stood out. He reached out to calm her, but she slapped his hand away. She pushed as hard as she dared.

The hair on his head and the back of his neck stood on end. A crackle sizzled through the air above them, signaling the crossing of a dhoshahezhan.

But then the long call of the akhoz abruptly ended.

Instead of using the trail, it charged down the slope, heedless of the scrapes along its legs and torso it received from the dry growth.

Nasim could feel the hezhan's hunger. It was angry, yearning more than ever to enter the material world. Rabiah eased her hold on it, but didn't release it completely. She kept it near in case they needed it once more.

Nasim took her by the arm and dragged her along the trail. They were nearly at the bottom, but the akhoz was gaining. With Rabiah as weakened as she was, Nasim thought of drawing on another hezhan. Whatever might happen to Rabiah, he could use one to protect them from the akhoz, but in the end he decided it was simply too dangerous. The veil was impossibly thin here; any serious bonding with the hezhan would draw them across, and that was something they could not afford.

Nasim realized the akhoz would be on them if they remained on the path. "Hold on!" Nasim said.

He took Rabiah by the arm and forced her down the slope as well. They slid, scraping against the uneven ground, the coarse vegetation and dry grasses cutting at their shins and knees and arms as they did their best to control their descent.

They came to the bottom at last, both of them stumbling, flailing their arms in a vain attempt to keep their feet. To no avail. They fell heavily to the ground, but they were back up a moment later, sprinting toward the water as the akhoz reached the valley floor behind them.

They crashed through the water. It was only shin-deep, but it slowed them, and the akhoz quickly caught up. In the short time Nasim spared to glance back he saw it rearing back, its dark skin pulling tight over gaunt ribs as it drew breath.

"Get down!" Nasim cried, pulling her beneath the water.

The cold water swept over them as a wash of flames lit the surface of the river. They swam downstream as far as they could, keeping to the swift, deep center.

When they surfaced, they saw the akhoz trailing them. It could cross, but the water would drain it of strength—perhaps too dearly.

It crouched, staring downriver, where a cluster of rocks stood, forming a navigable bridge, and then, like a hound on the hunt, it bounded toward the stones.

Nasim pulled Rabiah from the water. His muscles ached. Their drenched clothes were heavy.

The red face of the cliff lay achingly close. Water trickled down from it in places, and here there were flowering plants clinging to the rock, making it look like a massive, hanging garden.

Nasim ran toward it, the breath in his lungs burning, and for a moment he didn't realize that Rabiah was no longer running next to him.

He turned and found that she'd stopped. And her arms were spread wide. "Rabiah, don't!"

She didn't listen. She closed her eyes, and ahead, where the akhoz was leaping from stone to stone, the gravel near the edge of the water shifted. It rumbled. Then it lifted wholesale and sprayed against the water and the akhoz.

Though Nasim was not bonded with the vanahezhan, he could feel its closeness.

The akhoz was momentarily lost in the white, frothing water, but then it gained the bank. It shook its head like a rabid dog. After a moment it refocused on them and galloped, low to the ground, mouth wide, black tongue lolling.

Nasim and Rabiah raced along the base of the cliff. It was uneven terrain—rocky and treacherous.

He couldn't see the mouth of the cave.

But it was *here*. Somewhere. He was sure of it.

The akhoz reached the inlet.

Nasim and Rabiah came to a cleft in the stone. It was deep and dark, which was a vast relief to Nasim. They'd found the entrance at last. But the akhoz was too close. They couldn't simply retreat and hope the akhoz would lose their scent.

Before they'd even passed through the entrance, Nasim drew upon Rabiah and the nearest of the vanahezhan. He could sense its deep hunger for Erahm, and this time he was counting on it.

They continued, but when they were fully in the darkness of the cavern at last, Nasim spun and drew on the full strength of the hezhan. He felt the weight of the stone around him, felt it flow up through his legs, through his chest and into his arms. He felt solid and deep and immovable.

The earth rumbled. It shook. Dust sifted down from the roof of the cave. Chunks of it broke away. A stream of stone and dust fell between them and the akhoz. The sound of it was echoing, deafening within the confines of the cavern.

Then something changed. Nasim felt the hezhan drawing upon *him*. He coughed as his heart skipped a beat and he fell to his knees.

The akhoz was going to gain the entrance to the cave despite the falling stone. It was scrabbling forward along the ground, skirting the wall of the entrance. Stones were striking it, cutting into its pale skin and drawing dark blood, but it was avoiding the bulk of falling stone.

The feeling in Nasim's chest intensified. It felt as though the mountain itself were pressing down on him. He couldn't breathe. He could only exhale, until at last the edges of his vision began to glint.

He saw, by the bare light filtering in from the outside, Rabiah standing next to him. He felt the touch of her hand on his shoulder.

And in that one moment he felt a grand release.

No longer did he have any sort of connection to the earth. No longer could he feel the vanahezhan.

The akhoz had nearly gained the entrance to the cavern, but it stopped, perhaps sensing something. It stared to one side and crawled backward, staring at the opposite wall of the tunnel. It drew in a deep breath and released a gout of flame as a mound of earth with four arms and two legs the size of tree trunks pulled away from the wall. The flame blasted the emerging hezhan where the head was, baking the earth. It must have felt pain or discomfort, for it ducked and grabbed at the akhoz's ankle and pulled it away from the wall.

There was no way for the akhoz to survive this battle, not if it remained within the heart of the earth. It clawed furiously at the earthen hand that had grabbed hold of its leg, breaking free, then it darted for the light, heedless of the few remaining stones now falling.

The flow of earth, which had abated somewhat, resumed as the vanahezhan threw one arm forward, spraying the back of the akhoz with a gout of sharp rock and stone.

And then a great rumble shook the cavern.

Nasim and Rabiah backed away. It continued for long moments, the earth around them resounding from the force of it.

Until at last the rumbling died away, leaving only dying echoes in the distance.

And then all was silence.

All was darkness.

CHAPTER SEVENTEEN

Nikandr stood at the gunwales of the *Chaika*, staring at the horizon. It could barely be seen, but it was there—the island of Rafsuhan. Closer, less than a league from the *Chaika's* position, was a small island—little more than an inhospitable piece of rock that refused to yield to the sea's incessant waves.

These waters had been difficult to reach. As distant as the nearest spires on Rhavanki were, the ley lines were weak, and they succumbed all too often to random currents of aether, sending the ship twisting in the wind, or worse, dropping dangerously toward the sea. Still, it was better than open sea. There were still shallows that led eastward from Mirkotsk and the Northern Sea to the islands controlled by the Maharraht.

To the southwest, a silhouette against the bright yellow sunset, was the *Strovya*. Nikandr had ordered them to run as a decoy, hopefully pulling any ships away that might be watching. But so far the *Strovya* had not been approached. In fact, they'd not found any resistance at all, and so, as had been agreed, the *Strovya* would continue west to Mirkotsk and finally head south, toward Khalakovo, toward home.

"It isn't too late to reconsider."

Nikandr turned and found Jahalan approaching. His right leg ended in a wooden peg. The bottom of it was wrapped in triple-thick goat hide, and Jahalan had become quite accustomed to it, but even the small thump it made as Jahalan made his way across the deck reminded him of Ghayavand, where Jahalan's leg had been wounded by the serpents and they'd been forced to amputate in order to save his life.

Nikandr forced himself to focus on the winds. Jahalan had long become used to the wound. Why couldn't *he*?

"I cannot turn back," Nikandr said when Jahalan finally reached his side. The winds were in their favor, so there was no need for Jahalan to guide them.

"You can. You just won't admit it to yourself. Soroush will never turn, and neither will anyone else on the island."

"I'm not so sure."

"About the Maharraht?"

"About Soroush. He is a hard man, but above all he is loyal to his people."

"*Nyet*. He would sacrifice every last one of them if he could rid the islands of the Grand Duchy."

"This is my point. He is no closer to that than he was when he joined them, and if he loses more of his people, his goals are even further away, perhaps even unattainable. As much as he hates me, as much as he loathes the notion of helping one of the Landed, he will join us."

The ship was beginning to lower. Nikandr studied the smaller island they approached. It was still several leagues out from Rafsuhan, and it was an excellent place to hide the *Chaika* for the time they'd be on the island. It was craggy, with several small inlets where they could moor the ship.

"Even if you're right," Nikandr continued, "we cannot ignore the chance to learn more about the rift."

"Small chance of doing that if you're dead."

"You don't long for a chance to speak with them?"

"To what end? I don't approve of the Maharraht or their methods, and given the chance, I will admit that I yearn to learn more of them, but I'm a realist. It may be that none of them will learn in this life, or even the next. A dozen cycles may pass before they've undone the damage they're doing in this life."

"So you've said, but is it ever too late to start?"

"I see," Jahalan said. "You wish to be considered noble before you die."

"I merely wish to do what I can." Nikandr turned, trying to read his old friend's mood. "If you're so convinced this is the wrong path to take, why did you agree to come?"

Jahalan merely stared out toward Rafsuhan, a coal black rock against the indigo horizon.

"Jahalan?"

He turned then and looked Nikandr in the eye. "When one knows someone as well as I know you, and they see how the winds of fate swirl around them, they wish to watch, and perhaps learn."

"The winds of fate care not about me."

Jahalan smiled. "There you are wrong, son of Iaros." He turned and walked back to ward the starward mainmast, his leg thumping against the deck. "Come, we have work to do."

The small island was much closer now. "Pull in the topsails," Nikandr said to the boatswain, "and prepare to moor."

"*Da*, Kapitan!"

The following morning, under a gray and cheerless sky, Nikandr sat near the bow of the skiff as it bucked in the bitterly cold wind. They flew low to the water—so low that they were often struck by the salty spray. Nikandr refused to order them higher, though. He would not give the Maharraht warning if he could avoid it. Of the Maharraht, though, there had been no sign.

Jahalan and Anahid, one of Jahalan's distant cousins, guided the skiff. Neither seemed on edge, but the streltsi that had come were watching the island with something akin to horror in their eyes. He didn't much blame them. These were seasoned men, handpicked by Nikandr himself, and they had all seen battle, but it was one thing to fight the Maharraht in the shallows of home or another friendly duchy; it was quite another to search the Maharraht out on their own island, where they would defend it with a brutality and fierceness rarely seen, even among such ruthless folk.

Soroush sat aft, his hands tied to the thwart he was sitting upon. He wore a turban—something Nikandr saw no need to deny him—in the style of the Maharraht, the cloth ragged, the tail hanging down along his chest. His long black beard was more ragged than it had been after Mirashadal, and Nikandr wondered if he had been growing it in self-imposed penance. Perhaps he thought Nikandr's arrival, and his subsequent release, had been the fates shining upon him once more. That was fine with Nikandr so long as it didn't embolden him overly much. Nikandr watched him for some time, but not once did he look up. Instead, he kept his gaze locked on the island with an intensity that made Nikandr nervous.

They reached the rocky shores of Rafsuhan an hour after launching from the *Chaika*. They moored the skiff in a vale with a stream running down from the stark highlands. It was as good a place as any to begin their trek eastward toward Siafyan. It was one of two outposts on the island. Ashdi en Ghat was the larger of the two, but it was also the more militant. It was said that the leadership of the Maharraht were housed there. Those in Siafyan were still dedicated to the Maharraht cause, but they had come to realize that it may take years, generations, for them to reach their goal, and in that light they had forged from this cold, rocky island a village where they could raise their young, grow crops, and learn while they waited for their leaders to push the Landed from the islands once and for all.

Nikandr levered himself over the gunwales and down to the uneven terrain, watching himself carefully lest he twist an ankle on the sharp rocks. The beach, and much of the land leading uphill toward the peaks of Rafsuhan, was bleak and gray. It looked as if a host of drakhen had clawed their way up, the stone yielding and fracturing until all that remained was a sharp and deadly slope.

Soroush stared dispassionately as Nikandr approached the rear of the skiff. "Release him," Nikandr said to Styophan, his most trusted man and the sotnik of the streltsi.

Styophan, a tall, well-muscled man, reached inside and began untying the ropes around Soroush's wrists. With the cold wind gusting against the gray fur of his kolpak hat, Styophan worked at the knots. He did it casually while staring at Soroush, as if he wanted him to attack. Styophan's father and brother had both been murdered in the same week, in two separate and largely un-related attacks, one in the shipping lanes north of Khalakovo, the other in the shallow fishing grounds east of Ishal. Styophan had eagerly accepted the post when Nikandr had offered it to him, and Nikandr had nearly withdrawn it—he needed clear-thinking men on this mission, not those whose only goal was to taste the blood of the Maharraht—but in the end he'd decided to keep him. Styophan was too good of a soldier to leave behind.

While Styophan was somehow eager and calm, the five other streltsi were tense. They held pistols at the ready, alternating glances between Soroush and the boulders that loomed on the hillside above, as if at any moment the whole of the Maharraht would storm down to retrieve their leader.

"Easy," Nikandr said to them.

The expressions on their faces softened, and their shoulders lost some of their pent-up tension, but it was clear they were still wound tightly.

Soroush waited to be untied, and then he looked to Nikandr.

"Please," Nikandr said, "come."

He swung himself over the gunwales and down to the stones, steadying himself before facing Nikandr. It was strange to see him with no stone in his turban. It made him seem impotent, somehow, unmanned, yet when Nikandr looked him in the eyes, there was a completely different story to behold. Gone was the man who had seemed out of balance during their conversation on the *Strovya*. In his place was a man who seemed sure of himself, as if *he* had been the one who had summoned Nikandr to these shores.

"I have not changed my mind," Soroush said.

"I know," Nikandr replied.

Soroush blew several times into his cupped hands, warming them. "Then why? Why bring me here where I'm so close to those who would kill you at but a word from me?"

"Because I must." Nikandr turned and made his way toward the others, but when he heard no sounds of movement behind him, he turned. "Are you coming?"

Soroush stared, glancing toward the other skiff and then toward the harsh peaks above them. "I will not help."

"As you've said." Nikandr wanted Soroush to come, he was desperate for it, but in the end he could not force him. Soroush would come or he would not. Either way, there were many things to do while here, and he would prefer to be about it, one way or the other.

A moment later, he heard the sound of the rocks shifting behind him over the rush of the surf. He did not smile—the day was too grim for such things—but he was glad.

Nikandr ordered three streltsi and Anahid to remain with the skiff. After preparing shoulder packs with several days' worth of food, they were off. Styophan led the way. Two streltsi brought up the rear with Soroush, leaving Jahalan and Nikandr at the middle of the line.

They wound their way up through the treacherous rocks. There was no trail. Styophan had a good eye for climbing, yet there were still many places where it took them long minutes of careful navigation. Nikandr was apt to look after Jahalan, but he found that despite any reservations he might have of the man's climbing abilities, he was more than capable, wooden leg or no.

Soon the sounds of the surf were replaced with the sigh of the wind and the occasional call of the whistle thrush. Past midday, it began to snow. It was light, but after a while it made the going even more treacherous. One of the streltsi twisted his ankle, though thankfully it wasn't bad. Too much more of this, Nikandr thought, and they would be forced to stop until the snow abated.

But soon the snow had reduced to only flurries, and an hour later they reached a shallow stretch of land that would take them to the foot of the nearest peaks. If his information was correct, Siafyan lay in a valley between the nearest of them.

Along a ridge line above them, Nikandr noticed what appeared to be a convenient hole in a pile of rocks, and the closer he looked, the more unnatural the formation looked.

He pulled his pistol and grabbed Styophan's arm and pointed. A moment later, Styophan's gaze hardened, and he waved the two streltsi at the rear of the line forward. Together, the three of them climbed in lockstep, one of them always at the ready, pistol drawn, watching the rocks, while the other two climbed, quickly but quietly.

Nikandr stood to one side of the nominal trail they'd been following. He held his pistol at the ready, but left the hammer uncocked.

Jahalan watched all of this impassively, while Soroush fixated on the rocks as if he was sure that any moment a horde of Maharraht would begin firing down on them.

The streltsi finally gained the ridge and were lost from sight. Several minutes passed, and Nikandr grew nervous, but then Styophan emerged above the rocks and waved his hand.

"Come," Nikandr said, pointing Soroush to go on ahead.

After a brief pause, he complied, climbing ahead, and soon all of them had reached a narrow plateau that offered little in the way of protection except for the outcropping of rocks. Nikandr made his way there. It was certainly an outpost. The rocks, perhaps from some ancient fall, had positioned themselves in such a way that a small clearing had been created, as large as the interior of a skiff. The west-facing wall appeared to have been built by the hand of a vanaqiram, however. Stones had been fitted and fixed such that it offered good protection from the elements while providing an excellent view of the slope they'd just scaled.

There was evidence of a fire pit—caked soot and the charred remains of wood—and in a hole built into the wall they found several old apples, now shriveled and dark.

"Why wasn't it manned?" Nikandr asked Styophan after checking to make sure Soroush was out of earshot.

Styophan appeared as confused as Nikandr. "I know not, My Lord Prince. Perhaps they *did* see us and left for reinforcements."

Nikandr frowned and stared up at the two tall peaks, which now seemed much closer. "Perhaps, though they could have summoned any number of reinforcements by now. I imagine we'll find another, larger outpost not far ahead."

"As you say, My Lord."

"Come," Nikandr said, putting his pistol away. "Best we get moving."

Less than an hour later they came upon a tower made from the same gray rock as was found on the climb up. It was nestled behind a copse of larch, and was well hidden, but the top of the rounded and elegant structure had a clear view of the narrow canyon they were about to enter.

Nikandr called a halt, and for a time they merely watched for signs of movement. When there were none, he called for everyone to move together.

When they approached the tower, they saw that the door at the lowest level was open. It swung lightly in the breeze, knocking softly against the jam.

Styophan looked back to Nikandr, confused.

Nikandr shrugged and motioned for the three streltsi at the rear to remain with Soroush, then he continued on, bringing Styophan and Jahalan with him.

It felt as though eyes were upon them, from the nearby trees, from the darkened windows of the tower, from the rocky slope above. They reached the door and stepped inside, and a sour stench assaulted them. Nikandr knew what it was immediately—he'd smelled it many times before. It was the smell of the dead.

There was no one on this lowest level, but there were several bunks and a table with chairs, all of them disheveled or overturned. A curving set of stairs hugged the inside of the tower to their left. They went up slowly, carefully, pistols drawn.

The second level had a store of goods and munitions—baskets of potatoes and more shriveled apples, several serviceable muskets and a few pistols, all of them mismatched.

It was on the third level where the smell became markedly worse. Nikandr hid his nose in the crook of his elbow, which did little to mask the smell but made it somewhat bearable. Styophan and even the stoic Jahalan were forced to do the same.

On the far side of the room, just below a shuttered window, were two bodies. One looked like he'd died from a wound to his gut. He looked to be in his mid-twenties. He was still propped up against the wall, his dusty, rose-colored robes stained dark with blood around his midsection and groin. His arms were wrapped loosely around his wound, as though he'd lost the energy at the very end to stem the pain and had finally relaxed, allowing death to take him.

The other body was hidden in shadow further from the window. But when Nikandr approached, he sucked in his breath, unable to come closer. It was a woman. Her body was desiccated, blackened, shriveled like the apples still sitting in their baskets two stories down. Her arms were curled up near her head, and though Nikandr knew he could tell little from their dying postures, it appeared as though she'd died in much more pain than the man had.

These were not the most alarming, however. Near them, curled up into a ball, was the figure of a girl, perhaps ten or eleven years old. Her body was naked, and her skin was pale and sickly, but it was her face that drew the eye. She had no eyes to speak of. The skin had grown over, leaving her eyeless. Her jaw was elongated, and it was cast open, like the maw of a deep and dangerous cave.

"Ancients preserve us," Nikandr whispered.

He'd seen the like before. He and Nasim and Ashan had been chased through the streets of Alayazhar by creatures such as this. Akhoz, Ashan had named them. They had lived there, he'd said, since the early days of the sundering, ever tortured, ever hungry.

For long moments he could only stare. How in the name of the mothers and fathers had these abominations reached these shores?

CHAPTER EIGHTEEN

"**G**o," Nikandr said to Styophan, "and bring Soroush."

The officer's gaze darted to Nikandr, then back to the bodies. He blinked, his eyes hard but conflicted, as if this had been exactly what he'd been hoping to see, but now that he'd come face-to-face with it he wasn't so sure.

And then he caught Nikandr watching him, and he nodded and left.

As the footsteps upon the stairs faded, Jahalan approached the akhoz—his right leg thumping softly over the wooden flooring. He kneeled down by her side and leaned close, examining her face, her neck, her exposed hands.

"Are they the same as you saw on Ghayavand?" Jahalan asked. They had discussed his time on that island in detail many times. Jahalan remembered very little of that time, as feverish as he'd been after he'd lost his leg to the serpents, but by now he had a good understanding, at least of Nikandr's view of those events.

"Very much the same. But how?"

"The rift, of course."

"But even if it's wider than the others we've seen, how could there be such a drastic change? We've seen only the wasting, never something like this."

Jahalan leaned forward and sniffed the skin of the akhoz. "I cannot but think it has something to do with our heritage."

"Or the way you commune with spirits."

"Just so."

"And what of her?" Nikandr asked as he squatted next to the woman. "It looks like the wasting, only much, much worse." He couldn't help but think of the gnawing feeling in his gut when he'd had the wasting before the ritual with Nasim had saved him. He wondered what might have happened to him—or Victania—had the rift been wider. Would he have ended up like this?

"It worries me greatly," Jahalan said. "I only hope we can discover more."

He meant, discover more without interference from the Maharraht, of course. "I'll be back," Nikandr said.

With a vicious chill overtaking him, Nikandr took the stone rungs of the ladder that led up to the roof. He slid open the wooden door and stepped out to open air. After pulling his soulstone out and kissing it, he spread his arms wide and opened himself to the elements. He could feel the havahezhan immediately. It rarely took long to summon, but here it was especially close—as near as it had ever been.

"Do you feel it too?" he asked the wind as it whipped his hair and his heavy woolen cherkesska.

He had never felt the aether, never experienced it directly, but at the moment he felt as though he knew the boundaries of it: as a blind man senses a tree, not by the sound of the wind running through its branches but by the *feel* of the wind as it coursed over the bark. He felt, in fact, as though he could reach out his hand and touch the world of Adhiya, as if he could part the veil and draw the hezhan forth—something only the most gifted of arqesh should be able to do.

Despite the harrowing ramifications, it was exhilarating.

Would someone like Ashan feel the same? Or would he be horrified?

He nearly asked Jahalan to come up to speak to him of it, but just then he saw Styophan leading Soroush and the streltsi toward the tower. He took the ladder down again, and soon Soroush was coming up the stairs. Styophan followed behind, bearing his pistol.

"Leave us," Nikandr said.

Styophan paused, glancing at Soroush. He opened his mouth to protest, but Nikandr talked over him.

"Leave us."

Styophan nodded and complied, his eyes hard as they bored into Soroush.

When he'd gone, Nikandr beckoned Soroush closer. Soroush did so, staring down at the body of the akhoz, not with horror, but with morbid fascination. He was transfixed. His jaw worked. His nostrils flared. "How long—" He composed himself before trying once more. "How long has the rift been here?"

"Over a year."

He looked out to the window, which happened to be facing southeast, toward Siafyan. Then his attention was caught by Nikandr's soulstone, which glowed softly in the relative darkness. He set his jaw, and a tear slipped slowly down one cheek.

"What would you have me do?"

Nikandr had thought he would feel relief if Soroush ever decided to help him, and yet he felt as though he'd lost something today—he and Soroush both—and he couldn't manage to feel anything more than a profound sadness at the things that had come to pass, both here and elsewhere.

"I'm sorry for your loss," he said, motioning with one hand toward the dead.

Soroush did not reply, but the look in his tear-filled eyes hardened, as if Nikandr was somehow to blame.

"Come," Nikandr said, motioning toward the stairs. "We'll talk along the way."

The sky was still overcast, and daylight was beginning to wane when they came across a defile that would lead them to the valley that housed Siafyan. There was still no sign of resistance. The wind poured through the defile with no mercy, pulling all the warmth from their bones. Even Nikandr was forced to pull his cherkesska tighter.

When they came to a bend, Nikandr heard sounds from above, from the top of the defile. He thought surely the Maharraht were there, ready to fire down upon them, but as they waited, pistols drawn, staring up at the cloudy sky while the walls of the defile seemed to close in on them, they heard nothing more.

At last, when the mouth of the defile was clear before them, they saw movement above. A boy, small and thin of frame, stared down at them, but as soon as the boy saw them look up, he retreated.

"Wait!" Soroush called in Mahndi.

But the boy did not return.

They moved faster after that, hoping to catch him if he was headed toward the village. Ahead, the defile was coming to an end. Nikandr could see the gray skies beyond and the heavily shadowed valley.

And then he saw smoke.

Soroush did too. As he walked, a look of concern came over him. He picked up his pace. Then, before Nikandr could stop him, he slipped past Styophan and began to run.

"Halt!" Styophan called, drawing his pistol.

But Soroush didn't listen.

Styophan fired his pistol, rock spraying to the right of Soroush as he took a bend in the defile.

The other streltsi swung their muskets around.

"Hold fire!" Nikandr shouted as he ran forward.

Soroush, already well ahead, reached the mouth of the defile and darted to his right. Nikandr reached the mouth soon after. It was here that the valley opened up. It was dominated by a thick covering of larch that could easily hide those who wished to remain hidden. The trail out of the defile was little more than a switchbacked path that led down to the valley floor, and Soroush was already two turns of the trail lower.

"Soroush, stop!" Nikandr shouted.

Soroush continued, refusing to look up.

Nikandr ran after him, taking care lest he slip over the edge of the narrow path. He could see the edge of the village now. The buildings, most of them wood, not stone, were less than a half-league ahead, but the fire was not coming from there. It was coming from a clearing in the forest not far from the base of the path.

By the time Nikandr reached level ground, Soroush was already lost in the woods. Nikandr pulled his pistol and watched as he ran, his breath huffing, his thighs burning. He pushed harder, hoping to reach the fire before Soroush.

As he approached, a scent came to him from the woods. It was the smell of burning flesh, and it was accompanied by the heartbroken sound of a grown man moaning and weeping.

When he reached the clearing, he stopped and was again forced to cover his nose and mouth. In the center of the clearing was a charred pile of bodies, all of them shriveled and blackened nearly beyond recognition. Soroush was on his knees before the horrific scene, his hands lifted to the sky, shaking, quivering. He though Soroush was simply crying from the pain of facing such tragedy, but he realized it was much more. This was a dirge for his people, an appeal for the dead. A lamentation.

Nikandr stood there, helpless, as this hardened man, this murderer of Landed men and women, cried for his people. Nikandr found himself filled with sympathy, but also with satisfaction. Satisfaction that Soroush now felt what he had felt, what so many of the Landed had felt for those who had fallen to attacks from the Maharraht.

He cursed himself a moment later for being so heartless. Whatever Soroush might have done, whatever the Maharraht had done to the Landed, women and children did not deserve to burn.

It seemed at first as if the entire village lay within this pile of charred remains, but then Nikandr forced himself to estimate their numbers and realized that there were only thirty, perhaps forty bodies. This village was one that could house three or four hundred. So where had they gone?

His men reached the clearing behind him. They had clearly been running, but they slowed as they came near, staring wide-eyed at the horror before them.

Nikandr went to Soroush. "Come," he said.

When he did not, Nikandr laid a hand on his shoulder.

Soroush stood, slapping Nikandr's hand away. He stood face-to-face with Nikandr, anger in his eyes—hatred and revulsion—and for a moment Nikandr thought Soroush might reach for his throat, but then he cleared the tears from his cheeks, took several deep breaths.

And trudged toward Siafyan without saying a word.

They reached the edge of the village near nightfall. The structures Nikandr had seen from the defile towered over him. They were not so much built as *grown* from the forest around them. The larch had been coaxed, bent and shaped by gifted dhoshaqiram into towers that interlaced with one another. Walkways crossed high above them, leading to empty archways that yawned in the coming darkness. The smell of the larch was strong here, but also floral, and pleasant, as if this too had been coaxed from the trees by the hand of the Maharraht. The wind was the only thing to be heard. No people, no children. No sounds of cooking or laughter or quarrels. Nothing save an exhalation as Siafyan and the forest around it prepared for the coming night.

They came to what Nikandr took as the central square. A fountain stood there—as was common in nearly all Landless villages—though no water emerged from it.

Perhaps he was respectful, or perhaps fear was preventing him, but Soroush seemed hesitant to approach—much less enter—the towers. Nikandr, however, thought it foolish to wait. There was no telling what might befall them during the night; better to investigate now than allow something to come upon them while they slept.

"May I enter?" he asked Soroush.

Soroush stared at the fountain. He pulled his attention from it—regretfully, it seemed—and met Nikandr's gaze. After a moment of thought, he gave a motion of his hand, as if Nikandr were a child who had asked for a sweet.

Nikandr sent one of the streltsi and Jahalan to searching the lower levels of the village, and then he took to the towers himself, moving from room to room, which all seemed molded from the stuff of the trees themselves. The beautiful grain of the larch was revealed everywhere. Sculptures of stone and wood sat on shelves and mantles. Beds, chairs, blankets. All of it pristine.

All except the bark of the trees.

Nikandr almost didn't notice, but as he was taking a winding pathway down from a tower to head back for the fountain, he steadied himself against the bark. It powdered beneath his touch. He stopped and stared, brushed more of the bark away. There was solid wood beneath, but it was clear that the trees themselves were beginning to desiccate.

He thought back to his time on Ghayavand. His ship, the *Gorovna*, had withered beneath his touch. It was a similar effect to this, though there were differences. This wood was still living, where the windwood of the ship was dead wood. Still, Nikandr was sure it had more to do with the nature of Ghayavand—the rifts it contained and the hezhan it housed—than anything else.

Nikandr caught movement from the corner of his eye.

Turning casually, he saw a form hidden behind one of the towers some distance away. He wasn't sure, but he suspected it was the boy they'd caught watching them from the top of the defile.

He pretended as if he hadn't noticed as he strode toward another of the massive towers.

But the boy sensed his intent. He ducked behind the tree and ran, his footsteps crunching softly against the cold ground.

"Stop! I won't hurt you!" Nikandr ran after him, darting around the tree, losing him for a moment. But then he found him again, heading toward one of the tallest towers in the village. If he were to gain any height he could lose himself in the village for days.

Nikandr quickened his pace, but soon found that it wasn't necessary. The boy was already losing speed. He was weak, perhaps from lack of food, perhaps from sickness. He paused as he gained the walkway circling up and around the tower, and then he collapsed.

By the time Nikandr came near, the boy had turned onto his back and was scrabbling away, fear plain on his face.

"Please," Nikandr said, holding up his hands for the child to see. "I only wish to know what happened. Why are you—"

With night coming on, light was scarce, but Nikandr could see that he'd been mistaken. This was no boy at all; it was a girl. She wore a boy's clothes, and her hair was wrapped up into a dark turban, but the set of her eyes, her lips, the line of her jaw. It was unmistakable now.

"Why are you here?" Nikandr asked.

She spoke in Mahndi. Nikandr knew the language well, but she was speaking so quickly, and her accent was thick enough that he couldn't understand her.

He held up his hands to stop her. "Slower," he said in Mahndi.

"I left when they began burning..." She waved toward the scene in the woods, the pile of smoking bodies. "They'd taken memma."

"Why?" Nikandr asked. "Why were so many burned?"

"They'd been marked."

"Marked by what?"

"By the taint. They said those who had been touched would die."

"So they forced everyone there so they could burn them?"

She was already shaking her head. "*Neh*. They went—"

She'd spoken so quickly he couldn't understand her last word. "They what?"

"They went willingly."

Nikandr stared, confused, but then her words settled over him like a thick blanket of snow.

Willingly, she'd said. They'd gone *willingly*.

By the ancients, what was happening on this island?

CHAPTER NINETEEN

Bahett, dressed in a fine white kaftan and a red silk turban with a massive pearl set into it, stood near Atiana's door. "Someone will come within the hour," he said.

Ishkyna stood next to him, waiting impatiently and holding a mask with iridescent black feathers affixed to it.

"Bahett, I love my sister. But masks or not, you're making a mistake if you think that anyone will confuse the two of us."

"It isn't so hard," Ishkyna said. "All I need do is pout and bite my tongue no matter what is said."

Atiana fixed her eyes on Bahett, if only to avoid gazing upon Ishkyna's smug face. "You see?"

"She has promised her best behavior."

"I'm not yet ready," Atiana said.

"You must *be* ready. Arvaneh and the Kamarisi will both be occupied, as will nearly everyone else who's come to Baressa. They won't expect you to do something so quickly."

"That's because it would be foolish to do so. The aether is a storm here. I need time to assess it properly. This is no time to dive into the water like a child driven mad with boredom. We must take our time, or all of this will be for naught."

Bahett came to her and took up her hands. His skin was soft—the hands of a man well used to the life of a Kaymakam. "All I ask is that you try. If you cannot but step into the aether, then so be it. Can you do this for me?"

She squeezed his hands and released them. "I will do it for the Grand Duchy."

"Of course," Bahett said, bowing his head.

"Go," Atiana said.

"Come, Bahett." Ishkyna raised her mask to her face and widened her eyes at Atiana. "It's time I become as dull as I can possibly be."

After one apologetic smile, Bahett rushed out. Atiana stepped outside her room onto a small balcony. The hour was late, but far away on the southern horizon ships could still be seen heading toward the eyrie. Most would be bringing in provisions, and perhaps a few final members of royalty. Most of the dignitaries from the islands had already arrived and would be preparing for the reception.

It felt strange to be separated from them, and even stranger to be spying upon her hosts. She was not averse to it—the Kamarisi and his consort needed watching—but ties with Galahesh had always been strong, primarily between the Vostromas and the line of Kirdhash. In many ways, they had always seemed like the tenth Duchy—perhaps not to anyone who'd grown up on a more distant archipelago, but certainly to anyone who'd been raised on the shores of Vostroma.

A knock came at her door, and Yalessa stepped in. "He's come."

Atiana merely nodded. She followed Yalessa outside, and there, waiting for them, was a bald man, no older than Atiana. He stood meekly, clasping his hands together. He was a mute, and most likely castrated as well.

Atiana had always felt uncomfortable around the slaves of Yrstanla, but there was little choice in the matter now. Galahesh allowed few slaves, but with so many visiting from the capital, the kasir was thick with them.

They traveled down through little-used hallways and stairwells until they reached the ground floor. Throughout the walk, Atiana did not see a single other soul—clearly Bahett's doing.

They left the kasir through the door reserved for the servants and continued until they reached a high wall built from ragged, sharp stones. Atiana knew that inside lay the graveyard. She dearly hoped that this was not where the servant was taking them, but she knew in the same breath that it was.

They followed a stone-lined path. Near the top of the wall, spaced every few paces, were round holes, like windows meant to allow the dead to look out upon the living, upon the lives they once led. One section of the wall was marred by hundreds of pockmarks and several larger holes—signs of battle, Atiana knew, and somewhat recent, as the revealed stone was still bright, where the rest was dull and gray.

Even the walls have tales to tell, she thought.

They eventually came to a tall iron gate. The servant opened it soundlessly, and together they walked through the elaborate stone mausoleums. The early stars were out, the day having been reduced to a haze in the west. She had been to the cemetery only twice before. Both times had been for funerals, and she had found the experience unnerving, seeing so many houses for the dead crowding the landscape like crows before the feast. She had never been here at dusk, however, and it made the experience all the more chilling.

"How much further?" she asked.

The slave turned and motioned ahead with his hands, bobbing his head apologetically.

They turned down a row bordered by stone tombs with peaked roofs and crouching lions that stared hungrily down at them.

"Do you have a light?" Atiana asked.

The slave shook his head, this time not bothering to turn around.

Atiana stopped.

"What is it?" Yalessa asked.

Atiana stared down the row, feeling something crawl along her spine as she watched.

Something wasn't right.

The servant turned. She could no longer see his face in the darkness, only a patch of white where his face once was. He raised his arm and beckoned her.

She looked to the roofs, to places hidden by the corners of the mausoleums.

The servant gestured toward the end of the row.

She couldn't go. Something terrible awaited her there. She just knew it.

The servant stepped forward, holding one hand out to her.

The simple gesture drove fear through her like a knife. She grabbed Yalessa's wrist and ran, not the way they'd come, but deeper into the graveyard. She sidled between two of the tombs, and then ran toward the southeast corner.

Yalessa knew enough to keep quiet, but when they came to a rest behind a massive family tomb, she whispered to Atiana. "What is it?"

"I don't know," Atiana said.

Atiana's lungs and throat were burning, but she forced herself to slow her breathing. And she listened. There were no signs of pursuit. There were no sounds at all, except for the servant, far in the distance now, grunting something that sounded like *please* in Yrstanlan.

Atiana was beginning to feel foolish. It had only been a feeling, a premonition, but she had come to rely on such things in the years since she'd embraced the aether.

Yalessa began to speak, but Atiana placed a hand over her mouth. In the distance, at the peak of one of the tombs, there was a silhouette—a shoulder or a head outlined by the dim light coming from the west.

Atiana watched, and it did not move, and she thought surely it was merely another statue.

"Should we return?" Yalessa asked.

Atiana turned back to the tomb, a shiver running through her.

The silhouette was gone.

"Quickly now," she whispered.

"My Lady, we're going the wrong way."

She gripped Yalessa's hand fiercely as they ran, willing her to silence.

Atiana led her around the large tomb. They followed a haphazard trail, dashing through several more rows, cutting between tombs, then running and slipping down a narrow path between two massive stone statues, all in a desperate attempt to throw their pursuers off the scent.

At last they came to an area where there were no tombs. A circle of standing stones, no higher than Atiana's waist, stood around a small field of grass, and in the center of the field was a willow, tall and swaying in the breeze. Standing beneath the vine-like branches was a man, tall by the look of him. She could see no other details. It was too dark.

She slid sideways along the paving stones set into the mossy earth. Yalessa gripped her hand so hard it hurt.

Atiana heard a faint click, then again. It was soft, but the sound carried like a knife in the dark.

Moments later two more forms—one on either side of Atiana—slid out from between the tombs.

Atiana had only a short knife at her belt, useless here, but she drew it just the same and stepped toward the form beneath the willow.

"Who are you?"

"Be quiet," he said, "and come. Leave the girl with my men."

He spoke Anuskayan, though his accent was thick with Yrstanlan.

Atiana thought quickly. She did not want to leave Yalessa, as scared as the girl was—and Atiana herself felt hardly any braver—but these men could have already killed them had they wished to. "Go," she whispered to Yalessa, who continued to hold onto her hand for dear life. "Go," she said louder. "All will be well."

Yalessa left, shivering, as the men closed in beside her. Atiana stepped toward the willow. The man parted the vines and she stepped inside. The darkness became pronounced; the only thing she could see was the faint imprint of willow leaves swaying. The rustle of the leaves was just loud enough to cover their conversation.

"Who are you?" Atiana asked again.

The man was silent, making it clear this was not a question he would answer, at least not yet. "Let us speak instead of why you're here."

"Those are my reasons alone."

"Yours and Bahett's."

"It's no secret the Kaymakam and I are to be married."

"This has nothing to do with your marriage."

The wind blew the willow vines, tickling Atiana's ankles and the hem of her dress. "I would know with whom I'm speaking before I say one more word."

"Consider me a friend for now."

"That's not good enough."

In the darkness, she saw him shift his weight from one hip to another, perhaps choosing his words carefully. "I'm a man loyal to the Kamarisi."

"Then why are you sneaking about his cemetery?"

"It's not the Kamarisi's. It's Bahett's, the Kaymakam's, and it is *him* I do not trust."

"And by that you mean you do not trust *me*."

"I didn't say that."

"But you meant it."

Again he was silent for a time. "You've come here at Bahett's bidding, and if I didn't know who you were, I wouldn't think much of it. A princess from a foreign land, a woman who'll soon become his ilkadin, would have every right to visit the cemetery, perhaps paying respect to relatives who died here long ago. But it is known that you are Matra, and this is what gives me pause."

He was coming altogether too close to the mark for comfort. "Who was chasing me?"

"Men who wished to bid you good fortune for your wedding day." She could hear the sneer in his voice.

"I begin to wonder if they are allies of yours, meant to scare me into telling you secrets."

"A shrewd thought, My Lady Princess. They were allies once, and not so long ago. They are men fiercely loyal to the Kamarisi."

"And you are not?"

"We're every bit as loyal. We merely differ on *how* we think the Kamarisi should be protected."

"Why?" Atiana asked. "Why does the Kamarisi need such protection?"

A series of clicks came from beyond the willow tree. A moment later, more clicks came from the space before her. She could see little, but she thought she saw his shoulder and arm moving, perhaps from something he was manipulating in his hand, a device of some sort.

When he spoke again, his voice had risen in pitch, and it was subtly faster than before. "He needs protection because he is not himself. And do you know why?"

This was all strangely similar to the conversation she'd had with Bahett in Galostina. This man knew she had come here at Bahett's request. What he didn't know was how much Bahett had told her. She thought of lying. She also thought that telling the truth might give him reason to kill her. But she didn't think this was the case. His motives, strangely enough, felt sincere. And she needed to understand how his purpose differed from Bahett's.

"He needs protection because the Lady Arvaneh has enthralled him."

"Which is why Bahett brought you here. A Matra, from the shores of Anuskaya, here just as Lady Arvaneh arrives…"

Atiana didn't answer. He'd come close enough to the truth. It was she that had contacted Bahett, but now she wondered how much Bahett had looked upon the overture as good fortune. Suddenly it felt like she'd been manipulated into the whole thing, though she knew that wasn't the case. It couldn't be…

"It's said," he continued, "that the Matri cannot spy upon Baressa or beyond it because of the straits. Is it so?"

"Tell me first why the others, the ones you were so recently allied with, would wish me dead."

"It must be for the same reason," he said, more to himself than her. "They see you as a threat." She saw his head turn, focusing on her once more. There was a pregnant pause where she felt him staring at her in the darkness, his mind working through the implications. "Who is it you've come to spy upon?" He spoke these words slowly, the timbre of his voice low and resonant.

Atiana tried to swallow the lump that had formed in her throat. She had a primal urge to run. So strong was it that she'd taken a step back before realizing it. She composed herself, forced her breathing to remain steady, as she did in the drowning basin after submerging herself in the bone-chilling water. "I'm here to spy on no one."

"Come, My Lady." He took a half step forward. "We both know that isn't true."

And then she understood. He thought she was there to spy on him, or his allies, or both. He thought her an ally of Bahett, and Bahett a puppet of the Kamarisi. Surely he thought she was there to protect the Kamarisi. He didn't understand that Bahett was acting beyond the orders of his Lord.

"You don't understand," Atiana said.

He took another half step forward. "Who have you come to spy upon?"

She took one step back. The vines were at her back now, swaying, brushing against her hair.

Another series of clicks came. They were short, and very, very soft.

Atiana heard the unmistakable sound of a sword being pulled from its sheath. "You must go."

She shivered as he approached, but he merely guided her quickly, though not roughly, out from beneath the willow, spreading the vines for her as she went. "Go to the break in the wall. Tell Bahett you were attacked, and that you ran for safety."

"And if he asks who was chasing me?"

"Tell him the truth"—he stepped away, his form receding into the darkness—"that you don't know."

"I would trust the Kirdhash family a hundred times before I trust you."

Yalessa was brought to Atiana's side by two black forms. They left, speeding along the path behind the mysterious men.

"We'll speak again," he said. And with that he was gone, lost behind the pale echo of the tombs.

"Come," Atiana said, taking Yalessa's hand.

They fled, but before they'd gone twenty paces, there was the clash of steel, only a few rows away.

Atiana went as quickly as she could. The fighting reached a fervor, but it began to fade as they made their way slowly toward the break in the wall.

At last, they found it. It stood ahead of them like an open maw, the landscape pitch-dark beyond it.

"Ancients preserve us," she said softly as she and Yalessa climbed over the broken stone and made their way slowly but surely back toward the kasir.

As the sounds of battle slowed and then died altogether, she had no idea who might have prevailed, but she found herself praying.

Praying that the mysterious man at the willow had died.

CHAPTER TWENTY

When Atiana returned to the kasir, she summoned Bahett's seneschal, a wizened old man who seemed as likely to trip on the hem of his robes as take another step. She spoke with him for two hours, and he was nearly ready to pull Bahett from the masquerade, but Atiana begged him not to. She didn't want anything to seem amiss, especially since she and Yalessa hadn't been harmed.

When she finally made it back to her rooms, she downed a small carafe of warmed vodka to calm herself before bed. She did manage to fall asleep, but when she awoke a short while later the effects of the liquor had passed and she found herself wide awake. The words of the man from the willow kept playing through her mind. They had been laced with truth, and yet each time she worked it through, she decided he was lying. Clearly he was an agent of the Kamarisi, or Arvaneh herself, set to turn her against Bahett and his allies.

And still—

A knock came at the door to Atiana's apartments. Any trace of sleep vanished in an instant.

The knock came again.

In the outer chamber, Yalessa stirred and moved to the door. A soft click came, and the sounds of whispers drifted in to her. A moment later, Yalessa, carrying a lit taper, slipped inside her room and rushed to her bed.

"Bahett wishes to speak with you."

Atiana swallowed, remembering the words of the tall man from the cemetery. She maneuvered herself down from the bed and pulled on her night coat as Yalessa lit another taper. They moved to the outer chamber, and Atiana settled herself at a table with several opulent, padded chairs.

"Send him in," Atiana said, "and take my room. We may be a while."

"Of course, My Lady."

The dark form of Bahett slipped into the room. Yalessa retreated to Atiana's bedroom, closing the door behind her.

"I'm most sorry." Bahett moved to the table, his handsome face filled with regret. "Janissaries were stationed at all the entrances to the cemetery, but it is large. It's a mistake that won't be made again." He sat down, his face lit in soft, golden light. "The guardsman at the southern entrance said he heard fighting among the tombs. Did you hear it as well?"

She nodded. "Just as we were leaving through the break in the wall."

"And you saw no one?"

And now it came to it. She had told the seneschal nothing about the men near the willow, only that she had heard sounds of battle among the tombs, but she had debated ever since what she would tell Bahett. She did not trust the tall, dark man she'd spoken to, but he hadn't said anything that ran counter to what she knew of the Kamarisi and the Lady Arvaneh.

Atiana had always been good at trump, and one of the things she'd learned was not to play her high cards early. Not unless you knew you could run the trick. And she certainly couldn't do that, so for now she would protect what cards she did have.

"Ancients preserve me, I did not," she said to him.

Bahett's face relaxed. He lifted her hands and kissed them. It was a warm and tender gesture. "I'm so relieved, Atiana. I don't know what I would have done had they found you."

"Who were they?"

Bahett's eyes went faraway. "I wish I knew, but trust me when I say that no effort will be spared."

"And what of the servant, the eunuch?"

He focused on her once more. "An impostor. We found the one who should have been sent in his bed, his throat cut." He leaned forward until he was sitting at the edge of his chair, and then he reached out and took her left hand in his. It was not Nikandr's hand, but it was nice all the same. "Atiana, I will be blunt. It may be best that we abandon our plan. I would not put you in deeper danger, and the chances that Arvaneh will discover our plans are now too great. Clearly she suspects something, enough that she is willing to have you killed before you can learn more about her."

Atiana had been ready for him to say something completely different. She thought he would urge her to continue her efforts, no matter what the danger might be, but this was a side of Bahett she hadn't counted on. He had been so adamant in Vostroma, and now, here he was, asking her to back down.

"I have a duty to my family, Bahett, to the Grand Duchy as well."

"It may be that the Kamarisi will see reason. He may, perhaps, still be led out from under the shadow of Arvaneh's influence. I still haven't had the chance to speak to him at length, but when I do—"

"You said *Arvaneh* is the one pulling the strings. You said the Kamarisi is powerless. There's something strange happening, and I would learn its nature, danger or not." He looked as though he was about to speak again, but she talked over him. "My father arrives in less than a week. In order to protect him, to protect all our interests here, I will take the dark, as soon as can be arranged."

He smiled, the candlelight making him even more handsome than he was in the daylight. "My brave princess."

She felt herself blush as she pulled her hand away. "Go," she said, more strongly than she'd meant.

The following morning, Atiana went early to a terrace overlooking an expansive garden. Bahett was hosting a social for the Kamarisi and his retinue to meet the first of the dignitaries from the Grand Duchy who'd come. Atiana would be among the guests, of course, but so would Vaasak Dhalingrad, the younger brother of Duke Leonid and the man Father had chosen to act as his negotiator in the week before his arrival.

For Atiana's part, she was to meet Bahett's wives, or at least most of them. Some would be gone, tending to Bahett's estates around the island of Galahesh. But the most important, including Bahett's current ilkadin, would be in attendance.

Atiana met them, seventeen in all. They were all pretty, though in markedly different ways. Some were tall with bright eyes. Others had lustrous dark hair and strong cheekbones. Others still had full lips and fuller hips. Atiana felt strange upon exchanging pleasantries with them. They were real women, all of them. She had expected them to have nary a thought in their pretty little heads, but they were refined. They were well spoken. They knew much of the political landscape, if their subtle yet polite hints about her reasons for wedding Bahett were any indicator.

The last to come was Meryam, Bahett's ilkadin. When it was her turn to speak with Atiana, she clapped her hands. The other women, who had up until this point been sitting at intimate tables with mosaic inlays, stood and with their plates and cups in hand left the terrace.

In moments, Atiana was alone with Meryam at a single table, each of them sipping the strong coffee with the grounds still at the bottom of the cup. Meryam was a mature woman—she would be forty in three days, she told Atiana—and she was beautiful, a woman in her prime, a woman who commanded attention. Many of Bahett's wives wore bright dresses and jewelry at their wrists and ankles and throats. Meryam wore a ring in her nose, more in her eyebrows, more still in her ears. Her eyes were rimmed with kohl, and her dress was the color of her eyes, a brown so rich and bright it made Atiana think of beaten copper. The skin along the backs of her hands and wrists were marked with beautiful tattoos in the shapes of stars and whorls and bold, angular shapes that highlighted the landscape of her hands.

Meryam asked Atiana of Vostroma, of life among the islands. In return she spoke of Yrstanla and Alekeşir, her capital. They spoke of life on Galahesh, what the food was like, where the best cheese could be found. They spoke almost nothing of the thing that stood squarely between them: the fact that Atiana, once she was married to Bahett, would take the title that Meryam now claimed as her own.

The time was growing near when the social would begin, and still Meryam choose to speak of nothing but pleasantries.

Soon the other wives returned to the terrace—this time bearing trays with glasses and plates and silverware and food. Meryam stood and nodded toward them. "Ebru will be best to teach you."

Atiana stood. She felt dismissed and confused, both. She recalled Ebru as the short woman with the saucy tongue. "Forgive me, ilkadin, but wouldn't it be better if *you* taught me?"

"It might," she said, smiling, "but in two weeks I'll be gone."

"I don't understand."

"To my home, far to the southwest."

Atiana shook her head. "I don't understand."

"You will, in time. I've lived here in Baressa for twenty-five years. Not once in that time have I returned to my home. I was ilkadin. There was always more to do, and I've sired Bahett three sons and two daughters. I've earned the right to leave this place and run one of his households there."

"I thought we'd have time with one another, so I could learn more."

"That would be nice, wouldn't it?" And now a bit of the reception Atiana had expected revealed itself. Meryam stared at her coldly, as if she wished she could watch Atiana flail, watch as Atiana floundered in the myriad of tasks that lay before her. "Now forgive me, there is much to attend to." Meryam bowed her head, clasping her hands near her forehead as she did so. "Enjoy your time with the Kamarisi."

For a moment, Atiana could only stare. Meryam returned to the wives, ordering them around the terrace, making everything just so. She wanted to speak more with her, or perhaps Ebru, but in the end decided that Meryam had the right of it. The Kamarisi, and surely Arvaneh, would both be in attendance today. She needed to clear her mind before she met them.

The lords and ladies of Galahesh began to arrive in ones and twos. Atiana moved among them, greeting them, learning their names and where they were from. The talk was idle, and she soon found herself taking in more of the city, which was in full display. As high as the Mount was above the city, the terrace smelled of little more than fresh air and the late-blooming bluemists in the garden below. The western end of the city occupied the largest expanse of the horizon, but the northern run of the straits could also be seen, yet Atiana often found her gaze drawn northward, where the cemetery lay.

"My dear Atiana," Vaasak Dhalingrad asked near the noon hour, "what keeps drawing your attention so? And what turns your mood so sour? Did you have too much to drink last night? Or have you taken ill like your sister?"

"I have not taken ill," she replied, wondering when she would see Bahett again. "I only worry over what will come of these talks."

He smiled and patted her wrist. "All will be well. Do not worry."

She slapped his hand away. "There are troubled winds ahead, Dhalingrad. Best you remember it. Sihaş surely does, and the Kamarisi as well."

"The talks are proceeding smoothly," Vaasak said.

"Then you aren't paying enough attention."

"I have my orders, My Lady, and I'll see to them well. I suggest you see to yours."

He said the words as though he knew of her conversations with Bahett, as though he knew of what had happened last night. But he couldn't possibly...

Before she could respond to him, the golden doors to the terrace opened wide and out stepped four tall guardsmen dressed not in ceremonial armor, but hardened leather, the kind the men from the south of Yrstanla wore, the ones who trained with the sword day and night. They were the Kiliç Şaik, the Singers of the Blade, the Kamarisi's personal guard.

Shortly behind them came Hakan ül Ayeşe, the Kamarisi himself. He was young, several years younger than Atiana at least, and he was handsome. She could see why he was so loved, so protected—at least until now.

Behind the Kamarisi was Sihaş ül Mehmed, the tall envoy, the one treating most closely with Vaasak until Father arrived.

Atiana wondered where Arvaneh was, but she didn't have to wonder long. She strode out from the doors as Hakan began speaking with two old, bearded men from the north of Yrstanla, men wearing wide belts and large turbans with tall feathers pinned behind ornate brooches. Arvaneh did not tarry behind the Kamarisi. Instead, she walked among those gathered, conversing lightly, studying each carefully.

Atiana was surprised to see the Kamarisi break away from the two kaymakam—both of them bowing low—and come toward her and Vaasak.

"Good day to you," he said smoothly to Vaasak.

"And you, Kamarisi," Vaasak said as he bowed and stepped away. "By your leave, there are things I would discuss with Sihaṣ."

Hakan merely smiled.

Vaasak—his face coloring—bowed again and took his leave, leaving Atiana alone with the Kamarisi. He had a musky scent about him, redolent of sandalwood and open fields of hops. It smelled of confidence, of the assurance that all was as he'd planned. She was used to walking the halls of power, and yet before this man—several years her junior—she felt ill-equipped. She found herself shivering, though she tried to cover it, and unbidden, her throat began to close.

"Walk with me," he said in Yrstanlan.

He headed toward the northern edge of the expansive terrace, and he came to a stop when they were not only alone, but had an unobstructed view of the cemetery.

"Congratulations to you," he said, smiling and taking both of her hands. He kissed them quickly and held them out, regarding her as if he were a proud uncle.

"Thank you, Kamarisi." She cleared her throat. The language of Yrstanla was still thick on her tongue, but since her arrival on Galahesh it had quickly returned. "I'm lucky to have found a man like Bahett."

"Bahett is a good man, though I fear he has been placed in a difficult situation."

"How do you mean?"

"In these days of strife, these days of disease and blight, we are all put-upon, are we not?"

"We will survive, Your Majesty."

"I don't mean the islands. I mean us all. We are put upon in the west and the south. Our fields to the north have gone fallow despite all efforts to revive them. I fear the blight is moving west, for good or ill."

"And yet the Empire is strong. She will persevere."

"As will the islands." He smiled and turned to lean upon the white marble banister that lined the terrace.

"Of course, Your Majesty."

"But Bahett, he is caught between our two worlds, is he not? Galahesh has always had one foot among the islands, and another on the lands of the Empire. I'm glad he's decided to take someone from Anuskaya as his wife, and even gladder that he's chosen you."

Atiana smiled. "I was the closest at hand."

Hakan laughed. It was a pleasant sound. "You are more than that, Atiana Radieva Vostroma. Word of your exploits has reached even the halls of Irabahce."

"I would hardly call them exploits."

"My dear, you *saved* the islands. Surely much would have been lost had the Maharraht had their way. *We* would have lost much."

Atiana bowed her head, wondering why the Kamarisi was showering her with compliments, wondering as well what his consort would think of it. She glanced toward the crowd that was now surrounding Arvaneh. Bahett, though ostensibly watching Arvaneh as well, was clearly keeping an eye out for Atiana and her conversation with the Kamarisi.

"I thank you."

"I was ... disappointed when you did not come to the ball. I've heard much about your dancing as well, and was sad when it couldn't be put on display."

"Your Majesty?"

Hakan glanced sidelong at her. "It's difficult for your sister to go unnoticed, even when she's trying not to be. You, on the other hand, are more subtle. There's a quiet strength to you that may be overlooked by some, but not those with a more discerning eye."

Despite his simple words and his apparent indifference to her deception, she began to fear this man, as one fears the blackness in the depths of the sea. "I'm most sorry, Your Majesty. I didn't feel well. Travel has been difficult for me ever since Duzol."

"I hadn't heard. But why send your sister?"

"I didn't wish to disappoint."

Hakan smiled mischievously. "Did Bahett know?"

"He did not."

His smiled deepened. "Then we'll keep it between us. A secret between east and west."

"*Evet.*" Atiana smiled. "A secret."

CHAPTER TWENTY-ONE

"It's time you take the dark," Ishkyna said as she burst into Atiana's room four days after the meeting with the Kamarisi.

Atiana was penning a letter to Mother, but she looked up in annoyance. "What are you talking about?"

"The Lady Arvaneh, she's retreated to her tower."

Atiana returned to her writing. "What of it?"

"I've been watching her. She goes there often. At times she looks haggard when she enters and she returns refreshed. Other times she seems drained."

"You're making no sense."

Ishkyna flopped down into the chair across from Atiana's writing desk. "Set down your quill."

Her voice was so serious that Atiana complied. Ishkyna, so often ready to nip at her heels with a snide remark, was looking at her with a deadly serious expression.

"Go on," Atiana said.

"I may avoid taking the dark, Tiana, but it's provided me a certain amount of perspective that you and Mileva may lack. I can see the way Arvaneh is after her time in her tower. Often her eyes are dulled. Her words come more slowly. And her card play is, frankly, disastrous."

"I beg your pardon?"

"I've taught Bahett's wives trump. Arvaneh joined us one day. She's become quite enamored of it. I think at first she only wanted to learn more about you, but over the days she's become more and more wily at laying her cards, not unlike Mileva."

"What does this have to do with me taking the dark?"

"I didn't see her this morning, but Ebru did. She said that Arvaneh looked not just exhausted, but pale, her skin ashen, her eyes haunted, as if she'd aged thirty years in a week. She's done this before and returned rejuvenated, resplendent, as we saw her on our arrival here. I don't know what she does in the tower when she's like this, but she isn't taking the dark. It would be too dangerous, and besides, she would return looking even worse if that was the case. If there was ever a time to watch her, Atiana, it would be now."

Atiana considered this. "It doesn't make sense."

Ishkyna smiled a mischievous smile. "*Nyet.* It doesn't."

Although there were times that Ishkyna was too impetuous for her own good, Atiana would never deny that she was not sly, that she didn't know people. She knew them. She knew how to read their moods with but a word.

"Bahett wanted me to wait until his return from the hunt."

Ishkyna raised one eyebrow, her smile turning to genuine amusement.

"Wipe that grin off your face," Atiana said as she stood, "and tell Yalessa to begin preparations."

Ishkyna stood and sketched an elaborate bow.

When Atiana finally found Bahett, he was in the stable yard, preparing to leave with a dozen other men for a stag hunt in the forest south of Baressa. Before Atiana had even finished explaining, Bahett interrupted her. "It wouldn't do well to go now," Bahett said, looking over Atiana's shoulder to the servants, who were loading the last of the provisions to the coach that would accompany the men.

"You brought me here to help, did you not?"

He took her hands in his. "I did. Of course I did. But Atiana, I'll be too far away to help if anything goes awry."

She chose not to say that he didn't help the last time—the man at the willow did. "It's important to find her when she's in her tower. You said so yourself."

"I did, but not now. We'll return in three days. And we'll find a time—the proper time—on my return." He squeezed her hands, as a father might to a daughter he was trying to talk down from a foolish decision. "As we planned."

"Bahett—"

He squeezed her hands. Hard. "Atiana, I *forbid it.*"

She stared into his eyes. His face was as calm and pleasant as ever, but his eyes... They were not only fierce. They were fearful. He was *afraid* of what would happen were Atiana to take the dark.

Ishkyna's instincts were good, but Atiana hadn't been sure, up until that point, that she was right.

"Of course," she said, swallowing hard to make as if she were cowed by his actions. "Of course you're right. Please, forgive my eagerness. It's only that the islands..."

"Say no more." He stepped in and gave her a warm kiss on her cheek, one she immediately wanted to wipe off. "We'll speak soon."

She nodded and waved as he left to complete his preparations.

And then she returned to her apartments to make final preparations. They would go as soon as everything could be arranged.

That night, she left, though this time with Ishkyna instead of Yalessa. "You need proper looking after," Ishkyna had said, though it seemed more likely that she had only agreed to come because Sihaş had already left for the hunt.

She chose a man from her father's guard as well. His name was Irkadiy. Irkadiy Adienkov. And he was a man who had been in her father's service for fifteen years. He was a trustworthy soldier, and she felt far better for having him with her—not to mention foolish for thinking she could do without such protection the other night.

Bahett's servants were easy to manipulate, especially when they knew she would soon be his first wife. Bahett would find out upon his return, but that gave her three days to investigate.

A different servant came this time, of course—the impostor who'd taken her had never been found, and Atiana was sure he never would be. This one—small, bald, soft of voice—looked nearly the same as the first had, which gave her no comfort whatsoever. He led her through the kasir and out once more through the rear door.

As soon as she and Ishkyna stepped from the kasir and onto the lawn behind it, she scanned the sky and saw a rook flying in the air. The rook, spotting them, winged away, and was lost in the cemetery.

Atiana felt better knowing that Mileva was watching over them. Her sister had become quite proficient in the aether, and though taking the dark was dangerous so near to the straits, the danger was muted while taking the form of a rook. The animals had a way of deadening the ill effects that could come from treading the aether's currents.

Together, the four of them—the eunuch, Atiana, Ishkyna, and Irkadiy—wove through the cemetery, and soon they came to a different section than they had the previous night. Far off, she heard the caw of the rook, the signal that all was well.

Ishkyna couldn't apparently keep herself from a look of disgust as they walked past row upon row of mausoleums. "Isn't it dreadful?" she asked loudly enough for the servant to glance back at them.

For the moment, Atiana didn't care if he heard. "*Da*."

At a large marble tomb at the end of a row, he knocked thrice upon a heavy copper door thick with bright green patina. A moment later the door swung open on creaking hinges. Inside was a woman as old as Atiana's mother, dressed in white robes.

The woman glanced at them over the eunuch's head. She leaned forward and whispered softly, after which the eunuch bowed his head and left.

"Come," the woman said, and retreated into the darkness.

Ishkyna looked at Atiana seriously. "Pray to the ancients you never marry that man, Tiana."

For some reason that struck Atiana as funny. She laughed long and hard, and it did not ebb until they had made their way inside the darkened tomb, which was lit only with a small lantern held by the old woman. She stood by a stairwell that led down into the darkness.

"Careful now," she said as she made her way down, taking the light with her, "and close the door behind you."

Irkadiy, standing guard outside the tomb, nodded once before Ishkyna shut the door with a boom. After a cross look from the woman, the three of them descended the stairs down, down, down into the bowels of the Mount.

At the bottom of the stairs they came to a room with a copper tub at the center of it. Three covered wooden crates sat next to the tub. Ice was floating in the water, but Atiana could already tell that it wouldn't be enough.

"Prepare yourself," the woman said, motioning to marble shelves that were set into the well. Upon them were bolts of cloth the color of sandstone and a jar no doubt filled with rendered fat.

As Atiana began to undress, the woman opened the crates. Inside were fist-sized blocks of ice nestled within a thick layer of hay. She took all of the blocks from the first crate and dropped them into the water, then she took half of them from the second and dropped them in as well, until the surface of the water was covered like a frozen pond succumbing to the early warmth of summer.

Atiana took a deep breath as she folded her small clothes and placed them onto the shelf. Ishkyna helped her to spread the rendered goat fat over her body. The chill of it was welcome. She had too long been away from the aether, and she would welcome its embrace.

As she stepped into the tub, the cold water chilled her feet and shins. And when she sat down, she shivered for the first time, though she was able to quell this quickly. Several paces from the tub was an inlaid wooden door set into the wall opposite from the stairs. For some reason, as she stared at the door, she had the distinct impression that this tomb was connected to others—a maze of them interconnected deep beneath the kasir like an Aramahn village.

She took the breathing tube from Ishkyna.

"Dreams of honey," Ishkyna said.

It was something they used to say to one another as children before they went to bed in their shared room in Galostina. Atiana tried to smile, failed, and lay down in the tub, the ice parting and returning to place with dull clacking sounds. The water was cold, but there was something about it. It didn't have the bone-numbing chill that the water from the depths of Galostina or Radiskoye had. Perhaps it was the temperature, or the source of the water, or some quality of the water itself...

She stopped herself. She would never be able to take the dark if she allowed these doubts to fester. She had to accept the situation. She had to believe the water would hold her, would cradle her as she wandered through the aether.

She breathed through the tube, feeling suddenly self-conscious—like a girl taking the dark for the first time—but then she relaxed, forcing her breath to release more slowly, drawing it in with the pace of an achingly slow breeze, releasing once more, until inhalation and exhalation were equally measured.

Like the tides, she thought.

Like the measure of night and day.

Like the turn of the seasons.

And soon... Soon...

She floats through the aether. Already she feels drawn toward the straits. It tugs at her like a piece of flotsam among the waves.

She fights, realizing that it will mean her ruin if she is drawn to its center, the place the maelstrom was the strongest and most unpredictable. But try as she might, she cannot fight it. With the straits so near, so strong, she is pulled slowly but surely toward the gap in the island.

Knowing she cannot fight it—remembering as well the first tenet of life in the dark, that of submission—she allows herself to be pulled; she moves with it, faster and faster, until she whips past the straits, feeling the depth and power of the confluence below. How strong it is. How fearsome.

And how truly beautiful.

In the aether the tall cliffs are bright, blinding white. Chromatic whorls form and diffuse in moments. The water is dark as midnight, but above it the currents of the aether clash, driving their power high into the air. Lines of power arc over the straits as well. They shimmer and scintillate, towering high above Galahesh, glowing like the chromatic lights of the Great Northern Sea.

She remembers her purpose here.

Arvaneh. The tower.

She is on the northern side of the straits. As she drifts southward she once again finds herself at odds with the currents of the aether. They fight her every step, threaten to draw her downward. So she turns, using that movement to catch the whorls that are left in its wake. She slips like a salmon through a frothing white river.

At last, she approaches the tower. Arvaneh's tower. She feels threatened, as though touching its stones would mean the death of her. But this is one of Arvaneh's powers—fear, plain and simple—and Atiana will have none of it.

She crosses the walls.

And everything changes.

The typical silence of the aether is replaced by a low susurrus. The lights of the aether are dim, as if she's lost her ability to see in the dark.

She does not sense Arvaneh, but she senses another, someone like her, waiting and listening in the dark.

Who's there?

She receives no reply, but she feels them retreat.

It is not one of the Matri. Her mind is foreign, her movements clumsy.

Atiana moves quickly toward it. She catches up, and now she can sense the tendril that leads back east through the city, across the acres of towers and markets and homes, toward a hovel set among the battered remains of the Shattering.

She sees there a woman lying in a stone pool set into the earth. A feeling wells up inside her as she stares, wondering how this could be. The woman's form is the diaphanous white of all living things in the aether's midnight blue, but there are tinges of yellow and red and green. Most of all there is black. It is difficult to see against the aether's dark hue, but it is there. This woman is clearly a qiram. She may even be arqesh, one who has mastered every discipline.

And yet this woman has managed to enter the aether, a skill that has been the domain of the Landed alone for centuries. Of the Aramahn, only Fahroz has ever been known to take the dark, and yet here is another.

Atiana seizes the woman. She can feel her surprise. She doesn't know she's been followed, and she is weak, defenseless against such an attack.

I asked you who you were.

Still there is no response. She could force the woman from the aether now if she so chose, but why? She needs to learn more.

She tightens her hold, feels the woman squirm beneath her grasp.

Ushai!

Atiana eases her hold.

My name is Ushai. Ushai Kissath al Shahda.

Atiana remembers her. She was a servant of Fahroz. She was the one who'd led her from the lake deep below the village of Iramanshah. It made sense, then. If Fahroz knew how to take the dark, surely she would have taught others. It is something she'd have to give more thought to.

Why have you come, Ushai?

I've come for the same reason as you, I suspect, daughter of Radia.

And why is that?

To study her.

Arvaneh?

Sariya. The Scourge of Ghayavand.

Atiana feels her body jerk in the basin. *It cannot be,* she says. *Sariya is trapped.*

Trapped no longer, and better you become aware of it now before her plans are unleashed.

You're lying.

Arvaneh means "one of three" in Kalhani. She broke free of her bonds years ago, and when she did she returned to the desert where we believe she was born. From there she arranged to be purchased by one of the Kamarisi's men. After moving to Alekeşir to join his harem, she spent months watching him, creeping her way into his mind, and now she has taken him. She came with little, but now she has the resources of an Empire at her beck and call. It is her. Do not doubt these words. Now please, release me.

Atiana realizes that the hold she had on her would be painful. She releases her completely, confident she can find her should she choose to flee. *I would—*

Atiana feels a disturbance in the currents, a pressure that fills her, not with pain, but something akin to it.

I would speak with you. Face to face.

Ushai pauses. *What's happening?*

The pressure increases. Atiana expands her awareness, allowing it to encompass more of the ruins, more of Baressa. She knows it must be coming from the straits, but it doesn't feel like a simple disturbance or a clash of currents. It feels as though part of her is tearing, as though a part of her has begun to burn.

Memories and emotions come to her unbidden. Running through the halls of Galostina, bright with excitement. Unbridled fear while staring down for the first time from the gunwales of a windship. The drip of water in the drowning chamber. The earthy smell of rendered goat fat. Father staring sternly down at her, his sad eyes filled with disappointment. A candle that she touched with the tips of her fingers, heating them to the point of pain before yanking them away.

And on and on. She is in this moment completely and utterly at their mercy.

I do not—

And then the pain increases sharply, and her world goes white.

CHAPTER TWENTY-TWO

T he air around Nasim was chill and damp, but it had a mineral sharpness that did much to keep him alert. The tunnels seemed only big enough for the sound of their climbing, plus the occasional drip of water. Neither he nor Rabiah had spoken since heading out from the collapse at the entrance. They hadn't felt the need, and to speak felt as though they would give away their position—to whom, Nasim didn't know; it simply seemed wise to talk as little as possible.

The tunnel was complete darkness, but that didn't mean they couldn't move through it. Nasim taught Rabiah how to draw upon her vanahezhan to feel her way along the tunnels. Nasim thought of drawing upon the vanahezhan as well, but Rabiah was weak, and only one of them needed sight, so he followed her closely and obeyed her instructions when she gave them. If he was blinded in the meantime, he didn't mind. He had taken too many liberties with Rabiah already, no matter that it had been to protect them; allowing her to have sight and lead them both somehow felt proper.

Her earth sight was fouled when they came across water, even a trace amount of it. The first time it happened they heard only a trickle. The second time they heard nothing. The walls of the tunnel were damp—that was all. Nasim assumed there was a hidden stream within the earth, yet still it was enough to rob her of her newfound sight. They scrabbled, low to the ground, warding their hands in front of them to make their way beyond the deadening effects of the water.

They might have drawn upon a jalahezhan, but they were loath to do so. There were plenty around, but they might be drawn through the veil with even the smallest of contacts. The vanahezhan, however, seemed to be drawn to the collapse of the cavern, which now laid far behind them, leaving Nasim and Rabiah to choose from the lesser of them, the ones less likely to cross in this strange place where the worlds practically touched.

Nasim was somehow uncomfortable with the growing realization that he remembered this place. He could not recall Khamal walking these tunnels and warrens, and yet he knew with uncanny accuracy the path they needed to follow in order to reach the upper levels of the village, where the girl and the akhoz had surely been headed.

"Who do you think she was?" Nasim asked, growing tired of the silence. His voice echoed off into the distance.

"Someone Ashan brought to the island? A disciple?"

"Perhaps, but she was with the akhoz, going willingly."

Rabiah was silent for a time. "Do you think we'll find him?"

She meant Ashan. Nasim, shrouded in darkness, could only shrug. "Who can say? I had to try."

In the distance they heard a small splash. They stopped for a moment, but the sound wasn't repeated, so they continued on.

"There's something I don't understand," Rabiah said. "You said you thought Ashan knew you'd come here. That he had come in order to protect you."

"What of it?"

"Well, why would he do so alone? You said yourself that we needed to work together. That only in realizing our potential as arqesh could we close the rift here on Ghayavand. Neither of us believes the girl we saw has anything to do with Ashan. So what did he hope to accomplish?"

"I don't know. He may have come simply to prepare the way. Perhaps he hoped to discover more before coming to find me. Perhaps he planned to find a piece of the Atalayina, or even all three. Who can say?"

"*You* can. You knew him well, did you not?"

Nasim wanted to laugh, but somehow that didn't feel right in this place. "In truth I hardly knew him at all. I will love him always, but to know someone is to speak with them, to live with them, to cry and laugh with them. I did none of those things with Ashan. I was lost. He was a beacon—that much is true—but it's also true that from where I stood he was little more than a light in the distance. I know perhaps his heart, but little more than that."

"Then what is in his heart?"

"Care for the world that has come before. Care for the world that is yet to be. Care for that which has been lost and what might yet be gained." Nasim searched his mind for more, but as hard as he tried, he could only think of one more trait that had any bearing. "And kindness," he said. "These are the things that drive Ashan. These and little else. He is a selfless man, caring for others before himself."

"Then why did you not enlist his help?"

There was bitterness in her words. He didn't mind, though. He had asked this same question of himself many times, feeling that same bitterness sitting deep in his heart like a hardening cyst. But there was really only one answer to this question. "He has already done enough. This is *my* path to follow."

"Not just yours… *Ours*."

She meant herself and Sukharam. "*Yeh*, Rabiah. Yours as well."

They entered a cavern where the slow drip of water could be heard, and here the darkness was no longer absolute. Pale pink light suffused the cavern from veins of softly glowing stone in the ceilings and walls and floors. It was not so bright that they could see the natural features clearly, but it was bright enough to allow them to see a set of natural stairs that let up to another, higher tunnel.

In this place, lost among the hidden warrens of the earth, Nasim could not help but think about his time with Ashan. He'd been little more than a prisoner within the shell of his own body. He could remember the feeling he'd had around Ashan, even down to the individual stones he wore in his circlet and on his wrists and ankles, but as they took to the stairs, he realized that these were not memories. He could feel them now, and they were growing stronger.

"He's here," Nasim said, surprised at the realization. "I can feel him." It would be good—despite all his words of confidence of the need to come alone—to have Ashan at his side once more.

Rabiah said nothing, but he felt her prepare herself, felt her touch the walls of Adhiya.

"Be careful," he said. "Draw upon them only at great need. We'll not be so lucky as we were at the entrance to the tunnels."

They continued up, the light in the tunnels sometimes granting them some small amount of light by which to navigate, sometimes leaving them in complete darkness once more. The tunnels changed from the natural caverns to ones that were clearly formed by the hand of man. These had been hewn—or at the very least widened—by dozens of vanaqiram over the course of years and decades. Such was the care they had taken, for the detail—the intricacy of the traceries built into the walls—was immaculate.

And then they came to a space that was immense. He could feel it more than he could see, for it was pitch black except for the single siraj stone that was glowing far away on the opposite side of the cavern. It looked like it went on for a league, or more, though Nasim was sure this was a trick of the darkness and the odd dimensions of this place. Staring at it more critically, he guessed the stone was several hundred paces away, and as they walked toward it, he realized that the stone was sitting on a table of some sort.

The table was long, though even as long as it was it felt incongruous in such an immense space. Why was it here? Why had the siraj been placed on it?

And why were Ashan's stones sitting next to it?

"Can you feel them?" Rabiah whispered, clearly sensing the same thing.

"I can."

"I like this not at all," she said.

"Neither do I."

As they came closer, Nasim saw them. Sitting near the siraj stone was a circlet with a stone of alabaster set into it. The stone was dark, lifeless. Inside the circlet were a bracelet and two anklets, their stones similarly dark.

And in the darkness beyond—

Nasim shivered. How could he not have noticed?

—there was a shape. A man, sitting in a chair.

Muqallad.

Nasim had not sensed him on their approach. Neither had he seen or heard him, and he was unable to sense him in the aether.

Muqallad, his face lit in ghastly relief by the siraj, was possessed of a strong and imposing form. He had long black hair and ruddy skin. Rings of gold ornamented the braids of his long black beard. Like a wolf in the night, everything about him was striking, but it was his eyes, more than anything, that somehow pierced. They stared right through Nasim, ignoring Rabiah as if she didn't exist.

"Welcome, Khamal."

Muqallad's words were still echoing about the chill room when Rabiah shouted and fell to the floor in a flurry of hair and limbs. The sound of her head striking the stone made Nasim cry out. He dropped to his knees and felt for her pulse, for her breathing. Other than a welt and a cut on her forehead that trickled blood, she seemed well enough.

He stood and faced Muqallad, willing his fear not to show. "I am not Khamal."

Muqallad, nearly swallowed by the darkness of the room, smiled. "You may not feel so, but believe me, you are here because you planned it, even down to your forgotten memories."

Nasim could only stare. Khamal had planned this? All of it?

Neh, Nasim thought. Muqallad was lying. And yet the words had the ring of truth to them.

At the edge of his awareness, Nasim realized he could feel akhoz—many of them—approaching.

Muqallad motioned to Ashan's effects. "Do you know who these belong to?"

"They belong to my kuadim."

"Your *kuadim*..." Muqallad reared back and laughed, the sounds echoing off into the immensity of the room. The laugh was healthy and long, and it burned Nasim's ears to hear it. "You have the relationship backward, Khamal. It was *you* who taught *him*. And yet I will admit that he is learned. He could not have gained the island if he was not. He could not have dismantled the defenses around this village if he was not. He could not have learned that one of the stones had been hidden in the white tower if he was not."

Nasim tried to hide his reaction, but clearly he'd been unsuccessful, for Muqallad smiled. "You knew this already. Did you *send* him here?" He paused. "*Neh*, I see that you did not. He came then—what?—to find the stones for you? To prevent you from ever finding them? Tell me your thoughts."

"I haven't seen Ashan for five years."

"But you knew him well, and certainly he knows *you* well. What did he hope to accomplish with a third of the Atalayina?"

"I would imagine he merely wished to keep it from *you*."

Muqallad's eyes narrowed, and he smiled. "You may be right." He pushed back his chair and stood. The akhoz steadily approached.

"You came for Ashan, and you found me, and it makes me wonder whether the fates placed us here together. We all thought that we had failed those many years ago, that the fates had frowned upon our efforts. But I wonder now. I wonder if they truly thought this. I wonder if, rather than being disappointed in our *goals*, if they were instead disappointed in our *failure*. The fate of Ghayavand since the sundering has consumed me, Khamal. We came close—you and I and Sariya. We came *very* close, and I wonder why, after centuries, the rift has not been closed. If the fates did not shine upon us that day, why then have they not seen fit to close the rift once more?"

"To see if we have learned."

"Then you think it a lesson, a test of sorts, to see what we will do with our goals still within arm's reach."

"We cannot know their minds."

"That's where you're wrong, Khamal. It's where you've always been wrong. The fates are mighty, that is true, but they are not so different from you and me. And if that is so, then we can know their minds. It has been not only *your* failing, but all of ours, for generations beyond count: our inability to come to grips with the fact that the fates are neither all knowing nor all powerful. The knowledge is liberating. It allows me to ponder things I would never have considered before, such as completing our work despite the apparent displeasure of the fates."

Nasim could not yet see the akhoz, but they were close. He could hear their feet slapping against the stone floor at the edge of the room.

"I have a simple trade for you to consider." He glanced to one side of the room, then the other. "Speak to Ashan. Ask him where the stone in the white tower has been hidden. If you can find it, you may have both the girl and Ashan back."

The akhoz crept in. They seemed strangely fearful of the light coming from the siraj. They covered their lidless faces and crouched forward, crawling like crabs over the floor. One reached for Rabiah, but Nasim stepped forward and batted away its hand. Another came, ducking away from his strike and snatching Rabiah's robes.

"Leave her!" Nasim shouted. He kicked at the akhoz who had a hold of her, and the creature hissed like a mountain cat.

More crept in, a dozen or more.

"Leave her!" Nasim tried to call upon a vanahezhan through Rabiah, but found that he could not. He no longer sensed it at all. In fact, he could no longer sense Adhiya. It was simply gone.

One of the akhoz tilted its head back and bleated. Another joined in, and another, until all of them were sounding the same call, which made Nasim's stomach twist and churn. His mouth watered and he became dizzy, so much so that he fell to the floor.

The bleating stopped, but the effect did not, and he found himself unable to raise his head without a swooning effect storming in and forcing him to lie back again.

Footsteps approached. "Find the stone, Khamal."

Rabiah was lifted from the floor. The footsteps resumed and began to fade away.

"Find it, and we can finish what we started."

CHAPTER TWENTY-THREE

Hours passed before Nasim's dizziness faded. With a groan, he pushed himself off the cold stone floor onto his hands and knees. He breathed deeply, clearing his head, before standing and looking about the room. The akhoz were gone. Muqallad was gone.

Rabiah was gone.

He stood in the darkness, hands bunched into fists, fighting the urge to scream because he saw no point in it. In the end, though, he gave in. He released an unending lament for his foolishness, for his presumption, until his throat was raw.

He had brought them here on a fool's errand. He had hoped that through his renewed understanding of the island, and his teachings, that they would find the stones and enough knowledge to be able to close the rifts, something that the three arqesh who had torn it wide had been unable to do in the centuries following the devastation of the sundering.

Why? Why had he thought he could teach? Why had he thought he knew enough to overcome such obstacles?

Because he was foolish. Worse, he had valued their lives too poorly. Neither Rabiah nor Sukharam had had the best of lives before he'd found them, but that hadn't given him the right to uproot them, take them where he would. Better if he had let them choose their own path, or seen to it that they found their way into the hands of trusted Aramahn.

Such as Fahroz...

Who had only been trying to protect him. Who had only been trying to teach him the ways of the world, a world he still did not truly comprehend. Would that he had listened to her, stayed in Mirashadal until the time was right.

The only trouble was that the time may never have seemed right. He was terrified then of what he had to do, and by the time he'd stolen away from the floating village, he'd known that he would never overcome that fear, not without simply facing it.

And so he had gone. He had left, and he had traveled the world, and he had found two children that, given time, given the right sort of knowledge and insight, would have become great. But now he—not the fates, and not their cruel masters—had cut their lives short.

"Stop!" he bellowed into the darkness.

The words came back to him, softer and softer, until silence reigned once more.

"Stop," he said again.

He had to get a hold of himself. He had to make a plan. He had to find Ashan.

But where? Muqallad hadn't said. Which meant, of course, that he expected Nasim to piece together the clues in order to find him.

When he thought about it, though, the answer was simple.

He moved to the edge of the room, warding with his hands. He was blinded now, not only by the light but by his inability to call upon a hezhan. It was something that disturbed him—disturbed him deeply—but he couldn't afford to let his mind wander down those paths, and so he stepped forward, trusting to his memories.

Indeed, as he found the tunnel that led to the eastern reaches of the village, he had no trouble at all remembering the way to the lake. It was ingrained in him, infinitely brighter than the memories of his distant and oh-so-hazy childhood. As he wended his way through tunnel after tunnel, a fear took seed and grew within him, and soon the fear had turned into a certainty. Ashan was at the lake. He knew it. But what had Muqallad done to him? What tortures had he endured?

He shuffled forward, mindful of the darkness. Then he began to jog, and then run while touching his hands to the stone walls to guide him.

As he went, memories flooded over him, memories of walking through this village as Khamal. And they didn't feel like memories from dreams, they felt *real*, they felt like *his* memories. This had happened several times in the past several years—moments of lucidity of Khamal's life—but they had always been ephemeral and disjointed, and when he tried to guide them toward answers—what Khamal had done, how he had planned to pass his knowledge to Nasim—the memories had drifted away like dreams on the edge of waking.

This time felt different, however. The memories felt stronger, perhaps because of his return to the village, or perhaps because of his encounter with Muqallad. He coaxed the memories toward Sariya, toward the piece of the Atalayina Muqallad had mentioned. And more came to him. He remembered strolling the beach, climbing the rocks to the city proper. He remembered stepping up to the tall white tower. Sariya's tower. He remembered putting his hand on the black iron gate.

But there his memories faded, and the more he tried, the more distant they became, even those things that moments ago had been so clear.

He continued through the village, moving with foolish haste. He came to a stairwell and flew along the steps, heedless of the danger. At last the cavern opened up before him and a pinpoint of light shone in the distance. It was coming from the center of the lake. He continued down to the shore, and finally, his breath coming in ragged gasps, he stopped.

A trickle of water fell somewhere in the distance. The air was chill, and it smelled of copper. He stared toward the light, unable to see anything but the stone and the isle upon which it rested.

"Ashan?" he called. His name echoed into the distance.

There was no reply.

He waded into the water. It was frigid, but nothing like it had been centuries ago. Ghayavand had warmed since then.

He swam, feeling watched. He grew tired but pushed on, and as he did the water became colder and colder until he was numb from it.

When he gained the isle at last, he dragged himself onto it and stared at the source of light. It was no siraj. It was a pinpoint of light hanging in the air.

He turned to the water, scanning carefully beneath its surface. He found nothing. Ashan wasn't here. He despaired. This was the place. It must be.

He was nearly ready to give up when he saw something deep beneath the surface—something little more than a lighter shade of black.

The thought of returning to the water brought him no joy, but he had to be sure…

He dove beneath the surface, swimming in broad strokes, lower, lower, until he was able to feel for the shadow he'd seen.

He felt cloth. Then a limb. And a shoulder.

And then he touched skin.

And the world shifted.

Khamal swims below the surface of the bay, clearing his mind of the troubles that lay ahead. His long strokes pull him onward as the cold waves first tug, then push.

He breaks the surface. Far ahead stands the tower. Sariya's tower.

He swims toward it, seeing no further need to delay. When at last he reaches land, the sensation of the waves and the fluidity of the water fade like autumn rain, and he is left with the weight of the land beneath, the hardness of it, its brittle nature. It isn't jarring as it was so many years ago; it feels right, as if all the parts of the world are a part of him and he a part of them. Would that he had known as much before he had touched the surface of that deep blue stone.

Khamal steps toward the tower, he slips past the guards Sariya placed. Had her mind been with her in the tower above, she might have sensed him, but she is far afield, as she often is. As he touches the stone, he feels a sense of regret, not only for what he is about to do, but for allowing Sariya to see what he can now do. This too saddens him—the simple fact that the three of them have come to distrust one another to the point that they would hide information. At one time they had shared everything, all in the hopes of repairing what they had broken, but as the years had worn on, they had begun to form their own opinions on how that wound might be healed.

The stone he touches fills him. His skin hardens. His sight dims. A mineral scent assaults him. He does not feel himself move upward; rather, he feels the world move around him, and for a moment—a moment only—he is the center of all things. When he steps away from this state, it is with regret. He has come to love stone and earth more than any other.

He is within a room, standing on a red-and-umber carpet of the finest weave. Four windows set into the walls in the cardinal directions allow him to look upon the city and the land around it.

Sariya—

Sariya is here.

She lays upon a bed at the center of the circular room. Her hair is splayed over the rich blanket, making her look as if she has taken her final slumber.

But then his foot shifts in only the slightest degree.

And she wakes.

She sits up immediately, facing him with a confused and cross expression. She stares at the wall behind him, perhaps trying to determine its nature and whether Khamal has weakened it to allow him future entrance.

And then the stone hardens. He can feel it in his bones and in the core of his chest. She has altered the tower so that he cannot leave, and he fears that nothing within his power will be able to undo what she has just done.

She has learned.

And hidden.

Her blue eyes burn with anger. "Why have you come?"

"Has Muqallad not told you?"

"I would hear it from your lips, not his."

Khamal takes a step toward her. She slips off of the bed on the near side, watching him closely. Never has her expression or her stance been so defensive, as if she fears he would attack her. He, an Al-Aqim, attacking another. The very notion is mad, but then again, never had he stolen something from her.

"He tells me that you've convinced him to abandon his plans."

Her eyes search him. She is trying to sense whether the Atalayina is with him, but the Atalayina is curious this way. It cannot be sensed easily—even a stone one has held for centuries—as if the stone itself refuses to offer its allegiance to anyone. It remains neutral, always.

"Why did you steal it?"

Khamal takes another step forward. "I thought it best. For now."

She steps back, maintaining the distance between them. "I didn't need to convince him to abandon his plans. He'd already convinced himself."

"He told me as much."

"He no longer covets the stones. Neither do I. It's time we returned to working with one another."

"We did, for decades, and it only served to drive us apart."

Sariya licks her lips. "I didn't wish for that to happen."

"I know," he says.

This time when he steps forward, she does not retreat. Three gliding steps would bring them together. He found himself wanting to take another step. *Neh*. It was more than this. It was a desire. A need.

This is Sariya. Her tower. He has not come unprepared, and still she nearly managed to beguile him in moments. Indeed, she has learned. Even without the Atalayina she is fearsome.

He was prepared for this, but it saddens him that she has taken this step. She would never have done so if she and Muqallad weren't working against him. She would have felt resentment at what he'd done, but she would never have thought to enter his mind, to force his hand.

He shuffles forward, allowing a subtle confusion to show on his face. She steps forward as well. They could touch if they so chose, but they do not, but he can feel the heat from her, and he imagines she can feel his. He swallows, fighting the urge to take her into his arms.

But she is not so easy to resist.

When she opens her mouth to speak, he sweeps forward and takes her into his arms. He leans down and kisses her. Her lips are warm, though he knows it is only because she wills it so. Her heart beats slowly now, as does his own. They were all changed forever the moment the rift was torn between the worlds, but it did not take away their desires or their emotions.

He kisses her more deeply. He does this at first because he needs her mind elsewhere. He can feel her breath quickening, feel her tongue as it licks his parted lips, feel her hips and thighs as they press against him, and soon he is leading her toward the bed not for the reason he came, but because it has been so long since they were with one another.

He wonders if she understands his mind. Probably she does. Probably she knows that he will never give her the stone willingly. And she doesn't care. She wants this as much as he does. This is a bittersweet parting. A farewell.

They fall against the blankets as she bites his neck. He pulls from his robe the stone. He presses her down against the bed. Sariya, taken by the moment, grabs his hips and grinds against him. A rush of pleasure courses through him as he drops the stone from the edge of the bed. He summons a puff of air, enough to set the stone down on the floor soundlessly. He lifts himself onto his knees, staring down at Sariya as he pulls off his robes. As Sariya does the same, he spares one glance toward the floor and sees the stone being drawn into it.

He, too, has learned. Sariya will not be able to discern the disguise—she is not gifted in this way. Muqallad may sense the Atalayina, but he will not be able to remove it, not before Khamal's plans are triggered. And then the two of them will sleep until he returns.

He lowers himself down until they are skin against skin. He pulls her legs over his arms and slides downward. Sariya's breath comes in ragged gasps. She is like a summer storm now, hot and wild and wet. As he slips inside her and rocks, she grabs his hair and kisses him so deeply that he wonders if she will ever let him go.

He cares not what the answer is.

He feels her tightening around him. Her eyes are clenched, her head thrown back, leaving him to kiss her chin and neck and breasts. A long moan escapes her—an echo of his own—and as they reach their heights together, Sariya scratches his back and pulls him deep inside her.

They collapse, sweating and panting. Exhausted. Sated.

She turns to him, kisses his neck tenderly. Never has she looked so beautiful. "Will you stay?"

Her words are like honey, tempting and sweet. He wishes he could. He wishes none of this had ever happened, that they had continued toward their own enlightenment and allowed the world to proceed as it would. He wishes he had traveled the world with Sariya. He wishes he had made children with her. He wishes he could have passed his knowledge down to them before he'd stepped beyond the veil in preparation for his next life.

But all of this *had* happened. And here they were, two people who had been of one purpose now violently opposed to one another.

And so he gives her the only answer he can give.

"I cannot."

CHAPTER TWENTY-FOUR

Nasim shook his head, clearing the vision away. He was still below the surface of the freezing water. Precious seconds passed as he struggled to remember where he was and who lay before him.

At last the memories returned. He snatched a handful of cloth and kicked off the bed of the lake, and then he swam, holding Ashan with one arm, scissoring his legs. The surface was near. He knew this. And yet the seconds dragged on.

His breath was failing him. He began to exhale. He tried to stop it, but he couldn't.

Finally he broke the surface, spluttering and coughing. He heard nothing from Ashan, nor did he feel movement, but he could see him now, his hair plastered against his forehead and cheeks.

"Ashan!"

Nasim slipped his arm around Ashan's neck and swam for the isle. When he reached it he dragged Ashan higher, bit by bit, until he was halfway out of the water. Nasim was too exhausted to do any more than this.

"Ashan, please wake."

Ashan's cheeks were deathly cold—somehow colder than the water itself.

"Ashan, please!"

He slapped Ashan. Then again, harder. He rubbed his face and arms and chest and legs, hoping to warm him, to let him know that help had come, such as it was.

After placing his hand against Ashan's chest, he forced himself to stop, to feel, to simply *be aware*. He could feel the most telltale sign of his heart beating. It was impossibly slow, but it was there. How Muqallad could have done such a thing he had no idea.

Ashan suddenly spluttered, water spraying into the air and glinting under the dim light. Long wracking coughs escaped him, and for a good while that was all he could do. Then he turned toward the light, his face confused, and finally he looked upon Nasim.

"Are you well?" Nasim asked. A foolish question, but he could feel nothing but joy that Ashan was alive and awake.

Ashan looked at him, coughed, and then sat up and pulled Nasim into an embrace—a long, tender gesture that brought tears to Nasim's eyes. But after too long, Nasim pulled away, suddenly and inexplicably uncomfortable with it.

If Ashan was hurt by this he hid it well. He stared into Nasim's eyes with a look that spoke of relief and gratitude and confusion. "In truth, I had hoped you would not come, but I will admit now that I'm glad you did." He pulled himself backward, away from the water. "I'm not yet ready to see the next life."

Nasim didn't wish to burden him, but there was nothing gained in avoiding the truth. "Muqallad sent me here."

Ashan started, but then he crooked his neck and stretched his jaw. "Did he?"

"He claims that you went to Sariya's tower and that you know where her stone is hidden."

Ashan smiled, an expression so familiar Nasim nearly cried.

"He said the same thing to me, demanding I tell him where it was hidden. It's true that I went to the tower, and that I eventually found a way inside, but there was nothing there. For me, it was merely a gutted shell. Still, I can only assume it would not be so for Sariya. Or you."

Nasim didn't know. He didn't understand the tower completely, but he knew that it was the seat of Sariya's power. It was a place she had forged over the course of centuries, and if she had meant for those simpler than herself to see a gutted shell, then it would be so.

Ashan tried to get to his feet but fell backward instead. When Nasim moved to help him, he warded him away. "I'll be all right in a moment." He tried again, and though he did manage to stand, he seemed frail, like a foal newly born. "What I don't understand is why Sariya wouldn't deliver to him that stone."

"She cannot find it," Nasim said. "In the lake before I came to you I had a vision of Khamal going to Sariya's tower. He spoke with Sariya, but only as a way to enter the tower and to hide a piece of the Atalayina."

"Could it be that they still haven't found it?"

"Khamal seemed doubtful that they would be able to sense it, but he was sure they wouldn't be able to retrieve it."

"Why?" Ashan asked. "What did he do?"

Ashan was so eager to learn more, which seemed odd having just come from the depths. "The darkness and the cold weigh on me," Nasim replied. "Let's find ourselves away from this place."

"I don't know if I'm ready for another swim," Ashan said.

"Neither do I." Nasim dearly wished there were another way. A small amount of warmth was returning to him, but he was also shivering so badly it felt as though it would never stop.

Together they waded into the water and swam for the shore. Things were not so urgent as before, so it took longer, but it was no less tiring. By the time they dragged themselves onto the beach of stone and sand, Nasim could barely stand. Ashan was worse. After he'd crawled out he remained on hands and knees, his breath rasping. He spit from time to time, and the sound of it was thick, as if he was spitting up blood.

"The things Muqallad has done"—Ashan came slowly to his feet, and again he wobbled—"have not been kind. But all will be well. I need only time."

Those last words felt as if they were not meant for Nasim, but someone else.

"Come." Nasim pulled Ashan's arm around his shoulders and helped him walk. "Let's go up to the light."

They took to the stairs, though it was terribly slow going. Ashan could hardly take more than two or three stairs before he had to pause. Soon the light hovering above the center of the lake was hidden from them, and they were cloaked in darkness, but the memories of this place were as vivid as they had been before. Wherever Ashan wished to go, Nasim could take him.

"I'm worried over what's become of the city," Nasim said, if only to hear something in this cold, empty place. "Things feel more tentative since you and I were here last. Adhiya is so close I can practically touch it. Even the akhoz have changed. I saw one of them kill another in the city only days ago, near Sariya's tower."

Ashan stopped for a moment, catching his breath. "Things are worse than I thought."

"What do you mean?"

"In the months following the sundering, the arqesh who remained realized that the children might be bonded with hezhan, not just as you and I do, but permanently. They did so first to a girl named Yadhan. The ritual made way for the hezhan to inhabit her body completely, and with this, after one dark night, the first of the akhoz was made. As you can guess, more followed, and soon the island, especially the area around Alayazhar, was protected by their influence."

Nasim was already shaking his head. "They provide *protection* for the city?"

"Just so." Ashan nodded for Nasim to help him once more, and they continued their climb. "Even now they are preventing the rift from widening. So to hear you say that some are attacking the others makes me wonder just how long things can hold here. Though perhaps this should come as no surprise. In the early years after the sundering, the akhoz were of a single mind, united. Over time, as the last of the survivors left, the akhoz fractured and became aligned with the Al-Aqim. What you saw might be caused by Muqallad or it might be because without the presence of Sariya and Khamal, they are lost and left to their own devices."

"Why wouldn't Muqallad simply kill them and be done with it?"

"Why would he do that?"

"So that the rifts would tear wide, once and for all."

"Look further, Nasim. It isn't the destruction of the world he seeks. He believes the path to indaraqiram lies through the Atalayina. He believes, in fact, that the process was begun those three hundred years ago, and that what happened then and since is merely a test of our collective will, one that he will not allow us to fail. If I'm right he is close to achieving his goals. He has at least one piece of the Atalayina, more likely two, and though the third is lost to him, I suspect he now holds the knowledge for how to merge them together once more."

"He told you this?"

"*Neh*, but we've spoken at length. I told him much of my travels, if only to prevent him from resuming his torture, but he spoke as well. It was difficult for a man as prideful as he is not to share. He spoke of his travels before he came to Ghayavand. He'd spent nearly his entire life up to that point studying the Atalayina. He spoke of Kohor, an ancient village in the Gaji Desert. Tablets held in the archives there spoke of the Atalayina not having been found, but instead having been *made*—forged in some manner. He let slip that some of the guesses the writer of the tablet had put down were true, and he could only know this if he had had some success with the pieces of the Atalayina he already has."

Nasim nearly tripped as they reached the top of the stairs. They were in the circular room that housed entrance to the lake's stairwell. Here several passages broke off, one in particular leading to the upper passages and the way out.

The room, at least, was comparatively warm. Nasim's heart had already lifted, as if the last few hours had all been a bad dream. But of course the truth was sobering. "He wants the final pieces of the stone, and he's taken Rabiah to ensure that I'll deliver them to him. We must find her, Ashan, and we must find the others as well."

"You said he only wanted one piece of the stone."

"He did, but there is another."

"Which?"

"Khamal's."

"You know where it is?"

Nasim paused, feeling protective over this information. But a moment later, he felt foolish for it. "I found it in the celestia, where a secret compartment opened up for me. Khamal's doing, no doubt."

"And where is it now?"

"It's safe."

"Hidden?"

"*Yeh*," Nasim replied. He would divulge much to Ashan, but this didn't feel like a place to share this information, especially since Sukharam was still alone with the stone.

Perhaps Ashan sensed this, for he fell silent for long moments. "Nasim, how many others did you bring?"

"Two."

"Why?"

"The Al-Aqim were three, and so should we be."

"Is that the only reason?"

"What other reason should there be?" Nasim didn't like skirting the truth, but he didn't like this line of questioning either. Ashan's tone had become more aggressive, something he never remembered him doing.

"There could be many reasons," Ashan answered. "It's up to you to tell me the right one."

Something was wrong. Nasim could feel it. Ashan had changed. He had never spoken to Nasim in this manner. There was a hunger behind his words, an anger barely suppressed.

Nasim took a half step back, and the moment he did, a long, hoarse bray came from the tunnel behind him. It was followed by another, this one softer. The chilling sounds echoed away until silence once more reigned.

A pinpoint of light appeared in the air before Ashan, lighting his face and the tall, peaked room. The light continued to grow, revealing a large obsidian cross to which the form of a wretched, broken man had been lashed. The man's head hung low, his curly hair hanging over his face, preventing Nasim from seeing him clearly, but Nasim didn't need to see his face to know who he was.

Before him, the man he had thought to be Ashan transformed. His hair grew in length, became darker. The glint of gold appeared in his lightly curled beard. And soon, the handsome face of Muqallad was staring back at him.

As this transformation unfolded, the gathered akhoz shuffled into the room. They stood at the edge of the room, forming a circle around Muqallad and Nasim.

"Do you remember now what Ashan meant to you?"

Nasim felt a lump forming in his throat. He swallowed in a vain attempt at clearing it, but it was too late. Muqallad had already seen his weakness.

"Find the stone in the tower, Khamal, and bring it to me."

Behind Muqallad, Ashan lifted his head. His hair was matted and coppery brown and plastered against his forehead. His face was a mass of blood and bruises and cuts. He shivered from pain or cold or weakness, but unmistakable was the fact that he was pleading with Nasim to deny Muqallad his demand.

Nasim couldn't look. He couldn't look at Ashan and speak the words he was about to speak.

"I need Rabiah."

Muqallad stared. He was a tall man, but Nasim was nearly of a height with him now. Muqallad weighed Nasim, weighed his words and his intent.

In the end, he motioned with one hand, turned, and walked away, his footsteps echoing away into the immensity of the room. "You may have the one," he said as he passed beyond the akhoz.

Rabiah was dragged from beyond the circle of akhoz and thrown to Nasim's feet. She stirred, small moans escaping her as she rolled over and tried to lift herself with her arms.

Nasim helped her to her feet as the akhoz parted, allowing them clear passage to a hallway that sloped upward. They would not, however, allow Nasim any closer to Ashan. They crowded him and Rabiah until they were forced up the hall.

As they left, Nasim looked back, trying to catch sight of Ashan, but the light was beginning to fade, and he was already shrouded in shadow.

Eventually the akhoz stopped, allowing them to continue on toward the entrance to the village. The two of them were silent, Rabiah because she was in pain, Nasim because a growing dread was settling over him.

You may have the one, Muqallad had said.

The one, as if he had another.

He meant Sukharam, Nasim realized. He'd found Sukharam. He had him now.

And the second piece of the Atalayina.

He had two of the three. Only the piece in Sariya's tower that had been hidden so carefully by Khamal now stood in his way.

As he stepped out from the darkness of Shirvozeh's tunnels into the blinding light of the afternoon sun, Nasim wanted to admit this to Rabiah. He wanted to admit his failure. He wanted to ask her for forgiveness, for she'd been right. He should have brought Sukharam. Or he should have done more to protect him.

But he hadn't, and it shamed him like nothing had before in his life.

And so he couldn't speak to her. He couldn't face her judgment. Not yet.

So they walked together in silence toward Alayazhar, to their shelter that now lay empty as a dead man's hand.

CHAPTER TWENTY-FIVE

Nikandr sat near a fire in the woods of Rafsuhan. The sun had set and with the moon dark, the only thing Nikandr could see was what the small fire allowed: Soroush sitting on the far side of the fire, a half dozen tree trunks, the ground nearby, which was covered by larch needles. In the distance, a woodpecker rattled.

Jahalan and the girl, Kaleh, and most of the streltsi had already gone to sleep. Nikandr had elected to stay awake, at least as long as Soroush did. They would reach Ashdi en Ghat tomorrow, and for some reason he still didn't trust Soroush, perhaps because of the proximity to the village from which Soroush had for years schemed against the Grand Duchy. Though it appeared as though Nikandr had the upper hand, they both knew it was an illusion. The truth was that Soroush held the most powerful trump cards—Nikandr needed to speak with the elders of the Maharraht, and the only way to do that was through Soroush.

As the fire snapped, Soroush unwound his turban carefully, folding it into a tight circle in his lap. That done, he pulled his dark hair over his shoulder and began brushing away the tangles with his fingers. It was a personal moment, one that he would never have thought Soroush would allow him to see.

"Do you think of her?" Soroush asked without looking up. He'd chosen to speak Anuskayan—perhaps some small indicator of his mood. Or perhaps it was a small act of apology for how he'd treated Nikandr on the *Kavda*.

Nikandr knew he was referring to Rehada—it was not possible to be in Soroush's presence and not think of her. "I do."

"And what do you think, son of Iaros?"

Nikandr tried to smile, but the truth was that his memories of Rehada were still bittersweet. "I think the fates placed her in both of our paths for a reason."

And now Soroush did glance at Nikandr, his eyebrows raised. "So now you believe in the fates."

Nikandr had been struggling with that very thought for years. "I no longer know what I believe."

Soroush was staring at Nikandr's chest. His soulstone lay hidden beneath his shirt, but upon it he could feel the weight of Soroush's stare. "How long after Oshtoyets?"

"It began *before* Oshtoyets, on Verodnaya. Who knows why? Nasim, the cold, the rift, my broken stone, the wasting. *Something* allowed me to contact the hezhan. I didn't realize it at the time, but I think it had been with me ever since the ritual you performed on the cliff below Radiskoye."

Soroush's eyes went distant, as if he were reliving those moments again, piecing together the strange sequence of events that might have led to the ways of Adhiya being open to Nikandr.

If he was angered that he might have had something to do with it, he didn't show it. He merely seemed pensive, curious. "Do you commune with it?"

Nikandr understood the question, but the answer was not so easy. The Aramahn and the Maharraht communed with the spirits they bonded with. They believed it was a trading of breath, a trading of thoughts, a trading of their experiences of their respective worlds, a ritual that would slowly, eventually, bring the worlds closer together and lead the individual souls toward vashaqiram and the *worlds* toward *indara*qiram.

Nikandr felt as though he touched his spirit, felt as though his spirit touched him, but he didn't believe in vashaqiram. He didn't believe that one could ever attain perfection, in this life or the next. He *had* come to believe in reincarnation—he had experienced it firsthand with Nasim—but that didn't mean that the views of the Aramahn were correct in every way.

"I speak to it," Nikandr said, not wishing to offend. "I believe it speaks back as well, though my ears are deaf to its voice."

Soroush stared at him, perhaps measuring the sincerity in his words, but then he nodded, perhaps pleased in some small way. "Rehada spoke of you often."

"Of course. She was spying on me."

"That isn't what I mean. For years we spoke in letters only, and she would write of you longer than she needed to. She wrote of your family, your likes, your dislikes, your tendencies."

"Was that not her duty?"

"*Da*, but when one knows a woman as well as I knew her, one can tell the difference."

"Why are you telling me this?"

"Because you should know."

"You fathered a *child* with her."

Soroush paused in his brushing, staring at the dry earth in front of him as the light of the fire danced across his ruddy skin. "Does that mean she could never love another? Does that mean you cannot learn of her beyond her death? That you cannot perhaps love her more?"

Nikandr took a deep breath, releasing it slowly. It felt good, knowing this, though he had trouble releasing his feelings of distrust to allow it to sink in.

"Atiana told me of the time she crossed the fires in Iramanshah."

Soroush's back stiffened. It was sacred, what Rehada had done, and it was something Atiana should not have shared. But she had, and it was something he felt Soroush should know.

"She spoke of your daughter, Ahya. Of how she felt she had betrayed you when she told Ahya of your love for learning."

"Enough," Soroush said, staring at Nikandr with cold eyes.

"I say this so you'll understand how envious I am of you."

For long moment Soroush studied him with his deep, piercing eyes. "Envious of what?"

"You have lost much, son of Gatha, but you had much while it lasted."

Soroush stood, folding the cloth of his turban carefully and heading for space in the lean-to shelter they'd built from cut evergreen branches earlier in the day. "Go to sleep, son of Iaros. There's much to do tomorrow."

Nikandr watched him sit beneath the lean-to and lie with his back facing the fire. Nikandr could not sleep, however. His thoughts had turned to Rehada and Atiana, both. Long into the deepening night, as the owls called and the trees sighed beneath the wind, memories of them haunted him.

"My Lord Prince."

Nikandr woke from a deep sleep, blinking his eyes at the early morning light. Styophan was standing over him.

"My Lord Prince, he's gone."

Nikandr shot up, staring first at the lean-to where Soroush had gone to sleep and then toward the tree line. Only a few leagues away was Ashdi en Ghat.

"Send Avil to track him."

"I've already sent him, but there can be no doubt as to where he went."

Nikandr could only agree. He sent Styophan away and began gathering his things for the day ahead. Kaleh, the orphan girl from Siafyan, was watching him from the other side of the fire she was coaxing back to life.

"Did you see him go?" Nikandr asked in Mahndi.

Staring down into the fire, she nodded.

"Why didn't you go with him?"

She shrugged. "There is nothing for me in Ashdi en Ghat."

"Your people are there."

She looked north, back the way they'd come. "My people are *there*."

"I would not wish it, but you can go to them if you choose."

As she had many times over the past two days, she stared closely at his cherkesska, at his tall black boots. "Why have you come to Rafsuhan?"

Nikandr could tell it was something she'd been wanting to ask but had only now summoned the courage to do so. "I have come to learn of the rifts."

"Like Nasim?"

Nikandr was rolling his blanket, but he stopped when she said this. "How do you know of Nasim?"

"You spoke of him last night, with Soroush." She pointed at his chest. "He gave you your hezhan, you said."

"We didn't speak of Nasim learning about the rifts."

"We *do* know of him, son of Iaros, even here."

He stared at her a moment longer, and then let go of his distrust. Of course Nasim would be known here. He'd be legendary. "I said I didn't *know* if he'd given me my hezhan." He continued rolling his blanket, making sure it was tight and free of needles. "And it isn't mine. We share our lives with one another. That's all."

"Is there no other place you could do so?" Kaleh asked as she poked at the embers with a stick.

"Do what?"

"Learn of the rifts."

"There is something growing here. Something terrible. I can feel it."

"So you have come to study us. Nothing more."

Nikandr stuffed the blanket into his pack and slung it over his shoulder. "What would you have me say? That I came to save you?"

Her face grew cross. "We have no need of saviors, certainly not from Anuskaya, be he prince or no."

Nikandr bit his tongue as he finished his packing. He should have been more careful with his words. "What will you do, Kaleh, when we get to Ashdi en Ghat?"

Her eyes narrowed, curious and confused. "You will still go?"

"There is much to learn whether Soroush is willing to help me or not."

"The mahtar will not speak with you."

"As you've said." The walrus tusk cartridges on his bandolier clacked as he ducked into it so that it hung across his chest. He finished by slinging his musket across one shoulder. "But I will try."

"They will kill you."

He held his hand out to her. "As you've said."

She dropped the stick she'd been using to coax the fire and took his hand. "Not everyone who was taken to the fire went willingly."

She said it while staring down at the ground, and it came so softly that Nikandr barely heard the words. He knew immediately who she was talking about.

"There is no shame in fearing death."

"Is there not?"

He bent down so that their eyes were of a level with one another. "There is not."

The rims of her eyes were red, and her nostrils flared, but she did not cry. She nodded once, and then began walking, still holding his hand.

The entrance to Ashdi en Ghat was eerily similar to that of Iramanshah. It was dryer here, so the vegetation was more sparse, but like the valley leading to Iramanshah, the walls sloped up gently to two tall ridges that hid the village well. Nikandr practically expected the same sentries posted at the entrance, but here there were none.

When they reached the dogleg in the valley, the view changed entirely. Instead of a lush green valley like Iramanshah, he came to a gulch with a dry creek bed running down its center. It was bounded on both sides by inhospitable rock faces, and in these were built the houses of the Maharraht. Dozens of homes with oval windows were built into the steep gulch walls. On and on they went for hundreds of yards until they were lost at another bend in the land. Stone stairways connected them, though they were crudely made. They looked almost natural, which was not an indication of the ability of the vanaqiram who had carved them, but rather their aesthetic.

No one greeted them. No one stood in the windows. No one walked along the narrow pathways between homes. Just like Siafyan, it felt as though everyone had died in some ritual cleansing.

The call of a thrush sounded from somewhere ahead. Not ten paces away—as if he were stepping out of the ground itself—a man bearing a musket rose up from behind a scrub bush. He trained his musket upon them as four others stood behind him from places Nikandr wouldn't have thought could hide a man so completely.

Nikandr raised his hands. As ordered, the streltsi behind him did the same. Jahalan merely waited, watching calmly as the Maharraht approached. From a doorway in the stone at the base of the rock face came three more men. They were a good ways away still, but Nikandr recognized one of them immediately.

It was Bersuq, Soroush's brother.

CHAPTER TWENTY-SIX

Bersuq had been at the ritual in Oshtoyets, and he'd been taken, along with Soroush, by the Aramahn. Nikandr hadn't seen him since. He'd thought Bersuq was still in Mirashadal, but here he was, and by the looks of things, he was now a man to be reckoned with. Bersuq had always been a hard man, one who gave no leeway when it came to the Maharraht's objectives. Despite this singular focus, he had never seemed like a leader of men. Soroush, on the other hand, had seemed—no matter how distasteful the notion—a man who others would gladly follow.

Two things became clear with these revelations: first, Soroush had known of Bersuq's presence, and second, he had left to join his brother.

Bersuq walked straight up to Nikandr, staring at him with a look of contempt. He was tall and imposing, and though he was older than Nikandr's father, there was a fire within him that seemed inexhaustible.

Walking to his left, and just behind, was a man Nikandr had never seen before but who seemed important. He was older than Nikandr, but not by many years. Golden rings pierced his ears, but it was the two golden rings piercing his nose that marked him as a man from the southern sect of the Maharraht, the Hratha.

As was common among those islands far to the south of Bolgravya and Nodhvyansk, his clothes were drab—robes of leaden gray, ragged turban and tail of black. Still, as dull as his clothes may have been, his eyes were fierce. This more than anything was what made Nikandr take note—that and the fact that as far as Nikandr could tell he was the only one likely to claim allegiance to the southern sect. He seemed to take the entire scene in with but a glance, but then his gaze fell upon Kaleh, who met his gaze with something akin to fear. The man said nothing, however. He seemed content to allow Bersuq to deal with this as he would, but there was a clear note of judgment in the way he watched, as if he were preparing to weigh the words to come.

As Bersuq came to a halt, he looked at Kaleh strangely as well, as if he were uncomfortable with her presence. He pointed to her, and ordered his men in Mahndi, "Take her to the village."

Two of the Maharraht approached Kaleh. They stopped short of touching her, however. They seemed nervous to be so close to her. Kaleh went willingly, though her eyes darted between Nikandr, Bersuq, and the others.

Bersuq turned and bowed his head to Jahalan.

It was telling that only after Jahalan had returned the gesture did Bersuq allow himself to speak further. "We ask that you go as well, son of Mitra."

"*Neh.* I would stay, son of Gatha."

Nikandr thought Bersuq might become angry, but instead he seemed respectful, perhaps even a bit sad that the fates had seen fit to place one of the Aramahn on the island with Nikandr.

The man of the south, however, did not seemed pleased by this exchange. He remained silent still, but his jaw was tight, and though he tried to hide it he seemed to be looking upon Jahalan with something akin to disgust.

"So be it," Bersuq said, turning to Nikandr. "It is said that you've come to help."

This news could only have come from Soroush, of course, but it was telling that Bersuq refused to speak his name. "Where is Soroush?"

"My brother is no concern of yours."

"He is. I brought him here from Mirashadal."

"So he said, but for now it is just you and I. Be glad I've listened to his words, for if I hadn't, you and all of your men would already have passed beyond the veil." He paused, his lips tight, as if he were still considering that very thing. "You told Soroush you could help."

"I did."

"How? How could you help?"

"I know of the rift that has formed over Rafsuhan. I know that it is larger than what we saw on Uyadensk. I know that it will swallow you whole unless you leave or the rift closes."

As he spoke those words, Nikandr realized just how right they were. The men and women and children from Siafyan must have fled here, but if that were so, Ashdi en Ghat would be filled with life, and here it was, little more than a valley of ghosts. The lack of resistance as they'd come to the island, the lack of sentries, the dearth of people in both villages could only mean one thing: they *had* left. They'd left the island entirely, perhaps for farther shores, perhaps to join their brethren in the south. It all fit. In the last three years the attacks against northern Duchies had all but ceased while the attacks against Mirkotsk and Nodhvyansk and even Vostroma had increased in frequency and strength.

"We know this as well, son of Iaros. What I haven't heard is how you *could* help, if that is your aim."

"I've come to learn of the rift. To close it."

Bersuq's face twisted in disgust. "It cannot be closed. Not by one such as you."

More that Soroush had told him. "I can learn. I can try. I can heal."

"*Heal?*"

"I've done so before."

"You speak of Nasim. Nothing more."

"*Neh*. I've learned much, son of Gatha. You disregard it at the peril of your own people."

Bersuq studied Nikandr for a time, weighing his words. He looked to the streltsi, to Jahalan, and then back to Nikandr.

The single word that followed seemed to come with great reluctance, but he spoke it just the same. "Come."

Bersuq turned, presumably to head back toward the village, but the man of the south stepped in his way. Bersuq stopped, though he seemed ill pleased by it. "Speak, Rahid."

"He will not be allowed into the village."

Bersuq was silent for a moment. He seemed not angry, but composed, and he appeared to want those words to settle between them before he spoke again. Indeed, Rahid seemed unsure of himself for the first time.

"The Landed have never stepped foot in Ashdi en Ghat."

"In difficult times, we do what we must."

Rahid's eyes narrowed. His stance shifted so that he was facing Nikandr more than Bersuq. "Difficult times, but they don't call for this, Bersuq. I thought surely you would know the difference."

"How would I know?" Bersuq said. "I'm just a ruined old soldier."

With that he brushed past Rahid, forcing him to move out of his way. Bersuq's men shoved Nikandr and the others into a line, and together they marched toward the gulch. Rahid did nothing to stop them, but his sharp eyes studied Nikandr, as though it would be important to him later.

After passing several dark tunnels that burrowed into the earth, Bersuq led them into one of the open doorways. The temperature dropped. Siraj lanterns lit their way, revealing curving traceries on the floors and walls. It felt as though the earth itself had chosen all that Nikandr could see—not just the design, but the *structure* of the village.

Eventually they came to a massive room, and within it were scattered hundreds of cots, nearly all of them occupied. The cots held both the young and the old. Each of them looked to be sick—perhaps, Nikandr realized, too sick to be transported by ship. These people were the last remnants of the Maharraht in the north. The rift had all but wiped them out or chased them away, something the Grand Duchy had been trying to do ever since they'd dug in on this and the nearby islands.

There was a part of Nikandr that felt relief—relief that they no longer had the strength to attack Khalakovo and her neighboring duchies. But this also smelled foul, as if it would take but little before the same sort of scene played out on Mirkotsk or Rhavanki or, ancients forbid, Khalakovo.

"It will take time, but I will try," Nikandr said.

"*Neh*," Bersuq replied. "This is not the worst of it."

He led them deeper into the village, down, lower and lower. Nikandr realized they were heading to the lake, something he didn't think would exist in a village of the Maharraht, but of course the roots of Ashdi en Ghat dug much deeper than this splinter group of the Aramahn. Of course the village would have a lake, otherwise it would have been abandoned, even by these militant people.

Eventually they came to a stairwell that spiraled down into the earth. The sound of moaning—from many—traveled up from somewhere down below. The stairwell opened up into a cavern that swallowed the light of the siraj stones the Maharraht soldiers carried.

At the foot of the stairs, which ended in bedrock, more stones, fixed to posts that were fitted into the red-hued stone, cast a brighter light than they were now used to. It illuminated not only the black and utterly still surface of the lake, it illuminated the source of the moaning. Lying upon the hard stone bed at the edge of the lake were a score of children, all of them naked, all of them shivering, though none of them seemed of a mind to do anything about it.

Two women, both of them some years younger than Nikandr, chanted softly, their arms wide as if to encompass the children that lay before them. One wore a circlet with a stone of alabaster. The other wore a stone of azurite in a brooch pinned to her head scarf. Air and water, the spirits that stood in opposition to fire. If the same held true as it had on Ghayavand, the akhoz would be spirits of fire. Why this was Nikandr didn't know. Even Ashan hadn't known. But here it was again.

"How long have they been here?" Nikandr asked.

"Some only a few days. Some weeks. But the worst of them will turn soon." Bersuq turned to face Nikandr squarely. "If your offer of help is real, they may yet live. They may yet be returned to the arms of their mothers—not whole, perhaps, but alive. Can you do this, Nikandr Iaroslov? Can you heal these children?"

By the ancients, Nikandr thought, what was he to do now? He had hoped to learn of the rift, learn how to close it if he was lucky. But this... How was he to combat something even the wisest of the Aramahn had no answers for?

"I can try," he said weakly.

Bersuq walked past Nikandr and took once more to the stairs. "You have three days," he said, his words echoing and dying away as Nikandr stared at the moaning child at his feet.

CHAPTER TWENTY-SEVEN

"Why children?" Nikandr asked.

Jahalan, who kneeled next to him on the cold stone near the lake, shook his head. "Not *children*. Adolescents." Before them was a sleeping boy of thirteen, a boy who was early yet in his symptoms. He slept often, and when he woke he complained of aches and pains in his joints. The others—nearly two dozen in all—lay nearby, some moaning, some crying in pain, but most of them sleeping fitfully. "They are young men and women now. It is an important time in our lives. Most can now open themselves to Adhiya but few have learned which of the elements they most align with. They are, at this moment, open to all of them."

"Then why fire? Why are the akhoz all aligned in the same way?"

"Under normal circumstances, fire is rare among the hezhan, and so one of the least common among the qiram. But the rift may create conditions where the suurahezhan are the ones that come *nearest* to Erahm. For these youths, there may be no other hezhan with which to commune."

Nikandr reached for his spirit. This far below the earth, it was difficult, but he could still sense it. "There are other hezhan."

Jahalan shook his head, his gaunt face angry in the shadows thrown by the siraj stones. "You misunderstand me. Suurahezhan may be the only ones who approach such children. They may, in fact, force the issue. Normally this is a mutual decision. Our young choose their hezhan, and their hezhan choose them. One cannot happen without the other. But perhaps among the rifts, the conditions are right for the suurahezhan to choose in such a way that there is *no* choice for the children."

"Or perhaps it isn't that the suurahezhan become aggressive. Perhaps the other spirits become meek."

"This I doubt."

"Why?"

"Because none of the hezhan are meek. They all thirst for life. They all wish to experience Erahm through our shared bond."

Nikandr frowned while wiping the boy's forehead with a damp cloth. "Have you considered that we have the relationship wrong? Might it not be the children who search out the suurahezhan, ignoring the rest?"

Jahalan seemed disturbed by this thought. He studied the boy, and then looked around the shore of the lake as if seeing it again for the first time. "I will have to think on it"—something over Nikandr's shoulder caught Jahalan's attention—"but for now, you had better prepare yourself."

Nikandr turned and saw two women approaching. One was Nikandr's age, perhaps a bit older. She assisted the other, who seemed as old as the cavern that housed them. They wore stones of azurite. The Maharraht qiram—the few that remained on the island—had tried to commune with their spirits, had tried to fend off the suurahezhan from these children, but Nikandr and Jahalan had both reasoned that it made sense for them to try together. They would represent air, and the others would represent water, and hopefully they would be able to heal the boy who had been affected most recently, or, failing that, learn something that might help them in the future.

Bersuq had agreed, though grudgingly.

The four of them kneeled on opposite sides of the blankets upon which the boy slept—Nikandr above his head, Jahalan at his feet, the two women at his sides. The younger woman did not meet Nikandr's eye, but the elder watched him carefully, her gaze appraising. They all held hands and closed their eyes, the women singing a song. It sounded ancient to Nikandr's untrained ear, melodic and complex. He tried to allow the song to fill him, tried to commune with his hezhan in order to feel the world of Adhiya and through that contact the boy, but found that he could not. Perhaps it was the threat that hung over them—two of the three days Bersuq had granted them had already passed—or perhaps it was the sense that what was happening was preordained and nothing Nikandr could do would change it. He knew not what, but all too soon they had all woken from their trance and the women were kneeling, staring at him with hardened expressions on their faces. Even Jahalan looked grim, no doubt wondering if Nikandr could deliver on his promise.

"I need time. Time alone."

Without speaking, the women stood and made their way to a girl—one of the worst off. "Always more time," the young woman said to the other under her breath. The old woman glanced back, her face pinched, disappointed.

Jahalan hadn't moved. He still watched expectantly near the boy's feet.

"You may as well find food," Nikandr said.

Jahalan paused, but he had already given Nikandr plenty of warnings of how short their time was running. He nodded and stood, making his way over to the women and the moaning girl.

Nikandr scooted along the floor of the cavern until he could look upon the boy's face. He brushed away his hair. He felt how heated his skin was. It was a fever that never broke. How the children could live in this state for days on end he didn't know.

While humming a song his mother used to sing to him, he continued stroking the boy's hair, wondering what would come next—not for his own sake, but for Rafsuhan, for the Maharraht and the Aramahn and Anuskaya. The order of the world was changing, and he felt powerless to stop it.

Even his feeble attempts at healing the rifts seemed pointless in the face of what was happening here. With Atiana's help, he had learned to heal some who had the wasting; much as he'd done with Nasim in Oshtoyets when he'd drawn him toward Erahm and away from Adhiya, he could do the same with those who had only recently contracted the wasting. It was even more effective with Atiana. She could somehow drive the walls of the aether farther apart than they normally were, allowing Nikandr to save those who would have been too difficult to save otherwise.

But this... What could he do? What could Atiana do? It felt—instead of the victim slipping toward Adhiya—as if the arms of Adhiya were reaching out beyond the aether to affect these children, and he hadn't the first idea how to combat the effect. Surely it had something to do with the rift, but beyond this...

Nikandr tried twice more to commune with his spirit, and although he could feel it, something was preventing him from truly feeling the world through its eyes.

He left, disappointed in himself, and took the long and winding path up to the surface. The sun was lowering behind tall white clouds. Two Maharraht trailed him, their muskets at the ready.

"I would not leave my men," Nikandr said to them.

Still, they followed him as he moved eastward and into the hills there. The hills were small, but tall and numerous enough that they created a curving maze one could easily get lost in if care wasn't taken.

Ahead, movement drew Nikandr's attention—the brush of beige against the brown of the dying shrubs—and then it was gone behind the hill.

He ran toward it, but slowed when he heard "Halt!" behind him.

He turned back. "Did you not see it?" he asked in Mahndi.

The man nearest him, his beard dark and his clothes darker, stared at him coldly. "It is only the girl, Kaleh."

"What is she doing out here?"

"She refuses to live in the village."

"Why?"

He shrugged quickly and angrily, as if he were insulted at having to answer Nikandr's questions. "Who can say? Leave her." He had his musket pointed down, but he held it in both hands, ready to pull it up at any moment.

Nikandr didn't see that chasing after the girl was worth getting shot for, so he returned with the men to the village.

Nikandr woke to the soft moans of the Maharraht youth. The massive cavern had only one siraj lamp lit—an attempt to keep the time of the sun in darkness by the lake. He jerked his head, realizing someone was near, watching him. He sat up and found the old woman, the jalaqiram, who had attempted to help him with the boy earlier that day. She was staring down at him, the pits of her eyes and the crags of her skin heavy in shadow.

"I had three children once." Her voice startled him. It was as old as the stone around them, as old as the bones of the earth. "The first was taken by Mirkotsk over forty years ago."

Nikandr sat up, moving away. He stopped himself, however, after realizing how insulting this would be to her.

"What was his name?"

"You may not have his name. He died when he refused to sign his name to a ledger." Nikandr opened his mouth to speak, but she spoke over him. "My second became a beautiful woman. She had two daughters of her own before she was killed in a firefight between the Haelish and the Empire far to the west."

"What was her name?"

"You may not have that either. My third was a boy. He was killed on Yrlanda by your father's men when he was accused of stealing fish. It was in the early days of the blight, and it had struck the island hard." Before he could ask for his name, she continued, "His name was Iyesh, and he was good. He was kind. He would never have joined the Maharraht, which is what I chose to do after his death. He would be ashamed of me, but know this, son of Iaros: I would do it again in a moment. Fates willing, I would see you all driven back to your homeland."

She paused, her breath coming low and ragged, as if she were more agitated than she'd been in years. "But there are scales to be tipped, are there not? I will pay for my thoughts and actions, if not in this life, then in the next. I have come to terms with that. There are scales for you as well, whether you know it or not." By the shape of her silhouette he saw her point toward the boy they had tried to help earlier. "And you can tip yours back by reaching him."

He found himself unable to speak. He didn't know what to say, so he simply nodded.

"Can you do what you say you can?"

"I think so, but—"

"Do not *think*, Nikandr Iaroslov. You either can or you can't, and if you can't you should leave while the others are away."

"What others?"

The woman paused. He could see her wavering. A decision was being made before his very eyes, though he knew not what was at stake. "The men from Behnda al Tib. You've met one, Rahid, but there are more, and they will soon return."

Nikandr suddenly felt the weight of the mountain above them. His own breath sounded loud in his ears. "And what will they do if they find one of the Landed in their midst?"

"They will kill you."

She said it so baldly that there was little doubt that she was telling the truth. Clearly they had been here on the island already, and they'd gone for some purpose that none of the Maharraht would make clear to him. It was also clear that there was a struggle going on, not just for Ashdi en Ghat, but for the heart of the Maharraht themselves.

It felt strange to have not only Soroush, but *Bersuq* trust him in this way. It was a signal of their desperation as the horror of the wasting dawned on them. But now Nikandr saw that they were also fighting off a challenge from Behnda al Tib. How ruthless were the men from the south that these people were somehow afraid of them?

Nikandr took a deep breath if only to clear the suffocating feeling that the mountain was bearing down on him. He wondered again, as he did many times each day, if he'd done the right thing in coming here. Too late to worry about that now, he told himself. A man who looks constantly over his shoulder will miss the path ahead.

"I will do it," he said finally.

"Then come." She held a shaking hand out to him.

He took her hand and stood, and together they made their way to the boy. They kneeled on his blanket, the woman at his feet and Nikandr at his head.

"What is his name?" Nikandr asked.

She appeared ready to deny him this, but then the tightness in her shoulders softened and she said, "His name is Wahad."

Nikandr narrowed his eyes. "That's the name of Soroush's father."

The light was dim, but Nikandr could see the old woman smile sadly. "He was named after his grandfather."

Nikandr physically jerked back. "This is Soroush's *son*?"

"Just so," she replied softly, perhaps embarrassed over revealing this information.

He stared down at the boy. Even in the darkness, even in the deep shadows, he could now see the resemblance to Soroush and Bersuq, both. How could he have missed it?

The information did not help. It made things infinitely worse. To have the life of Soroush's son in his hands... Why would Bersuq have allowed it?

And then he understood—why Bersuq had allowed him to come to the village, why he had granted him time among their dying children. Despite his anger over Soroush leading one of the Landed to the home of his people, he wanted to save his brother's son from a fate that was worse than death.

"Are you ready?" the old woman asked.

"I am."

Instead of holding Wahad's hands, she placed her hands on his ankles, pulling them and fixing them in place. Nikandr mirrored her movements, gently pulling his head to elongate his neck and spine. Then he touched the boy's forehead. Together, he and the old woman closed their eyes, and their breathing fell into sync—slowing in pace, deepening—as each of them began to slip toward the other world, the world of the spirits, the world where life was renewed. He felt his vanahezhan clearly now, and he even felt the woman's jalahezhan. Both were near; both were bound by stones and the common bond to their host in Erahm.

Nikandr allowed himself to be taken by the hezhan. It was not so different from the way in which the hezhan feed from the living. He was simply turning the relationship around, using *them* to see into the world beyond.

And soon...

Nikandr feels as the hezhan feels. Its senses are not the same as those in the physical world. Instead of sight and taste and sound, there are impressions, emotions, senses that live beneath the surface, senses long forgotten by the minds of men.

He feels discomfort from the boy, or more accurately the creature that feeds upon him. He has come this far before, but this is different. He practically feels the emotion running through them—boy and hezhan, both. A seething. An anger. A yearning. It feels worse than any disease, for it both nourishes and feeds upon Wahad. He has become a conduit. A tool to be used and one day—if the boy is lucky—tossed aside.

And then he senses something beyond. In the world of Adhiya, it is difficult to determine distance and direction, but he knows it is near. It is something he has felt before, an ancient presence, and not simply a hezhan. It is something else, a man that walks between worlds, as Nasim once did. But how can that be? Nasim was unique, alone in the world with his abilities.

Suddenly he remembers. He saw this man on an island far away in a sea hundreds of leagues away. But he was trapped. How could he have escaped? How could he have come here? And why?

The understanding shakes him, and he is thrown from the dream.

A wind blew through the cavern, unbidden, but very much of his doing.

Nikandr stood, confused and angry and sick.

"Where are you going?" the old woman asked.

With the shades of Adhiya still upon him, he ignored her and staggered to where his old friend kneeled. He shook his shoulder. "Jahalan." He shook him again, harder.

Jahalan woke, squinted up at him.

"We must go. Quickly."

"Why?"

"Muqallad is here. He has come to Rafsuhan."

CHAPTER TWENTY-EIGHT

Atiana is still in the aether when her senses return to her.

When a Matra becomes overwhelmed, there are usually only two outcomes: she wakes exhausted and confused or, more rarely, she becomes lost, never waking from her time in the aether. Atiana wonders if *she* has become lost. Fear builds within her, but she can feel her body back in the drowning chamber beneath the cemetery. She nearly follows those fears to the point of wakefulness, if only to reassure herself that she is not lost.

So to be aware of herself as she floats through the straits comes as a strange surprise. The great standing cliffs to either side of her scintillate in the black. The Spar, a structure that has taken nearly five years and thousands of craftsmen to build, is nearly complete. It looms before her. She still feels some of the same raw and immense power she felt earlier, but there is a distinct feeling that it has ebbed, as if the pressure built to the bursting point, released, and finally receded. What caused the buildup and the eventual release she doesn't know, but she is sure that her surge of feelings were caused by the peak of energy.

Surprisingly, she no longer feels the fear she once did. She feels as if she's treading water; the depths below her are dangerous, and the waves may yet pull her under, but for the time being they have come to a mutual understanding.

She becomes aware of the spire to the south, the one that allows for the ease of travel between Galahesh and Vostroma. She knew of this. What piques her interest is the fact that she feels something similar to the north. This makes no sense, however. The northern side of the island has never *needed* a spire. Galahesh didn't have the Matri to maintain one, but more importantly, the ley lines flowed naturally from the massive continent, through Oramka, and to the northern end of Galahesh. It was only at the straits that the aether clashed against the currents coming from Anuskaya to form an unpredictable maelstrom.

She widens her mind, casts herself outward, and attunes herself to the spires. The aether flows between them, just as it does along the islands of the Grand Duchy. The flow is little more than a trickle because of the straits, but she can sense it running from the north, down along the Spar until it bridges the gap at the center, and then continuing to the south. She wonders if she can guide the aether as she does in Galostina. She tries, coaxing the aether, and it responds. It flows faster. And when she releases it, the effect continues. It makes sense—this was what the spires were built to do—but it doesn't answer the question of why the northern spire was built in the first place.

She feels something, a feeling similar to when another Matra is near. She casts outward, but feels nothing, and yet the sense that another is near continues. The memories of Ushai return. She pulls herself inward, focusing instead on Baressa and the Shattering. As she does, the feeling fades, and then is lost altogether. It must have been Ushai, and yet Atiana wonders if Arvaneh has woken.

She studies the tower again, but it is empty, as it was before.

The urge to continue the search for Ushai is strong, but exhaustion has long since set in, and she finds herself making small mistakes, slips of the mind. She must return and heal before attempting to do more.

Atiana woke coughing and spluttering even though the breathing tube was still in her mouth.

Ishkyna, reading a journal by the light of a small lantern on a nearby table, stared down at her, her mouth turned down in disapproval. "Control yourself."

Atiana sat up, having more trouble orienting herself than she had in some time. She should be in Galostina, not in this cramped space beneath a cemetery in Baressa. Shouldn't she?

"How long?"

Ishkyna stood and held out a towel for Atiana to step into. "Eighteen hours, Tiana. You've been gone for nearly a day. You were to take only two or three hours."

Atiana's feet slipped on the slick stone tiles as she stepped out of the copper tub, but Ishkyna caught her with practiced hands.

Atiana looked at Ishkyna, and then she was overwhelmed by a surge of emotion. She took Ishkyna into a sudden, tight embrace.

Ishkyna yelped and tried to shove Atiana away. "You're freezing!"

Atiana held her close for a moment more before stepping back and shaking her head, spraying Ishkyna with the chill water from the tub.

"Stop it!" Ishkyna cried. She took up Atiana's robe from a shelf nearby and threw it at her. "This is serious business."

The robe struck Atiana in the face. "Listen to yourself," Atiana said as she shook out the robe and slipped into it. "Serious business..." She knew Ishkyna was right, but for some reason the real world felt far away. It felt good, like it was just the two of them when they were young, waking from a session in Galostina's drowning chamber.

"It *is*. Now tell me what you found."

Atiana took up the towel and began drying her hair. "Little enough."

"Eighteen hours had better result in something better than that."

She told Ishkyna about Arvaneh and Ushai and her time at the Spar.

Ishkyna sniffed. "Little enough, indeed."

"Long journeys start with small steps, Shkyna."

"And *slow* journeys may end in disaster." Ishkyna pulled on her coat for the cold walk above. "Best you quicken your step."

Dawn had yet to break when Atiana rode through the streets of Baressa with the strelet, Irkadiy. He was a logical choice for her escort; he had already been trusted once with her protection and the knowledge of her mission in the cemetery. He was a crack shot with a musket, and the best huntsman and tracker in Galostina. Best of all, he knew the area. He'd spent many summers here as a youth, visiting his family on his mother's side. He still took dinner with many of them when he could, and raised glasses with old friends besides. It gave Atiana a sense of comfort that she had someone that knew not just the lay of the land, but the people as well.

Irkadiy rode a healthy black gelding and wore the garb of a Galaheshi merchantman—a round turban and billowing coat and brown woolen pants with black boots that stopped halfway up his shins. His musket was slung in a holster affixed to the saddle. It was behind his left leg, mostly hidden, especially from someone viewing them from the front.

Atiana rode a pretty roan mare. Her garb was that of a merchantman's wife—an ornamented headdress with a yellow veil that hid her face. The dress she wore was intricately embroidered velvet with ermine accents. It was rich clothing, to be sure, but not so rich that it would mark her as a noblewoman.

The streets near the Mount were nearly empty, giving the city much the same feel as the cemetery, but as they approached the famed Baressan market, more and more people populated the streets, most of them with small carts or wagons clattering along to set up their stalls for the coming day. Some eyed Atiana and Irkadiy, but most bowed their heads in greeting, and those that didn't took little notice.

Not far beyond the market, the cobbled street they rode along ended abruptly. Ahead there was little more than a curved edge to the street and a strip of green land before the straits opened up before them. They turned left and headed up the street toward the Spar.

Atiana had heard stories of, but was still surprised to see, especially at this hour, a long line of merchantmen and landsmen waiting to cross the water. Goods were heading out from Baressa to Ramina, the port city on the northern end of the island. They would typically be bearing goods meant for windships bound for Oramka or the Empire proper. They waited their turn, and eventually came to the front of the line, just before the pulley houses, where the tariff master asked them questions about their destination and their purpose. He saw them as easy pickings, which was what Atiana had been hoping for. The more he felt they were a normal part of his day, the more quickly they'd be forgotten.

They managed to gain passage while losing only a handful of coins, but the way the master watched Atiana as Irkadiy paid him was unsettling.

Seven pulley houses stood at the edge of the cliffs. They were built outward into the air over the cliff such that strong ropes could be lowered below them. Outside of each were massive capstans, each with eight or more mules harnessed to them. The pulley masters called "Hiyah!" and whipped the ponies when it was time, and the ponies trudged, causing the ropes that ran above them and into the pulley houses to turn and force the inner workings to raise or lower the wooden cage that contained either cargo or people.

Atiana and Irkadiy were led to the third pulley house, one of the smaller ones meant for a handful of people.

The pulley master approached Irkadiy and held out two burlap cloths with ropes tied to them. "Blinders, for the ponies." He stared at Atiana and smiled, revealing teeth stained brown by tabbaq. "You can wear one, too, if you like." He laughed at that, but stopped when Irkadiy waved him away.

"They're good climbing ponies," Irkadiy said.

"Good or not, put them on. If they're not used to it, they'll be skittish. They won't enjoy it, and neither will you if you're caught in the cage without these." He waggled the bags again.

Irkadiy accepted them with a nod and put one over each pony's head so that their eyes were covered. Only then did the pulley master swing open the large door, and allow them into the cage. The cage swung slightly as they stepped onto it, giving Atiana a strange feeling—as if she were stepping onto a small waterborne ferry.

Her pony stamped her hooves loudly and threw her head back, perhaps trying to knock the mask from her eyes, but Irkadiy took the reins and ran his hand along her neck and spoke into the pony's ear softly until she calmed down.

The doors came closed with a creak and a bang. A bell was rung, the massive ropes and pulleys began to turn, and then they were headed down and out into open air.

Atiana had ridden in dozens of windships and yachts and skiffs. She'd been a passenger on a waterborne ship a handful of times. She had never been bothered by them, even while she was sleeping in a cabin, unable to see much of the outside world. But riding in this contraption made her stomach churn. It felt as though the rope would snap at any moment. The cage itself was little more than four wooden fences, head-high, built onto a wooden platform. The platform seemed fragile, as though her feet, or their ponies', might crash through at any moment.

When it happened—and she was sure it would—they would plummet and buffet against the ivory cliff before plowing into the lower pulley house in the split second before their deaths.

She closed her eyes and shook her head, moving to the edge of the cage if only to pretend she was standing on the deck of a windship.

To her right, two more sets of pulleys were drawing their cages up, or perhaps down. She wasn't sure; she couldn't see either of the cages yet. To her left four more moved, their cables swaying gently in the wind. As they neared what she judged as the halfway point, she saw a crowd of people packed like fish into a single cage—there must have been thirty of them, rising up along the cliff. Most of them wore the simple clothes of workmen. Nearly all of them took it as easily as taking a stroll, but one young man near the corner watched Atiana with a look of barely concealed terror. The two of them watched one another silently—one rising, the other falling—until he'd passed out of sight.

She had wanted to study the Spar on their descent, but she found herself unable to. She could focus on nothing but reaching the bottom. Her foot began to tap of its own free will.

"My Lady, please," Irkadiy said. "You're making them nervous." He was standing at the reins of her pony, rubbing her neck, staring at Atiana's foot.

Atiana had to concentrate to stop it, but that just made her fears resurface.

Ponies be damned. If she wanted to tap her foot, she was bloody well going to.

Only after they had finally landed and boarded the large ferry did the terror leave her. She and Irkadiy shared the deck with dozens of others, a handful of ponies, and twenty cords of wood. She stood at the bulwarks, staring up at the bridge as the ferry's drum beat time and the twelve oars below her cut into the blue-green water.

"Can they have built the Spar in only four years?" Atiana asked Irkadiy.

"It doesn't seem possible," he said.

Far above, dozens of Aramahn stonemasons were moving along the bridge and the supports beneath the open section that had yet to be joined. It was stout, and massive, and yet Atiana couldn't get the notion out of her head that after a surge of tide water below or a squall above, it would all topple into the sea.

"I saw it in the dark," she said.

"And what did you see?"

"An edifice. A structure every bit as impressive as what we see before us."

"It's nothing more than a bridge, My Lady."

"If you could see the world through my eyes you would not say such things. This is a place that has been anathema to the Matri for centuries. To have it spanned so, and in such a short amount of time, smacks of hubris."

Irkadiy snorted. "The line of the Kamarisi is nothing if not proud, My Lady."

Atiana shook her head. "I speak not of Hakan, but the Lady Arvaneh."

They made it to the other side of the straits, passing two ferries as they did so, and they gained the top of the cliffs after another harrowing ride—though Atiana had to admit that it wasn't so bad as the first.

It was freeing to move beyond the straits and into Vihrosh, Baressa's smaller sister that stood on the northern side of the straits. It was much smaller than Baressa. An eighth-league beyond the cliffs and it was little more than a village. They were through it and into the hills beyond well before the sun had reached high noon.

The land sloped downward beyond Vihrosh. They made good time, passing into the lowlands and into the wide plateau that covered much of the northern half of Galahesh. There was little breeze and the day was unseasonably warm. They both found themselves unbuttoning their clothes to let in a bit of air. Irkadiy seemed overly conscious of her exposed neck and arms—she caught him glancing at her more than once—but Atiana didn't care. If she didn't get some air she was going to pass out.

Atiana had told Irkadiy that she wasn't sure what they were searching for. She could tell from his sidelong glances that he dearly wished to ask her of their destination, but he was a good man, and he kept his questions to himself.

Atiana wished she knew herself. She only knew after the experience she'd had in the aether, the feeling of being drawn westward as if a spire lay in that direction, had forced her hand. There was no choice now but to go to the area and see what she could see. She had considered coming while taking the dark, but the truth of the matter was she didn't know how far beyond the straits she could travel, and she was still weak. It would take days before she would trust herself in the aether once more. Were Bahett not returning from his hunt tomorrow, she would have waited, but he would soon learn of her transgression. She'd gone to the drowning chamber and spied on Arvaneh without his leave, which made this ride all the more important.

They came to an area that was lightly wooded with pine and oak, and shortly after that the woods thickened until they were traveling a road that cut through a thick forest.

"Wait," Irkadiy said.

He reined his pony over and trotted back. He sat in his saddle, considering a road that ran off through the forest.

"What do you suppose this is?"

Atiana shrugged. "A homestead?"

"Look at the ruts. Dozens of wagons have passed this way, and recently."

The inference was clear. If so many had passed, it may very well be what she was looking for.

They took to the trail. Irkadiy was on edge. They could not see far on the road ahead, and the undergrowth was thick, making it difficult for them to forge a path through it.

After they passed a ridge and the land took them downhill, Irkadiy guided their ponies into the forest until the trail was lost from view. After tying their ponies behind a copse of alder, Irkadiy retrieved his musket from its holster behind his pony's saddle, and they began walking eastward on foot.

The going was slow, but Atiana felt better for the cover of the forest around them. Clouds had moved in while they rode. A light drizzle fell over the forest, the sound of it like rashers of ham frying over a fire.

Atiana watched the landscape ahead closely. She was aware of her surroundings as she had rarely been, and for a long while she wrote it off to how on edge Irkadiy was and how acutely aware of it she was, but the further they went, the more she realized there was something more.

She had been a Matra for some time now. She had spoken at length to the other Matri about their abilities, and she had tried to learn as many of them as she could. She paid particular attention to her stolen time with Saphia when the others were far away and she could work closely with her. She had tried to attune herself to the aether while outside the drowning basin, with some small amount of success. She could feel the draw of the aether, could feel the presence of the rooks that were placed in or near the drowning chamber, could feel the receding presence of other Matri. She could even feel the subtle shifts in the currents caused by the spire high above Galostina, and this, as strange as it seemed, was what was causing the sharpening of her senses.

And so she knew, well before she saw, that ahead of her lay a spire, and yet it was still strange to look upon it. As she and Irkadiy came to a stop beneath an ancient larch and he parted the lower branches, she saw it.

A tall black tower of obsidian.

CHAPTER TWENTY-NINE

"Why would they build such a thing?" Irkadiy whispered.

Why, indeed? The empire had no need of such things. The lines between the mainland and Oramka and Galahesh were strong. They were naturally guided by the land itself and the relatively calm seas between. And there was no need for one between the northern and southern ends of Galahesh—the straits saw to that. So why? Why would they spend all these resources to build one?

Atiana became suddenly aware that Irkadiy was ignoring the obelisk, his eyes narrowed and distant, as if he were listening more than looking.

Then he grabbed her arm and pulled her toward the trail they'd forged coming in. He said nothing, so neither did she.

The sound of the rain—as well as the soft forest floor—covered their retreat, but by the time they'd reached the top of a nearby rise, Atiana became aware of forms mirroring their movement to her right. On her left there were more.

Irkadiy sprinted downslope, trusting Atiana to keep up so they could stay ahead of the pursuit. She followed, nearly keeping pace with him. They came to the trough of the shallow vale and then attacked the incline on the opposite side, which was steep, much steeper than Atiana was used to climbing.

Soon she began to flag. Irkadiy took her wrist and pulled her along, helping her to take the hill.

"Stay!" a voice called from behind them in Yrstanlan.

They pushed. Atiana's legs were already burning, but fear was driving her onward.

A musket crack sounded as bark exploded from the bole of a nearby tree. Another dug into the dirt near their feet.

"Go on," Irkadiy said as he shoved her and then spun around.

A glance behind showed him sighting down the length of his musket. The musket fired, white smoke coughing from the muzzle, and one of their pursuers dropped, clutching his chest.

Irkadiy reloaded as he ran, but grunted in pain as a musket shot grazed his leg.

They reached the crest of the hill and were beyond it as several more shots whizzed over their heads. Further down, the slope leveled off at the edge of a marsh. Stands of cattails hugged the edge of the green-coated water.

"Hurry," she said softly.

They ran and reached the edge of the marsh where Atiana snatched two of the cattails up. She motioned for Irkadiy to follow her and then she stepped into the water, being careful not to splash. She waded deeper into the water and wended her way into the cattail stand. As they slipped through the tall grasses—the cool water rising to their shins and then to their knees—she ripped off the base of the cattails and did the same a goodly length up. "Lie down," she whispered while handing one of the cattail tubes to Irkadiy. "Breathe through this."

He took the cattail, doubtful, but they could already hear the pursuit approaching the top of the rise behind them. He swallowed hard, glancing toward the rise, and then lay down, setting his musket in the water next to him. After taking a huge breath, he inserted the makeshift breathing tube into his mouth and lay back. Atiana lay down as well, trying to calm herself as she inserted the tube and breathed through it.

The stands of grasses and cattails would, she hoped, suppress their ripples, and the green muck on the surface would hide the mud they'd kicked up.

She breathed slowly as the fetid water filled her nostrils and her body pressed against the slick muck. She calmed herself as she did in the drowning basin. She slowed her breath, slowed her heart, so that she could hear. She heard little at first except the patter of rain on the water and the weeds. But then she heard a pounding, as of men running. It approached—very close—and then stopped. She dare not open her eyes. The water was much too murky, and she didn't wish them to sting. So she breathed, and she waited.

Then the pounding resumed, slower this time.

Soon she heard only the pattering. The men had gone on, searching ahead. They would not be fooled for long, though. She waited until they would have moved well beyond the marsh before reaching over and squeezing Irkadiy's hand and poking her head above the water.

Seeing that they were indeed alone, they stood and cut across the path they had taken earlier during their flight, making their way quickly but quietly toward their ponies.

Atiana whispered, "They may have taken them."

Irkadiy shook his head and whispered back. "We hid them far enough. They won't have found them yet."

The tone in his voice sounded more hopeful than certain, but they found both ponies right where they'd left them. They mounted and kept the ponies at a walk for some time. Atiana felt muskets being trained on them, felt something at the nape of her neck and the small of her back, phantom pain in the center of her wet bodice where the musket ball would strike. She resisted the urge to touch the scar where the musket shot had torn through her chest five years before. It still ached from time to time, and it was doing so now, worse than it had ever been except for the days that had followed Soroush's failed ritual on Oshtoyets.

In the end they made their way back to the road and then pushed hard for Vihrosh. They stopped outside of the city and found a clear stream that ran over gray rocks. While Irkadiy watched the path for signs of pursuit, Atiana stripped and washed the worst of the marsh stench from her clothes and skin. It wasn't perfect, but it would prevent anyone from asking of it—or more importantly, remembering it. As she washed the clothes, she kept glancing toward the tree Irkadiy was hiding behind, wondering if he was going to pop his head around to steal a look. But he never did.

They switched places, and Atiana was not so resilient as Irkadiy had been. She did steal a look, and Irkadiy was looking right at her when she did. He smiled, and when she ducked back behind the tree, he laughed.

She was too embarrassed to look again, but the sound—the healthy laugh of a naked man in an idyllic place like this—did much to drive back the terror she'd had in her heart since finding the spire.

They didn't wait for their clothes to dry, but instead trusted to the wind to do that for them, at least as much as it could in the light drizzle. By the time they reached the straits and took to the ferry that would bring them back across the water, the Spar looked vastly different than it had that morning. The sun had already set, casting it the blue color of wet slate. The Spar had never looked anything but imposing, but now it seemed bellicose as well, like a hand upon the hilt of a knife.

What would Arvaneh or the Kamarisi want with a newly built spire? Clearly it would be to control the aether in some manner, but this made no sense. Unless she considered the presence of Ushai. Years ago she had been learning the ways of the dark from Fahroz in the depths of Iramanshah. Clearly in the years since she had learned much. In all likelihood she had surpassed Fahroz herself in ability. And now she had turned up here, in Baressa, in a place where it was imperative that someone with the abilities of a Matra be found and used.

But toward what end? It seemed likely that it was to control the flow of aether between the northern and southern halves of the island. And if that were so, then it would seem to make sense that the bridge would have something to do with it. Why else would both have been built at the same time?

"Irkadiy, you said you know your way around Baressa."

"Like the back of my hand."

"Good, because there's someone you need to find for me. An Aramahn woman. It's most important, Irkadiy."

"Yes, My Lady."

When Atiana returned to her room, she was shocked to find not Yalessa, but Bahett in her apartments. He was sitting in a padded chair, watching the fading light of dusk through the nearby window.

"You've returned from your hunt," Atiana said with as much nonchalance as she could muster. She thought of trying to bully him away, to force him to speak with her tomorrow, but there was something about him—the angled way he was sitting in the chair, the tilt of his head—that shed light on not only how furious he was but how desperately he was trying to hide it.

"Good thing that I did," he said, turning to look at her. The shadows were heavy across his face, somehow turning his refined beauty into something wicked. "You're wet."

"I left with Irkadiy to take in Vihrosh."

"Irkadiy?"

"A strelet in my Father's service."

"Why?"

"Why what?"

"Why did you go to Vihrosh with a lone strelet?"

She thought at first he knew of the spire, but then she caught herself. Was he *jealous*? "His family is from Galahesh. He wanted to visit the city before the Spar was complete."

"Why?"

Atiana shrugged. "Because the lifts will no longer be needed. He remembers it fondly and—"

"*Nyet*. Why did *you* go to Vihrosh?"

She gave him a stare that made it clear that this was a subject she no longer wished to discuss. "I went because I needed to clear my mind. And I wanted to see more of Galahesh."

"With one man. Alone."

"*Da*," she said, daring him to accuse her of anything more.

His eyes bore into hers. His whole body was tight. Eventually he broke his gaze and stood, pacing to the far side of the room. "You disobeyed me. After

I explicitly forbid it, you spied upon Arvaneh. Why?"

"Because she needs spying on. You said it yourself in Galostina."

He stopped his pacing and faced her. "I will not stand for this from a wife of mine."

"I'm not yet your wife."

"You are, Atiana. You represent me now. I had to tell my servants that I had agreed to your trip so they didn't think you were scheming. But some no doubt heard me in the courtyard. They'll talk. My authority will be questioned."

Atiana stared, feeling the anger radiating from him. He really was affronted by what she'd done. "I'm sorry," she said. "You're right. It was disrespectful. I only thought... I only thought I could catch her unaware, thinking her guard would be down with you and Hakan and the other men gone from the kasir. It won't happen again."

The anger remained in his face, but his body relaxed. And then he seemed to soften. "In any case, we know that you can take the dark here." He looked at her more closely. "You can, can't you?"

"I can, though the straits make the aether swirl in unpredictable ways. It's difficult, but I can manage."

"And what of Arvaneh? What did you find?"

"I found nothing. When I went to the tower, she wasn't there."

"Where was she?"

"I don't know."

"In the kasir? The bazaar?"

"I don't *know*. She was simply gone."

"She can't have disappeared. You must have missed her."

"I didn't miss her, Bahett. She was gone, or she was able to hide herself from me."

Atiana felt her fingers go cold.

Her hands began to shake and she was forced to cross her arms so Bahett wouldn't see.

Or she was able to hide herself.

The words struck a memory, like the feeling a low chord from a harp made in her chest.

While she'd been in the aether, her memories had played through her mind as if someone were sifting through them.

She realized now that they *had* been... Arvaneh had not been the one to be searched. *Atiana* had. She had entered the dark here, in Baressa, and she had searched Arvaneh out. And Arvaneh had found her.

Her mind started working backwards. Bahett's insistence she not go. The hunt. Ishkyna's insistence that Arvaneh would be vulnerable.

Had it all been a ruse?

And if so, why?

Because they wanted her relaxed. They could not have her on her guard.

And it had worked. She had gone, confident that beyond the difficulty of taking the dark so near the straits she would be able to handle anything.

Arvaneh had found her and sifted through her memories.

But why? What could she have wanted?

She didn't know, but she knew this: Bahett had been lying to her from the beginning. The man beneath the willow had hinted as much, but she hadn't quite believed it. Bahett had lied about Arvaneh. Lied about Hakan. And he had manipulated her masterfully at the stables. He'd forbade her to take the dark, knowing full well that it would force any one of the Vostroma sisters to do the opposite.

Most importantly, he'd lied about the reasons he wanted Atiana to come to Galahesh. It hadn't been so he could learn more about Arvaneh. It had been so Arvaneh could learn more about *her*.

Bahett was staring at her. "Are you quite all right?"

The concern in his voice sounded genuine, but she was beginning to learn just how good an actor he was. It also made it clear what would happen if she were to let on that she knew what had happened. She would be killed, as simple as that. And it would happen as soon as could be arranged. This very night, most likely.

"I'm sorry," she said. "I was merely trying to think where I might have gone wrong, but I swear to you, Bahett, she wasn't there. I felt her not at all."

"You were—" Standing near the mantle, he visibly calmed himself. "I'm sure you tried, but she has magics we do not understand." He stepped forward, the light of dusk casting his face in stark and desperate relief. "This is merely one small hint of what she can do." He was so close now that he was towering over her. His hands shook as he spoke. "There is time yet. I have made arrangements." He turned and walked back to the chair.

"What sort of arrangements?"

"Your father arrives in two days. The following night we will have a grand celebration, and the day after that, your father and Hakan will be wrapped up in negotiations. That night, in Arvaneh's drink will be placed a tincture. It will do little at first, but it will muddy her mind. She will retire early. It is then that you must watch her."

Atiana already knew he was lying. "There's to be a dinner that night with the wives who've come from Anuskaya. My absence will be noticed."

He was already shaking his head. "You will take ill early in the meal."

"I require Ishkyna."

"Your caring sister will escort you from the room, making your apologies for you."

"And what is it about this night that makes you think that it will be easier to watch her?"

"Your father's arrival demands it. Hakan will rail against her control. He will need to be controlled more than ever. And," Bahett continued, "there's also the chance she will attempt to do the same to your father."

"It cannot be so easy as that."

"Who are you to say? This is exactly why we need you, Atiana." He came to her and rubbed her shoulders, the old Bahett once more. "The Grand Duchy needs you. Galahesh needs you." He took her hand and held it tenderly. "*I* need you."

His touch made her skin crawl, and before she knew it she'd snatched her hand away. Too quickly.

He stared down, a glimpse of his other self returning. "Forgive me. The Kamarisi... I have seen much over the past week that makes me think that he considers Galahesh little different than the islands of the Grand Duchy."

"A fruit ripe for the plucking," Atiana said.

"Just so." He swept to the door. "Three nights, Atiana. This may be our last chance."

And with that, he left, leaving a rush of wind and a chill in Atiana's heart.

She waited for a time, but then left the room and moved down to Ishkyna's apartments. Ishkyna opened the door a crack, but when she saw who it was, she opened the door and allowed Atiana in.

Atiana could hear from the next room the bed creaking, blankets rustling.

"We must speak, Ishkyna." She glanced at the bedroom door. "Alone."

Ishkyna stared at Atiana for a long moment, then rolled her eyes. She stormed over to the bedroom door, opened it wide, and said, "Out!"

A minute later, a young man—a stablehand, if Atiana wasn't mistaken—bowed his head and fled from the room.

"Now, what is so important"—Ishkyna fell into a chair across from Atiana—"that you need to interrupt my sleep?"

"There's trouble, Shkyna." Atiana told her everything Bahett had said.

"And this couldn't wait until morning?"

"He was lying."

She paused. "How do you know?"

"Because he was eager. *Too* eager. It's a trap. They *want* me to watch Arvaneh."

"But why?"

Atiana shook her head. "I think Arvaneh has what she wants from me, but

I'm too big a prize to simply throw away. I think she's planning on beguiling me as she has the Kamarisi."

"Why wouldn't she have done so already?"

"Because—" Atiana stopped. She couldn't because she needed Atiana's mind to be her own. But Arvaneh had given Atiana a suggestion. She was sure of it now. The urge to control the spires. She'd done so at Arvaneh's bidding.

"What?" Ishkyna asked, concern coming to her face for the first time.

"You're right. She *has* done so already. In the aether, she put a suggestion in my mind to work the aether through the spires. And when I did, she watched. That's what she's wanted all along, the knowledge of how to control the spires."

"And now she has it?"

"Perhaps not. That may be why she wants me to take the aether again."

Ishkyna shook her head, her long blonde hair swaying against her shoulders as she did so. "You can't be thinking of going."

"I am. But we will not be unprepared."

CHAPTER THIRTY

Khamal steps into the celestia. Standing along the edge in a wide circle are dozens of men and women, Aramahn one and all. They wear their robes of summer solstice, flax and lemon and gold. Outside the celestia, rain falls in sheets. The air is thick with the smell of it. The skies are dark, with lightning striking bold across the sky, the thunder soon following, raucous and fey.

By way of protest, Sariya and Muqallad have not come. The same can be said for some of their disciples, but by and large the people have been persuaded by Khamal's words—that this is the only way.

In the center of the celestia stands a girl. Her name is Yadhan. She is thirteen, but she looks no older than ten. She, of all the children that remain in the city, seems most prepared for what Khamal is about to do.

He approaches her, motioning to the celestia floor. The girl glances toward her father, who merely nods. She stares with uncertain eyes at Khamal. Khamal smiles for her, though there is regret in doing so. He does not wish this upon her, but there is no other way, not if they are to halt the steadily marching progress of the rift.

"Lie down," Khamal says, annoyed at the need to speak.

She does. She closes her eyes. Her nostrils flare. She swallows uncontrollably.

Her mother watches, her tear-filled eyes alternating between her daughter and Khamal.

Khamal does not acknowledge her. Doing so would give the impression that there is something wrong, that this is something to be consoled. It isn't. This sacrifice is what Yadhan was made for—of this Khamal is sure. There is a part of him that wishes it didn't have to be children, but they had already tried this ritual with five adults of varying ages. All of them had died. Only near the change to adulthood was it possible to create a vessel where the soul of the child and the soul of a suurahezhan, a spirit of fire, could coexist.

Khamal kneels by Yadhan's side. When he does, twelve of the most gifted suuraqiram step forward and surround them. They begin a chant, a dirge from the Gaji that is often sung during vigil—a mourning period of three days and three nights in which a loved one's death is honored and their procession to the life beyond is made easier.

Khamal chose this song not for himself, but because it holds meaning for Yadhan. She was born in the Gaji Desert, and so it will bring some sense of normalcy to this island and this city that has become little more than anathema to life.

As the dirge continues, Khamal takes his piece of the Atalayina from his robes. He holds it in his hand, feels its heft. He studies the delicate striations running through it and wonders once more if the fates are watching him. He has tried to do right by them. He thought—as did Sariya and Muqallad—that the world was ready. They were not so foolish as to believe *everyone* was ready—certainly that wasn't the case; he did not even believe that the three of *them* were truly worthy—but he thought that by ushering in indaraqiram the rest of the world would follow, that they would *become* enlightened, as it was meant to be.

How wrong they'd been. How many had suffered.

And now there would be one more.

Yadhan watches with fearful eyes as Khamal places one hand on her chest. With the other he places the Atalayina upon her forehead.

With this she tightens. Her body rigors. Her neck muscles grow taut, and her arms and legs shake as though she's been struck dumb.

Khamal can feel the hezhan now, the one that chose her. It is near. It's so close it could cross the threshold into Erahm any time it chose. And yet it does not. It is drawn to Yadhan, but more than this, it is drawn to the stone. It wishes to touch it, to have it, to experience it, perhaps as it did on that night nearly one moon ago when the Al-Aqim ripped the world asunder.

Yadhan screams, shaking the stone, but Khamal keeps it in place, and though the throes of her agony seem to shake the very dome of the celestia above them, he does not yield. This is unfortunate but necessary.

A shift in the aether takes place.

The suuraqiram feel it too. Every one of them pauses momentarily before picking up the chant once more.

Yadhan goes silent. She falls slack to the stone and lies unmoving. Her breathing slows, but her eyes are moving beneath her lids, back and forth, as if she dreams. As if she's having a nightmare.

"Leave us," Khamal says.

The crowd stirs, but does not move.

"Leave us!"

The dirge abruptly ends, and the crowd begins to disperse.

Soon Khamal is alone with Yadhan. He watches her, but there is nothing to be seen in this manner, and so he places his hands upon her heart and head once more.

Inside, she has changed. She is no longer a soul being fed upon by the hezhan. She is something else. She is of both, and neither.

He knows that this has done more to her than simply bind her to a spirit. They have been bound to Erahm as an anchor, preventing Adhiya from approaching. It is working, but it brings Khamal little joy. This girl—her soul and the soul of the hezhan—have both been sacrificed. Truly sacrificed. Neither will return to Adhiya. Neither will resume the cycle of birth and rebirth.

They are lost, and some day, they will both be forgotten.

It is something he knew would happen, but to stare it in the face was something entirely different.

"Come," he says.

Yadhan takes a deep breath. She releases it in a huff, not like a child, but like a winded animal.

Khamal swallows, wondering if the fates are watching him now. Wondering if they are laughing.

"Come," he says again.

And this time the akhoz rises.

Nasim woke in their makeshift home. He stared up at the stone ceiling, covered in leafy vines.

He felt sick.

He had long tried to convince himself that he had no connection to Khamal, that he was not at fault over what happened on Ghayavand those many years ago, but as more of Khamal's past was revealed, he felt a stronger connection, and it sickened him.

Khamal had not only been the one to come up with the idea of the akhoz, he'd been the first to transform a child into one. He had sacrificed them so that the rift might be halted, but that didn't make up for the fact that he'd taken those children against their will. They might have agreed, but Khamal knew better. They were only putting on a brave face for their parents and for Khamal. With this ritual he was taking the soul of each child—and the soul of the hezhan that fed upon them—and sacrificing them like saplings to keep a dying fire aflame.

They would never return to Adhiya. They would never be reborn. They would simply be gone, one problem to hide another.

Nasim could no longer shy away from the fact he was Khamal and Khamal was he. Did the Aramahn not preach that one builds upon himself to make better his next life? And if that were so, then one has a responsibility for what had occurred in his prior lives. The two lives were the same, facets of the same jewel.

"Rabiah," he said softly.

He turned over and realized she was not in the house.

He said it again, louder.

He made his way outside. The sky to the east held a high, thin layer of clouds, colored bright yellow with the coming dawn. He called for Rabiah, shouted for her, and still she didn't reply.

They had returned from Shirvozeh near sunset last night. They had searched the house and, as Nasim had told her, had found no sign of Sukharam. Muqallad had taken him.

You may have the one.

Rabiah had been furious. "How could you have let Muqallad take him?" she'd spat.

"I didn't—"

"You did! You wouldn't allow him to join us. You brought us here for a reason, but since we've come you've been hiding behind your past. Hiding behind your fears. We are young, but we are strong, and you chose to throw that away so you could go after Ashan yourself."

Nasim had stared at her. Rabiah had always been so protective of him, and it was unbalancing to see that same fierceness turned against him.

And what could he say? She was right. He'd failed them, and now he'd failed Ashan as well.

She rushed forward. "Stop it!" she shouted, and using both hands she pushed him backward, hard.

He fell onto the ground, staring up at her wild-eyed. "What are you doing?"

"You're *hiding*, Nasim. Hiding within your own walls. You can't do it anymore. Not this time, not when Sukharam needs you so badly."

He'd shaken his head. "I can't save him."

"You must!"

"I can't."

She stood there, arms at her side, shivering with impotent rage. She spat at his feet and turned away, and in moments she'd stalked off, lost behind the grassy hill to the south.

A cold wind blew in off the sea that night. Nasim had gone inside the house, allowing Rabiah the time and space she'd needed. She'd returned hours later, well after the sun had gone down, well after true night had fallen over Ghayavand.

He'd lain there in their stolen home, his back to her, pretending to be asleep. He didn't know what to say. He didn't know how to make it better.

He was not Ashan. He was not Nikandr. He was no leader of men, to inspire with words and deeds. He was a child who had opened his eyes five years before to discover he was already eleven years old. He was an infant still. He never should have convinced them to come. He should have stayed with Fahroz and let her tell him what to do.

Eventually, his thoughts still churning but his body exhausted, he'd fallen asleep.

And now that he'd woken, Rabiah was gone. She'd abandoned him, and it was painfully clear what she'd gone to do. After gathering a few necessities, he began jogging toward Alayazhar.

And then he began to run.

His chest still heaving from the run into the city, Nasim paced the streets, moving swiftly but warily, ever closer to the tower. The wind was bitterly cold, a strange thing for Ghayavand. It seemed to be keeping the akhoz's movement lower than it might otherwise have been, and for this he thanked the fates.

He could feel them and their movements, and he used this knowledge to wend his way forward. He realized nearly two hours into his journey that he was taking nearly the same route that he had with Ashan and Nikandr and Pietr on their way to the very same tower. The central portion of the city did not look the same, though. Then, Sariya's enchantments had still cast a glamour over the buildings and streets nearest the tower.

Not so now.

Now the streets were broken and decayed. The stone buildings lay shattered, ghosts of their former selves.

At an intersection where three roads met, a marble statue of a woman, naked from the waist up, stared down at him. He paused, feeling as though it was one of the fates.

Beyond the statue lay a wide thoroughfare, one of the primary spokes that radiated outward from the harbor. Broken stones with weeds growing between them lined the road. Buildings on either side—mostly stone, none with surviving roofs—watched him pass. They seemed angry at Nasim's intrusion, or perhaps they were somehow protective of the akhoz, the only residents they'd known for the past three centuries.

Here, at last, Nasim felt the one he'd been searching for.

Most of Khamal's memories were hidden from him, but he had found that once he'd had a dream, he could not only recall it well, he could remember the days that led up to the memories that filled the dream; he could remember the days that came after. After his dream that morning, the days beyond the ritual performed beneath the celestia's dome opened to him, and as he'd run toward the city his plan had fallen into place.

Two akhoz were somewhere ahead, perhaps in the great stone building he was headed toward. The building had housed, as near as he could tell, a bazaar, but now, despite the grandeur it had once laid claim to, it was little more than a broken shell.

A form stalked out from under the archway that stood at the center of the bazaar's grand facade. A girl, naked and dirty. She dropped to all fours, crab-crawling along the ground, her black lips pulled back, revealing dark, broken teeth.

Nasim's heart began to thrum. He had masked his presence, and still the akhoz caught his scent. It raised its head and released a long, sickening bleat to the sky above the city. An answering call came only a moment later, and soon after, another—this one a boy—entered the same archway.

Together they crawled toward Nasim, sniffing the air, bleating softly as they came.

And then they stood and charged.

CHAPTER THIRTY-ONE

The akhoz galloped more than ran, their long limbs loping over the ground faster than it appeared they could. Their lips were drawn back, their dark tongues hidden behind blackened teeth, making them appear vengeful and ravenous.

Nasim's sandals scraped over the ancient stone. His nerves willed him to flee. But he would not. This girl, this very girl, was the first of the akhoz. There was little that remained of Yadhan, but he recognized her by the shape and tilt of her head, her delicate features, and the small scar at the nape of her neck.

And he'd also felt in his memories that a connection had been made to each of the akhoz that Khamal had created. In the nights that followed, Khamal had gone on to perform the ritual again and again, sacrificing more and more children to the grisly fate that awaited them. And they had held a bond with him, a loyalty. Surely part of this was borne from the piece of the Atalayina Nasim had found, but it was also a bond to Khamal, and if Nasim were right, that bond would still exist with him. It must—Khamal wouldn't have allowed it to happen any other way—but that didn't stop Nasim's heart from beating like a blacksmith's hammer.

The akhoz were nearly on him when Nasim spread his arms wide. It was a gesture of supplication that Aramahn gave to hezhan before they communed.

Both of the akhoz slowed, and when they came within four paces, they stopped. The girl, Yadhan, watched him with sightless eyes, while the other, the boy, shook his head so vigorously that Nasim wondered if he was tearing muscles.

"I have need of you, Yadhan."

Yadhan shivered. She craned her neck back like a rook and released a bleating call into the chill morning air.

Nasim kneeled, still holding his arms out wide. "I have need."

Yadhan pulled back her lips. Her tongue lolled like a freshly cut piece of meat.

She crawled forward.

The other, the boy, craned his head back, back, until Nasim thought his neck would break. Then brought it down hard against the stone before him. He did it again and again—black blood leaking from the many wounds he was inflicting upon himself—and it soon became clear that he was fighting against some hold Yadhan had placed on him.

Nasim could not remember the boy's imprint, nor could he feel any sort of loyalty from him, so he wondered if this was one of Muqallad's or Sariya's. It must be so, but if that were true, why would it bow to Yadhan? As foreign as it seemed to him, there must be some sort of hierarchy among the akhoz. Perhaps they followed the rule of the hezhan in the world beyond, or perhaps they followed the customs of the Aramahn from centuries ago. Whatever the reason, Nasim was glad for it, for it seemed to be keeping the akhoz at bay for the time being.

Yadhan's breath came sharply, quickly. She wheezed as she came to a halt at Nasim's feet. And then she stood and faced him, crooked limbs and gaping maw. It was all Nasim could do not to retch from the stench that came with each exhaled breath.

"I go to the tower," he said. "Will you accompany me?"

Yadhan seemed to consider these words. Her nostrils—more akin to a lizard's than a girl's—flared. She twisted her head around and waggled it back and forth in the direction of the tower.

And then she turned back and bowed her head ever so slightly.

The moment she did this, the other akhoz attacked.

Time slowed.

The akhoz reared back, pulling in a huge breath and releasing it toward Nasim. A great gout of fire blossomed from his mouth.

As it hurtled forward, Nasim was transfixed, rooted to the spot.

But Yadhan pushed him out of the way and stood in the path of the fire. It enveloped her—black smoke trailing up from her skin—and yet it only seemed to enrage her.

She took two loping steps forward and then leaped upon the other akhoz. The boy fought, using his arms to try to bat her away, but Yadhan was a mongrel dog, jaws snapping, teeth bared. One hand was locked on his forehead, muscles as taut as cords, while the other grabbed his wrist and pinned him. Ignoring the boy's free arm that clawed at her face, she lunged forward and bit deeply into his neck. Skin and flesh so dark it was nearly black was pulled away. She bit again and again, and soon the other's attempts at fending her off weakened.

And then stopped altogether.

Yadhan's chest heaved as she straddled him. She twisted her head around at an inhuman angle. Her gruesome look beckoned Nasim, telling him it was now safe to approach.

Nasim did so, but he was forced to pull one arm across his mouth and nose to fight off the reek of rotted meat. As he kneeled next to the boy, Yadhan merely waited, her lungs working like a bellows, the wavering of heat coming from her mouth and nostrils.

After kneeling and shrugging out of his robes—leaving the skin of his torso and arms exposed to the bitter wind—Nasim pulled his knife from the sheath at his belt, one he had carefully sharpened before returning to Alayazhar.

The akhoz, perhaps sensing what was to come, began struggling once more. His head thudded against the stone beneath him and a mewling sound came from his throat, but Yadhan was strong—much stronger than Nasim would have guessed—and she held him still.

Quickly, Nasim told himself. *Quickly, but with a steady hand*.

He took a deep breath, his lips curling, and he leaned over the thing's chest, mindful of Yadhan's shriveled breasts and dark nipples.

He pressed the tip of the knife against the boy's throat and cut downward. The akhoz screamed, arching its head back and railing against Yadhan's hold. Nasim drew the knife down toward the gut, exposing red flesh and white cartilage. Exposing bone. He sawed against the joints where rib met the rightmost portion of the sternum, taking care not to allow the knife to slip free and damage the beating heart beneath.

One rib. Two. Three.

Soon, all of them were free, and Nasim set the knife aside, which clattered with a metallic ring against the stone. Using both hands, he pulled the ribs apart, using all his strength until he heard a crack. All while the akhoz screamed.

One more pull, another snap, and at last the heart was exposed. It was a shriveled thing, nothing like what a living heart should be. It pumped, the thing's darkened blood now pooling within the cavity. He retrieved his knife with his right hand and with his left held the still-beating heart. It felt like malice, like hatred. Like regret.

He turned away, still holding it.

He coughed, then retched.

Contain yourself, he told himself.

He breathed deeply and turned back. As the akhoz writhed, screamed. It shook its head maniacally as he picked up the knife and used it carefully to slice one of the major arteries away. He did so again, and again, until at last it was free.

He dropped the knife, sickened by it.

The heart pulsed. Black blood pattered against the stones. It gathered in the spaces between them and ran like veins.

Then the beating began to slow, as did the movements of the akhoz. He turned back and forced himself to watch. He owed the boy this, at least. He was once a child, no matter what he might be now.

Finally, the beating stopped, and the body of the akhoz came to a rest.

In that moment, the moment the akhoz passed, Nasim felt something, a shift in the aether, as if the strand of a spider web had just been plucked. The web still stood, but it had been weakened, and even if it was clear that there were dozens—hundreds—of other strands supporting it, it was just as clear that the web would never be repaired; it would only become worse, until eventually it would fail altogether.

Nasim's eyes began to water as he studied the heart. It was already shriveling, shrinking, hardening into a small, misshapen lump. It stopped when it was the size and hardness of a walnut.

This, he knew, would allow him to reach Sariya's tower. With the heart, the other akhoz aligned would not sense him, or at the very least would think him one of them. Who knew what might happen when he reached the tower? But at least he now could. It was the key to everything that lay before him. Muqallad had two pieces of the Atalayina. In Sariya's tower lay the third, and it was imperative that Muqallad not gain it. Rabiah had known this as well, and surely she had made for the tower, hoping to retrieve the stone and take control of her life once more since Nasim—in her eyes—refused to do so.

Nasim stood, leaving his robes as they were. It wasn't that he didn't need the warmth, or that he didn't want it, but that he felt he didn't *deserve* it. It was small penance for what he'd just done, but he would pay it just the same.

"Come," he said to Yadhan, shivering from the cold of the wind and the chill of drying blood on his arms. "There is one more we must gather."

With Yadhan at his side, Nasim treaded along the streets of the lower city. He could feel the akhoz nearby. Here there were many—the streets were thick with them—and they were aligned with Sariya—sentinels set to protect her demesne and the secrets that lay within.

The two necklaces hanging around his neck and the shriveled hearts they held were a burden the likes of which he'd never shouldered. They rubbed against the skin over his own heart, making his skin crawl and his back bend.

It was repulsive not only because of the way the hearts had been harvested, but because of the similarity he felt between this and the way the Landed wore their soulstones. He still had trouble sorting all of his memories from his time before Nikandr had healed him, but most of what he remembered of the Landed made him either angry or deeply, deeply sad.

They were a selfish people. Thoughtless. They could no more see into the future than they could swallow the sea. And yet there was Nikandr. His memories of the Prince of Khalakovo were not altogether pleasant, but he held a certain empathy for him. He knew Nikandr like he knew no other, including Ashan, who had spent years trying to communicate with him when he could hardly tell the worlds apart.

He thought about opening himself to Nikandr again. He could do so any time he chose. Part of him would welcome it. Even though he'd done it willingly and consciously, he'd felt hollow ever since, as if a part of him had been stolen when Fahroz had taken him to Mirashadal.

Feeling the bitter weight of his necklaces, he decided once again that allowing Nikandr back into his life would be a foolish thing. It didn't matter what Nikandr's intentions were; he was not his own man. He was controlled by his family, by the Grand Duchy, and for that reason alone he couldn't be trusted.

He approached the tower, and it made him wonder how Sariya and Muqallad had come to be at odds. It was clear that they were. If it were not so, Muqallad would have already had free access to the tower. She had left the island, or had been forced to, leaving Muqallad free reign over the city, and yet Muqallad had so far been unable to gain entrance. It was proof of how truly powerful Sariya had become, and also an indication of how little the Al-Aqim had trusted one another in the days or weeks or months leading up to the division that had formed between them.

He also wondered how he was able to come so near the tower without her traps triggering. Did it hold meaning? It may simply be that the surprises still lay ahead, hidden, and revealed only when he came near—knowing Sariya as he did, Nasim thought this likely—but there was nothing to do now but move forward. He needed the remaining piece of the Atalayina. What he would do with it once he found it he wasn't sure, but he knew he couldn't leave it for Muqallad or Sariya to find.

As he came to the street that surrounded the tower, many akhoz met him. They closed in, moving their heads from side to side, sniffing both Nasim and Yadhan.

Yadhan craned her neck. Her nostrils flared, and Nasim thought surely she was about to attack, but he touched her arm, and she seemed to calm.

Nasim scanned the area around the tower. He had expected to find Rabiah's dead form on every turn of their journey here to the tower. Some small amount of relief greeted him at each turn when he didn't find her, but there was still a certainty that he *would*, if not on this street, then the next, and if not the next, then certainly the tower grounds. But Rabiah wasn't here, and it gave him hope that he would soon find her.

They neared the wrought-iron fence surrounding the tower. The akhoz— dozens of them now—became more animated. When Nasim touched the gate, several of them opened their mouths and released their sickening call.

Nasim grit his jaw. He pushed open the gate. The hinges squealed, and more of the akhoz shook their heads violently. One even attacked another, but many more moved in and subdued the one who had attacked.

Yadhan stepped inside the gate, at which point Nasim closed it. Immediately the akhoz outside calmed. Their bleating ceased. And some of them began to wander away. Many did not, however, and Nasim wondered whether they would still be here when he returned.

He walked to the large wooden door set into the imposing gray stone of the tower wall. The handle was dark iron as well—black, rusted, threatening in a way he couldn't define. He flexed his fingers before reaching out, and even then he was unable to complete this one simple motion.

He breathed deeply, flexed his hand once more, and then touched the handle.

CHAPTER THIRTY-TWO

He stands alone in a field blanketed in snow. He turns, scanning the land around him. The fields go on and on beneath an overcast sky, gray and oppressive. Only on the horizon is there any change in the terrain. Dark mountains loom with black clouds above.

He sees nothing else, and he is nearly of a mind to begin walking for the mountains when the sound of footsteps breaking through the ice-rimed snow comes to him. When he turns, he finds a girl and a boy trudging over the top of a shallow rise toward him. Their footsteps mar the otherwise perfect layer of snow. This seems like an affront—though to whom, and why, he is not sure.

Nasim shivers as they approach. Rarely does he feel cold, even in the wind, but here somehow the chill sinks beneath his skin, draws the warmth from his bones.

The girl is young, perhaps only twelve. Her hair is light brown, almost golden, and she is fair of face, and if she cannot be considered beautiful now it is only because there is still so much youth in her features. One day not far from now, she will blossom, and men will look upon her with awe. The boy watches Nasim from behind unkempt hair. He is dark of expression, as if he has come against his will.

It takes him time, but he realizes that the girl is Yadhan, as she was before she was sacrificed—or perhaps how she might have been; he is unsure. And the boy is the other akhoz, the one who fell to Yadhan.

When at last they stand before him, Yadhan holds out her hand.

He does not take it, and she stares at him, her expression turning severe. And then her gaze is drawn downward to the place where the hearts of the akhoz lie beneath his shirt. She frowns, and Nasim becomes conscious of their weight. He can feel, as the wind blows softly over the snow, a telltale pulsing. They are not in time; somehow this is more disturbing than the fact that they are beating at all.

Nasim takes her hand, and together the three of them head toward the rise, except now the footprints are gone, and they are trudging through virgin snow.

The going is slow and arduous, for the snow is deep, but they continue until they reach the ridge. Below them rests a lake, its surface frozen over. Though the surface is marred by cuts of white, the water beneath is dark and foreboding. Nasim stops, feeling suddenly worried over what he might find should he continue. The boy turns and walks back toward him with grim intention until the girl steps in his path. The boy stares at Nasim over her shoulder, but then he lowers his head and stills. Only then does Yadhan turn to him and take his hand.

She is warm, warmer than she was only moments ago.

She seems to notice, for she meets his gaze and smiles, as if to console him. What is happening he doesn't understand, but he knows they have little time left together.

The three of them continue toward the lake, slipping down the slope, which becomes steep closer to the lake's edge, and soon they are out among the ice, the snow dancing in circles as the wind plays. Nasim feels something at the center of the lake. There is an aberration there among the dark undersurface of the ice.

He drops Yadhan's hand and begins to run. He knows what he will see, but he is still horrified when he slides to his knees over Rabiah's form. She rests beneath the surface, her eyes open, her hands splayed against the underside of the ice, hoping for release while knowing it cannot be.

Yadhan steps beside him. The boy is near but seems reluctant to approach.

"How do we free her?" Nasim asks Yadhan.

Her eyes are drawn to the horizon.

"*How do we free her?*" he yells, and at last she pulls her gaze downward. She kneels next to him and places her hands on the surface of the ice. It melts at her touch, but then, as if in response, a hissing and cracking sound comes. She jerks her hands away. Shards of ice fly from where her hands once were. In moments, all signs of her presence are wiped away as the surface freezes over once more.

As it has always been since his awakening, Nasim feels Adhiya. He feels the hezhan who stand just beyond the veil. They would come willingly if he only could pierce the thin shroud that separates them. But try as he might, he cannot. As always, there is something that holds him back.

He slams the surface of the ice, hoping it will yield. He beats his fists raw, and still there is no change.

Rabiah stares at him. Her eyes take in the sky and the girl next to him, and as she spreads her hands wider, the weight of the ice, the immensity of it, seems to dawn on her, and she becomes frantic. She claws at the ice. She pounds at it, but her movements are slowed, a fly caught in sap.

Nasim stands and stomps upon the ice. A surge of fear wells up inside him. Rabiah came at his bidding—*his* choice, not hers—and now she sits below him, separated by ice as thick as the world itself.

"Help her!" Nasim screams.

Yadhan tries. She places her hands against the ice once more. It melts in an area much wider than it had the first time. She sinks until her knees and shins and feet and hands are below the water. Her strength flags, and the ice begins to encroach. It moves quickly, the entire surface of the lake cracking as the water solidifies around her limbs. She pulls one arm free, but she is becoming trapped.

The boy stands by, staring only at the horizon.

Nasim moves to him, slipping on the slick ice. He grabs the boy's robes, shakes him and points to the girl. "You must help!"

The boy turns his head and stares vacantly at Nasim's hand upon his shoulder, and then he looks to Yadhan, who has begun to whimper from the cold. In response to Nasim's plea, he merely returns his longing gaze toward that which lies beyond.

Nasim slides back to Rabiah, who has sunk lower beneath the surface.

Yadhan pulls at her arm. She is losing what strength she has left.

Nasim shivers with rage, but he realizes in his moment of panic that he can feel Adhiya. He can feel it through Rabiah. He coaxes the feeling, and it grows. It seizes his gut, and soon it is all he can do to remain standing. He grabs his midsection and curls inward, a gesture he's intimately familiar with.

The aether, so present moments ago, vanishes, and he feels as though here in this one place the world is not divided. There are not two worlds. Only one.

He can touch the hezhan. They are not separate from him. They are part and parcel of his existence, and he of theirs. He does not bid them to come. He does not demand. It is *they*, it seems, who voice a call to action, and it is *he* that responds.

The place that lies at the center of him begins to warm. The feeling grows as the landscape around him brightens. The sun, which had been cold and cheerless, is now bright in the sky, piercing. The feeling swells until the blue sky peels away and all that is left is a searing brightness that fills him and the land around him.

Suddenly the world falls away.

He plunges into water.

The darkness of the lake surrounds him, as does the suffocating water.

He sinks, searching for Rabiah, as the surface above begins to mend, threatening to trap him here. He swims downward, and sees her reaching up toward him. He grabs her arm—giving her some small amount of the fires that rage within him still—and propels them both up toward the surface.

The ice has closed over, but he will not be denied. He breaks it with his fist, and soon he is at the edge, pulling Rabiah up and into the air.

She gasps, coughing and retching, but she is here, alive.

Yadhan helps them out from the lake. They gain the solidity of the ice as Nasim releases much of the heat within him. He does not, however, release it completely. He is afraid to. If he cannot retain his hold on it, he will lose it once more—of this he is sure.

Rabiah stares at him, unsure of herself, unsure of this place. Nasim knows she cannot stay. There is work to do yet, but she will die if she goes on.

"Take her back," Nasim says.

Yadhan, her face serene and inscrutable, looks to Rabiah, and then she goes to the boy and guides him to Rabiah's side. The boy seems surprised that Rabiah is here, but after a moment this passes, and he takes her hand.

"Go," Nasim says. "I will find you."

Rabiah does not argue, and as the boy leads her away, shivering and shaking, she nods.

Soon, they are lost behind the nearby ridge.

Nasim already knows that the boy will travel to the horizon after he returns Rabiah to Erahm. He will go, and it will not be to Adhiya. He will be lost to the world, lost to the next—and not just him, but the soul of the hezhan that had occupied him for so long. In a way it is a blessing—the two of them locked together, struggling with one another for so long, was cruel and inhuman—but in another it is sad. Profoundly sad. They will not learn or grow or teach. They will not be reborn to learn from their mistakes. They will never reach their higher plane.

Yadhan waits. She was able to lead Nasim here, but now she doesn't know where to go. Neither does Nasim, but it seems probable that the stone would lie ahead, so they go on, to the far side of the lake and up the hill. When they reach the top, a plain lies before them and beyond it a forest, much of it towering spruce and larch blanketed in snow.

As he walks toward the forest, there is a hint of movement near its edge. A woman steps from behind the trees and walks through the snow, though as she comes nearer it is clear that she is not hampered by the snow's depth as Nasim and Yadhan are. Instead the snow bears her as if she weighs nothing. Her feet draw from its surface only a dusting of snow, which swirls in her wake.

Her golden hair flows, and as she comes close, her blue eyes shine, bright against white fields and gray sky.

Nasim is worried at first, but when the woman smiles, his worries seem to melt.

"You are Nasim," she says as she comes to a halt. Her eyes are for Nasim only; she does not glance at Yadhan, who, so brave before, now hides behind Nasim.

"Sariya," Nasim says into the silence. His breath, soft and white, is taken upon the wind. "I didn't think to find you here."

CHAPTER THIRTY-THREE

When Nikandr finally reached the entrance to the village and stepped outside, they squinted against the morning light. Even though it was early, and the sun little more than a wash of pale yellow in the east, it was still almost unbearably bright after being underground for so long. Jahalan stepped next to him and stretched, breathing deeply of the chill air.

There were often guards stationed near the entrance, but today there were none. Nikandr thought this a favorable sign, but before he'd gone ten paces he realized he was wrong. From the shadows of another doorway came four men, all of them wearing dark robes and turbans the color of night. They did not bear muskets, but each of them wore a curved shamshir and a khanjar at their belt, and they wore these weapons easily, as if they were old friends.

At the lead was Rahid. He stepped into Nikandr's way, much as he had Bersuq's the other day, and waited, his hand on the hilt of his sword. "And where does the man from Khalakovo think to go?"

Nikandr came to a halt. Jahalan, so often a man of calm, stood stiffly, his eyes watching Rahid and the other Hratha closely.

"We will return, if that is your fear," Nikandr said.

The rings in Rahid's nose glinted as he sniffed in a short, sharp breath. "Do the Landed find it so difficult to answer questions?"

"Bersuq gave us leave to go as we would."

"Bersuq is not the only voice in Ashdi en Ghat."

"What does that mean to me?"

"It should mean much." Rahid took a step forward. If he drew his sword now, he could easily cut with it. Rahid looked him up and down, as if he was still offended at having to suffer a man such as Nikandr in the village, but Nikandr knew he was just trying to bait him.

"Speak your troubles to Bersuq." Nikandr made to walk past him. "We have work to do."

Nikandr didn't wish to provoke, but he could not give a man like Rahid the upper hand. Men like him were ruthless, but they were also simple. Push them hard enough and they would often back down.

Rahid stepped back and drew his sword. He was fast, Nikandr realized. Very fast.

Rahid's men drew their swords as well as Rahid leveled the tip at Nikandr's chest.

"Enough, Rahid."

Nikandr turned and squinted into the darkness of the tunnel, unable to find the source of the voice. A moment later Soroush stepped out and into the light, limping badly. His left forearm was bandaged. The area above his left eye had an angry red wound still scabbing over, and it was surrounded by a mass of bruises.

Soroush stepped in front of Nikandr, placing himself between him and Rahid. "Lower your weapon."

Slowly, Rahid complied, his gaze alternating between Nikandr and Soroush. "Thabash will not be pleased, Soroush."

Thabash was a name he'd only heard in reference to the attacks on the southernmost duchies, most often organized from Behnda al Tib, the Hratha stronghold. Nikandr shouldn't be surprised to hear his name, but he was. Why had so many of the men from the south come to Rafsuhan? And why now?

Soroush merely nodded and guided Nikandr and Jahalan away. "Tell me when Thabash *is* pleased, and that will be a new day."

Rahid stepped forward and placed his hand on Jahalan's chest. "One will remain here."

Jahalan began to protest, but Soroush held up his hand. "Don't worry, son of Mitra"—he stared down at Jahalan's wooden leg—"I will go with Nikandr."

Jahalan looked abashed, even angry. His leg, and the troubles it caused him, was one of the few things that got Jahalan's blood moving quickly. Nikandr wanted his old friend with him, but he could already tell that the Maharraht would not bend. "Stay," Nikandr said to him. "Work with the children, and I will share anything we learn when I return."

Jahalan finally relented, and Nikandr left with Soroush, who brought with him a musket and a bandolier. They left the confines of the valley and headed down the trail back toward the forest in which they'd hidden before coming to Ashdi en Ghat. Nikandr felt strange, walking in silence this way, a certain trust now implicit between them where only months ago each had considered the other an enemy. It was not merely the war they were waging—albeit in different ways—against the changes in the world. That merely gave them understanding of one another. They were bound instead by Wahad, Soroush's son, the boy Nikandr had sworn to protect.

"What interest has Thabash in the north?" Nikandr asked.

"You can ask him when he arrives."

"Thabash will most likely let Rahid do what he will with me, which means I'll be taken to the nearest cliff and shot in the back."

"Then best you hurry."

"Are the Maharraht fighting?"

Soroush was silent as they walked, the only sounds their steps over the narrow trail they were following and the morning calls of the nearby thrushes. "Where do we go, son of Iaros?"

"Soroush, the lives of my men are at stake."

Soroush whirled and stabbed his finger at Nikandr. "The lives of my *people* are at stake. You've seen the sick. You've seen the children."

"*Yeh*, and I've seen your son."

Soroush bit back his reply. He walked in silence, but his stride seemed to ease, as if he were thinking wistfully over the pleasant memories of his son. The Maharraht were strange this way—with the people of Anuskaya, Nikandr knew how they would react about death, but with the Maharraht, or any of the Aramahn, it was simply impossible.

"How is he?" Soroush asked.

"Not well, but I'm hopeful. Jahalan and I are doing what we can."

"You see them, then. You see them, and still you would cast them aside so that your men would be safe."

By *see*, he meant seeing them as real people. And he was right. Nikandr was beginning to do just that. "I do not *cast them aside*, Soroush. But I will do little good if Thabash—or worse, Rahid—runs a length of steel through my chest. We could take them away. We could try this elsewhere."

"It would never be allowed."

"It might…"

"*Neh*," Soroush spat back. "Have you not guessed why the bulk of the Hratha left the island?"

"I assumed to return with those who left the island."

"Not to return with them. To kill them. To make an example out of them."

Nikandr worked this through. "They would kill their own sons and daughters, their brothers and sisters, because they seek a better life?"

"In the eyes of the Hratha, they're spurning their old life. *That* is what cannot be allowed."

Nikandr felt sick to his stomach. "Bersuq would listen to you if you asked."

Soroush laughed. "Who do you think gave me these wounds?"

"What? Why would he *do* such a thing?"

"You are *Landed*, Nikandr."

"He took me into the village. He showed me the children himself."

"Because I asked that he did."

Nikandr paused as these words sunk in. "And what did you grant him in return?"

"A simple request," he said as he turned and began walking once more. His limp was still noticeable, but it had either warmed up or he was ignoring the pain. Likely it was both. "I was to take breath on Baisha"—he pointed to their right, to a tall black mountain—"and find my true answer."

"The answer to what?"

"Whether or not you would be allowed to live."

Nikandr let him walk in peace. The answer at which he'd arrived was clear, and he saw no need to reopen a wound that was clearly still fresh.

"Will you explain to me now," Soroush asked after a time, "why there was such a burning need to leave the village?"

"I must go to Siafyan."

"Why?"

"Because I saw Muqallad there." Nikandr had never shared with Soroush his time on Ghayavand, but he did so now, sparing little. He went into great detail describing the dreams he'd shared with Nasim, particularly the ones involving Muqallad, and he told of their mad dash through the Alayazhar in the hopes of avoiding him. But Muqallad had found and nearly trapped them. If it hadn't been for Nasim, they would surely all have died.

Soroush glanced at Nikandr as they turned and headed down the narrow trail that led to the forest and beyond it the defile that would take them to the other village. Dark clouds covered the sky, and the wind was blowing with vigor, tugging at Nikandr's hair and his clothes. "And now you think he has come here, to Rafsuhan?"

"I felt him, when I kneeled with... When I was near the lake."

"It is only a name, Nikandr Iaroslov. You may say it."

"I only thought that you might feel..."

"Beholden? And so angered? Incensed? I would have been in years past, but time"—Soroush glanced sidelong at him—"time has a way of humbling a man. Wahad is a wonderful son, and I pray to the fates that they allow him to live, even if the way of salvation lies through one of the Landed."

"Did Rehada know?" In many ways Nikandr was hesitant to speak of her, but there were so few he could actually speak to of the woman he had loved, about her death and what she'd meant to him in life. Soroush was no friend to confide in, but something inside Nikandr wanted to know where Soroush had stood with her in the years before her death because, strangely, it would tell him something about his own relationship with her.

They took a steep decline through tall swaying grasses and entered the forest. Only then did Soroush speak once more. "I never told her."

"She would have accepted him."

"You know her so well"—his voice had risen in volume—"that you can tell me what she would do?"

"It would have been painful, but she would have loved him."

"She might have accepted him, but she would never have forgiven herself. She always blamed herself for Ahya's death. It ate her from within, as much as the wasting, or more, for it was a wound she would not die from. She would go on living, torturing herself until her end of days. Had she known about Wahad, it would have been worse. I was only protecting her."

"She didn't need protection. She needed caring and love."

"You speak to me of *love*? She came to you at my behest, son of Iaros. She wheedled from you secrets that she fed to me through messengers you never suspected, and I in turn guided our efforts because of it. People died because of what you told her. And she hated herself for it"—Soroush spat on the ground ahead of them—"nearly as much as she hated you. You knew *nothing* of her needs."

Nikandr felt his face flush. His heart galloped within his chest. "*Neh*? She may have stolen secrets, son of Gatha, but she loved me, and I was there for her when she needed me. I never abandoned her."

"You would have had you known."

"Early on, perhaps, but in the end I found out, and still I loved her. Perhaps you'll do for Wahad what you couldn't do for Rehada."

Soroush's face went red. He stepped forward, sliding the khanjar from its sheath.

Nikandr backed up, knowing he had pushed Soroush too far.

But from the corner of his eye he saw movement. Moving among the trees was a form, small and bright among the dark trunks of the larch and spruce.

Nikandr held up one hand and with the other pointed over Soroush's shoulder.

Soroush, nostrils flaring, took a half step toward him, but then stopped and turned, scanning the forest behind him. The form was nearly out of sight, but he saw it and cocked his head. "Kaleh?"

"I saw her yesterday among the hills. They said she refused to live in the village."

Without speaking another word, they both began to jog over the soft bed of the forest, weaving through the trees to keep Kaleh in sight.

When she walked down a decline, they lost her for a time, and both of them began to sprint, hoping not to lose her. When they found her again, she was treading downhill toward a thin stream. She moved with speed, but not so quickly that they couldn't keep pace. She came to a clearing at the base of the hill, and she slowed, taking deliberate steps while studying the ground carefully. Her head was tilted, as if she were listening, though Nikandr could hear nothing above the wind and the high chatter of snowfinch somewhere in the distance.

Near the stream, she dropped to her hands and knees. She crawled forward, moving her ear closer to the ground each time, until at last something seemed to satisfy her and she lay down flat and placed her ear against the ground.

She lay like this for long moments, and Nikandr became progressively more aware of the forest—the oppression of the tall trees surrounding them; the curve of the land and the stream that cut through it; the air, which smelled of rain, and the slow, rhythmic ticking of the bark beetles. He debated on whether they should approach. He looked to Soroush, asking him silently, but Soroush shook his head gently.

For no reason Nikandr could see, Kaleh got back to her feet and padded over to a nearby hillock overgrown with moss and ferns. She kneeled before it and placed her hands on the ground, and then she kneeled forward and placed her forehead on the backs of her hands, as if she were praying to the earth.

Mere moments later, the moss bulged near the top of the hillock. It rose and split, spreading wide like the petals of a gazania blossoming in spring. The cleft it created was wide and deep, large enough to fall into.

Kaleh took from a bag at her belt something small and shriveled and black. She held it between her fingers for a time, merely staring at it. As she did, Nikandr swore it was pulsing.

Then, like a doe that had heard something amiss, her head turned ever so slightly to one side.

She dropped the blackened thing into the cleft.

And then sprinted like a cannon shot over the hillock.

CHAPTER THIRTY-FOUR

Nikandr and Soroush immediately gave chase. They hurried down the slope, sliding among the tree trunks as Kaleh fled. Kaleh was like a fawn, swift and fairly bounding over the landscape. Still, she was young, and the two of them began to shorten the distance between them.

She glanced back once, her eyes wide, not with fear, but with exhilaration. As Nikandr ran, he saw a root rise up before him. He leapt over it, and a branch swung in his way, forcing him to run wide.

Soroush grunted as the bough of a young tree struck him. He slid along the slick slope, but regained his footing.

"Stop!" Nikandr yelled in Mahndi. "We only wish to speak."

She kept moving and began to widen the distance. Nikandr increased his pace, but the moment he did a sapling bent nearly in two and struck him across his face and chest. He fell to the ground, slipping on the damp layer of autumn leaves.

Soroush fell as a thick, knotty root rose up and caught his ankle. He shouted in pain as his ankle twisted on it and he fell face-first to the ground.

The sound of Kaleh's flight faded as Nikandr pulled himself up, his face and chest throbbing, and made his way over to Soroush. Soroush flipped over, holding his ankle for long seconds as Nikandr waited. "It's unwise to chase after a deer," he finally said, holding out his hand.

Nikandr took it and pulled Soroush up to his feet.

"Shall we track her?" Nikandr said.

"With *this*"—Soroush nodded meaningfully to his injured ankle—"I couldn't hope to outrun a hedgehog. Let's return to the cleft and see what she dropped into it."

Nikandr nodded and they made their way slowly back. They easily found the place where the cleft had opened. Digging a hole, however, was much more problematic. Nikandr broke a thick branch of deadwood in half and the two of them used the relatively sharp ends to dig into the ground, but the earth seemed whole, compact, which was more than strange since it had lain open only minutes ago.

Still, they made progress, and as they came to the depth where they thought the object might lie, they moved more slowly, took greater care.

"There," Nikandr said, seeing movement.

As he watched, one spot in the dark, loamy earth pulsed like a thing alive. He kneeled down and carefully scraped the dirt away. Slowly, more and more of it was revealed.

"Ancients preserve us," Nikandr said as he stared at it. He reached in and took it up. Though the urge to drop it back into the hole was great, he held it up for Soroush to see.

It was small and misshapen, looking more like a walnut than anything else, but there was no mistaking it. It was a heart. A blackened, beating heart.

Soroush swallowed once before reaching out and taking it. As he examined it, the thing seemed to beat more heavily. "What under the dark heavens is she trying to do?"

Nikandr looked around the forest. "I don't know, but is there any doubt it has something to do with the fire?"

"That was no fire, son of Iaros." He was shaking his head, staring at the beating heart with naked revulsion. "That was a sacrifice."

The more Nikandr stared at the heart, the sicker he felt. He thought at first it was mere disgust, the same as Soroush, but it soon became clear that it was something else entirely. Much as he could feel Nasim those many years ago, he felt *this* heart. It was as if a soul were still attached to it. It was a notion that seemed foolish at first, but the more he thought about it, the more sense it made.

"What do we do with it?" Nikandr asked.

Soroush stared at it for a moment, considering, then he dropped it onto the ground and kneeled. He took from its sheath at his belt his khanjar. It was a curved blade that had seen its share of use, but it gleamed under the overcast sky as he set the tip against the heart and pressed downward with all his weight.

Nikandr felt a sharp pain within his chest. His *own* heart could feel the knife slicing through the dark, inhuman flesh of this shriveled and blackened thing. He bent over, clutching his chest, holding himself up by propping one arm against his knee. And then the pain lessened, and the heart began to beat slower, until at last it had stopped altogether and the pain had gone away.

"You felt it," Soroush said. It was a statement, not a question.

"I did."

"If there was one, there will be more."

His meaning was clear. He wished Nikandr to help him. "I will try," he replied. "We're less than a league from Siafyan. We should continue in a circle, and perhaps we'll find more."

A light rain had begun to fall against the canopy. It was soft, the raindrops striking lightly against the forest around him, and yet it felt ominous.

Soroush wiped his knife against the pine needles that blanketed the ground. As he stood and sheathed it, he looked to Nikandr with a mixture of gratitude and confusion. "Why do you stay, Nikandr Iaroslov? Why do you help your enemy?"

"Are we enemies?"

"We are."

Soroush spoke the words with conviction, and yet there was a softness in his eyes that spoke of hope—hope for a better future, perhaps, hope for a world that did not contain such complications—and yet both of them knew such a world could never exist, not while the Grand Duchy and the Maharraht fought for the same land.

"Come," Nikandr said, striking a path northward. "We have a long walk ahead."

They had been traveling northward for the better part of an hour when the feeling returned. It was faint at first, but he was becoming attuned to it. They continued until the feeling faded, at which point they backtracked and took a path through a section of wood that was marked for the tall white birch that dominated the area. They came to a place that looked nothing like the previous mound to the south. It was simply a piece of ground, indistinguishable from the area around it. After clearing away the layer of yellow and brown leaves, there were no obvious signs of it having been opened. There was even a light covering of moss beneath the leaves that appeared completely undisturbed.

But Nikandr could feel it, that same discomfort. As the two of them began to dig with their makeshift shovels, he began to feel it *beat*, and shortly after that he realized that it was falling in time with his own heart.

"Faster," he told Soroush, wanting this to be over and done with.

How many might have been buried like this? And for what purpose? Perhaps Muqallad wished to widen the rift, though why he would do this he had no idea. He had some memories of Muqallad through Khamal's dreams, but it had always seemed as though Muqallad searched for what all three of them had hoped and for centuries failed to do—to close the rift over Ghayavand. Why then would he come here, to a place thousands of leagues from Ghayavand? What was it about Rafsuhan that made it so valuable to him? It could not merely be the rift.

Perhaps, Nikandr thought, it was the people. The Maharraht. Were they not a resource, something Muqallad could use to his benefit? But in what way? And what would the fire have to do with it?

As they dug deeper, Nikandr could feel the heart more fully now. Even Soroush looked uncomfortable.

"You can feel it as well?"

He nodded. "It is—"

He never finished his thought, for just then the beating of the heart changed. It became stronger, more pronounced. Nikandr coughed. He felt lightheaded for a moment. Soroush seemed even worse, blinking his eyes and staring at Nikandr as if he didn't know who he was.

"Get away from it," Nikandr said.

Soroush did not respond.

Nikandr pulled him away. The effect lessened but was still present as he guided Soroush along a wash in the sloping land that led to a creek below. The heartbeat quickened, and Nikandr suddenly felt another presence, far beyond where the heart lay buried.

Soroush must have felt it as well, for he was staring northeast, the same direction as Nikandr. They slid to their right until they were hidden behind a thicket that gave them a good view of the land in that direction. Nothing lay before them, however, save the white trunks of the birch and their golden leaves upon the ground.

From beyond the trees a tall man strode. He was muscular, and his light robes were more suited to summer than they were the chill days of autumn. Even at this distance, and even though it had been five years since he'd seen him, Nikandr knew it was Muqallad.

A girl followed, speaking to him. Kaleh.

And then came the akhoz.

Two, then three more. Another on a tall stone to their right. They snuffled low to the ground like dogs. Several craned their necks at the same time, perhaps sensing something, while the others turned their eyeless faces on Nikandr and Soroush's position.

The akhoz froze. They strained against some unseen bond—their muscles flexed, the tendons in their necks stretched taut like rigging lines as they craned against some hidden leash—and then, at no more than a flip of Muqallad's hand, they surged forward, loping across the ground at an alarming rate.

Nikandr and Soroush turned and ran, flying through the trees and down the slope toward the creek. They splashed through the water and used the speed they'd built to hurry up the far side, but making progress on the incline demanded much more effort, and they began to slow. By the time they reached the top, where level land led them deeper into the forest, the akhoz had reached the thicket where they'd been hiding a short time ago.

"Take this," Soroush said, and he tossed the musket to Nikandr. He followed a moment later with his bandolier, which Nikandr slung over his shoulder.

He swung the frizzen back to check the pan. Seeing what little powder was there was too damp, he blew it clear while grabbing one of the wooden cartridges from the bandolier. He filled it with dry powder, and when he heard the akhoz clear the top of the rise behind him, he stopped and turned. Only two of the akhoz had crested the rise. The light rain fell against their loping bodies and immediately steamed, making them look like infernal machines plowing through the undergrowth. He sighted along the barrel, aiming for the nearest, and pulled the trigger.

The musket bucked, and the first akhoz crashed to the ground, leaves billowing up around it.

It was up again a moment later, a gaping hole leaking dark blood from its chest. Nikandr had hoped to strike the heart, but the ball had struck too low.

Pulling the wooden stopper from another cartridge, he loaded the pan and closed the frizzen. As he put more powder into the barrel and dropped the ball and wadding in, the second akhoz caught up to the first and galloped ahead of it. His hands shook as he used the ramrod to drive the shot home.

He raised the barrel and fired without thinking.

The shot took the closer akhoz full in the chest. Skin and black blood exploded as it released a gout of flame toward Nikandr. It was too far away, however, and the shot seemed to take its breath away. It fell to the earth in a heap. Its hands clutched at the earth, leaving deep furrows. And then it was still.

The second akhoz had reached Soroush. The akhoz was on all fours, wary of the khanjar Soroush held in one hand. Soroush, perhaps sensing its weakness, darted in. The akhoz raised and tried to attack, but Soroush ducked and slashed it behind the knees.

The akhoz fell and in a blink Soroush had raised the khanjar high and driven it down into its chest.

Nikandr reloaded as the remaining three akhoz charged forward. He got off only one more shot, striking the akhoz closest to him in the neck, before the other two were on him.

He swung the musket like a club against the first to reach him, a girl with stringy hair and a deep scar across the skin where her eyes should have been. The musket came down against her right arm, which she used to ward against the blow. He heard and felt the bone give way beneath. The girl mewled but grabbed for Nikandr's neck with her free arm. Nikandr darted back, but it gave the other akhoz time to snatch the musket and rip it from his grasp.

Soroush hobbled toward him and from behind drove the knife into the one with the broken arm. The thing arched its neck back and released a sickening call. She sounded as if she were calling for help, and perhaps she was. She fell to the ground, clutching at the wound to her back as her other arm lay useless at her side.

Nikandr retreated as the last akhoz advanced. He tried to draw it away from Soroush. It worked, but Nikandr soon realized he'd made a grave mistake.

The akhoz crawled along the ground toward Soroush, closing the distance quickly. Soroush squatted into a swordsman's pose, preparing for the charge, but he was too close to one of the wounded akhoz.

The girl with the broken arm stood and grabbed him from behind. Soroush stumbled backward, and the other fell upon him from the front. Nikandr ran, shouting, when pain exploded at the back of his skull. It sounded like windships breaking.

Stars danced in his vision as he tipped toward the ground. His arms were suddenly leaden, unable to break his fall.

He struck the ground...

And woke some time later.

He managed to pick his head up off the damp earth, and when he did he saw three akhoz surrounding Soroush.

The sixth akhoz, Nikandr thought. He'd lost track of how many there were and the sixth had crept up from behind.

Soroush stabbed the wounded akhoz in the chest and managed to wrest himself free and scrabble backward along the ground, but the other two jumped on him.

"*Neh!*" Nikandr tried to get to his knees. He lifted himself off the ground, but that's as far as he got. He became dizzy, nauseous, and seconds later the stars closed in around him.

Soroush's cries of pain were the last thing he remembered.

Nikandr woke staring up through the boughs of the trees. Rain was falling, stealing warmth. The back of his head felt like it'd been mauled by a blacksmith's hammer. The left side of his face ached. The skin there was abraded and tender, but it was only from his fall, which had been onto soft earth. The wound behind his ear, however, was different. It was matted with blood and hair, and it flared like a brand as he probed it gently. His hand came away bloody, but he was satisfied that it was no longer bleeding much, and if that were so, he judged that he'd been unconscious for fifteen minutes, perhaps twenty.

Next to him lay a musket, useless now that rain had seeped into the pan and the barrel. For a moment he thought it was his own, but it looked nothing like his. It was Soroush's, the one he had brought from the village before...

Before the girl... Kaleh. They had chased her through the woods. The rest came rushing back as he pushed himself up to his hands and knees. He could go no further; the screaming inside his head and the waves of pain that washed over him saw to that. He grabbed the musket and used it to lever himself to his feet. It may be useless, but it felt good to be holding a length of steel.

He stood there, bowed over, leaning against the musket, squinting against the pain not merely from the wounds but the light pummeling him as it filtered down through the trees.

He found signs of Soroush's struggle with the akhoz nearby. Matted plants, furrowed earth. Blood.

There was a trail that led eastward. He followed this, staring ahead for signs of being watched, but as he climbed the short rise toward the thicket where he and Soroush had hidden themselves, the ground tipped and he fell. He barely managed to bring his arms up to fend off the worst of the fall. He thought surely he was being attacked again, but as the rain pattered against the forest floor, he realized the disorientation was a symptom of his wounds. When he tried to reach his feet again, a fit of nausea overcame him. What little he had in his stomach came rushing up, burning his throat as it went.

He spit to clear his mouth and found, strangely, that he felt better. He moved with a slow steady pace and found the nausea beginning to ebb and his breath coming easier. He could see straight again, and although the light was still bothersome, it was becoming less of a problem as nightfall neared.

The trail led him up the rise and down a long hill. Ahead, the trees of Siafyan towered high above the surrounding forest.

When he came to the edge of the village, the earth was more packed, more well worn, and the trail he was following vanished. It was with a growing sense of dread that he entered the village proper. It had felt empty before, but now it felt ancient and forgotten.

He had felt something like this before, though he could not place the memory. Perhaps while walking the tunnels of Iramanshah, or while strolling through the streets of the Mount in Baressa.

He realized he was walking toward the northern end of the village, toward the burning site. Without quite knowing why, he began to hurry. Then he began to lope—at least as well as he was able. Soon the sense of dread was so strong upon him that he began to run, heedless of the intense pain in his head.

He passed beyond the village and ran through the trees, worried that he was losing his way, that he would forget where the clearing had stood.

After rounding a rocky promontory where a massive tree created an archway of sorts, he came to it. The rain beat down against the blackened circle, striking the burned remains of the dozens who had given themselves that their brothers and sisters—their sons and daughters—might yet live.

Nikandr walked to the edge of it, stopping when he came within several paces. He could not find it in himself to come closer. It felt like sacrilege, as though treading upon this hallowed ground would cause irreparable harm—though whom it would harm, and in what ways, he did not know.

And then he saw it. A glint of metal among the ashes, buried beneath the bones, nearly hidden.

He swung back and forth, trying to determine what it was, but he couldn't—not from this distance.

Swallowing heavily, he dropped the musket and took one step forward. Then another. Soon he stood at the edge of the ashes.

"Forgive me," he said softly, and stepped onto the remains. He moved as carefully as he could, but he could feel the brittle crunch of bone, the slurp of the wet ashes as he went.

At last he came to the source of the glinting. He reached down and picked it up.

It was Soroush's dagger. The khanjar, the one he'd drawn against Nikandr when they'd fought over Rehada. There were patterns in the ashes that spread from the place the knife had rested. Four large furrows radiated outward, and he though immediately to the hillock that had opened for Kaleh. He wondered if Soroush were dead, buried beneath this very place where he now stood.

But that made no sense. They wouldn't have dragged him this far simply to kill him. Soroush was alive. Of this he was sure. He just had no idea where they might have taken him, nor why his knife had been left behind. Perhaps it was a sign from Soroush himself. Or perhaps it had been left as a warning for Nikandr to stay away.

Staring at the blade, feeling its heft, Nikandr recalled the source of the half-hidden memory he'd had at the edge of the village. He'd felt the same way five years ago on Ghayavand while walking the streets of Alayazhar. It had been the strongest as he'd stepped toward the tower. Sariya's tower. It had happened when he'd realized the depth of the illusions that ran through the entire city.

The same thing was happening here—not an illusion, but the influence of one of the Al-Aqim. Muqallad's power was spreading. Why, and why *here*, he didn't know. He only knew that Soroush was now an integral part of it.

CHAPTER THIRTY-FIVE

With a guard on either side of him, Nikandr walked along a wide hallway in the upper reaches of Ashdi en Ghat. They led him to an empty room—more of a cavern. It had taken him hours to return to the village. Light filtered in through several natural breaks in the roof high above them, where Nikandr could hear the rain still falling. Along the floor were deep etchings in the stone. The gaps above carefully guided the water to the floor and into the etched channels. The water made hardly any sound at all. Barely a trickle.

The water rippled as it moved through the channels, creating a hypnotic effect. It felt as if the floor was moving, or that *he* was moving over the floor. The movements seemed purposeful but unfathomable until Nikandr realized that the course of movement mimicked the shimmering northern lights. Even here among the Maharraht there was beauty and art. As Nikandr watched, the floor shimmered like a veil, with certain spots glinting like stars in the northern sky. How long had it taken the vanaqiram to craft such a thing? How long must she have studied the sky in order to recreate it with such accuracy?

On the far side of the room, from some passage hidden behind a curve in the cavern's wall, came Bersuq. He wore a brown turban. The cloth was crisp and richly colored, but Bersuq looked old and used and near to breaking. He bore with him a ledger. He was poring over it closely, flipping back and forth between two pages, but then he seemed to remember the business at hand, and he closed it with a snap. After setting it down on a shelf built into the stone, he walked across the room, taking care not to step in the channels of water.

The soldier on Nikandr's right bowed his head and held out Soroush's musket and his khanjar. Bersuq accepted them with stoicism, and yet, as Nikandr watched, he could see emotions playing subtly in his eyes and the set of his jaw.

"Leave us," Bersuq said.

The soldiers did, their footsteps fading as Bersuq returned to the shelf and set the musket upon it.

"Where is he?" Bersuq asked without turning around.

"Taken. Taken by Muqallad, who has come to your island."

Nikandr expected surprise at these words, but Bersuq merely stood where he was, his back to Nikandr as he cleaned Soroush's knife with a kerchief he'd retrieved from his robes. "Soroush knew what he was doing when he left this village."

"He *knew* Muqallad was here?

"*Yeh.*"

"Are you saying he *wanted* to be taken?"

Bersuq turned and regarded Nikandr with weary eyes, his voice hoarse, his posture hunched, as if the mantle of leadership weighed too heavily upon his shoulders. "He only suspected, but I think he wanted it to be so."

Nikandr stepped further into the room, careful not to step upon the cracks where the rainwater flowed. "For the love of those who came before us, why?"

"Because he wished to see him. He wished to know Muqallad for himself before he decided."

"Decided what?"

"Whether the children would be given to him. Whether those who still follow and believe in Soroush would be given as well."

Nikandr stood there and stared, trying to piece together all that Bersuq was saying, all that he was implying. Clearly there was friction among the Maharraht. He had thought that the men from the south had been the cause—a power struggle for the mind and soul of their movement—but now he realized it was much deeper than this. Muqallad had come, and he was making demands, and few, it seemed, could agree on the right course of action. Bersuq and Soroush had already fought over it. The majority of the men from Behnda al Tib had left their island, most likely for the same reason. Even the men and women at the shore of the lake deep below where Nikandr now stood, the ones who hoped to heal the children, clearly could not quite bring themselves to side with the decision to hand these children over to Muqallad.

"His *son* lies below," Nikandr said.

"What is one boy, even a son, against all that we have lost?"

"And yet you've given me leave to heal them."

Bersuq stared down at the khanjar he held in his hands. He scraped his thumb against the tip absently. "I say 'what is one boy,' but he is bright. A shining star. Perhaps he will be the one to lead us to greatness. Perhaps he will be the one to lead us back to the path of learning. It's a difficult thing to give up—not just Wahad, but all of the children."

Nikandr lowered his voice. "But the men from Behnda al Tib."

Bersuq's eyes shot up. The fierceness Nikandr remembered had returned. "Do not speak of it outside of this room, son of Iaros, or I will have no choice but to give Rahid his wish."

"They've aligned themselves with Muqallad."

Bersuq shook his head. "The men who are here, *yeh*. Those that Thabash left behind in Behnda al Tib, who can know?"

"Why don't you fight them?"

"Because there are too many who would join them. Muqallad is persuasive. He has told us that the time of enlightenment is near. How can we ignore those words from a man such as him, especially when it's exactly what so many of us want to hear?"

"And yet you harbor doubts."

The blade in Bersuq's hands glinted from the incoming light. He stared at it, twisting it slowly back and forth. "I don't know what to believe. He came those many months ago, just as some were taking sick." He looked up, then, meeting Nikandr's gaze with piercing eyes. "You've met him?"

"I have," Nikandr said.

"Then you know the weight that surrounds him. The gravitas. He need but speak, and the world around him answers. He told us that we had been chosen, that our struggles all these years had not been in vain. He told us there were trials yet ahead, and that if we saw them through, we would be rewarded. We would all be rewarded.

"And then the sick became sicker, and the young—dozens of them—fell to the plague you saw at the lake. We came to Muqallad begging for his help, but he merely said that it was the first of many steps. He said those children had been chosen by the fates themselves, that they were now only one step from Adhiya, one step from vashaqiram. All we needed to do was give them to the fire, as they clearly wished."

Nikandr shook his head. "The fire in Siafyan. It wasn't meant to rid you of the wasting, was it?"

Bersuq was having trouble meeting Nikandr's gaze. "It was done in preparation for a greater ritual, one that involves the children. Muqallad was pleased when it was done, but I"—he glanced toward the open doorway and lowered his voice—"I was sickened. How we could have..." He looked up to Nikandr, his eyes regaining some of their fierceness. "It is why you must hurry, son of Iaros. If you can heal them, then it will be clear to all that Muqallad was lying. They will believe me then, or enough will that the others won't matter, and Muqallad will be cast aside."

Above, from somewhere outside, came the soft fluttering of wings. Nikandr knew who it was immediately; he could feel her through the soulstone that lay against his chest.

"Muqallad will not take kindly to being cast aside."

"If the fates will his vengeance against us, then it will be so, but I will not grant him children if his words are proven lies." He held Soroush's knife out, hilt first, until Nikandr took it. Then he raised his eyebrows as the sound of beating wings came again. "Speak with your Matra. Have her help if she would. You have one more day."

After retrieving his ledger, Bersuq strode toward the tunnel.

"I need more time," Nikandr said.

Bersuq stopped at the entrance to the room and spoke without turning. "I don't have it to give. In one more day, perhaps two, Thabash will return."

"*You* lead the Maharraht."

"*Neh*, son of Iaros, I do not. That mantle belongs to Muqallad now. But with your help, that may all change."

And with that he left.

As his footsteps receded, a rook hopped down to a natural stone ledge above him. It surveyed the room and then winged down to land on the floor near Nikandr's feet. It cawed and pecked, and Nikandr worried over the sound, but when the rook shivered and flapped its wings, he realized that Atiana would have already searched the upper reaches of the village for prying ears.

"*Privyet*, Atiana," Nikandr said.

"*Privyet*."

The rook cawed and was silent for a time, and Nikandr wondered whether she was giving him time to speak.

"Atiana, I pray you, forgive my words on—"

"I haven't come to discuss our past, Nikandr. I've come bearing news of Galahesh. News you should know."

"But Atiana—"

The rook spread its wings, cawing fiercely, over and over again. The feathers shivered, as if from barely contained rage.

Nikandr sighed, crossing his arms over his chest. "Go on."

"Arvaneh is not who we thought. She is none other than Sariya."

Nikandr could only stare as a deep pit opened up inside him. Muqallad here, and Sariya on Galahesh.

"She's pulling many strings, Nikandr. It was she that built the Spar, and now I've found a spire to the north of the straits."

"To what purpose?"

"I don't yet know. It's all happening so quickly. But know this… We need you. You must leave Rafsuhan. Take to the winds and come home. Khalakovo must be prepared."

"Would that I could, Atiana, but I can't. I'm needed here."

"You're needed by the Grand Duchy."

"Which is the exact reason I'm staying. This is too important to set aside."

"They are *Maharraht*." Even through the voice of the rook Nikandr could hear her disgust. He tried to explain. He told her of the children. He told her of Rahid and the Hratha and Muqallad's manipulation. He told her of Soroush and Bersuq and their confessions to him. But nothing would sway her. "All of that means little if Hakan is preparing to sweep down on Vostroma when morning breaks."

"He cannot. The straits stand before him."

"Don't be so sure. I know not what the spire is for, but I suspect... I *fear* that I've given Sariya more than I should have."

"What could you have given her?"

"One of the times I spied upon her, I thought she wasn't there, but I believe now that she was watching me, studying how I manipulate the currents of the aether."

Nikandr worked it through in his mind. "And if she can learn to do the same..."

"She can control the storm that sits above the straits. To allow ships, for the first time, to fly over them. To give Hakan what he and the centuries of Kamarisi before him dearly wished they could have—a clear path to the islands."

The rain outside fell harder. The water spilling into the channels was quickening. Thunder rang as he paced along the room, no longer caring if he stepped upon the channels.

"Have you told your mother?"

"Of course, but they are ill prepared. Three attacks from the south were orchestrated over the past week alone, and Father fears more. Ships are being brought in to help, but we are weak, Nikandr. You know this. Father will not ask it, but it would do him good to see you commanding a wing of ships. Even Hakan would pause if he knew you were near." The rook arched its neck, then ducked low and tapped the stone softly with its beak, an act of supplication. "Come home, Nischka. Leave Rafsuhan behind. Let them quarrel amongst themselves. Let them weaken while we prepare for the coming storm."

"Don't you understand? This is *part* of that storm. We cannot ignore it, Atiana."

"*I* can. And you can, too."

Nikandr paused, knowing the words he was about to say would drive a wedge between them—even more than their argument had, more than her pending marriage had—and yet he said them anyway. "*Nyet*, I cannot."

He expected the rook to caw, to flap around the room as Atiana lost control as her emotions flew high. It did not, however. What it *did* do was much more disturbing. It stood completely still, one eye trained upon him, blinking once, twice, as thunder shook the air outside the chamber.

"You are needed, Khalakovo."

Nikandr shivered at those words.

"I'm needed here."

After one more brief pause, the rook flapped up to the ledge where Soroush's musket lay, and then was gone in a rush of wings through the driving rain.

CHAPTER THIRTY-SIX

With three streltsi walking ahead and another three behind, Atiana and Ishkyna strode among the stalls of the bazaar. Irkadiy was leading the guardsmen. He watched Atiana closely—making her feel overprotected—and yet it did little to silence her fears of being out in the open among so many in so foreign a place.

She'd finished speaking with Nikandr only that morning, and her anger was still high. But really, she should have expected it. He'd been invested in this—the rifts and the healing of those afflicted by the wasting—for so long he'd become blinded by it. He thought that what he needed to do to protect his homeland was to solve the riddle of the rifts, but there came a time when one had to fight the threat that lay directly before you. Later he could return to that if he so chose, but not now. Not when the Grand Duchy itself was threatened.

And yet, he was a grown man, a stubborn man at times, and there would be no changing his mind. Not until the events on Rafsuhan played themselves out.

As they wended their way toward the granite edifice that marked the center of the bazaar, Atiana watched among the dozens of stalls she could see, wondering who might be watching them, wondering if anyone was following or lay in wait ahead. The vendors behind their tables looked up as they approached, sensing money. Their hawkers bowed, displaying wares in their extended hands—trinkets of every imaginable color; kaftans and slippers of fine silk; kolpaks of worsted wool; glass pitchers, red or golden or blue, bright from the sun shining down through the cloth over the stalls; weapons and shields and armor, most of it decorative or so old they would be useless on the battlefield; the skins of animals, supple leather or striped fur or scaly hide. There were even curious inventions—clocks that struck the time on the hour; miniatures that when wound properly would play a lonely, foreign tune upon a tiny mechanical harp.

Atiana saw all of this, but she also found herself studying the vendors and buyers for things amiss. She never saw anyone openly staring at her, but she became convinced that they were watching her from the corners of their eyes, or spying upon her once she'd passed.

Only the food made her pause. There were spices and herbs and roots. There was smoked fish, sweetmeats, pickled goat's feet. There were grapes and melons and beans, braided garlic and a sea of onions and potatoes. Nearly every stall that sold food—and a good many that didn't—had hanging from their tents clusters of bottles filled with wine the color of garnet and ruby and evening primrose. It was a wonder that there was any shortage of food whatsoever among the islands, but no sooner had the thought occurred to her than the sheer number of people walking through the bazaar registered. There were hundreds of thousands in Baressa, and nearly as many on the island of Oramka to the north. There was food, but there was no shortage of mouths to feed, either.

The bazaar's central structure was closer now, and it was more massive than Atiana had realized. It was called the Kirzan, the rock, and it had once been the seat of power on Galahesh, abandoned after the War of Seven Seas. The men of Yrstanla had always been a suspicious lot, and they had practically given it away after the peace treaties with the young Grand Duchy had been signed.

Early this morning she and Ishkyna had received a note from Vaasak Dhalingrad to come to the Kirzan at midday *to discuss the arrangements of the new treaty*, but Atiana knew it was no such thing. Something had happened. She just didn't know what.

Beside her, Ishkyna walked soberly. She had looked at hardly a thing since entering the bazaar—she'd merely matched Atiana's pace, staring straight ahead, allowing the sights and sounds and smells of the bazaar to wash over her like rain—but then she came to a stall selling matroyshkas, and she stopped. There were dozens of them, red and green and purple, but she looked at only one. A bright yellow doll with a patterned blue babushka. She opened it slowly, almost reverently, to reveal the second doll hidden within. She set the larger one aside and opened the others, each one smaller, hiding within the larger doll, until she came to one that was as small as her thumb. Her hands shook as she opened this last. She stared within the empty confines as Atiana came to her side.

"What is it?" Atiana asked.

Ishkyna ignored her. "How much?"

The old woman sitting behind the table, clearly a woman of the islands, had a scar along her throat. She did not smile nor stand up from her stool where she was carefully painting another matroyshka. She held up three fingers for

Ishkyna to see, and then she went back to her painting.

Ishkyna carefully put the matroyshka back together again and reached inside the purse at her wrist. She pulled out a medallion of gold. It was a coin of Anuskaya, but it could easily buy every doll in the stall. Ishkyna placed it on the table. The dull thump the coin made on the cloth-covered table made the woman look up. She stared at Ishkyna, her eyes hard but not harsh. She glanced at Atiana then, and then the streltsi around them.

Ishkyna put the matroyshka in her cloth purse and walked away. The streltsi looked to one another, worried, but without saying a word the three ahead followed Ishkyna while the other three remained.

When Atiana looked back to the table, the coin was gone, and the woman had gone back to her painting.

When Atiana had caught up to Ishkyna, she asked, "Do you mind telling me what that was about?"

"It's none of your business."

"I know, but it's important to you." She meant that it would therefore also be important to *her*, but Ishkyna merely sniffed and kept walking.

Finally the bazaar fell away and the bulk of the Kirzan towered over them. It stood on the highest point of the bazaar, watching the land around sleepily, as a lynx watches the snowy field. At the top of the stairs, beneath tall colonnades, were brass-bound doors and two city guardsmen. The guardsmen took note of them, but little more than that, and they were soon through doors and into the interior, which held more stalls. These stalls, however, housed glass cases and refined men standing behind them. They stood wearing bright silk turbans and fine kaftans, waiting and smiling patiently if they weren't already speaking with a patron, of which there were few.

Irkadiy led the way to a curving set of marble stairs that led to the second floor. There was a wide, open hall. The floor was covered in a variety of mismatched carpets that somehow complemented one another. Sitting at a large, round table in the center of the room were Vaasak Dhalingrad, Atiana's father—

And Grigory Stasayev Bolgravya.

Atiana stared for long, confused moments, unable to comprehend Grigory's presence, here of all places. Galahesh felt so foreign. To find someone so rooted in her past, someone so vile to her, was as jarring as falling from the rigging of a windship. Nikandr's refusal to return to Vostroma was even more infuriating than only moments ago. To have Grigory here only served to remind her of the distance that stood between her and her love, a gap as wide as the straits and getting wider.

Father rose after speaking low to Vaasak and Grigory. "Welcome, daughters."

As Atiana and Ishkyna approached, the other men rose and bowed while Father granted them a smile. He stepped in to kiss Ishkyna. The two of them touched stones, and then he turned to Atiana.

"What is *he* doing here?" Atiana asked before he could move to embrace her.

Ishkyna had not moved toward the table. She was staring at Grigory with a look of unbridled disgust. Ishkyna—even more than Mileva—had been protective of Atiana after learning what he'd done.

Father's sleepy eyes glanced back to one side, toward the table. "Atiana," he said, his voice low. "Had I been able, I would have strung him in the courtyard of Galostina for all to see, but such a thing *wasn't* possible, nor is it possible for me now to tell his brother, the Duke, whom to send to represent him."

"A dozen others could have taken his place."

"Konstantin would beg to differ, and his stakes are high in this. There are few enough Bolgravyas left after what happened on Khalakovo. I would think of anyone *you* would understand this. Now come"—he held his stone out for her to touch—"we have much to discuss, and the sooner we have it done, the sooner Grigory will be gone."

Atiana swallowed her next words, for they were petty. She detested that Grigory had crawled his way back into her life, but there was little enough to do about it now. She took her soulstone and touched Father's. She felt the warmth within her chest expand ever so slightly. They had touched stones only weeks before, but it was nice to do so again after feeling so alone in this foreign place.

Father led them to the table and waited until she and Ishkyna had taken their seats. Grigory and Vaasak, who had stood at her approach, sat, followed at last by Father.

"Now," Father said, motioning to Vaasak, "finish what you were saying."

Vaasak bowed his head. There were empty glasses before Atiana and Ishkyna. Vaasak took up a blue bottle of vodka and poured healthy servings for them both. "I was saying, Your Highness, that the papers are nearly ready. I've been dealing closely with Sihaş, and I believe that they're nearly ready for your signature. Only one obstacle remains."

Father straightened himself in his chair. "And what would that be?"

"The Kamarisi wants an additional tribute of gems each year. One thousand more of each."

Vaasak and Grigory watched closely as Father considered these words. Atiana could tell he was tense. The forefinger of his right hand tapped against the inlaid mosaic of the table. Atiana was not privy to all of the numbers from the mines, but a thousand more of each would be nearly impossible. They could barely conduct trade with such a hit to their yearly totals, much less fend off the Maharraht and their incessant attacks, especially considering how viciously they'd been attacking Bolgravya and Nodhvyansk.

"A thousand cannot be allowed," Father said. His voice was breathy, as if he were speaking only to himself, as if he knew exactly what this demand meant.

Vaasak was already nodding his head. "Of course, Your Highness. I pushed him. I tried to maneuver to half that. I offered windships, iron, gold." Vaasak lowered his voice and leaned in toward Father. "I even offered him his choice of brides, but Sihaş would have none of it. On this the Kamarisi is adamant."

Father's chair creaked as he slumped further into it. He stared at the table, mesmerized, while continuing to tap his finger. "He knows we have no choice."

"You can't be considering this," Atiana said. "The Kamarisi is setting a trap."

Father turned to her calmly, his heavy eyes weighing her before he spoke. "Your mother told me of your warnings, but what if you're wrong?"

"What if I'm right?"

"If you're right then I may very well be making a poor decision this day. But if you're wrong, and we pull away from the table, we will not be able to find our place at it again."

"He will take you, Father, or kill you."

"We are not enemies, Atiana. He has a war raging to the west. He has unrest brewing in the north. He has discontent festering in places he thought to be his most loyal. He has nothing to gain by attempting to retake something that has been out of the Empire's reach for generations."

"If he can gain the islands, he will have more than enough resources to win to the west, to stifle whatever uprising might be brewing in the north. With a victory over the islands, discontent will turn to satisfaction. Do not risk yourself—"

Father pounded his fist on the table, rattling the bottle and tipping over one of the glasses of vodka. As the vodka pattered onto the carpet, he spoke with an intensity that shocked Atiana. "I *must* risk it! We are dying, daughter! Vostroman, Bolgravyan, Khalakovan. Mirkotski and Rhavankan. We are being dragged beneath the waves. By the blight. By the Maharraht. By the wasting, still, no matter what your beloved Nikandr might think he is doing for hearth and home. We are pulled low as the tide rises. Yrstanla makes demands. They wish for stones. They wish for wood. They wish for liquor." He looked at her closely. "They wish even for our daughters. And what am I to do?"

"We can fight!" Grigory said.

Father snapped his head toward Grigory. "Mind your tongue!"

"Forgive me, Your Highness, but I will not! Send the ships across the downs. If they're not needed, I'll return them home."

Atiana knew what he was speaking of, but she thought it complete folly.

He spoke of a path from Nodhvyansk to Yrstanla's mainland that windsmen called the downs. Before reaching it, ships would need to cut northward across some of the deepest waters in the ocean. It was a dangerous path he suggested taking, but it was the implications that made her back straighten. He was suggesting they circle around and secure Galahesh from the north, where their ships would be unhindered by the wild currents around the straits. More than this, he was suggesting they take the Kamarisi captive. With the northern end of the island secured, it would be all too easy to sweep in from the south and take Baressa.

Atiana had never seen Father so angry. His eyes were bright with emotion, and his jaw was clenched so tight he was shaking. His chest pumped like a child working a blacksmith's bellows.

But then he collected himself. He began to breathe easier, and his jaw relaxed. "The riots have begun again, Grigory. They've become more organized, even in these last few months. If we do not have ships to sustain order, we may fall to *them*, never mind the Empire."

Grigory made a face and waved toward Vaasak. "What order can there be with demands such as these? We won't last two years, Your Highness. Never has the Kamarisi come so close to our shores. This is a chance we must take."

"We cannot," Vaasak said.

"Why can't we?" replied Grigory. "They've as much as declared war on us already."

"If we take Hakan, a new Kamarisi will come, and he will bring with him the whole of their might."

"Grigory's right." Atiana turned, stunned, at these words from Ishkyna. She had been so hostile to Grigory when they'd first arrived, and here she was supporting his foolhardy plan. Ishkyna continued to stare at the tabletop, as if she were still working all of it through, and then she nodded to herself, apparently satisfied. "The Kamarisi is begging us to do it."

Atiana could not remember a time when her father had been indecisive. Ever. He had always been a man who knew just what to do no matter what the circumstances. But sitting before her now was a man on the brink of defeat. The mantle of the Grand Duke had burdened him heavily ever since he'd taken it up, but never had it made him seem small. It did now, and she felt for him—caught between difficult choices, none of which seemed likely to save the Grand Duchy.

His gaze moved between Ishkyna and Atiana, to Grigory, and then Vaasak. "You have dealt with Hakan the most. How do you weigh him?"

Vaasak looked nervous to speak. He knew his words would determine much. "In truth, he has seemed earnest. Perhaps too much so."

Father digested these words. He picked up his heavy glass and downed the last of his vodka. As he set the glass down on the table with barely a sound, he turned to Grigory. "Return to your brother, Grigory. Tell him to send the ships." He stood and looked down upon Atiana. "And you, daughter." She had not felt so much the child in years. "There's no time to spare. Find what Arvaneh is about."

With that he and Grigory and Vaasak left, leaving Atiana alone with Ishkyna.

Ishkyna stared at her glass of vodka, which she hadn't touched once. "Dangerous business, sister."

Atiana hadn't touched her drink, either, but she took it up now and downed it in one big gulp. "*Da*," she said, setting the glass onto the table, rim-side down. "Best we get to it."

CHAPTER THIRTY-SEVEN

As snowflakes the size of petals fell over Baressa, Atiana strode along the edge of a pool that had not quite frozen over. A thickening blanket of snow was building around the edge where ice had formed, but in the center, white snowflakes fell against the water's black surface, melting in the blink of an eye. They looked like souls falling against the aether, slipping through the dark to the other side, and it made Atiana wonder if this was indeed what it was like when souls reached Adhiya and when they returned once more to Erahm.

How might *she* go? How might Nikandr?

Would it be quick, like these snowflakes? Or might it be slow and painful and filled with misery, like those dreadful hours on Duzol after she'd been shot in the chest?

The sound of approaching footsteps, muffled by the snow, pulled her attention away from the pool. Walking down the path between two broken buildings was Irkadiy.

"My Lady Princess," he said bowing his head. "Please, come."

She followed along a path that led her down a row of stone buildings that were now little more than gutted shells. They were deep in the Shattering, the swath of Baressa that had been left as it was after the greatest and final battle of the War of Seven Seas. It was a land that had been considered fouled, for it had been one of the few great battles the Empire had lost over its long, grand history.

They followed tracks in the snow that were already becoming obscured by the heavy fall. They came to an area that was not nearly as devastated as the one they'd just come from. They made for a depression circled by columns. Many of the columns were intact, whole, but those nearest Atiana were broken, little more than white fingers clawing skyward. As Atiana and Irkadiy walked through it she realized it had been a celestia, which made it clear that this had once been an area where Aramahn had lived.

Beyond the ruins lay a stone building that bore the mark of the Yrstanla stonemasons from centuries past—it was grand, but it was also stark and serious. Inside, the light was dim, and at the northern end the roof was broken, snow swirling within and piling in the corners. At the other end stood three streltsi in dark gray cherkesskas and kolpak hats, and between them, sitting on the ground, was Ushai, the Aramahn woman who had been treading the dark the last time Atiana had been searching for Arvaneh. She did not cower, but she watched the men closely as Atiana approached. Then she seemed to recognize Atiana, and her eyes went wide.

As Atiana neared, the bruises and cuts on Ushai's face came clearer. Ushai stared up at her defiantly, but she shivered as she did so, and not from the cold.

Atiana turned to Irkadiy. "What have you done?"

Irkadiy bowed his head. "My Lady Princess, she tried to escape."

"So you *beat* her?"

"*Most important*, My Lady. Those were your words."

Atiana lashed out and slapped him.

The muscles along his jaw worked, but his eyes were impassive. "We do what we must."

It was a common saying among streltsi. "We are not at *war* with the Aramahn," she said.

He bowed his head. "As you say, My Lady."

"Go," she said.

Irkadiy looked back to the broken section of the wall where they'd entered, but didn't otherwise move.

"Go!"

"Forgive me, My Lady Princess, but your father said never to leave your side."

She swallowed, wishing she'd shown more self-control. "You can watch from the entrance, but I will speak with her alone."

She waited as he stared, perhaps calculating just how far he could push his orders, but then he nodded to his men and they trudged away, leaving her alone with Ushai.

"Ushai, I'm sorry." Atiana kneeled and stared closer at her wounds. There were abrasions along one cheek, a cut on her lip. One eye was red and swollen. It would blacken within a day. "Did you resist them?"

Ushai's jaw worked. She stared over Atiana's shoulder to the streltsi beyond. "Why shouldn't I?"

Atiana's head jerked back before she could think to stop it. This was something she hadn't expected. The Aramahn cherished peace. Or they *had*. She wondered if this was an indication of what the Aramahn had been driven to or if this was yet another splinter that was forming, one that was not bellicose like the Maharraht but would defend their interests more vigorously. Even a year ago most Aramahn would not lift a hand to defend themselves, even if it meant death for themselves or another.

Atiana paused, feeling small in the face of Ushai's pain. "I sent the streltsi because I need your help. I go tonight to confront Sariya."

"That would be unwise, daughter of Radia."

"Which is why I needed to speak to you. You know of her, and I would have you share it"—she glanced back toward the soldiers—"if you would have her stopped."

"You will not be able to stop her. She *wants* you to take the dark."

"I know."

Ushai shook her head. "She is no simple qiram who has learned the skills of the dark."

"Which is why I need your help so desperately. Come with me. Come with me tomorrow night, and together, you and I will break down the walls Sariya has put in place."

Ushai hesitated. Her eyes were angry, indignant, but after a pause she steeled herself and nodded.

Atiana smiled and held out her hand. Ushai took it, and together they made their way out and into the cold of the Shattering.

The dinner meant to honor the arrival of Atiana's father was as grand an occasion as she had ever seen. It was held in a room four times the size of the largest ballroom in Galostina, and twice as tall. The light from twelve golden chandeliers cast a warm glow against the filigreed ceiling. Hundreds of men and women milled about the room. The servants—all of them women, many of them Bahett's wives—had jewels worked into their hair, and wore dresses of the most supple silk. They held trays filled with food. Some offered skewered medallions of cooked antelope with dark red centers, harvested, they said, from the steppes of central Yrstanla. Others brought mouthwatering fruit, bright with color, or cooked tubers—nothing like the potatoes of the islands—marinated in oil and capers and dill. There were dozens of other delectables, but Atiana found herself unable to eat. She was studying the crowd, watching for one particular man that would allow her to complete her preparations for the following night.

She saw him enter as a bell was rung softly from the center of the room—Sihaş ül Mehmed, the Kamarisi's personal envoy. The bell was struck again, and the conversation began to die down as people made their way toward their seats. Atiana intercepted Sihaş at the stairs that led up to the raised head table.

When Sihaş realized that it was he Atiana wished to speak to, he stepped aside to allow the others access to the stairs. "My Lady Princess," he said, bowing his head.

"My Lord," Atiana said, smiling, "I wonder if you might do me the honor of allowing me to sit by your side."

"You don't wish to sit with your family? Or with Bahett?"

"Father is always a bore at such things. Of Ishkyna, it may surprise you, I've had my fill. And Bahett?" Atiana leaned to her left, allowing Sihaş to see where Bahett sat, or more to the point, who sat next to him. It was Meryam, Bahett's ilkadin. "We are not yet married, and as this is her final dinner with her title, she will sit at his side."

He smiled and offered her his arm. "Then I would be honored."

After a slight shuffling of chairs, she and Sihaş were seated. Once everyone was settled, the bell was rung again. Shortly after, Father and Hakan and a select few others entered the room and made their way to the head table. Bahett was among them, and he watched Atiana curiously when he saw her sitting with Sihaş. She wasn't sure whether it was because she wasn't sitting next to *him* or because Sihaş was the man she was sitting next to. Either way, the look was gone a moment later, and he gave her a pleasant smile.

She smiled back, but her attention was soon drawn to Arvaneh. Her golden hair was tied behind her head in a complex braid ornamented with bright amber jewels. The bodice of her dress was aubergine, the skirt layer upon layer of deep reds. It was not her beautiful raiment that drew the attention, however. It was the band of gold across her forehead and the string of crystals that hung down from it, covering her eyes like a veil. Rather than make her seem hidden, it made her stand out. It seemed as though she could look upon anyone without reciprocity. Indeed, she seemed to be staring at Atiana even then. She nodded, and Atiana was forced to do the same.

Arvaneh and Hakan were the last to be seated. As soon as they were, the woman at the center of the room—Ebru, Bahett's second wife—struck the bell one last time. With her higher vantage, Atiana could see that there were no tables where Ebru stood; they had been cleared in a circle around her. She wore a beautiful, formfitting dress of red. Her fingers bore rings that sparkled under the light of the chandeliers. Dozens of bracelets circled her wrists. She stood, back straight, chin high—the pose of a dancer—and brought the mallet high above her head, ready to strike. As she snapped her arm into place, the bracelets made a sound like the rattle of coins, and when she did, others around the room did the same. Bahett's other wives, now free of their trays, had bracelets as well, and they had brought their arms high in time with Ebru.

Small gasps of pleasure came from the room as the guests looked around them, understanding at last what was happening.

Ebru struck the bell—it rang more faintly than before and yet still filled the room—and then she snapped her arm to the ready position. The others snapped their arms in response, taking a long, sinuous stride forward.

Again the bell was struck, and again the women strode. As they moved in unison toward the center, more servants, all of them men, wound through the tables, bringing the first course—an intoxicating mixture of sugared sage and salted pear. As the head table began to eat, Atiana leaned in and spoke low to Sihaş. "I know it was you who came to me by the willow."

The sounds of forks clinking against plates, of the bell and the *shink* of the dancers' arms, came to Atiana clearly, almost dreamlike, as she waited for Sihaş to respond.

When he did not, she spoke again, "I know it was—"

"I would not say that so loudly if I were you."

Atiana had made sure that those to her right and to Sihaş's left were engaged in conversation. "If I speak too softly, good Sihaş, it will attract *more* attention."

Sihaş seemed suddenly disinterested in his meal. He merely pushed it around his plate with his fork. "I know what you plan to do tomorrow night as well."

"Then you also know a trap has been laid for me."

His silence was telling.

"You were willing to let me walk into it," Atiana said.

"I wish you no harm, but there is more to consider."

"Such as?"

"We must know Arvaneh's plans. It was decided that you would be allowed to go, and that we would watch."

"With no intervention from those who claim to be mindful of Hakan's true purpose."

Bahett's wives had reached the center of the room. There, they began a slow but complex ritual, moving around one another, hooking arms and spinning about, as men standing at the corners of the room beat large skin drums. The beat was thunderous at times and subtle, almost tender at others. It was a rhythm that felt deep as the ocean or light as summer rain, and the dancers echoed it well.

"In truth, I hope that you will come to no harm, but there are casualties in war, My Lady."

"This is why we need to speak, Sihaş. I will not offer myself as a sacrifice."

"I cannot help you in the dark."

At those words, Atiana glanced over to the head table, the same point at which the drumbeat quickened and the intensity of the dancing increased. Arvaneh seemed transfixed by it.

"That isn't the sort of help I require," Atiana continued.

"Then what?"

"I need protection, both during and once it's done."

"You have your streltsi."

"Hakan has allowed few enough in the kasir, Sihaş. You know this. We need *others* to watch over us as we study Arvaneh."

"If you do it in secret, there will be no need."

"It will hardly be in secret. In all likelihood Arvaneh will know we have come."

"It is not the time for boldness, My Lady."

"It is, My Lord. My father has arrived on these shores, and there is something afoot. I can smell it. And Arvaneh is the key. Isn't this what you've been searching for as well?"

"*Evet*, but we are not ready. Hakan has begun to fear those close to him. He sent a kaymakam away from the kasir two days ago, and we found out this morning that he has been lost on the road to Ramina. He was one of our most careful, and still Hakan found him out."

The beat of the drum had become frenetic, even ardent. The dancers swung about, dresses flaring, legs arcing. They had surrounded Ebru in her red dress, she with the bell and the rings of gold. They began to lean in and scratch at her. Only one or two at first, but as Ebru tried to escape the circle, the others pulled her back in and more began to feed upon her. She fought, rising above the tide, but there were too many, and she was drawn back down. She fell to the floor, and as she did, the men, who had been beating their drums furiously, raised their mallets up and struck once. The note reverberated around the room. All eyes were fixed on the dance.

"You must *be* ready," Atiana said. "There is no time to wait."

The drums beat again, and one of the remaining women—the women in white—fell to the floor.

"Two more days, My Lady Princess. That's all I ask."

Another beat, and another woman fell.

"I cannot delay. We go tomorrow night."

The drumbeats continued. Each one, each collapse of a dancer, felt like a heartbeat, like blood dripping upon the floor, like her last chance was slipping from her grasp.

"Then you go alone."

Atiana stared at the floor, where not a single dancer remained standing.

"So be it."

CHAPTER THIRTY-EIGHT

N asim stares into Sariya's deep blue eyes.

"Why would you not think to find me here?" she asks.

"Because you were not on Ghayavand."

She motions to the forest, and Nasim falls into step alongside her. Unlike Sariya, who moves like a bee over a field of wildflowers, the going is difficult for him. He trudges, the deep snow thumping as each footstep breaks the surface.

She glances down—no more than this—and Nasim's steps are light upon the snow. Yadhan, however, continues to struggle, and she appears more and more uncomfortable with this exchange. Sariya pays so little attention to her that Nasim wonders if Sariya knows she's there.

With a simple but elegant motion, Sariya sweeps the air with one hand, as if to indicate the entirety of this place they walk within. "Does the aether stop at the borders of Ghayavand? Is it bound by land or sea?"

Nasim takes in the terrain once more. He thought this a place that Sariya carved from her dreams, made real by her will over the course of centuries and the peculiarities of the aether that Sariya had managed to uncover, but now that he looks, he realizes how similar it is to the land of dreams that embraced him in his younger years. The aether is the land of dreams, after all, the place where Adhiya and Erahm touch. If Sariya tried hard enough, could she not have unraveled its secrets?

"Where are you?"

"Why, do you wish to join me?"

"I don't know where I wish to go."

Sariya smiled. "Then come."

They continue into the woods. They pass well into the trees before Nasim realizes Yadhan has not followed. She watches from the edge of the forest, ducking beneath the lowest branches to watch him, unwilling to take even a single step into the trees.

254 • BRADLEY P. BEAULIEU

Nasim doesn't want to continue alone, but he cannot allow Sariya to sense his worry. If she senses weakness, all will be lost.

They come to a rise, and soon the trees part, revealing a white monolith standing tall and proud, as if it considers itself the lord of all it surveys. It is taller than any of the trees that stand outside the clearing.

Sariya considers the stone, for the time being ignoring Nasim.

And then Nasim realizes.

The stone. The piece of the Atalayina. The one he'd hidden in Sariya's tower. He feels it within the strata of rock that forms the monolith, and he is sure that Sariya feels the same. He is confused, for his memories tell a different story. Khamal dropped it onto the floor of Sariya's bedroom within her tower. How, then, had it become trapped within the monolith that stands before him?

But of course, this place, its nature… He stands in the aether, true, but he also stands in a place of Sariya's making. This is her demesne. By Sariya's hand it would have been formed and reformed until—as improbable as it seems—the tower and everything within it would have expanded, bringing into being all that surrounds him, including this monolith.

Now it is a riddle to be solved. Sariya has isolated the Atalayina, separated it from the rest, giving her time to remove the stone without damaging it. Surely she sensed the stone in the weeks after her awakening. Had she the power, she would already have retrieved it, making it clear she hasn't yet unraveled Khamal's spell. This is why she brought him here, to retrieve the Atalayina for her.

But of course, this is also a trap. Sariya will not let him have it. "I must return the stone to Ghayavand," Nasim says.

"Ghayavand is Muqallad's now. Take the stone and come with me to Galahesh."

Nasim turns in the snow and looks back through the trees the way they'd come. "There are those on Ghayavand who need me."

"Ashan?"

"Among others."

"You may think him a bright star, Khamal, but had he been alive when we were at our height, he would have shined no brighter than a wisp."

"I am not Khamal," Nasim says sharply, "and you may all have been bright— you may be bright still—but look at what has come from your radiance."

She smiles, the expression calming, so much so that Nasim grows afraid. "We can return to our greatness," she says. She isn't merely implying that they *could* return, but that they will. "But if you feel the path lies through Ghaya-vand"—she bows her head and motions to the monolith—"then so be it."

With that she turns and walks through the woods. As she passes between two larch, their branches part and the snow upon them falls soft and forgiving to the blanket of white beneath. And then she is gone, leaving Nasim alone with the wind and the tall white stone.

He waits a long time, thinking surely she watches from afar, but try as he might he cannot sense her.

With his feet still floating upon the snow, he steps forward and touches the stone's white surface. It is not cold, but warm, like a slab of obsidian at sunset.

He thought that when he found this piece of the Atalayina that it would reveal itself to him, that it would be granted when he came near. Did not Khamal plan for this, after all? He hid the stone mere days before his plans came to fruition, when Sariya and Muqallad together drove the khanjar into his chest, so why would he not have made it such that the stone would be revealed upon his return?

But of course it couldn't be as simple as that. The easier it was for him, the easier it would be for Sariya and Muqallad to retrieve it.

In the end he decides that more likely than not Khamal never meant for him to inherit any sort of key to pry the Atalayina away from its hiding place. Passing this knowledge on is difficult, but more than this, whatever he did might have been altered by the other two arqesh. For good or ill, Khamal expected that Nasim would be able to rely on the abilities he would inherit. What he hadn't anticipated was Muqallad's final spell, the one that crippled Nasim upon his birth.

The notion of being on his own—unable to rely on anything from Khamal—is freeing in a way that Nasim hadn't expected. Through his dreams and the history of the time of the sundering, he had felt responsible for Khamal, responsible for his legacy. To now be left to his own devices made it feel as though the future, at least some small part of it, now lay wholly in his hands. Not Khamal's. Not Ashan's or Nikandr's. Not even Soroush's. His own.

He touches the stone gently. The warmth after so long in the cold makes his fingers tingle. For a long time he merely listens, waits for it to tell him something—anything—of its nature, but when this proves unfruitful he tries to sense the structure of the monolith: whether the Atalayina is high or low, whether it is truly within the stone or whether this is all some ruse on Sariya's part to draw information from him. The presence of the Atalayina is strong and distinct. It is exactly as he remembered. The feeling sits deep within him, like an animal eager to leave its den. It is worry and satisfaction and hope. It is substantial, as if something weighty forms within him. It is the feeling one gets when standing on the edge of a precipice—the wonder and fear and exhilaration. These things are the Atalayina, and there is no mistaking it.

Why, then? Why is it so difficult to isolate?

It is important to realize that this place is not of the material world. It is largely a place of Sariya's making, though there *are* still pieces that are real, like Nasim himself and the Atalayina. Not knowing its true nature, Sariya has folded the stone into her world to keep it safe from everyone, even Muqallad, for despite her words, she desperately wants the stone to be hers.

He will use this to his advantage. He must, or he will never be done.

And then an idea comes to him. Instead of drawing upon a vanahezhan to try to draw it forth—which is something Sariya would have tried over and over—he summons instead a dhoshahezhan, a spirit made from the stuff of life. Of all the hezhan they are the least understood. Qiram use them to grant lift to their skiffs or to the ships of the Landed, but there is so much more that has been forgotten: the way things grow, the way they die, the way souls interacts—all of this is due to the flow of life that runs through and between them.

He uses this now and focuses not on himself, not on the stone, but on the world Sariya has created. The aether normally acts as a medium through which the hezhan can experience life in Erahm, but they are now *in* the aether, and this place is tied to Sariya herself. It isn't so difficult, then, to act as a conduit himself so that the hezhan can feed upon *Sariya*—at least this one small part of her.

He gives himself to the hezhan. It feels like sunlight running through him, or the sound of the sea, or the darkness that swallows the stars. He revels in it, for it has been so long since he has touched the hezhan without the need for another.

He feels it begin to feed on Sariya. She is here. She is everywhere. This place *is* her, and the dhoshahezhan draws upon her mightily.

He also feels—for the first time in this place—something familiar, a presence, a woman, and one he's felt before. She was on the skiff that bore him and Ashan to Ghayavand as Nikandr chased them. The Duchess of Khalakovo, their Matra, had attempted to assume him like some crow she hoped to command, and Nasim was deeper into his dreams than he'd been in a long time. There on that skiff, a woman came to save the Matra. Her name is Atiana Radieva Vostroma, and she is here now.

He wonders if Sariya can sense her. Perhaps she can. Perhaps Atiana's presence is somehow for Sariya's benefit.

Nasim, Atiana calls. *Nasim, you cannot do this.*

He wonders where she is, how she came to be here, watching him, and he knows that it cannot be without Sariya's blessing. It cannot. How else can a Landed woman, even a Matra, end up here?

He allows the dhoshahezhan to continue to feed as he focuses upon the stone. The Atalayina becomes more real. It solidifies within the stone before him.

She knows what you're doing. She's allowing it.

This gives him pause, but really, it's too late. The discomfort Sariya was feeling has risen to pain, and the Atalayina is now close enough to touch.

He reaches out with trembling fingers, but as he does, the stone loosens. It powders away as if it is made not of stone, but so much dust.

The wind heightens. The trees sway and sigh and creak. The top of the stone high above him begins to ablate. It flies like a swirl of snow at the crest of a drift. The gust becomes a gale. It swirls around the stone, sending biting sand downward into the trees, into the snow at Nasim's feet, into his face and scalp and skin.

He cowers as the wind reaches new heights.

Nasim, run!

This time, he listens. He turns and bolts through the trees, but as he does he can feel clearly for the first time the Atalayina. It is at the center of swirling sand behind him. It nearly makes him pause, but the sand has begun not only to bite, but burn. It sears his skin where it touches.

Sariya knows what's happening. She's known all along, but was waiting for Nasim to release the stone that she might have it.

But Nasim is not so young as she might think, nor as callow.

He still touches the dhoshahezhan, he still allows it to feed upon Sariya, but instead of trying to intensify this connection, he shifts it to the stone, the piece of the Atalayina that now lies behind him.

As the sand falls among the trees and the needles burst into flame, he shifts this world around the Atalayina. Sariya hopes to take it, to have it land in her very lap, but Nasim alters its course. He instead guides it toward another.

He guides it to Atiana.

If all goes well, *she* will be the one who ends up with the stone, not Sariya. He only hopes that he was wrong to have mistrusted her earlier. He hopes she is not in league with Sariya, for if she is, Sariya and Muqallad will have what they've wanted all along—all three pieces of the stone—and then they will have it remade.

The burning sand and fire have spread. Smoke chokes the forest, and the burning branches bar his way. He cannot breathe. He coughs, using his hands to fend off the heat, to fend off the branches, but it's too much.

He falls to his knees, and though he tries to crawl, he is too weak. He collapses, his lungs gasping for breath.

It is then that he hears footsteps crunching through the snow. Hands lift him and pull him onward. He can hardly breathe, his chest wracking with painful coughs, and he can see nothing, so blinded by tears and smoke are his eyes, but the hands that guide him are strong and sure, and soon he has broken through to the plain beyond the borders of the forest.

Yadhan has found him. She drags him farther and farther away, until at last he can go no more and he collapses into the snow.

He coughs until his chest hurts. His hands grow numb as they sink into the snow, but after the heat from the forest, it is a gift granted by the kindness of the fates.

Hearing the roar of the flames behind him, he rolls over, and what he sees takes his breath away.

The entire forest is ablaze. From horizon to horizon, it burns. It boils. Flames of gold and amber and rust twist and meld and part. Black smoke roils high into the sky like a wall both amorphous and impenetrable.

With Yadhan's help he manages to stand. It cannot have happened so quickly, but he reminds himself that this place is not real. What's more shocking is that Sariya tried to kill him. It was something he thought her incapable of without Muqallad at her side. Then again, if she's convinced the world is about to end one way or another, toward what extremes might she be pushed?

This, Nasim says to himself as he stares at the forest.

But at what cost? She may have thought the risk worth it, but he knows that this has cost her dearly.

Cost her dearly, indeed.

CHAPTER THIRTY-NINE

When Nasim released the rusted handle of the iron gate, he looked up to the tower and saw a fresh gap in the stone. It ran the full length of the tower—from the base, where it was wider than his hand, to the top, where it disappeared into an indiscernible crack.

Around him, he saw only the emptiness of Alayazhar. Yadhan and the boy were missing. Their souls had been freed, but their bodies were gone as well. Perhaps, he thought, they'd been taken by the other akhoz to a place they thought sacred.

A fallen form drew his attention toward the lone, dead tree in center of the tower's yard.

"Rabiah!" He ran to her and dropped to his knees. "Rabiah, please wake up!"

He recoiled the moment he touched her skin. She was cold. Her eyes stared up toward the cloudless sky and the bright, noontime sun. Her face was slack. And she looked nothing like the girl he'd known. Nothing.

He took her hand up in his and stroked it gently. He kissed the back of her hand as tears fell to the dry ground. "I've failed you in so many ways," he said to her softly. "I couldn't even get the Atalayina. It was right there in front of me."

He wanted to be strong for her, even though she was gone, but he couldn't stop himself from falling across her chest and crying until his tears ran dry.

"I'm sorry," he whispered to her. "I'm so sorry."

When he pulled his head up at last, he wasn't sure how much time had passed. His sadness had left in its wake a cold, hard anger that he hadn't felt in years, not since the days when his emotions were as out of control as the autumn winds. It was time, he thought, time to find Muqallad. He had to save Ashan and Sukharam, but he wouldn't leave Rabiah. Not here.

He looked up to the celestia on its hill above the city.

Yeh, he thought. He would bring her there, and he would build a pyre and set her to the winds.

He picked her up in his arms—by the fates, she was light—and walked up the long sloping hill toward the celestia. On his right, the ground fell away, leaving only a steep slope and a short, rocky beach before the waves of the sea stretched out toward the horizon. He remembered that beach. He had dreamed of it many times. He would go there, he decided. After he'd laid Rabiah to rest, he would go there, and the beach would whispers secrets to him.

By the time he reached the top of the hill sweat rolled down his forehead and his arms burned. He brought Rabiah to the center of the celestia's floor, where he could still see the outline of Ghayavand. As he laid her gently down, he caught movement from the corner of his eye. Standing at the edge of the stairs leading up to the celestia floor was a man wearing the ragged robes of a Maharraht. He was tall with dark hair and piercing, gray-green eyes.

It was difficult to remember the people and events from before Oshtoyets, but this man he recognized. This was Soroush, the man who had sought to use him to tear open the rift that ran through Khalakovo. In his black turban was a stone of jasper. His beard was long and black, and the earrings along his ruined left ear glinted beneath the cold winter sun. It was as it had always been, and somehow this enraged Nasim.

Before he knew what he was doing, he had stood and charged forward. He beat Soroush with his fists. Soroush gave ground, but did not otherwise defend himself. This only enraged Nasim further. He swung, over and over, pummeling Soroush's shoulders, his arms, his torso, his head, and Soroush took it all, his face calm and accepting, as if he knew this was just punishment.

In the end, Nasim couldn't keep it up. The anger in him ran deep, but it was not in him to harm others, not when they refused to raise a hand to defend themselves. He realized then, even though he'd not been with Ashan all that long, how much he'd been affected by the kindly old arqesh, and how little he'd been affected by Soroush.

Thank the fates for small favors.

Nasim's breath came in ragged gasps. "What are you doing here?" It was all he could think to say, though his emotions were still so close to boiling that his hands shook.

Soroush stared into Nasim's eyes. Nasim was not as tall as Soroush, and it made him feel insignificant. It made him feel as if he was eleven all over again. It made him feel as though the days of dreaming between the worlds had returned. It felt—staring at Soroush with sudden clarity—as if he were experiencing one of those rare moments of lucidity in his younger years, and that at any moment he would revert to being confused, to walking Adhiya and Erahm simultaneously, his mind and senses in a constant state of war.

"I asked what you were doing here," Nasim said, more forcefully.

Soroush motioned to Rabiah. "I don't know who she was—"

"Speak not of her." Nasim's fists were bunched so tightly it hurt.

"I speak not of her, but of your loss. I am sorry for it."

"Tell me how you came to be here, son of Gatha, or begone."

Soroush's jaw went rigid as he considered Nasim, perhaps wondering whether he should push Nasim or not. "I've come from Rafsuhan. It is where Muqallad has gone. Did you know this?"

"What of it?"

"He's preparing to perform a ritual to fuse two pieces of the Atalayina."

Nasim had known this, but his fingers still tingled to hear that it would happen so soon.

Soroush continued, "He's taken many children, including my son, and created more of the akhoz." Soroush's voice... It was strange. His voice was filled not with regret, but wonder, and pride. *Pride*, as if the loss of his son was somehow something he would cherish for the rest of his life.

"Do you not love your son?" Nasim asked.

Soroush's head jerked backward. "Of course I do."

"In one so vengeful as you I would have thought to find anger."

"Do not mistake my actions for vengeance, Nasim. I am an agent of change. Just as the Landed were centuries ago. It is our time now."

"Then why not let Muqallad have his way with the world?"

"Because he would undo all we see around us. He would have me believe that the world is ready for indaraqiram when it is not. To force it upon the world would be to send us back to the beginning. We would lose whatever progress we have made—however slight it might be, however grand, he would ruin it."

"As you would ruin your own life."

"I darken my soul that others' might brighten."

"You speak of the Aramahn, but what of the Maharraht? What of their lives? Their future selves? They are people as surely as those who live today, are they not?"

"I don't expect you to understand my sacrifice, Nasim. It's merely something I must do."

Light glinted from Soroush's stone of jasper. Nasim took note, not of the stone, but of his own growing awareness of Soroush's connection to Adhiya. He had been so lost in his grief of Rabiah, and then his surprise at Soroush's presence, but over the years he had become adept at telling who might be able to commune with hezhan. Soroush, he knew, had been burned. He'd had his abilities taken from him by the Aramahn for his conversion to the Maharraht's cause. His burning was a great source of shame for Soroush, and yet here he was with a stone of jasper and a clear ability to commune with the spirits of the earth.

Not only this, Nasim realized; other spirits as well, and the deeper he looked into Soroush's soul, the more he realized how wrong all of this was.

This wasn't Soroush at all, he realized.

This was Muqallad, and just like in the village by the lake, he had come to trick Nasim. He had come to fool him into believing he was something he was not.

"Can you not face me as yourself?" Nasim asked. "Did Khamal strike such fear into your heart that you would hide from *me*, a mere echo?"

Soroush's eyes narrowed. He paused, and then his face began to change. It broadened. And his ear was healed. His beard became longer and darker and squared at the end. And soon, Muqallad stood before him once more.

"Have you come for the stone?" Nasim asked. "For if you have, it is too late. It is gone from this isle, slipped from the reach of Ghayavand, slipped even from the reach of Sariya."

"Regrettable," Muqallad said, "but it will come, and there is more to discuss."

"There is nothing for us to discuss save the freeing of those you've taken."

Muqallad smiled. He seemed somehow larger than he'd been only moments ago. He seemed darker, as if his eyes could peel Nasim's skin. Muqallad took a step forward, into the circle of the celestia. This was as clear a challenge as Nasim was likely to get.

"Do you remember when you came here with Ashan and the men from the islands? I was still in the throes of the spell you'd cast upon me and Sariya." He took another step forward. "You managed to slow the world around us. You managed to banish me from this plane, send me back to the place you'd prepared for us until your return. I hardly think you even knew what you were doing then, but I wonder if you do now."

Nasim knew exactly what Muqallad was talking about—he'd thought on it often—and the truth was there had been little he'd done consciously while on this island. He'd felt as though he were walking in someone else's dream. Surely Khamal had hoped that a man in control of himself and his mind would make his way back to Ghayavand. He couldn't have been prepared for a boy who barely understood the world around him.

Muqallad approached, and Nasim could do nothing but step back. Muqallad raised his hand and Nasim froze in place. His muscles would no longer respond. Muqallad stopped when he was face-to-face with Nasim.

"You've grown in many ways, Khamal, but you are still as a babe in the ones that matter most."

Muqallad reached out and grasped Nasim's head. As soon as Muqallad's warm skin touched Nasim's ears and cheeks, pain coursed through him like a red-hot iron.

CHAPTER FORTY

Nasim's mind was lit afire. Memories played through him, things he hadn't thought of in years, things he couldn't recall ever happening to him. What Muqallad didn't realize—or disregarded—was that Nasim could read *his* thoughts as well. It was difficult to understand, but Nasim knew this: Muqallad was searching for something. He was desperate for it.

Through the haze Nasim recalled the sense of clawing from Muqallad in the depths of the village. He remembered as well his yearning to be free from the trap Khamal had laid for him when he'd last been on the island.

And then it struck him.

Muqallad was not yet free.

Khamal's trap was still in effect, and Muqallad needed to unlock its secrets to free himself from this island once and for all.

This was something Nasim could not allow. At all costs, he had to prevent Muqallad from attaining this information. But Muqallad was already getting closer. He was sifting through Nasim's dreams, his memories of Khamal. There were glimpses of Khamal's life that Nasim couldn't remember dreaming.

Time passed. Just how much Nasim had no idea, but he began to understand what Muqallad was doing, and *how* he was doing it. He could sense the hezhan Muqallad was bonded to, five of them at once.

It was these that Nasim called upon now.

He drew upon Muqallad's havahezhan to raise the wind. It blew through the celestia, pulling dust and dirt and fallen leaves into the interior of the dome. It swirled around Muqallad, confused him.

Then Nasim caused the stone beneath Muqallad's feet to soften, to become little more than mud, and the moment Muqallad sank to his ankles, he firmed the stone up once more.

He drew upon the jalahezhan to slick the surface of the celestia's floor and he used the dhoshahezhan to draw himself away from Muqallad.

But then it all stopped.

Muqallad cut him off. He knew of Nasim's limitations, and had devised his defenses accordingly.

Muqallad ripped his feet free, and the stone—solid once more—cracked and clattered and skittered over the floor. As the wind died, the leaves settled onto the wet floor like pattering rain.

"Come," Muqallad said as he neared, "I would have thought you'd *want* me to uncover these things. Is it not what you've been searching for for years?"

Nasim worked desperately to force himself to move. He railed against Muqallad's will, trying to gain access to the hezhan once more, but it was impossible. Muqallad was too aware of what he was trying to do, and he stopped him at every turn.

But then, as Muqallad tore through Nasim's mind once more, Nasim felt something—someone—at the edge of his awareness. She—for Nasim was certain the presence was a girl—reminded him of Rabiah at first. But of course that was impossible. Rabiah lay dead at the center of the celestia floor. And then he thought it was Sukharam, for who else could it be?

In a flash a vision came to him—the memory of the girl walking across the bridge toward the village's entrance. She had been leading the akhoz—he was sure of this—and yet here she was, watching as Muqallad came closer and closer to finding what he needed, and it seemed as though she was *asking* Nasim to use her abilities, *asking* him to stop Muqallad.

It seemed strange.

It felt like a trap.

But in his desperation he couldn't deny himself this chance for escape. He drew upon her, as he had with Rabiah and Sukharam, as he had Muqallad, but this time was so much easier. It was like picking up a pen to write. Like strumming the strings of a lute to make sound.

The wind came again, and this time there was nothing Muqallad could do to stop it. He was pushed away. The debris from around the celestia struck him. He fell to his knees, arms up, warding against the attack.

Nasim freed himself. It was not like he had broken bonds, but rather as if he'd *stepped to one side* and the bonds had fallen away.

Muqallad was already recovering. He drew upon his own hezhan, perhaps more than he had in decades. He was angry now. Nasim could feel it, could see it in his face. He stood and summoned water to envelope Nasim. In a flash, Nasim was pulled up from the floor until he floated within the muddy water.

He had been weakened from the pain Muqallad had inflicted, but this would not stop him. Not now.

He drew upon a vanahezhan, called it to action.

And it obeyed.

The floor shook. The columns began to crack. The sound of it resonated beneath the high dome.

Nasim demanded more.

Muqallad knew what was happening, knew that he had to leave, but Nasim drew upon a dhoshahezhan to force him to remain in place. He had not expected something that he had used so effectively against another to be used against him. He stood frozen, and the water around Nasim fell in a loud rush.

Nasim stumbled back, the ground beneath him rising and bucking, shifting and sliding. And then a crack resounded above him. It was followed by another and another. The high dome focused the sound, making what was already loud deafening.

He ran, but a chunk of stone struck his shoulder and sent him sprawling. Smaller pieces of rock and scree bit into the skin of his scalp and forehead and hands. Rock dust billowed around him, making it nearly impossible to breathe.

Gathering himself, he called upon the wind to blow the dust away. He sprinted forward as a crash moved the ground. He slipped on the slick marble floor, half crawling and half running from the crumbling structure.

As he reached the edge of the circular floor, the fluted columns nearby groaned and bowed and finally gave way. He ran as quickly as he was able, but he was still thrown forward onto the ground. It sounded as if the island itself was being swallowed by the world.

As the sound began to fade, Nasim got to his feet. Though he could sense the girl standing not fifty paces away, he found his path to Adhiya cut off.

Nasim approached her while the ruins of the celestia grumbled and groaned. The dust parted and flowed around her like a weathered stone in a long-forgotten stream.

"Who are you?" Nasim asked.

She looked over Nasim's shoulder to the destruction beyond. "He will not remain for long." She held out her hand to him and turned, waiting.

"Where do we go?"

"Do you not wish to find your friends?"

"Who are you?"

"Kaleh. Now come," she said, shaking her hand for him and glancing again toward the ruined celestia.

He took it, and together they ran. Fear drove them, and it took little time to reach the streets of Alayazhar and to pass beyond Sariya's broken tower, but they had gone only halfway through the city when they heard a resounding boom from the hill behind them. Nasim turned and saw on the celestia's hill, above the shattered remains of the buildings, a pillar of dust flying high into the air.

They pushed themselves harder after this. Nasim was too worried to speak, to ask Kaleh questions. He felt as though breaking the silence would also break this spell of good fortune and reveal it to be yet another trap.

Kaleh was just as silent, though whether this was simply her nature or a symptom of her own fear he didn't know.

They raced through the city and reached the outskirts. The road through the hills led them up toward the peaks and the bridge that led to the village. The bridge itself, tall and white and ill kept, was empty. It looked fragile, as if adding their weight to it would force its collapse. As they crossed, holding hands, Nasim looked down toward the river, to the place he and Rabiah had run from the akhoz. It felt strange to be looking down upon it, walking on the bridge with the same girl he'd seen from that lower vantage. It felt as if he'd allied himself with Muqallad, as if Rabiah's death had been a plan in which he'd played an integral part, and each step he took cemented these feelings until it felt like little more than betrayal.

"I'm sorry," he whispered.

"What?" Kaleh asked.

"Nothing."

They entered the village and wended their way down through the tunnels. Nasim did not see any of the akhoz, but he could feel them lurking in the darkness. They did not bar their way, however. It made this strange situation feel even more surreal, and soon Nasim couldn't take the silence any longer.

"Why are you helping me?" he asked.

"Because Muqallad is using me. He would use you as well, and that, at least for now, I will not allow."

"*How* is he using you?"

"You of all people should know. You were what gave him the clues he needed."

"Clues to what?"

"Finding the way Adhiya and Erahm are linked."

"They are linked through the aether."

"That doesn't answer the question of *how* they're linked."

"Then tell me."

She pulled him down a tunnel where several siraj stones lit the way from sconces set into the walls. "That I cannot say."

"Why not?"

"Because I don't yet know whether I will allow Muqallad to use me further."

"You have a choice?"

"Do you?" she asked, her eyes flat and judgmental.

"I don't know."

"And neither do I." They came to the doors. "Get them, quickly. Muqallad is coming."

Before Nasim could move, he heard the braying of one of the akhoz, far in the distance. It was picked up moments later by others, dozens of them. They were closing in already.

Nasim took a siraj from a sconce and went to the nearest door, which opened at his touch. Inside, sleeping, was Sukharam. He stood from his bed of matted hay, blinking at the light.

"Come," Nasim said. "We have little time."

Sukharam's eyes were wild with fear, darting to the hall behind Nasim, and yet he stood his ground. "What of Rabiah?"

Nasim waved him to leave the room. "Not now, Sukharam."

"Where *is* she?"

"She's gone, Sukharam. Dead. Killed in Sariya's tower."

Sukharam lowered his arm, allowing the light to strike him full in the face. His look of anger became one of disgust, a mirror of Nasim's own feelings.

The wails of the akhoz approached. They sounded hungry, and it made Nasim's stomach turn. "We must *go*, Sukharam!"

Sukharam walked past Nasim, the cold air of the tunnels wafting by as he did so. "We'll speak of this again."

Nasim rushed into the next room. Ashan was lying on the floor, his face a mass of cuts and bruises and half-healed burns. Soroush was already standing, and looked as though he'd received no ill treatment whatsoever. Seeing him next to Ashan, who looked as though he'd been beaten for weeks, was strange indeed.

Soroush and Sukharam slipped Ashan's arms around their shoulders and half carried, half dragged him from the room.

"This way," Kaleh said as she continued down the tunnel. There, however, they came to a dead end.

"What have you done?" Nasim cried.

"Be quiet," Kaleh said. With a touch of her finger, a small hole opened in the wall and widened.

Behind them, the akhoz rounded the corner. They went mad when they spied the five of them.

The hole widened until it looked like the open maw of an earthen beast.

"Step inside," Kaleh said. "Quickly."

They did, without hesitation. As soon as the last of them were in, the walls began closing in again. The world darkened, and the stone pressed in around them.

Sukharam shouted in fright.

Nasim's last thought was that Kaleh had betrayed them.

What followed was darkness and a freezing embrace as the cold stone pressed ever more surely against their frames. Nasim could not draw breath. He could not move.

A panic as deep as the earth had just begun to set when the earth shifted——and opened before them.

Light flooded into the space, making Nasim cringe like a newborn.

Ahead was a short, earthen tunnel that led to a forest of white birch. Nasim could see the trunks and the bed of fallen leaves that covered the forest floor.

"By the fates, where are we?" Sukharam asked.

In a croaky, long-neglected voice, Soroush replied, "We are returned to Rafsuhan."

CHAPTER FORTY-ONE

Nikandr waited in the dark halls of Ashdi en Ghat, listening for the sound of footfalls. He heard them at last near midnight, the hour at which the Maharraht changed watches. One man—one of Bersuq's most trusted—walked past with a siraj stone hanging from a leather cord. He turned his head toward the hallway where Nikandr lay in wait, but then continued on as if he'd seen nothing, as if he didn't know that Nikandr was there.

"Is it time already?" the guard further down the hall asked.

"*Neh*," said the other, "but I haven't been able to sleep in days. Go. Get some rest. The ships will most likely return tomorrow."

A pause. "What will become of *them*?"

"To that you already know the answer."

When the first guard spoke again, his voice was lower. "There are times when I think Thabash's arrival was an ill omen."

"Silence," hissed the one who had carried the stone past Nikandr. "Rahid has ears everywhere."

"But sending ships to attack our own…"

"They weren't sent to attack, merely to return the children that were taken away."

"If you believe that, you're a fool."

"I do believe them."

A short laugh echoed down the hall. "Listen to the words of Bersuq if you must—listen even to Rahid's—but do not try to tell me that no harm was meant to those who fled."

"We lead the life we lead."

"We do, but why is it we must kill even amongst ourselves?"

There was a long, uncomfortable silence.

"Go. Find rest. You'll think better under the light of the morning sun."

Footsteps approached Nikandr's position again. He made himself small as

270 • Bradley P. Beaulieu

the Maharraht approached. "This will look no better under the sun," he said. "It may in fact look worse." He passed the tunnel entrance with no stone in his hand, and soon his footsteps had faded.

All was silent for a time, then sounds came of the remaining soldier pacing further and further away in the opposite direction.

The light, however, remained.

With cautious steps Nikandr made his way forward, finding the siraj sitting on the stone floor of the cool, vacant tunnel. He picked up the siraj and made his way deeper, taking the directions Jahalan had given him earlier that day, and at last he came to a door set into the wall of the tunnel. He turned the handle and swung it soundlessly inward.

Resting on three pallets were his men: Styophan and Avil and Mikhalai. They looked to the doorway not with fear, but something akin to it. No doubt they understood that something was about to happen.

"It is well that you're here, My Lord Prince," Styophan said in Anuskayan. "Are we to leave?"

"*Da*, the three of you will go, and quickly." Nikandr hugged Styophan and kissed his cheeks. "You will take the *Chaika* and return word of these events to Khalakovo."

Styophan sent a confused glance back at Avil and Mikhalai. "My Lord Prince, we cannot leave you here. There's talk of the Hratha returning."

"I know, but I cannot leave."

"Then we stay as well."

"*Nyet*," Nikandr said, raising his voice as loud as he dared among these tunnels. "Khalakovo has need of you. The Grand Duchy as well. There will be need of ships, and soon. But first, you will return to Ranos. Tell him what has happened here. Bid him send no men, and tell him I will return to Khalakovo as soon as I'm able."

"You try to heal them, My Lord, but they don't deserve it. They—"

"I will not speak of it!" Nikandr's words echoed off into the distance. "Believe me when I say this is necessary. Ranos must understand what is happening. He must know of Muqallad and the rift. Tell him, and tell him to speak with the Aramahn. We will need their guidance in the weeks ahead."

Styophan looked into Nikandr's eyes, anxious, but willing to do as Nikandr bid him. "What will you do?"

"If I'm able, I will heal. If I'm not, I will leave."

They both held the other's gaze, knowing that in all likelihood it wasn't in Nikandr's power to do this. With Thabash came a singular mind, no matter that some of the Maharraht may doubt his purpose.

Styophan stepped in and hugged Nikandr. "Fare well, My Lord."

"And you," Nikandr said.

He hugged and kissed Avil and Mikhalai as well, and then they were off, taking the turns Nikandr gave them to reach the upper exit from the village.

Nikandr returned to the place where he'd found the stone and set it down.

"You should have gone with them."

Nikandr spun around and found the guard who had walked past him, the man Bersuq had sent to clear the way while Nikandr freed his men. He was one of the older Maharraht. Grizzled. Though most of his face was hidden in shadow, his eyes twinkled as he studied Nikandr.

"You no doubt heard my answer."

"I did, but why would you consider such a thing for a boy that will most likely turn no matter what you do?"

Nikandr stepped forward and placed the stone into the man's hand. "Have you so lost your way that you need to ask me the question?"

The Maharraht swallowed, incensed, but he stood taller a moment later. "I know *why*, I merely question why *you* would do it."

"He is only a boy," Nikandr said.

"Who will grow up to become your enemy."

Nikandr, after one last pause, turned and walked away. "Perhaps he will."

Nikandr, kneeling at the shore of the lake, touched Wahad's shoulders.

Nikandr represented wind.

Near Wahad's feet were Jahalan and Zanhalah, the old woman who had helped him with Wahad before.

Together they represented water and life.

The two others—a man and woman who had fathered three children together—kneeled by Wahad's arms.

They were fire and earth, and they completed the circle.

Ever since returning from Siafyan and his encounter with the akhoz, Nikandr had considered the approach of bringing only the opposing elements of water and air against the fire that raged inside Wahad. Though he didn't wish to discount the wisdom of these qiram, he found the strategy lacking. The boy was being taken by a suuraqiram—it seemed that it would take all of the elements, not just those opposing, in order to save him.

The dying children had been moved far away in hopes of giving Nikandr and the others the room they needed to complete their ritual, but their coughs, their moans, could still be heard. This didn't bother Nikandr. If anything, it was a simple reminder of why he was doing this, one that did not fluster, but in fact *calmed* him. Thoughts of Atiana and Galahesh and Khalakovo and his mother and his father had hounded him in the hours since his men had escaped, but the moment he'd reached the cavern of the lake, he had calmed. The sounds of pain from these children had allowed him to push all the other thoughts away, until all that remained was a singular focus toward a singular aim.

Save one child.

He stared down at Wahad, brushed the hair back from his forehead. His skin was hot to the touch, but he did not sweat. His eyes were closed, as they had been for days, and there was a crust over them. They had tried once to open his eyes, and Wahad had thrashed and struggled against the men holding him and beat his head against the ground. They'd released him shortly after, and he'd cried and moaned for hours afterward.

Nikandr brushed Wahad's hair one last time.

Just one, he thought. That was all he wished for.

"Let us begin," he said.

Together, they closed their eyes.

Nikandr calmed himself, breathed deeper. He felt the touch of his vana-hezhan on the far side of the aether, and through this bond he drew himself deeper into its world, drew it deeper into his. Other than this one spirit, he'd rarely felt another hezhan, but now he felt all four of those that were near. He suspected it was because of the rift and how wide it had grown on Rafsuhan, perhaps especially so here in Ashdi en Ghat on the shores of the lake.

He did not ignore these other hezhan, but he focused his mind primarily on Wahad, on the pain he was feeling. After a time, he felt heat, like the touch of the sun on those rare days of summer when the wind was low. The feeling heightened until it was more like the heat from a bonfire burning nearby. Still it built, and he allowed it to take him.

He wanted to scream, so strong was the sensation, but he did not. He simply accepted it, allowed it to *become* him. He could feel the hezhan that was taking over Wahad's soul now. It was impossible not to once he knew what to look for. It was not merely sharing the experience of life in Erahm, as most hezhan were content to do. It was devouring him.

But there was more. The boy was devouring the hezhan as well. They were becoming part of one another. They were forging something new from the substance of their souls.

Nikandr let the knowledge wash over him, as well as the fear that followed, and soon he felt as though *he* were the one being devoured, not Wahad.

The sun is bright among the walkways of Siafyan. Wahad takes them toward the home of Mehjoor, who is to join him on his watch. He stops short, however, when he sees the girl, Kaleh, at the end of the swaying bridge.

She stands in his way, staring at him with a look of challenge, as if *she* ruled here, not the Maharraht who had been on this land for forty years.

"What?" he asks, though he feels ungracious in being so blunt. In truth he knows her not at all, only that she came with the tall one, Muqallad.

"Come with me," she replies, and with that she turns and walks away.

He hesitates for only a moment. She has done this before—spoken to children around the village, brought them to see the man that everyone assumes is her father. When they returned, they would not speak of their time with him. They would only say that they were sworn to secrecy, but Mehjoor and Wahad hide nothing from one another. Eventually Mehjoor spoke of his visit with Muqallad, of standing before him, of hearing his words.

"What words?" Wahad asked.

Mehjoor would not reply, but Wahad thought it was not because he chose not to, but because he couldn't remember. Such is Muqallad's power, and it makes Wahad fear him, but he cannot refuse this summons. Things are happening to the village; things are happening to the Maharraht. Everyone can feel it. Surely the rise of the Maharraht and the fall of the Landed is nearly upon them.

They climb down the curving stairs built into the side of the great trees to reach the ground. From there, Kaleh heads south. When they enter the village circle, Bersuq is standing there with Thabash and Rahid and several others from the south. Thabash hardly notices him. Rahid watches with something akin to hunger. But Bersuq...

Wahad nearly stops, but he doesn't want Bersuq to know what he sees in his eyes. And yet at the same time Wahad doesn't understand, for Bersuq is looking upon him with pity.

Pity.

Why? Why does Bersuq, the man who is hardest on him—especially since his father is still in the arms of the Aramahn—look upon him with *pity*? He had thought these visits to Muqallad some sort of honor, or perhaps some sort of test. But if that were so, Bersuq would look upon him with pride, or if not that he wouldn't look upon him at all. He certainly wouldn't look upon him with pity.

The expression leaves as quickly as it came, and Bersuq speaks in low tones with Thabash and the others. Rahid continues to watch, however. It makes Wahad shiver.

Eventually they move beyond the borders of the village square, and then the village itself. They hike through the forest, through the shorter larch and pine that cover the land here, and soon Wahad's nerves are starting to tingle.

"Where do we go?"

Kaleh glances back, but does not otherwise respond.

He grabs her arm and spins her around. "Where do we go?"

"To the clearing."

"Why?"

She stares up at him, her blue eyes bright. "You do not have to come."

He pauses. "I merely wish to know why. Why is it kept secret?"

"You can ask Muqallad when you see him."

"I'm asking you."

Her eyes are hard, but as she studies him they soften. She glances over her shoulder, toward Siafyan, and then licks her lips. "The end is near, Wahad. Very near. Muqallad is choosing those who will be granted the honor of leading the way." She peers into his eyes. "Are you ready for such a thing?"

Wahad pulls himself straighter. "Of course I am."

Kaleh smiles sadly. "We all think this. But there are trials ahead, and when they come it is not so easy to remain steadfast. To remain silent."

"I am ready. I've been ready since my naming day."

"You will become one of the chosen, you and the others who've already gone. You will pave the way for what is to come." Her look becomes sober. "It requires sacrifice."

Though he tries to control it, Wahad finds his breath coming faster. His fingers tingle, and his chin quivers. A mix of fear and elation runs through him, something he's never experienced and has no idea how to handle.

"I'm ready," he says again, glad that his teeth do not chatter as he speaks these words.

"There's no turning back once you enter the clearing."

"I understand."

She seems to measure him, but then nods. "Then come, and no more questions."

They reach the clearing, the one used most often for mid-winter vigils. Within it stands Muqallad, wearing light robes and boots of soft, white leather. His robes are brightly colored, and he is tall and muscular. He looks young—younger than Wahad's own father—and yet his gaze is ancient, as old as the earth he treads upon.

Wahad feels small. He feels as though he stands before one of the fates, not a man like his father or his uncle.

"Has she prepared you?" Muqallad asks.

"*Yeh.*"

"This is no easy thing I ask of you," Muqallad says.

Wahad shakes his head. "It is. My lives have been led so that I could arrive at this moment. I am sure of it."

Muqallad smiles. And shows Wahad a blue stone he holds in the palm of one hand. "This, Wahad Soroush al Qediah, is one piece of the Atalayina. Do you know of it?"

Wahad stares, confused at first, but then elation fills him and threatens to bubble over. He grips his hands to keep himself from looking like a small child before his grandfather. "I do."

"Tell me what you know."

"The Atalayina was the first stone, and it will be the last. It was created by the fates, each of them shedding one tear to create the three pieces. It was taken to the shores on Ghayavand and lost during the sundering."

Wahad seems pleased. "Good," he says simply. "This is but one, and I will soon have the other two. And you, Wahad, will help unite them."

He begins walking to the center of the clearing. Wahad follows, more nervous than ever now that the moment draws near. He dearly wishes to ask questions, but does not. Muqallad will tell him what he needs to know. Of this he is sure.

Muqallad stops in the center of the clearing and faces Wahad. "Spread your arms wide."

Wahad obeys.

"Look to the sky."

Wahad does.

Blue shines through among tall white clouds. They are majestic, towering. They are vengeful, not out of spite, but justice. It is proper, Wahad decides. This day has always been the right day for this.

Muqallad raises the piece of the Atalayina. Wahad's breath comes faster and faster, and nothing he does seems to quell it.

"There are difficult days ahead, Wahad."

The blue stone arcs down toward Wahad's forehead. Though it has not yet touched his skin, he can feel it—the power within, the power it draws from within *him*. He can feel as well the walls of the world growing thin. He can feel a hunger from beyond the veil, a hunger deeper than he ever expected.

"At times you will feel confused and lost, but cast these doubts aside."

The stone touches his forehead.

"You are bringing the world to its proper end."

The world rips.

And Wahad screams.

A searing brand touches his soul and fills him. Unbidden, his hands bunch into fists. His arms tighten until they shake. His body spasms in the throes of pain that wash over him and through him.

It is a thing more beautiful than he has ever beheld, has ever experienced.

He realizes that this is what it must be like. This is what vashaqiram feels like for those who achieve it. So few have done so, and yet Muqallad, fates bless him, is bringing this to them all.

He is a man to be honored.

A man to be cherished.

He is the one who will bring the world to its final resting place, as the fates have decreed.

Soon the pain begins to fade, begins to ebb, begins to shed from his soul like water. All too soon it is gone, and he begins to cry.

He wishes for more. Already he aches for it.

Muqallad touches his shoulder, and only then does he realize he is hunched over, hands on his knees, supporting himself as his lungs heave and tears shed from his eyes.

"Stand, Wahad."

For long moments he cannot. The beauty. Gone. Gone...

"*Stand.*"

He does, and he stares into Muqallad's strong face and knowing eyes.

"Do not fear," he says. "The end is near. Return to the village now. Go about your life. You will feel drawn here, but do not come again. Not until it is time."

Wahad nods and turns to leave. He makes it to the edge of the clearing.

"Wahad?" Muqallad calls.

He turns.

"Speak of this to no one."

He leaves, knowing that this final command will be the most difficult to obey—not withholding the knowledge from those who do not know, but not speaking of it to those who *do*.

He would share this. He would ask them of their experience and share with them his own. He would ask them if they, too, hunger for more.

In the end, as he walks away from the clearing, he resolves himself to his fate, and as the gnawing feeling in the pit of his stomach grows, he relishes it, for it is a reminder of what he has seen.

And what is yet to come.

CHAPTER FORTY-TWO

Nikandr woke, though it was long moments before the notion of who he was and where he was had any meaning. These dreams were very much like the ones he'd had of Khamal through Nasim, but they felt much more real, much more present, perhaps because they were Wahad's own memories.

He knew already that he had failed to heal Wahad. Wahad, unlike so many of those with the wasting, did not *want* to be saved, and without that help there was nothing he could do.

At Wahad's feet, Jahalan stirred. The others did as well, but Nikandr waited until Jahalan met his eyes. "Did you see?"

Jahalan nodded. He looked to the others, who did not answer, but they had shocked looks on their faces. Perhaps they had worked out Wahad's past already, and Muqallad's involvement in it, but to see it for themselves was something else entirely.

At the entrance to the cavern, there was a commotion. A group of a dozen men, led by Rahid, strode in amongst the Maharraht children and those tending them. Bersuq was not with them, which was reason enough to give Nikandr pause, but then he realized who the man walking next to Rahid would be. This was Thabash Kaspar al Meliyah. Nikandr knew him by reputation only, but had never seen him until Wahad's dream, and now he had returned to Rafsuhan. He was at least ten years Nikandr's senior, but he was built like a bull. Despite his physical appearance, it was his eyes that stood out the most. They were nearly as dark as his clothes, which along with his reddish beard gave him the appearance of an animal of the night with wide, searching eyes that could dig into one's soul if he wasn't careful.

Nikandr found his fingers itching to hold a sword, or better yet a pistol.

As Rahid and the others came near, he stood, as did the four other qiram with him. Jahalan raised his hands, but it was Zanhalah, the old woman who had shared with him the name of her son, that stepped in Rahid's path.

"He has come to heal."

Rahid stopped only for a moment. In a blink he raised his hand and struck Zanhalah across the cheek so hard that she spun and collapsed to the ground. Jahalan moved to help her, but Rahid grabbed him and shoved him away. Jahalan stumbled on the sandy shore and fell as Rahid rounded on Zanhalah.

"They are not *sick*. They are chosen."

"They are *tainted*," Zanhalah said, "touched by a man who failed to destroy one island, and so has come to try again."

Rahid pulled the khanjar from his belt and made to move toward Zanhalah, but it was Thabash that grabbed his hand and held him.

"Now is not the time for judgment," Thabash said. "Nor is it the time for punishment."

"I have suffered this"—he waved his hand about the cavern as if to implicate the whole of Ashdi en Ghat—"long enough."

"Their time will come, but not here, and not now. The children are nearly ready."

Rahid stared at Thabash's hand and ripped his arm away. Then he sheathed his knife and stalked back toward the stairs. Three of the Maharraht that had accompanied him followed.

Thabash stepped forward and faced Nikandr. He was shorter than Nikandr, but more heavily built.

"You are the son of Duke Khalakovo?" Thabash asked.

"I am."

"And you have come to heal these children."

"In a way."

"What way?"

"I came to learn more of the rifts. These children were here, suffering, and I thought it my duty to help them if I could."

"Your *duty*..."

Nikandr said nothing, which only seemed to anger Thabash.

"Your father sent you, then?"

"He did not."

"Of course," he said, pacing in front of Nikandr. "Your father is still an honored guest in Galostina. Surely, then, your mother sent you."

"She did not."

"Is that so? Is she still hidden away in the bowels of Iramanshah?"

Again Nikandr did not speak. He did not like how very much Thabash knew, but he wasn't surprised. The Maharraht had spies everywhere, and many of those in Iramanshah knew of his mother's presence.

"It's interesting how often we hear that we lost that day on Duzol, that you stopped Soroush from completing his goal, but what you fail to understand is that there is never a single goal in what we do, and that the fates watch over us, no matter how low the Landed might bring us."

"To say that we bring you low are the words of a fool," Nikandr replied. "You bring yourselves low."

Thabash stopped his pacing. "Do you think yourself above us because you've come, as you say, to heal?"

"I merely wish to save those that can be saved."

"And if they don't wish to be saved? Were you to heal any one of these children, they would spit upon you for the curse you've laid at their feet. They would tell you that they went willingly, and that to bring them back would be an indelible stain upon their soul."

Nikandr could only think of Wahad, how proud he was of Muqallad's faith in him. "They were lied to."

Nikandr could tell that these words made Thabash bristle, but he could not simply attack. There was a battle being waged here in Ashdi en Ghat for the minds of everyone involved. Few knew the truth, but many suspected Thabash and even Muqallad were leading them astray.

"They were not lied to. They were freed. Freed to make their own choice. Freed to bring this world to a higher place and a higher plane."

"They were given no choice. What could they choose but to please Muqallad? He is no savior, Thabash. He spells our doom, not just the Landed, but all of us."

Thabash waited for those words to settle over those nearby, waited for the echoes to die. "Not our doom, son of Iaros. Our *salvation*." He motioned to the men behind him, at which point they strode forward and took Nikandr and Jahalan by the arms. "And you will have a chance to see it firsthand. At the equinox, these children will allow Muqallad to take another step forward, and Muqallad has asked that you be there to see it so that when you die, you will know the fate of this earth. You will know the fate of the world beyond."

"He doesn't care for the Landed."

"*Neh*, he does not, but of *you* he cares. You, the chosen of Khamal."

"Khamal did not choose me."

Thabash's eyes opened wide. "You're blinded if you believe it was luck."

"Blind or not, Khamal is nothing to me."

"Nothing?" Thabash asked. "The two of you are bound so tightly in this life that there can be little doubt you were bound in another." He waved his hand, and the men hauled Nikandr by the arms.

Looking back, Nikandr saw Thabash standing over Wahad. Wahad could not see him anymore—most likely he would never open his eyes again—but somehow he knew Thabash was there, for he was shaking his head back and forth. When he began to pound his hands against the stone, Nikandr could watch no more, and soon he had lost sight of the cavern altogether.

Before he was placed in a cell, Nikandr's soulstone was taken from him. When the soldiers left, they took the light and locked the heavy wooden door behind them. The light from their siraj bobbed as they left, growing dimmer and dimmer, until all was darkness.

He lay on the pallet he'd been given, wondering where they'd taken Jahalan. It was likely they'd brought him to another cell somewhere else in the village, but it was just as likely that they'd simply asked him to leave, or allowed him to stay as long as he agreed to interfere no longer.

It was a symptom of their grief that they dealt with the Landed ruthlessly, and yet treated the Aramahn with respect, even reverence. The Maharraht claimed they were doing this for their brothers and sisters who could not find it in themselves to take the same path they did. They didn't hold it against the Aramahn for not taking up arms—the Aramahn, after all, were the ones they were trying to protect. It was not *in* the Maharraht to harm them as long as they didn't stand in their way.

Whether Jahalan remained or not, it didn't change the fact that something momentous was about to happen. It was clear that Muqallad had been working for months, perhaps years, toward this very thing. The girl, Kaleh. The beating hearts in the wilderness. The fire in the clearing. And now the children who were slowly but surely being consumed.

He couldn't help but think that if he could have healed one of the akhoz—just one—he could have swayed opinions, enough to overpower the men from the south, who, though smaller in number, seemed to be exerting undue influence over their brethren from the north.

And yet Wahad had been so adamant in his beliefs. He had believed everything Kaleh and Muqallad had fed him, and this was a thing that would build upon itself. When a select few children believed that Muqallad was their savior, more would believe, and that in turn would make more follow, until all that remained were silent skeptics.

If only he could show Wahad what *he* had seen.

But he could not. He was too late to save them, and now he was powerless to stop Muqallad.

When morning came, the men who came for Nikandr—seven of them—all wore the black robes of the Hratha. They put manacles around his wrists and hobbled his legs with rope. They did not allow him his cherkesska, but instead forced him to wear only his pants and shirt and boots. They pushed him from the village and walked him southward. There were others far ahead on the road that did not wear the dark robes of the south. Surely this was something momentous. The plans Muqallad had been making were coming to fruition.

Nikandr watched for someone, anyone, he might be able to speak to. He watched the road behind, hoping a parent of one of the children would catch up with them—until the Hratha nearest him thought ill of it and struck him on the back of the head with the hilt of his dagger.

Nikandr cringed, expecting another blow, but the man only held the gleaming blade close to Nikandr's face and said, "Look again, and I use the other end."

Nikandr was careful to make sure the man was busy with something else before stealing a glance behind, but he never saw anyone. He assumed they would be the last to reach Siafyan.

They came to a rest only once. With his stone taken, he was unable to ignore the cold so easily. He shivered as three of the men broke away and began speaking in low tones. They had been in Ashdi en Ghat since Nikandr had arrived. Surely they were either loyal to Rahid, or at the very least not favored by Thabash. That they were speaking alone gave him no comfort at all.

They did not rest long, and soon they were into the defile and heading through the woods toward the tall trees of Siafyan. When they neared the village, Nikandr could feel a distinct demarcation. It was a subtle thing—no more than a slight pressing within his chest, a souring of the tongue—but he knew immediately what it was. It was the ring of hearts around the clearing. They felt stronger and fouler than before.

As they continued, the feeling grew, until Nikandr became nauseous from it. He stole glances at the men around him. They did not seem to show it on their faces, and he wondered whether it was only he that could feel it.

As they moved through the village, Nikandr felt watched. He looked up to the walkways, to the windows worked into the trees, but he found nothing and no one. Still, his skin crawled, until finally they moved beyond and into the trees once more.

When they came to the clearing, however, his heart stopped.

Sitting within the ashes and bones of the fire were dozens of tall wooden posts spaced in three concentric rings. Chained to these were the children. Many towns of the Grand Duchy did such thing to murderers and rapists. The convicted men were strung high for all to see, to spit upon as they froze to death, but what had these children done to deserve such punishment? Nothing more than being of a certain age and having the misfortune of being born Maharraht.

Strangely, the children were all facing inward, toward the center. Their faces had transformed in the past day. Their eyes were now completely closed over. Many of them still had their hair, but from the patches of skin Nikandr could see along their scalps it was clearly falling out in tufts.

They were no longer moaning, either. They hung, their arms at painfully awkward angles, without uttering a sound. The silence was eerie. It made his skin crawl. Worse than the silence, though, was the distinct impression that the children knew the end was near.

And that they welcomed it with open arms.

CHAPTER FORTY-THREE

Atiana waits in the dark, willing Ishkyna to hurry. Her awareness is drawn outward until it encompass the Shattering, where her body— along with Ishkyna and Ushai—lies in an ancient and abandoned stone pool. Other than the streltsi who guard the building, there are very few Baressans brave enough to live in the Shattering, but even they stay along the edges, afraid to step too far into the cursed lands.

Atiana's awareness expands even further, until she's pulled toward the straits. It is difficult to remain near the Shattering, but it is important that she do so to guide Ishkyna and prevent her from losing herself, and so it is with a growing sense of unease over the strength of the swirling aether around the straits that she strengthens her footing until she *can* remain close. About Ushai she is not as worried; while she is young in her craft, she has managed the dark here in Baressa before.

At last Ishkyna's presence comes to her, tentative and scared. It is so unlike her sister that Atiana nearly loses control. That one moment of weakness is all it takes. The weight of the city presses in, and it is all she can do to control it. As she restores her tentative balance, her senses become more attuned, and she realizes there is one place in particular that presses her the most.

The tower.

Sariya's tower.

The fear within her grows, and her balance is once again thrown off. Like a hulled ship taking on water, she begins to list, leaving her vulnerable to the growing strength of the waves.

Soon the tower is the one thing she can focus on. The only thing. She is being drawn toward it. This is Sariya's doing—a trap set for the unwise, the unskilled in the dark—and yet knowing this does her no good. She is power-less to prevent it.

But then she feels Ishkyna's touch, feels her guiding hand. She feels Ushai's as well. Even though she cannot pull her attention away from the pure white of the tower against the blackened landscape of the aether, her awareness begins to expand.

Like a drowning woman, she clings to the lessons of her mother. She strengthens her bonds with the other two. Together—especially as close as they are to one another in the physical world—they are able to do so quickly. She can already tell that Ushai is unskilled in this, but not so unskilled as Atiana might have guessed. She has come far.

This is ... difficult, she hears Ishkyna say.

Atiana expected a biting response from her, an admonishment over her lack of control, but instead here is Ishkyna, humbled.

You become used to it, but the influence of the straits is stronger today, so take care.

I can feel the tower even now, Ishkyna says.

Da. She is there, waiting for us.

The fear within Ishkyna and Ushai grows. Atiana can feel it like a glowing brand moving closer to her skin.

Do not worry, Atiana says. *We are prepared.*

Before they begin, Atiana reaches out to the south, toward Vostroma. She feels the other Matri there, waiting. She does little more than this. It is understood that they will approach Galahesh en masse at this signal.

Atiana waits, holding tight to Ishkyna and Ushai for the time being, until she feels the attention of the tower shift. The pressure on her fades, and she knows that Sariya has taken the bait.

We go, Atiana says.

They move as one toward the tower.

It is a beacon that stands upon the Mount, staring down over the city below. The emotions of so many people—more than Atiana has ever experienced at once—come to her. They assail her, and again it is Ishkyna more than Ushai that provides shelter against this unexpected storm.

What's wrong? Ishkyna asks.

I don't know, Atiana replies.

Ushai and Ishkyna have ceded control to her. There is no other choice—they aren't strong enough to lead—but her inability to master the aether, even knowing how turbulent the straits are, scares her. This day of all days she cannot allow her mind to betray her.

Beyond the tower, the ceremony at the bridge is about to begin. There are wooden cranes and scaffolding at the gap, which is now only several yards wide. Four keystones swing beneath the armature of the cranes, awaiting the masons who stand stoically nearby to lower them into place. A pavilion stands on the southern side of the gap, its canvas walls blowing in the gusting wind. A gathering of thirty nobles stand within it, waiting as Bahett delivers to them a speech.

Atiana feels Ishkyna tug upon her. *Come, sister. It is time.*

The tower is difficult to approach. Rather than shy away from it, however, Atiana opens herself to it. If it wishes to shed light, she will let it. She allows it to fall upon her, allows it to fall upon the others as well, and when she does, she finds it bearable.

She approaches the tower wall, and though there is part of her that pleads for caution, she ignores it. She is done listening to her fears.

The structure of the tower is echoed here in the aether, but she realizes that it is also echoed beyond the veil, in the world of Adhiya. Never has she seen such a thing, and she wonders how Sariya could have created it.

She is born of a different age, Ishkyna says.

And wise beyond our reckoning, Ushai echoes.

This is something she must remember if she is to continue.

As she passes through the wall, she knows she is doing something that cannot be undone; she has taken a step into a world of Sariya's making. Sariya herself is here. She sleeps in a bed at the top of the tower. She is alone—unguarded—which gives Atiana pause.

Atiana moves to the bedside. Looking upon Sariya is unsettling. She has looked upon Matri as they tread the dark, but this is strangely different. The Matri are her sisters. Even Ushai—though Aramahn—follows the ways of the Matri that have been passed down from generation to generation. Sariya is something else entirely. She is a woman who has lived to see centuries pass. She was trapped on Ghayavand for most of those years and knows little of the world as it is today. She knows more of the old world, the world she left behind—that and the never-ending nightmare of her time while trapped on Ghayavand.

The strikingly beautiful woman lying on the bed seems foreign. Not at all like Mother, or Mileva, or Saphia. She is more like a wasp—venomous and filled with ill intent.

It is then that Atiana realizes Ishkyna and Ushai are no longer with her. She immediately expands her awareness, searching for them, the terror of the early moments of the aether returning to her.

She cannot allow this. This is but the first of the traps Sariya has laid for her. The worst thing she can do is to give in to her own fears. And yet already she can sense nothing outside the tower. She can feel neither the Matri nor the straits. She cannot feel the city, the bridge. She cannot feel Father.

She can feel Sariya, however. Her mind is focused to the northeast, toward

Ghayavand. Within that room in the tower, Atiana moves to the window facing north. It looks out over a wide sea.

Atiana touches the glass.

And it is bitterly cold.

She turns.

And the world around her has taken shape. The walls of stone are gray. The sky outside is blue. The blanket upon the bed is a rich brown.

She knows she's been taken by Sariya—taken by her tower—and she has no idea how to return. This creates a sudden need to leave this place. She feels it in her throat, a tightening that takes hold and threatens to cut off her air. She swallows and runs down the spiraling stairs. She picks up her pace, faster and faster until she's flying down them to the lowest floor where a thick, ironbound door bars her passage to the outside.

She pulls the handle, but the door refuses to yield. She tries again and again, jerking at the handle, and all the while, welling up inside her is a fear that she will fall to the cold stone floor and never wake up.

She tries once more, not yanking, but pulling with all her might, and at last the door groans open and she is out into the cold, fresh air.

She sprints away from the tower, her feet thumping through the thick cover of snow. She does not stop, but continues into the nearby woods until at last the tower is lost from view. Only then does she pull up, gasping for breath, steadying herself against the rough bark of an ancient larch.

The forest—now that she's able to consider it—stands serene. The wind blows, cold and biting, and yet she herself is not cold. The trunks of the trees sway, they creak. The sound is sharp and confusing, as if there is some infernal purpose behind it.

She heads northeast. She knows not why.

The way is slow, even beneath the trees, for the snow is thick. She tires as she trudges her way down a gentle slope, but then she hears voices, and she slows.

She recognizes one—Arvaneh, Sariya, who knows how many other names she might possess? And the other? A man's voice, rich and light with the cadence of the Aramahn. There is something familiar about his voice, but she cannot place it.

She approaches carefully.

The forest opens up into a clearing, and within it stands a white monolith. The top of it stands tall over the tops of the ancient trees.

Sariya, her golden hair flowing softly in the breeze, stands near its base. As does a young man.

Atiana jerks as she recognizes him at last.

Nasim.

But what can he be doing here?

As Sariya and Nasim stare up at the monolith, Atiana feels the power emanating from within it. She feels it in her heart, in her gut. She feels it at the back of her throat. But it is not the power of Sariya. *Nyet*, this is something different, something foreign to this place. It is strong and ancient as the bones of the earth.

"There are those on Ghayavand who need me," Nasim is saying.

"Ashan," Sariya replies.

"Among others."

"You may think him a bright star, Khamal, but had he been alive when we were at our height, he would have shined no brighter than a wisp."

Nasim's face turns angry. "I am not Khamal, and you may all have been bright—you may be bright still—but look where things have come from such brightness."

"We can return to our greatness, Khamal. But if you feel that the path lies through Ghayavand"—she motions up to the monolith—"then so be it."

And with that Sariya turns and leaves. Atiana hides behind the trunk of the tree, waiting until Sariya is gone. Atiana worries that she is allowing Sariya to gain access to her tower once more, but she cannot leave. Not yet.

Nasim watches Sariya go. Only after her form is lost through the trees does he consider the monolith once more. He reaches a hand up and places it against the white surface of the stone, and when he does, she feels the response from within. The power there knows him. It *wants* Nasim to find it.

But there is something else. A noose is closing around this place. She can feel it.

Nasim, Atiana calls out. *Nasim, you cannot do this.*

Nasim stops, looks through the forest, wondering where her voice is coming from.

But she cannot reveal herself. If she does, Sariya will know.

She knows what you're doing, Atiana tells him. *She's allowing it.*

He ignores her. When he reaches out to touch the monolith again, it begins to powder, white dust falling and blowing with the wind like the finest of snowfalls.

The wind blusters through the forest.

The stone crumbles, more and more of it sloughing away as the tops of the trees dance with the wind.

Nasim, run!

He does, and Atiana is ready to as well, but the scene before her gives her pause. The white dust of the monolith swirls like a dervish at the center of the clearing. She can feel its unfettered power, and it is terrible.

What in the name of the ancients has Nasim unleashed? And what might happen were Sariya to get her hands on it?

Atiana readies herself. She prepares to sprint forward to see what might be waiting when the swirling dies away, but the wind does *not* die away. The sand is drawn up. It spins and twists, and where it touches the trees, they spark. They smoke. They burn.

Some of it strikes Atiana's skin, and like hot ash it scorches her. She staggers away, but the forest above her is now ablaze. She wants to follow Nasim, but already this place is beginning to falter. She cannot follow him, not if she wishes to live.

She heads back toward the tower.

And stops.

For in her hand is a stone. It is unlike anything she's ever seen before. It is blue—the blue of the ocean shallows—and striated with bronze and copper and nickel. It is beautiful and heavy and deep. Holding it is like holding a piece of the world in her hands.

The fire is spreading. It has moved beyond her along the tops of the trees, and the wind now carries the smoke down to her. It chokes her, makes her eyes water.

She runs, but she is weak, and soon she begins to stumble and fall, coughing until her chest burns and her throat is raw. She can breathe better here, but she is so weak she can hardly move. The stone sustains her, however. She can feel it, lending her its strength. There is more hidden beneath its surface—much more—but she has no idea how to unleash it.

This is enough for now, she decides.

At last the winds shift. The thick haze of smoke is pulled away, and she sees standing just beyond the trees the tower she left to enter the forest.

As she watches, a crack forms near its foundation. It runs up the tower's length, the stone shattering as it goes. Other cracks form. And widen. Stones along the topmost edge break and fall away.

With the stone lending her its strength, she stands—still coughing, still unable to catch her breath—and shambles forward, knowing she must get inside before the tower crumbles completely.

Larger pieces of stone, and even sections of the tower's wall, fall away, striking the ground before her. Scree bites into her skin, drawing blood along her arms, her forehead, her cheeks. A larger piece cuts into her shoulder and knocks her down. She gets up, realizing she has lost the blue stone.

She looks for it frantically, feeling faint and afraid, until she sees a glimpse of it beneath a heavy stone.

She pushes it, but it is too heavy, and she cannot move it.

Nyet! she screams.

She gathers herself and tries again. And slowly the stone tips.

As the sound of the crumbling tower reaches new heights, she grabs the stone and sprints for the tower door. The door twists unnaturally. The supports buckle as she leaps toward the frame.

And then she is through.

Atiana knows immediately she has returned to Baressa. No longer is she caught by the spells that surround Sariya's tower.

She cannot for the moment feel Ishkyna's presence, nor can she feel Ushai's. She reaches out for them, but as she does she senses a disturbance near the Spar.

The ceremony.

The ceremony Father is attending.

She rushes toward it and is relieved to find that little has taken place since she left. Either the ceremony has crawled at a glacial pace or little time has passed since she entered Sariya's tower. Whichever the case, dozens are still gathered beneath the pavilion. The keystones have been set into place, and the Kamarisi is speaking to the assemblage on a platform carpeted in red and trimmed in gold.

Father stands at the front of the crowd. Vaasak Dhalingrad and the men of their retinues stand patiently behind him. Near the back of these gathered men and women, spaced along the balustrade, are the men of the Kiliç Şaik, the Kamarisi's personal guard. They stand at attention, legs spread, arms behind their backs, the plumes attached to their rounded turbans tossed wildly by the winds.

The Kamarisi seems to be finishing. Many begin to clap, and in the manner of Yrstanla, Hakan raises the back of one hand to all who stand before him.

Near the balustrade, one of the guardsmen steps forward toward those who stand at the rear of the tent—the streltsi of Vostroma and Dhalingrad. Before Atiana can understand what is happening, the lone guardsman has pulled his sharply curved kilij sword. This seems to be a signal of sorts, for in a flash, all of his men—a score of them—have pulled their kilij as well.

Father, behind you!

Her father reaches for his chest, grasping for his soulstone, which lies hidden beneath his coat.

Turn, Father, now!

But it is too late.

The men of Yrstanla cut the streltsi from behind.

Many in the crowd scatter, their eyes wild and their mouths wide with shock.

Father pulls his shashka, as does Vaasak and many of the men of Anuskaya, but the streltsi have already fallen, and they are faced with impossible odds.

Do not fight! Atiana urges.

She doesn't know if her father heard her, but he lowers his sword at the command of the Kamarisi's guard.

Most of those who ran are herded back into the pavilion. All are relieved of their weapons.

And then Father is led away from the pavilion by three guardsmen. Hakan follows. His face is serene, as if this all has gone according to plan.

Father is brought to his knees with a sharp strike from the flat of one of the guardsmen's blades. It is the one who first drew his sword, a man who Atiana saw with Sihaş in the kasir but does not otherwise know.

As the two other guardsmen pull Father's arms wide, holding him in a kneeling position, the first steps to Father's left side.

Hakan watches this. He speaks, eyes closed, as if reciting a chant.

Or rendering judgment.

And then Atiana realizes. Father has been positioned over the keystones. He's been positioned over the centermost of them, the one that lies at the true center of the Spar.

This is not a simple act of war. This is a sacrifice.

They are *consecrating* the bridge.

Father, fight them! Do not allow this!

But he makes no move against them.

She assails Hakan's mind, trying to assume him as she would a rook, but the currents of the aether are too wild. Each time she tries, she nearly slips from the aether.

Vaasak! she calls. *Save him!*

She calls to others, but she already knows it is too late.

The sword is lifted high.

Hakan finishes his speech.

And the sword swings low.

Atiana sees the sword strike home, sees it sever the neck of her father. Sees his head roll across the stones.

His blood spills, staining the central keystone.

In the aether, Atiana stares. The world, so often wide and expansive in the dark, focuses tightly on her father's body, on the blood still pumping from his neck, on his *head* as it rocks to a stop.

Atiana is frozen. The scene before her is frozen, imprinted on her mind like blood upon stone. Shock gives way to horror. A thousand implications swirl through her mind, but she can focus on none of them. She can only think of one thing.

Her father is dead. Gone forever. Taken from her by the whims of a sick and twisted emperor, the lord of a slowly dying state.

And then Atiana's mind fills with rage. Her emotions—vengeful and primal and brutal—make it more and more difficult to remain.

She wants to stay, wants to rend Hakan's mind to shreds, but in the end, her emotions run too high, and she is thrust from the aether as if it were repulsed.

CHAPTER FORTY-FOUR

The clack and thunder of stones falling, the tower rumbling, woke Atiana from a deep sleep.

She sat up, the water of the pool splashing around her.

Her entire body clenched. She knew she should relax, but she couldn't. She gripped her legs tight, shivering. She was colder than she had ever been. Another boom shook the building. And another.

By the ancients who watch over, what was happening?

The tower... The tower had been crumbling...

She looked around, eyes wide.

There was no tower here. She was in a pool of water. A young woman wearing the dress of a servant stood at the edge of it. "Can you hear me, My Lady Princess?"

Atiana stared, unable to understand how she'd come to be here. Two soldiers wearing the stripes of Vostroma stood by an open doorway leading outside.

"My Lady," the woman said again, her voice more urgent. She waded into the pool in her black boots and rich wool dress and took Atiana by the shoulders and helped her to her feet.

Only then did Atiana realize that there were others in the pool. They were submerged, naked, their breathing tubes still in place. For the life of her she couldn't remember their names.

"*Please*, My Lady, come."

As Atiana prepared to stand, she realized that she held something small and hard and smooth in one hand. She looked down and found the stone. The stone Nasim had liberated from the monolith. The stone Sariya had wanted at all costs. And here it was, with her.

The events that had occurred outside Sariya's tower came clear. She didn't understand how it could have been, but she did know that it had been no dream. That had been Nasim himself, drawn, as she had been, into a world of

Sariya's making. And he had wrested from Sariya the thing she most desired.

It did not sit well with Atiana that he could do such a thing—it seemed like too much power to rest within one soul—but Nasim was a special child. He'd spent years straddling the aether, walking between worlds. Could he not then walk the dark as she did? Perhaps he would even be better at it, as gifted as he had been with hezhan.

She stared down at the blue stone. It was both beautiful and terrifying.

When she looked up she saw the woman staring at it. Yalessa... Her name was Yalessa.

Atiana palmed the stone—making it clear it was something not to be questioned—and took Yalessa's hand to step with shaking legs from the pool. As she did it registered with her how broken this building was. She knew this place. It was the very same building where she'd first seen Ushai in the Shattering.

Another boom shook the building. Atiana allowed Yalessa to put Atiana's thick winter coat around her shoulders, and then she walked toward the open doorway. The streltsi held their muskets and berdische axes at the ready. They bowed their heads as Atiana approached and stepped outside ahead of her, both with their muskets resting at the top of their axes, ready to set them down and fire should the need arise.

"My Lady," Yalessa said, "don't go outside!"

"Wake them," Atiana replied calmly. "It's time we leave."

Yalessa seemed relieved by this. She bowed and moved to comply as Atiana stepped outside and into the adjoining courtyard. Within it were withered trees and a disused garden. Above, there was gray sky, the monotony broken only by the dark forms of windships sliding below the clouds. A dozen circled about one another. Almost directly overhead, cannon smoke belched from the side of one of them. Windwood flew from the hull of the ship it had targeted, the sound of the blast falling upon her moments later.

Debris rained down over the courtyard, and the streltsi pushed her back beneath the overhang.

As chunks of wood pattered onto the stones, Atiana remembered the events she'd seen from within the aether.

Father.

The ceremony at the Spar.

Dozens of her countrymen had been there along with the Kamarisi and his courtiers. Father... Father was dead, but what about the rest? Had they all been killed?

Six streltsi came running into the courtyard, boots stomping, bandoliers rattling in time. Two stopped at the archway that led to the streets of the Shattering. The remaining four continued with Irkadiy at their lead.

"My Lady Princess, we must go. Now."

"The others aren't ready."

"We're as ready as we'll ever be."

Atiana turned and found Ishkyna standing in the shadow of the doorway. Ushai was there as well. Both of them looked as if they hadn't slept in days.

"My Lady," Yalessa said, holding Atiana's clothes and motioning to the interior.

No sooner had Atiana nodded her head than musket fire broke out from the archway.

The leg of one of the streltsi standing there buckled. He grunted in pain, aiming and firing his musket. Blood stained his pant leg where it was tucked into his tall leather boot, and then it began to spurt.

"The Kamarisi's men have come, My Lady." Irkadiy's face was hard, but as he glanced toward his man, she saw the pain and worry that roiled just below the surface.

Atiana took time only to pull her boots on. The coat would have to do for now. She pulled it tight around her and cinched the belt and they were off, running toward the courtyard's other exit.

As they ran into the Shattering, Atiana looked back and saw a dozen janissaries dressed in the red turbans and the black coats of the Kamarisi's personal guard. One of the soldiers spotted their escape, but he did not shout. He merely whistled and pointed, and his comrades ran up the street, half of them peeling away, heading southward to cut them off.

Irkadiy led them into a round building, a scriptorium. They took the stairs that were just inside the foyer and went up three levels. Shelves were built into the walls, and were visible in many other rooms they saw as they ran. The shelves were largely empty, but every so often she would see a thick book, dusty with mold, and she wondered distantly why those particular books had been abandoned, why they had survived the scavenging that had taken place over the course of generations.

At last they reached the highest level. A wooden ladder stood at the ready, one that had been prepared three days before. Irkadiy and one other strelet climbed the ladder first.

Yalessa, eyes wide and movements rushed, made to follow them, but one of the streltsi put himself between her and the ladder. "They will make sure it's safe," he said.

Five of the streltsi lined the balcony and brought their muskets to their shoulders, aiming their weapons down to the foyer below.

Sounds came from the entrance three stories down.

Two quick shots came from the streltsi, the sound of it deafening in the enclosed space. The other three fired shortly after, and they heard moaning and a cry of pain cut short by the musket fire.

Irkadiy returned, waving them up. "Quickly now," he whispered.

As Yalessa took the ladder up, a musket shot struck the stone ceiling. Yalessa screamed as the shot scattered powder and bits of rock everywhere.

Below, bootsteps could be heard running along the scriptorium halls, and then along the stone stairs leading to the second level.

"Hurry," Irkadiy called.

Ishkyna gained the roof quickly, as did Ushai.

As Atiana made her way up, another shot came from the streltsi behind her. And another. They were staggering their shots, delaying the chase. When she reached the roof at last, the streltsi came quickly behind her. Just as the last of them reached the top of the ladder, a shot rang out from below. The strelet arched back, his face twisted in pain. He was hit by another shot before the others could pull him to safety.

They pulled the ladder up immediately and dropped two heavy boards into place over the hole. A shot tore into the wood, followed quickly by two more.

She watched as the men helped the wounded soldier away and checked his wounds.

"*Nyet*," he said, waving them away. "Leave me my musket and one other."

He was young, younger than Atiana. Irkadiy glanced ahead, to the building they were headed toward, and then he slipped his musket over his shoulder and gave it to the wounded man. After kissing his cheeks tenderly, Irkadiy said, "Go well."

"Go well," the young man replied.

They padded over the tiles of the roof to an adjoining building, one whose roof was only a short drop from the scriptorium's. It was the first in a connected series of buildings that had once been part of a grand estate.

Atiana silently thanked the ancestors for Irkadiy.

He and his men had blockaded all of the entrances, all except the rooftop garden—which they reached in short order—and three others, leaving them several choices of escape routes.

They entered the building, blockading the garden entrance behind them. They found themselves in a long, marble hallway.

"Which way?" Atiana asked, her breath coming heavily. She removed her belt and motioned for Ishkyna to hold it up so that she could change.

The men turned away, several of them reloading their muskets with quick efficiency.

"They will expect us to run west," Irkadiy said, "toward the bulk of the Shattering."

"And so you plan to go south." Warmth was beginning to return to Atiana's extremities, but this only served to make her aware of how cold she truly was. She began to shiver fiercely as she allowed the coat to drop and pulled a shirt over her naked frame.

"*Da*," Irkadiy replied. "We'll be able to see them pass along the grounds. Once they do, we will make our way and—"

"*Nyet*," Atiana said. "We will head north."

"My Lady," Irkadiy said, lowering his voice, "that way lies the city."

"I must see what became of the Spar."

"We will be trapped."

"My Father, your Lord, was there on that bridge, Irkadiy." She accepted the leggings from Yalessa and pulled them on quickly. "We will see what became of it."

"My Lady—"

"They will have the ground from here to Svoya covered," Atiana continued, "both by land and by air. Our only real choice at this point is to head south by sea."

"You may be right, but to go there now would be foolish. We might as well give ourselves up to the Kamarisi's guard."

She slipped back into the coat and belted it, feeling more herself than she had in quite some time. "We go, Irkadiy, and we go now."

"Forgive me, but we will not."

Atiana stepped up to him. "Who gave you your orders, Irkadiy, son of Adienko?"

"Your father, the Grand Duke himself."

"The Grand Duke is dead, Irkadiy. He died on the Spar. Beheaded by the Kamarisi."

Irkadiy's nostrils flared, and he swallowed reflexively. He snapped his heels and bowed his head to Atiana. "I'm sorry, My Lady Princess." He turned to Ishkyna and snapped his heels again. "Most sorry."

Atiana sent an apologetic glance at Ishkyna. She hadn't wanted her to find out this way, but she needed to shake Irkadiy's resolve. Ishkyna seemed rigid as she met Atiana's gaze. She'd seen. She'd seen in the aether, but she'd only just now remembered.

Atiana turned back to Irkadiy, waiting until he calmed himself. "Who would you take orders from now?"

He measured her, and then Ishkyna. No doubt his orders had been to protect them at all costs, but so much had changed.

"We go to the Spar," Atiana continued, "as secretly as we may. If you deem it too risky to take a cage down to the sea, so be it. We will hide in the city until we're able to make plans to reach Svoya another way."

He paused another moment, his men looking to him, ready to act however he decided. The silence was lengthening, and then, in the distance behind them, they heard the report of a musket. It was followed quickly by another. And then there was shouting and several more shots in tight sequence.

Irkadiy looked back the way they'd come.

"*Kozyol!*" he breathed to himself. "Come."

And they were off again, heading through the connected buildings until they reached a half-ruined wall in a grand entryway to the north of the estate.

"Ancients," Irkadiy said as he came to a stop.

The others stopped as well, all of them staring up through a massive hole in the wall before them.

When Atiana reached their side, she felt the blood drain from her face. She could feel her heartbeat pulsing in her neck, pounding as the scene over the city came clear.

A column of smoke, wide and thick, rose up from beyond the city's center—certainly somewhere close to the Spar. But this was not what had shocked her. It was the scores of ships she saw heading south across the straits. Some were small ships—yachts and the like. Others were larger barques. But there were at least two dozen massive galleons flying with them. And none of them seemed to have any trouble at all with the straits even though they were passing directly over it.

"How many?" Ishkyna asked.

Irkadiy glanced back at her. "With the others I saw earlier, perhaps fifty or sixty."

Atiana was shaking her head. That matched the ships they had available in the south. But only thirty or so were ready to come quickly to their aid. With this many ships heading toward Vostroma, her homeland would be overwhelmed in days, perhaps less.

"Did you warn them?" Atiana asked.

Ishkyna looked to her, angry at hearing the accusation in her voice. "Did *you?*"

"I was—"

She wasn't able to finish the thought, for just then a meaty thump struck Yalessa in the chest. Her young handmaid spun and fell as the sound of the musket-fire reached them.

It had come from outside.

Their pursuers had found them. They hadn't been fooled at all. They'd either guessed where they'd been headed or there were enough of them that they could cover all of the exits from this massive estate—Atiana wasn't sure which scared her more.

Atiana dropped to Yalessa's side as Irkadiy and the others fanned out and moved to the holes where windows once stood. Yalessa gasped wetly for breath. The wound bubbled red. She stared up at the ceiling blinking rapidly as Atiana held her hand and called her name.

No one on the islands was a stranger to battle. Atiana knew what this wound meant for Yalessa. She leaned forward, kissed her forehead, and whispered into her ear. "Your story will be told."

She didn't know if Yalessa had heard, for by the time she straightened, Yalessa's eyes had gone lifeless and the blood had stopped pumping so fiercely from her wound.

The streltsi had positioned themselves and were just then peering around the corners.

They pulled back just in time.

A handful of shots came whizzing in, several striking the stone window frames.

They returned fire, and immediately another of the streltsi was felled.

He did not scream, for the shot had caught him in the throat.

He lay there on the dirty marble floor, staring up at Atiana, holding his neck as bright red blood coursed from between his fingers. His eyes were scared. As the firefight continued, she smiled, trying to console him, but the fear never left him, not until he slumped to one side.

Atiana took up his musket and moved to another window. She looked out carefully and saw, standing behind a low stone wall not thirty paces away, two dozen soldiers.

"They may not kill you if we lay down arms, My Lady," Irkadiy called.

Atiana was already sighting down the barrel of the musket, training it on a man near the center. She knew what Irkadiy said was true, but the two of them—two princesses of Vostroma—would only give the Kamarisi another tool to use against the Grand Duchy.

She swallowed hard. She could not allow herself or Ishkyna to be used this way.

She squeezed the trigger.

The pan flashed and the musket bucked like a skittish colt.

She'd been trained long ago, and she'd been a fairly good shot, but she had forgotten just how powerful these weapons could be.

Her shot missed.

She pulled back as a musket shot struck the wall outside her window.

She reloaded as quickly as she was able, and when she brought the weapon up again, she saw that several men were running low toward the base of the wide marble stairs that led to the entrance.

She aimed and squeezed.

The musket kicked again. This time a man fell.

And then she heard the bootsteps coming from behind. There were many, coming from the hall they'd run down only a short while ago. The soldiers that had chased them from the scriptorium had found their way here at last.

Atiana was in the midst of reloading when seven of them reached the bannister overlooking the entrance hall.

Irkadiy turned and raised his musket.

But he was too late. One of the janissaries fired and struck Irkadiy in the shoulder.

He crumpled to the ground.

"Irkadiy!"

Two more shots came in, one striking the marble floor near Irkadiy's head, the other missing another of the streltsi.

"Lower your weapons," said one of the Kamarisi's men. He was the same one Atiana had seen earlier, the one that had spotted them as they ran from the courtyard.

There were tense moments as the streltsi neither fired nor lowered their weapons.

Atiana was nearly ready to tell them to comply when a trickle of water came down from the ceiling above the soldiers. The trickle increased to a stream, and then a deluge. No sooner had the men looked up than a section of the roof collapsed.

It crashed down on them, stone and ancient wood crumbling, wounding one of them and causing several others to back away. This did them little good, however, for the water was slithering over the floor like a snake.

One of the soldiers fired his musket at the twisting column of water, which did little but spray water in a wide fan. A moment later, the water had wrapped around his legs, then his chest, and then it drove against his face, entering his mouth and nose. He reared back, flailing his arms, trying to bat the water away.

Atiana looked to Ushai. She wore a circlet with a stone of azurite, which glowed dully. It seemed strange for the gem to shine so little. As hungrily as the jalahezhan was taking the lives of the soldiers on the balcony above, it felt as though it should be as bright as the sun, not idly glowing like a bedside candle.

Two of the Kamarisi's guard drew their kilij swords—blades with a sharp bend halfway down their length—and used them to cut at the twisting jalahezhan. Another drew a pistol and aimed it at Ushai.

Before he could draw the trigger, the snake flicked its head, and a tendril of water splashed across the pistol. When the guardsman squeezed the trigger, the weapon merely clicked, the powder wet.

Three shots came in quick succession against the heavy wooden door. The door was stout, but the wood was brittle. A moment later, it crashed inward, bringing three men with it.

One was felled by a point blank shot from Ishkyna.

Three of the streltsi charged, screaming the names of their fathers and bringing their berdische axes arcing downward. Both of the Kamarisi's men were felled, but more came in after—five, then six, with more rushing forward now that the door had been breached.

Atiana watched only for a moment. It was going to be a slaughter unless she did something.

She raised her hands, but before she could shout their surrender, she heard the sounds of a renewed firefight. A handful of musket shots fired. Then more, and more, until it seemed that an entire war was being fought outside the doors. She could see outside the windows several dozen men advancing quickly across the estate grounds from the west. The men they were attacking—the Kamarisi's guard—had been positioned to defend against fire from the estate. They weren't at all prepared for an attack along their flank.

"Hold!" Atiana called. "Hold, for help has arrived."

More gunfire rained in near the entrance, and several shots flew in through the nearby window. She could see men in dark garb and ivory-colored turbans.

"Pull back!" the leader of the Kamarisi's guard called.

His men obeyed, retreating quickly up the stairs. Another of them dropped from gunfire, but the rest reached the second level and retreated down the hallway from which they'd come.

The men in dark garb rushed in through the open doorway, firing at the retreating men. They saw Atiana and the streltsi, and one of them with a thick moustache and black beard waved to her. "Come quickly," he said in thick Anuskayan.

They were soon out and onto the grounds as the firefight was pushed ever eastward.

"Stay low," the man with the thick beard said. "The danger is not yet over."

They crouched as they ran, some shots still coming in from the Kamarisi's guard, but soon they were beyond the grounds and into the northern buildings of the Shattering. They reached one—a domed building—and were led inside.

At last Atiana saw who her savior had been, for Sihaş stood there among several men.

Seeing Atiana, he spoke low to the others and then came to her. "You should have left the city while you had the chance," he said.

"I would not have. The fight is here."

He stared at her soberly. "It is, My Lady Princess, but it's much larger than you could have guessed."

CHAPTER FORTY-FIVE

As Nikandr was led around the edge of the clearing, many of the children—the akhoz—on the outermost row of posts craned their necks and followed his movement. They could no longer see, and yet they seemed drawn to him. He had no idea why this should be, but it made his skin crawl.

The men of the Hratha led him to a tree where a spike had been nailed into the trunk. He fought, but the Hratha yanked the chain between his wrists viciously when he did, the shackles biting deeply and drawing blood. When they reached the tree, the Hratha threw the chain up and over the spike, securing Nikandr. Just as the akhoz were.

Bersuq watched all of this with dispassionate eyes. He seemed to acknowledge that he had betrayed Nikandr, that he had allowed the Hratha to do this to him, but then he turned his head back toward the clearing, making it clear that in the end, they were on different sides of a conflict bigger than the one playing out here in the clearing.

The Hratha that had brought Nikandr here to the clearing moved to another group of men. Rahid was there, and when his men arrived, he looked back at Nikandr, tilting his head to listen to the quiet words of his men.

The day grew longer, but nothing happened. Midday passed, which would have been an auspicious time to perform this ritual. There seemed to be some concern among those gathered. Most watched through the trees to the west, waiting expectantly. A group of men were dispatched, presumably to search for Muqallad.

And then at last, as the sun was beginning to set, Muqallad came. He was flanked by many of the Hratha, and a few of the men from Siafyan. Kaleh was with him as well. They reached the edge of the circle, and Muqallad stopped. He turned to Nikandr and walked toward him. Strangely, he had cuts along his forehead and on one side of his nose. His left eye was half red where it should be white, and a host of bruises marked the left side of his neck and jaw.

When he stopped a few paces away, Nikandr realized that Muqallad was staring at Nikandr's chest, where his soulstone should have been. Nikandr realized in this instant that he could feel Nasim. It was weak, very weak, but he could feel him. It was the first time in years he'd felt anything like it.

Muqallad must have sensed it too, though how this could be he had no idea. "We will speak when this is done," Muqallad said, and with that he turned and strode into the clearing.

The sun was touching the tops of the trees now, a time that was perhaps more auspicious than high noon, for he could think of nothing more apt than the setting of the sun for what was about to happen to these children.

Muqallad walked over the ashes, over the bones, to the center of the clearing. He held up his hand and in them held two stones, both of them blue and brilliant even under the setting sun. "Who will take them?" he asked.

After only a moment's hesitation, Bersuq strode forward and bowed his head. Muqallad handed him the stones, and without returning the bow walked from the clearing to stand at its edge.

Bersuq situated himself at the center of the posts. After taking in the faces of the akhoz, he held the stones aloft and began to chant. The rest of the gathered men and women—including Muqallad—soon picked the chant up. The roots of the words were both familiar and foreign, but the cadence drove a spike of fear through Nikandr's heart. Surely the words were Kalhani, the mothertongue. It was an ancient language, and indeed, this ritual felt as if it were tied to the making of the world, as if the fate of Erahm hinged upon it.

With so many eyes turned toward the clearing, Nikandr was able to look up to his chains. He pulled down upon them, hoping to pull the spike free, but it had been driven too deeply into the wood.

The akhoz began to moan. The sounds came louder at the end of each recitation of the chant. Bersuq held the stones high above his head, pressing the two pieces together. The stones seemed to draw in the breath, draw in the voices and guttural calls of those nearby. There came a tugging within Nikandr's chest, and his heart skipped a beat as the first of the children burst into flame. It was a girl on the outer ring. As her hair singed and burned and her skin lit like burning scrolls, the pitch of her moaning rose, as if the pain somehow excited her.

Soon the two next to her were aflame, and then the two beyond them. And so it went, more and more of the outer ring lighting like torches, until the circle was completed. The flame then leaped to the middle ring, and at last the innermost ring. The chanting rose higher as the akhoz burned bright like beacons. Nikandr could feel it now, even from this distance.

The smell of it—burning hair and burning skin—filled the clearing. It made him retch. His mouth filled with saliva, and he spit to clear the taste of it.

Bersuq had somehow been spared from the flames. Surely he was protected by the suuraqiram nearby, but it could not last long. His body twisted from the pain, but he continued to hold the pieces of the Atalayina above him.

The chanting rose higher. The calls of the akhoz became little more than inhuman screams rising above the sound of the roaring flames.

Bersuq could not last forever. Soon it became too much. He screamed, still holding tight to the Atalayina. His robes caught fire, and then his hair and his beard. He shivered from the pain as his screams became a piercing cry that rose above all other sounds.

Nikandr followed the black smoke up and into the sky, if only to be free from this horrific vision for a few moments. That was when movement among the clouds caught his eye. Flying low, above the trees to the north, was a ship. He recognized it immediately. It was the *Chaika*.

A moment later, the ground near the outer ring of akhoz blossomed into a high plume of fire and dirt and ashes, a resounding boom coming a split-second later. Three of the posts flew up and outward, the akhoz still attached. They twirled lazily until they struck the ground near the feet of the chanting Maharraht.

Muqallad raised his hands, but as he did another cannon shot shattered the ground in front of him. Two Maharraht nearby were thrown wide of the blast. What happened to Muqallad, Nikandr didn't see, for the crowd was now in disarray. Some were taking up muskets and firing on the ship while the qiram drew upon their hezhan. Others continued to chant, so lost in the ritual were they. But most took cover in the nearby trees.

Nikandr looked up to his chains. He jumped and tried to fling the chains up and over the spike. But he was weak, and the motion caused the sockets of his shoulders to scream in pain after remaining stretched and immobile for so long. As the *Chaika* slipped over the clearing and began heading over the far side and beyond the trees, he tried one last time, and this time the chain came rattling down.

He lost his balance and collapsed. When he finally managed to come to his feet, he found four men standing before him—Rahid and the three Hratha that had brought him from Siafyan.

Rahid's men bore muskets, while Rahid, his sword held loosely in his right hand, used his free hand to grab Nikandr's chains and pull him into the forest. Nikandr resisted, pulling on the chain in a vain attempt to remain in the clearing, until two of Rahid's men struck him with the butt of their muskets, forcing him onward.

A sudden rise in pitch from the clearing made all of them turn back. The akhoz burned white, their voices adding to one another, driving those closest to put their hands over their ears. A moment later, Nikandr did the same, as did Rahid and the Hratha. Bersuq fell to the flames at last. The Atalayina slipped from his grasp and was lost.

Only then did the sound of the akhoz begin to wane. The moment that it did, Rahid ordered his men to continue. They moved beyond a rise, and into a stand of trees. They could still hear the flames and the akhoz and the occasional snap of musket fire, but they were effectively hidden.

Rahid's men fanned out behind him. Rahid stepped forward, facing Nikandr, the tip of his sword swinging back and forth, as if he were itching to swing it.

But then Nikandr saw hanging around Rahid's neck a chain. *His* chain. The one that held his soulstone.

Rahid noticed Nikandr's lingering gaze. He pulled the stone out and held it up for Nikandr to see, and then he let it fall against his black robes. The chalcedony stone glimmered dully in the waning light. "They say you can feel those who've worn your stones. Is it so?"

Strangely, these words served only to calm Nikandr's coursing blood. What Rahid said was true. Grigory had done this to him years ago, and for the short time he'd worn the stone afterward—before placing it in Nasim's mouth to draw him away from Adhiya—he'd felt the taint, felt Grigory's hatred of him. There was no doubt that the same would be true now, but he had come to accept that the ancients worked in strange ways. If this was something they had chosen for him—to have his stone worn by a Maharraht—then he would accept it.

"A pity you won't be afforded the chance." He spat at Nikandr's feet. "It is long past time I put an end to your presence on these shores."

"Tell yourself what you wish," Nikandr said, "but *you* were the trespassers here, not me. You came and you raped your sister tribe. You're worse than anything the Landed ever did, for you did this to your brothers and your sisters. You did this to their children."

Rahid stalked forward and raised his sword high with both hands. He brought it down and Nikandr, who'd been hoping for such an attack, dodged backward. He was still hobbled by the rope, but he knew its length well and was able to compensate with short, quick steps. Rahid swung again, and again. He came closer, for he was pressing the advantage of his longer strides, but Nikandr was still able to outpace him.

And then Rahid became too bold. He came in fast, his sword swung in at an angle. Nikandr spread his manacled hands wide and allowed the sword to strike the chain, allowed it to yank his arms sideways.

This simple action halted the blade. Nikandr twisted his arms, twisted the chain around the blade, and while he did he lunged forward and grabbed Rahid's wrists and slammed his forehead against Rahid's face.

Rahid turned and tried to pull away, but Nikandr had hooked his foot behind Rahid's, and Rahid went sprawling.

A quick jerk of his arms and the blade was free. Before Rahid's men could react, Nikandr twisted it around and brought it down in one fierce motion. The tip drove down through Rahid's chest and into the cold earth beneath him.

Rahid's eyes went wide. He shivered and grabbed for the sword. The blade cut his fingers deeply, but he didn't seem to notice. He stared into Nikandr's eyes, coughed once, twice, and then his head fell back as he stared at the sky, unmoving.

Nikandr yanked the blade free.

By now the men in their black robes and turbans had pulled their muskets up. Nikandr dodged as one fired. The shot went wide and Nikandr brought the sword down sharply across the rope tying his ankles together.

He dodged another, but the shot bit into his thigh. He tried to roll to his feet, but he put too much weight on his wounded leg and fell back down.

He scrabbled away on the soft floor of the forest until the third man pressed him down with the barrel of his musket. He was young, this one, the youngest of the three. He stood there, staring at Nikandr, glancing back at the other men, before turning back to Nikandr, his eyes hard.

The man's head jerked back sharply as a musket shot took him in the face. A burst of skin and red flew from the back of his head, showering his comrades. They both blinked and stepped back, their eyes shocked as they watched him fall to the ground. Then they looked beyond Nikandr, the direction from which the shot had come.

Nikandr turned and found Soroush charging forward with seven others—six Maharraht, and Jahalan.

Jahalan had a stone in his circlet. He stopped—allowing the others to continue—and spread his arms wide.

The Hratha pulled their shamshirs and advanced. Had Nikandr's allies not been barreling forward, they might have been more sure with their weapons, but as it was, they were rushed and clumsy. Nikandr fended off their first hasty swings. A musket shot zipped in and narrowly missed the one closest to Nikandr. A moment later, the wind whipped up through the boughs of the trees above them. Pine needles swirled through the air, stinging the skin. Nikandr was not the center of the wind's attention, however. It focused on the Hratha, forced them to hide their faces or lose their eyes to needles and pinecones and fallen bark.

They had just begun backing away when Soroush and his Maharraht arrived and drove swords through them.

Nikandr pulled himself over to Rahid and slipped his soulstone necklace from around his neck. When he slipped it over his head, he could immediately feel his hezhan. He ached to draw upon it, to summon it, but he did not. It felt too close, and for the moment things seemed to be in hand. Better to commune with his hezhan when he had the time to be patient.

Soroush and another of his men helped Nikandr to his feet, and then put Nikandr's arms around their shoulders and helped him to shamble eastward. They moved as quickly as they could, but Nikandr was slowing them down. Eventually the forest thinned and left them on the edge of a meadow. Hidden behind a rocky hill ahead of them was a ship, one of the Maharraht's. Beyond it, floating low on the wind and well out to sea, was the *Chaika*.

Dozens of Maharraht were already aboard the moored ship, and more were boarding now. Many of the parents Nikandr had seen along the lake in Siafyan were there, as were others—men and women with younger children, children that hadn't yet been affected by the wasting. Zanhalah was there was well, watching their approach with a small but satisfied smile on her face.

Soon they were loaded and into the air. Nikandr stood by the gunwales, watching the forest closely as they rose higher and higher. They had risen only an eighth-league when a column of fire broke high into the air over the clearing to the west. It shot straight up and into the cloud cover leagues above. The bright column—orange and yellow and white—turned and roiled, but it did not twist. It was as if the ritual of the akhoz had sent a spear of fire up in the hopes of piercing the sky.

Nikandr thought it would end quickly—he *wanted* it to end quickly—but it continued on and on as they headed north and eventually west. It hung on the horizon, all through the night until at last it was lost from view.

PART II

CHAPTER FORTY-SIX

Khamal steps out from under the celestia's dome. It is the hour of the new day, and the stars are bright, bright enough to guide his way down from the celestia toward Alayazhar. He has not gone far before he realizes that there is someone waiting for him on the road ahead.

It is Inan, the mother of Yadhan.

"Peace to you," Khamal says, and tries to pass her by.

He hopes that she has come to visit the celestia, to meditate upon the stars, but he knows that she has not. She falls into step alongside him, and together they make their way down toward Alayazhar. The light of the quarter moon illuminates the sea below, makes it glimmer and give shadow to the crescent bay at the edge of the broken city. Years ago the city would have danced with light. Dozens would have come to the celestia on a night like this. But now most have left. Most have abandoned the island and her Al-Aqim. Some have come to mistrust or even fear them. It is a strange position to be faced with. It has been years—since his childhood among the wastes of the Gaji—that Khamal has dealt with such.

"What is it you wish?" Khamal asks.

For a while the only sound he hears is that of their soft leather boots sighing over the low grass of the trail.

When at last Inan speaks, it is with a heavy heart. "Yadhan is lost to me, Khamal. Dozens of others have lost their children as well. And yet the rifts are beginning to grow again."

"You knew your children would be lost."

"*Yeh*, you explained everything so well, down to the last detail."

"I did," Khamal says. He spoke the words harshly, much more harshly than he'd meant to. The months since the sundering have worn on him greatly, but he takes a deep breath and begins again, careful to keep his tone soft, understanding. "The rifts may grow, Inan, but not nearly as quickly as before."

"So of course more must be taken."

Khamal stops in his tracks and turns to Inan. By the moonlight he sees her face, the tightness there, the anger. She was once his most devout disciple. She left with his blessing and after her time on the wind—a mere two circuits of the world—she returned to him, her eyes bright, her mind sharp, ready to learn more.

How much has changed.

After the sundering, she did not offer Yadhan to him—he suspects she knew all along that her daughter would be one of the children able to become akhoz—but she accepted his request that Yadhan be given. That day in the celestia, though, when the first akhoz had been born, something inside of her broke. She lost her faith in him, lost her faith that the rifts could be closed, and she infected others. There were only a few at first, but the idea took root among his followers and grew like creeping vines.

Until they came to this: a woman who would have done anything for him now stands ready to defy, to take from him the salvation of the world.

If she thinks he will let that happen, she is mistaken.

"I know you've been speaking to others, Inan. I know you've been asking them of their will to leave."

"You said the way was open."

"It is—of course it is—but we have need of everyone. This is no time to abandon hope when there is time yet to save everything."

"*Neh*, Khamal. The tide has turned against us. It has turned against you. It is time to do what Yadhan's father suggested."

"I cannot give you your daughter back, Inan."

Inan's face goes hard. She spits at Khamal's feet. "I would have my daughter back, but I know better than you that she is gone. Gone forever, lost to the world." She spits again. "I trusted you, Khamal, but now I know you are a fool. You thought the world ready for indaraqiram. You think it's ready still, or if not that you can *force* it into being. You are not *enlightened*, and neither are Sariya and Muqallad. You are little better than mules, braying and tugging at your tether. The world has spoken—the *fates* have spoken—and here you stand, telling *me* that there's still time."

Khamal feels his face flush. Nearly, nearly, he allows his confidence to slip, but he has been down this path before—not from any doubts Inan might foist upon him, but those he has placed upon himself. In this way lies ruin. He knows this. He cannot allow himself to dwell upon the question of whether he has chosen wrongly. If he does, even for a moment, it will be the ruin of them all. He must continue, and so must the others, no matter what their disciples—the men and women of Alayazhar—might say.

And then he realizes. Had he not been so tired he would have seen it before as he left the celestia.

The city. It is dark. Too dark.

He reaches out to find them, the men and women who still call Alayazhar home. They had remained after the sundering after many had died. They had remained after many more had left. They were the few that he thought surely would be able to help stem the tide of their ever growing failure. And they've left. All of them.

Only Inan remains.

"Go, then," Khamal says, and resumes his walk down the path. "Follow the other children."

"I cannot follow. And neither can you. The paths have been closed to you, Khamal."

Khamal stops.

He feels his heart race. He opens his mind to the land beneath him, to the air above him. He feels the city below, the hills above, and the mountains beyond. He feels the bay, and the river that feeds it. He feels the trees and the grass and the voles and the goats. He feels even the rifts that run deeply through the island.

What he *cannot* feel is anything in the sea beyond. He feels only Ghayavand, her small sister islands, and nothing more.

"What have you done?"

"You have taken enough, Khamal. You have taken all that we have to offer, and still you ask for more."

His heart beats madly. "It won't work, Inan. You know it won't."

"It will for now. Until we have time to learn more."

"You're fools. All of you. The rifts cannot be chained. They will find the cracks in your walls, and when they do they will spread among the islands. They will spread to the motherland."

"Save your breath, Khamal, and do not think that you may use your stone."

Khamal feels for the stone, his portion of the Atalayina. It is safe where he left it in the celestia floor, but something is wrong. It feels dim, a candle in place of the sun. Inan and the others have somehow managed not only to trap the Al-Aqim, they've dulled the Atalayina as well.

His hands clench. His throat tightens. For the first time in ages he considers killing another.

"You cannot leave," he realizes.

"How astute of you, Khamal."

"Why? Why have you remained?"

"*One* had to remain, Khamal. *One* had to ensure the walls were closed. I accepted the honor. Gladly."

"*Neh*," he says, opening himself to the world beyond and drawing upon the spirits of fire that hover close, always close. As his hands shake with rage, he feels the fire build within him. "You stayed so you could be the one who told me."

She smiles sadly. "I will pay for it in the next life, but you're right. It shames me, but I'm not afraid to tell you that this is the most gratifying moment of my life."

She speaks those words with such pride, such smugness. It burns Khamal's ears to hear them. He finds his hands bunching into fists. Finds the muscles of his arms and chest tightening so fiercely that he shivers from it.

"Look at you." Inan smiles, showing her perfect white teeth. "The great Khamal, humbled at last."

Before he knows what he's doing, he releases the power built within him, feels the suurahezhan revel in the gout of flame that flows from his fingertips. It cuts through the cold air, brightening the hillside, brightening the underside of the celestia, making it sparkle against the nighttime sky.

How long he allows it to continue he isn't sure. He only knows that when he stops, all that remains of Inan is a blackened pile of soot on the ground above Alayazhar.

Nasim woke sweating as the hammock he slept in swayed. The room was dark, but he could see light coming through the shutters of the nearby porthole. He reached out and flicked them open. Through the small window he saw only driving white snow swirling and collecting at the window's edges.

He rocked himself out of the hammock and onto the cold deck as Khamal's memories faded.

He began to shiver. But of course it was not simply the cold of the ship or the dampness in his clothes. He had known that Khamal was rigid in his views. Even ruthless. What he hadn't known was that he could be brought to murder.

As he changed into dry robes, Nasim wondered: could *he* be driven to such violence? He knew little of Khamal's life before the sundering, but he knew from his time on Mirashadal and his travels around Erahm that he was revered, and it was not merely because of some perceived sacrifice on the part of the Al-Aqim. He had apparently been a man pure of heart and mind before meeting Sariya and Muqallad. His writings could still be found in the libraries of Alekeşir and in the secret holds of the Aramahn. So what had happened? What could have driven him to this, to murder a woman who sought only to protect the world?

If there were answers, they refused to come.

He slammed the lid of his chest closed, cursing himself immediately after for his lack of control.

He needed fresh air. He always thought better when he stood among the elements.

As he left the confines of the hold and headed toward the stairs leading up to the forecastle, he realized that his dream answered at least one burning question. The Atalayina, while not powerless, had certainly been muted by the spell that kept the Al-Aqim on Ghayavand. This was surely why Muqallad was trying to leave the island. With the Atalayina muzzled as it was, he had no choice but to try the ritual elsewhere. And the only logical place to do it was Galahesh; the patterns on the floor of the celestia had shown him this much. With so much aether channeling through one place, it would allow him to complete his ritual and let the worlds do the rest. It also explained why the piece of the Atalayina he'd found in the celestia had felt so lifeless. He'd thought it a combination of its inscrutable nature and his ignorance of the stone's nature, but now he knew the cause, and he wondered what it would feel like away from Ghayavand. What would it feel like if all three were combined?

He stopped near the small cabin Ashan had been lying in since their flight from Rafsuhan. He held his hand above the handle, willing himself to open it and look upon the kindly old arqesh. His hand remained. He gripped it, once, twice, still unable to summon the courage to look upon Ashan.

In the end, he walked on by and continued up to the forecastle deck. There, while stepping out into the driving snow, he saw Sukharam standing amidships, looking out into the storm. He turned and locked gazes with Nasim for long moments. Then he turned and began climbing the shrouds of the starward mainmast, up and up until at last he'd reached the rook's nest, where despite the driving snow he settled himself and began to take breath. He'd done this each day they'd been on the winds since leaving Rafsuhan—nine days running.

"He does it so that he doesn't take revenge on you."

Nasim looked to his left along the gunwale and found Soroush standing there, watching him. White, fluffy snow fell against his beard and turban, both the color of burnt autumn leaves. He'd chosen not to wear his stone of jasper. Nasim didn't know why, nor did he care to ask, but it was telling that he'd had it when they'd fled Ghayavand together.

"Revenge is not in him," Nasim said softly.

"Man can be driven to many things, Nasim. Things we never thought possible." Soroush stepped closer, but seemed to sense Nasim's discomfort and stopped some paces away. This was the first time Soroush had spoken to him since they'd left Rafsuhan. Nasim would never have guessed it, but he seemed shamed, somehow, of their shared history, though in truth Nasim remembered little of it. "He was angry with you for leaving him in your home outside of Alayazhar, but furious when he found out what happened to the girl, Rabiah."

"I would have come had I been able."

"I know," Soroush said, "and I think he knows as well, but for now, perhaps it's best to let his anger burn itself out."

He joined Nasim at the landward gunwale and together they looked ahead of the ship, westward, toward the *Chaika*. The falling snow obscured it, but they could see its silhouette, gray in a haze of white.

Nasim had thought of nothing but Rabiah since they'd left Ghayavand. He should have been more careful. He should have been more prepared. Only, it felt as though there was no time. Every day on Mirashadal had felt like one more day closer to the end. For him. For the islands. For the world. By the time he'd left he felt as though he was years behind. He had to hurry. He *still* had to hurry. There was no time for preparation. He simply had to *do*.

"Nikandr has asked to see you."

Nasim saw no reason to answer, so he remained silent, watching the snow fall between their ship and Nikandr's.

"Shall I send you to him?"

"Where was I found?" Nasim asked. He meant where Soroush had found him—either as a child or as a babe.

If Soroush was bothered by the change of subject, he didn't show it. "What does that matter now?" he asked.

"I'd like to know. I think I deserve that, at least."

"Will that somehow help you to see your way ahead?"

"Where did you find me? Was I stolen away from my mother? Was I born of the Maharraht?"

"Those things don't matter, Nasim."

"They matter to me!"

Soroush stared at him, his face sad but stern. The look was so paternal it made Nasim want to shout, to rage against this man that had stolen him away from some unknown shore and put him to use as a tool, as a weapon, to cause destruction to the Landed.

"You are a small man, Soroush Wahad al Gatha."

He turned at movement among the rigging. Sukharam was making his way back down to the deck.

Soroush turned back to Nasim, his eyes still sad, but now also full of regret. "This I know," he said, bowing his head to Nasim. "This I know."

He stepped away as Sukharam approached.

Sukharam looked confusedly between the two of them, but when Soroush retreated below decks, he approached Nasim and seemed to steel himself.

"Where do you go?" he asked.

It was clear that he was asking out of some sense of duty. He wanted nothing to do with Nasim, but he still believed in the cause Nasim had described to him on that hillside overlooking Trevitze.

"You should return home," Nasim replied.

"Where is home but here?" he said.

It was a phrase common among the Aramahn, but Nasim knew that his heart didn't stand behind those words. "Return home," Nasim said again, "or take to the winds."

"I came," Sukharam shot back, "because the world is torn. Is it not so?"

Nasim was taken aback by his fierceness. "It *is* so, but it is bigger than you or I."

"*Neh*, you were right, Nasim. You are bound to Muqallad and Sariya. You are bound to the tear that runs through Galahesh. And *you* must be the one to overcome it."

Nasim wanted to dismiss him, but at that moment, he seemed wiser than his years. He reminded him more than a little bit of Rabiah, and it shamed him that another was pushing him to do what must be done.

He could feel Sukharam's connection to Adhiya. He could feel those of the vanaqiram and dhoshaqiram who guided the ship as well. He could even feel, as weak as it was, Soroush's, who had had his abilities burned from him by the Aramahn years ago. And yet he could not feel his own. He could not find his way to Adhiya. It had, through the misfortune of his return to this earth, been lost to him. Surely it had to do with the spells Muqallad and Sariya had cast upon Khamal in their haste to prevent him from escaping Ghayavand. Or perhaps it was his own lack of confidence, which had begun on Mirashadal but had since only grown. Or it might have been Khamal's plan all along, his condition somehow vital to his connection to the rift or the Atalayina.

There was one more possibility that Nasim didn't really want to consider, but consider it he did—refusing to do so would not only be cowardly, it would be a grave disservice to the world. His limitations might very well have something to do with the ritual that had saved him on Oshtoyets. He could feel Nikandr standing somewhere on the deck of the *Chaika*. Perhaps a piece of the puzzle lay with him. Why, after all, had he connected to him so strongly on Uyadensk? Nikandr's broken soulstone was coincidence, but there was something there that seemed to be planned.

If only he could unravel how...

He thought of speaking with Ashan, of speaking with Fahroz, or even Nikandr, but the truth was he was sick to death of talking. It only seemed to confuse things further.

The wind gusted, twisting the ship until the pilot corrected their course.

His thoughts pushed him deeper and darker. "You should not follow me, Sukharam."

"Why?"

"Because I know not where I go."

After a pause—a pause that felt as long as the day—Sukharam turned and walked away.

CHAPTER FORTY-SEVEN

Within the kapitan's quarters of the *Chaika*, Nasim sat behind a large desk in the swiveling kapitan's chair. The sun had set over an hour before. A brass whale oil lantern hung by a chain from the beams running along the ceiling, lighting the cabin in a golden glow.

The ship twisted slightly in the wind. The calls of windsmen could be heard outside the cabin door. Men walked about the ship, footsteps thumping against the deck.

Nasim could feel Nikandr striding across the deck, his soulstone a bright flame. He had brought Nasim to the cabin himself, but just as he was readying to close the door the boatswain had come to tell him of a shape they'd spotted along the horizon. Fearing the Hratha, Nikandr had gone to investigate.

Nasim had wondered why Nikandr hadn't summoned him sooner, but the conversation with Soroush had made things clear. Nikandr had asked for Nasim, and Soroush had declined. Why Soroush had declined to allow Nikandr access to Nasim, and why he had eventually relented, Nasim didn't know. Nasim wasn't even sure he wanted to speak with Nikandr, but Sukharam, with his disappointed, sidelong glances, had made his mind up for him.

Nasim leaned forward, the chair creaking beneath him. A number of maps lay across the surface of the desk. Thanks to Fahroz he could read Mahndi, but Anuskayan was still beyond him. The letters were strange and the endless combinations and rules surrounding them made no sense to him. Still, he had seen many maps in Mirashadal, and he knew the islands of the Grand Duchy well. He could point out all of them on the largest of the maps before him. In the upper right corner was Rafsuhan, and though he also had trouble with leagues, he could judge distance well enough from the shape of the islands and the relative distances from others he knew, like Samodansk in the archipelago of Rhavanki, and Uyadensk in Khalakovo. And Ghayavand.

What was clear to him by looking at these maps was that he had traveled thousands of leagues with Kaleh. Thousands. She'd somehow opened up a tunnel between the village in Ghayavand and the outskirts of Ashdi en Ghat. But how? It was something he'd been asking himself over and over since they'd left Rafsuhan.

There were some clues. She was gifted in many of the same ways he was. She needed no stones to commune with Adhiya. She could control any of the hezhan, as he could. It may be as simple as finding the right child. After all, if Nasim had found gifted children, why couldn't they? It seemed improbable, but not impossible.

In the end, it didn't much matter how they'd found Kaleh. What mattered was that they had her, an ally to … do what?

Nasim stared at the map, tracing the line between Rafsuhan and Ghayavand. Why did Muqallad need Kaleh? And what did it mean that she'd helped Nasim escape? Was there now some hope that she would turn away from Muqallad's path of violence? Or had it simply been a moment of weakness?

A tapping behind Nasim made him start. He turned in the chair, but could see nothing beyond the rectangular window but the blackness of the night.

He moved to the window and levered it open. With the bitterly cold wind blowing, a rook hopped inside. It flapped over to a wrought-iron perch in the corner of the room behind the desk, where it walked along and beat its wings and pecked at the crossbar. Nasim stared at the golden band about its ankle, wondering which of the Matri had come.

"Are you still dumb, child?"

Nasim shook his head, confused. "Nikandr isn't here."

"And that's well. We have things to talk about, you and I."

There was no doubt now that this was Saphia Khalakovo. Not only could he hear it in the way she spoke, he could feel her distantly in the aether. He was curious to know what she wished to speak about, but more than anything he was worried that she would try to assume him if he didn't cooperate. It hadn't worked out well for her the last time, but neither had it worked out well for him. He'd been struck by vivid, debilitating dreams in the days that followed, and he had often wondered whether something different might have happened on Ghayavand had he not been so incapacitated on his arrival.

The rook cawed. "You're sure you're well…"

"I am," he answered simply, waiting for her to get to the point.

"Then tell me how you came to Rafsuhan."

"Why?"

The rook arched its neck and flapped its wings. "Don't be impertinent, boy. You're better than that, unless I've missed the mark…"

Nasim took a deep breath and released it noisily. He didn't wish to speak to this woman, but he saw no reason to withhold the information, so he told her what he could of his arrival on Ghayavand, his battles with Sariya and Muqallad, and his eventual flight. He glossed over Rabiah's tale—those memories were his and his alone—but he told her of Alayazhar and Sariya's tower and the akhoz. He told her of his flight through the village of Shirvozeh. He told her of Kaleh as well, a girl he wasn't sure just how to measure. Was she friend or foe? And did it even matter now that he'd left Ghayavand?

"And what of the stones, the Atalayina?"

"What of them?"

The rook cawed again and flapped over to the desk. It turned its dark eye on him. It was not an easy thing to look at, that staring, unblinking eye. "You may be angry with me, Nasim, for what I did to you those years ago, but I don't care. I did what I thought was right for my family, for my Duchy, and for Anuskaya." Finally the rook blinked. "This is important. Vostroma is set upon by the forces of the empire. Galostina may not last the week. The woman, Sariya, was close to having a piece of that stone, but thanks to you it has fallen into the hands of Vostroma's daughter. We have much to thank you for, it seems, but we have need of more—most likely *much* more by the time all is said and done—so grant me this one favor: answer my questions. It may very well help to protect the islands you seem so intent on saving."

"I don't care what you consider important, Matra. It isn't your counsel I seek."

The rook flapped its wings—hopping along the desk and shuffling the maps—and the caw it released sounded strangely like laughter. "And whose *do* you seek, pray tell?"

"My own."

"Poor counsel, indeed. You may think you know what's happening, but you don't. I know this because *I* don't know, and if I don't, I'm sure that *you've* fared little better. We need one another, boy. You, the Landed, the Aramahn—even, it seems, the Maharraht. Muqallad will have his way with the world if given his way. Don't let your wounded pride stand in the way of the greater good."

Nasim had no wish to speak to the Matra, but what was worse, he didn't *trust* her. She said she was concerned over the world and Muqallad's plans for it, but that wasn't true at all. She was concerned over the future of the Grand Duchy, nothing more.

He was saved from answering by Nikandr's entrance. He closed the door and shook snow from his black cherkesska as he removed it and hung it on a hook. "I told you I wanted to be present if you were to speak with him," he said to the rook.

"There are conversations I would have alone, Nischka."

An uncomfortable stalemate followed, in which Nasim suddenly became conscious of where he was sitting. He stood, but Nikandr waved him back down.

"Stay," he said, sitting across from him in the chair that would usually be reserved for guests in this cabin. "Are you well?"

"Well enough," Nasim said.

"Would you care for tea? Or araq?"

"Get on with it," the rook cawed.

"We've had no chance to speak, Mother."

"And our time is short, Nischka."

Nikandr glared at the rook, and then returned his gaze to Nasim as he sat deeper in his chair. "She speaks of our arrival on Uyadensk. There's a delicate matter we must speak of."

"The Maharraht," Nasim said.

Nikandr nodded. "In part. It's an important thing that's about to happen. Something that's never happened before. Nearly everyone on the *Bhadyar* have decided to offer themselves to the Aramahn in Iramanshah, hoping they'll be allowed to rejoin their brothers and sisters."

Nasim shook his head. "The Aramahn won't allow it, not unless their qiram are burned. Even the children may be burned for what their parents have done."

Nikandr nodded soberly. "They realize this, and yet all have still agreed to come."

"Because of Muqallad?" Nasim shook his head. "They've lost their home, and they can't head south to Hratha strongholds. Have you considered that they're only looking for a place to rest and regroup?"

The rook released a harsh laugh.

Nikandr glanced over at the bird, a calculating look in his eye, but then he studied Nasim once more, weighing him. "You've grown, Nasim, but I wouldn't have guessed you'd become so cynical."

"I am older than my years, son of Iaros."

Nikandr stared at him with a strange expression. Unlike so many over the years who had regarded him as if he were a callow youth in need of protection, Nikandr looked deeper, as if he considered Nasim an equal, as if *he too* were older than his years.

"The path to Iramanshah is not as easy as it first may seem," Nikandr continued. "Borund Vostroma still sits the throne of Khalakovo, and he will not take lightly or kindly the landing of a Maharraht ship without his permission."

"And still you will disobey?" Nasim said.

The rook pecked the table. "*Da*, boy, we will disobey. Vostroma has enough to worry about."

"What we need to know is where you wish to go," Nikandr said. "If you wish to join the Aramahn in Iramanshah, you will be allowed to go. But if you wish to remain with us, or go elsewhere, you will be allowed to do it with our blessing."

"What my son neglects to tell you is the depth of our need. The Empire has apparently grown tired of leaving the islands in peace, and Muqallad…" The rook cawed. "Who knows what Muqallad is about?"

"If you would remain with us," Nikandr said, "we will gladly accept your help, but you have earned the right to choose your own way—at least among the islands of Khalakovo, if nowhere else."

Nasim felt off-balance. He felt as though Soroush and Nikandr were going to war over him again. He had been preparing to find his way on his own once more. Leaving Sukharam behind. Leaving all of this behind. And now here was Nikandr and his mother, the Matra, trying to manipulate him, no matter how subtle it might be.

He could not, he decided, allow them to do so. "I will go my own way," he finally said. "I require only a skiff."

"Think well on this child. Do not choose brashly."

Nasim turned calmly to the rook. "I've had all the time I need."

The rook let out a ragged, disgusted sound.

Nikandr glanced at the rook, but then returned his gaze to Nasim. He was surprised. He was disappointed. But in the end he simply nodded. "A skiff you shall have, Nasim an Ashan, and more if you wish for it. You need but ask."

The rook hopped between them on the desk, shuffling the maps beneath its talons. "I ask you to reconsider, child. We—"

"Enough, Mother," Nikandr said. "He's made his decision. Go in peace, Nasim."

"I would go now, if we are so close."

"Of course." Nikandr nodded. "But where? Where will you go?"

Feeling watched, feeling pressed, Nasim stood and moved to the cabin door. "Wherever the fates take me."

CHAPTER FORTY-EIGHT

Upon his return to the *Bhadyar*, Nasim stepped off the skiff and found Soroush waiting for him.

"Come," he said. "There's someone who wishes to speak with you."

"Who?"

Soroush merely turned and headed to the stairs leading down into the forecastle. He came to Ashan's door, motioned to it, and began walking away.

"I've thought on what happened since we last talked," Nasim said.

Soroush stopped and without turning said, "You have?"

"I forgive you for what you did."

"I don't want your forgiveness, Nasim."

"I know, but you have it just the same."

Soroush paused for a moment, and then continued on without saying another word, leaving Nasim standing alone before Ashan's door.

Nasim reached out and held his hand above the handle once more, and this time, though his hand shook, he was able to grasp it, to open it.

Inside the tiny cabin was a bed, a small table with a lit lamp, and a chair. Ashan sat at the edge of the bed, leaning forward with his head in his hands. As Nasim entered, Ashan looked up and smiled broadly, though the physical act of it seemed somehow to pain him. "By the fates who rule above, it does my heart good to see you, Nasim."

Nasim backed the chair up until it rested against the far wall. Only then did he sit down.

Ashan's smile faded. "I don't blame you. I've done little to gain your trust."

"That's not true," Nasim said. "You were the one who showed me the most kindness."

"Kindness, perhaps, but in the end I think I was little better than anyone else." Ashan held his forehead tighter and grit his teeth against the pain. "I searched for you," he said after he'd finally recovered.

Nasim smiled. He almost wanted to laugh. "You won't remember, but we've had this conversation before."

Ashan looked confused but intrigued. "We have?"

Nasim explained the talk he'd had with Muqallad in Shirvozeh, the village near Alayazhar. "We spoke of your travels after I'd been taken to Mirashadal. We spoke of the Atalayina. And many other things."

Ashan frowned. "It makes a certain sort of sense. He was trying to make you believe that it was truly me you were speaking to, and of course a man like Muqallad would find it difficult to lie."

"He spoke to me again at the celestia as Soroush."

Ashan's frown deepened. "Did he?"

"He caught me like this and was rifling through my mind. For what, I do not know. It was Kaleh that saved me from his attentions, and she may have unwittingly done more damage to Muqallad than she knew of."

"Because she prevented Muqallad from finding what he sought."

Nasim nodded. "Still, we were harmed much that day. Muqallad followed us to Rafsuhan to fuse the pieces of the Atalayina together, and if the column of fire we saw above Rafsuhan was any indication, he succeeded."

"Soroush said as much." Ashan sat back in the bed until his back was propped against the wall, though judging by the look on his face it gave him no comfort. "Muqallad wants the Atalayina whole, which was why the three pieces were split among the Al-Aqim those many years ago. Each of them knew that none could be trusted with all three pieces."

"The third now lies upon Galahesh with Atiana Vostroma." He told him of his encounter with Sariya in her tower, how he'd spoken with Sariya, how the monolith had crumbled before him, how he'd prevented Sariya from taking the piece of the Atalayina by giving it to Atiana instead. What he didn't share with Ashan was the story of Rabiah. His memories of her, particularly *those* memories, were still much too raw.

Ashan took this all in and worked it through, as he always did. "It's too bad you couldn't have brought it to Ghayavand."

"If I'd done that, Muqallad would most likely have it now. Better that it lies hidden on Galahesh for now. With any luck she may think that I still have it." Nasim worked at the problem further, more than he had at any time since leaving Rafsuhan. "What I don't understand is what the two of them are doing. Why is Sariya pulling strings on Galahesh when she could be with Muqallad, helping him?"

Ashan drummed his fingers against his knee absently. "I wonder if they're working together at all. Had it been so, they might have been able to find the stone in her tower. Which makes me wonder if they now oppose one another."

Nasim shook his head. "There was a map on the celestia floor. Did you see it?"

Ashan nodded.

"What you probably didn't see was that it showed the progression of the ley lines and how they were compressing around not only Ghayavand, but Galahesh. The straits are certainly the cause, and now Sariya has built a bridge over them. Saphia Khalakovo told me just now that Sariya's using it to attack the islands. She wouldn't do so merely to take Anuskaya, to rule over the Duchies, for to do so would be to ignore Muqallad's plans."

"Perhaps she's fooling herself. Perhaps she wishes to live the life she gave up those many years ago." Ashan said these words with a mischievous glint in his eye. This and the beginnings of a smile that made it clear that he was impressed with Nasim. Perhaps he'd thought Nasim would still be simple, or callow, or at least confused in certain ways like he'd been years ago, but Nasim had grown. He'd left so much of that behind.

"Sariya may be many things," Nasim replied, "but she is no fool. The fact that Galahesh is the very place Muqallad will bring the Atalayina nearly rules out the possibility that she's planning to oppose him. The greater question is how Muqallad hopes to widen the rift once he's made the Atalayina whole. It troubles me that he posed as others, and that he searched through my mind as he did. What could he have been looking for?"

"As for the disguises, it seems to me he was merely trying to get what he wanted," Ashan said.

"Perhaps, but he could have done so merely by forcing my hand. He had you. He had Rabiah and Sukharam."

"Meaning you would have handed the Atalayina over?"

Nasim looked into Ashan's eyes, but couldn't hold them. He was too ashamed. "Of course I wouldn't."

"There's no need to be ashamed, Nasim. That would have been the right thing to do."

"That doesn't make it easier, Ashan."

"I know..."

"And then there is Kaleh to consider," Nasim said, more to change the subject than anything else.

"There is Kaleh," Ashan echoed. "She is the one who caught me. Or at least, allowed Muqallad to catch me. I saw her near the celestia, and I was so confused as to how a child could have come to Ghayavand that I didn't notice Muqallad until it was too late."

"She helped us once," Nasim said. "She may help us again."

Ashan reared back, stretching his ribs and grimacing. "Perhaps she will, but we cannot count on it. So the question remains, where do we go?"

"We?" Nasim asked.

"I would join you. I learned much about the Atalayina before I made my way to Ghayavand. If we find the pieces, I hope to teach you."

"Are you offering to be my kuadim?"

Ashan smiled, showing his crooked teeth. "I suppose I am."

There was a part of Nasim that wanted no one near him. A part that wanted simply to run. But these were not things he could run from, and it would be good to stand at Ashan's side once more, no matter how confusing or painful it might have been in the past.

"Then I think," Nasim said slowly, "I accept."

Ashan laughed. "You think?"

"I accept, Ashan. I accept."

"That's good. And I have an idea of where we can learn more, from people who may, in the end, decide to do more than simply teach us."

Nasim didn't understand what Ashan meant, but when he put his mind to it, the answer was obvious. "Mirashadal."

Ashan's smile widened. "You were always very bright."

Nasim shook his head, nearly laughing. "It would be good to see Fahroz once more."

"You are wise, Nasim." Ashan stood and rubbed his head, as he had many times when he was young. "You are wise, indeed."

Nasim woke at dawn the following morning. He prepared himself to leave, packing away his few belongings into a bag and slinging it over his shoulder. He went quietly through the room as many of the refugees from Rafsuhan slept. A small girl, no more than five, opened her eyes at his departure. She watched him go, brushing away her black bangs from her eyes, but she didn't call out.

He made his way up to the deck. Soroush was manning the helm, adjusting the keel levers, watching Nasim from the corner of his eye. When he finally did look at Nasim, he didn't nod and he didn't smile; he merely watched and then turned away, his attention returning to the attitude of the ship.

Nasim headed aft, to the windward side of the ship where a skiff sat waiting. Sukharam sat in the confines, watching him with a serious expression that was also the tiniest bit hopeful.

Nasim shook his head as he approached. "You cannot come."

"It isn't up to you." This came from behind Nasim. He turned and found Ashan approaching. "It's his choice," Ashan continued. "He deserves to learn from those who would teach him, the same as you."

Ashan stepped into the skiff as Sukharam stared up at Nasim with a hardened expression and said, "I go despite you, not because of you." With that he shifted away on the thwart and hugged the far side of the skiff.

Nasim balanced himself against a nearby belaying line as the sting of their words settled in. *He* should have been the one to teach Sukharam. But he had failed utterly.

Ashan waited, his hand held out, smiling. When Nasim didn't accept his offer of help, his smile faded and his eyes grew serious. "It's your choice, Nasim. You don't have to come."

You're wrong, Nasim thought.

Yesterday when Ashan had made the offer, he'd *felt* like he was making a choice. And here, standing near this skiff, felt like another. But there really was no choice. He'd been trapped from the moment Khamal had died. Despite what had happened on Oshtoyets—or perhaps because of it—he felt as though he'd been walking his entire life in the footsteps Khamal had left for him.

And this was merely one more step.

He nearly turned away, nearly considered returning belowdecks. But he did not. He was trapped, well and truly.

He took Ashan's hand and stepped into the skiff.

What could he do now but find out why?

CHAPTER FORTY-NINE

Two points off the landward bow of the *Chaika*, by the bare light of the moon, the coast of Uyadensk came into view at last. Nikandr had hoped the snowstorm had enough strength to cover their arrival, but it had abated shortly before nightfall. Still, movement around the palotza would be low, and if Victania's plan had worked, she would be the one in the drowning chamber tonight. And even if she wasn't, the attention of the other Matri would be focused on Vostroma as the battle with Yrstanla widened and intensified.

The ship reached the shores of the island and headed inland toward the valley that housed Iramanshah. They plotted a course that avoided the villages on the northern side of the island. It made their approach painfully slow, but it was necessary. He couldn't risk Borund hearing about this, at least until it was too late for him to do anything about it.

The *Chaika* and the *Bhadyar* continued until they came to the meadow east of the valley's entrance. As the *Bhadyar* filled their skiffs with the men, women, and children who would be left here in Iramanshah, Nikandr took his own skiff down.

When he reached solid ground and slipped over the side of the skiff, he saw the outline of two men near the entrance to the valley. One was hunched with age. His name was Hilal, and he was one of the seven mahtar of Iramanshah. A younger man stood by, holding his arm. Hilal was blind and infirm and needed help to walk, yet when Nikandr approached, the young man bowed and stepped away, leaving Nikandr and Hilal alone.

"I thought they might not come, son of Iaros," Hilal said.

"Your thoughts echoed my own," Nikandr replied.

The skiffs were just now dropping from the *Bhadyar*. Nikandr wondered what those men and women would be feeling. To say it was difficult would be to insult their sacrifice. But he had wondered often since learning of their decision: would this be freeing for them after following the path of violence for so many years? Or would it taste bitter? Would they hate themselves for falling back into a life they had long ago rejected?

"These last many months on Rafsuhan were trying for them," Nikandr said as the skiffs touched down.

"Of this there can be no doubt." Hilal was silent for a time. "Did you know that Fahroz came to the village?"

Nikandr felt a chill run through him, and he wondered if Hilal could sense such things. "Did she?"

"*Yeh.* She left only days ago."

"And what did she want?"

"She wanted to speak with you. She hoped to see Nasim as well."

Nikandr shook his head, laughing lightly. "Nasim left my care only days ago with Ashan. He wouldn't tell me his destination, but I suspect he's gone to find Mirashadal."

"The fates work in strange ways," Hilal said in his faraway manner, leaving Nikandr to wonder whether his words were meant as question or statement.

The Maharraht approached. "I must go," Nikandr said, "but I hope we can speak again."

"I hope so as well. Fare well, son of Iaros."

"Fare well, son of Sadira."

Nikandr turned and headed down the well-worn path toward the Maharraht skiffs. He stopped when he recognized the form of Zanhalah. She looked toward him, but she did not call out, she did not wave, and if Nikandr had been close enough to see her face, he was sure that she would not be smiling. Many more came, few of them acknowledging Nikandr's presence.

He did not feel like a savior to these people, but he felt he deserved more than cold shoulders and suffering silence. But the Maharraht were proud, and this was a difficult step for them, so he let it be.

The last to come was Soroush. It was difficult to tell his mood, as dark as the night was. Nikandr thought he seemed regretful, though for what Nikandr wasn't sure.

"Will you still return to Rafsuhan?" Nikandr asked.

"There are more who would come, hiding now in the hills and the forests. I would see them home."

Nikandr found it interesting he used the word *home* to describe the Maharraht returning to the fold of the Aramahn, but he said nothing of it.

An uncomfortable silence hung in the air between them. Nikandr thought of asking him of his intentions. He wanted to ensure that Soroush wouldn't return to wage war against the Grand Duchy; a part of him still wanted to take Soroush back to Radiskoye, to see him hung for what he'd done, but these were empty thoughts at best. He owed Soroush his life, and what was more, he'd never thought to see the Maharraht splinter as they had. They'd been so resolute since their formation, and yet here they were, dozens of them, not only turning their backs on the Hratha, but forsaking the ways of violence.

Only the ancients knew if it would hold, but he hoped it would.

Nikandr was ready to break away when he felt a presence through the soulstone at his neck. He reached for the stone as a chill washed over him. It was not Mother, nor was it Victania. It was another of the Matri, and the presence felt strong, which meant it was most likely Nataliya, Borund's wife.

"What is it?" Soroush asked.

"You must go," Nikandr said. "Quickly. Head west for a day, as we agreed."

Soroush did not question, nor did he linger. The two of them merely nodded to one another and went their separate ways.

As the bulk of the Maharraht walked down the path toward Iramanshah, Soroush's skiffs returned to the *Bhadyar*, and soon the ship was away. The *Chaika* took wing and headed back out to sea the way they'd come. They rounded the island and approached the eyrie from the south, so as to pretend that they had come directly from Rafsuhan. Nikandr thought surely there would be a ship sent to find them, but none came, and by the time the sun rose in the east, he hoped that the Matra he'd sensed had not understood what she was seeing. Perhaps she was too far away to see clearly. Or perhaps she'd seen Nikandr and reasoned that whatever was happening was innocent.

The sun had risen fully by the time they approached the eyrie. Early morning light shone bright against the massive cliffs and the long stone quays. The eyrie held five dozen perches, but there were only a dozen being used, and these only by smaller crafts unfit for flying between the duchies. The ships of war had already flown westward toward Vostroma.

After the eyrie master had signaled them their berth and they'd moored to the perch, Nikandr left the ship, planning to head for the stables to fetch a pony, but he hadn't even finished navigating the quay when he saw his brother Ranos and several men in gray cherkesskas and square woolen caps—the uniform of the Staaya—approaching him.

He knew immediately. He knew that Nataliya had seen him. Knew that Ranos had been alerted. Knew that he and his men were now in grave danger.

Ranos looked haggard. His beard and mustache were trim, as always, but his eyes were dark and the skin along his cheeks and neck seemed to sag, giving the impression of a man who was eating less and drinking more. These past few years serving under Borund had not been kind to him.

"Quickly," Ranos said as he put his arm around Nikandr—not in a brotherly way, but as he might do for someone he was trying to shelter—and led him toward the square that housed the eyrie's offices.

"What did Mother tell you?" Nikandr asked.

"Be quiet until we can make it out of this square and to the—"

Ranos's words trailed off as two full desyatni—twenty soldiers—wearing the uniforms of Vostroma entered the square. As it had been since Father had ceded the Duchy to Borund, the Khalakovos had nominal control over the larger cities and the eyrie. The Vostromas lorded themselves over just about everything else.

The desyatnik of the soldiers, seeing them, called a halt and slipped down from the saddle of his pony. He walked purposefully across the square, as nearly everyone else—windsmen and landsmen alike—cleared the way.

Nikandr groaned inwardly. He knew the officer. His name was Feyodor. He was old, burly, and angry that he'd been passed up for promotion for years, and though he seemed to know that his failure to rise among the ranks and his quick temper both stemmed from his drinking, it did little to stop him from taking it out on anyone who found themselves in his way. Borund was in a foul mood indeed if he'd sent Feyodor to detain Nikandr.

Feyodor held up his hand as Nikandr and Ranos approached. Ranos, however, held Nikandr's arm tightly and guided him toward a handful of ponies, where two more Khalakovan streltsi stood.

The Vostroman soldiers dismounted, most of them ordering themselves into ranks, weapons at the ready, as the others gathered the ponies.

"Nikandr Iaroslov Khalakovo, halt!"

Ranos kept on pulling Nikandr along until they both heard the sound of a pistol being cocked. Even then Ranos was still determined to continue, but Nikandr feared that if Feyodor were pushed too far, he might indeed fire, and as poor a shot as the man was reported to be, he might hit Ranos, so he stopped and turned.

Ranos immediately stepped between him and Feyodor. "He is *my* charge, Feyodor. He's returning with me to Volgorod."

"The Duke requires your brother's presence, Boyar." Feyodor's eyes were bloodshot, and he looked like he dearly wished to be still sleeping, not standing at the eyrie in the day's early light. He took one step forward, past his men, and spoke low to Ranos, the pistol still pointed toward Nikandr. "I don't know what he did, but I've not seen Borund so angry in years. Best he come now. Things will simmer down before nightfall and you'll have him back, safe and sound in the Boyar's mansion." He glanced once over his shoulder. "I'll bring him myself if you'll only step down."

"I won't, Feyodor. He is a Khalakovo, and we stand on Khalakovan ground.

He'll not be taken like a criminal to stand before an interloper."

Feyodor's watery eyes hardened. "He will, Boyar. Trust me in this."

Ranos was prepared to press the issue. The tensions between him and Borund had always run high, but the last year had been filled with a series of escalating incidents. The palotza would levy new taxes from Volgorod so that Borund could funnel more of Khalakovo's money to Vostroma. Ranos would find ways to *tilt the books* so that the levies produced only a quarter of what Borund had hoped. Borund would levy more in turn, forcing Ranos to become even more creative.

It had gotten to the point that armed men from the palotza were escorting tax officials to businesses without leave from the Boyar, who by the strict reading of the treaty needed to approve their presence.

Nikandr stepped in front of Ranos.

Feyodor was edgy, and worried about losing face, a terrible combination in a man such as him, but he lowered his pistol when Nikandr raised his hands.

"I'll go," Nikandr said, more for Ranos's benefit than Feyodor's.

Ranos breathed heavily, his gaze alternating between Feyodor and Nikandr. He seemed shocked at what Nikandr had done, betrayed, but as the seconds ticked by his shoulders dropped and he released a slow breath.

"Treat him well, Feyodor," Ranos said, "or I'll come for your head."

The muscles along Feyodor's jaw worked. He looked like he wanted to reply, but he merely pointed Nikandr toward his ponies.

Nikandr mounted up, and in moments they were off, heading along the eyrie road toward Radiskoye.

CHAPTER FIFTY

Nikandr waited as the door to his cell clicked and opened.

As far as he could tell it was the afternoon of the next day. He'd been given only water and slim bits of dry bread since he'd come. He'd been famished since waking, but now the hunger had faded, replaced by a gnawing emptiness in the pit of his stomach.

Outside his cell, the rustle of a dress came. A moment later, the door clanked, and in strode Victania. Nikandr stood immediately, and as the guard closed the door and locked it, Nikandr embraced her.

"You look well," he said.

And she did. Her cheeks were healthy and full, her eyes bright and sharp. He still marveled when he saw her, half expecting her to have succumbed to the wasting once more, but the ancients had been kind in this at least. Not only had she recovered physically, she'd regained her abilities with the dark. She'd become one of the strongest of the Matri, rivaling even Mother's great strength.

"I'll sit," Nikandr said. "I fear this won't be pleasant."

"Don't smile, Nischka, because it won't. They know of your trip to Iramanshah."

"I'd rather guessed, Tania. What happened? Mother said it was all arranged, that you'd be the one in the drowning basin."

"Nataliya came and relieved me early. Somehow they suspected. Perhaps one of the other Matri warned her." Victania paused, gathering her thoughts before speaking again. "They know of the Maharraht. They know you gave them safe passage to the island."

"They were not Maharraht. They were Aramahn."

"Don't lie to *me*, Nikandr."

"I'm not lying. They've forsaken the path of violence. The qiram among them are going to ask to be burned."

"And the ones who left on the ship?"

"The same. Believe me, Victania. We've come from Rafsuhan, and trouble is brewing, trouble that will eclipse what's happening in the west."

"Don't change the subject. They've convened a tribunal, Nikandr. They're discussing your transgressions now in Father's hall. They will find you guilty. The only real question is the punishment that awaits."

"They won't hang me, if that's what you're worried about."

Victania's features grew fierce, a look she rarely leveled against him. "Watch your tongue. You don't know what it's like here anymore. Did you hear what I said? They've convened a *tribunal*, and they very well *may* decide to swing you from the end of a rope."

"Such things can only be decided at Council."

"We are at war, Nischka. And Borund has been licking his gluttonous chops at the seat he already holds in all but name. Think… Think what Ranos would do if his brother were hung in the very courtyard of Radiskoye."

Nikandr considered this. Perhaps the war with Yrstanla was more serious than he'd guessed. Vostroma might even fear for its very welfare, and with Khalakovo in thrall, they might just use this incident as an excuse. And if he *were* hung, Ranos would rally the streltsi of Volgorod and he would come for blood, and then Borund would have two traitor brothers of Khalakovo to present to the other dukes. Many of the duchies, certainly those in the south, had already begun to refer to Khalakovo as the northernmost island of Vostroma. Father's honored place at Zhabyn's side or not, the dukes might very well decide to grant Vostroma their wish—for permanent assumption of Khalakovan lands.

"It will take the northern dukes less than a minute to see through this. They know what a bully Borund is."

"If this had happened three years ago—even one year ago—I might have agreed with you, but they are weakened, Nischka. They are tired. And the last thing they want to do is go to war with the South again, especially with the Empire standing on our very doorstep with bloodied swords in their hands."

"Go to Ranos," Nikandr said, "and tell him this. All of it."

"He *knows*, Nischka. But he's been pushed to the brink. Borund takes and takes and takes, no matter that Father stands at the Grand Duke's side. He will not allow himself to be pushed further, no matter what you or I or even Father says. And if you cared to spend more time on the shores of your homeland, you'd know that."

"Don't preach to me, Tania. We each find our own way to help. The Maharraht saved my life, and they may very well have saved many lives from the threat building in the east."

"Muqallad and the stone—Mother told me of it—but really, how is this different than what we've faced from the Maharraht for generations?"

"Don't underestimate him, Victania. He is no less strong than Nasim was those years ago, and he now has the Atalayina."

"So Mother has said, but when a wolf lies before you in the field…"

"Don't throw proverbs at me. The wolf that lies in the woods could feast on our flesh as well, and mark my words, Muqallad will not remain beneath the shadows of the boughs for long."

Three soft knocks came at the door.

Victania glanced over and stood. "I must go. Ranos and I will speak to Borund, Nischka. In the meantime"—she reached the door and knocked on it softly—"don't do anything stupid."

In moments she was gone, leaving Nikandr alone with his thoughts. He waited hours more, wondering what might be happening in the *tribunal* being held several floors above him.

He found out as he was beginning, at long last, to nod off.

The door opened suddenly and jolted him awake.

Viktor Avilov Vostroma, husband to Atiana's sister, Mileva, strode into the room, coughing heavily as he came.

Viktor was a heavyset man, and though he was barrel-chested and older than Nikandr's father, he had always seemed strong, like a prized mastiff. His pepper-gray beard was trim, and he had a sharp look in his eye that meant he felt he had the upper hand—Viktor had always been a terrible player at trump.

Had it been Borund himself who'd come to visit him, Nikandr would not have been quite so worried. Borund was taken with the occasional fit of anger, but Viktor was a different sort of animal. He was a minor noble in House Vostroma, a man due little. The only reason he'd been given the hand of Zhabyn's daughter was because, at the time of the arrangement, Viktor owned the rights to three mines that had become suddenly important when rich veins of jasper had been discovered. Ownership of the mines had been formally transferred to Zhabyn and Viktor had taken Mileva. Knowing Mileva as he did, Nikandr was sure it didn't take long for Viktor to figure out which end of the bargain had been worse.

He'd been pushing ever since—if the stories of his bellyaching were to be believed—for a larger title and more holdings, things Zhabyn had been ever more reluctant to grant, but when Khalakovo had been ceded to Vostroma, Viktor had quickly found himself on the next windship to these shores. He, like many on Vostroma, thought it a permanent change in the structure of the Grand Duchy. He'd been vying for Ranos's title, to push him from the Boyar's mansion so that he could move in and pull on the Boyar's coat, and if things continued as they had been, Nikandr wasn't so sure Borund wouldn't do it.

As Nikandr pulled himself up from the bed, Viktor pulled a chair out from the nearby table and fell into it. He scratched at his beard and clasped his hands around his ample belly, his jaundiced eyes glaring at Nikandr as if he'd just caught a hound escaped from the kennel. Nikandr refused to sit. Instead, he leaned against the stone wall and stared down at Viktor as if he were a boy.

Viktor frowned and coughed again before speaking. "Do you know what they say of you in the halls of Radiskoye?"

Nikandr stared, keeping his expression relaxed.

"They say you've forsworn vodka in favor of araq. They say you keep the stones of a qiram and wear them in your cabin at night." Viktor paused. "They say you find solace only between the legs of the Aramahn. People talk, Nischka. The truth grows twisted in the telling, but with you I wonder if they've not struck truth."

"What do you want, Vostroma?"

Viktor chuckled, pleased with himself. "Three sotni were sent this morning to round up the enemy you brought to these shores."

"Iramanshah will not give up their own."

"In this case"—Viktor grinned, a ghastly affair filled with yellowed teeth and baggy eyes—"they just might. The real question is whether you'll admit to helping them."

"What difference would that make? You've already had your trial."

Viktor frowned and glanced back toward the door—clearly wondering who had told him of the proceedings but unwilling to ask—but then he relaxed and a satisfied smile came over him. "It may matter, Khalakovo. If you admit to it, perhaps some will be spared, the children, perhaps the women."

A vision of Zanhalah and the others from Ashdi en Ghat came to Nikandr, and his stomach sank. "They won't give up their own," he said again, more to convince himself that none would die on account of his actions.

"Say it, Nischka. Say that you aided them. Surely there are some you wish to save, and if you confess, I'm sure that can be arranged."

Nikandr nearly did. He hated that Viktor, this jackal, this carrion crow, had come in place of Borund himself. He hated that he had to sit before an interloper in his own house and debate whether to trade the lives of the Maharraht—a people he had been raised to hate—over his own. But then he began to wonder why the question was being asked at all. Just how much had Nataliya seen while she was in the drowning basin? She had taken over some time during that night, and from what Victania had said, she would have had plenty of time to watch, but perhaps she'd been too late. Perhaps her blood had been up and she'd had trouble slipping into the right state of mind to take the dark.

Nikandr decided he'd been wrong earlier. Sending Viktor to exact a confession had been the perfect choice. Keep Nikandr off balance and angry so that something might slip.

Viktor began coughing again, and this time it didn't stop for a good long while. He leaned forward and coughed heavy and long into his closed fist, his back heaving, his body rocking back and forth. When Viktor raised himself to a sitting position once more, his eyes were red, and the yellow at the corners of his eyes stood out even more.

By the ancients, why hadn't he noticed it before? Yellow eyes were common enough, especially among aged men who itched when their vodka glass grew dry, but it was one of the early signs of another condition.

"How long have you had it?" Nikandr asked.

Viktor stared at him. "What do you mean?"

"You know what I mean." He placed his ring finger over his lips, the not-so-subtle signal one used in social situations to indicate someone had the wasting.

He stared at Nikandr's finger as if he was going to deny it, but they both knew Nikandr had had the wasting for nearly a year, and now that Nikandr was on to him, it was as plain as day.

Viktor stood and stalked over to the door and rapped on it three times.

"You were right, Khalakovo. The Aramahn refused to identify the Maharraht you delivered to them, but Borund's orders were clear. When they refused, ten Aramahn were lined up at random outside the entrance to Iramanshah. Muskets were trained on them, and we would have killed them, and ten more every hour—"

The muffled sound of keys jingling filtered into the room, and the door swung wide.

"—but the mahtar volunteered." With that, Viktor made to leave.

"Wait! Viktor, what do you mean?"

Viktor turned back. His face was once again satisfied, but now it was grim as well. "The mahtar. All seven of them. They volunteered themselves to be hung in the place of the Maharraht. And Borund agreed."

CHAPTER FIFTY-ONE

Nikandr slept fitfully, thinking of Hilal. He knew the other six mahtar as well, but he knew Hilal the best. He'd taken Fahroz's seat after she'd left with Nasim for Mirashadal. He was a gentle man. A learned man. But most of all, he was a caring man. He, much like Ashan, seemed to embody the calmness of center that the Aramahn were ever searching for.

Had it been Hilal who thought of the idea of offering themselves for the lives of the Maharraht? It had been a day Hilal most likely thought he'd never see: so many Maharraht forsaking their ways and taking up the life of an Aramahn once more. Many of the children would never have been exposed to any other life, and here they were being offered to the people their parents had betrayed in their quest to drive the Landed back to the Motherland.

And now, in order to protect them, Hilal had given himself. He and the other mahtar. In a way, it made sense—the Aramahn were quick to sacrifice themselves for the greater good—but that made it even more discouraging. This was an unprecedented event. One or two Maharraht had returned to the fold of the Aramahn over the years, but never so many at once. It might even have become a bridge to peace. But not now, not if those six men and women were killed.

In the end, Nikandr couldn't sleep. He woke well before the four Vostroman streltsi came for him. When they did, he pulled on his cherkesska and followed them, hoping to speak with Borund away from others where he might at least listen to reason.

When he came at last to the long hall that led past Radiskoye's central garden, he could see through the leaded glass windows that a gibbet had been stood in the center of the courtyard. He could see men gathered there, but he didn't realize that none of them were Khalakovan until he stepped out from the hall and into the chill morning air. The smell of the sea filled the air, and the sound of the surf rose up from the base of the cliffs far below the eyrie of Radiskoye.

A handful of Vostroman royalty watched him pace forward. Borund and Viktor were among them, and they were flanked by two dozen streltsi wearing the seal of Vostroma. Their faces, to a man, were judgmental, angry, as if Nikandr had somehow called down the fury of Yrstanla on their homeland. He thought surely there would be at least one representative from Khalakovo. Ranos or Victania or Yvanna. But there were none.

As Nikandr was led forward, a portion of the courtyard previously blocked by a jutting corner of the palotza came into view. Here the gallows stood, and when he saw it against the backdrop of the eyrie and the cold gray sky, he stopped, his fingers going cold. Through the shrubs in the nearby garden, the wind whined before dying down once more.

Four men and three women stood on a raised wooden platform, Hilal and Amra and Saeeda and the rest. Black woolen sacks covered their heads, and nooses hung loosely around their necks, trailing up to the stout wooden beam above them. A hangman, a stout, hard-looking man whose left arm ended in a stump, stood on the far side, waiting with his hand on the lever that would drop the trap doors beneath the mahtar.

The courtyard was a study in silence. The sigh of the surf and the distant call of gulls were the only sounds to be heard. Knowing Borund as he did, Nikandr was sure that he'd ordered it so to let the scene sink in.

At last Nikandr's escort of streltsi bowed and stepped aside and Borund broke away from the gathered royalty and stepped close to Nikandr, most likely so they could speak for a moment in peace. He held a rolled proclamation in one hand, but Nikandr could spare no time to wonder how it might read. He was too struck by how much Borund had changed. The Borund of five years ago was large, healthy, vibrant if a bit headstrong. This Borund looked beaten and crooked, even defeated.

"Don't do this," Nikandr said to him, loud enough for only Borund to hear. "These are innocent men and women."

"They sheltered our enemy."

"So you would *hang* them?"

"Some must pay, Nikandr."

"*Nyet*. They are innocent. They need not die."

"They are *not* innocent." Borund's face became splotchy with anger. "How could you bring them here, Nikandr? They were Maharraht."

"They have forsaken their ways. Don't you see?"

"They were *Maharraht*," he repeated, loud enough for many of those gathered to hear.

"They *weren't*," Nikandr said, softly but sternly. "Not any longer. They were going to allow themselves to be burned."

"What is burning when their minds are still willful and full of hate?"

"They were not willful!"

Borund looked at Nikandr with naked disgust. "You have been among them too long, Nischka. Too long by far."

"Those Maharraht were ready to lay down arms. More might have followed. It might have been a path to peace, Borund. But none will do so now, and any that had thought to rejoin their brothers will redouble their efforts to harm us, to kill and to slaughter."

Nikandr glanced to the gallows, where the Aramahn stood serenely. He turned back to Borund, his mind wild with possible ways to change Borund's mind, none of them likely to succeed.

Until he came to one.

He stared Borund in the eye, willing him to listen. "What if I confess?"

Borund's eyes went wide. His hand adjusted its grip on the proclamation. "Nischka, be quiet."

"Borund, what if I—"

Borund's fist came so fast there was nothing Nikandr could do to stop it. It connected across his jaw, sending him sprawling to the stones.

Borund's footsteps crunched over the river stones. Nikandr tried to rise, but Borund leaned down, the bulk of him blocking the light of dawn, and placed one meaty hand against Nikandr's chest, pinning him in place. "Say nothing, Nikandr, or I'll be forced to put you on the gallows next to them."

Then Borund took the front of Nikandr's cherkesska with his two massive fists—the rolled proclamation crumpling—and pulled Nikandr to his feet.

Nikandr turned his head and spit to clear his mouth of the blood that was welling from the cut inside his cheek. He stared into Borund's eyes. He was shocked—not by what Borund had done, but the reason behind it.

By the ancients, Borund was *protecting* him.

He wondered, then, why Viktor had been sent. Perhaps Borund's place on the throne of Khalakovo was not so strong as Nikandr had imagined. Or perhaps Viktor had come of his own accord.

Whatever the reason, it was clear that Borund thought it certain that Nikandr would need to die as well were he to confess to bringing the Maharraht to the shores of Khalakovo.

Borund turned to the gallows, finality in his eyes.

"Bora, I would not have brought them if I feared they would harm us. You must know this."

Borund licked his lips. He swallowed.

"I brought them to the very doorstep of Radiskoye. Why would I have done this if I thought they meant us harm?"

Borund raised his arm.

"Borund, don't!"

And brought it back down.

The hangman pulled the lever.

The trapdoors swung, and seven mahtar fell, jerking against the ropes. Their arms flailed. Their legs kicked. And then one by one, they all went still, while the wind sighed through the garden's short trees and the surf called up from the cliffs.

Nikandr didn't know how long after the hanging Borund began to read, but he heard his low voice, reading in somber tones the contents of the proclamation. "Let it be known that as of this day, the sentence of death for Nikandr Iaroslov Khalakovo is to be stayed, pending his duty to the Grand Duchy, which takes precedence. Upon successful execution of those duties, the stay shall be writ permanent."

Upon this, the expressions of the Vostroman royalty turned to distaste. Viktor stared hard enough that Nikandr thought he might pull his pistol, shoot Nikandr in the chest, and be done with it once and for all.

While Nikandr stared at Borund, confused, the royalty and the streltsi began to disperse.

Borund turned to him. "You are to take command of the *Lihvyen*."

Nikandr stared, the words of Borund's proclamation still swirling in his mind. "For what purpose?"

Borund gripped the scroll so tightly it creased in the middle. "They're attacking the spires, Nikandr. Last night, they destroyed the one on Ildova, and Mother fears they've done the same thing to the spire on Tolvodyen."

Nikandr was numb. He could hear the creaking of the ropes as the bodies swung in the wind. The notion that Yrstanla was attacking the spires didn't make sense, and he could only think to ask one simple question. "Why?"

"We don't know. It's sent a wave of storms through the islands of Vostroma and Nodhvyansk… We've never seen the like." Borund stared deeply into Nikandr's eyes. "If you want to protect the Grand Duchy, as you say you do, then go. Use the gifts the ancients have given you. What few ships we've held back in the North are gathering. More ships will be outfitted from the merchants, but you must go now. Take the *Lihvyen*. Stop them from taking Vostroma."

Nikandr looked up to the men and women swinging from the ropes of the gallows. "We are not done with this, Borund."

"We're done for now," he said as he turned his back on Nikandr and began walking away. "If you're still of the mind, take it up with me on your return."

The sky was gray and the wind was blustery. A scout ship had been sent out in advance of the wing of ships Nikandr now flew with. He commanded the *Lihvyen* and seven other ships—all that could be cobbled together from the ships that hadn't already been sent to defend Vostroma.

Nikandr stood at the *Lihvyen's* helm, working the levers of the rudder while Jahalan and Anahid stood amidships summoning the wind and controlling the *Lihvyen's* heft. Near the helm stood a wooden perch. Upon it, tethered with a leather cord, was a black rook. It had been silent for nearly a day. Over the last three days, Victania and Mother and Borund's wife, Nataliya, had assumed the form of the rook and spoke to him of the latest news—such as it was. None of them had so far been able to penetrate the storm surrounding Vostroma, and when the ships had approached the nearest of Vostroma's islands the rook had gone silent. No doubt the Matri were trying to penetrate the storm, but had so far been unable to do so.

Nikandr reached up and pulled his soulstone out. It had been resting against his skin, the way he preferred it, but he had taken it out every few hours to see if he could sense something—anything—from the Matri. While holding himself steady against the helm and gripping the stone in his right hand, he opened his mind to the darkness between worlds. He called to his mother, to Victania. He called to Atiana, hoping in vain that she would hear him, that she would know that he would come to find her when he could. But as it had been every other time since the rook had gone silent, he felt nothing. Nothing at all. It left him feeling cold, colder than the bitter winter wind could account for.

Elykstava, the first of the islands in the Vostroman archipelago, sat east of their position. They had bypassed it on their way south, reasoning that the forces of Yrstanla would not have come so far north. There was part of him that wanted to continue past Vostroma and on to Galahesh, but he'd heard no word of Atiana or Ishkyna or their father, the Grand Duke. Another part of him wanted to go to Galostina to find his father, but this would be a foolish course of action as well. Yrstanla was attacking *here*, and if they'd learned anything in the past few days, it was that their spires must be protected at all costs.

Something caught Nikandr's attention near the horizon. He took his telescope and studied the western sky carefully. He soon found it—a small, six-masted cutter flying well beyond the safety of the ley lines. It was most likely a ship of the Grand Duchy, one that had fled the battle or been sent north to bring news. As he watched it became clear that the ship was adjusting course to meet them.

They allowed the ship to approach, and indeed, they saw men of Anuskaya standing at the gunwales, waving their arms, cheering. And no wonder, Nikandr thought. Their ship seemed barely held together. Massive holes from cannon shot marked the hull, and the sails had been hastily repaired—no doubt only in the last few days—from innumerable tears and holes. The masts were generally in good shape, though its two starward masts both had lengths of iron buckled along sizable cracks to prevent the upper lengths from snapping entirely.

"It's good to see you," Nikandr called across the distance to the kapitan, a man of Vostroma, as it turned out.

"Not as good as it is to see you," he shouted back. He held a canister in one hand, a tube of wood they transferred to the *Lihvyen* with a length of cord.

Nikandr opened it and found a note contained within—news from Andreya Antonov. Ranos and Father had squared off against him during the Battle of Uyadensk, but Nikandr was glad to see him still alive, for he was a shrewd tactician. He wrote much the same news as they knew already—that the spires on Ildova and Tolvodyen had indeed been destroyed. He feared that the next to go would be Pradosht, for the forces of Yrstanla had landed and positioned themselves well. No doubt they would soon take the fort there and destroy the tower with gunpowder, either from the stores they'd brought or the stores in the very fort they sought to take.

He asked that the Duchies of Khalakovo and Mirkotsk and Rhavanki spare no effort to send all the ships available and to connect to the fleet that had formed around Kiravashya. They hoped to stop Yrstanla there before they could get to Palotza Galostina, and so they asked all ships to make haste there to receive orders from Andreya.

Nikandr read it again before rolling it up and putting it back in the tube. No doubt ships had been sent with similar messages eastward for Dhalingrad, Lhudansk, and Khazabyirsk, and southward for Nodhvyansk and Bolgravya.

"Have you more to deliver?" Nikandr called loudly to the other kapitan, holding up the tube.

"I do, My Lord Prince," he shouted back.

"Then go. Bring news to Khalakovo and beyond."

"I will, My Lord."

The ship continued on, and Nikandr wondered about the wisdom of Andreya's words. It made sense to band the ships together in defense of Vostroma's largest island, her largest cities, and her seat of power, but Yrstanla didn't seem interested in taking land. Their purpose was apparently only to destroy the spires, and if that were so, why would they take their forces into the teeth of the lion? Why wouldn't they bypass Kiravashya altogether and take out as many spires as they could throughout the undefended islands?

In only hours, Nikandr and his wing of ships might reach Alotsk, but in doing so they would leave Elykstava defenseless. What if Yrstanla had targeted the furthest of Vostroma's islands? Were *he* after the spires, that's where he would go.

He looked to the southwest, toward Kiravashya, toward Galostina and his father.

I'm sorry, Father.

"Styophan," he called.

"*Da*, Kapitan." Styophan—as he had on the *Chaika*—was the ship's acting master.

"Send word. The four trailing ships will continue on and report to Kiravashya."

"And the lead ships?"

"We head east to Elykstava," Nikandr said. "If all goes well, we'll return to Kiravashya shortly."

Styophan paused, but only for a moment. "*Da*, Kapitan."

The *Lihvyen* turned and with the two trailing cutters—both of them small and ill-equipped but fast and maneuverable—headed east. Nikandr's stomach churned as they sailed toward Elykstava and the small fort that stood upon her northern shores.

It took hours, but eventually they saw her, a hard black jewel among the ocean blue. As they came closer, he could see a small fishing village along the southern shore. He could see farmland on the higher plateaus.

And then the fort and her spire came into view.

Still standing, Nikandr thought, and not another ship in sight.

They'd come for nothing. They'd delayed their arrival to Kiravashya by as much as a day, all because he thought Yrstanla would send some token force here.

"Shall we turn back, My Lord Prince?" Styophan called.

"*Nyet*," Nikandr said. "Circle the island and let's return."

"You're sure?" Styophan said softly.

"Call the orders, Styophan."

"*Da*, Kapitan."

They continued around the northern side of the island. As they went, Nikandr felt his stone. It had felt dead before, but here—perhaps because of his proximity to the spire—he felt something at last. It was not the feeling that a *presence* was near, as he felt with the Matri, but instead a yawning emptiness, as if he stood near the edge of a great chasm, and the closer the *Lihvyen* came to the spire, the more pronounced it became.

"Prepare for battle," Nikandr said to Styophan.

Styophan snapped his heels and bowed his head, and then left, giving hand signals to the crew that were quickly passed around the ship and to the trailing cutters.

Nikandr met Jahalan at the mainmast. "Can you feel it?" he asked.

"I feel *something*," Jahalan said, "though I know not what. It feels strange here. My havahezhan is distant, and it grows more so the closer we come to this island."

"Anahid?"

Anahid sat at the base of the mainmast, her arms out and her hands barely touching the surface of the windwood. It seemed as though she hadn't heard him, but then she answered, her voice hoarse. "The same, son of Iaros"—she swallowed—"though for me it is much worse than Jahalan describes."

Nikandr moved to the fore of the ship and stared at the fort, which was now in easy view, and he realized that though the flag of Vostroma was flying, there were no signs of life within the keep.

He raised his telescope to his eye and studied the fort closely. There was no one. Along her tall gray walls. On the road leading eastward. No one.

He remembered a cove that was set into the northern shore of the island, a place surrounded by steep hills. It had harbored, he recalled, many ships during a famous battle during the War of Seven Seas.

He swung the telescope along the coast, searching for it.

He might not have found the cove as distant as it was if he hadn't noticed the tops of the masts and rigging that could barely be seen above the hill that stood between the cove and the *Lihvyen*.

"Rise!" Nikandr called. "Rise, and pass the signal!"

No sooner had he said these words than the first puff of smoke came from the nearest of the fort's cannons.

CHAPTER FIFTY-TWO

Atiana was awakened by a hand on her shoulder.

She sat up in her bed and found Sihaş standing over her. "What?" she asked, rubbing her eyes and pulling the thin blanket off her.

"The guards are coming this way."

Ishkyna, lying nearby, woke and groaned. "Let them come."

Atiana shoved Ishkyna's backside with one foot. "Get up, unless you wish to wait for them alone."

"If it means I can sleep longer, I will."

Atiana kicked her again, harder. "Get up."

Ishkyna slapped her foot away and rolled up in bed until she could rest her head in her hands.

Atiana pulled on her boots and raked her fingers through her grimy hair. She already wore the Galaheshi peasant dress she'd worn for the past week. It was properly grubby, to the point that she looked like half of the women that dared wander about the city.

In little time all of them were ready. Ushai, Ishkyna, Atiana, plus Sihaş and Irkadiy and two of their streltsi. The other streltsi had been quartered in a farm to the south. There had been no sense in keeping so many in one place—too much chance of discovery.

They slipped out the back door and into the cold night wind. The street was filled with small homes built close to one another, most of them narrow and built to two or three stories. Atiana studied the windows closely, wondering who might be watching. In one she thought she could see the silhouette of a girl behind white curtains. When they came closer however, the silhouette was gone. Perhaps she'd gone to tell her parents, but that only made Atiana wonder whether her parents would suspect who was walking down their street, and, more importantly, whether they'd run and tell the city guard.

They continued on, and the feeling of being watched grew until Atiana's skin itched from it. In more and more homes she thought she saw faces, or watching eyes, and though she came to understand they were merely hallucinations brought on by too little sleep, it didn't make her terror any less real.

For seven days they'd been in this city, being woken at all hours, slipping from one section of the city to another, all in hopes of staying one step ahead of the Kamarisi's men.

Twenty minutes into their walk, one of Sihaş's sentries returned to tell them that the guardsmen had come to the room they'd just left and were questioning the mason who owned it. Atiana prayed to the ancients that they would be spared. So far, the people that had sheltered them had come to no harm, but it was only a matter of time before one of them was taken to the city square at the base of the Mount and hung.

In time they came to a servant's home behind a large house in a section of Baressa that had once been affluent. Hard times had come and some of the buildings had fallen into disuse.

Ishkyna dropped into a chair covered by a sheet and leaned back, closing her eyes immediately. Ushai sat on the floor, crossed her legs, and took long, measured breaths. Meditating. Again. It had begun to grow on Atiana's nerves.

Unable to watch her any longer, Atiana investigated the small home. It was bare, but she could tell it had once been quaint, a place she would have been pleased to have tea in, to visit relatives in. Now it seemed lost and forgotten among the immensity of Baressa.

They could not stay here, she knew—this had been planned only as a temporary hiding place—but she hoped it could shelter them for a few days at least. They were running out of places to go. The Shattering was off-limits to them now; it had been from the moment Sariya had discovered that they'd been hiding there, that they'd used it to attack her. Since then, they'd been wandering the neighborhoods of Baressa, never staying in one place for more than a night, biding their time until Sihaş found a way to reunite them with his countrymen.

The days after the keystone ceremony on the bridge had been brutal and bloody. Hakan had made examples of those he thought had been plotting against him. In some cases, he'd been right; in others, Sihaş had said, he'd merely been using it as an excuse to right a wrong that had been festering in Hakan's mind for years. And once Hakan's bloodlust had taken hold of the Lords of Galahesh, it had spread like wildfire. Hangings and shootings had been commonplace in the days after the attack.

Only after the fifth day of terror, when Hakan had lined seventy-two men and women along the tallest section of the kasir's curtain wall and pushed them to their death one by one, had the killing subsided. For the past several days, things had been quiet, though whether this was due to a natural bleeding of tension or a simple dearth of anyone else to accuse and summarily hang Atiana didn't know.

Irkadiy and Sihaş stood by the window, watching the empty row outside. There were no guardsmen visible, but the sentries Sihaş had posted were good. They would have warning should the guard find them again.

"Where will we go?" Atiana asked.

Irkadiy turned to Atiana, his face haggard under the light of the lone lamp on the far side of the room. "My cousin has found a new home."

"We won't be going there," Sihaş said.

"We will," Irkadiy said.

"We will not. The homes your cousin finds have received too much attention."

"My cousin is worthy of our trust. I'd stake my life on it. I already have."

"That may be," Sihaş said, walking away and gathering up his woolen coat, cut long and straight in the style of Yrstanla, "but anyone he speaks to might sell our location to the guard."

"They wouldn't do such a thing. Not for Hakan."

"They will if they think overly long on the bounty on our heads."

"I said"—Irkadiy took two long steps toward Sihaş, squaring himself before he spoke again—"they would not."

"Then you're a fool."

Irkadiy bristled, but before he could do anything foolish, Atiana put her hand on his chest. He looked angry enough to slap her hand away, but he did not, and slowly his anger drained. "Forgive me, My Lady Princess. The days…"

"Have been long. And difficult, I know. Speak no more of it." She turned to Sihaş. "Where would you have us go?"

"To the village."

This came not from Sihaş, but Ushai, who still sat cross-legged on the floor. There was a village of the Aramahn deep beneath Baressa, near the straits. In fact, the northernmost ends of the tunnels—dozens of them—ended abruptly at the sheer cliffs. They looked down on the churning water, and gave an impressive view of the opposite cliff face. Ushai said they'd been little used in the last century, but there were still some that came there to study and to rest for a time before the winds took them elsewhere.

Atiana sat in another chair. Dust rose from it, irritating her nose. She pulled from her coat the stone that had been given to her by Nasim. A piece of the Atalayina, a stone—Ushai had told her—that had been used by the Al-Aqim to open the rifts on Ghayavand.

She looked up to Sihaş, who still watched by the window. They had discussed the possibility of going to the village in the days following the battle. It had seemed like a foolish place to go. The wiser course of action had seemed to be to hide among the throngs of the people of Baressa so as to make it more difficult for Sariya to find them, but now—she held the heavy blue stone in her hands—it was becoming clear that they had to act. And soon. With no resistance, Sariya would have free reign to do as she would, and that was something that couldn't be allowed.

As she twirled the stone, it caught what little light there was and brightened it, made it glint.

"We will go to the village," she said.

Within an artfully carved room of stone deep beneath the city of Baressa, Atiana sat with three Aramahn, the mahtar of this village, such as it was. There were less than thirty here now. Most Aramahn had stopped coming to Baressa, preferring to move on to the villages of the Grand Duchy and then westward on their journeys around the world. Those that did come spoke of discomfort in this place. When asked, they couldn't say why—only that it felt as though the land here was not proper, as if it were a place that had somehow gone overlooked by the fates for too long. Some came here for that very reason. They chose to study not those things that brought peace, but those that brought pain or anguish. Such was the case with the two men and one woman that sat at the table, looking at the wondrous stone Atiana had given them.

They had discussed its history, from its legendary history with the Al-Aqim and backward to its origin. In many things they disagreed heartily, one saying it had come from the wastes of the Gaji, another saying it had fallen from the heavens, the third saying it had been left behind when the first of the Aramahn—the first truly gifted in the ways of communion—passed from this world to the next.

In the end, Atiana left them to discuss it unobstructed. She spoke Mahndi fairly well, but their rapid speech, using old terms she had trouble keeping up with, was beginning to give her a headache. And also, she felt that they were holding back because of who she was, and she would rather they discuss the stone without fearing what she might think.

As she left to walk the halls of the village, she had a passing thought that the mahtar might work against her to keep the stone, to make sure it made it into the proper hands, but she rejected this out of hand. When she had brought the stone to them, and when they'd finally come to grips that it may indeed be one piece of the stone that had brought about the sundering, it was clear that they thought the fates had given it to her for a reason. Theirs was now to play their part in the stone's history: to help Atiana along the path the fates had set for her. And so she left it with them to do so.

She walked for a long while, and grew lost, but she didn't care. It felt good to be in a place she'd never been before. It made her feel as though what was going on above in Baressa wasn't really going on at all, and for a little while at least, that was a very comforting thing.

She came to the sun-brightened end of a tunnel. It stopped at a short ledge—a *natural* ledge—that overlooked the straits. To the east towered the bulk of the Spar, stretching its way across the great expanse between the two tall cliffs that faced one another like enemies waging some long-forgotten war. At the center of the bridge were the wooden cranes that were used to drop the keystones to the centermost arch. It was the place where Father had met the Kamarisi, where he'd been betrayed.

Where he'd been killed.

She still didn't know what had happened to the rest. Some said everyone from Anuskaya had been slaughtered on the Spar. Others said they had fled, but had been found shortly after and shot by the janissaries in the streets. Others reported hangings in the high gardens of the Mount. The most likely story, however, was the one that had been repeated most often—that Father's retinue had been taken to the Mount after a short but bloody skirmish. Surely many of the streltsi in attendance had been killed by the Kamarisi's guard, but beyond this it would be foolish to kill men that would be invaluable as bargaining chips.

With Father now gone, who would the Grand Duchy rely on? Borund might be able to fill the void, but the other dukes would speak through the Matri to find a stand-in among those who held scepters, not a regent like Borund. So who? Certainly not Iaros Khalakovo. Despite working himself to a place of honor at her father's side, too many in the south distrusted him, especially Leonid Dhalingrad. Most likely it would go to Leonid, if only for his age, though she hoped it wouldn't be so. Among all the dukes, he was the most bellicose by far. He would have the Grand Duchy throw its resources against the might of Yrstanla, odds be damned.

Atiana was pulled from her thoughts by the tunnels at the far side of the straits. There were more like the one in which she was standing. They were easy to see; the late morning sun was striking them brightly. In one of the dark tunnels she saw a figure robed in white. She wondered how many were on the far side. Probably no more than those on this side, but it still felt strange, a stark contrast, as if the far side were still visited by the Aramahn—alive, not dead like this side of the straits.

A line of wagons making their way across the Spar drew her attention away from the cliffs, and by the time she turned her gaze back to those distant tunnels, the figure was gone.

CHAPTER FIFTY-THREE

When Atiana returned to the room with the mahtar, only Ushai remained. She sat at the long table in the cavernous room, studying Atiana as she entered. Atiana sat on the opposite side of the table so that the piece of the Atalayina lay between them.

"What have you learned?" Atiana asked in Mahndi.

"Much." Ushai stared into the depths of the stone. "And little." She smiled sadly, as if she didn't really want to speak on the subject. "We discussed the origin of the stone at some length. As you may have already guessed, there is much that lies in the past that may now never be recovered."

"Is there no one who knows?"

Ushai shrugged. "There may be some in the Gaji who know more, but the tribes there are secretive. In the Towers of Tulandan, or the libraries of Alekeşir or Thend or Kahosh, you might find more, but even then all you will find are pieces of recorded conversation buried among hundreds and thousands of texts. The people who would know the most, though, are the Al-Aqim."

Atiana smiled. "Perhaps they can spare a moment of their time."

Ushai, instead of showing amusement, stared into Atiana's eyes with a look of fierceness that she'd rarely seen on the face of an Aramahn. "I doubt you would like their demands for doing so."

"You're too serious, Ushai."

"You're not serious enough."

"Then tell me"—Atiana picked up the stone, felt its weight in her hand—"what shall we do? Sariya wants this for a reason."

"*Yeh*, to hand it to Muqallad."

Atiana shook her head. "I've wondered over that. Why is Muqallad to the east, with the Maharraht, while Sariya is here?"

"It only makes sense. They divide their efforts, and we're forced to divide ours as well..."

350 • BRADLEY P. BEAULIEU

Atiana rubbed the smooth surface of the stone. "Why not remain together and overwhelm the Grand Duchy before focusing on the Maharraht?"

Ushai seemed amused by this. "Do you have the sense that things have gone beyond Sariya's control?"

"*Neh*. Which brings me back to my question. What shall we do?"

"The stone," Ushai said. "While we may not know its history to our satisfaction, its history on Ghayavand has not been lost. It is said that the Al-Aqim used it in an attempt to bring about indaraqiram. They failed, and at that moment—as the first of the rifts was created over the island—the stone broke into three pieces. If what your Nikandr says about Muqallad is true, he now has two of the three pieces. I suspect they will try to fuse the stone, to make it one so that they can finish what they began three hundred years ago." She pointed to the stone. "Even broken, it will have strong powers. Were you gifted in the ways of the hezhan, you would no doubt be able to use it to great advantage, communing with elder hezhan, perhaps even summoning one to this plane. Your gifts lie elsewhere, but I suspect it will enable you to touch the aether like you never have before. In this lies our greatest chance."

"To stop Sariya?" Atiana scoffed. "How?"

"I've heard the story from Fahroz of how Nasim, when he was taken beneath Radiskoye, drew upon Saphia Khalakovo's soul. He nearly killed her."

Atiana shivered at the memory. Nasim had done the same to her, as if she were nothing more than water to be poured from an urn. "He did."

"Can you do the same?"

"To Sariya?"

"Would that bother you?"

In truth it would not. What shocked her was the fact that one of the Aramahn had suggested it. And not just any Aramahn; Ushai had been a disciple of Fahroz herself. Which raised the question: would Fahroz condone such a thing? The Aramahn had always been peace-loving, had always stood aside and waited for the fates to intervene on their behalf, but Fahroz had taken a stand on Oshtoyets, inserting herself and the Aramahn of Iramanshah into the affairs of the Landed and the Maharraht, and now here was Ushai, not merely suggesting, but *condoning* murder.

"Don't be so surprised," Ushai said. "There are those of us who have come to believe that we are all of us tools of the fates, and that where we know their purpose, we should use whatever is at our disposal to achieve it."

"You claim to know their purpose?"

"How can I not? The fates would not wish the end of the world in this manner. Of that we can be sure." Ushai's eyes were deadly serious, her expression fervent. It sent a chill down Atiana's frame, but she could not deny the wisdom in her words. With this stone—Atiana hefted it, felt its weight in her hand—she might be rid of Sariya, and then, perhaps, the tide might be turned against Hakan and Muqallad.

"Is there a lake within the village?" Atiana asked.

"*Neh*, and we can't go back to the Shattering."

Atiana knew there was little choice, then, as to where they would have to go. Taking the dark was not a simple matter of submerging oneself in cold water. The water itself had to have a certain quality. It had to be connected in some way to the earth, as it was in the drowning chambers of the Grand Duchy's palotzas, as it was in the Shattering within the deep wells Ushai had found.

As it was in the cemetery, in the mausoleum Bahett had prepared for her.

She wondered whether they would suspect her return. If so, they might have dismantled the fountain.

She hoped not, because if so, their plan would be ruined. But there was really no choice in the matter.

She had to take the dark.

And she had to kill Sariya.

Irkadiy was the first one over the cemetery wall. Four streltsi in black cherkesskas and kolpaks followed. After a soft whistle, Sihaş approached with ten of his men. They brought a rope ladder, which they flung over to the other side. After his men had weighted it down with two men and Irkadiy had done the same on the other side, Atiana climbed the ladder with Ishkyna following right behind.

They were along the far eastern end of the massive cemetery, a place few traveled save the caretakers. They wound their way through the rows, moving up toward the hill where the mausoleum they needed lay. The morning was bitterly cold, but that only helped. The royalty of Baressa liked to visit the graves of their forebears, but on a day like today fewer would be out.

As they walked, Ishkyna fell into step beside her and took her hand. Atiana nearly thought it was in jest, but when she glanced over, Ishkyna was staring straight ahead, refusing—for the moment at least—to look at Atiana. Atiana did not smile. The day was too grim for this. But she felt her heart lighten at this rare show of solidarity from her sister.

"Be careful," Ishkyna whispered.

"I shall," Atiana whispered back.

They reached the mausoleum without incident, though the kasir on the Mount—less than a quarter-league away from their position—looked like a sleeping beast. It felt, as Atiana gave it one last glance before entering the tomb, as though it would wake at any moment, and when it did, all would be lost.

The mausoleum had felt so foreign the first two times she'd come, but she had been here on Galahesh for some time, and now—the small rooms, the trickling fountain, the strangely shaped basin—it all felt familiar. It felt as though it were an old friend, this room deep below the earth, and she just hadn't recognized it before. It was a comforting thought, but she didn't allow it to lull her into any sense of security. What she was about to do was dangerous, and there was a good chance she would never again take to these steps to return to the light.

Irkadiy and the streltsi accompanied her down to the lower rooms. In the closeness, the sound of their muskets rattling, their bandoliers clacking, was loud. When they reached the bottom of the stairs, Irkadiy inspected the rooms carefully, much more carefully than he needed to, and then he stood before Atiana, asking her with a nod, one last time, whether she was ready.

"I'm as ready as I'll ever be," she said.

He smiled at her awkwardly. "On this—" He cleared his throat. "On this day, My Lady Princess, I am proud to be Vostroman."

She took his hand and waited for him to look her in the eye. "I'm sorry I didn't say something when Sihaş spoke ill of your family."

"Think nothing of it."

She shook her head. "Don't dismiss my words. I was thinking the same things as he was." She waited for her words to settle, and indeed, as she'd known would happen, his eyes looked at her in shock, in pain. "But your family was nothing short of heroic for what they did for us. They *saved* us, and I will never forget it."

His eyes softened, and he smiled. A handsome man indeed was Irkadiy. "Thank you, My Lady Princess."

Atiana stepped in and kissed him on the cheek. "Thank *you*."

Ishkyna watched as Irkadiy and the streltsi left, their tall black boots clopping against the stone stairs at they spiraled their way up.

"You were right, you know," Ishkyna said once their bootsteps had faded.

"About what?"

"His family probably did alert the Kamarisi."

"The family his cousin married into is large. Perhaps one was tempted to speak to the guard, but the rest were loyal and brave. Had they not been, we would have been found before the sun had set on that first day."

Ishkyna shook her head. "You're too sentimental, Atiana. It's going to be the death of you one day."

"You're not sentimental enough, Ishkyna. You're going to die rigid and lonely and lost to the world."

Ishkyna's face was not angry at these words. It was instead thoughtful, as if she'd been thinking the very same thing, and Atiana's words had merely reinforced the idea. "Best we begin," she said at last, motioning to the basin.

Atiana undressed and with Ishkyna's help began rubbing the rendered goat fat over her body.

"Be careful," Ishkyna said as she worked Atiana's back. "There's no telling what's become of the aether now that the Spar is complete."

"I know."

"Sariya had a plan, and there's little doubt it included the Matri."

"I *know*, Shkyna." She turned and found, by the golden light of the two small lanterns, tears welling in Ishkyna's eyes. Had this been Mileva, she might not have been taken aback, but this was Ishkyna, a woman so unused to sharing her emotions that this was akin to a deathbed confession in its seriousness. And then Atiana realized. Ishkyna thought Atiana wouldn't wake once she'd taken the dark.

She reached up and with the backs of her fingers brushed the tears away. "I have no plans of leaving just yet."

"Be serious. You need to be careful."

"And as you've said it thrice, there's no longer any doubt that I shall be."

Ishkyna held up the stone, the Atalayina. It glimmered beneath the soft light. It was usually bright, but here in the bowels of the earth it looked deep and dark and dangerous. "Use *this* as your anchor. Avoid the spires, for I think she'll sense you if you do."

Atiana nodded and took the stone. She stepped into the basin, and when she did, the cold of the water felt proper. She welcomed it, welcomed the drawing of her warmth, welcomed the icy touch as she sat and then lay back with the breathing tube in her mouth. This, she decided, this subtle strength granted in part by the Atalayina was a welcome thing.

A welcome thing indeed.

As the water enveloped her and her breathing slowed, her mind became more and more aware of the aether, so near she could nearly reach out and touch its soft, gauzy veil.

And soon… Soon…

She feels the small room. Feels the earth bearing down on it.

She searches immediately for the Atalayina. She thought it would be bright in the dark of the aether, but it isn't. She cannot see it. She cannot even see it in her hands as she lies in the basin.

Though she tries to stop it, her awareness expands. She feels the cemetery with its rows of mausoleums. She feels her loyal men standing guard above. She feels Kasir Yalidoz and her servants within, her guardsmen and her royalty.

She feels the Mount and her winding roads, her proud and ancient estates. She feels Baressa and her thousands upon thousands of children, many of them cowering from the attentions of the Kamarisi. She feels the Spar, and the ley lines being drawn through it from the spire to the north to its sister in the south.

Then, at last, she feels the Atalayina. It is just as deep and dark as it was in the chamber where she lay. It is an anchor every bit as strong as the spires. She tries to bind herself to it, but it is not easy, and she feels herself thrown by the winds. The harder she tries to stop it, the more the aether gusts around her. It draws her thin. The aether rages in her ears, in her eyes, in her mind. She is lost in a wind-tossed sea, adrift and moving further and further from shore.

She feels now not only Baressa, but the whole of Galahesh. She feels Oramka to the north and the islands of Vostroma to the south. There is familiarity among the islands of her homeland. She became a woman there. She learned to tame the aether there. She spent hours, days, carefully tending to the ley lines between the spires of the Grand Duchy.

And she knows immediately that something is horribly, horribly wrong.

The spires…

Some are missing. Ildova to the west, her sister spire to the south, on Tolvodyen. And Elykstava to the east. It is there, on Elykstava, that she feels a momentary pang of familiarity.

Nikandr… Nikandr is there. She desperately tries to reach out to him, but her mind is drawn away, tossed among the waves.

She knows she is losing herself. There were times when she was able to bring herself back from the edge of such madness, when she reined herself back once she knew that she was spreading herself too far and too thin. But this is different. She had always been able to rely on the spires, like mooring lines to anchor a windship. Not so now.

As her mind drifts outward, she remembers Ishkyna's words: *Be careful.*

She had, but she hadn't been careful enough.

The last thing she feels is the well of darkness in the distance—the Atalayina—calling to her like the sirens of the southern seas.

But it is too late, and much too far away.

CHAPTER FIFTY-FOUR

Khamal watches as the boy—the *akhoz*, he reminds himself—shuffles along the lip that leads to the massive rock. Below, the waves roll in, pounding against the far side, sending the spray into a blue sky. Khamal glances up at Sariya's tower and wonders if she watches him.

At last he reaches the top of the rock. The akhoz cowers and looks away when Khamal motions to the flat surface of the rock.

"Lie down," Khamal says, and reluctantly the akhoz obeys.

Somehow he knows. He knows what lies ahead, and in these moments of realization, Khamal nearly changes his mind, nearly orders the boy away, nearly prepares to climb down from this rock to return to the celestia to meditate on what he and Muqallad and Sariya might do to close the rift.

But there are no other paths. He knows this.

He stares down at Alif. The boy cranes his neck, releases a mewling sound like a weak and wounded calf.

"Fates forgive me," Khamal says as he kneels.

He pulls his khanjar from its sheath at his belt. It gleams both wicked and hungry in the sun.

Alif squirms, moves away from Khamal. His mewling becomes louder, more raucous in his ears.

"Nasim!"

Nasim opened his eyes, expecting to see Rabiah kneeling over him.

But he didn't find Rabiah. Rabiah was gone.

He found Sukharam instead. He was staring down at him with a look of concern, but not of caring, and certainly not of love.

Nasim pulled himself back along the flat bottom of the skiff and leaned against the bulwark. Sukharam moved back to his regular seat, the rearmost thwart, and began scanning the westward skies. Ashan was manning the sails.

He took note of their exchange, but said nothing of it.

They were sailing the winds over the Sea of Tabriz. Nasim looked to the southern skies, shaking away the remains of the dream. This dream, the dream of the akhoz and the massive rock, was by far the most common of Khamal's memories. He knew it was significant, he just didn't know how.

He tried to remember more, for he knew that what happened to that boy on the top of the rock was the key to remembering the rest of Khamal's memories, but as always what came after was lost to him, and eventually he gave up.

His thoughts turned instead to the Atalayina. He wondered where the pieces now lay. He hoped that Atiana still had the one he'd given to her. He hoped, in fact, that Sariya had been wounded in some form or another. He couldn't quite bring himself to wish for her death, but if the fates had seen fit to do so, he wouldn't find himself weeping.

He turned west, the direction in which they were headed.

Sukharam looked up to Ashan, who was manning the sails. "How do you know where the village will be?"

Ashan glanced down. "They won't be far from Galahesh, and given that they were flying the Great Northern Sea only weeks ago, it makes sense that they will be found here. Somewhere."

"We are in a place as large as Yrstanla. How can you hope to find them?"

Ashan smiled, showing his crooked teeth. "The fates will show the way, son of Dahanan."

"That isn't an answer," Sukharam replied, his face sour.

But it was as much of an answer as he was going to get. Sukharam had asked much the same thing over the past four days, and received much the same answer from Ashan.

"Leave it be," Nasim said. "If he says we'll find Mirashadal, then it will be so."

Sukharam twisted in his seat to face Nasim. "If his foresight is no better than yours, then I'll have my answer."

"There are ways," Ashan said, interrupting them, "to sense the movement of other hezhan through the bond with your own."

Though his face was still angry, Sukharam went silent. He was gifted, but still callow in the ways of the Aramahn; this wasn't something he'd been formally taught. No doubt he was already trying to do the very thing Ashan had spoken of. Nasim could feel him touching Adhiya, communing with a havahezhan. As Sukharam's anger faded, Nasim could feel him reaching out to the skies around them, waiting for the telltale sign of shifting winds. He scanned westward, then southward, and then westward again. The moment he felt it, Nasim did too—like a shifting of one's attention in the moments following the snap of a branch in a dark forest. Moments later, as if it were a hezhan summoned from Adhiya, Mirashadal floated out from a massive white cloud far in the distance.

It had been nearly three years since Nasim had seen Mirashadal. He had thought that it would have little effect on him were he ever to see it again, but as it neared, he found that an anxious feeling had settled within his chest, and it was getting worse by the moment.

"They won't eat you, if that's what you're worried about."

Nasim looked up at Ashan. "I know."

Ashan laughed. "Do you?"

They continued, and the bulk of the village was revealed. They were below it, which gave visibility to the ballast, the long tower-shaped limb that hung from the center of the concentric rings of the village proper. The windwood glowed brightly under the sun, making it look like one of the iconic paintings of the Landed. As they floated upward and came even with the perches built into the outer ring, Nasim saw smoke rising from the far side of the village. Above it, rain was falling, though it resolved from the very air over the village. No doubt jalaqiram—those who could bond with spirits of water—were summoning the rain to douse the fire, but that didn't explain the fire itself.

He also noticed women, dozens of them, wearing double robes of white and yellow, each with a stone in the circlets upon their brows. They stood on the perches circling Mirashadal. Each had eyes closed and arms spread wide as if they were welcoming the wind, but their stones were opals, not the alabaster of havaqiram, and strangely, they were all facing inward, as if the singular focus of their attention was the tower that stood at the center of the village.

Why would dhoshaqiram, masters of life, be communing in this way around the perimeter of the village? They must be guarding the village, though from what, and why, Nasim had no idea. He looked up to Ashan, but the face of the old arqesh was confused as well, his brow furrowed with thought and worry.

When they came at last to the perches built into the outer ring, Fahroz was already there. She and several others—some of whom Nasim recognized, but many he did not—greeted them as they disembarked.

"The fates work in strange ways," Fahroz said to Ashan as she stepped in and gave him a hug.

"Indeed," Ashan replied, "but please, is all well?"

Fahroz turned and glanced back at the steam and smoke rising in the distance. "Well enough, son of Ahrumea, but we'll have time to discuss that soon." The implication was that she wished to speak with Ashan alone, away from the ears of children—or from *Nasim's* ears in particular.

Fahroz greeted Sukharam, hugging him deeply and welcoming him to Mirashadal. And then she turned to Nasim. She stared at him, maintaining a respectful distance. They were near enough to reach out and hold one another's hands, and yet the gulf between them seemed impossibly wide. There was hurt in Fahroz's eyes, and disappointment, but there was also surprise. Perhaps she thought never to see him again. Perhaps she was surprised he'd gone to Ghayavand and found his way back again. Whatever the reason, Nasim couldn't help but feel like a son to this woman. Even though he had resented her for taking him here to Mirashadal, she had done so with love in her heart—love for him and love for the world.

He stepped forward and took her into a tight embrace. "You were right to give me shelter." He said the words softly, so that only she could hear.

"And perhaps you were right to leave. In the end, we must all follow our hearts." She pulled him away, holding his shoulders and staring deeply into his eyes. "Is it not so?"

Nasim smiled weakly. It was all he could manage, because for reasons he could not quite define, he was on the verge of tears.

Fahroz motioned to the perch, and together, with the other Aramahn that had come to greet them, they made their way toward the center of the floating village. "There is someone who's come," Fahroz said to Nasim as she walked by his side. "She wishes to speak with you."

"Who?"

Fahroz studied him. She used to do this often. She was weighing just how much information she should give him, weighing how much he could handle. His instinct was to look away, as Sukharam was so apt to do, but he was a boy no longer. He would not shy away from such things.

"Tell me who's come," Nasim said.

"You'll see soon enough."

They passed over several arching bridges, through narrow walkways bounded by trellises and boughs and houses, all made of living windwood. They came to the center of the village, where a tower with a winding staircase stood. At the top, upon a platform, stood dozens of men wearing white and yellow robes and stones of alabaster. They were facing outward, each a mate of sorts to the women who stood at the edges of the village.

Fahroz caught his eye. She knew he was wondering just what had happened, but she seemed content to let the answers go unsaid, so he kept his questions to himself.

They took a set of stairs down and finally came to a round structure with oval windows set into it. He couldn't see inside; the windows were covered by drapes the color of coriander. They came to a door, and Fahroz stopped. She motioned to it. "You can speak with her alone for a time if you like. Or you can join us." She pointed to another, similar structure further along the path they were following.

Nasim nodded and the rest continued on, leaving him alone. He turned to the door, feeling suddenly anxious. Who could be here waiting for him?

He reached out, his hand hovering above the simple wooden handle.

Foolish, Nasim told himself. *You're being foolish.*

He pushed the handle to one side. It struck home with a hollow thud, and he opened the door.

Inside was a room with carpets upon the floor and two small lamps upon the wall shedding the barest amount of golden light. He could not see anyone yet in the dimness, so he stepped inside. Only then did he see the form of a girl at the rear of the room. She was sitting, facing him, but his eyes had not yet adjusted to the darkness, so he could not see her features.

He closed the door and at last recognized her.

By the fates… It was Kaleh, the girl from Ghayavand, the girl who had helped him escape.

She was kneeling on the richly colored carpets, hands on her knees, eyes closed. Ages seemed to pass before she finished drawing breath, ages more before she finished her exhalation. She was young, perhaps only eleven, but there was something in her—especially now that she was tranquil and unmoving—that seemed ancient.

Nasim watched her for a time. She was taking breath, a ritual he had never managed to find peace with. It brought only memories of his younger years, when everything was confusion, everything was chaos. He envied those that had mastered it. It seemed to bring them such peace, a peace he hoped to one day find, but in the years since leaving Mirashadal, he had begun to wonder if he ever would.

"It's taken you time to reach the village."

Her voice made him jump. "What are you doing here?"

She opened her eyes slowly—as though she didn't wish to disturb her own breathing—and gazed upon Nasim with emotionless eyes. "I've come to find you."

For a moment, Nasim could not find words, and when he did, he could only manage one. "*Why?*"

"Sit," she said, motioning with one hand.

He did, crossing his legs instead of kneeling as she was. Only then was he able to see the bright red burns along the right side of her face. It traveled down her neck and was lost beneath the simple white shift she wore, but he could see red skin along her right wrist as well.

"I'm sorry for your loss," she said, forcing him to pull his gaze away from her wounds.

The words registered, but Nasim couldn't comprehend her meaning.

"The girl in Alayazhar."

Rabiah. She meant Rabiah.

"Were you close to her?" she asked.

It seemed so distant now, and it felt strange for Kaleh, a girl who barely knew him, to console him for the death of his friend, one that he loved so dearly. "Does it matter if we were close?"

She stared at him, her face unreadable. "I suppose it doesn't."

She said these words with such lack of emotion that it made Nasim's blood boil. It felt as if she were dismissing Rabiah, dismissing what she had done in her life.

He stood and jabbed his finger down at her. "Why are you here?"

"I came for you."

"Why?"

"Because I've come to believe that Muqallad is wrong."

"Just like that?"

There was sadness in Kaleh's eyes. "Sit."

Nasim wanted to scream at her, and he didn't even know why. She was someone who had helped him when she stood to gain little. He looked at the burns on her face and wondered if it had been punishment of some sort. As he stood there, her ancient eyes boring into his, the anger drained from him like snow beneath the summer sun.

When at last he managed to sit and face her, she said, "It's not so simple as you think."

"Things always seem that way, but what could be so complicated about leaving a man like Muqallad?"

"It is *complicated*, as you say, because he is my father."

CHAPTER FIFTY-FIVE

Nasim felt the blood drain from his face. His fingers tingled and a ringing like struck crystal sounded in his ears.

"Muqallad is your *father*?"

She nodded, holding his gaze. She looked like a doe, ready to bolt.

If Muqallad was her father, then Sariya was her mother. By the fates above, a child borne of the Al-Aqim. What power she must hold. He had seen it with his own eyes, and still the possibility seemed ludicrous. Impossible.

"How old are you?"

She looked down at her hands, which she wrung for several moments before speaking. "I don't know."

"Sariya and Muqallad were awoken only five years ago."

She stopped wringing her hands long enough to stare at them as if they belonged to someone else. "My mother tells me that I've grown faster than a child should. She thinks it's because of Ghayavand." She looked up to Nasim. "Either that or the spell Khamal cast over her before I was born."

Nasim looked at her wounds again. They somehow seemed redder than moments ago. Angrier. "How did you get those burns?"

Kaleh turned her cheek to hide the burns from Nasim. "I came here to find you, but my father guessed my purpose. He followed through the doorway I created and fought the Aramahn to find me. I think he hoped that you would be here as well, for he stormed through the village, searching for you. In the end, he killed three before he fled under the threat of the others who came to protect the village."

Nasim thought back to the men and women stationed around the village. "Will he return?"

"*Neh*. He's hampered by the bonds of Ghayavand. He can create doorways of his own, but not this far from Ghayavand, and with so many qiram warding the village, he won't be able to break through again."

362 • Bradley P. Beaulieu

"He has two pieces of the Atalayina now, doesn't he? He's fused them."

"He has, which was why he was able to follow me, but even so, the bonds placed on all the Al-Aqim are strong. He will not be able to come again."

"I've dreamed of those times, when the bonds were placed on the three of them."

Kaleh smiled. She shifted from her kneeling position—wincing so badly Nasim cringed in sympathy—until she was sitting cross-legged like Nasim. For the first time, she seemed a child of her age. No longer were her eyes deep and ancient. Instead, they made her seem humble, as if she knew what she was about to ask was unreasonable.

"There's a reason I came here, of all places," she said softly. "I had hoped to find you. I had hoped to learn more of you, more of Khamal."

"Why?"

"So that we can stop my father."

Nasim stared. "Forgive me, Kaleh, but you have been with your father, preparing the way for the akhoz, for months and years. I know this."

"I have done those things." Her eyes went far away, as if she were reliving the ritual that took place on Rafsuhan, the one that had consumed the children of the Maharraht. "But I was fooled. Tricked."

"Then what changed your mind?"

"I'm no fool," she said sharply. "I've read texts—books and scrolls hidden away by my father. They spoke of his desires when he came to Ghayavand. They spoke of the desire of all who came to Alayazhar—for higher learning, for raising humanity above pettiness and anger and war. They spoke of a desire to find within ourselves the capacity to welcome all that we are, and to share. Our knowledge and our love and our pain.

"For years I was afraid to speak of these things, but months ago, I told him what I'd done. He wasn't angry, but he told me that what we were doing *was* bringing the world to that higher place. I tried to believe him, but when I saw what he was doing to you that day at the celestia, it all changed. It cannot be what the fates wanted." She shook her head. "It cannot."

Nasim wanted to believe her, but could not. Still, if she were able to help him find his memories, it may shed light on the key to unlocking his own potential, or at the very least removing the walls Sariya and Muqallad had placed on him.

"How can Khamal's memories help Muqallad?" he asked.

"Khamal left the island and was reborn. In a way my father hopes to do the same, for even with the Atalayina, he is bound to Ghayavand."

"Sariya isn't."

"It mightn't seem like it, but she is. She has her tower in Alayazhar. She took another in Alekeşir, and yet another in Baressa. They are linked. They ground her to Ghayavand, but do not mistake this for her being free of it. She is bound as tightly as Muqallad is. The only difference is the way in which they pay for the small amount of freedom they've found. Only Khamal truly escaped."

He didn't escape, Nasim thought. *He died, and I was born.* "Why do *you* want to know Khamal's secrets?"

"Because my father is close to doing the same thing. He hinted at it, but he refused to tell me details. He may have found what he needed from you at the celestia. But if *we* can find the secret too, we may be able to prevent him from escaping. We may even be able to bind him to Ghayavand forever."

"He is your *father*."

"Can a father do no wrong? Can he not be misguided?"

"Of course."

"Then that is enough. I have been blinded, I will admit, but I will allow it no longer. Help me, Nasim. Help me to find Khamal's secret, and together, we can stop him."

"I've tried," Nasim said, thinking of the horror contained within that dark place inside him that he'd never been able to go. "I've dreamed of him many times, but never the ritual he completed to be reborn and to grant me his power."

"Then we will try together, but not today." She glanced down with tired and haggard eyes at the burn on her wrist. "Perhaps not tomorrow, either."

"Rest," Nasim said as he stood and backed away toward the door. "I'll see you again soon."

Nasim didn't see her again for days. He wandered the halls and paths of Mirashadal, reliving his past. He'd spent over two years here, but those first months had been confusing. He had been healed, but after walking between the worlds for so long, being relegated to only the material world was difficult. And then, when his mind had finally acclimated to Erahm, he *longed* for Adhiya. He wished for ways to touch it, but it had been cut off from him, and he grew despondent. Angry. He lashed out at all of those who tried to help.

But the Aramahn were patient, Fahroz especially so. She helped him to realize that he could touch Adhiya through others. He thought she was mistaken at first, for though they tried, he was unable to do more than *sense* Adhiya through the learned men and women that came to work with him. They tried and tried and tried again. And finally, it worked. The qiram acted as a conduit for him, after which he could begin to commune with the spirits, he could almost—almost—touch the stuff of Adhiya itself. For a time, he was appeased, but he still felt as though he'd been robbed of much on Oshtoyets. That anger had festered as it became clear he would never again have the ability to walk through the glorious plane of the spirit world. It had been that anger as much as his desire to mend the wounds Khamal had inflicted on the world that drove him from Mirashadal.

Now, as he took long walks around the village, feeling the sway of the walkways, smelling the scent of the sea, he realized just how much he owed Fahroz. She had done so much for him, and all he had done was spurn her.

He tried to speak with her during meals in the great hall, to apologize. He stood before the door of her home so that he could share these thoughts. She would like them, he thought. He even saw her once, alone, walking down the winding ballast tower path, but then, just like every other time, he had backed down, embarrassed over what he'd done.

Four days after his arrival on Mirashadal, Kaleh found him sitting in one of the village's many arboretums. It was a hidden place, more like a courtyard than a garden. The ground, such as it was, was a gnarled pattern of tightly packed roots. The trunks of the trees that circled the space stood side by side, with hardly a gap between them. The boughs curved up, moving amongst the other trees, until the branches reached up toward the sky, a crown of green leaves and swaying branches that made this place feel separate, hidden from the rest of Mirashadal.

There was only one archway leading into the arboretum, and it was through this that Kaleh came. She was limping, but she looked much healthier than she had days before.

"Good day to you," she said, smiling.

"Good day," Nasim said, smiling back.

He was sitting on a bench, another mass of roots that had been painstakingly shaped by the dhoshahezhan who had grown this village. Nasim patted the space next to him. Kaleh limped over and sat down.

"Are you well?" he asked, motioning to her right hand.

"Well enough. How are you?"

"Miserable."

She frowned, shaking her head quizzically.

"Never mind," he said. "I've been thinking about what you said. I'd like to try, if you're still willing."

Her blue eyes searched his, perhaps surprised, perhaps pleased. Perhaps both. "Where?" she asked.

Nasim looked down at the roots beneath his feet. They looked hard and gnarled, but he knew that here in the arboretums they were soft as rabbit ears. "Here, if you don't mind."

She motioned for him to lie down. "Then sleep," she said. "Dream, and I'll guide you."

He hesitated, but only for a moment. This had been a thing that he'd been dreading for too long, and it was time to be done with it. Strangely, Kaleh, even though they were not related, felt like a sister, a child born of Ghayavand, linked to it just as inextricably as he was.

The tightness that had been inside him since seeing Mirashadal on the horizon fell away, and he smiled at her—a gesture she responded to in kind. He lay down on the roots. Kaleh chanted softly as he closed his eyes and stilled his mind. The words she spoke felt as old as the world itself, and somehow, despite his fears, he found himself falling quickly and deeply into sleep.

Khamal walks along the edge of the water. The surf rolls over his feet, the frothing water cold against his feet and ankles. The sound of breaking waves is all that he hears. Ahead of him, two akhoz walk. They are side by side, but they do not acknowledge one another. For all he knows, they do not even know the other is there.

Beyond the beach, beyond the shallow cliff dividing city from sea stands Alayazhar, cold and empty and haunted. He can see the telltale signs of other akhoz as they wander the city, lost.

Lost, Khamal thinks.

The akhoz are lost in so many ways. They anchor the city, preventing the rift from widening, but those children have been lost to this world. They are lost to the next as well. They are lost to their loved ones—their parents and sisters and brothers. They are lost to the children they might, in a different world, have borne.

Worst, though, is the fact that they are lost to themselves. To save the city—to save the world—they had been forced to remove them from Adhiya. No longer would they travel to the world beyond, to be reborn brighter. They would live out whatever existence the fates had in store for them, and then they would die. Truly die.

Ahead lies a massive rock, dark gray against the white beach and blue-green waters of the bay. The two akhoz stop near it, waiting obediently. Khamal approaches. The first, the one nearest the rock, is Yadhan. She was the first of the akhoz and so seemed, at least in the hour of her choosing, like the proper one for the ritual about to take place, but as he approaches, he knows that he cannot take her. He still remembers her face in the celestia as he performed that first ritual. She was brave, but within she feared. She feared like nothing her scant years on Erahm had prepared her for, and in his heart he knows that she made that sacrifice for him. She revered him. She viewed him as a savior. And he took advantage of it.

"Go," he says to Yadhan, more harshly than he meant to.

She turns, her eyeless face looking up at him, her mouth pulled back in a feral grin.

"Go!"

She scuffles along the beach, away from him. A wave surges up and sizzles as it rolls across her feet. She bounds away from the water, looks back one last time, and then gallops toward Alayazhar. Perhaps she feels rejected, or confused. Or perhaps she feels nothing at all. Who can say what the akhoz feel?

Khamal turns to the other. His name is Alif—the one, the lone. It is not his given name. Alif was found after the devastation of the sundering, alone and able to speak but little. He had a wound to his head and was never able to say the names of his parents. He was a simple child. Quiet. And like the name Khamal gave him, he often spent his time alone.

Khamal is not sure why, but it is somehow easier to take *this* child. It shames him. Why is Alif worth less than Yadhan? It should not be, but one must be chosen, one must be sacrificed, if his plan is to have any hope.

As he takes to the rock, he feels the sun-warmed surface and wonders how it will feel when he returns to the world.

Stop, he tells himself. *Do not think of it.*

He shuffles along the lip leading up to the top, glancing at Sariya's tower. He wonders if she watches him, wonders if she cares. She still wants him to bring Muqallad back, to allow him to return to Alayazhar, but Khamal can't. Not yet. Once this is done, it will be time to lift the veil he'd placed around the island that prevented Muqallad from returning.

He reaches the flat surface at last. Alif is close behind. He cowers and looks away when Khamal motions to the center of the rock face.

"Lie down," Khamal says.

Reluctantly, Alif obeys. Somehow he knows. He knows what lies ahead, and in these moments of realization, Khamal nearly changes his mind, nearly orders Alif to follow Yadhan, nearly prepares to climb down from this rock to return to the celestia to meditate on what they can do to close the rift.

But this ritual had occurred to him years ago, and he'd been pondering it ever since, slowly coming to the realization that this was the only way. He had to break free of the bonds his people had placed on him if he were to have any hope of finding sway against the rift. He knows that it is not without risk. It will weaken the bonds around Ghayavand. The rifts will spread, causing havoc among the nearby islands, perhaps even the motherland. But what choice is there? The bonds would not hold forever, and if they fell when no one was prepared for them, it may well mean the destruction of the world.

Sariya reasoned that perhaps this was what the fates had envisioned, but he could not believe that this was what they had in store for Erahm. He could not.

And so it comes to this.

He stares down at Alif. The boy cranes his neck, releases a mewling sound like a weak and wounded calf.

"Fates forgive me," Khamal says as he kneels.

He pulls his khanjar from its sheath at his belt. It gleams both wicked and hungry beneath the sun.

Alif squirms as he moves away from Khamal. His mewling becomes louder, more raucous.

"Silence!"

Alif's moans grow quieter. He shivers, but otherwise remains still as Khamal holds out his wrist, the Atalayina gripped tightly in one hand. He places the knife against his skin, where blood pulses in dark veins.

Before he can change his mind, he runs the edge of the knife over his skin, stifling a groan from the pain of it. He draws on the Atalayina. He draws on himself, much as he does when creating the akhoz. As his blood drips into Alif's open mouth, he feels himself detach from Adhiya. Slowly but surely, as his lifeblood drips away, his soul is drawn from the world beyond.

Never to return.

This is the most difficult part by far, knowing that once his plans are complete he will never return to Adhiya. If he succeeds in maneuvering Sariya and Muqallad, he will return, he will be reborn, but it will only be once. That child, when he dies, will be as dead as Yadhan. As dead as Alif.

As the flow of his blood slows, he feels Adhiya slip from his grasp. It is gone, and he nearly cries from its loss.

But he cannot. There is work to do yet.

Gritting his jaw so hard it hurts, he takes the knife with shaking hands and raises it high.

Alif lies below him, crimson red spattered across his face and lips and teeth. He knows what's coming. He goes rigid, muscles tightening, frame going taut, but he does not move away. For this Khamal is proud.

As Alif cries out to the noontime sun, Khamal plunges the knife through the center of his chest.

The cries reach a violent pitch as Alif convulses.

And then he falls still.

And the sounds of the surf return.

Khamal carefully wipes the blade of the dagger against his robes. Black blood, foul smelling, comes away from the blade, indelibly staining the persimmon-colored cloth. He places the tip of the khanjar into its sheath and slides the blade home. Only then does he reach down and pick Alif up into his arms.

He stands, tears streaming down his face, and tosses Alif into the waves. The current here will take him away. Sariya will not see. Not unless she is looking down upon him now.

And if that is as the fates will it, then so be it.

CHAPTER FIFTY-SIX

Nikandr heard the boom of the fort's cannons shortly after the white puff of smoke.

A black, twirling chain shot ate the distance between the fort and the *Lihvyen*. It missed, flying low beneath the ship. The next two shots, however, spun through the air with a whirring sound and crashed through the seaward rigging. Nikandr felt it in his boots as the sound thundered through the ship.

The ship was rising, but too slowly.

"Faster, Anahid!"

Nikandr could see men at the turrets of the fort now, and more along the walls, and within the courtyard.

As Anahid and Jahalan worked to bring the ship higher, Nikandr stood at the bow of the ship and called upon his havahezhan to give it extra lift. He spread his arms wide and closed his eyes. The bottom dropped out from his stomach, and his awareness expanded. He felt the currents around the ship, felt the wind that Jahalan's hezhan was summoning. His own hezhan now added to it, but the spirit felt distant somehow.

Still, it helped. The wind buoyed the ship, lifted it higher than Anahid and Jahalan could do on their own. The *Lihvyen* took one more cannon shot, but no more. The men in the fort saw the *Lihvyen* moving out of range and began targeting the cutter behind them, which had so far been slow in adding air.

Nikandr called upon the wind to help the trailing ship, but the fort had now measured their shots. The next two took out a section of her seaward mizzenmast. The ship tilted forward as another shot took her in the fore.

The entire forward section of the ship, from the foremasts to the bowsprit, exploded in a cloud of fire and smoke and flying wood.

The rear of the cutter was thrown backward from the blast. Bits of it struck the *Lihvyen* with the clatter of wood and the patter of debris. And then, having lost its heft the instant the magazine had been struck, tipped it over like a bottle tipping off the edge of a table. It flipped backward, end over end, picking up speed. Men and rigging and planks of wood flew free, all of them spinning with their own particular rhythm before crashing into the churning green sea a quarter-league below.

"Signal the *Opha* to send a skiff for survivors!" Nikandr shouted to Styophan, and then he quickly turned his attention back to the fort. There were few men in the open, but to take a fort like this there must be dozens at the very least. The front gates had been shattered, most likely with cannon shot from the enemy ships.

He looked ahead to the cove. The ships were in a very vulnerable position. He couldn't allow the forces of Yrstanla to return to them.

"Ready the pots, men! We make a line for the ships!"

A cry came up from the crew. They were seasoned, and now they were thirsty for blood.

As the ship made its way eastward toward the cove, a deep iron brazier was filled with wood and lit with a healthy splash of whale oil. Several dozen clay pots filled with cotton were filled with more oil until they were nearly full.

As they flew above the hill hiding the ships and the cove came into view, the three ships—all twelve-masted schooners—were on the move. They'd spotted the *Lihvyen* and had certainly heard the cannon shots, but they'd begun to flee too late. They could not prevent the ships of Khalakovo from passing over them at least once.

Nikandr took one of the clay pots, as did Styophan and a dozen more of the crew. They positioned themselves around the deck in places where the path downward was clear of rigging and sails. The enemy ships tilted their cannons to fire straight up. Everyone hunkered low as the *Lihvyen* caught two more shots along the forward hull.

"Now, men! Let's send them to the sea!"

As the crew raised up a cry, releasing their fury, Nikandr dropped his pot. The flames were bright against the wood and rigging of the ship below. It struck the deck at the aftcastle, the oil splashing over the side of the ship, engulfing it in flame. A few other pots were dropped too quickly and missed, but a good dozen struck home. Flame blossomed about the ship, some of it splashing against the crewmen of Yrstanla. They tried desperately to smother the flames, but it was already too late.

The *Opha* had steered toward the windward ship. Their pots struck the second enemy ship, engulfing it in flames as well.

The remaining schooner had gained enough altitude that it could challenge them if they weren't careful.

"Fire!" Nikandr called.

The forward cannons of the *Lihvyen* and *Opha* let loose. The chained shot cut through the upper rigging of the enemy galleon. Both shots caught the starward mainmast at two different points. The mast snapped halfway. As the upper sails crashed down to hang loose against the mizzen rigging, the *Lihvyen* gained more altitude.

It didn't take long from there. They dropped more pots against the last of the ships, and soon all three of them were aflame. As the *Lihvyen* and the *Opha* wheeled windward and cut back toward the wide plateau below the fort, the first of the ships they'd struck was little more than a burning torch twisting down toward the sea.

Nikandr ordered skiffs readied. Fifteen men from each ship loaded into two skiffs. They broke away and made their way to the ground, nervous that the enemy would be difficult to reach now that they'd taken the fort. They landed on the grassy plain below the fort and ran forward, each man bearing a musket, watching the fort for any sign of the enemy. There were none, however. They weren't along the walls. They weren't manning the towers.

But there was smoke on the wind. It rose up from the courtyard and drifted, a thin streamer floating up and away.

As they approached the keep, all muskets trained on the shattered remains of the doors or the top of the wall, Nikandr heard a hissing sound.

The hiss of gunpowder.

"To the courtyard! They've set gunpowder to blow!"

No sooner had the words left his mouth than a bright flash lit the interior of the fort. A bare moment later, something struck Nikandr in the face and chest and limbs.

He flew backward. A roar unlike anything he'd ever heard assaulted his senses.

He struck the ground, losing his musket. He stared up at the sky, his ears ringing.

And then he heard the crumbling. A sound like a landslide. A sound like the earth itself was opening up beneath him, beneath his men, ready to swallow them whole.

He rolled over and managed to make it to his knees.

The rumbling grew louder.

He looked up and saw the spire—seventy-five feet of obsidian standing tall and black against the blue of the sky—begin to tip. It tilted toward the courtyard's interior. Toward Nikandr and his men.

"Away!" he shouted, though it was weak and caused him to begin coughing. "Away!" he shouted again through his coughs.

He helped the nearest of his men to his feet. It was Styophan, he realized. And then the two of them helped another. Soon all of them, including one they were forced to drag, were moving away from the walls of the fort as quickly as they could.

The rumble increased yet again. Nikandr glanced back and saw the top of the spire plummet. The tower crashed down, fell against the nearest wall of the fort, crushing it as if it were made of ash. Like leaves in autumn, the stones of the wall blew outward, pounding into the men on his right. In an instant seven of them were dead.

Some hidden force pushed at their backs, though it was not so strong as the explosion. Dust billowed outward and enveloped the entire area. In moments all of them were coughing and hacking and wheezing, and it was nearly impossible to see.

At last they made it out and away to clear ground and clear air.

They stopped and turned, looking at the cloud of dust that was still settling.

That was when Nikandr felt the wind. He felt it in his chest first—his chest and his soulstone, both.

He pulled the stone out and held it in his hand. He closed his eyes and opened himself to Adhiya. He could feel the havahezhan, the one that had been with him since Soroush's men had summoned it forth on Uyadensk. But now it grew distant. It slipped further and further away. And then it was gone, ripped away, leaving an empty feeling that made him double over with a nausea he hadn't felt since the worst of the wasting was upon him.

At last, all had grown quiet—all save the settling of stone within the broken walls of the fort. The area around him—the narrow plain, the sparse trees, even the tall brown grass dusted with snow—felt expectant, as though it knew what was coming.

The nausea began to ease, and Nikandr stared up at the sky. There had been only a few clouds high up before the fall of the spire, but now they began to form before his very eyes. Like cream poured into water, the clouds billowed and grew in odd, lurching increments. A rumbling came from above. Lightning lit the clouds, which were already beginning to darken. Soon the entire sky was covered in a thick layer, and it was settling over the island, lowering like a great woolen blanket thrown over the world by the fates themselves.

When the wind began to pick up, Nikandr realized that the sky was no place for his ships to be.

He turned east and scanned for them. They were told to hold position further inland, well away from the range of the fort's cannons, but they were now approaching with speed.

And yet it felt as though they were leagues away.

Nikandr began to run. "We must warn them," he said, waving his men to follow. "They must moor the ships in the cove!"

As he ran he waved his arms over his head. Styophan and Jonis and a half-dozen others followed, doing the same.

But already the wind was high and swirling. There were times when it robbed him of breath. The moment he was able to clear it, he shouted, higher and higher, as high as his raw and aching throat would allow him.

The ships twisted in the wind. They were blown north and then east. Nikandr could see crewmen standing on the deck, could see them in the rigging. Some of them saw him as well, for they waved back and seemed to then call toward the master to come to the gunwales.

Nikandr never found out if the master had heard, for just then, the *Lihvyen*, the closer of the two, twisted, nose down, until it was nearly standing on end. They had pulled in a good half of the sails, but the spars were beginning to snap. The rigging was ripped away from its belaying pins. White canvas flapped like burial pennants in the wind.

And then the *Lihvyen* shot down with such speed that Nikandr knew it was going to crash.

A pattering sound could be heard, coming from behind them. Nikandr glanced back and saw sheets of hail falling from the sky. It rushed toward them and fell upon them like wolves. It stung their face and hands and shoulders. It caused them to slip and fall, so thick was it in moments.

They continued on as they could.

The *Lihvyen* rushed toward the ground. Through the haze of hail, Nikandr could see men falling—or perhaps leaping—from the ship. Most flew wide, but several were caught in the whipping sails and rigging.

But then Nikandr saw a form flying free from the ship, not downward, but to one side. It was Jahalan. His robes whipped fiercely about his frame as the wind held him aloft. The alabaster gem glowed brightly upon his brow, much brighter than Nikandr had ever seen one become. He was like a bright star, his arms wide—taken, perhaps, by the havahezhan he'd bonded with.

"*Nyet*, Jahalan." It was too much, Nikandr knew. He was giving too much.

The wind changed. It became less chaotic, more focused on the *Lihvyen*. By the ancients who protect, the ship was *slowing down*.

But there was only so much Jahalan could do.

Nikandr wanted to add his own effort to Jahalan's, but he still couldn't feel his havahezhan.

In the sky, as the ship plummeted past Jahalan, he arched back as if he were offering all of himself to the hezhan if only it would save the ship.

The alabaster gem upon his brow burst in a spray of scintillating light as the *Lihvyen* crashed. The speed was not as great as it might have been, but still the forecastle crumbled beneath the weight of the ship's impact, perhaps lessening the blow to those who remained. Snow and earth erupted as the bow gouged deeply. The stern tilted high and then tumbled over, snapping masts and rigging as it went.

Jahalan's body plummeted and was lost among the rubble of the *Lihvyen*.

In the distance, dropping much faster than the *Lihvyen* had, the *Opha* struck the crest of the angled plain they stood upon. Nikandr knew immediately that everyone onboard had died.

CHAPTER FIFTY-SEVEN

While Nikandr and his men searched through the wreckage of the *Lihvyen*, the hail continued to fall mercilessly. The sound of it was deafening, and for a time it grew so bad that all they could do was huddle beneath the wreckage of the ship as fist-sized hailstones broke and sprayed against the earth.

For nearly an hour it continued, sometimes stronger, sometimes weaker, but then at last the hail—if not the wind—subsided and they were able to search once more.

They found six men alive, though all had sustained terrible wounds, and most likely two of them would not last until morning.

As the others searched the surrounding land for bodies that had flown free of the ship, Nikandr climbed the *Lihvyen's* deck, which was tilted at a sharp angle. As he came amidships, he heard moaning coming from the lower square sail of the starward mainmast. He slid down to it and hiked up to the Spar until he reached the source. After pulling the sails away, he found Anahid, unconscious. He called to her, but she would not wake, but thank the ancients she seemed to have sustained little damage. She must have been thrown into the sail as the ship crashed. Or it may have been Jahalan's final act, protecting his cousin before he was consumed by the spirit of the wind.

Nikandr called men over to help him get her down. It was easy enough. They simply pulled the remains of the sail taut and allowed her to slip slowly down to the ground.

As Nikandr slid along the canvas himself, he saw something lying near the wreckage. He recognized Jahalan's peg leg immediately, but the rest of him was lost beneath a section of the ship's bulwark and hull that had broken away. As he pulled the wreckage away, his jaw tightened to the point of pain.

Jahalan lay there in the snow and the hail, broken and twisted. Just like the *Lihvyen*. Everyone would have died, Nikandr thought, had Jahalan not slowed its descent. Because of him, seven souls had been given a new chance at life.

"Goodbye, dear friend," Nikandr whispered.

"My Lord Prince?"

Nikandr looked up. Styophan stood several paces away, staring down at Jahalan with a sadness that Nikandr wouldn't have expected from him. He had never spoken with Jahalan with anything akin to friendship, but the ties of the crew—Landed and Landless alike—grew deep over time.

"What is it?" Nikandr asked.

"There are men coming." He pointed eastward. "Men of Anuskaya."

Nikandr stared eastward. The hail was beginning to abate, allowing him to see further down the gentle slope leading toward the sea. Two dozen men wearing not the uniforms of the streltsi, but the heavy, oiled coats of farmers and shepherds, were marching toward them. Many bore muskets, but some had only swords and axes to hand. Their muskets were held at the half-ready, and they were scanning the landscape as they came, as if they expected the forces of Yrstanla to leap from the boulders that dotted the landscape.

"Tell them what's happened," Nikandr said. "Have them help if they would, but otherwise let them stand aside while we finish."

Styophan nodded, glancing down once at Jahalan before turning away and heading for the men.

Nikandr kneeled by Jahalan's side, wondering if he'd already crossed over. He combed Jahalan's wet hair from his forehead, brushed the dirt and grime and ice from Jahalan's gaunt face, until at last he looked like the man Nikandr remembered.

Many things could have gone through Nikandr's head—they *should* be going through his head, he thought—but he could think of nothing more than the time Jahalan had nearly died on the shores of Ghayavand. He'd been saved by the *Gorovna's* windsmen that day, and whether it was borrowed time he'd been living on since or whether Nikandr should be furious that he hadn't lived longer, he wasn't sure. He only knew that his dear friend was gone, and that he would miss him.

After leaning down and kissing his forehead, Nikandr said, "Go well," hoping dearly Jahalan could hear him.

The windows rattled as Nikandr entered the office of Dyanko Kantinov Vostroma. Sleet struck the diamond-paned glass so harshly that Nikandr wondered whether they were going to shatter from the force of it. As Nikandr took a seat before Dyanko's desk, the wind died down, but it seemed only to be taking an inhalation in preparation for another onslaught. The wind had not let up since they'd left the wreckage of the ships and returned here to

Skayil, Elykstava's only sizable village.

Nikandr looked to the rook on the iron stand in the corner of the room. Telling was the fact that the rook had a golden band around its leg. A man like Dyanko—even though he was the Boyar of Elykstava and the Posadnik of Skayil—would not normally be afforded such an honor. The golden band marked it as one of Galostina's, which meant that it had probably been sent when the hostilities with Yrstanla erupted, or perhaps when the first of the spires had been felled.

"What news from Galostina?" Nikandr asked as he accepted a healthy serving of vodka from Dyanko.

Though his round cheeks and flat nose were already flushed from drink, Dyanko took a drink himself and poured another before sitting down and facing Nikandr. "The bird has not spoken since it arrived two days ago." Dyanko squeezed his eyes shut tight and then reopened them, blinking several times before focusing on Nikandr once more. He looked as though he could slump forward onto his desk at any moment, snoring before his head hit the wide leather blotter.

"When did you sleep last, Dyanko?"

"I'll do well enough, Khalakovo." He took the last of his vodka in one fierce swallow and focused on Nikandr carefully. "Now would you please tell me what happened to the spire?"

Nikandr sat deeper into his chair. "I don't like your tone, Vostroma. I was sent by your Lord to assist in what ways I could."

"And a fine job you've done of it."

"I came upon a keep that had already been taken. Where were your men?"

"Sent to the fighting, as you should have been. Why were you, the vaunted Hawk of Khalakovo, so far behind them?"

"My business is my own."

"Would that your business had led you away from Elykstava."

"I destroyed three ships that lay off your coast." Nikandr stood, slapping the glass of vodka onto Dyanko's desk untouched. The liquor splashed over his desk, wetting the disheveled pile of papers that lay there. "I found your keep taken and risked the lives of my crew to stop the Kamarisi's men from destroying your spire. Three of my ships are lost, dozens are dead, and you wish that my business had led me *away*?"

When Dyanko answered, his eyes were heavy and bloodshot. It was only with difficulty that he looked up to Nikandr. "Trouble follows you, Nikandr Iaroslov. Even you must admit that."

"You're drunk," Nikandr said, turning away. "Sleep it off if you would, but you will first authorize a ship for me to take to Kiravashya. I intend to leave at dawn."

Nikandr headed for the door but stopped when the rook suddenly cawed in the corner. Both he and Dyanko turned to the bird. For long moments the rook craned its neck backward until its beak was digging into its dorsal feathers. It shivered and its eyes fluttered. A clucking sound emanated from its throat as if a hunk of rotted meat were stuck in it.

Then, without warning, it fell from the perch and landed on the floor with a hollow thump. It tried to flap its wings, tried to regain its footing, but the bird was either too weak or too disoriented to do so.

Nikandr moved toward it until Dyanko scooped the bird up and fell back into his chair. He stroked the bird's head and back tenderly and made soft clucking sounds into its ear, and strangely the bird calmed itself.

The bird stopped rubbing its head against Dyanko's fingers. "I come for Nik…" It was quiet for a time, but then it seemed to regain itself. "I come for Nikandr Iaroslov Khalakovo."

Nikandr knew immediately it was Mother. He could hear it in the way even those few words had been spoken, and he could feel it in his chest, though it was terribly faint.

"I'm here, Mother."

The rook did not respond. It returned to its bestial self, blinking slowly, making a creaking sound like the hinges of some ancient and forgotten chest. But then it began flapping its wings furiously. It bit Dyanko's fingers. He howled and dropped the rook, and the moment he did, it flapped into the air, cawing loudly over and over again.

It landed on Nikandr's shoulder and from this position stared at Dyanko. "He has men in the donjon, Nischka. Two of them. Men from Yrstanla."

Dyanko looked up at the rook, and then met Nikandr's eyes. There was a look of uncertainty there, as if he was no longer sure how far he could press his authority, even if it *was* with an unfavored prince and a fallen Matra.

"Is this true?" Nikandr asked.

Dyanko swallowed, eyes shifting, but then he nodded slowly and spoke carefully. "Nearly a dozen found their way to Skayil shortly after the spire fell. They stole a skiff, but we captured two of them."

"Why wasn't I told?"

"They are on Vostroman ground, My Lord Prince." He glanced sidelong at the rook. "They will be given to the Grand Duke to do with as he would."

Nikandr stood, his chair scraping loudly backward. As he did, the rook flapped to its perch. Nikandr could already tell that Mother had left. He was surprised she'd been able to do this much so shortly after the spire had fallen. No doubt Elykstava's proximity to Khalakovo helped, but Mother had always been strong in the aether, particularly with assuming rooks and the like.

"Take me to them," Nikandr said.

"I take no orders from a Khalakovo, certainly not this one."

Nikandr rounded the desk, pulling his khanjar from his belt as he did so. Dyanko tried to stand, but Nikandr was too quick. He grabbed Dyanko by the collar of his coat and shoved him back into the chair, scraping it across the floor until he was pressed against the shelves filled with ledgers in the corner.

"I don't know the sort of problems you might have in giving information to me, but I was sent by the Grand Duke's son, Borund. I am a son of the Duke of Khalakovo. I am a prince of the realm, and we are at war." He pulled Dyanko back and slammed his head hard against the shelves. "Put aside your superstitions, Dyanko, son of Kantin, or I swear by the ancients that preserve us I'll run you through and deal with the rest later."

Dyanko's skin went porcelain. His breath came like a rabbit's. He stared, eyes bulging, first at Nikandr, then at the khanjar leveled against his throat, and finally at the door, as if he wished to flee or call for help. Nikandr wondered if he might faint.

"You wouldn't dare draw the blood of Vostroma."

"I know the Grand Duke, Dyanko, better than you. My wrists might be slapped, but do you think he will do anything beyond this over a man he's relegated to Elykstava?" He let these words sink in. "Or will he be glad to find your seat vacant and offer it to another who's owed favors?"

Dyanko blinked. He seemed, for the first time, to consider what might come after his death. His breathing began to settle. He closed his eyes, and when he opened them again, the anger had left, as had the fear.

Slowly, he nodded. "I will take you to them."

After talking with the soldiers who'd captured the two Yrstanlan windsmen, Nikandr spent an hour questioning the first. His name was Sayad, and he eventually admitted—after several whippings from Styophan—that his rank on the ship had been that of boatswain. Only after threatening worse to the second prisoner had Sayad admitted that his shipmate was named Fuad and that he'd been the ship's carpenter.

They left Sayad and traveled to another part of the donjon, one separated by distance and two heavy doors. When the gaoler opened the cell door, Styophan went in first, holding a short whip still wet with Sayad's blood. Nikandr waited for a minute as silence settled inside the cell. Only then did Nikandr step inside.

The space was cramped and wet and cold. Fuad had seen perhaps fifty winters. His dark hair was long and wet and hung in matted locks down his cheeks and neck. His turban had been removed from him, making him look more like a wet rat than a windsman.

Nikandr sat on a bench, while Styophan stood above Fuad, gripping and re-gripping his whip.

"Why the spires, Fuad?" Nikandr asked in Yrstanlan.

"I would not know."

"You must have heard something."

"The Kamarisi ordered it."

"For what reason? It would seem if he wanted the islands he would want the spires as well."

"Perhaps he wishes simply for you to be gone."

"I didn't ask what you *thought*, Fuad. I asked what you'd *heard*."

"I am a carpenter on a ship of the Empire. What would I have heard?"

"The men who took you," Nikandr said. "Two of them spoke Yrstanlan." Nikandr let the words sit between them. "When you fell from the skiff and your comrades returned for you, you were heard ordering them to leave."

"You would do the same in my place."

Nikandr smiled. "I very well might, and as the kapitan, I would expect them to heed it. I would expect them to do it smartly as well, as your men did."

Nikandr watched as Fuad swallowed once, then again. "They are not my men."

"Are they not?"

"I am a carpenter."

"Perhaps you once were, yes." Nikandr had noted his hands. They were large, and supple, and bore more than a few scars that looked similar to the cuts and scrapes a carpenter might receive from his tools. "Why the spires, Fuad?"

"I don't know."

Nikandr nodded to Styophan, who whipped Fuad across the shoulders twice. Fuad pulled himself back up from the whipping, staring fiercely into Nikandr's eyes.

"How many ships has the Kamarisi set upon the wind?"

"I know only of the three that came here."

Nikandr waited as Styophan whipped him again.

"Your Kamarisi would understand, were you to give us such simple things, Fuad. He would not want you to suffer, no matter what your station."

Fuad licked his lips, pulled himself higher against the wall. He glanced at Styophan, but did not speak. His eyes were steel, and full of hate.

"I spoke with the boatswain at some length," Nikandr said. "You may have heard it… Like you he was loath to speak of anything beyond his duties to the ship. But then I remembered something the men told me, the ones who took you. They said that Sayad was already on the skiff. They said that he leapt from within it despite your orders. Why would he do that, Fuad? Why would he have leapt to help you while the rest remained?"

"He is young," Fuad said.

"Young indeed," Nikandr replied. "I will admit that I don't know much of the customs of Yrstanla. I've had little enough use for them. But those of the military? Those of ships? *Those* I have paid attention to." He stood and began pacing in front of the bench. "It is said that many sailing men—kapitans, especially—will take their sons to war. On their own ships. They give them titles of coxswain or boatswain or quartermaster if they're able men. It's a right of passage, *evet*? If something like this war had come along, I wonder if a kapitan wouldn't take his son along with him. It would be something difficult to pass up, I would imagine."

Nikandr stopped and turned to face Fuad. "Had *I* a son, Fuad, I would have taken him on *my* ship."

Fuad stared. No longer was there hatred in his eyes. No longer was there steel.

Now there was worry, though he was clearly trying to hide it.

"Shall I return to the other cell? Shall I speak again to Sayad?"

Fuad did not reply.

Nikandr made his way to the door, raised his hand, ready to knock so he and Styophan could leave. "Though I promise you, once Styophan and I enter his cell, only two men will be leaving it alive."

Fuad was breathing more heavily. His nostrils flared as he looked between Nikandr and Styophan.

Nikandr knocked on the door.

The jingle of keys could be heard, the sound of a key rattling home.

"Fifty-seven."

The words had come softly, like words spoken in the middle of the night.

"Pardon?" Nikandr said, still facing the door.

"The Kamarisi sent fifty-seven ships."

CHAPTER FIFTY-EIGHT

As Atiana floats in the darkness of the aether, the storm rages around her. She doesn't know how long it's been. It feels like lifetimes, especially when she's tossed by the hidden currents. The loss of the spires has made the aether more unpredictable than she's ever seen, so much so that she can hardly control her thoughts. She feels the currents in the Sea of Khurkhan, feels the wind sighing through the meadows of Kiravashya, feels the roots of the oldest spruce on Galahesh. She feels the fear of a windsman on the deck of his ship as he and his comrades fly toward battle, feels the hopelessness of a mother as she holds her frail, sickened child, feels the building of a man toward release as he clutches his lover's hair and thrusts desperately into her.

But then, like the tides that drive the water through the Straits of Galahesh, time slows. The images of the world around her fade, and like honey on the steps of winter, time moves so slowly she wonders whether it will stop altogether.

She knows that this is a time most dangerous. It is a time when she runs the risk of becoming so attuned to the world—the islands, the water, the air itself—that she might soon release her hold on her body and float freely through the paths of the aether. She wonders whether her soul will cross the veil to Adhiya, or perhaps it will remain, forever trapped. Is this what happened to the Matri who became lost? Will she find them when her soul slips free? Will it take only moments to do so, or will it take years or centuries or eons? Perhaps when she returns they'll be so foreign to her that she'll never even sense them.

Her mind begins to dull. She feels the weight of the earth and little else. It presses down on her, forces her—slowly but with ever growing strength—to succumb, to leave the world she once knew behind. It tempts her. She recalls vaguely that she has a body, that blood runs through her veins, but she doesn't care. She would rather feel the stone as it rests in layers, slowly shifting, supporting the weight of the world.

It is here, in this torpid state, that she first feels the signs of another. A woman. Her scent is immediately familiar, and she thinks that perhaps another of the women from the islands—she forgets their names—has been taken. But as the presence coalesces, she thinks not. This one is old—not as old as the earth, but certainly older than the children that have spread themselves throughout the islands.

The woman is not aware of her until she reaches out, and then, like a taper set to the wick of a candle, she brightens. It is through this act—the creation of light in another—that *she* is illuminated as well.

She remembers herself.

Atiana...

Atiana Radieva Vostroma.

She is a child of the islands, a child of the Grand Duchy, and she lies now in the bowels of the earth on the island of Galahesh.

She remembers the other as well.

Sariya, who once called herself Arvaneh.

Sariya Quljan al Vehayeh.

She is one of the Al-Aqim, a child of the desert wastes of the Gaji, and she lies now in her tower in the city of Baressa.

This realization strikes Atiana as strange.

She lies in her tower...

When Atiana last took the dark, she saw Nasim destroy *another* tower, a tower Sariya had built for herself in her years of exile on Ghayavand. And now, here she is, lost among the aether as Atiana is.

Was it the destruction of the tower that laid her low? Or was it the destruction of the spires?

Does it even matter?

Nyet. What matters is that she is lost.

And yet, in that glimpse she had of her only moments ago, Atiana saw something else. A plan. Sariya wishes to destroy the spires, not in preparation for Muqallad, but in defiance of him.

In *defiance*.

Why?

It is a question that needs answering.

She calls to Sariya, and receives nothing in return. She reaches out, feels for her. She finds her and draws her closer.

Sariya is weak, but she finally responds, and slowly the two of them buttress one another. The weight of the earth begins to recede. The islands come into focus, as does the sea, the air. And the life within it.

Only then does her sense of purpose return to her. For so long she had been little more than her senses, little more than the life that runs through this world and to the one beyond. She remembers now. She remembers that she was here not to *help* Sariya, but to murder her. These thoughts return to her, as does the feeling of desperation she had when she entered the cemetery.

Yet in remembering this, Sariya knows as well—they are too closely linked for it to be otherwise—and it sparks in Sariya memories of her own. She remembers the unfolding of her plans, and through their bond, Atiana remembers them too.

As Sariya waits in the dark of the aether, the last stones of the Spar are lowered into place. She assumes the form of a rook. She is new to such things, but she's watched the Matri of the islands closely, and she's learned from them how to control the simple beasts. She tells the windships lying in wait to the north— nearly three score in all—that it's time. They approach the straits, the kapitans fearing what's to come, but as she told them, they pass beyond the white cliffs with little more trouble than they'd have approaching the cliffs of an eyrie.

And then the telltale sign of something old, something familiar, alerts her. It is in the tower, in the aether. Sariya approaches and finds Nasim, and the Atalayina. This is unexpected. The stone has never been key to her plans, but she can't pass up the opportunity to gain it, to prevent Muqallad from attaining it.

She pushes, hoping to retrieve it if only Nasim can reveal where it was hidden. Nasim does, but he is stronger than she would have guessed, and he has help from the woman, the Matra from Vostroma. In the end she pushes too hard—she allows her emotions to overcome her—and she is lost in the aether. It is a mistake she won't make again.

These memories fade, and Atiana realizes just how strong Sariya is becoming. She tries to retreat, but Sariya pins her down, prevents her from returning to her body deep in the bowels of the cemetery. Atiana fights, but Sariya will not be swayed. She drives Atiana so deep that Atiana begins to fear that she'll never be able to return.

And then she feels the stone. She holds it in her hands. Part of it is smooth, the inner faces rough. It is just as cold as the numbing water that surrounds her, but there is life within it, a well of power that waits to be tapped.

She has gained some of Sariya's knowledge of the Atalayina, and she draws upon it for the first time. She uses it now to push Sariya away.

Sariya tries to fight, but for the moment she is too weakened from her ordeal. She releases Atiana, and then her presence is simply gone.

Atiana knows she has resurfaced. She has regained consciousness in her tower, and there's no telling what she'll do now that she knows where Atiana lays.

Atiana swims toward the surface, tries to return to her physical self.

She moves slowly...

But eventually she returns.

When Atiana woke, spluttering in the basin, she was numb. Her hands would not respond when she willed them to move. All she could do was to curl like an infant and shiver while cold water dripped from her hair.

Ishkyna was there, but she was sleeping.

Atiana tried to speak, but her mouth refused her commands.

"Shkee—" she eventually managed to say.

Ishkyna did not wake.

"Shkyna..."

Ishkyna opened her eyes, wild and confused. Her gaze finally settled on Atiana.

"H-how long?"

It took some time as Ishkyna looked toward the next chamber, toward the stairs, but she finally seemed to understand. There was a sound coming from above, something like the pop of a campfire filled with unseasoned wood. She stood and moved over to the basin, preparing to help Atiana out. "Nearly two full days."

"N-not yet," Atiana said, knowing that to pull her out now would cause her joints to flare in pain.

Ignoring her, Ishkyna slipped her hands under Atiana's arms and began pulling her up. Even this small movement was excruciatingly painful.

"Not yet!"

"Can you not hear it?" Ishkyna asked.

The sound was louder now. It wasn't the snap of burning wood, but the report of musket fire.

"What's happening?" she asked.

"I'll wager you know a good deal more about it than I do, Tiana."

Atiana grunted, stifling the pain as best she could, as Ishkyna pulled her out and onto the stairs that surrounded the basin. While Ishkyna used soft cloth to dry her off, Atiana tried to piece it all together. She remembered entering the crypt, remembered becoming lost in the winds of the aether, but little else.

Until she felt the stone in her hands.

With shaking arms she raised the Atalayina up. She stared at it. She felt, in the darkness beneath the earth, as though she could look *through* the stone, as if it were a window that gave her view of the aether. Indeed, she could feel Ishkyna much as she could in the aether. She could feel Irkadiy far above them, his men as well. She could feel the soldiers advancing through the cemetery toward them, firing their muskets as they began to outflank them on two sides.

"Sariya," Atiana said.

Ishkyna helped her to pull on her clothes. "What of her?"

"She's awoken."

"She was asleep?"

Atiana shook her head. "She was lost. We need to get to the surface."

"*Nyet*. Not until the fighting is over. Irkadiy will lead them away."

Atiana warded away her sister's attempts to pull a coat over her frame and stumbled toward the stairs.

"Atiana!"

She ignored her calls as she took the winding staircase up toward the surface. Her knees and ankles and hips screamed from the abuse, but she pushed on, knowing there was little time left. She wouldn't let them die, not these loyal men.

As she wound her way up, higher and higher, the sound of musket fire came clearer. She heard men screaming, others shouting orders.

At last she came to the cold metal doors. She unhinged the latch and pushed them open with a mighty heave.

"Stop!" she shouted in Yrstanlan. "I'm here!"

She stood in a row of mausoleums similar to hers. Snow was falling and drifting. Men wearing the uniform of the Kamarisi's personal guard stood nearby, aiming weapons past the mausoleum entrance where she now stood, but at her shouts they all turned to her, several of them leveling muskets at her chest.

A musket shot cracked against the marble column of a mausoleum across from her.

"Irkadiy!" she shouted in Anuskayan. "Drop your weapons! Go with them peaceably!"

At last the firing stopped.

One of the Kamarisi's guardsmen, the one wearing a dark brown turban, stepped forward and took a knee before Atiana. "My Lady Princess," he said in heavily accented Anuskayan, "Arvaneh üm Shalahihd would speak with you."

Atiana stared at these hardened men, confused by the silence around her. But then she understood.

"Take me to her," she said.

CHAPTER FIFTY-NINE

With the snow still falling and the bitter wind gusting, Atiana was led by twenty janissaries across the cobblestone expanse surrounding Sariya's tower. The tower stood at the foot of the Mount. Ancient stone buildings created a ring around the tower. They stood shoulder to shoulder, frowning down at Atiana, as if they blamed *her* for what had befallen their city.

Atiana had forbidden Ishkyna and Irkadiy from accompanying her. She doubted the guardsmen would have allowed it in any case, but there had still been something about this meeting that felt as though it should be shared only between the two of them—Sariya, as strange as it seemed, felt like a sister of the aether, a Matra of sorts.

They came to the base of the tower. It felt odd to be here at last, a place that had occupied her mind both here in the material world and within the dark. She realized that this was not the same tower that she had built while on Ghayavand, but by the same token she knew that *this* tower, the physical tower that stood before her, had changed since Sariya's arrival. It had been transformed—not only in Erahm but in the aether as well—into the seat of Sariya's power.

As the guards knocked thrice and the doors were opened from within, Atiana wondered if there was an echo of this tower in Adhiya. Surely there was. Surely Sariya had found a way for it to reach into the spirit realm as well.

She stepped inside and found a wide room every bit as opulent as the kasir. There were granite floors and marble columns, gilded furniture, and rich portraits hanging from the curving interior wall. She was led to a set of stairs that climbed up into the cavernous darkness. As the doors boomed shut behind her, the guards motioned for her to continue up. Only after Atiana had taken the stairs did she realize that the guards would remain here.

The room on the second level was richly appointed, but not nearly so rich as the room below. The next several floors were simpler still, but the sixth was the one that startled Atiana. It had little more than patterned carpets upon the floor and ironwork trees that held siraj stones to light the dim interior. It felt as if she were in an Aramahn village.

She continued up to the seventh floor, and here she found a circular room with four windows set into it. When she saw the windows and the bed and the carpeting, she knew that she was no longer in a tower within the city of Baressa. She had entered another place entirely—a place of Sariya's making. Nikandr had spoken of the tower he had entered in Alayazhar, and surely what she saw before her was little different from what he'd seen. She wondered about the tower's nature, whether it was something that granted her strength or whether it was something else entirely. Perhaps it was necessary. Perhaps Sariya could no longer exist without such a thing.

Sariya stood by one of the windows, the one facing east. When she turned, Atiana was struck once again by her beauty. Her long golden hair swayed with her movement. Her blue eyes fixed on Atiana. Her expression was not one of amusement or thinly veiled disgust—as it had been when Atiana had first arrived in Baressa—but was instead something like respect or admiration.

"It's interesting, is it not?" Sariya asked. "No matter how carefully we lay our plans, the fates toy with us."

She meant, perhaps, how she'd become lost in the aether after years of planning. Atiana didn't know how to respond, so she remained silent.

"Interesting as well how greed can be our undoing." As she said these words, she glanced at Atiana's belt, at the purse that hung by her left hip. It was where Atiana had placed the Atalayina.

Seeing no reason to keep it hidden, Atiana took it out and held it up for Sariya to see.

Sariya underwent an interesting transformation as she stared. She had been calm since Atiana's arrival, but also reserved—perhaps guarded, unsure how the coming conversation would unfold—but as she stared at the glittering blue stone, a subtle fierceness overcame her, like an owl at dusk.

"May I hold it?" she asked.

Atiana was loath to do this, but she had known this request would come, or if it didn't, that the stone would be taken by force. She nodded and held the stone out. When Sariya stepped forward, Atiana could smell the scent of cardamom.

"Do you know," she asked, taking the stone from Atiana's palm, "what Muqallad hopes to do with this?"

Her words implied that *she* was not part of Muqallad's plans. Atiana still worried that this was simply not true, but she had felt Sariya's mind. She had, for however short a time, become a *part* of Sariya—just as Sariya had been a part of her—and there was no denying that her fears were unfounded.

"He wishes to create more akhoz," Atiana replied.

"The akhoz had nothing to do with the stone," Sariya said. "They acted as sacrifices only, providing him with a way to heal the stone. *Neh*, he wishes to bring about indaraqiram. Do you know what this is?"

"It's the end of the world."

Sariya could not seem to prevent herself from giving Atiana a patronizing smile. "In one sense it is the end of the world, but in another it is the beginning. We hope, through our efforts on this mortal plane, to learn, to attain higher wisdom, to become as perfect as we can be so that one day we might achieve vashaqiram—a perfect state of enlightenment. And if we can do this, we can teach others, so that they might do the same. And if enough can do so, we can bring the world to its next stage."

"You sound as though you pray for his success."

Sariya did not seem perturbed by this comment, but rather, thoughtful. "Any brightness in my eyes, daughter of Radia, stems from the hope that we can one day achieve indaraqiram. I do not, however, believe that Muqallad can deliver us to this goal. He hopes to force it, as if this world and the next can be bent to his will. It cannot, but there is a desperation that comes from standing face to face with your greatest failure for three hundred years."

"And what of you?" Atiana asked. "You were in the same position as Muqallad and Khamal. What would *you* hope to do?"

"I?" Sariya stepped to the window and beckoned Atiana closer. "I merely hope to set the world right, so that I can leave it in some semblance of peace. I yearn for the other world. I desire it deeply. So deeply I dream of it. Some days I feel as though Adhiya touches my skin. I smell it on the wind and sense it in the skies. There are days where I swear I can taste it."

Atiana approached the window. "Then why not go?"

To suggest suicide to an Aramahn was a grave insult—they believed that even in the lowest circumstances there are things to be learned, knowledge to be gained—but she needed to know this woman better if she were to have any hope of judging her.

Sariya's face turned cross. "I stay because Erahm has need of me, and I would give her those things I have to offer, regardless of the pains I may suffer."

Atiana reached the window. Outside stood the straits and the massive white arches of the Spar. The sun shone brightly upon much of it, but the far side and the city of Vihrosh were caught in a light fog that glowed brightly, as if the ancients themselves were shining down upon them. The scene was beatific, until Atiana noticed the wagons moving across the span of the bridge. They were supply wagons, she realized. Dozens of them. Those nearing the southern edge of the Spar bore munitions, and behind them were teams and teams of ponies pulling canons.

As a mixture of confusion and anger and—strangely—betrayal welled up inside her, Atiana shook her head. "You're sending them to Vostroma."

"You asked what I hoped to do. After the tearing of the aether on Ghayavand, the wards that were put into place held for some time. But over the years they weakened. Rifts were formed elsewhere. They were small at first, but over time they grew and spread until the worlds themselves became threatened. Muqallad hopes to use that to his advantage." Sariya held the stone out to Atiana. "And all he needs is this."

Atiana accepted the Atalayina, and when she did, it felt ten times heavier than it had moments ago.

Sariya seemed to sense this, for she nodded to the stone. "If he can fuse this, the third piece, to the other two, he will be able to rip the aether asunder, a thing from which neither world would, I fear, ever recover. Eons would pass before we could begin anew."

"What does this have to do with bringing war to the islands?"

"Not *war*, Atiana. I do no more than I need to."

"If not war, then what?"

"I have come to learn what happened on Khalakovo five years ago. You and Nikandr healed the boy—he who was Khamal. When you did this, it also healed the rift, did it not?"

Atiana merely stared, fearing to speak.

"It was one of many rifts that were open at the time, which were but a few of the ones that have opened and closed since. If Muqallad is to succeed, he needs to find a place where using the Atalayina will cause the rest to open wide."

"That could only be Ghayavand," Atiana said.

"*Neh*, the wards around the island are weakened, but they are still very much in place."

The answer, of course, was standing right before her.

She stared out the window.

At the Spar.

She thought of the confluence of aether centered here at the straits. It was a place of concentrated power, so strong that for centuries neither the Matri nor the Grand Duchy's windships had ever been able to cross it.

"This may be the place he seeks," Atiana said, "but that doesn't answer the question. Why wage war against us?"

"Because the pressure that has built up here at the straits must be relieved. It is not war, but a means to an end. Hakan watches for him—he will prevent Muqallad's arrival if he can—but Muqallad needs but little. With only a few of his servants he can perform his ritual anywhere on the island. The only way to stop him is to relieve the pressure, as Nasim did on Oshtoyets."

"But how?"

"The spires, Atiana Radieva. The spires of the Grand Duchy. They must fall."

Atiana swallowed, felt the world around her recede. "What?"

"It has already begun. Three spires have been destroyed, and more will follow."

"But if more of them fall… The storms will worsen. It will cost more lives."

"It has, and it will, but it is worth it."

"We *depend* on those spires."

"That may be true, but it is just as true that they cannot be allowed to remain standing. If you would save lives, I would ask you to take the dark, speak with your Matri. Tell them to agree to destroy the spires before we are forced to do it ourselves."

"I cannot do that."

"You are a daughter of the islands." Sariya spoke these words like an accusation. "If you care for them at all, you will do this."

Before Atiana could react, Sariya snatched the Atalayina from her hand. Atiana tried to take it back, but Sariya drew her hand away, her eyes fierce. Atiana grabbed her wrist, but cried out and pulled away immediately. Sariya's wrist had become as hot as a glowing brand.

"Go, Atiana," Sariya said. "Think on this carefully. Return to me if you change your mind, but make no mistake, one way or another, I will see them fall. Better that it be orderly, don't you think, than to see so many die?"

Atiana turned at the sound of the bootsteps upon the nearby stairs. Two guardsmen stood there, ready to lead her from the room. Before she left, Atiana looked back and saw Sariya staring out the window at the wagons moving steadily southward.

As the guards led her down the tower stairs, Atiana's emotions began to cool, and she found herself surprised not at what had happened but that she was seriously considering Sariya's offer. By the time she had gone three levels down, she'd made up her mind.

She stopped. The guards did not seem surprised. In fact, they parted easily as she took one hesitant step after another back up toward the top of the tower. It felt like a betrayal, walking back up those stairs, but she knew Sariya wasn't lying—she'd felt it when they'd shared one mind—and she forced herself to continue, step after confusing step.

When she once again stood on the topmost level of the tower, Sariya turned from the window to regard her. She did not revel in Atiana's return, nor did she seem expectant. She merely waited for Atiana to speak.

"I will do it," Atiana said. "I will speak with the Matri, but I require help."

CHAPTER SIXTY

When Nasim woke from his dream, it was to the feeling of warm tears streaming down his own face.

Strong were the sounds of the surf. Strong was the scent of the sea. Stronger still were the memories of Alif, the boy Khamal had murdered to secure his release from the island. Khamal had *murdered* him, and now his soul was gone. Lost to the world. Khamal had not only made it possible by turning him into akhoz, he'd been the one to drive home the blade.

It made Nasim sick to his stomach.

How many had Khamal sent to this undeserving fate? Dozens, certainly— dozens of children taken by Khamal in order to protect Ghayavand, to prevent the rift from spreading.

What made Nasim's fingers shake was the fact that Khamal had sacrificed more than just Alif. He'd bled his own soul, and in doing so he'd bled Nasim's as well. He'd taken all that Nasim could one day have been with the simple thrust of a knife.

"Nasim?"

He looked up, startled.

Kaleh was kneeling near his head, as she'd been when he'd begun to dream—

If only it *had* been a dream. It was a memory—a memory he knew to be all too real.

In Kaleh's blue eyes—her mother's eyes—was concern, but there was hunger as well, hunger for the knowledge he'd gained. Surely she'd seen what he'd seen—her look was too knowing for it to be otherwise—but she didn't know everything. She didn't understand.

Her face turned sad and apologetic. She shifted until she was kneeling by his side and pulled him into an embrace. The simple gesture spoke of apology, of asking him for something he wasn't yet ready to give. For a time they simply held one another, but Nasim began to feel smothered—not by her, but by this place, and the village around it.

"Come," he said, taking her hand.

He led her out from the arboretum and together they walked for a time.

The wind was unnaturally strong. It made the hems of their robes snap. It pushed them as they walked.

Nasim thought he was leading her aimlessly through Mirashadal, but he soon realized he was taking a familiar path. They wound through the bulk of the village proper and came eventually to the ballast, the long spire of wood that dropped down from the upper portion of the village. Around the ballast was a railed walking path that wound its way lower and lower until at last they came to a platform—the lowest place in the entire village. He used to come here and put his head out over the edge of the platform. He would sit there for hours at a time, wondering what would happen if he simply leapt. Would Erahm save him? Would Adhiya?

Many times he had slipped over to the other side of the railing and leaned out over open air. A simple slip of his hands was all it would have taken, and all the confusion and madness and pain and even ecstasy he'd experienced in Oshtoyets as he'd swallowed the stones would have been gone. Back then, all he'd wanted was a moment of peace. He had thought death would deliver him to his next life, and he'd begin again, perhaps poorer for resorting to taking his own life but at least free to begin again without the curse that Khamal had laid upon him.

Dropping Kaleh's hand, he sat on the planks, putting his legs out between the railing. Kaleh did the same, and for a short while it felt as though they were simply two children, sitting and measuring the wind.

"I wonder why I cannot touch Adhiya," Nasim said.

"Because you prevent yourself from doing so."

"If that's so, how is it that I can manipulate others?"

"You were lost as a child, Nasim. You floundered in the sea. Is it any wonder you grabbed for that which might save you? Is it any wonder you would do the same after you woke?"

In the distance, lightning arced within black clouds, lighting them from within. Long seconds later, the thunder came, rumbling and ominous.

"Khamal bled himself," Nasim said to her, hoping more than anything that she would be able to help unravel this mystery.

"What do you mean?"

"He cut his wrist. He fed his blood to one of the akhoz. It bled from him his power. It bled from him his soul." The lightning arced again, longer, brighter. "He bled mine as well."

"You hadn't even been born," Kaleh said.

"He took it just the same. He and I are connected. We're practically one, and he sacrificed our most precious gift so that he could return unfettered by the bonds the survivors of the sundering had placed on him."

"Then what happened?"

Nasim, unwilling to share so much, listened to the wind. A gull called, flying up from below the village to fight the gusts and land on a ledge above them.

"I don't blame you for keeping it to yourself," Kaleh said. "I know what it's like to hide secrets. The Landed man, Nikandr Khalakovo. I lied to him. I lied to Soroush as well. I led them to my father."

"Why?" Nasim asked.

"Does it matter?"

Nasim looked over, realizing that she was crying. Tears slipped along her cheeks and fell upon her robes.

"I suppose it doesn't," Nasim answered, returning his attention to the horizon. "Did you know that Muqallad cast a spell over Khamal?"

"*Neh*, I did not."

"It's the reason I couldn't return fully to Erahm, the reason I was caught between worlds. When Muqallad and Sariya conspired to murder him on top of Sariya's tower, Muqallad drew upon Khamal, preventing me from being born fully. And so, while I know that Khamal wished to heal the rift, I don't know how he meant me to do it."

The dark clouds were closer. A cold sleet began to fall, the sound like rashers in a frying pan.

"Isn't that what we all struggle with?"

"What?"

"Our purpose."

"That may be true, but most people have free will."

She stood and kissed the top of his head. "You have more choices than you realize, Nasim."

She took to the stairs, leaving him alone at the bottom of the village. Somehow he couldn't find it in himself to rise, so he sat there and let the sleet bite him.

When he was sure Kaleh could no longer see him, he stood and stepped over the railing as he'd done so many times before. He leaned out, wondering if the fates would cause his hands to slip on the slick wood. Below, the sea churned. If he fell, he would fall to his death—there would be no one to save him—and unlike those early days on Mirashadal, he knew now that he would not return. Death would not be a release. It would not lead to a new life. It would not be a beginning, but an end.

As his breath flew white upon the wind, he felt as if he were the world itself.

It, too, would one day cease to exist, and he wondered whether Muqallad's plans would bring that about. He wasn't even sure it would be a bad thing. After eons, perhaps the fates thought it time to slumber at last.

Nasim's grip tightened when someone spoke behind him.

"Will you jump?" It was Ashan's voice, and in it were notes of both forced amusement and hidden concern.

"I don't know," Nasim replied.

Ashan approached, his soft leather boots crunching over the sleet-covered platform. "It would be a shame. We haven't had much chance to talk."

Nasim didn't know what to say, so he remained silent.

"I would like to work with you tomorrow."

"To do what?"

"To heal you. I've spoken to Fahroz, and she believes we might be able to do it." He said it so plainly, but the words held power, like thunder felt in one's chest.

Nasim's grip began to loosen despite himself. He swung himself back over the railing and looked at Ashan, looked at his kind face, wondering if he could believe him. "How?"

"Through Sukharam. You may not know it, but you chose wisely, Nasim. *Very* wisely."

The following day, Nasim headed toward the center of Mirashadal. At the wooden tower that stood there, women stood on the platform, not men. He didn't understand the need to change, but he trusted that it was necessary.

When he entered through doors at the base of the tower, he found an empty room. Thick, wavy windows were set into the wood, allowing in the yellow light of the morning sun.

The only other person in the room was Sukharam. He looked over Nasim's shoulder, perhaps wondering who else might have come. He seemed uncomfortable being left alone with Nasim, but then his face hardened.

He'd changed... This was no longer the boy he'd found in Trevitze. *That* boy had been young and impressionable. He'd been a mere shadow of what he might become. This young man standing before Nasim was confident and brash. His back was straight, and he stared into Nasim's eyes with a look bordering on defiance, a look that said he would no longer be used.

Nasim didn't blame him. He'd enticed Sukharam and Rabiah with promises of greatness, promises of saving the world. And what had he given them? He'd given them pain. He'd given them death. He was utterly undeserving of their trust.

But he needed it now. He needed it desperately.

"Rabiah died because of you," Sukharam said. "We all could have died because of you."

"You're right," Nasim replied, "though I told you there was danger involved."

"You also said you'd be there for us."

Sukharam's eyes were filled with so much hate. Nasim didn't know what to say. What *was* there to say? Sukharam was right. He *had* abandoned them on Ghayavand. No matter how he might try to fool himself, he had abandoned them.

He was saved from responding when Ashan stepped inside the room. He knew there was tension, for his gaze darted between them, but then he merely smiled his toothy smile and said, "Come."

"Where's Fahroz?" Nasim asked.

"Kaleh asked to speak with her. But it's better that it's just the three of us in any case."

He led them outside and down through the warrens of Mirashadal. The sky was overcast, the wind bone-chilling. Nasim knew the village well, but after a while he realized he no longer recognized the path they were taking. They wended their way down a long and winding walk to a massive, open space. Nasim's mouth fell slack. It was like walking into a yawning cavern. The structure of the village surrounded them on all sides, but it was ingenious enough that wind and light flowed through the space. It was not so different from the feeling of hiding within a thicket—difficult to see into, not so difficult to see out. In all his months here, he'd never found this space. He marveled at it. It lifted him, made his heart open wide.

"Sit," Ashan said.

Nasim did, choosing a spot such that he and Sukharam could kneel in the center of this grand place. "What are we to do?"

"You will allow him to enter." Ashan moved until he was standing behind Sukharam. "Open yourself to the world, Nasim. And open yourself to Sukharam. He will do the rest."

Sukharam seemed uncomfortable, but he placed his hands gently upon his knees. His eyes were still full of anger, but he composed himself. He breathed, his chest becoming full. After three measured breaths, three measured exhalations, he lifted his gaze to look on Nasim once more.

The transformation was complete. He was calm. His eyes were gracious. His expression forgiving. He had many of the qualities that Nasim found so endearing in Ashan.

Had Ashan done this in only a mere handful of days with Sukharam?

Neh, Nasim realized. This was the real Sukharam. This was the Sukharam he should have seen long ago.

Knowing it was time, feeling it in his bones, Nasim closed his eyes, allowed himself to take breaths that filled him with the brightness of day.

He found no peace—thoughts of Rabiah kept invading his mind—but he somehow forged a cool and calm accord with the world, something he'd never managed to do before.

This, he thought, was the way Ashan must feel all the time. If only he could become so wise.

He felt a soft touch upon his shoulders. "Go further," Ashan said.

And with that touch he did. He realized that his constantly moving mind had prevented him from feeling Sukharam. He felt him now, felt his presence, felt his calmed thoughts and the doubts that stood behind them.

And then something strange happened.

The two of them settled into a rhythm. Their breathing began to match one another. Their thoughts faded until they were little more than one being, present in this place and time.

All as the wind whispered through the boughs of Mirashadal.

CHAPTER SIXTY-ONE

Nasim feels Sukharam's lives, not only those from his past, but his future as well. They do not come and then go like dreams half remembered; they build upon one another—dozens of lives, their memories and loves and regrets falling like leaves upon the forest floor.

It is not disconcerting. It is, instead, enlightening. It feels like the coming day, like the brightening of the dawn. It feels like vashaqiram must feel. It is true enlightenment, and Nasim realizes at once that he has felt it before. He felt it as Khamal, when the world nearly ended three hundred years ago.

Never before had he dreamt of the sundering—not once—but here a memory from Khamal is revealed to him. Sariya and Muqallad were there as well. They stood upon Sihyaan, the tallest mountain on Ghayavand. No one else was present—only the Al-Aqim.

Between them, sitting on an obsidian pedestal, was the Atalayina. It was whole, pristine, impossible to look upon without feeling like one stood at the center of all creation. By the fates, it was beautiful. He wanted to hide this memory away, to return to it when he was more prepared, but it quickly began to fade. More of Khamal's life came to him, some things he could remember dreaming before, some things he could not.

Faster they came, until, like the lives of Sukharam, he remembered more of his *own* lives. Khamal's memories overshadow the others at first, but this feeling recedes, and soon these lives, his past lives, are little more than links in a chain that drift into the dim and distant past.

He feels nothing of his future, however. Nasim knew that he would die— truly die—when he faded from this world, but to see it like this, so stark in comparison to the fate of Sukharam, makes him feel small, makes him feel powerless to affect the world.

As bleak as this realization is, it sheds light on his prior life, and more importantly, his connection to it. For the first time he can feel the spell of

Muqallad weighing down on him like a stone. It presses against him like the depths of a hidden lake, preventing him from touching Adhiya.

There is another link as well. This one he recognizes immediately. His link to Nikandr, still strong after all these years.

As he reflects upon this a realization comes to him, one he never would have expected. By the fates who weave, the link to Nikandr acts in *opposition* to Muqallad's. It saved him on Oshtoyets. Nasim knows this. What strikes him like a thunderclap is the fact that it has been doing so ever since. Every minute he doesn't slip back into madness is due to his link to Nikandr. He acts like a length of driftwood, preventing Nasim from sinking beneath the waves.

This bond had always felt like something he should be ashamed of—partially because Nikandr was Landed, but also because it had felt like it was keeping Nasim from standing on his own two feet. His shame is like a glowing brand, and it grows brighter as he thinks not just how he treated Nikandr, but Ashan and Sukharam and Fahroz and nearly everyone he'd come to know. Everyone except Rabiah. And Rabiah is now dead.

He focuses on Muqallad's spell, tugs at its threads, which are tied around him so tightly that the effort feels futile. As he pulls the threads away, new ones form like spider silk. He tries harder, becomes desperate to rid himself of Muqallad's taint, but soon his efforts bring pain—they disturb the delicate balance he's found—and he retreats.

He is about to pull away, buoyed in defeat by the notion that he'd finally found the source of his inability to touch Adhiya, when he feels something in the village far below where he stands now.

In the ballast tower, near the place where Soroush and Bersuq were kept prisoner for long months and years.

Fahroz is there. She lies on the floor of the room.

And Kaleh stands over her.

A knife gripped tightly in one hand.

Nasim woke.

He stood immediately and began running for the nearest of the paths. "We must go! Fahroz is in trouble!"

Ashan looked like Nasim had scared him nearly to death. "What did you see?"

"Send help to the lowest section of the ballast tower!"

"Wait!" Ashan called.

Nasim heard them chasing after him. The paths here were not familiar, but he soon found some that were. In little time he was bolting through the village's warrens, heading ever lower. On a wooden deck, a qiram kneeling with her young disciples stood as he ran past. She looked worried, even angry, when she heard the calls behind him, but Nasim moved on before she could react.

He reached one of the lower entrances to the tower. He took the spiraling staircase downward, moving as fast as he dared.

He came at last, breathless, to the room he'd seen in his dream, a dark place no longer used as a prison. A lone siraj lit the room. It cast deep shadows against Kaleh, who kneeled above Fahroz with the khanjar held over her chest.

Nasim froze in the doorway. "Please, Kaleh! Stop!"

Kaleh looked to him, her expression resolute.

Then she turned back and thrust the knife into Fahroz's chest.

"*Neh*!" Nasim screamed.

Fahroz jerked. Her eyes went wide, but she made no sound, as if she'd just been awoken from a vivid and horrifying dream.

Kaleh turned back to him. Nasim shivered at the emotionless expression on her face.

"Why?" Nasim asked, his hands shaking in front of him.

The answer came moments later.

The wall behind her, made from some of the stoutest, thickest wood in the entire village, opened like a wound. It yawned, wider and wider, until it was large enough for her to step into. He knew then that she'd killed Fahroz so she could open this portal. She was fleeing Mirashadal, and the qiram at the edge of the village had surely prevented her from doing so.

Despite her words the day before, she was returning to Muqallad. That much was clear.

Kaleh stood and squared herself, as if she thought he might attack. She glanced over his shoulder. She could hear—as Nasim could—others coming down the stairs. "Goodbye, Nasim an Ashan."

She took a step toward the gap in the wood, but the notion that she would leave after what she'd done so incensed him that he felt the blood pounding through his veins. His heart beat powerfully. Madly. An anger welled up inside him—an anger so intense it threatened to blind him with white rage.

As Kaleh took another step, the world around him slowed.

Her movements decelerated until they matched the pace of the tides, the pace of the seasons.

Kaleh halts short of the opening. A shimmering curtain surrounds them, contains them.

Nasim takes one stride forward. And another. Soon he stands just short of her.

She holds in her left hand the knife, the blade still slick with blood. He reaches out to take it. Her hands are cold and stiff.

As he touches them, he feels a stirring within her.

Whether it is because of his touch, or because she's learned what he's done to her, he does not know, but her motion accelerates. Like a hare in spring, she is rousing from Nasim's spell.

He has an urge to back away, to protect himself, but it is distant and small. Much larger is the desire to plunge the khanjar deep into her chest, doing the same to her as she did to Fahroz.

And then he realizes. The khanjar... He's seen it before.

By the fates above, it's the same knife that Muqallad and Sariya used to murder Khamal.

"Will you kill *me*?" she asks. She turns slowly, ever so slowly, toward him.

Nasim stares into her eyes. "Why would you follow him?"

"I follow him because he is right."

"He brings us to ruin."

"He brings us to our better lives."

"You're a fool if you believe that."

Kaleh's eyes soften. She looks upon him with pity—with *pity*, as if *he* is the one who will never understand.

"I had hoped you could join me, but when I saw what happened to Khamal—saw your reaction to it—I knew that you were not ready." She stares down at the khanjar. "Kill me if you would."

Nasim grips the handle, feels the braided metal dig into his skin. He feels the weight of it, and a part of him—a part he is only distantly aware of—feels the keenness of the blade.

Were he to use the blade, he would kill her. She would die and would never deliver the knowledge she'd gained to Muqallad.

He considers this. He actually *considers* killing another. Is he so like Khamal that he could be brought to such a thing? Killing in cold blood? It triggers a memory of Khamal when he hid the piece of the Atalayina in Sariya's tower, when the two of them had made love.

And Kaleh... Nasim looks at her anew.

She has none of Muqallad's features.

She isn't Muqallad's daughter at all. She's *Khamal's*.

A shiver runs through him as the implications work themselves through his mind. He is *not* Khamal. He is *Nasim*. He is his own, linked to Khamal only by the whims of the fates and the threads of souls. He knows this, and yet Khamal feels like his sire. Kaleh feels like his kin. A sister, a cousin, blood of his own blood, though he knows this isn't true.

As he breathes, he stares into her pitying eyes and finds that he cannot do this. He isn't made for such things, and yet it feels, however disturbing the notion, like failure.

What have things come to that the lack of will to kill another feels like *failure*?

He finds—perhaps through his confusion, perhaps because of the simple awareness of it—his control over the curtain around them slipping.

As the world returns to normal, Kaleh turns and walks into the opening, and as the sounds of footsteps upon the stairs resume, the opening closes around Kaleh.

Nasim stood near the village's central tower. The qiram still stood at the edge of the circle facing outward, protecting the village against another attack though everyone knew Muqallad had already done what he'd come to do. His retreat after Kaleh's arrival had all been a ruse so that she could remain in the village and become close to Nasim once he arrived.

How easily he'd been fooled, Nasim thought. How quickly he'd believed her story. He'd been so desperate to speak to someone similar to him—someone who understood at least in part what it was like to be of the Al-Aqim—that he'd overlooked all else. That Fahroz and Ashan and the wisest of the village's mahtar had also been fooled was no consolation. He should have known better.

On the platform, Majeed, the mahtar that would take Fahroz's place as Mirashadal's leader, held a burning torch. It guttered in the wind but remained lit as he touched it to the skiff that held Fahroz's body, which was wrapped carefully in a white shroud.

The wood within the skiff lit. Another mahtar touched the wood. The skiff lifted and floated eastward.

Nasim could see Fahroz lying within, the white cloth catching fire.

"Fare well," he said softly, his words taken by the wind.

Ashan, standing next to him, put his arm around Nasim's shoulder. He allowed it to remain for a moment, but such closeness still discomfited him, and he shrugged it off.

He remained while many left. He watched the skiff drift away as the smoke trailed black against the incessant gray of the high clouds. He remained until he could no longer see the skiff against the sky.

"There was so much I wished to say," he whispered, "and now you're gone."

Dozens of memories played within his mind, each of them begging for a voice. But anything he thought to say sounded weak and miserable, unworthy of being spoken in Fahroz's honor.

He caught, near the horizon, one last wisp of smoke. A tear slipped down his cheek as he watched it disperse, Fahroz's final farewell.

"I don't know who my parents were," he said softly, "but surely, if Ashan is my father, you are my mother." He took a deep breath, and while he released it, his chest shook with the emotion he was keeping inside. "Thank you," he whispered.

He cried then. Cried for a long time, but in the end, he knew this was no time for lamentation, or for grief.

He left without another word, retreating to his room. He began gathering his few belongings into a bag, but before too long, a knock came at his door.

He sighed, closing his eyes, wishing he could leave without seeing another soul. But he knew he would have to speak to Ashan. It might as well be now.

When he opened the door, he was surprised to find not Ashan, but Sukharam.

"If you've come to lecture me, you can leave now."

"I wish to speak."

"*I* don't."

Nasim tried to close the door, but Sukharam held his hand out, preventing Nasim from doing so. After a glance behind him, he forced his way into the room and closed the door behind him. "I know what you're doing."

Nasim went back to his bag, putting the last of his clothes into it. "I suppose you'd like a ribbon."

"I want to go with you."

Nasim cinched the bag, refusing to turn. He didn't want help, and he certainly didn't want it from Sukharam, who would only be a constant reminder of his failures.

"You can't control a skiff," Sukharam continued. "Not in these winds. Not alone."

"I'll be fine."

"You won't. Whatever you did in the tower with Kaleh, we both know it was only in passing. If you leave alone you'll die before you reach Galahesh."

Nasim turned to face Sukharam. "How did you know I'm going to the straits?"

"Because that is where Muqallad must go."

"The question was how *you* knew."

Sukharam was pensive for a moment. He looked around the small room, looked toward the dying light through the window over Nasim's shoulder. "I never thought your goals were foolish, you know."

"You merely thought me incapable of achieving them."

Sukharam laughed sadly. "I was upset because you refused to include us. You refused to let us in, including Rabiah. You refused to ask for help."

Nasim grit his jaw. He wanted to walk past Sukharam, wanted to leave this room and take the skiff as he'd planned, and trust to the fates that he would be able to reach Galahesh on his own.

But he couldn't. Sukharam was right. And there was a part of him that knew it would be a grave disservice to Fahroz and Rabiah if he were to refuse Sukharam's help.

Especially Rabiah.

In the end, there was nothing for him to do but step forward and embrace Sukharam for all he was willing to do. After all Sukharam had been through, after all he'd risked already, he deserved the chance to see this through. He kissed Sukharam's cheek and pulled him away. "I'm glad to have another."

CHAPTER SIXTY-TWO

Nikandr, blinking sleep from his eyes, stood on the deck of the old six-masted yacht he'd taken from Elykstava. He was standing in Jahalan's position near the base of the starward mainmast. It felt wrong—like a dishonor to Jahalan—but in his heart he knew Jahalan would be proud. It was something they'd rarely talked about—his ability to commune with spirits of the wind—and now that Jahalan was gone, Nikandr was sorry for it. Jahalan could have taught him much, and now he'd squandered the opportunity.

Would that you were here, Nikandr thought.

The ship bucked, sliding this way or that under the fierce winds that howled through the rigging, stole warmth from the skin, threatened at all times to upend the ship. Only through Styophan's skills as a pilot, and Nikandr and Anahid working together, had they been able to come this far. This storm was the strongest he'd ever seen in his time on the winds. He knew it was due to the spires falling. The seas and the winds seemed to be in a rage, seemed to be vengeful, as if the spires had controlled them too long and they were now taking their revenge.

Nikandr pinched his eyes, shook his head vigorously. This did little to shake the feelings of sleep that stole over him every time he began to relax. They'd been sailing for nearly two days, plotting a course wide of Alotsk and Balizersk, the next two islands in the Vostroman archipelago.

He'd felt craven in doing so, but the information he'd received from Fuad, the Yrstanlan kapitan, had been too valuable to do otherwise. He could not risk meeting the enemy and being killed or captured—not with information like this—and so they'd gone wide with only Anahid and Nikandr to act as dhoshaqiram and havaqiram. He wasn't comfortable with more people learning of his abilities, but enough rumors had spread from what had happened to him in Oshtoyets that it would surprise few, and would merely confirm their fears of him as a Landless sympathizer.

At last, just as dawn was breaking, the mountains of Kiravashya appeared on the horizon.

"Where are the ships?" Anahid shouted above the wind.

Nikandr looked down at her. She hadn't spoken in over a day, so lost in her duty was she. She was a slight young woman, and quiet, but she was diligent and gifted in the ways of a dhoshaqiram.

Nikandr returned his gaze to the massive island ahead. "I don't know."

He thought surely he would have seen windships scouring the island, destroying what was left of the resistance from the Grand Duchy, or at the very least he thought he would see ships patrolling—either Yrstanlan or Anuskayan—but to his surprise there were none. None at all.

As they came near, and they saw Beshiklova, the mountain that housed Palotza Galostina, Nikandr started to get the impression that this was all planned—the attacks on the outer islands. Word was that they had attacked Ildova and Tolvodyen first. He had seen the spire on Elykstava destroyed with his own eyes and now he wondered if they hadn't already destroyed the ones on Alotsk and Balizersk, leaving only Kiravashya—the largest of Vostroma's islands with the largest of the spires. If that were so, he wouldn't be surprised to see the winds as wild as they'd been these past few days. It would probably continue for days, even weeks.

Strangely, Yrstanla's gambit attacking the outer islands might have given the Grand Duchy time in which to recover.

Best we use it wisely, he thought.

When they neared land, the bulk of Galostina and its towering black spire came into view. Three ships launched to meet them far from the palotza's grounds. Nikandr ordered the men to hoist the white pennant so that it flew below the Vostroman flag.

As the ships neared, Nikandr could see battle scars—holes in their hulls, rips in their sails, missing rigging—and they were clearly recent. How many enemy ships had been felled, he wondered. How many lives had it cost? How many ships of Anuskaya had been lost?

The kapitan of the lead ship seemed relieved to find them an ally, but his face turned sour when he realized it was Nikandr who commanded the ship.

"Follow me to the palotza," he shouted across the gap as they were readying to leave, "and do not straggle."

Their approach to the rocky coast of Kiravashya brought with it more evidence of recent battle. A trail of flotsam could be seen among the waves, and when they came within a half-league of the coast, he saw the aft of a ship pointing up from the waters, the bow wedged in the rocks below the water's surface. Within a shallow vale on the rising snow-swept landscape the remains of two ships lay. It was clear that they'd collided, their masts caught in the rigging of the other. How many had died when they'd fallen? Forty? Fifty?

As the sun rose fully, they approached Galostina's eyrie, which looked down upon a wide green valley. It would be idyllic, Nikandr thought, if it weren't for the wind threatening to uproot the trees. The island's primary eyrie was higher up the mountain. The eyrie on its cliff face seemed to crouch, ready to leap and strike should the enemies of Vostroma approach, but the ships lashed to the perches spoke of the grievous wounds Yrstanla had inflicted. Even from this distance Nikandr could hear the sounds of industry—the hollow sound of wood being pounded as the ships were repaired, gang leaders calling out orders to their men, the *whoo-haa* call of men working a massive mast saw.

And then came Galostina. She had a larger eyrie than Radiskoye—ten perches in all. And seven of them were filled. As the escort ships flew toward the mountain, Nikandr guided them toward the berth where a man waved two black flags. A woman stood near the perch, waiting. It took him time to realize it was Mileva Vostroma, Atiana's sister. She wore a fine white woolen coat and an ermine cap. The hem of her coat blew fiercely, making her look like a qiram summoning the winds that howled among the crevices of the massive palotza.

When Nikandr leapt down to the perch, Mileva met him and took him into an embrace. "The ships told us of your decision to head for Elykstava. We thought you'd been lost."

It felt strange to have Atiana's sister hug him, and perhaps it was the same for her, for she hugged him stiffly, awkwardly.

"I feared it was *Galostina* that had been lost." Nikandr looked up to the signs of cannon fire that marked several of the palotza's towers. The spire, both wider and taller than the spire over Radiskoye, was strangely intact. No cannon fire marred its surface, which was strange, considering the state of Galostina.

Mileva turned and looked at the damage as well, perhaps remembering the battle from the halls. "She nearly was." She guided Nikandr toward the palotza. "Come," she said as they entered through a set of brassbound doors. "There's ill news, and someone you must see."

"What's happened?" he asked as they walked down a long central hallway. There were dozens of military men walking to and fro. Their conversation filled the space, making the tense atmosphere somehow more tense. Some noticed Nikandr and Mileva and bowed their heads, but most were too busy to take note. Mileva led Nikandr to a winding set of stairs that ran along the edge of a massive domed intersection of the two largest halls of Galostina. The dome towered six stories high, its gilt mosaics shining down on the marble balusters and golden lantern holders.

"Mileva, what's happened?"

Still she waited until they'd reached the next floor before speaking. "It's your father. He was wounded during the last attack two days ago. A colonnade collapsed, killing three of my father's advisors and wounding seven others, including your father. He is sound of body, but he suffered a head wound. He's woken only sporadically, and he's become weaker over the last several days."

The news was better than he'd feared, but his gut still churned, and it only became worse as Mileva led him up to the fourth floor and down another long hallway. There were more streltsi stationed here—nearly a dozen of them—all of them Khalakovan. They all bowed their heads low, reverently, as Nikandr approached.

Mileva stopped in front of an ornately carved door.

"I'm glad you've come." Mileva stepped in and kissed his cheek. "We have need of stout men at times like these."

Her words were spoken with a sincere admiration that shocked Nikandr. What had been happening in the halls of Galostina?

"Thank you," he said.

"I'll wait, and do not tarry. You'll need to speak with Andreya when you're done."

Nikandr nodded and squeezed her hand, glad to have an ally in this place. He entered the room and found his father in a large bed. The bandages around his head were stained with blood. Most of it was dark, but the center was red, making him wonder how well the wound was healing. He sat in a chair by the bedside. The light coming from the windows behind him lit the landscape of his father's face in bas relief, making it clear just how much pain he was in, even in slumber. Nikandr sat there for some time, knowing he should leave and speak with Andreya, but he could not. Not just yet.

Father never woke. His breathing was shallow, so shallow that the added time did nothing to make Nikandr's feelings of unease settle. In fact, it made them worse.

At a soft knock at the door, he stood and kissed his father tenderly on the cheek.

Mileva was standing in the hall when he left the room, looking small and apologetic. How much she'd changed, Nikandr thought. The Mileva of old would never have acted like this.

"All will be well," she said, though she knew no such thing.

"I know," Nikandr replied, realizing in that one moment what might make her act this way. "Where is your father, the Grand Duke?"

"Taken," she said, "by Hakan the Betrayer." Her tone was bitter, and little wonder. With one barbarous act, Hakan had changed from provisional ally to sworn enemy.

"Can you sense him?" Nikandr asked, motioning to the soulstone that glinted in the dim light of the hall.

She pinched her lips before replying. "I cannot."

"It's the storms," Nikandr said. "You'll find him when they die down."

"I know." She smiled, an unconvincing gesture, and then motioned back the way they'd come. "Please."

She took Nikandr down to the ground floor to a location in Galostina that was one of the earliest structures built. The original keep—which had over the centuries been absorbed by the larger palotza—was being used as the headquarters for the war. The room was windowless—the original windows having long since been bricked up. At the center of the room, surrounded by a dozen massive brass lanterns on tall stands, was a table with several men standing at it, all of them looking down at the maps arrayed there. Nikandr recognized Andreya Antonov, the polkovnik of Vostroma's stremya, and Betyom Nikolov Vostroma, Zhabyn's cousin and the admiral of the staaya. Duke Leonid of Dhalingrad was there as well, and when he realized Nikandr was approaching, he motioned to Andreya, who nodded toward his men. Most of the gathered men left the table, though not before they'd stared at Nikandr as if he were a deserter, and soon Nikandr was alone with Andreya, Betyom, and Leonid.

"I will leave you to it," Mileva said, smiling and bowing her head before taking her leave as well.

"Well met," Duke Leonid said to Nikandr. Leonid's long white beard fell down his black kaftan. With his dark eyes, it made him look wild, a wolf in goat's clothing. His expression was wholly uncharitable, which gave Nikandr pause. He had thought his presence here might be looked upon with some relief, but now he could see that at least for these men, who had always been loyal to Zhabyn, that wouldn't be the case.

"My Lord Duke," Nikandr said. He turned to Andreya, all but ignoring Dhalingrad. "I come bearing news."

Andreya was a tall man. He was Father's age, but he looked as fit as Nikandr. His trim beard was gray, darker near his jowls. His hair was lost beneath the fur cap he wore. "When have you last slept?"

Nikandr shook his head, unable to remember. "It's been days."

Andreya paused before speaking again. "The ships sent from Khalakovo arrived well ahead of you, My Lord Prince."

"I was diverted to Elykstava—"

"Diverted," Leonid scoffed, "with *three* of our ships."

Duke Konstantin of Bolgravya reached the table. He bowed his head to Nikandr. It was an awkward gesture, more so than the other men, no doubt because of the history Nikandr had with his family, Grigory in particular. He said nothing, content for the moment to listen as the others questioned Nikandr.

"It seemed important," Nikandr said carefully, "to determine the state of her spire."

Andreya stared intently into Nikandr's eyes, his expression stark and serious though not unkind. "When you had been given orders to come to Kiravashya."

"Forgive me, Polkovnik, but the ships were mine to command."

Duke Leonid bristled. "Those ships were needed *here*, Khalakovo, a fact I'm sure the Duke of Khalakovo shared with you before you left."

"My Father, the Duke, lies upstairs."

"He is the duke no longer," Leonid said.

"A mongrel might leap upon the throne, Dhalingrad. Would you call him duke if you came across him lying there?"

The potbellied Betyom looked on this exchange in silent acceptance, but Konstantin jumped in. "My Lord Duke. My Lord Prince. Please, we shouldn't waste time bickering. We don't know when Yrstanla will return."

"Very well," Leonid said slowly, as if he were humoring Konstantin, who was twenty years his junior. "What news from Elykstava?"

"We captured a kapitan of one of the ships that attacked the spire. He confessed that their admiral was worried over an attack on the Spar. He recommended they not overcommit their ships, but the Kamarisi would not allow anything other than a full attack."

"What of it?" Betyom asked.

"They're overextended, admiral. If we can destroy the bridge, we can cut off any hope of reinforcements arriving."

"This is senseless," Leonid said, motioning to the map before him. "Their ships are *here*. What good would destroying the Spar do now?"

"Reinforcements could still be moving toward Galahesh, and it would cut off their lines of supply and their route of escape."

Leonid frowned. "We need not worry about their *escape*, Khalakovo. We need to save Galostina and *her* spire, not the spire on Elykstava, which we had already decided to give them if they chose to take it, nor the spires on other, nearby islands, *nor* a bridge a thousand leagues from where we stand. *Galostina's* spire. That is all that matters, and you've lost us three ships in her defense."

"I would not give up the spires so easily," Nikandr said. "They lost three ships on Elykstava as well, and we found critical information. If we could send ships, we might stand a good chance of taking the Spar."

"We have no ships to spare," Andreya said.

"I would need only five or six—"

Andreya's flat look made Nikandr stop. "Have you come to serve," he said, "or have you come to dictate?"

Nikandr looked at each of the men in turn, who looked at him as if he were a raw strelet who had yet to learn the ways of the wind. He had hoped that they might be convinced, but now he saw that they never would be. They might trust him to fly a ship, but beyond this they trusted him not at all.

"I've come to deliver vital information, and to serve in a way that helps the Grand Duchy."

Andreya stood taller. "With the Grand Duke gone, *I* decide what helps the Grand Duchy."

"*Nyet*, Polkovnik." Nikandr couldn't help but think of the proclamation that Borund had read in Radiskoye. He had stepped over a line by saying these words, but he was done with hiding from men who sought to control him, a prince of the Grand Duchy. "With my father unconscious and my brother out of reach, I am Khalakovo."

Duke Leonid looked as if he wanted to spit at Nikandr's feet, but Andreya seemed to be weighing his words carefully. His eyes were not angry—there might even be a touch of respect in them—but it was also clear that if it came to it, Nikandr's claim to authority or not, he would take from Khalakovo the resources he needed. "I understand that you hope to protect us, My Lord Prince. But you fail to understand the situation. Yrstanla has retreated, most likely to weather the storm they've unleashed. But have no doubt—the moment the storm abates, they will return for the spire, and when they do, it will be all we can do to stop them. We have need of men like you, men who can command a ship and command a wing. I cannot afford to have you missing from the coming battle."

"We might save the island only to lose the Grand Duchy."

"Just now, My Lord Prince, Kiravashya *is* the Grand Duchy. Now leave. Think on what I've said." He returned his attention to the maps before him. "And find some sleep. You look terrible."

CHAPTER SIXTY-THREE

Nikandr woke in the chair sitting next to his father's bed. The room was dark. Only the smallest amount of light came from the crescent moon through the high window. As he rubbed the sleep from his eyes he realized he'd slept through the entire day.

He was ravenous, but he didn't want to leave his father. Not just yet. He'd barely had any time with him before he'd fallen asleep.

He lit the small lamp at the bedside and for a time simply stared as his father's chest rose and fell slowly. He looked old. He looked weary and white, as if he'd already begun taking small but unyielding steps toward the beyond. Nikandr was proud of him, though. He'd been brought to Vostroma little more than a thrall, but as his counsel had proven more and more invaluable, he'd risen in Zhabyn's circle, even among the misgivings of men like Leonid Dhalingrad, to become the Grand Duke's most trusted advisor.

He felt bad for Mother, who despite spending nearly all of her time in the aether had come to cherish her time with Father outside of it.

Still, they were born of the islands; they were hard, and they spent time with one another as they could, speaking when Mother took the form of one of Galostina's rooks. Though her ban from using the aether had never formally been lifted, it had eased to the point that two years after the ritual of Oshtoyets, Nikandr had brought Yrfa here to Galostina so that Mother could assume her favorite bird to speak with Father.

A soft knock came at the door.

Nikandr rose and opened it, and to his surprise found Mileva standing in the hall.

"May I come in?" she asked.

"Of course."

She took a padded chair near the fireplace and warmed her hands as Nikandr moved his own chair over from the bedside. Mileva's pale skin turned ruddy under the light of the low fire, making her look, momentarily, like one of the Aramahn. She leaned, elbows on knees, staring into the fire. In that small instant Nikandr could see the young Mileva. Many a night had he seen her do the very same thing among the halls of Radiskoye or Zvayodensk or Belotrova.

But then Mileva seemed to catch herself. She turned sharply, though not unkindly, toward Nikandr, and sat back in her chair. She crossed one leg over the other, and now she seemed like little more than a Duchess upon her throne, elegant and beautiful and cunning. Her eyes twinkled under the firelight.

"Has Atiana found you?" Mileva asked.

"I haven't spoken to her in weeks. Not since leaving Rafsuhan."

"She's contacted no one on Kiravashya, nor any of the Matri we spoke to before we lost contact. Mother has tried to find her, but with the storms…"

"My mother found me near Elykstava, though I think it cost her dearly."

"Thank the ancients for women like Saphia."

"You speak so reverently, Leva."

"No matter what you might think, I've always held your mother in high regard." Nikandr chuckled, but Mileva seemed offended. "How could I not? Especially now?"

She meant, of course, because she was now a Matra herself, not just in name but in deed. She had become strong—not as strong as Atiana, but strong just the same. Nikandr had often wondered what the Matri shared with one another among the aether. It was completely foreign to him, but there could be little doubt the aether created a sense of sisterhood that could never have been born in the waking world.

"You're worrying over Atiana and Ishkyna," Nikandr said.

"Of course I am," she snapped, a bit of the old Mileva returning.

"They yet live."

"I know, Nischka, but I wonder under what circumstances? Surely the Kamarisi has them. What might he do to get what he needs? What would he stop at to find the weaknesses of the Grand Duchy?"

"Little."

"Little, indeed. And here we sit while Leonid and Andreya rule in my father's place." She glanced over at the bed. "Your father, were he to wake, might have made a difference, but without him there is nothing to keep Leonid in check. I think he prays for Father's death that he might take the Grand Duke's mantle."

"There is Konstantin."

She paused before speaking. "*Da*, there is Konstantin." The way she spoke those words, and the way she looked into Nikandr's eyes, he knew. She and Konstantin were lovers. Konstantin had long been married, and for all who saw him with his wife, they would say he was happy, but here he was, a thousand leagues from home… Perhaps it was simply a romance of convenience, but the way Mileva had spoken those simple words, it made him think that she wished her mother had chosen another for her hand in marriage.

Mileva's eyes narrowed, as if she realized it was time to come to the point. "They didn't tell you of Grigory, did they?"

"What of him?"

"He was sent weeks ago with ships. He was to position them along the coast of Yrstanla such that they could be called to attack the northern stretch of Galahesh, should the need arise."

"So why didn't he?"

"He was sent across the downs, around the Sea of Khurkhan."

"That's madness!"

"It was dangerous, true, but Father needed leverage should things go sour with the Kamarisi. We know he arrived on the southeastern shores of Yrstanla. He was headed north, but the winds were rough and getting rougher. I wasn't able to find him again before the first of the spires were felled, and now… Now it's impossible."

Nikandr leaned back, making his chair creak. In the fireplace, a log crumbled, the embers releasing sparks into the air. "Why are you telling me this?"

"Do you believe the words of the kapitan from Yrstanla?"

He nodded carefully. "I do."

"Do you believe Andreya is right in keeping you here?"

Nikandr glanced over to his father. This was treasonous talk. He hadn't agreed to join Andreya—not yet, anyway—but Mileva certainly had.

"You don't have to answer," Mileva continued, "but you could use Grigory's ships. You could find the men you need to destroy the Spar, and Konstantin might have his brother back."

"And you your sisters and father."

"The Grand Duchy needs them, Nischka. You can't deny it."

"I need no incentive to find them."

"And yet Andreya's words hold you back."

"They make sense."

Mileva stared at him. One moment the firelight was playing against her porcelain skin, and the next she was standing in a rush, as if she found this conversation suddenly distasteful.

"The *Yarost* is the first ship on the third quay of the eyrie." She turned and strode toward the door. "It will be empty and unguarded, but only this one night. And I will be in the drowning basin." She opened the door, pausing for one brief moment on her way out. "Choose wisely, Nikandr, and quickly."

And then she was gone, leaving Nikandr alone with his thoughts.

He sat alone, wondering how wise this could be. The ships of Yrstanla would return soon. They could not give the Grand Duchy too much time to recover, and the wind, though still strong and unpredictable, was beginning to subside, at least enough that stout ships of war could be put to sail. In a day, perhaps two, they would return, and Nikandr didn't want to be missing when that happened. As Andreya had said, they could focus on Galahesh after the battle.

"Nikandr."

Nikandr turned, realizing the softly spoken name had come from his father. He moved to the bedside and took his father's hand in his.

"I'm here, Father."

"Go," Father said.

"Go where?" Nikandr had spoken the words before he realized that his father had heard everything that he and Mileva had talked about.

Father coughed and turned his head, though even this simple act seemed to pain him. "Go. Find Grigory. Find the others if you can, but at all costs destroy the Spar."

The moon was a sliver in the nighttime sky, giving Nikandr and the others plenty of cover as they slipped quietly from the halls of Galostina and into the frigid air. A dozen, they numbered: he and Anahid, Styophan and nine of his best men. Nikandr felt his hezhan and called upon it to still the winds as the men unlashed the lone skiff from the ship they'd flown in early that morning. Was it truly the same day? It felt like he'd been here for a week.

As they filed in and released the mooring ropes, Nikandr watched the palotza carefully, particularly the doors and the towers along the curtain wall that protected Galostina everywhere except at the eyrie, where the protection was a sheer drop of hundreds of feet to the valley floor.

He saw no one. Relief began to fill him as they dropped below the level of the eyrie, but when they began to rise and fly toward the mountain, he could see clearly a doorway of the palotza and within it, framed by the faint light coming from within, the silhouette of a man. They were too far away for him to have any idea of who it might be, but a moment later, the door closed, leaving the palotza in darkness save for the handful of lantern-lit windows.

"Who was it?" Styophan asked.

"Who can say? But best we put the wind beneath our sails as quick as may be."

And so they did. As the wind blew fiercely—tossing the ship about—Nikandr drew upon his hezhan as he'd rarely done before, partially to combat the winds but also to hasten them toward the eyrie. He felt it in his gut, in his chest, the hezhan hungering, feeding off of him. He coughed, stifling the discomfort. They needed this speed.

They reached it before fifteen minutes had passed, but it still felt too long. A swift pony could have reached the eyrie by now.

He brought the skiff up beneath the *Yarost*, the ship Mileva had told him about. He was sure it would be well outfitted—the threat of Yrstanla required it—but he was also sure Konstantin would have had it provisioned with extra rations and extra munitions in case Nikandr took this bait.

They came even with the deck, and though the wind was still strong—especially as it swept up along the mountainside to blow among the moored ships—Nikandr and the others moved quickly and efficiently. They had discussed this over and over before leaving the palotza. One by one, they leapt over to the ship as Nikandr and Anahid held her steady.

Then Anahid was over and finally Nikandr made the leap himself, his men catching him and steadying him as he used his hezhan to reverse the wind and push the skiff away. It twisted like a leaf on a pond, floating away until he was sure that he could release it and leave the winds to do the rest.

By then the men had already begun preparing the ship, most moving to the perch to release the mooring ropes. They were only half done when lights appeared above at the eyrie master's house and an alarm bell began to ring.

Clang-clang-clang-clang.

"Quickly, men!" Nikandr called.

He joined in, forgetting the winds as he leapt over to the perch and helped Styophan with one of the last three mooring ropes. They were heavy, and though they worked as fast as they could, he could already hear the shout of men, hear their footsteps as they worked their way down from the upper quay. They would arrive in little time, and when they did, Nikandr and the rest wouldn't stand a chance.

Nikandr moved to the middle of the perch. The first of the streltsi, each bearing a musket, were already rounding the last of the switchbacks. Nikandr allowed his hands to fall to his side. He closed his eyes and tilted his head back. He felt the rage of the wind, felt it course up along the hills and valleys until funneling up toward the snowcapped peak of Beshiklova with an energy he'd rarely felt.

As the bell continued to clang, Nikandr bid the wind to give him all that it could. He directed it as the walls of a valley would. He bid it to heave itself against the quay.

It did. It rushed against the streltsi as they were leveling their weapons. The wind blew them like autumn leaves, pushing them against the cliff at their backs. The sound of it… Nikandr had never heard the like, the shrieking as it ran through the rigging of the eyrie's ships, the pound of canvas as sails came loose, the hollow thudding as ships were thrown against their perches. The insistent and fearful orders of the sotnik were nearly lost among the gale, but Nikandr knew they were readying themselves.

"The ship is free!" he heard Styophan shout.

Nikandr didn't care.

Rarely had he felt so deeply connected to his hezhan. Perhaps he'd felt this way in those first few encounters on Uyadensk, when he'd not known the nature of the hezhan, nor his bond to it, but those times had been brought upon by his link to Nasim. Since then he'd been nervous to draw too heavily upon the spirit, but he did not feel so now. Whether it was an abandon that came from desperation or a trust that had been slowly built over the years he didn't know, but he allowed the hezhan to take more of him than he ever had before.

"We're free!" Styophan shouted, this time at the top of his lungs.

He knew he should release the hezhan, at least enough that he could move to the ship, but for the moment he couldn't. He was lost. Lost among the winds. Lost in the in-between space between Erahm and Adhiya.

Had Jahalan felt this way when he'd communed with spirits? Did Atiana feel like this while taking the dark?

Had he been more aware, he might have seen the men on the perch to his left. He might have seen them train their muskets. He might have seen the flare as the gunpowder flashed in the pan.

Searing pain sliced across his shin, just below the knee.

He cried out, buckling and falling to the stone perch.

He heard the buzzing sound of a musket shot whip past his head.

The wind died in one final gust as his men dragged him toward the ship.

The Vostroman streltsi along the quay set their muskets on the top of their berdische axes and sighted along them.

Nikandr's bond was not yet broken, however. It had been shaken, but he was able to draw upon it again, forcing it to assault the streltsi before they could fire.

Too late. The crack of four muskets rose above the howl of the wind.

One of his men cried out. Nikandr heard him fall to the deck.

"Help me," Nikandr asked Styophan. "Quickly before they can reload."

With his arm around Styophan's shoulder, he managed to stand, managed to call upon the wind to push the Yarost away from the perch. A lantern came arcing from the ship next to them. It dropped against the deck, spilling oil and lighting the deck in a wide swath.

"Douse those flames!" Styophan called.

The fire was bright enough that Nikandr could see the streltsi clearly now.

And they could see him.

They paused, all of them frozen. They had thought that Yrstanla had come. They thought themselves under attack from the West. They had not expected men of the Grand Duchy, much less a prince of the realm, to steal into the eyrie and take one of their ships.

Two of the men had finished reloading. They lined up their muskets once more, training them on Nikandr.

But their sotnik stepped in the path of their shot, waving his hands, forbidding them to fire.

Reluctantly they lowered their weapons, but the looks of shock and disgust on their faces were telling. Nikandr's abilities were not common knowledge, but they could clearly see that he was summoning the winds.

Only his hand-selected men had known before. But now…

Now the entire Grand Duchy would know.

CHAPTER SIXTY-FOUR

Atiana climbed the stairs to the top of Sariya's tower. She had expected basins with women to attend to her and Ishkyna and Ushai, but there was no one besides Sariya herself.

Sariya turned from the window she was examining. Outside, Atiana thought she saw the view of another city entirely beyond the pane of wavy glass, but when she blinked, it was gone. Sariya walked forward, her simple white robes trailing softly over the stone floor. "Lie down," she said, motioning to the center of the room where four pallets with brightly colored blankets lay.

Ishkyna, standing next to Atiana, scoffed. "We need basins."

Sariya regarded Ishkyna anew. She glanced to Atiana, perhaps weighing just how different the sisters were, but then the look was gone, and she was cold indifference once more. "The tower will see to your needs. Prepare yourselves as you have always done, and we will reach the dark together."

Ishkyna paused, looking to Atiana for her answer.

Atiana nodded to Ishkyna and moved to the furthest position, the one facing the westward window. Ishkyna approached the southern position, Ushai the eastern. Ishkyna seemed at ease, though it was easy for Atiana to tell from the stiff way in which she walked, the way her eyes took in the room, that she was nervous. Ushai was openly fearful. She swallowed constantly. Her gaze darted about the room, particularly to the windows and Sariya.

As Atiana kneeled upon the bedding, Sariya closed her hand around the empty air between the four pallets. She had grabbed at nothing—Atiana was sure of it—but a moment later something twinkled bright and blue in the palm of her hand.

It was the Atalayina. Ishkyna stared at it openly, transfixed. Ushai, however, had somehow managed to calm herself, and the longer she stared at the stone, the more composed she seemed to become. She caught Atiana watching her, and some of the nervousness returned, as if laying her eyes on Atiana had reminded her of their purpose.

Atiana widened her eyes at the Aramahn woman, asking if she was all right. Ushai nodded once, carefully.

"Lie down." As Sariya spoke these words, she spun the Atalayina in the air. It remained, spinning, twirling on some unseen axis, equidistant between the four pallets.

Sariya lay down, motioning for the others to do the same.

Atiana complied, and finally, so did Ishkyna and Ushai.

It took time—Atiana was not used to taking the dark without the help of the bitterly cold water of the drowning basins—but she found, as Sariya had said, the tower drawing her toward the aether. She had barely reached a level of calm when...

She wakes. She sees the form of the tower cast in the darkest blue. Sees herself and the other three women. Sariya has already crossed over. Her presence is strong. Her emotions ring clear. There is a certain pride in her heart that warms Atiana, though why she should care about the feelings of Sariya, she isn't sure.

Ishkyna joins them soon after. The three of them pull one another near. Like strands in a braid they strengthen their mutual bond, and when Ushai joins them, they pull her closer. Ushai had always seemed, if not strong in the ways of the dark, at least competent. She had never seemed like a foal still learning her legs, but she did now.

Control yourself, Atiana says.

Ushai tries, but this only seems to make things worse.

Leave her, Ishkyna says. *We'll be fine on our own.*

Don't be so sure, Sariya replies. *The storms over Galahesh are strong.*

We will groom the paths between the spires, Atiana says, stopping them before they quibble. *If she is still unable to come, she will remain.*

They give one another silent assent, and together, they expand their awareness. They move beyond the boundaries of the tower. They feel the city of Baressa below them, quiet for the time being. They feel the Spar, the conduit it creates between the northern and southern land masses.

They have chosen their time well. It is low tide, and the way from the spire on the northern half of Galahesh to the one on the far southern tip is easy to groom. The ley lines toward the center of the island are guided, and these in turn guide the others until the way is made stronger. It strengthens the path to the spire on Kiravashya far to the east. It is the only spire that remains on the islands of Vostroma. It holds open, barely, the path northward to Khalakovo, and southward to Nodhvyansk. Take this one spire away, though, and it would be impossible to sail windships for months, perhaps years.

They've long since lost the art of grooming the ley lines without the help of the spires. It might be done, but who knows how to do it now? Perhaps Saphia can learn—perhaps Polina Mirkotsk, but even they will be able to do little against the strength of the storms that would follow the destruction of the spire above Galostina.

Together, they reach outward, toward Kiravashya. The storms over Galahesh are manageable, but when they move over open sea it becomes infinitely worse. Here the storms rage. It draws their minds outward, forces them to take in the full extent of it, and it is humbling. Even Sariya is cowed.

They try to move on, but the further they go, the more difficult it becomes, and it's soon clear that Ushai is the cause. She's lost her nerve, and if she tries to go further, she'll drown in these waves, and she'll take the others with her.

Go, Atiana snaps. *Return to the tower and await us.*

Ushai is shamed by this, but there is relief as well. Her presence soon dwindles and is eventually lost altogether.

Without speaking, they move forward once more. They can feel Kiravashya's spire now. Like a bell in the distance, it rings, calling to them, and together they wend their way through the storms.

A presence grows in the distance. It is one of the Matri, but this woman is tired beyond any boundaries Atiana can fathom. She has been pressing to keep the connections alive between Vostroma and the distant archipelagos. Through her, Atiana can feel—barely—the touch of the other Matri. The connections are still alive then. The duchies, at least for the moment, are able to speak, to warn one another.

Mileva, Ishkyna says.

Atiana realizes that Ishkyna is right. Why didn't she recognize her? Perhaps because, even in these few weeks since they'd seen one another, Mileva has grown in strength. The Mileva she'd known before leaving Vostroma for Galahesh—how long ago that seemed—could not have done this.

Sisters, comes Mileva's weak reply. *You've come. But how?*

Mileva's confusion is palpable, but then she feels the third presence. She doesn't know who it is at first, but then it dawns on her.

How dare you bring her near!

We've come to warn you, Atiana says. *Stand down. Prepare the island, and the others as well. The spire must fall.*

She feels the shock within Mileva as she says these words, but she shares with her what she knows—her experiences, her memories, her fears and her hopes for the islands once the storm has passed. Again Mileva surprises her. She sifts through these memories quickly. She absorbs. She understands.

But she is vehement in her denial.

We cannot, Mileva says. *We* will *not.*

Through Sariya, Atiana feels—and she knows her sisters can feel as well—the dozens of ships that lie in wait far to the south of Kiravashya. They hold position near the edge of the shallows before the sea deepens and the currents of the wind and the aether become uncontrollable, unpredictable. It is a glimpse of the remaining strength of the Empire. It lies in wait for the hour when the winds have died down sufficiently for the battle to resume.

Atiana feels Mileva's shock. In that moment, Atiana can sense how truly weak the remaining forces of the Grand Duchy are. They have not a third of the ships the Empire has. And once the last of Anuskaya's ships fall, it will only be a matter of time until Galostina herself is taken.

And then the spire will fall.

Hundreds will die. Thousands. The seat of Vostroma's power will fall to enemy hands. It is a bitter leaf to chew, but they all know what will happen if Anuskaya doesn't surrender. Muqallad is coming—they know this now—and when he does, the scene upon Oshtoyets will be as child's play.

The decisions made in the aether are not made alone. One is entwined, and it is sometimes difficult to pull away, to make decisions clearly. It is why the Matri often do not make decisions when they first meet; they merely discuss. Only after they remove themselves from the others—either by leaving the aether entirely or retreating to their own corner of the world—can they think clearly. With the three of them sharing so much, it is hard for Atiana to focus her mind on notions of loyalty and patriotism for Anuskaya.

Not so for Mileva. She pulls away easily, her anger flaring.

I will not bow and offer up our spire to Yrstanla like a lamb for the slaughter.

We have no choice, Atiana says.

There is always choice, Mileva replies, her mood cold. *Yrstanla can pull their ships north of the straits, and then we can talk.*

Sariya's response is felt before she speaks. *You have few ships, and the winds are beginning to quell. In another day we will attack. This is the only chance I granted to Atiana in the interest of avoiding further bloodshed, but make no mistake. I won't hesitate to bring those ships to bear—all of them. The threat of Muqallad demands no less.*

Whether we lie upon the ground wounded or not, I will not treat with the likes of you while a sword swings above our necks.

Her words are meant for Atiana as well. Mileva's blood is up, and it seems to strengthen her will and revive her strength. She pushes the three of them away.

And strangely, it works. Atiana feels a gap form, a distancing, as if Mileva can no longer stand to be so closely tied to them. Even knowing Mileva's strength in the aether, Atiana is surprised. Sariya is Al-Aqim, Atiana's abilities still outstrip Mileva's, and though Ishkyna is the weakest of the three, together they should have been able to prevent Mileva from doing so.

This is when Atiana first senses the bitter cold through the haze of the aether. It is a draining, like a trickle of blood from a wound she didn't know she had.

The feeling grows. It saps her strength. It takes from her what little warmth there is in the aether, until all around her feels like the coldest and darkest part of winter.

Atiana knows only moments after Sariya does that it comes from the tower, and the moment that realization comes to her, she knows it happened because of Ushai.

Sariya withdraws so quickly Atiana and Ishkyna cannot follow, and soon they are left alone. And now, not only is the supporting presence of Sariya gone, but so is the Atalayina.

Ishkyna!

Atiana can feel her slipping away, blown like a feather on the wind by the forces of the aether.

Ishkyna, hear me! Follow my voice!

But she can't. She drifts further away, her mind drawing and thinning like smoke.

Atiana feels the same happening to her. She's cast adrift over the Sea of Tabriz.

How massive it is. How dark and deadly. She can feel its depths, feel the cold touch of its embrace. It pulls her downward, no matter how much she might like to reach the surface.

But there is one thing that brightens the borders of her mind. Anger... Anger over what has happened. Anger that—however improbably—Ushai *arranged* for this to happen. Her emotions were so plain when they entered the tower, and now Atiana knows why: betrayal was on her mind, not the imposing presence of Sariya nor the task that lay before them.

Only betrayal.

And it spurs Atiana to find her way back.

She detects the barest of scents—Sariya. She moves toward it, pulling herself inward slowly but surely. The sea retreats. The mass of Galahesh lies before her. And then Baressa.

And finally the tower.

When Atiana woke, she remembered everything. Never had she recalled her time in the aether so completely, so vividly.

But as sharp as her memories were, her body was dull. It did not respond to her commands. For long moments all she could do was stare at the stone ceiling of the room she lay within—she and Sariya and Ishkyna.

At last she was able to roll her head to one side, toward Sariya.

Sariya was staring at Atiana with wide blue eyes. Blood stained her dress along her chest and ribs, a puddle collecting there and slowly expanding across the stone floor toward Atiana.

Sariya coughed. Blood slipped from between her lips, slid lazily along the dark skin of her cheek. Her eyes were the eyes of a frightened child.

One of the Al-Aqim, Atiana thought, brought to this...

She had not been afraid, but she was now.

Sariya's lips moved. She was trying to speak, but Atiana could not hear her words.

Then, finally, her voice reached Atiana's ears.

"*Istizhar.*"

It was a single word, spoken not in Mahndi, but in the mothertongue, Kalhani. It meant, simply, *help*.

CHAPTER SIXTY-FIVE

Atiana watched as Ushai hunched over the Atalayina, which spun in the space between the four pallets. Ushai glanced at Atiana—nothing more than this—and then returned her attention to unraveling the spells Sariya had placed on the gem. Why she hadn't simply killed Sariya, Atiana didn't know. Perhaps she feared that the stone, as it had been in Ghayavand, would be lost in the tower. Perhaps she feared *she* would be lost as well, unable to escape unless she was able to leave before Sariya perished.

Atiana realized this was an altogether too real possibility. Worse, though, was the knowledge that she had been betrayed by a woman she had come to trust, a woman she had believed to be one of the Aramahn.

"You may not have it," Atiana said.

Ushai glanced again. "There you are wrong." With an opal glowing brightly within the circlet upon her brow, Ushai reached out and grasped the Atalayina.

The hair rose along the back of Atiana's neck and along her arms. A sizzling sound rent the air, and Ushai was thrown backward. She struck the granite floor and slid toward the far wall.

A sound came like leaded crystal tinkling against stone.

The smell of burned flesh came to Atiana as she rolled over. Her body was sluggish, and it was a mighty struggle to simply prop herself on hands and knees. She looked around, confused. Sariya was gone. She had simply vanished.

Ushai, grimacing in pain, made it to her feet. The fingers of her left hand were blackened. Blood oozed between cracked skin. It dribbled on the floor, the sound of it like the last pattering of rain after a sudden summer storm. The pain she was experiencing was plain on her face, but she seemed to think Atiana posed no threat, for she strode forward and kneeled next to her.

The Atalayina lay on the floor, not spinning, but lifeless. Inert.

Ushai had grasped the stone knowing she would trigger the spells that protected it. She had done so knowing she might be harmed, but she'd clearly thought the risk worth it.

Ushai shivered as she reached down and picked up the stone. Her lower lip quivered and her eyes watered from the pain. And then she met Atiana's eyes with a defiant gaze that reminded her of another who had done so in the same manner. Rehada... Rehada had looked at her this way on the mountain above Iramanshah, and she had done so knowing Atiana had discovered her secret.

"You are Maharraht," Atiana said, the words thick on her tongue.

Ushai blinked. Tears sped down her cheeks and fell to the floor to mingle with her blood. Atiana knew the tears came from more than her pain.

In the end, Ushai merely grit her jaw, glanced to where Ishkyna lay, and took the nearby stairs, down and out of sight.

As Atiana slid over the floor toward Ishkyna, she heard no sounds of resistance, no cries for help. But she cared nothing for this, nor did she care that Sariya had vanished; for the moment all she cared about was Ishkyna, who still breathed but would not wake when Atiana shook her.

"Ishkyna?" Atiana called, shaking her harder. "Ishkyna!"

But nothing she did mattered. She would not wake, because her mind had been taken. She was lost among the aether, and there was no telling when, or if, she would find her way home.

The following day, Atiana stood in the opulent receiving room of Kasir Yalidoz, less than a quarter-league from Sariya's tower where the horrific events with Ishkyna had occurred.

At the head of the room, seated in Bahett's throne of office, was Hakan ül Ayeşe. Beside Atiana was Vaasak Dhalingrad, the envoy father had appointed, and beside him Sihaş ül Mehmed. Both had been freed from their cells in the lower levels of the kasir.

Bahett stood to Hakan's left, watching this meeting with great interest. The rest of the expansive room was empty. No others would be allowed to witness this meeting. Were it known that Hakan was treating with the Grand Duchy after murdering the Grand Duke, there would be chaos in the courts of Yrstanla.

Atiana had just finished relating the tale of the tower. It was the third time Hakan had heard it, but the repetition was necessary. He had trouble remembering what had happened. He would ask her to repeat the simplest of things, and even when she had, she doubted he fully understood. She had little doubt now that what Sihaş had told her—that Sariya had beguiled him—was true. What was unknown was how long her spells would remain, and what he would do when finally he returned to himself.

And this was the true danger. The Kamarisi had always been bellicose; it simply hadn't, until now, been directed toward the Grand Duchy.

As Atiana's story came to a close, and she spoke of Sariya's departure, Hakan seemed to understand at last. He was handsome, and the gleam of brightness had always rested within his eyes, but now there was something more—perhaps calculation over what all this would mean for Yrstanla as he weighed the choices before him.

"What of Arvaneh?" Vaasak asked. "Has she not been found?"

"There's no need for pretense," Hakan replied. "She is Sariya of the Al-Aqim. And she has not been found."

"One might wonder, were they in my place, where that leaves us."

"In a difficult position."

Vaasak stared at Hakan, his hard eyes evaluating the man who still had the power to ruin the islands. The question wasn't whether he wanted the islands. The question was whether he would risk it.

"I don't wish to admit it," Hakan said at last, "but I was not of my own mind. Even *you* will admit that you would be hard-pressed to stand against one of the Al-Aqim."

"The Grand Duchy already has."

He was speaking of Nasim, a subject that had come up early in the conversation.

"Then you know their power," Hakan continued. "Sariya may be gone, but Muqallad is coming. As Atiana has told us, she is Maharraht, and there are certainly more about the city and the countryside." He paused, bowing his head in Atiana's direction. "Would that I had Matri of my own to look for them."

He refused to meet Vaasak's eyes as he spoke these words. He would be asking for many things over the course of this conversation, but begging the man he had effectively imprisoned—whether he had been sound of mind or not—was not something he could do.

Vaasak considered this, his head lifting, but his face clearly relieved. "If the Grand Duchy can be set aright, Kamarisi, there may be some aid that could be lent."

It was the first hint Vaasak had given that he would be willing to bargain with Hakan for the safe return of the peoples of Anuskaya.

Hakan considered this for a time, glancing not at Bahett, but *Sihaş*, for confirmation. This was a strange shift in power, indeed, but it shed some light on just how much Hakan valued each of these two men.

Sihaş bowed his head ever so slightly, at which point the Kamarisi turned his head to Vaasak and smiled.

"What ships we have will be set to scouring the land and sea around Gala-hesh for the Maharraht, but certainly a few can be spared to return you and your countrymen back to Vostroma."

"And certainly, assuming the storms have died down enough for me to speak with the Matri, the ships of Yrstanla will be granted safe passage in their return to Galahesh."

The problem standing before Hakan was a difficult one to solve. He had ships amassed that could attack Vostroma. They could defeat the remains of the staaya now housed in the eyrie of Kiravashya, but he had no way to reach them, no way to issue them orders. He had no way to order them home or to continue on to the other islands. They were, for the moment, isolated from his command, at least until such time as Sariya returned—*if* she returned. Add to this the fact that Hakan clearly didn't believe in Sariya's cause—he had, after all, been cast under her spell unwillingly—and it all added up to a powerful man who simply wished to retreat, to return to the things that had occupied him before the building of the Spar had begun.

Hakan, of course, knew this. Everyone in the room knew it. As strange as it seemed, *Vaasak* was now the one who stood in control of this conflict.

"A grant that would be most appreciated," Hakan said, not deigning to tip his head in thanks, but with a subtle expression of contrition that did much the same.

"We're missing the point," Atiana said. "We must look beyond the return of ships."

Hakan turned to her. "You speak of Muqallad, of course."

"He's here, or soon will be, and he will then have all three pieces of the Atalayina."

Hakan sniffed. "It is not clear that he will come to Galahesh."

"There can be no doubt."

"Who can know the will of Muqallad? Who can know where he will go?"

Atiana wanted to grab his silver kaftan and shake him. "I tell you, he comes *here*."

"If he does, we will find him. We will root him out, he and his Maharraht."

"As you rooted me out?"

Hakan nodded, a gesture so patronizing Atiana wanted to scream. "If you hadn't noticed, good princess, you have been in the care of the Kasir for days now."

"You are a fool if you ignore the threat Muqallad poses."

The words echoed into the far reaches of the room. Hakan's face reddened.

Atiana knew she had crossed a line when she spoke those words, but she didn't care.

Vaasak stood stiffly beside her.

Hakan's eyes narrowed as he stared intently at Atiana. Suddenly it felt like the two of them were alone to fill the immensity of this room—she representing the Grand Duchy, he the Empire.

"A shadow was laid over my mind for years—such is the power of the Al-Aqim—but the shadow lingers no longer, Atiana Radieva. *I* am the heart of Yrstanla. *I* am her thought. Her blood. And now that I can see, I tell you that Muqallad will be found."

Atiana did not speak. There was nothing to say. The Kamarisi would try to find Muqallad or he would not, but she bore no illusions that Muqallad would allow himself to be found. He was too careful, and they knew too little of his plans.

She did know one thing, however.

She couldn't leave. She couldn't return to Vostroma while this was still undecided. Vaasak would leave on the morrow, and though she wasn't sure how she would manage it, she knew, as surely as the winter winds blew cold, that she wouldn't be going with him.

CHAPTER SIXTY-SIX

While Sukharam slept, Nasim manned the sails. The coastline of Galahesh lay ahead. They had flown in toward the northern half and so Nasim could not *see* the straits, but he could feel it. In fact, he'd been able to feel it for days, but it had since grown tenfold, starting as a tickle in his chest and growing to a constant burning feeling. He could feel the closeness of Adhiya as well, and further inland, where he supposed the massive bridge stood, there was a yawning hole that felt large enough to swallow the island whole.

These things were similar to what he'd felt on Ghayavand, which was surprising. The island was still protected by the wards, and Galahesh was not so protected, which made Nasim wonder just how close to the edge this place was. How little might Muqallad have to do to open the rifts once and for all? Then again, Nasim knew that Muqallad considered it insufficient to simply call down destruction upon the world. He wished to bring about indaraqiram. Whether or not he could do this wasn't the point. Muqallad believed it was possible, so he would try to bring Erahm and Adhiya together. He would try to merge them. Anything else would be abject failure. And so he would be careful. He would ensure that conditions were perfect. This, more than anything, convinced Nasim that there was still time to thwart his plans, even though he now had one of the secrets he'd been searching for ever since Khamal had died at the top of Sariya's tower.

Drawing upon Sukharam's abilities, Nasim raised the skiff. He could see over the top of wooded land the southern cliffs. He wondered if Kaleh was there with Muqallad. She had betrayed him, and yet she felt more like a sister to him than anyone ever had. He hoped, though he knew it was foolish, that if he could talk to her, he might be able to lead her from the path Muqallad had set her on.

Nasim shifted the ropes tied to the lowest corners of the billowing, triangular sail. He called upon the winds to shift and the skiff began to turn as it headed for land.

When he did, Sukharam woke and pulled himself up and sat on a nearby thwart. He crossed his arms over his stomach and leaned over his knees.

"Should I stop?" Nasim asked.

Sukharam shook his head. "I can feel him," he said after a time, his voice scratchy.

"Muqallad?" Nasim asked.

Sukharam nodded, pointing toward the straits. "He's there… Somewhere."

"And the Atalayina?"

His brow creased in thought. "Of the stones I feel nothing."

"They may no longer be separate. By now Muqallad might have recovered the third piece and fused it to the other two."

Sukharam shook his head. "We would have felt it."

"Perhaps, and perhaps not. The Atalayina has always been difficult to sense, even for those who know how."

"Have you considered—" Sukharam coughed and shifted to ease his discomfort. "Have you considered whether you'd like it to be or not?"

Nasim stared westward. They were close enough now that the gulls were visible as they flew near the mouth of the straits. They'd discussed the Atalayina for days now, and what it might mean if it were whole. If they were able to retrieve it—and there was no guarantee they could—they might be able to use it to free Nasim. And then, if the fates were kind, they might be able to stop Muqallad once and for all.

As tempting as the thought was, he also knew the Atalayina was the key to Muqallad's plans. So what would he wish? That the Atalayina was whole so that he might be able to ensure *his own* victory, or that it remained broken in the hopes that it was the only way in which Muqallad might achieve *his*?

"I think," Nasim said at last, "it is a decision I will leave to the fates."

The winds blew more fiercely for a moment, drawing Sukharam's brown hair across his face. He stared intently to the forest far north of the straits.

Nasim felt it as well, a presence, though he couldn't define it any better than that. It was already fading, however, and soon it was little more than a scent upon the wind. It faded so completely that Nasim wasn't sure whether it had been real or not.

"What was it?" Sukharam asked.

"It's strange," Nasim said, more to himself than Sukharam. "It felt like Khamal did upon the shore, just before he drove the knife into Alif's chest." Nasim was so taken by the memory of Alif's cries that he had to shake his head to clear them. "It feels as Khamal did, when he had one foot in Adhiya and one in Erahm."

"Is it not what you felt when you were young?" Sukharam asked.

"*Neh*. The world was new to me yet. On the beach, it felt…" Nasim stopped and started over. "*Khamal* felt as though he had lived all the years of the world. It felt as though he would live to see the end. It was timeless and ancient. Nothing about it was new."

"What, then, could it mean?" Sukharam asked as he stood and took the sail from Nasim. Nasim released the havahezhan and Sukharam bonded with another. He called upon the winds to halt their progress, the skiff floating in place as he waited for Nasim's answer.

"I don't know, but we shall go there."

"We should find the Atalayina," Sukharam said.

"The path to the Atalayina may very well lie through those woods."

Sukharam studied the gap of the straits, then the woods. He seemed unconvinced, but in the end he nodded and called upon the winds to blow them northward.

They landed in the forest an hour later. The sun was a bright brass coin behind a cheerless layer of clouds. They left the skiff and set a path through the woods toward the feeling that Nasim could once again feel in his gut. It grew worse the further they went, until Nasim was dizzy from it.

The tall spruce trees gave way to a downward slope of larch and alder. A stream could be heard running to their right, hidden behind the tall grasses and cattails that hugged the streambed.

"I don't feel right about this," Sukharam said.

Nasim looked over and realized he was holding his stomach. His face was white, his eyes wary of the way ahead.

He cannot come.

Nasim started. He looked around the forest, wondering where this voice had come from, but then he realized that it had been called from within him. What chilled him to the bone was the knowledge that he'd heard this voice before. Many times. He'd heard it in his dreams.

"Remain here," Nasim said.

"*Neh!*" Sukharam said. "I won't be left behind again."

He cannot come.

The voice was insistent, desperate.

He felt upon him the same feelings that he'd had in the ballast tower of Mirashadal. He felt as though he could slow the world, to deal with it as he would. He could leave Sukharam behind, and so keep him safe. But as he looked at his friend, this youth he'd plucked from his previous course in life, he knew he couldn't abandon him again. Rabiah had died, and he would give anything to have her back, but he couldn't leave Sukharam behind. He would give Sukharam to the fates.

"Come," he said. "She's not far."

If he wondered who Nasim meant, he didn't ask. Perhaps he already knew. He was bright, after all, brighter than Nasim gave him credit for.

Near the bottom of the slope, the trees fell away, leading to a tall black spire. It was not so high as the ones on the islands, probably so that it could remain hidden—insomuch as a tower like this could *be* hidden.

"What's this?" Sukharam asked.

Nearby, tracing a trail along the dark gray stones, were drops of blood, long since dried. They were little more than black stains now that led to the entrance to the spire.

Nasim couldn't recall an *entrance* to the spires of the Grand Duchy, but his mind was so muddied then he couldn't be sure if there were any or not. Still, he thought not, and he wondered why this one would have been built with one.

He may not enter!

"He will," Nasim spoke aloud.

Sukharam looked worried and confused, but he remained silent.

Nasim walked up to the short corridor leading into the stone. He could feel wards against them, but Sukharam raised his hand and spelled them away.

Sariya was weak, Nasim realized. Much weaker than he ever would have guessed.

They came to a set of winding stairs, and they climbed, up and up, much further, it seemed, than the tower was tall. All was darkness for a long time, but at last they saw a golden light coming from above. The stone here was not dark gray and opaque as it had been outside. It was like blackened crystal, or burnt honey, and the edges were as sharp as knives.

At a landing, they halted. A room lay ahead. From it came the source of the light, a beautiful golden siraj that spun at the center of the room.

Nasim stepped inside, not slowly as he might have in years past, but confidently. He knew who he was, and it gave him a strength of purpose he'd never had before. Sukharam followed closely. He seemed to take heart in Nasim's stature, for he stood taller, and strode with confidence.

In the corner they found a layer of black and gray animal hides—wolves, Nasim thought—with a woman lying upon them.

"Sariya," Nasim said.

It seemed to take a supreme effort for her to turn her head and gaze upon him with her bright blue eyes. She was covered by a wolf pelt, and there was a dark stain at the center of it. By the fates, she'd bled so much it had leaked through the hide.

She didn't speak. Nasim wondered if she *could*. Her eyes considered Sukharam. She seemed to weigh him, seemed to weigh Nasim's decision to bring him, and then she came to peace with it, for she looked upon Nasim once more and smiled. It was a smile filled with pain. It was a smile that said she knew what lay in store for her. It was a smile that said she would take what might be offered to her, but also that she would do what she could before she passed beyond these shores.

"How?" Nasim asked as he kneeled by her side.

"I was betrayed," she said.

Nasim pulled away the pelt.

She was naked beneath. Her chest and stomach were smeared with blood, and there, between her breasts, was a wound shaped like a mouth, parted like lips in the release of a gentle sigh. And the flesh inside… Nasim had difficulty looking at it, for it was a deep, deep red. And it was bottomless.

CHAPTER SIXTY-SEVEN

Nasim, holding the wolf pelt, reeled from the sight of the wound, from the pain Sariya must have been experiencing.

He wanted to drop the pelt and leave her here—he wanted to leave this place and find Muqallad and the Atalayina and finish what he'd come to do—but there was an undeniable feeling of kinship with this woman, a woman he'd never truly met in this life—only in his last. But do not these things last? Do we not take what's been given from our former lives? Do we not give what we can to the next? He couldn't turn away from her—no matter that she had tried to deny him on Ghayavand, no matter that she had tried to take his life. They were alike in too many ways, and if she would help him before she passed, he would accept it.

As he stared at the wound, he wondered how she could have lived so long, but then he felt her connection to the world beyond. It was subtle, and it was foreign to all he had learned about such things. He didn't know if the spire afforded her a way to do this, but it was clear she was bonded to an elder spirit, but instead of the dhoshahezhan feeding upon her, *she* was feeding upon *it*. It was not so different from what the hezhan did with qiram or those afflicted with the wasting, but Sariya had somehow twisted the relationship around.

If she continued in this way, she would feed upon the hezhan to the point that—just as those struck by the wasting would eventually die—it would be lost forever. Just as Nasim would one day be lost.

"You cannot take the hezhan," Nasim said. "I won't allow it."

Sariya smiled, though it was a tremulous thing, and her eyes brimmed with tears and misery. "I will release it before the time comes."

"Sukharam is gifted—"

She was already shaking her head. "It cannot be healed. The blade Ushai used was tainted."

"Ushai?" Nasim remembered her, remembered her attempts to join him as he flew toward Ghayavand.

"She is Maharraht. She found her way to Atiana Vostroma, and from her to me." Sariya's smile deepened, though this simple act cost her. "I should have known."

"It's difficult to guess the heart of another."

She seemed to consider these words as she pulled the pelt back into place. "Muqallad has arrived on Galahesh. He has the third piece of the Atalayina. And soon he will make them one. And then, Nasim an Khamal, he will have it done."

He ignored the use of Khamal's name in the place of his father. "There is time yet."

"There is." She coughed, a wet and sickening thing. "You must find him—this much is clear—but you will not go alone."

Nasim glanced down at the bloody pelt. "Stop. You're too weak."

"I will join you."

"You can't even stand."

She glanced above her, indicating the spire itself. "The tide has finally started to turn. I am gaining strength. I will be able to join you when the time is right."

"And when will that be?"

"It will begin on tomorrow's eve."

Tomorrow was *Abistan*, the day Iteh had been given his harp by the fates. Given that Muqallad had performed his last ritual on the autumnal equinox, it made sense that he would choose another important day to make the Atalayina whole.

"You know where he is?"

"*Neh*," Sariya said.

"Then how are we to stop him?"

"Because I know where he *will* be."

Hours later, Nasim pulled on the oars of the boat. The freezing water sprayed against him as the boat rocked up and down, plowing through the waves. On either side of the boat, the walls of two massive white cliffs rose. They were strong and imposing, but there was a note of fragility, as if a part of them might shear off at any moment and come crashing down on top of them.

Sukharam sat at the rear of the craft. His arms were wide and his eyes were closed. He was open to the churning waves funneling through straits. He was bonded with a jalaqiram, which he used to quell the waves, but not to any great degree; they could not afford to be capsized, but neither could they afford to be seen or sensed.

Sariya lay wrapped in blankets at the bottom of the boat. She looked weak, and white, but she insisted that she be allowed to remain where she was. "Concentrate on the waves," she'd said as they started. "Concentrate on the tide."

If all went well, they would be able to study the Spar for any signs of Muqallad or the Maharraht, for this was the place, Sariya was sure, that they would come. To the Spar. No other place afforded such a confluence of the aether. No other place was such a wellspring of power save Ghayavand, but there the spells that still stood would prevent the Atalayina from doing as Muqallad wished.

It would be here, but Muqallad would have prepared for them. They had to be careful.

They made slow progress, Nasim pulling at the oars, Sukharam quelling the waves, and Sariya using her bonded elder to cover their approach. There were no boats in the straits this day. The conflict was still too tense for trade to flow, and what there was would be moved along the Spar, not shuttled down to the water by the mule-driven lifts.

Nasim had seen the Spar once, years ago, when the building of it had just begun. He remembered thinking how foolish it seemed to attempt such a thing, that the Kamarisi would most likely abandon the plan once he realized how much it would sap the Empire. Now he knew that the Kamarisi had been in thrall to Sariya, and the completion of the bridge had never been in doubt.

It was more grand than Nasim could ever have imagined: as tall as the broad white cliffs of the straits, arch after magnificent arch towering up from the waves and holding the bridge as straight as the flight of a kingfisher.

"It is there," Sariya said, looking up toward the center of the Spar. "When the sun goes down, he will come."

"Why not simply alert the Kamarisi?"

"Because the Kamarisi cannot help. Muqallad has had spies in Baressa for years, many I have yet to root out. If there is any chance Muqallad will have warning of our approach, it is a chance we cannot take."

They continued on in tense silence and after a long stretch of rowing came to a shallow inlet. At the end of it was a rocky beach.

"There," Sariya said, pointing toward a large set of boulders, most of them caked in ice from the spray of the waves.

They landed the boat and approached the boulders, beyond which, Sariya said, lay the entrance to the tunnels that ran through the cliffs. The boulders were large, and their faces tricky to climb with the ice, forcing them to go slowly. Sariya grimaced as she climbed, even with their help.

But at last they reached the top and found an easy climb down to the tunnel. It was dark and cold, but they carried small siraj stones to light their way. They walked for what felt like hours, though Nasim was sure it was little more than one. Somehow the closeness of the walls and the uncertainty about what lay ahead made time seem to slow.

As they continued upward, Nasim sensed a faint presence. It took him a while to place it, but eventually he knew that the akhoz were here—somewhere far above him, and ahead.

He was reminded of the tunnels in Shirvozeh, the village near Alayazhar. He felt as if he'd once again entered Muqallad's demesne, as if he was granting him the upper hand before they'd even met on this island so far away from that other place.

Nasim felt dizzy. He became aware of Sariya's breathing, of Sukharam's trek up the slick stone. He became aware of the earth and stone surrounding them. It felt oppressive as it never had before. He wondered what would happen to it if Muqallad had his way. Would Erahm itself be gone? Or would it simply be wiped clean of the souls that inhabited it? And what of Adhiya? When the aether was lost, would the two worlds become one? Or would they be permanently divided from one another like ships lost in the wind?

He had often wondered what it would be like to bring about an age of enlightenment. Khamal had tried with Muqallad and Sariya. They had failed, but might they not have learned from this? Might they not still succeed?

It was a noble goal, Nasim thought. A noble goal, indeed.

When they came to a large cavern, Nasim recognized the constellation that had been worked into the stone of the floor—Almadn, her amphora cradled as she dipped it into the spring of life. It was lit by a bright shaft of light that came down through an opening somewhere along the cliffs.

Nasim reached the center of the room. He stood upon the constellation and looked up, blinking, his thoughts suddenly confused and wild and directionless.

He turned and looked to Sariya, who favored her left side but otherwise seemed unaffected by her wound. He looked to Sukharam, who was staring at him with a look of confusion, as if he too were questioning those things he had been certain of only moments ago.

Nasim thought back quickly, wondering how Sariya could have done this. He realized in a moment what he should have known immediately. The spire in the forest vale. The interior was hollow. The entire structure was a tower—another manifestation of her tower in Alayazhar. It was Sariya's haven, her source of power and strength.

Sariya met his eye. She still had a look of pain—the wound, at least, had been real—but there was a look of triumph as well, and a clear note of sadness, as if she'd hoped things wouldn't have come this far, or that she and Muqallad might have found another way.

Neh, Nasim said to himself. She wasn't sad over what had come before, but that which had yet to come.

Nasim heard footsteps approaching from one of the other tunnels. He turned and saw the shapes of forms in the darkness. As their images brightened from the shaft of light, Nasim's breath caught in his throat. The sound was sharp, guttural, and it echoed about the cavern like the sound of chittering laughter.

Muqallad strode forward and into the wide space. Near his side, only a step behind, was Kaleh, and behind her were the akhoz, three or four or more— Nasim couldn't tell; his eyes were drawn to Muqallad's, and the two of them stared at one another for a good long while. Nasim remembered staring into those eyes many times before. These were Khamal's memories, but at that moment they felt so much like his that he started to wonder *who* he was, and *where*. This place might be on Ghayavand. It might be on Galahesh. It might be in the desert wastes of the Gaji, where he and Sariya and Muqallad had traveled together to first find the Atalayina and then unlock its secrets.

He didn't know who he was anymore, nor when he'd come to this place or why.

"Have you found the final piece?" Sariya asked.

He knew this was the third piece of the Atalayina, but he couldn't remember when it had been lost, or who had taken it.

"We will have it soon." As Muqallad spoke these words, he held his hand out and looked to Nasim.

It was a beckon, a summons, and Nasim knew that if he stepped forward and accepted his hand, he will have given up all he had striven for, all he had fought for since regaining himself in the keep of Oshtoyets.

"Nasim, stop!" This came from Sukharam, a boy he hardly knew.

He paused, his breath coming rapidly, his pulse beating heavily along his neck. He swallowed once. Twice.

"Nasim!" Sukharam called again. "Listen to me! You cannot do this!"

And then he stepped forward.

And took Muqallad's hand.

CHAPTER SIXTY-EIGHT

Nikandr woke as a hand shook his shoulder.

He blinked as the sounds of the wind and the feel of his weight upon the deck returned to him.

He stood before the *Yarost's* starward mainmast, his arms hanging at his sides. Every part of him felt as if it were weighted with lead.

Anahid stood beside him, and after long moments he realized she had been the one who had touched his shoulder.

"Where are we?" he asked.

"Off course," she replied. Her face was dour, as if he had disappointed her in some way, perhaps because he was not Jahalan. "If you can find the strength, another day will see us to land, and then we can begin skirting it eastward."

"I don't know if I can stand another day."

"You will, son of Iaros, or we'll never reach Yrstanla."

Nikandr took a deep breath. He stretched his jaw. He shook his head until his neck hurt. But none of it managed to drive away the sleep.

Anahid evaluated him with a long, searching look.

"I'll make it."

She looked doubtful. She appeared tired as well, exhausted even, but there was grim determination in her eyes. How the Aramahn managed to stay awake for such long periods, he would never know. "The winds will be stronger today as we reach the edge of the storms."

"How do you know?"

"The tightness in my chest is finally leaving. I first felt it on our way across the neck, and it has been with me ever since."

"I'll be ready," Nikandr replied.

"See that you are," she said, nodding over his shoulder.

He turned sluggishly and found Styophan approaching with a steaming mug in his hand. Nikandr accepted it gratefully. It was filled with *pyen*, a tea that contained the fermented bark of a tree that grew in the lowland swamps of many of the Grand Duchy's islands. They'd found it in the physic's chest in the galley.

He took one large swallow. The scalding liquid burned its way down his throat, but he didn't care. The pain served to wake him up, and the sooner he got the liquid into his gut, the better.

He was nearly ready to begin calling on his havahezhan when something caught his eye far out to sea. He moved to the windward gunwales and steadied himself while drinking his *pyen*. His eyes refused to remain steady, however, and no matter how forcefully he tried to remain awake, his eyes began to close.

And then it came again.

"Do you see it?" he asked Styophan when he stepped up to the gunwales at his side.

"What?"

"The darkness against the sea. Three leagues out"—he held his arm straight out—"there."

Styophan stared. "*Nyet.*"

After downing the last of his drink, Nikandr used his spyglass to watch for minutes more, but it never recurred. He didn't like it, though. It was dangerous to fly so close to the sea. Any loss in lift or an unforeseen gust might drive you down on top of the waves, so Landed windships rarely did so, but the Maharraht would often fly this way because it made them more difficult to spot against the dark sea. Many of their ships' sails were dyed gray to add to the effect.

In the end, there was nothing he could do about it. Even if he'd wanted to, there was no way he'd be able to catch up to the ship. He'd be lucky to bring them safely to the shores of Yrstanla.

"Son of Iaros?"

"Coming, Anahid."

He returned to the mainmast and drew once more upon the wind, using it to guide the ship and her sails. As he had for the past seven days, he drove them onward, fighting the prevailing winds. Their only saving grace was that though the winds were normally unpredictable over the Sea of Khurkhan, they were generally heading northwest—an oddity he could only assume was due to the storms centered on the Vostroman archipelago—so all he need do was correct so that they were headed due north.

Were Jahalan with them, the two of them could have traded time at the mainmast.

But Jahalan wasn't...

The image of his old friend often played through his mind when he was at his weakest. It did so now, haunting him as he fought to keep the ship headed in the right direction. Tears welled up in his eyes as snow began to fall, but he blinked them away and bent his will to the task ahead.

At least, he thought grimly, the memories of Jahalan were keeping him awake.

Past midday a fog rolled across the sea, dropping visibility to little more than an eighth-league.

"Keep close watch," Nikandr ordered Jonis, a sharp young officer who'd proven to have excellent eyes.

They moved slower, partially because of the fog but also because Nikandr was nearing exhaustion. He found it progressively more difficult to commune with his spirit. It was not only growing tired, its demands upon him were also growing. Nikandr could feel his heart beat heavily, could feel it skip and his breath grow short if he drew upon the winds too fiercely. And the winds were starting to shift against them. They eddied for several hours past midday and then began to push against the ship head-on, stunting their progress. The best Nikandr could do was to slip northwestward as the wind tried to push them east. If the winds picked up any further, they would be lost, and the ship would be pulled back over the heart of the sea, and if that happened, there would be no returning.

Nikandr drank more *pyen*, but it was having so little effect that he asked Styophan to bring him the last of it. He took the final pinch and packed it between his cheek and gums.

He began to shake after this, and yet he felt no less tired. Then again, maybe he would have simply collapsed if he hadn't taken it.

An hour later, he leaned his head against the mainmast, his eyes closing of their own accord.

He woke, only vaguely realizing that Styophan was holding him up.

"Not yet," Styophan said, rolling Nikandr's shoulders to try to get his blood moving again. "We're nearly there."

"I can't," he said, but the words were so soft he barely heard them. "I can't."

"You can, My Lord."

When Nikandr didn't respond, Styophan pressed him up against the mainmast and struck him across the cheek. Nikandr barely felt it.

Styophan struck him again. "We are not yet done, My Prince!"

A third time he struck, and Nikandr vaguely tasted something warm and slick in his mouth.

Blood, he realized.

He shook his head, which did nothing, and fell to his knees.

But then he heard something else. Something new.

The sound of cannon fire coming off the windward bow.

He dragged himself to his feet and looked, able to stave off some small amount of the clutching weariness. The way ahead was still cloaked in fog, but it seemed not so thick as it once was. The sound of a cannon came again, accompanied by a brief flash.

"Ready cannons, men," Nikandr called as he resumed his position at the mainmast. "And prepare the muskets."

"The coast is near," Anahid said. "I can feel it."

Nikandr could as well, but not in the same way. The air smelled different. It smelled of earth, of the cold loamy scent of a forest in winter. And now that he put his mind to it he could hear gulls far below, off the landward side of the ship.

As they approached, the cannon fire intensified. And then it was mixed with musket fire.

"Follow the cliff line," Nikandr ordered, speaking only loud enough for the master to hear, "but stay above land."

Orders were passed about the ship. The keels were reengaged by the pilot. The land mass would provide them ley lines to work against once more. They would not be as strong as those that ran among the islands, but they would be strong enough in this meager wind.

As Anahid lowered the ship, the pilot brought them in line with the cliff so that it was only a few hundred yards off their landward side. The fighting intensified, men shouting orders or crying out in pain.

And then they saw it. A dozen ships, all of them moored to the cliff. Their landward masts had been disengaged, and spread apart until they were positioned like three-legged stools against the cliff face. It was not ideal, but all ships made for fighting were constructed so in case the ship couldn't reach the safety of an eyrie.

Nikandr could already tell that they were the ships Konstantin had sent. He didn't at first understand why they would be moored, but the reason came clear when he noticed that the nearest three ships had been gutted. They'd stopped here for repairs, perhaps after a battle with Yrstanlan ships that had been sent to intercept them, or even because of damage sustained during the crossing of the Sea of Khurkhan.

Further west, stationed at a gentle curve of the snow-covered cliff, were a dozen janissaries wearing white uniforms and rounded turbans with tall, colorful plumes, but there were also several dozen ghazi with them, the militia of the Empire's outlands that heeded the call of the Kamarisi when it came. While the ghazi fired muskets, the janissaries manned three cannons, which had been maneuvered behind a low rock formation that provided them protection against return fire from the Grand Duchy's ships. But they were completely open to attack from the rear, and so far, thank the ancients, they hadn't spotted the *Yarost* approaching through the fog.

"Lower the ship even more," Nikandr ordered Styophan. "Reload the cannons with grape, and have no one fire until I do."

Styophan went quickly about the ship, passing orders, while Anahid used her bonded dhoshahezhan to gradually increase the heft of the ship and bring them closer to the level of the cliff ahead.

As the musket fire continued and the three Yrstanlan cannons belched black smoke one more time, Nikandr moved to the bow and took a musket from the ship's master, Vlanek. Eight others stationed themselves along the landward gunwales, each man loading his weapon smartly.

Nikandr's exhaustion began to lift as he loaded his musket. No sooner had he finished and laid the musket against the gunwale when one of the janissaries turned and began shouting to his men. Nikandr waited for one of the men to pick up on the danger and to begin issuing orders.

It came a moment later. A tall janissary wearing a large red turban. They were close enough that Nikandr could see the black, iridescent feathers pinned to the front of the officer's turban with a large jeweled medallion.

He aimed his musket for this man as the first scattered fire came in from the rag-tag ghazi. Several shots bit into the hull. Others flew high, punching through canvas.

Nikandr released his breath and pulled the trigger.

The musket kicked.

Through the puff of smoke he saw a spot of blood appear on the chest of the man with the feathered turban, just above his heart. The tall man tipped backward, eyes wide, trying to catch himself with flailing arms, and then he was lost among his men and the rocks and snow at their feet.

The rest of Nikandr's men fired in tight sequence, followed by the forward cannon.

At the cliff, all six men stationed at the two nearest cannons were thrown to the ground in a mass of red. More fire came in from Grigory's ships, dropping some that had risen to face the threat bearing down from their rear.

The ghazi were not well organized, but they did manage to maneuver themselves to have decent cover against both the *Yarost* and the ships lashed to the cliff. Nikandr and the others reloaded quickly, firing upon any that took to the cannons, but then the *Yarost* flew past, and the ghazi were able to hide behind their rocks once more.

"Take her up," Nikandr called, "and circle back."

The fighting continued as the *Yarost* swung out to sea and arced westward, but by now two of Grigory's ships had freed themselves from the cliff. They were heading up, and it was clear to everyone that the men of Yrstanla had long lost their advantage. They began to retreat, taking ponies that were tied a few dozen yards from the cliff.

Still, the *Yarost* and the other two ships harried them until the two dozen that remained had ridden northward into the fog.

Nikandr stepped off the skiff and onto the deck of the *Drakha*. Grigory stood on deck, flanked by three of his kapitans. By now Grigory could no longer be surprised that Nikandr had found his way here on the shores of Yrstanla, and yet as he studied Nikandr—glancing occasionally up to the *Yarost*, which was now lashed to the cliff above them—he looked more surprised than if Nikandr had stepped onto deck wearing the Grand Duke's mantle.

Breaking from custom, Grigory did not welcome Nikandr onto his ship. He merely stared, waiting for Nikandr to state his business.

For Nikandr's part, he was surprised at how quickly and vividly the memory of Grigory firing a shot into the chest of his man, Ervan, came to him, and more than this, his actions on the shores of Duzol... He'd left Atiana for dead after she'd caught a stray bullet in the struggles on Uyadensk.

He had tried to prepare himself for standing face-to-face with Grigory—he'd been imagining the scene ever since learning of Konstantin's wish for Nikandr to find him—but now that he was here he found it difficult not to reach for the pistol hanging from his belt.

"Your brother has sent me," Nikandr said at last.

"Has he now..." Grigory looked doubtful, as if he was sure, even before Nikandr presented evidence, that this was all some lie on Nikandr's part to deceive him.

From the inside of his cherkesska, Nikandr pulled out the folded paper that had been waiting for him in the kapitan's desk. It had Grigory's name written upon it in Konstantin's hand, and it had a red wax seal of Bolgravya holding it closed. After taking one deliberate step forward, he held it out for Grigory.

Grigory was too far away to accept it, and there was a clear note of reluctance on his face to meet Nikandr halfway, but his curiosity seemed to overcome any revulsion he still harbored for Nikandr, and he stepped forward and took it. He examined the seal carefully—more than was needed—and then cracked it open. He unfolded the note and read it twice before raising his gaze and staring at Nikandr. His face had already flushed, but now it was positively red.

He remained this way, his eyes boring into Nikandr, and then he turned his head and stared up at the cliff and the ships that were lashed to it.

When he turned back to Nikandr, something cold and hard had settled within him. Gone was the emotion. Gone was the redness of his skin. They had been replaced with a cold calculation that made Nikandr nervous.

"Take him and the others belowdecks," Grigory said as he tucked the letter into his long black cherkesska and began walking toward the stern of the ship, "and place them in chains."

CHAPTER SIXTY-NINE

When Nikandr woke in the hold of the *Drakha*, he had no idea how much time had passed. It had been near sunset when he'd been taken down and—as Grigory had ordered—placed in chains in the holding cell. He could see little outside the barred window set into the door, but he could see some light.

He vaguely recalled his own order to Styophan that he and the rest of his men comply with Grigory's demands—there was no need for the duchies to be warring, not when they needed one another so desperately—but it all seemed so distant, so dreamlike, that he wondered if it had happened at all. Yet here he was in a cell, his legs manacled, the chain between them running through a stout ring set into the angled hull that acted as one of the cell's four walls.

Despite the chains, despite lying on the floor, he'd fallen asleep nearly instantly once the streltsi had left him alone. He was still drowsy now, even though he was sure that he'd been asleep for over a day.

It was clear that they weren't flying. The ship was too stable for that, though there was a creaking as the wind rocked the ship against the three landward masts. They couldn't remain long, however. The janissaries would return. Had they been near a city of any size, they already would have, but they were at the eastern edges of the Empire, a region that hadn't seen real war since the War of Seven Seas. It was a place that would have been drained of its fighting men long ago, leaving only the untrained and undisciplined ghazi in place with a handful of janissaries to command them when the need arose.

Much to the Grand Duchy's advantage, as it turned out.

Nikandr wondered where his men were. Most likely they'd been spread among the rest of Grigory's ships so that no resistance could be formed.

Nikandr took his soulstone in his hand and gripped it. He could not sense his havahezhan, but as tired as he was, as far as he had pushed it, he refused to do more than simply search for it. Surely if Grigory had known of his abilities he would have taken the stone from him. Even without this, he was surprised Grigory hadn't taken it as he had years ago. Perhaps after doing so he had thought better of it. Or perhaps he didn't care. They both knew they were far from the reach of the Matri.

In a few hours, the sun went down, and darkness reigned. He heard men coming and going, working on the ship in preparation of launching, most likely in the morning. Nikandr wondered when Grigory would come to see him, but then he thought that perhaps Grigory had decided not to. He had already ignored his brother Konstantin's orders, and though he hadn't apparently been able to bring himself to kill Nikandr outright, he'd decided to leave him where he would raise the fewest number of questions.

With that realization, and his continued feelings of exhaustion, Nikandr laid back on the floor and fell asleep.

When he woke again, he was not alone.

Grigory sat on a stool near the door. Light was coming in through the window. By the ancients, he'd slept through the entire night.

In his lap Grigory held a clay mug. When Nikandr had pulled himself up and propped himself against the hull, he leaned forward and set the mug near Nikandr's feet. Nikandr could smell Grigory's unwashed scent, even from this distance. It was the smell of a man who refused even so much as washing himself down with a wet rag as a proper windsman should.

As Grigory returned unsteadily to his stool, Nikandr noticed the pistol at his belt. His first thought was that it was only for show, that it was unloaded, but the more he thought about it, the more he doubted this. A sober Grigory might come with an empty pistol in an attempt to cow Nikandr. A drunk Grigory would bring a loaded one.

When Grigory fell onto the stool, Nikandr took the mug and drank the water within it quickly. After he'd set it down with a heavy thud against the deck, he met Grigory's haunted eyes.

"How long have you been here?" Nikandr asked.

Grigory didn't answer. He merely stared into Nikandr's eyes as if trying to find the answers to the questions he dearly *wished* to ask but couldn't ask of *Nikandr*.

"If you don't wish to speak, leave. I can't suffer to be in the room with a traitor to his own brother."

"Why would he send *you*?" Grigory asked. His words were not slurred, but they were slow in coming.

"Did the letter not say?"

"Would I be asking if it did?"

"He sent me because no one else would come."

"Because they didn't believe you."

Nikandr pulled himself higher. "Would *you* have?"

Grigory paused, his hand moving momentarily to the handle of the pistol before returning to rest on his thigh. The gesture was so casual Nikandr wasn't even sure Grigory knew he'd done it. "The kapitan you found on Elykstava... Was he telling the truth?"

Nikandr nearly sighed, but he had to tread carefully with Grigory. He could not act dismissive or brash, but neither could he allow Grigory to bully him. "I pushed him hard, Grigory. If he were lying, I would have known."

"But the Spar," Grigory said. "If it were destroyed, would it... Do you think it would make a difference in the war?"

"*Da*," Nikandr said. "I think it would."

Grigory's eyes closed, and for long moments Nikandr thought he was falling asleep, but then they snapped open and focused on Nikandr once more. "Are you so great a kapitan that you could lead us there? Are you so great that you could destroy it with only a handful of ships?"

"I only know I must try."

"Ah. Nikandr Iaroslov... Ever the comrade."

"Grigory, you're drunk."

Grigory stared down at Nikandr, his face suddenly angry. He stood, his hand moving to the butt of his pistol. "Do you think I cannot do the same?" And then he drew it, pointing the barrel at Nikandr's chest. "Do you think you're the only one who can command a ship?"

"Of course not. Grigory, put the pistol away."

He pulled the hammer back to full cock. "You can't even keep your bride."

"That was five years ago."

"It was yesterday! I remember it! Zhabyn Vostroma remembers it!" He pointed eastward with the pistol. "My brother, the *good Duke*, certainly remembers it!"

Nikandr didn't dare open his mouth. Grigory's face was red. Spittle flew from his mouth as he spoke. One wrong move and Grigory would pull the trigger and be done with it, the son of a duke or not.

"Where did the kapitan say to attack the Spar?"

"What?"

Grigory shook the pistol inches from Nikandr's face. Despite himself, Nikandr cringed and turned his head away from the gaping maw of the pistol.

Grigory shouted, "*Where* did he say it would be *weakest*?"

"In the center, where the keystones have only just been laid into place."

Grigory stood there, half crouched over Nikandr, the pistol unwavering, and then he brought himself to a stand. He did not adjust the pistol's aim, however, and a smile came over him. "I'll take these ships, Khalakovo. I'll take the *Yarost* as well. It's Bolgravyan, after all. You and your men, however, will remain here. You will guard the remainders of the ships."

"Those husks? They're useless, Grigory."

"They are ships of the Grand Duchy, and you will guard them with your life."

"The janissaries will return."

Grigory turned to the door and turned the handle. "Then best you get to your preparations."

"You're a coward."

Grigory turned and aimed. Pulled the trigger.

The pistol roared in the small space. Wood bit deeply into Nikandr's cheek. The shot had gone wide, just next to Nikandr's head and into the hull.

Grigory stared at Nikandr, then the hole where the musket ball had struck, and Nikandr was not at all sure he'd meant to miss. He appeared unsure of himself, perhaps sensing through the haze of liquor that he'd gone too far, but then it was gone, and he stormed out of the room.

Shortly after, Nikandr was taken by the Bolgravyan streltsi to the worst of the ships. Styophan and Vlanek and Jonis were all there. Everyone but Anahid.

The nine windworthy ships, plus the *Yarost*, departed soon after, leaving Nikandr and his men standing on the deck of a ship that had been stripped of everything valuable. Grigory had given them each a musket, and granted them twenty rounds of ammunition apiece. The rest they had taken.

As the ships flew off into the morning air, Nikandr stared up the cliff, wondering when the men of Yrstanla would return.

Nikandr glanced at Styophan, then to the men beyond him. Nikandr was glad that Grigory hadn't in his rage decided to have any of them killed—or worse, killed them himself—but he'd left Nikandr alone on the shores of Yrstanla with no real hope of returning to Galahesh or Anuskaya.

"Take stock," Nikandr said. "Search the ships and find if there's any way we can make them windworthy." Even as he spoke, Nikandr was shaking his head. Their ship, a six-masted brigantine, was the smallest of the three ships. He had hoped to find enough canvas to sail her, but he was nearly as worried as not that he *would* find the canvas. The ships were nearly worthless; it was a wonder that any one of them still held their loft. "Send Jonis and Mahrik to the top of the cliff. Have them prepare defenses."

Nikandr paused, for Styophan was looking over his shoulder to the cliffs behind him. Nikandr turned and saw a large black bird sitting on a small outcropping near the ship's stern.

"Go," he said to Styophan without turning his head.

Styophan snapped his heels and left.

Nikandr walked along the deck slowly, keeping his eyes on the bird.

The bird was larger than a rook, and along its breast and wrapping around to its back was a streak of bright white feathers, but it had the same intelligent gleam in its eye that so many of the island rooks seemed to possess. By the time Nikandr reached the stern, he was within a few paces of the bird. It remained, watching him. He was sure that it had been assumed. He took out his soulstone necklace and held it in his hand. He cast his mind outward, as he did when he knew his mother or Atiana were near. He felt so little that he thought perhaps one of the Matri he hadn't spoken to in years might have come—Duchess Rosa of Lhudansk or Ekaterina of Rhavanki.

Then he sensed something familiar, but it was so faint he thought surely he was merely *wishing* it were so.

"Atiana?" he said.

The bird studied him with an unblinking eye. It arched its head back and ran its beak down one wing and flapped its wings. He thought surely it would speak, that he would hear the cadence of Atiana's words, but then the rook cawed—its voice much lower than the rooks of Anuskaya—and took wing. As it flapped and headed up and over the cliff, heading inland, he wondered whether he had imagined it all.

The day became bitterly cold, so cold that it was impossible for the men to work on the cliffs above. He called them in after midday, and bid everyone to stay within the ship. The enemy would not brave this weather in any case. They would be safe at least until the cold snap broke. But the winds became so fierce that he began to wonder about the wisdom of remaining within the ship. The hull was stout enough, but it was lashed to the cliffs, and the landward mainmast had received damage during whatever storms Grigory had experienced on their way north. With that and the constant rocking against the cliff—something that was never meant to be done for very long—he worried that remaining here would doom them as well. At least on the winds, assuming they could break away from the cliff, they could brave the weather. Here they would eventually be crushed against the stone rock face like grist in a mill.

He went up on deck as the sun began to set. The winds grew stronger the longer he watched. It forced him and the rest of the crew to hold to the ropes and the gunwales wherever they went. The farthest ship, a twelve-masted galleon, was rocking so badly he wondered whether it would last the hour. As its landward mainmast cracked, the ship's stern twisted inward toward the cliff, then the wind shifted and threw it forward.

They couldn't release from the cliffs—not in weather like this—and they couldn't remain here. "Up, men!" he called down the hatch. "We go up to the top of the cliffs." It was not something he relished, remaining out in the open in this weather, but there was no longer a choice.

Styophan ordered Jonis up the rope first to help those who would come next.

Level ground was only fifteen paces above them, but it was taking Jonis minutes to make the climb. The wind threw the rope back and forth, bashing him into the rock face as he climbed. He tried to fend it off with his legs, and they also tried to steady the rope from below, but the wind was howling so fiercely now there was little they could do.

Nikandr felt for his havahezhan, but for the first time in years he felt nothing. Nothing. He had often wondered when the bond with the spirit might be broken, and he was sure that it now had been after the days and days of a constant, draining bond.

Snapping and cracking sounds rose from the fore. The galleon two ships ahead was beginning to break apart. A large crack in the hull formed and widened. The gravel ballast spilled from inside as the ship was thrown back and forth.

"Hurry, Jonis!" Nikandr bellowed above the wind.

At last Jonis reached the top. As he slipped over the edge, Mahrik took to the rope, moving little faster than Jonis had. When he had made it two thirds of the way up, their ship tilted sharply, the landward side dipping down as the mizzen cracked neatly in two. The deck was nearly impossible to stand upon now. The men looked to one another, eyes wide, trying to hold back the fear but finding it impossible with the elements raging against them.

The ship directly ahead of theirs, a ten-masted barque, broke free of its mooring lines and floated out toward sea, but then the wind brought it rushing back again.

"Hold!" Nikandr yelled.

Just before the barque smashed into their ship.

CHAPTER SEVENTY

Atiana sat in a hard, unforgiving chair with a pillow beneath her and a blanket across her lap. Ishkyna lay in the nearby bed, her skin pale, her breathing shallow. Atiana leaned forward and took her sister's hand in her own. Ishkyna's fingers were so cold—colder, it seemed, than the evening winds blowing outside the kasir.

Atiana held Ishkyna's hand tighter, willing her to warm, as the memories of those few precious moments in the aether haunted her. She should have sensed what was happening. She should have tried harder to save her sister, but Ishkyna had never been strong in the ways of the dark, and she had paid for the inexperience. She was lost now, perhaps forever.

Atiana wondered if she had joined the other Matri that had become lost over the centuries. Many believed that those who became lost never died, even if their bodies perished. Atiana hoped not. The idea of living in such a state forever was not a pleasant one.

As she'd done every waking hour, Atiana pulled the soulstone necklace out from beneath Ishkyna's nightdress and touched it with her own. She felt nothing—no momentary brightness, no glimpse of emotion, no sense of Ishkyna at all. It had been the same ever since their return from the tower, but that hadn't kept Atiana from performing this one small ritual. It might be the very beacon Ishkyna needed to return to herself.

She held Ishkyna's stone tenderly, ran her hand over its smooth, glasslike surface. It was not dark like Nikandr's had been years ago, but instead dim, as if she were merely lost and would one day find her way home. Such stones would remain this way forever, except in those rare cases where its owner would return. This was yet another possibility Atiana hoped would not come to pass, for most who returned were never the same.

It had happened to Atiana's great-great-grandmother. She'd become lost for eight days and seven nights. She'd returned, screaming and thrashing in her bed for hours until finally she'd fallen asleep for two days straight. When she'd woken again, she could speak, but no more than a child of three. She was petulant, emotional, her moods swinging wildly between exuberance and rage. Often when the moon was full she would become inconsolable, and once she'd even taken a knife to her wrist. She'd been found, bloody and near death, crying to herself softly on the floor of her room.

She had been confined to a wheeled chair after that, and was rarely allowed outside her room in one of the high towers of Galostina.

Atiana took Ishkyna's hand again, struggling with this cold reality. To be lost among the aether forever or to return a shell of what she once was seemed no choice at all. If it had to be one of these, she silently hoped Ishkyna would simply pass.

She watched the bedcover's rise and fall slowly, wondering if the ancients would take her right then as punishment for such thoughts. The very thought—*hoping* for her sister's death—shamed her greatly, but she also knew it was the very thing *she* would wish for in Ishkyna's place.

Atiana shivered as a tapping came at the window.

She turned and saw by the golden light from the lantern at Ishkyna's bedside the silhouette of a rook and the barest gleam from its eye. It tapped again and she heard a muffled caw, nearly lost among the sound of the wind scouring the towers of the kasir. It was Mileva. Atiana could feel her, even from this distance. It was not only an indicator that the storm was finally dying, but of just how strong Mileva had become. It had been only two days since her time in Sariya's tower, and though the storm had abated somewhat, Atiana still wouldn't have thought that Mileva could make her way here.

Atiana moved to the window and levered it open. The frigid wind entered the room as the rook flapped in noisily and dropped to the floor. It hopped forward and with three swift beats of its wings flew up to Ishkyna's bed.

"How did you know?" Atiana asked.

"Vaasak told me."

Of course, Atiana thought. Of course she would have spoken to Vaasak first. She fell into a nearby chair, the exhaustion she'd managed to stave off these past many days catching up to her at last.

The rook hopped along Ishkyna's chest, swiveled its head to look closely at her soulstone, and then Ishkyna's face. "How does she fare?"

"You saw her in the aether," Atiana replied. "You would know better than I."

"In the aether she is lifeless, as black as the bed she lies upon."

"And yet she breathes, and her soulstone glows."

"Of her stone I see little, but you are right. There is something, a single ember in a long-dead fire, and when I focus upon it, there are times when I feel as though I can sense her, as if she's calling to me somewhere in the fog."

Atiana felt her emotions getting the better of her. Being here with Mileva and Ishkyna both—one in the form of a rook, the other not really present at all—only served to remind her of brighter times. Always when they came together after being apart they slipped into a comfortable routine that felt—despite the biting remarks and rows that inevitably arose—like a comfortable blanket on a cold winter night. And now one of them had been taken away, perhaps never to return.

She'd been hiding these feelings since returning to Sariya's tower, but now it was too much, and she broke down, sobbing uncontrollably into the palms of her hands.

Mileva said nothing. The rook remained on Ishkyna's blankets, blinking those deep black eyes and watching.

"Have you no heart?" Atiana asked.

"It's too soon to give up hope, and there's little time to grieve."

Little time, Atiana thought. Little time, indeed. There was still a host of ships sitting far off the coast of Kiravashya. "You have kapitans to speak to, do you not?"

"I do. More than you might guess."

Atiana paused. She didn't care for the way Mileva had spoken those words, nor the not-so-subtle meaning behind them. She was supposed to have spoken to the Kamarisi's ships, to pass them messages that could only have come from the Kamarisi himself. But if she were speaking to more than just them, it could only mean one thing.

"You will betray the Kamarisi," Atiana said softly.

"I made no promise to the Kamarisi."

"*Vaasak* did. He guaranteed them safe passage."

"They cannot be allowed safe return, Atiana. You should know that."

"I know no such thing."

The rook arched its neck back and released a series of mighty caws. "You speak of Sariya's lies."

"You know they're not lies."

"What I know is that Sariya is Al-Aqim. She is one of the three who broke the world. She, like no other Aramahn since, has found the way into the thoughts and emotions of men and women, both. There's no telling how slyly she might place a thought or command into any one of us."

"Including me."

"Of course *you*!"

"She was lost in the aether, Mileva. When I found her, she didn't know herself. She was spread as thinly as Ishkyna is now. She knew not who she was, nor where she was. She was laid bare."

"Be not a fool, Tiana. Can you say for sure she wasn't lying in wait? Can you say for sure she didn't do this so that you would find the thoughts she wanted you to see? She desires the destruction of our spires. What better way to do it than if we were to lay down arms?"

"She had more than enough ships to do so."

"Don't be so sure. They were waiting for the winds to die down after the destruction of the lesser spires. Could she know that more ships would not arrive in time to aid us? Could she be sure they wouldn't turn the tide?"

"There is still the matter of Muqallad."

"Nikandr may worry of Muqallad, but I do not, not when there are so many threats that stand before us."

"*Be not a fool*, you say. Well, be not dismissive. Nikandr spoke the truth when he warned you of Muqallad. He could destroy us all. You need only look at Nasim to see the sort of destruction the Al-Aqim might cause. He was but a boy, Mileva, an echo of the man he once was, and he nearly destroyed Khalakovo."

"Muqallad is still a man, and he will be found, little thanks to Sariya *or* the Kamarisi. Yrstanla must be neutered and driven beyond the shores of Oramka. Then and only then will we have hope of defeating Muqallad's plans."

"You're playing with fire."

"Something you're all too familiar with. It's time to return home, sister. It's time to recover and gather our strength and begin the rebuilding. We have plenty to worry about."

Atiana had known it would be difficult to convince Mileva, but now she knew it was impossible. "You're right." Atiana collapsed back into the chair, allowing the exhaustion she felt to show through on her face. "You're right."

The rook hopped and flapped its wings. "Just like that, Tiana?"

"I'm not happy, Mileva. I'm worried more than I can say, but what can I do?"

The rook stared, its eyes boring into her. In the end, it hopped down to the floor and flapped up to the windowsill. Using its beak it pushed the window open, which Atiana had left unlatched. "When you see the devastation on Kiravashya, you'll not be so quick to speak lightly of Sariya."

Atiana remained silent as the bird leapt out and into the night. She waited until she could no longer feel Mileva's presence in her soulstone, and then she stood and returned to Ishkyna's side. She took her sister's hand in hers, hoping, however irrationally, that Ishkyna would wake with this one insignificant gesture, but her eyes remained shut, her hand cold, and Atiana was somehow sure that Ishkyna would never wake, would never find herself.

She had always thought—foolishly, she knew—that she would be able to say goodbye when the time came. But there had been no time at all, and now it seemed there would never be.

She slipped her soulstone from around her neck, held it in the palm of her hand. The stone itself and the stout chain felt incredibly light. She couldn't keep it, not if she were to leave the kasir and have any hope of remaining hidden in the streets of Baressa or the hills of Galahesh.

She had to leave, for there was no other choice. She would find no allies to the south of Baressa, so she would look to Sihaş, and perhaps the Aramahn if she dared to return to them.

She leaned forward and slipped the necklace around Ishkyna's neck, hoping it would comfort her.

She kissed Ishkyna on the forehead and whispered into her ear, "Go well, sister."

And then, through her tears, she left Ishkyna's room.

Atiana watched the sleet fall against the stones of the courtyard. It was the worst storm since the spires had fallen. Warm wind blew in from the southwest, from the deserts of Yrstanla, which brought with it some warmth, but only enough at this time of year to alter the snow into something equally unpleasant.

She had been watching for nearly an hour and she feared that something had happened to Irkadiy. She waited for minutes more, eyeing the ramparts of the kasir's inner keep for any signs of being watched. There were none, however; with so little to fear from within, every available man had been sent to the outer defensive wall.

Just as she was about to give up hope, a form resolved from the darkness. It moved quickly, threateningly. She opened the eye of her lantern and shined it ahead of her. She breathed a sigh of relief when she recognized Irkadiy's face.

"Quickly," he said, holding one hand up to block the light from her lantern. "The Kamarisi has stepped up the watch."

"Then how will we escape?"

He held up an oiled canvas coat. "I told them I'd be bringing another, to help with the watch."

As she slipped her arms into the heavy coat and pulled the hood over her hair, Irkadiy continued. "Don't speak, even if spoken to. I told them you're my countryman, a good man, though you lost your voice to a sliver of wood when the Maharraht attacked your ship years ago."

"A pity."

"Be quiet," Irkadiy said.

He led her through an open sally port. As the sleet pattered against her canvas hood, they crossed a larger courtyard between the stables and something that smelled like an abattoir. She slipped in a pile of manure before they made it to the stairs leading up to the top of the rampart.

As they neared the last of the steps, Atiana felt something deep within her. She felt dizzy, and she was barely able to hold herself up against the wall.

Irkadiy came rushing back down the stairs. "What is it?" he whispered.

The feeling—not unlike the first few moments in the aether—was still present, but she was growing used to it. "I don't know."

"Can you go on?"

A spike of fear drove through her as the effect intensified. She stared out over the edge of the stairs, somehow feeling the wall itself and beyond it the steeply sloped hill that dropped down from Kasir Yalidoz to the city proper.

"My Lady," Irkadiy whispered.

Her awareness began to expand even more, spreading beyond the borders of the Mount and into the city.

And then it struck her. She was slipping into the aether.

By the ancients, what was happening?

She didn't understand, but she was no child dipping her toes into the icy waters of the dark for the first time; she was a Matra, and she had tamed worse than this.

She halted the outward progression and drew herself inward. She focused on the sound of sleet, on the way it crackled against the stones of the stairs, the way it splattered in the mud of the courtyard below. And slowly, she regained herself.

Irkadiy had just started leading her back down the stairs when she waved for him to stop. "It's all right," she said, holding his cold hand to ground herself even further. "Let's go on."

"My Lady, we can try another night."

"*Nyet*. It must be tonight."

A sudden flapping of wings frightened her. She *felt* more than saw a large bird land on the crenelations near the top of the stairs. When she swung the lantern toward it, she found what she thought was a massive rook, the largest she'd ever seen, but then she noticed the bright white cowl that ran down its breast. When it flapped its wings, more white feathers were revealed.

It cawed once, the sound low and foreign to her ears. It stared at her, one eye blinking under the light of the lantern.

"Dim the light," Irkadiy whispered harshly.

"One moment," Atiana said.

She stepped forward. The feelings within her intensified, making it clear that this bird—or the one who controlled it—was the reason she'd been drawn into the aether.

"Who are you?" Atiana asked.

She took another step forward. The rook bobbed its head up and down. It twisted its neck, its beak opening and clacking shut several times. Atiana could tell it was trying to speak, but nothing came out.

Suddenly an alarm bell came from the inner keep. It rang insistently, over and over again, and the call was picked up by others.

The bird flapped its wings, and then it leaned out beyond the battlements and dove out of sight. The beating of its wings was the last thing she heard before several men came running along the wall. The first of them called out to Irkadiy, telling him to halt in Yrstanlan.

"It's only me, Irkadiy." He motioned to Atiana. "I've brought the help I promised."

The Galaheshi soldier used a dim lantern to look Atiana up and down. He was about to say something when more men entered the courtyard below. "Wait here," he said, motioning five of his men to remain. He nodded to the sixth, and together they went down to the courtyard.

Atiana couldn't see the newcomers well enough, even by the lanterns they held, but when the first of them spoke, she knew immediately who it was.

It was Bahett.

CHAPTER SEVENTY-ONE

"The Princess Atiana is missing," Bahett shouted into the muddy, pattering courtyard below.

Atiana's heart pounded in her ears. She was painfully aware of the soldiers standing just next to her. The nearest of them watched the scene play out in the courtyard below, but he was close enough to reach out and touch her.

"She's most likely gone to the cemetery," Bahett continued. "Ten have been sent already. Gather twenty more and join them. The rest will watch the walls."

The soldier Bahett was speaking to bowed his head. "*Evet*, Kaymakam."

Bahett turned and strode away, his tall boots slurping in the slush and the mud. The men that had accompanied him followed, leaving only the two who had come down from the wall. The heavyset one spoke low to the other. He'd guessed her identity. Atiana was sure of it.

As they finished speaking and trudged toward the stairs, Atiana shifted her stance so that she was incrementally closer to Irkadiy. "I won't return," she said loudly enough for Irkadiy to hear. She didn't care if the guardsmen heard. The only reason they didn't already know was that their commander thought they could be caught with little or no bloodshed.

Irkadiy looked into her eyes. He was asking—for her sake—to reconsider. She shook her head.

After one more pause, and a brief nod of his head, Irkadiy grabbed the lantern from her hand, swung it high over his head in a blur of movement. It came crashing down on the rampart. Fire blossomed across the stones, spreading quickly and engulfing the walkway.

Seeing Irkadiy's intent, Atiana turned and ran, Irkadiy close on her heels. "Stop them!" the commander called.

Upon passing a turret in the wall, Irkadiy called to her. "This is far enough." Atiana stopped and turned as Irkadiy unbuttoned his heavy canvas coat.

He undid his cherkesska next, and finally he began unwinding the length of rope he had hidden there.

Far behind them, the flames were already beginning to subside. One of the guardsmen removed his coat and threw it down against the oil, creating a bridge for them to pass over. Three of them did, with ease. The fourth caught fire.

Irkadiy had finished unwinding the rope and was looping it around a battlement. He moved with quick hands. Sure hands. He was so calm, where her heart was beating so madly she thought it would burst.

"Quickly," he said, taking her hands and forcing her to grab the rope.

The soldiers were nearing. "Halt!" they called.

Atiana would be able to make it down, but Irkadiy wouldn't. There wasn't enough time.

"Go!" he cried.

Atiana stepped up between the battlements—realizing only then she'd forgotten to wear gloves—and swung over the side. As she began to slide down, the sense of vertigo she'd experienced earlier returned. It was all she could do to hold on. She knew if she loosened her grip on the rope, she would fall to her death. She could do nothing but hold tight.

Above her, Irkadiy turned and drew his shashka.

Just as he was about to engage, a low, ragged caw cut through the night. By the light of the dying flames Atiana saw black wings streak between the two soldiers.

Both paused.

The feeling of dizziness intensified. The air filled with the sound of wings. Dark figures cut above the curtain wall. A dozen. A hundred. A thousand black, fluttering forms.

They chattered, their myriad voices collecting in a cacophony that forced Atiana to duck her head and hide her face against her shoulder.

She thought it would end quickly, a freak passage of birds over the kasir, but it did not. She felt them against her face, against her hands. They flew about her legs, some of them thudding against her coat before flying off again.

"Come, Irkadiy!" she managed to yell, though whether he heard her she wasn't sure. "Irkadiy, follow me!"

She allowed herself to slip downward. She moved slowly at first, but then, blessedly, she felt the rope above her shift. Irkadiy was coming.

Hand over hand she moved as the wings beat around her and the birds continued to screech.

At last, bless the ancients, she found herself below the cloud of wings, and soon after that, her feet touched ground.

Her nausea began to ebb. Finally the effect brought on by the gallows crow was starting to pass.

As soon as Irkadiy slid down beside her, they moved away from the wall and slid down the steep slope. Standing in their way were an army of thickets and scrub trees and tall stands of wiry grass, making the going arduously slow. They hadn't gone twenty paces when the sound of the birds faded into the distance.

"There's a path ahead," Irkadiy whispered.

They came to it as the sound of pursuit heightened. Again the bells were ringing among the kasir, but this time at a different pace and rhythm—*clang, clang, CLANG... clang, clang, CLANG*—no doubt calling help to this section of the curtain wall.

The path for a time seemed no less dangerous. They struck as many clawing branches as they had during the slide down from the wall, but they were more sure on their feet. They were adding distance between themselves and the guardsmen, but the location of this path was no secret. Their only hope was to reach the bottom of the hill and lose themselves in the city before Bahett's men could find them.

Lights shone against the wall as the slope leveled off at last. They took one last look up as they reached a dirt road that continued downhill, but as they did they heard the first sound of approaching hooves.

She and Irkadiy ran, but they could already tell that dozens of ponies had been dispatched from the kasir. Bahett's men knew where this path emptied into the streets of Baressa, and they would start their search there.

The sounds of hoofbeats echoed through the streets. The air was so cold it numbed Atiana's fingers. It sapped her warmth through the dampness of her coat.

In an alley running between two rows of tall stone buildings, they huddled in a deep, arched doorway. The clop of ponies approached, and soon three men wearing Galaheshi uniforms—red coats with white turbans—came abreast of the mouth of the alley. They rode tall brown stallions, and each carried a lantern.

While Atiana and Irkadiy pressed themselves against the door and made themselves as small as possible, the guardsmen swung their lanterns along the alley.

The light had just fallen upon their archway when a cawing sound came. It was distant, and it echoed in the cramped spaces of the city, so Atiana could not tell the direction from which it had come.

"There!" one of the guardsmen called. A moment later, the ponies clopped further up the street.

As the sounds died away, punctuated by the cough of a pistol being fired, fluttering wings fell through the night and landed in the street. A low caw, loud enough for only them to hear, beckoned them. They approached, and the old gallows crow took flight, heading southwest over the nearest buildings.

They followed the course the crow had set for them. The sound of hooves approached, but each time they did a caw would come again, drawing the soldiers away from their trail. As they made their way toward the poorer sections of the city, the caws came again and again, steadily further away from their current location.

They heard it once more as they came to a large circle where six streets met.

"We should not go through here," Irkadiy said.

Atiana, taking the circle in again, agreed—there were too many windows, too many eyes—but just as they were preparing to head back, the sound of ponies came again, this time from the west, the direction of the kasir.

The rain had finally stopped and the moon shone down through thin clouds. The wings of the gallows crow flapped from the west. It cawed twice and then landed on the edge of the fountain at the center of the circle.

Atiana and Irkadiy hid among the shadows and watched as five men rode into the circle. They bore lanterns, and they shone them on the crow, making it seem as though they'd been following it for some time. The crow took wing, flying not *away* from Atiana, but *toward* her. It flew straight to their position and landed not five paces away.

The ponies approached.

The light from the lanterns darted toward them like hawks.

The crow hopped closer. It stood just before them now.

The desire to stand and run was overpowering, as was the desire to take a knife to the gallows crow.

"There!" one of the men called.

They pulled swords, and three kicked their ponies into action. All were well trained. The ponies had them surrounded in moments.

"My Lady Princess," one of the men called in Anuskayan. "Please come with us."

"Sihaş?" Atiana asked, holding her hand up and squinting against the light of the lanterns.

"*Da*, My Lady."

Before Atiana could wonder why *he* would have been sent to find her, the gallows crow flapped its wings and hopped and cawed.

All eyes turned toward the spectacle. The bird swung its head back and forth in rhythmic patterns that seemed both painful and uncontrollable.

After one more caw, a single word escaped the bird's throat.

"Hakan."

No one moved. A chill ran down Atiana's already-numb skin.

"Leave us," Sihaş said in Yrstanlan.

"My Lord," one of his men replied.

"Go to the far side of the circle," Sihaş said, more insistently. "I'll call you when needed."

They complied, but Atiana could see by the grisly light shining against their faces that they were not pleased.

Sihaş swung a leg over his saddle and dropped down to the cobbled street. "What is this about?" he said to Atiana while motioning to the bird.

It was the crow that responded, however. "Hakan is not yet freed."

"What do you mean?" Atiana asked.

It seemed so distraught, so in pain, that Atiana crouched down in order to touch the crow. It deftly avoided her touch, however, and hopped away. "He is still under Sariya's spell."

Atiana stood.

She looked to Sihaş, whose face was every bit as shocked as hers. But his look was calculating as well. He had placed much on the notion that Hakan—once Sariya had been wounded and subsequently disappeared—was once again whole. His loyalty to Yrstanla, and even Hakan, had driven him to act against the wishes of the Kamarisi. No doubt he had been relieved when Sariya had fled. But now, if what the crow was saying was correct, he might still have to act against his lord in order to protect his empire.

"There's more," the crow said. It cawed once, sadly, and its eye never seemed to leave Atiana.

"What?" Atiana asked.

"You..." The crow cawed several times and twisted its head and flapped its wings. It hopped away, and Atiana thought it was going to take wing and leave them. But it didn't. It recovered and approached once more, eyeing Atiana carefully.

Atiana stared at the bird, fearful of what it would say when it spoke once more. She swallowed. Something large and raw was caught in her throat, and nothing she did seemed to clear it.

"What about me?" she finally managed to ask.

"You're caught as well." The crow pecked the cobblestone near Atiana's foot. "You have been from the moment you entered her tower."

Atiana began to shiver. First her arms and shoulders, then her entire body.

"Who *are* you?" Her words were swallowed by the night.

The crow opened its beak and its tongue lolled out. It shook its head and shivered violently. One long, mournful sound escaped its throat, and though

Atiana knew it was trying to speak, it sounded more like the sad, soulful cry of a little lost girl.

It tried once more, and then with a noisy flutter of wings lofted itself into the sky. In mere moments, the dark shades of its wings had faded into the night.

Irkadiy and Sihaş stared at Atiana with confused looks. They didn't know who had assumed the bird's form. But Atiana did. The crow hadn't needed to say.

As the last of hints of its wings were lost over the buildings beyond the circle, Atiana whispered her name.

"Ishkyna..."

CHAPTER SEVENTY-TWO

Nasim walked down an empty street toward the center of Alayazhar. He was near the top of a long sloping hill. The empty shells of the buildings cast long shadows beneath the golden light of the lowering sun, and in the distance he could see Sariya's tower.

How had he come to be here? It must be a dream, he thought. It must be.

Yet when he turned to his right, he realized he was holding hands with Muqallad. As he had when he stood within the cavern near the towering white cliffs of Galahesh.

He had realized something in that cavern just before Muqallad had entered.

"He's waking."

This had come from the voice of a woman.

He looked to his left and found her. Sariya. She walked with a hitch, blood still leaking through her robes, but she was also strong. Her *will* was driving her to finish what she'd started.

At this, a spark of memory came.

In the cavern within the cliffs of Galahesh, with the light shining down on his face, he had looked into Sariya's eyes.

And he'd remembered the tower. *Her* tower. The spire in the forest, linked to the tower here on Ghayavand. He had entered, and from that moment on had been under her spell.

"It need only hold until the sun sets."

"He's strong, Muqallad." Her voice was strained, desperate.

"You will overcome," was all Muqallad said in return.

They continued down through the city, walking along the empty thoroughfare. Strangely, they turned off the street well before Sariya's tower. Nasim didn't understand why, but he *did* understand that they were avoiding the tall, white tower itself.

Nasim tried to work it through, but his mind wouldn't allow it. All he could focus on were the broken stones of the street and the utter silence that greeted them throughout their long walk down to the sea.

They passed beyond the city proper and took a set of stairs carved into the dark gray slabs of stone that lined the sandy beach. The sound of the surf rose. Ahead, he saw a massive black rock. The incoming waves splashed against it high into the air, catching the light against the distant clouds of the dying day. This was the stone he'd seen in so many of his dreams. Khamal had come to this stone. He'd brought Yadhan and Alif—unsure, perhaps, which he would use to free his soul from this place.

In the end he had chosen Alif. Khamal had cut his own hand and spilled his lifeblood into the opened mouth of that forgotten boy, linking the two of them, and then he had driven a knife deep into his chest, severing his ties to Ghayavand once and for all.

And all it had cost him was his future lives.

Save one, Nasim thought. He was the last. And now Muqallad had come to do the same.

He looked down to Muqallad's belt and saw a khanjar. *Khamal's* knife. The one Muqallad and Sariya had used to slay Khamal at the top of Sariya's tower.

The one they would use to slay Nasim.

Muqallad glanced down, and then returned his attention to the road ahead, as if acknowledging the weapon would acknowledge not only the atrocities he'd committed, but the one he was about to commit. To Muqallad this sacrifice was necessary. Khamal had trapped them. He had murdered Alif and then forced the Al-Aqim to slay him, but in those last moments Muqallad had realized what Khamal was about to do, and he had foiled, at least partially, Khamal's plans. Nasim had been linked to them from that point on, and it felt as if every step he'd taken had been leading toward this: this dark stone and this sighing sea and this bright blade.

They came to the stone at last. The frothy water rushed up to their feet with every exhalation of the sea. Muqallad climbed, but Sariya, sensing Nasim's hesitance, turned and held out her hand. "Come, Nasim."

Nasim stared at the stone, then back to Sariya's hand.

Dread filled him. He didn't want to die.

And yet he knew he deserved it.

The things Khamal had done… The hubris he and the other Al-Aqim had shown was reprehensible but perhaps forgivable. What was not forgivable was the sacrifice of the first akhoz, Yadhan, and the others that had followed. What was not forgivable was the sacrifice of Alif to allow himself to pass beyond the protections that had kept the rifts in place for so many years. Or manipulating Sariya and Muqallad so that they might take his life. Or knowingly allowing the rifts to spread beyond Ghayavand so that he might have a chance to repair the damage he'd caused.

Sariya waited expectantly. Her hold on him had failed. She was too weakened from her wound, and something had happened to her tower, barring her from the kind of power that had once come so easily.

She shook her hand, waiting for him to take it.

Muqallad merely stared down from the top of the rock, his dark eyes and strong face commanding.

Nasim could walk away. He could refuse them what they sought.

But why should he? He had only ever failed in his life. His touch was death. He was nothing, and he would have this life done with.

He took her hand and together the two of them climbed up to the top of the rock.

"Lie down," Muqallad said.

Nasim complied. He stared up to the sky, where yellow clouds caught the last rays of the sun beneath an indigo sky. The first stars shone along the eastern horizon. His mind was afire with the things he'd done in his life, and he wondered if Alif had thought the same things. He wondered if he had given up, or perhaps, behind the veil of the nightmare in which he lived, he had come to believe in what Khamal was hoping to do.

Did Nasim himself now believe in what Sariya and Muqallad hoped to do?

He still felt the tug of the enchantment upon him. It held him down. It prevented him from raising a hand against Muqallad.

He wondered whether it had been Khamal's lack of interest in studying the ways of the mind. Khamal, after all, had always been focused on the rifts and the barrier around Ghayavand that prevented him from leaving. Perhaps if he hadn't been so singularly focused, Nasim might have been more aware of such things. Or perhaps if he hadn't been hobbled for so many years, he could have broken Sariya's hold on him.

But he couldn't. All he could do was watch as Muqallad kneeled to one side of him, Sariya to the other. He listened to the waves and smelled the sea and felt the warmth of the black rock through the skin along his back.

Muqallad took from his robes the irregular shape of the Atalayina. Two pieces had been fused, but one piece was still missing, making it look like a knife had cut away a third of it. They placed it on his chest. The weight of it... It was difficult to comprehend. It felt as heavy as the world.

Muqallad pulled a khanjar from its sheath at his belt. With deliberate care he cut the palm of one hand. Sariya did the same, and then, holding them above Nasim's mouth, they allowed the blood to drip down. Nasim did not wish to partake of their blood, but neither was he willing to prevent it. The salty taste entered his mouth, made him feel heady with power. Through blood, they hoped to lift the curse Inan and her followers had lain upon them, just as Khamal had with Alif.

How apropos, Nasim thought.

Alif had been lost, a soul that had perished forever when Khamal plunged the knife into his chest. Was Nasim any different? He was also a boy who had never truly lived, who would be lost to the worlds when his heart no longer beat within his chest. Khamal had taken Alif's life, and now justice would be meted, for this, it seemed to Nasim, this ritual, was little more than a weighing of the scales in which his life stood forfeit in recompense for Alif's.

The time was growing near. Sariya and Muqallad took the knife in their hands, not unlike the way they'd done with Khamal, though this time, instead of surprise on their faces, they had looks of sorrow and grim determination.

They raised the knife together. For a moment the edge caught the light of the setting sun, making it gleam, golden and bright.

It did not look angry, or vengeful, as Nasim thought it might.

It looked merciful.

He was ready to be done with this life, so when the blade was brought down, when it pierced his chest with white-hot pain, it felt like little more than bittersweet release.

The pain rose. Climbed high. Climbed well beyond the stars, beyond even the resting place of the fates.

It grew distant as he felt the warm flow of blood seep along his robes and along his rib cage. It pooled in his navel before tickling down his sides.

And all the while he breathed shallowly, watching the hands of the Al-Aqim as they closed their eyes and felt—as Nasim felt—the restrictions lift from them. These were bonds that had been with them for three hundred years, and now they were being lifted entirely.

They released the knife and stood.

Muqallad stared at his hands, then down to Nasim's chest, then out to sea, where the sun was slipping beneath the horizon.

Sariya stared at the knife, at the blood. She swallowed, her blue eyes wavering. A tear slipped along one cheek, and when Muqallad turned and began climbing down from the top of the rock, she did not follow.

"Come," Muqallad said when he was halfway down.

Sariya met his eyes. Tears continued to stream down her face. She seemed remorseful, but also curious, as if she were wondering how things could have come to this.

"Fare well, Khamal," she said, and then she turned and followed Muqallad.

Over the sounds of the sea he heard the soft scrape of their boots on the rock, and then the crunch of their footsteps against the beach as they walked away. Softer and softer they became until at last he was alone.

As his lifeblood spilled, he felt the barriers around the island. They had been placed by the dozens of qiram, the followers of the Al-Aqim. What power they had held to keep them for centuries. But Khamal's departure had weakened them, and soon—perhaps weeks from now, perhaps months—they would fade entirely. And then the fears of all who had stood upon Ghayavand when the rift had been formed three centuries before would at last be realized.

The rifts would spread. They would consume the islands. They would consume the sea. They would consume, in the end, even the motherland, Yrstanla, and the desert wastes to the south, even the plains of the Haelish and the wide, barren steppes that ran up to the Great Northern Sea.

The pain in his chest began to fade.

His fingers felt cold.

A high-pitched ringing filled his ears.

He stared up to the skies, wondering if the fates would embrace him or spurn him. Perhaps Khamal's plans had been so complete that he was beyond even *their* power.

The light was fading as a soft crunching came from the beach. It grew louder and louder, but he could not find it in himself to turn his head.

Sounds of soft scraping came, as of someone climbing the rock, and soon he saw a form standing above him.

It was not Muqallad, nor Sariya.

He could not at first understand who it was.

But then he realized.

And he nearly cried.

By the fates who shine above, it was Rabiah.

CHAPTER SEVENTY-THREE

Nasim looked up into the beautiful face of Rabiah. She'd come to take him. Of this he was sure.

She kneeled, and the moment she did, the numbness that had been spreading through him stopped. Then it receded, and the pain began to return.

She touched the knife, and pain seared through him—white hot at the center of his being, like embers hidden deep beneath the ash.

"I can't! Let me go!"

He couldn't go back. He was ready to leave this world, one way or another.

She leaned close to his ear. "You cannot go," she whispered. "Not yet."

He could do little more than draw breath, though each one fluttered in his throat and caused so much pain he felt as though he were merely holding his breath. He had been prepared to leave, but staring into her eyes, the eyes of a girl he had come to cherish, he realized he couldn't do it. What a poor man he would be if he gave up now—on himself and Rabiah and the world itself—simply because of pain.

He swallowed, staring into Rabiah's beautiful eyes. He swallowed again, not sure if he could go on.

She nodded to him with a smile on her lips, a smile as wide and deep as the sky.

With that one simple gesture, his nerves began to calm. He could not go, he told himself. He could not.

There was still much to do.

Rabiah waited for him to nod in return, and then in one sharp motion pulled the knife free.

His body rigored. His muscles tightened like catgut. His head convulsed, heedless of stone beneath him.

And he screamed for the first time. He screamed to the sky above, to the seas below, to the mountains beyond and the fires beneath. He screamed, unable to understand who he was, what he was, until he felt cool hands touch his forehead, urging him to stillness.

He thought it impossible, but the more her palms pressed downward, the more he was able to control the pain. It did not fade, but he found that with that one simple touch of skin against skin he was able to master it, and himself.

"How did you find me?" Nasim asked.

Rabiah did not respond. She merely helped him to sit up.

When he did, he realized the pain was not so great as it had been only moments ago. He looked down and saw that the flow of blood was merely a trickle. The wound was beginning to close as if drawn by purse strings.

She helped him to stand. Her hands were warm. They were wonderful. It was so glorious to have her near.

If she noticed his rush of emotions she didn't mention it. She held his hand as they stepped down from the rock—as Muqallad and Sariya had done only a short while ago—and together they trekked along the sand back toward Alayazhar. They went beyond the beach, and by the time they'd climbed the path up to the city proper, his wound had closed entirely. It felt strange, though. Tender. But more than this, it felt as though it would never heal. Not completely.

Rabiah led him toward the tower until Nasim stopped and pulled his hand away.

"We can't," he said.

She turned and regarded him. "There's no other way."

Nasim shook his head. "We cannot place ourselves in her power again."

"We will not," Rabiah said.

As she said these words, he felt souls about the city, the souls of the akhoz that still remained. He knew that these were those that had remained to keep the rifts stable. They were also those that Khamal himself had sacrificed. Though Nasim himself had had nothing to do with them, he also knew that they were attuned to him—yet another effect, intended or not, of the circumstances surrounding Khamal's death.

Through the broken streets and alleys of Alayazhar, the akhoz approached. Their presence made him aware of the aether and of Adhiya beyond. By the fates, they felt closer than any time since the ritual on Oshtoyets, a time when he'd barely been aware of himself or the worlds around him. His mind had been only a shadow of what he would become, and yet he had lost so much since then. Had it been because of Khamal, or had it simply been because he'd tried too hard? Had it all been self-imposed?

He longed to reach beyond, to commune with the hezhan. He longed for their touch. He wanted to give of himself so they could learn from him. But he knew that such a thing would be foolish here. Now was not the time.

The akhoz were near. They approached the tower, not with rage or hunger, but with reverence. They shambled, their arms to their sides, their faces slightly uplifted, as if they were basking in some unseen glow.

"Come, my children," he said to the crisp air. "Come, and we will go where we are needed."

They moved more quickly now, but with no lesser sense of awe and deference. There were dozens, all of them ready to do what Nasim asked of them. He was saddened—their lives had been cut short so long ago, and they'd been forced into an existence infinitely worse than beasts of burden—but at least their lives might have some meaning in the end.

Rabiah tugged Nasim's hand. She nodded toward the tower. "Time grows short."

He did not want to enter the tower, but he would trust her. He would trust her, he thought, as he had not trusted her in life.

As they walked toward the iron fence, the smell of the air changed. The wind calmed. The clouds in the sky paused.

"What's happened?" Nasim asked.

"What do you mean?"

"The sky," he said. "The wind."

"Nothing is different…"

Nasim looked to her, wondering how she couldn't have known, but her gaze was fixed on the tower ahead, as if that and that alone was what mattered.

Nasim felt it, though, and it was growing worse, this feeling of pregnant intent. It felt like the time before a great storm, but this one, thought Nasim, was going to be worse than any other.

They walked through the open gate, the akhoz following. Rabiah stopped at the door to the tower. Nasim didn't understand at first, but it soon became clear she was waiting for him to open it. Why she refused to touch it he didn't know, but it seemed important that he not ask of it, so he took the handle and opened it himself.

Inside it was dark and foreboding, but beyond this he could not sense Sariya's presence. He stepped within, and immediately the akhoz swept into the room behind him. They moved like a pack of animals. Nasim didn't know what had changed, but they seemed hungry—hungry for blood. Some climbed the stairs as if their hunger drove them to hunt, to move, even knowing there was nothing to find in the upper levels of the tower, but most of them remained in the room, crouching, their eyeless faces trained on him and the door.

It felt strangely comforting to have these forgotten souls join him, but the one he most dearly wished would join him—Rabiah—remained just outside.

"Will you not come?" Nasim asked her.

She did not respond.

He nodded, not wanting to close the door, for he knew that when he did, she would be gone forever.

Rabiah seemed to hear something, for she turned and looked deeper into the city. What had attracted her attention Nasim couldn't guess. Rabiah glanced back once through the doorway, her eyes searching, confused. She didn't seem to notice him.

And then she turned and walked away.

Nasim held the door open, hoping she would return, knowing she would not.

Then, knowing he had to leave now if he was ever going to, he closed the door until the latch clicked shut.

In that moment, he felt a boom. The earth shook and stones of the tower rumbled above him. He heard shouting and screams. Musket fire erupted, rising to a fierce intensity as men shouted and the clash of steel rang out. When Nasim opened the door again, he saw outside a completely different city filled with bloodied men waging war against one another.

Beyond the tower stood dozens of men wearing dark woolen cherkesskas. They held berdische axes in one hand, muskets in the other, and when they prepared to fire, they dropped the butt of the axe to the ground and placed the barrel of the musket at the crook of the axe head before sighting along the length of the barrel and pulling the trigger.

It all seemed as it should be, as if these men were merely a force of nature unleashing their vengeance upon another.

Another boom shook the tower. Grape shot tore through the forward ranks of the streltsi. Dozens of them spun and twisted and arched backward, as if they were men made from cloth and sticks, not blood and bone.

He thought at first that this was all happening in Alayazhar, but of course it was not. This city looked nothing like Alayazhar. Rabiah had transported him, or rather, the magic of Sariya's tower had.

But where had he come? Kiravashya? Had the war stretched so far?

Neh, he thought as he took in the imposing form of the Mount. He was in Baressa, and the streltsi were warring against the men of the Kaymakam and the Kamarisi.

There were hundreds of Anuskayan soldiers along this length of road. The akhoz had gathered behind him. They watched, mouths open, tongues lolling, as if they tasted the battle that raged only paces away. They strained at their leash. They hungered for battle. But Nasim would not allow it. Not yet. Not here.

Among the cries of the wounded and the crack of musket fire and the sound of a charge in the distance, he heard the cawing of a rook. He saw the bird fly over a tall stone building and come winging down straight toward him. It landed and pecked at the ground. A young man of Anuskaya lay dying nearby. His fur-lined kolpak had fallen away, revealing dirty blond hair. He blinked several times with a look on his face that made it clear he thought the bird had come to save him. He tried to speak, but words failed him, and then he fell slack.

The rook beat its wings against the air and cawed over and over again, but then it regained itself and hopped toward the open doorway as the battle continued to rage.

"I have looked long and hard for you, Nasim," it said in Anuskayan.

"Matra Saphia," Nasim said, bowing his head though he knew not why. "I've just returned."

"Returned to *her* tower."

It was a question, one he could not in any way answer fully. "They took me," he said simply, staring down at his robes, which were still bright red with blood.

The rook clucked three times. "So they did."

The tower shook as another shot thundered into it. Stone and sand rained down. He could feel the entire structure begin to shift with several piercing cracks breaking through the sounds of war.

Behind the rook, riding on ponies from the same direction in which Saphia had come, were four streltsi wearing red kolpak hats.

"Quickly," she said. "We must get you to safety."

More screams of the dying came. As he stepped out of the tower, musket fire tore through the line to his right. A roar was taken up, and dozens of janissaries wearing tall turbans came rushing forward. Their strangely bent kilij swords were drawn, and they broke into the double line of streltsi. The shouting intensified as men were shifted from other parts of the line, but as soon as those orders were passed, another roar was heard. More men of Yrstanla counterattacking along the right flank.

All four ponies galloped forward. One was felled a dozen yards from Nasim. Another broke away to meet the charge of three Yrstanla soldiers. The pony rammed one, and the soldier took out another, but the third swung his kilij high over his head and down against the strelet's thigh. The pony reared and clubbed the soldier, but the strelet was lost, blood poring from his nearly severed thigh before he struck the blood-slick stones of the street.

Before Nasim could stop them, the akhoz streamed out of the tower. Three ran like hounds toward the soldiers of Yrstanla. The soldiers' eyes went wide.

They warded the akhoz with their swords just before two gouts of flame were released from widened maws, catching them across their chests and heads. The third akhoz leaped upon one of the flaming men, taking him down and tearing into his neck with its teeth.

This one was shot point-blank by two other soldiers. It reared back, baring its teeth and blackened gums and leaping at another soldier despite the black blood seeping down from its chest and shoulder. It was caught by another musket shot in the temple, and a vicious slice from a sword across its neck, and it fell twitching to the ground.

Its brothers and sisters bayed in sickening tones, bringing the battle to momentary silence. Soldiers of both sides turned, weapons lowered, as they looked on with fear plain on their faces.

"Come!" Nasim called to them as the streltsi on the ponies rode near. One of the remaining two streltsi reached down. He and Nasim locked forearms, and then Nasim swung up into the saddle behind him. "Hear me! Come!" he called again.

And now they obeyed. Slowly, reluctantly, they turned away from the battle and followed the pony that bore Nasim southward.

The rook flew silently up and over the same buildings, guiding them. The streltsi followed, the hooves of their two ponies ringing, gaining in volume over the sounds of the battle as they wound their way through the empty streets.

As the sounds of battle faded, the relative peace allowed Nasim to notice what he hadn't before. The sky. The wind. The taste of the air. It had that same feeling that it had had in Alayazhar.

And it felt worse.

The time was growing short.

CHAPTER SEVENTY-FOUR

Wood thundered as the barque crashed into the bow of their brigantine. The deck bucked and slid beneath Nikandr's boots. Three of his men fell, scrambling for handholds.

Nikandr's attention was caught by a dark shape in the sky above him. It was a ship, gliding not thirty paces above them. There was another higher up, and another. Four in all.

Before he could identify them, the barque slammed into the cliff again. Gaping cracks formed in the hull, running jaggedly from top to bottom, and the ship was beginning to lose its loft. As the ship dropped, its seaward masts got caught up in their brigantine's starward rigging.

"To the masts!" Nikandr cried. "Cut the barque free!"

The men responded, slipping down the deck to the foremast and climbing it quickly and expertly even in the wind and the shaking of the ship.

Nikandr looked up to the ships. His first thought was that the forces of Yrstanla had arrived, but these ships did not look new like the Kamarisi's. These ships were old and weatherworn, and the sails were heavily patched and dyed gray as the Maharraht would do.

The barque pulled away, tugging on their lines, stretching them taut until the only thing that was holding them in place were the twelve mooring spikes that had been driven into the rocks of the cliff.

One of them snapped free as Nikandr watched. And another.

The bow of the ship swung wide, snapping another line, and soon all twelve had been pulled free and their ship was sliding out to sea.

As Nikandr moved to join the men, Mahrik's rope was caught. He was climbing quickly, but before he could reach the top, the rope was pulled taut, snapping him like an arrow on a string. He flew out beyond the deck, flailing his arms uselessly as he plummeted through open air down toward the sea.

Three of the newly arrived ships continued their eastward course, but the nearest altered its course to hover above them. The men aboard were Ma-harraht: small turbans dully colored, tails hanging down their chest, their double robes ragged, their beards long and whipping in the wind.

It was the *Bhadyar*, Nikandr realized, and Soroush was standing at the gunwale. His men were lowering ropes, but there'd be no chance to climb if the barque continued to pull them down. Nikandr reached the shrouds and climbed up as quickly as he could. He came to the nearest halyard that had been caught beneath the lowest of the foremast's yards. He cut the rope as quickly as he could manage, but there were many more, and as they managed to cut some, the two ships would shift, pulling more of the barque's rigging against their own.

He could feel the havaqiram aboard the ship above them trying to slow the descent of their ships, but these winds were beyond anything a lone havaqiram could hope to outmatch.

Nikandr tried to feel for his own hezhan once more, but again felt nothing, so he climbed further, to the uppermost reaches of the foremast where he and Vlanek sawed furiously at the ropes.

Suddenly the mast was pulled sharply windward. One of the galleon's yards had slipped beneath the foremast's shrouds.

"Cut the shroud!" he yelled.

Only Styophan remained on deck. He pulled his shashka and sliced it across the heavy ropes of the shroud. With four quick swings the shroud snapped up and away, and at last they were free.

Their brigantine floated out to sea, twisting in the wind like the seed of a sycamore. Nikandr leaned forward and kissed the mast, silently thanking the ship for its kindness.

By the time he'd climbed down to the deck, the *Bhadyar* had moved directly above them. The havaqiram above was skilled—Nikandr knew this much—for he was able to match both the pace and the slow spin of their ship. Nikandr and the others grabbed and steadied the rope ladders the Maharraht lowered, and in short order they were up and onto the deck of the *Bhadyar*.

Nikandr sat in Soroush's cabin at the rear of the ship, sipping bitter araq from a sandalwood cup.

Soroush had asked him here once Nikandr's men were all safe. He'd given him the araq to warm him up, but then had gone to see to the safety of the other ships. Nikandr had never been inside a cabin such as this. He'd been involved with the capture of four Maharraht ships; three of them had previously been Grand Duchy ships and one had been a ship built by the Maharraht themselves, but he'd never been inside one of the kapitans' cabins. Colorful glass baubles hung from the ceiling, their colors mirrored by the carpets layering the floor. In one corner, a shisha was held in place by twine, and next to it was a shallow box with a hinged lid that no doubt held a variety of tabbaq.

Soroush returned some time after Nikandr's second cupful, and by then Nikandr was finally beginning to feel the effects of the strong, fragrant liquor. "Your man from the cliff is safe," he said, "but we could not find the one who fell."

Nikandr nodded grimly. He wished they could have gone to the base of the cliffs to search for Mahrik, but it would have been foolish to do so with the storm as strong as it was. Most likely he'd fallen against the rocks below, or if he'd somehow made it to the sea he would quickly have been overwhelmed by the crashing waves.

"My thanks to you for saving us," Nikandr said in Mahndi.

Soroush sat in the kapitan's chair and poured himself a cup of araq. His turban and his beard twinkled with the gleam of melting snow. "A pity Mahrik could not be saved."

Nikandr looked at him closely, surprised he remembered Mahrik's name. He wondered just how heartfelt those words were, but he could sense no deception, and it made him wonder just how much the experience on Mirashadal and Rafsuhan had changed Soroush. This was a man that had led the Maharraht for years. He had always seemed ruthless, steadfast in his belief that for the Aramahn to be free the Landed must die. And now here he was, lamenting—genuinely—a Landed windsman he hardly knew.

"How did you find us?" Nikandr asked.

Soroush, staring beyond his cup of araq, took long moments to formulate his response. "We were skirting the edge of the Empire's lands when we came upon a bird. A gallows crow."

"A black bird with a white hood."

"*Yeh.*" Soroush's eyes were distant, as if he were reliving the moment. "It landed on a shroud and stared directly at me. One of the crew tried to scare it away, but it remained. Only when a musket was trained on it did it take flight, but it returned shortly thereafter and landed near the helm. Again the men wanted to kill it—fearful it was a bird sent by the Matri—but I forbade them." Soroush's voice became softer, almost reverent. "I came to the helm, and the bird pecked at the levers. I realized it was always pecking at the leftmost. Slowly, I pushed it inward, and the crow cawed furiously, but as I pulled it out, and the ship turned windward, it remained silent. Until we were heading on the bearing that took us directly over your position." Soroush paused, shaking his head. "It must have been one of the Matri, but it never spoke. Why would this be?"

Nikandr shrugged. "I saw it as well, less than an hour before you came upon us. I thought I felt one of the Matri as well, but it was faint. Very faint. And then the bird left."

"Whoever she was, you owe her your life. We would not have come upon you in the direction we were headed."

"But why? Why are you here?"

"We've been skirting the Sea of Khurkhan for over a week, and the days before that we were watching the islands to the east."

While giving Soroush a questioning look, Nikandr took a swig of his araq, swirling it around in his mouth before swallowing.

"We had hoped to find the Hratha," Soroush said. "After leaving you on Uyadensk we returned to Rafsuhan, but found almost no one. They had murdered any they could find before leaving the island."

"What of Muqallad and the children?"

Soroush grit his jaw. There were tears welling in his eyes, but he blinked them away. "They were no longer children. They were akhoz, and of them we could find no sign. Those few that survived by hiding in the woods said that Muqallad left the island the day after the ritual."

"With the Hratha?"

Soroush shook his head. "Thabash returned to Siafyan and there gathered more ships and men. And then he headed northwest, across the Sea of Khurkhan."

Nikandr thought back to the glint he'd seen on the sea days before. It must have been Thabash and his men. "They're headed for Galahesh," Nikandr said, knowing it was true.

Soroush nodded and finished his araq, his lips pulling back from the bite of it. "I believe they go to meet Muqallad."

"And to find the final piece of the Atalayina."

"Perhaps," Soroush said, "but they will not find it."

"What do you mean?"

While drawing in a deep breath, Soroush glanced toward the door, then down at his desk. He seemed to come to some decision, for he leaned down, opened the drawer, and retrieved from it a satchel of the softest goat leather. After setting this on the desk and closing the drawer, he opened the satchel's drawstring and pulled out a stone that was unmistakable. He set it on the desk near Nikandr. The knock it made against the wood sounded as though it were made of lead, not stone.

Nikandr picked it up. It was indeed heavy, more like pure gold than stone. The copper lines that ran through the blue stone lent it a raw beauty and an undeniable feeling of age, as if the stories about the fates having created it along with the worlds were true. He remembered Bersuq as he'd held the other two pieces—sisters to this one—above his head. He remembered Bersuq's *will* as he'd kept himself from crying out, until eventually it had become too much and he'd released his pain to the uncaring sky.

He was also uncomfortably aware of what this stone would mean to Soroush. His brother had died in fusing the other two for Muqallad. Nikandr wasn't sure in those waning moments whether Bersuq had questioned his decision. Surely he must have, and if *he* had thought this way, what must *Soroush* think? If he believed Bersuq had been misled, it would only fuel Soroush's determination.

"How did you come by it?" Nikandr asked.

Before Soroush could respond, soft footsteps approached the cabin door. The door opened, and in stepped a woman in robes of blood red. She wore a simple headdress of silver and pearls, and at the center of her brow rested a stone of alabaster, softly glowing in the dim light. She was striking, especially her eyes, which were bright and piercing, as if she could understand one's very nature with but a glance.

She stared down at the stone Nikandr held in his hands. One of her hands was heavily bandaged, but with the other she stepped forward and snatched it from him. "You would share this with *him*?"

Soroush leaned back in his chair, as calm as a frozen lake. "You would rather I kept it hidden?"

"*Yeh*! He has no right to even look upon it."

As she said these words, Nikandr realized he knew this woman. "You are Ushai. You were once a disciple of Fahroz."

She glanced at Nikandr, then turned her gaze back on Soroush. There was deep betrayal in her face, more than this stone could account for. And then Nikandr understood. She and Soroush were lovers. Or had been at one time.

"Whether you want to admit it or not," Soroush said, "he has done much for us."

"We don't need him."

Soroush shrugged and looked to Nikandr. "The fates have seen fit to bring us together once more. Who am I to deny them?" Ushai made to speak, but Soroush raised his hand. "Enough. He is here, and he will help us when we reach Galahesh."

Ushai's face turned to one of disgust. "He is a forgotten prince, lost among the seas. He can do nothing to help."

Soroush stared up to Ushai and held out his hand. Ushai seemed angry at first, but then she softened and gently laid the Atalayina into the palm of Soroush's hand.

"We shall see, Ushai." Soroush stared into the depths of the Atalayina and smiled briefly. "We shall see what he can do."

Three days later—days filled with merciless winds and snow and hail—they approached the shores of Galahesh. Nikandr and Styophan stood at the bow of the *Bhadyar*, staring out into the gray fog that lay ahead of the ship. They flew low, close enough to see the white-tipped waves of the sea.

Nikandr was tense—tense because of the weather and the landing that would take place a little more than an hour from now. Soroush had brought seventy fighting men, a dozen of them qiram. They would land far to the north of Baressa and head south, some scouting ahead to find Muqallad's hiding place, which they hoped would be somewhere near the Spar.

Visibility was down to a quarter-league, and the fog was becoming thicker. More than this, there was a source of discomfort in Nikandr's chest. He'd woken with it this morning, and it had taken him some time to realize it was due to Nasim. He was to their southeast, somewhere on Galahesh.

The burning at the center of his chest told Nikandr something was wrong. It was akin to the feelings years ago on Uyadensk and Duzol, but this was different in that he'd felt nothing like it since Nasim had been healed. He didn't know what this meant, but he was sure Nasim was in danger.

"The Spar will not be easy to bring down." Styophan was leaning against the bulwarks, staring aft toward the three trailing ships.

"The keystones, Styophan. If we can destroy one, I hope it will be enough."

"As you say, My Lord, but if it's as simple as that, the Kamarisi will not leave it untended."

"*Da*," Nikandr replied, "but we will try."

Styophan, as if taking silent inventory of the men they had at their disposal, chose not to reply, but it was clear he considered their mission suicide.

Soroush, after passing out final orders, joined Nikandr and Styophan and looked beyond the sails and into the fog.

"Where will we land?" Nikandr asked.

They had decided that attacking the Spar directly—while containing an element of surprise—would be unwise. They had munitions aboard the ships, and they might fire them all at one point along the massive structure, but it was still questionable whether this would be enough. It would most likely only damage the bridge, and that was an unacceptable outcome.

Soroush pointed out into the fog. "There is a deep vale ten leagues northwest of the Spar. We'll moor the ships there and head inland toward Vihrosh. Bahett, the Kaymakam of Galahesh, keeps several small storehouses filled with munitions. One is particularly vulnerable. It is there that we will go."

Revulsion flared up within Nikandr. This was the sort of information the Maharraht painstakingly collected. No doubt they had similar details for each of the Grand Duchy's cities. That it helped Nikandr now didn't change the fact that Soroush and his followers were still enemies of Anuskaya.

Soroush must have known this as well, for he was watching Nikandr closely, as if he expected Nikandr to say something of it, as if *he too* knew they were still enemies and that if they lived beyond the days ahead their hostilities would resume.

It reminded Nikandr of their time on Rafsuhan, when the two of them were still feeling one another out. It reminded him, too, of Soroush's abduction. "Why did Muqallad take you?"

"What?"

"On Rafsuhan. He took you and left me. Why?"

He shrugged. "Who knows the mind of Muqallad?"

"What did he want with you?"

"Can you not guess?"

"My guesses are worth nothing."

Soroush's jaw set, and his eyes flickered with anger. "Why he took me is of no consequence."

Nikandr's first instinct was to bark back a reply, but the two of them, if not allies, had at least come to understand one another, and it was through this lens that Nikandr began to understand. "He wanted the hearts of the Maharraht."

Soroush's expression turned dark.

"He wanted the hearts of the Maharraht," Nikandr repeated, "and Bersuq wasn't delivering them."

"My brother was loyal to his people."

Nikandr bowed his head. "He was loyal, but also torn."

"As I am torn." Soroush said it so flatly that it took Nikandr aback. Muqallad had no doubt tried to convince Soroush that his cause was not merely worthwhile, but righteous. And Soroush had listened. Even now, there was doubt in his eyes.

A distant boom drew Nikandr's attention. It drew Soroush's as well. It had come three points off the windward bow. Another boom sounded moments later, and more as they continued on their southeastward heading.

"Come about," Soroush ordered.

They did, followed by the three trailing ships.

But the sounds of battle continued to approach. They could hear the calls of men now, orders shouted in haste and fear. Given the cannons' rate of fire it was clear that a ship was being chased by at least two others.

Soroush used hand signals to pass orders to his men—an upheld fist for absolute silence, an upturned palm to the pilot to bring the ship higher, three tight circles with the index finger to bring guns to the ready. The signals were similar to those used by the windsmen of Anuskaya, used when silence was absolutely necessary.

It was a near thing, but they were rising fast enough that they would most likely avoid being seen, but then Nikandr heard a voice in the fog, a call made in desperation to his men.

It was the voice of Grigory.

CHAPTER SEVENTY-FIVE

Nikandr stood at the bow of the *Bhadyar*, his eyes fixed down toward the sea where the sounds of battle still raged.

He considered leaving Grigory to his fate—it was important they reach land without being discovered by the Hratha or the Kamarisi's men, and Grigory's betrayal still stung, more than he'd realized until now—but he couldn't do it. He couldn't abandon his countrymen.

"Soroush, we must turn back."

"*Neh*, it cannot be risked."

The report of a cannon shook the air.

"They are my *blood*."

"I'm sorry, son of Iaros."

"We must rescue them! They can help us!"

"What will help is to land and to worry about Muqallad. Blood or not, the Atalayina cannot be risked."

Nikandr's desperation turned to anger. He was ready to fight if need be, but as he stood there staring into Soroush's stony eyes, he realized that his touch to Adhiya had returned. He could feel his havahezhan once more. Where it had gone he didn't know, but for the time being he didn't care. He drew upon it, more sharply than he had for some time.

The winds responded, snapping the sails and pulling the *Bhadyar* off the course the Maharraht qiram had set for them.

Soroush, realizing what was happening, pulled the khanjar, a dark length of steel, from his belt and stalked forward. "Stop, son of Iaros."

Styophan shouted, "*Kozyol!*" and rushed forward to meet Soroush, but before he could take three steps, two Maharraht rushed in and grabbed his arms.

The winds increased. The ships slowed.

Soroush drew his arm back. The earrings along his ruined ear glinted, even in the dim light. He could easily swing it and cut Nikandr's head from his shoulders. "Stop!"

"I will not!"

Soroush breathed heavily. His shoulders heaved; his eyes were aflame. At the boom of a cannon, much closer now, he glanced over to the gunwales. The battle was raging just below them. It would be easy now to slip behind the enemy, especially in the fog that had continued to thicken, but any moment now someone on those ships would hear the rhythmic pounding of the *Bhadyar's* canvas.

Soroush, eyes still aflame, lowered the sword and stepped so close to Nikandr that they were practically nose-to-nose. "This is a foolish choice, son of Iaros."

"I cannot leave them."

He nodded and spoke so that only Nikandr could hear. "I know."

And then he spun around and sheathed his sword and began sending hand signals to the rest of the crew.

Nikandr immediately released the call of his havahezhan. Though the spirit obeyed, it did so only reluctantly. Instead of drawing on the world, it drew instead upon Nikandr, made him cough, reminding him of nothing more than the wasting disease he'd had years ago.

Orders were relayed to the other ships via hooded lanterns as the Maharraht crewmen prepared the ship. They were a crack crew, these men, nearly a match for the best crews Nikandr had sailed with.

The ships swooped down like eagles. They found one ship in pursuit, and then another, both of them crewed by men wearing the black robes of the Hratha.

As the battle was joined, Nikandr struck the bell in a sequence that he hoped Grigory would hear. It was a call to allied ships that help was needed. If Grigory or any of his men heard it, they would hopefully understand that help had arrived.

Nikandr felt winds blowing against the ship—the havaqiram calling upon their spirits to delay them. Nikandr worked against them, keeping the winds as steady as he could. They tried to fly above the enemy to drop fire pots upon their ships, but the Hratha—like Soroush's men—were too cunning. These men had been fighting Bolgravya and Nodhvyansk for decades; they were battle tested, and it showed.

For nearly an hour they tried unsuccessfully to catch them at a disadvantage. Even with four ships, they couldn't manage to pin them down, and suddenly the *Bhadyar* was caught too far from their allies.

As the Hratha ships approached—one to the landward side and one to windward—Nikandr realized he could see only a few crewmen among the rigging.

"Get down!" Nikandr called.

Just as he ducked behind the starward foremast, the Hratha rose from behind the bulwarks, muskets at the ready.

The crack of musket fire rang across the deck on both sides. Cries of pain rose above it, some cut short by added fire.

The Maharraht crew manning the two small cannons was decimated. One returned fire, but it was hasty, the cannon ill-aimed.

"Boarders!"

Nikandr looked over the edge of the ship. Along the enemy ship's seaward yards were four Hratha. As Nikandr watched, they swung down and across the open space between their ship and the *Bhadyar*. One of them had a stone of opal that glowed, making it clear he was bonded to a dhoshahezhan. All four landed in the *Bhadyar's* seaward rigging and were lost from sight.

It was a risky maneuver, but smart if it worked, for the seaward sails were the least manned. They might try to set fire to the ship from there, or cut what rigging they could before men could arrive to stop them.

"Come," Nikandr said to Styophan.

The two of them slipped over the side and dropped to the landward shrouds. They moved quickly along the rigging, seeing one of the Hratha sawing at the ropes of the seaward mainmast. Nikandr hooked his arm around a rope and slid along it to the crow's nest.

They were just below the Hratha.

Seeing them approach, the lone Hratha stopped sawing at the ropes long enough to pull a pistol from his cloth belt and fire it.

Nikandr felt it tug his cherkesska just beneath his rump.

Another pistol shot came from Styophan at Nikandr's side. Blood welled up along the Hratha's ribs, below his heart. He dropped his pistol and fell groaning from the rigging and plummeted into the fog.

Nikandr scanned the underside of the ship for the other Hratha. Three more Maharraht had joined him and Styophan, but of the enemy he could see no sign.

And then he looked straight up.

The mainmast had a ladder that led from the crow's nest, along the mast, and through the hull and into the lowest deck. It would normally be secured.

But the dhoshaqiram...

He could use his spirit to work at the wood, to warp it and allow him entrance.

But why? Why would they steal into this ship of all ships when so many men stood against them?

And then it was crystal clear.

"Come!" he shouted to Styophan.

And he took to the ladder, climbing as quickly as he could.

"Tell Soroush!" Nikandr shouted to the Maharraht, waving them back up to the deck. "They've come for the Atalayina!"

They nodded and climbed up toward the deck as Nikandr reached the dim interior of the ship.

He could see little, but he pulled his own pistol—

—and managed to raise it just in time to block the sword thrust of the Hratha that stood over him on the ship's lower deck.

He heard something click on the pistol as the blade struck. Nikandr aimed and pulled the trigger, but nothing happened.

The Hratha, expecting the pistol to fire, was momentarily stunned. But he recovered quickly. He pulled his sword back and swung down fiercely. He was cramped by the low ceiling, however, and the motion was unnaturally compact.

Nikandr slipped as far as he could to his left. The sword bit into the wood just to his right.

The Hratha was close now, allowing Nikandr to reach forward and grab his leggings. He pulled with all his might and the Hratha tumbled forward. Nikandr pulled his kindjal from his belt and stabbed it into the man's throat. Blood spurted and immediately the Hratha's hands went to his neck, trying to stop the flow of blood.

Nikandr pushed him away, allowing himself and Styophan to gain the deck.

They moved quickly to the stairs, but just as they reached the top, where the men slept, they heard the sounds of ringing steel above. A musket was fired as they climbed the stairs toward the main deck. Then another, as men shouted in Mahndi, "Stop them! Stop them!"

Nikandr made it back to deck just in time to see the two Hratha running along the windward mainmast. They moved with sure steps, as if their feet were glued to the wood—an effect, no doubt, of the qiram's bonded hezhan.

A half-dozen Maharraht, including Soroush, were lined up along the windward gunwales, each of them bearing muskets. One fired, catching the Hratha that was closest to the ship, but immediately after the boom of a cannon came and grape shot tore into them and the wood of the gunwale. The shot was not well aimed, but it caught four of them. Blood and bits of wood flew outward from the men gathered there.

As cries of pain fell across the deck, Nikandr rushed to the gunwales. Another Hratha ship was passing just below them along the windward side.

Nikandr dropped as he noticed, from the corner of his eye, the forward cannon pointed up toward him.

A boom shook the ship, and more grape shot bit into the bulwarks, spraying his side with splinters of wood.

He made it to his knees in time to see the dhoshaqiram, a knife in one hand, leap from the end of the windward mainmast. He flew downward and used the knife to punch into the other ship's mizzen mainsail. Downward he slipped, slowing himself with the cut of his knife against the canvas. The sail flapped free as he reached the foot of the sail and crashed against the deck.

He held his ankle tightly, grimacing in pain, but when he looked back up at the *Bhadyar*, there was a clear note of satisfaction in his eyes.

They fired more muskets. They fired their cannons as well, but the Hratha had caught them completely off guard.

Soroush, whose left arm was bloody, stormed over to Nikandr. "What have you done?"

Nikandr could only stare.

"He's given them the Atalayina."

Nikandr looked over and found Ushai, standing near the helm. Her expression was one of anger and cold hatred.

And he couldn't blame her. All he could do was stare, and nod.

"You're right," he said softly. "I've given them the final piece."

They looked for the Hratha ships, but they had had superior angle and speed. It was soon clear the enemy would not be caught. With the fog as thick as it was, they could not give chase, so they turned back. Soroush was still loath to return for Grigory, but the chance to add more fighting men to theirs was too important to pass up.

It took a little more than an hour of ringing their brass bell to hear Grigory's reply. As they approached, Nikandr saw how badly the *Yarost* had been damaged. There were many men on deck. More than there would usually be. Most likely—however they'd managed it—Grigory had ferried as many men as he could to his ship before fleeing.

As his skiff drifted in and Nikandr threw the mooring ropes over, the crewmen eyed him with a mixture of wonder and awe. He had expected perhaps distrust or anger, but not a single windsman looked at him this way. Except for Grigory.

Grigory stalked forward across the deck and met Nikandr as he stepped down onto deck. Grigory looked tired, he looked angry, but the thing that made Nikandr worried was the fact that he looked embarrassed.

"How did you find us?" Grigory asked.

Nikandr stared over Grigory's shoulder to Avayom Kirilov, a man who—despite flying in battle against Khalakovo five years ago—had been a true soldier and a stout kapitan for both Stasa Bolgravya and his son, Konstantin, after Stasa's death. Avayom looked to Nikandr with an expression of apology, but Grigory was his commander. He could do nothing but pull his hands behind his cherkesska and wait for Grigory to play this out.

"Would you rather I hadn't found you at all?"

Grigory's face reddened. "You were flying with Maharraht ships. We saw you descend."

"They have allied with us. They would not have Muqallad destroy Galahesh and the islands with it."

Spit flew as Grigory shouted, "And I would?"

"Grigory," Nikandr said softly. "Let us retire to your cabin. There are things we should discuss."

"What we must *discuss* are your traitorous actions. First, you *stole* this ship from Kiravashya's eyrie."

Nikandr looked to the helm. Behind it, at a post made for the purpose, was a rook. He had seen it as he approached the ship, but he thought it merely a rook ready to be used, separated by a distance too great for the Matri to assume it and communicate with Grigory. But now he realized the storm must have died enough for the Matri—most likely Radia Vostroma or Iyana Dhalingrad—to tell him what had happened on Kiravashya.

"Your brother gave me that ship."

"A right he no longer had, Khalakovo. It was a ship needed in the defense of the realm, a ship he had already given to the Grand Duke in our time of need."

"With his own, a duke can do what he will. Is it not so?"

Grigory raised his voice until he was practically shouting. "And though I ordered you to guard our ships, you've come, and you've done so arm-in-arm with the Maharraht."

"There are strange things afoot, Grigory."

"Strange things, indeed, but I tell you this, Nikandr Iaroslov, I will suffer no traitors on this ship."

Nikandr stepped forward until the two of them were close enough to strike blows. "I am no traitor, Bolgravya."

Before Nikandr knew it Grigory had pulled the kindjal from its sheath at his belt. The knife shook in his hands, and his eyes were wild as he stalked forward.

Nikandr backed away, ready to grab for Grigory's arm should he lunge. Styophan was ready to jump in and grab Grigory, but Nikandr waved him away. If he did that, there would be no turning back.

"My Lord Prince!" This was from Avayom. "There is another way to solve this."

Grigory's eyes lost none of their craze, but he stopped. He waited for Avayom to continue.

"*Bazh na bazh*," Avayom said. "Settle it once and for all and be done with it."

Grigory looked to Avayom, and then back to Nikandr.

Bazh na bazh was a duel—pistols, usually, followed by swords if neither had been felled. Nikandr was confused why Avayom would offer this solution—Grigory could, after all, merely order Nikandr belowdecks as he had before, with no consequences—but then Nikandr realized that perhaps Avayom *wanted* Nikandr to win. Grigory was known to be a decent shot, but in his state he would probably miss. And if it came to swords, there was little doubt as to the outcome. It made Nikandr wonder just what had gone on since Grigory had abandoned them on the cliffs.

Grigory, after glancing to the faces of the men around the ship, nodded sharply. There was really no choice in the matter—not any longer. Once Avayom had stated that the challenge could be made, it was implied that Grigory would accept. If he didn't, he would lose face, and that, for whatever reason, was not something Grigory would allow himself to do.

Nikandr nodded as well.

In the minutes that followed, the two of them were each allowed to prepare their pistols. Grigory loaded his carefully. Nikandr had to replace the flint that had been lost on the *Bhadyar*. It was still loaded, so he merely lifted the frizzen and added powder to the pan before closing it once more.

The crew cleared the windward side of the ship. Nikandr and Grigory paced to opposite ends. They turned and faced one another, each holding their weapon toward the sky.

Nikandr refused to lower his pistol. Grigory held his steady as well, waiting for Nikandr to fire first. Nikandr would not, however. If Grigory felt the need for this duel to continue, he would need to take the opening shot.

Realizing Nikandr's intent, Grigory lowered his pistol and aimed.

Nikandr's heart pounded in his chest.

Grigory fired.

The report of the pistol resounded over the ship.

The shot struck the bulwarks behind Nikandr.

Nikandr released his breath, realizing how mad this was.

He lowered his own pistol and aimed wide of Grigory. When he pulled the trigger, the pan flashed and the shot flew harmlessly over Grigory's right shoulder.

In a moment Grigory had pulled his shashka and was stalking forward.

Nikandr pulled his own and the two of them met amidships. Nikandr beat off a flurry of hasty sword strokes. He retreated as Grigory expended a furious amount of energy. Their blades rang, and for a moment he wondered what Soroush must be thinking, hearing these sounds coming to them through the fog.

Nikandr baited Grigory over and over again, and eventually Grigory accepted. He lunged too deeply, and Nikandr sidestepped the thrust and brought the pommel of his sword across Grigory's forehead.

Grigory was dazed, but he managed to nick Nikandr's leg while falling backward.

Nikandr grit his teeth and stomped his boot onto Grigory's sword. He dropped to one knee, keeping the blade firmly pressed against the deck and allowed Grigory to grab his sword hand. With both of Grigory's hands occupied, Nikandr brought his fist down and across Grigory's cheek. Grigory's eyes fluttered for a moment.

Nikandr struck him again, the sound of it resounding through the deck. On the third strike, Grigory's eyes went up in his head and his arms went slack.

CHAPTER SEVENTY-SIX

Atiana rode behind Sihaş on his pony over a snow-covered plain. After a night that had seemed endless, the sun was rising, and Atiana could see through the morning mist a keep that stood at the edge of the tall white cliffs.

It brought Atiana no relief whatsoever. They had ridden throughout the night, weaving through the cold streets of Baressa, skirting the Shattering and heading west as quickly as they could manage. They heard sounds of pursuit several times throughout the harrowing ride, but when their pursuers had come too close, the gallows crow had led them safely through danger. Once they had reached the city's outskirts, they had found the streets not just empty and silent, but eerily so.

They may have found shelter, but Atiana's mind was still afire. It was clear that Ishkyna wasn't completely lost, and yet Atiana knew there was something deeply, deeply wrong. Ishkyna wasn't acting normally, and she appeared to have risen in power sevenfold. To do what she'd done on the walls of the kasir and throughout the city… Ishkyna could never have done this. She was too undisciplined. Too uninterested in the aether to plumb its depths to such a degree.

But even Saphia Khalakovo could not have done what Ishkyna had done with apparent ease, as if she were *part* of the aether.

Perhaps she was. Atiana couldn't know for sure, but she doubted Ishkyna had found her body lying in the upper reaches of the kasir.

Nyet, Ishkyna had changed, perhaps for good.

As they reached an escarpment and began taking a narrow but gently sloped path down toward the keep, Sihaş glanced back at her. He'd been doing such things ever since there had been enough light. The look in his eyes was not one of distrust, but of judgment. It was a weighing look.

He doesn't trust me, she thought. He was wondering whether she should be left so that he could return to the Kamarisi and free his lord. He might come to the conclusion that killing her would be wisest. Her mind went wild with the possibilities, but Sihaş merely turned back and guided their pony onward.

His thoughts were anything but misguided. Ishkyna had revealed the truth. She had said that Atiana was still under Sariya's spell, that she'd been under it for some time now—ever since the two of them had communed with one another in the aether—and yet, even knowing this, Atiana wasn't sure. Ishkyna could be wrong, could she not? Atiana had been so close to Sariya. She had *known* her mind. Known it fully. As well as she knew her own.

She shook her head vigorously.

Had she been doing this all along? She couldn't remember.

Sihaş glanced back.

"I'm fine," she snapped in Anuskayan.

His face grew incrementally more grim.

"I'm fine," she said, softer, this time in Yrstanlan.

"You're troubled."

"Of course I'm troubled."

"I only mean to say it's understandable."

She didn't respond, and after a time he cleared his throat. "The Kamarisi. I don't know how I can reach him."

She didn't know Sihaş well, but she knew him well enough to know that this was a plea for help, for understanding. He was a man of cold steel and hot blood. He knew nothing of the Al-Aqim and the Matri and their powers of the dark.

Atiana's attention was caught by movement near the top of the keep. Over the edge of the cliff, carried by the updrafts, was the gallows crow, its wings spread wide, motionless as it glided back and forth. For a moment it seemed like pure joy.

Atiana hoped it was.

Sihaş noticed her shift in attention and turned to look.

"We will speak with her," Atiana said, "and we will see what can be done for the Kamarisi."

They reached the keep, and Sihaş's men took the ponies. Irkadiy joined Sihaş and Atiana on the second floor of the keep, a room filled with four beds and several old wooden chests. No sooner had they levered the lone window of the room open than the gallows crow flapped to the stones of the sill and rested there, taking in each of them in turn.

It flapped down to the floor, cawing once, long and lonely.

"Do not—" The crow cawed several times and pecked at the musty carpeting, kicking up dust to cloud the low sunlight coming in through the window.

"Do not speak her name."

Atiana felt her fingers tingle, felt her insides twist.

Do not speak her name. She meant Ishkyna, of course. Her sister was lost, and by the ancients, Atiana was not even allowed to speak her name.

"The Kamarisi moves to secure the city," the crow continued.

"From whom?"

"The men of Anuskaya have arrived by sea. One hundred sotnik or more, led by Iaros Khalakovo. They've brought ponies and cannons; even the hussar have come. They've already taken Baressa's southern quarter, and they're moving now to secure the Shattering."

Sihaş opened his eyes wide. "Ten thousand men..." The look on his face was one of wonder and respect and no small amount of relief. "Perhaps there's hope yet."

Ten thousand, Atiana repeated to herself. It would leave the islands defenseless, not only against the Maharraht, but against the hordes of diseased and dying that were rioting among the cities of Kiravashya and the other islands. Surely Iaros and the other Dukes realized how dangerous it was to leave Vostroma unattended, but this was still a surprise.

"There is more. The Hratha have arrived as well. They, along with Muqallad and the akhoz, have taken the old keep on the eastern end of Vihrosh." The bird turned a cold eye on Atiana. "They're preparing something, and it will happen soon, perhaps today, no later than tonight."

"What?" Irkadiy said. "What are they preparing?"

"They have the third piece of the Atalayina. They will fuse it, or attempt to."

"Can we stop them?" Atiana asked.

"Not by force of men," the crow said, flapping its wings and craning its neck up toward the ancient wooden beams running along the ceiling. "Bahett's men, and the Kamarisi's, have moved to intercept the army of Anuskaya."

Upon saying the word *Anuskaya*, the crow devolved into a slow cawing. It sounded like the wracking cough of an old woman on her deathbed.

Atiana felt a tear come unbidden to her eye. Dear Ishkyna, to not even be able to speak the name of your homeland...

"Then how?" Atiana asked sharply, not only to draw back the attention of the crow, but to strengthen her own resolve.

The crow was silent for a time. It seemed purposefully to be looking away from Atiana.

"*How?*" Atiana said, louder.

"There may be a way." The crow met her eye with a baleful stare. "I believe Sariya needs you. The wounds inflicted by Ushai in the tower were deep. She is weakened, and can no longer complete the ritual as she planned."

Sihaş leaned forward. "What does she—"

"Silence!" the rook cawed.

Atiana held her hand up, a request for Sihaş and Irkadiy to remain silent. "What does she plan?" Atiana asked.

"She and Muqallad will come to the Spar, but she can no longer draw upon the aether as she once did. You can get close to her, for she desires your power. She would use it to do what she cannot."

"And if she cannot have me?"

"Come," the crow said with some of Ishkyna's biting tone. "You know better. The noose is tightening. It will be done in a day whether they have you or not."

"But if they cannot complete the ritual—"

"They will still do it in the hopes that indaraqiram can be brought about. But believe me when I say that she would welcome you. I can bring you close, but it is not without danger."

Atiana knew the danger well. It was all she'd thought about since riding out from Baressa. If she returned, she would once again fall under Sariya's spell.

"If we can," the crow continued, "we will deceive her. It is the only way you can come close enough."

"Close enough to kill her, you mean."

The crow twitched and released a caw that sounded like low laughter. "Is there any other choice?"

"How, then? How will we find her?"

"With you in tow, the Kamarisi will welcome Sihaş with open arms. And then he will take you to the Spar."

"I don't like it," Sihaş said.

"Nor do I!" echoed Irkadiy. "My Lady Princess, we should go to our countrymen. Let us join the push to take Baressa and the Spar and let Sihaş and his men work from behind the Kamarisi's lines."

Sihaş, his dark brows pinched, glanced aside at Irkadiy. "He may be right. The time may have come to admit that the Kamarisi can no longer be saved, and if that is so, you would be safer with your people."

"If you do this"—the feathers along the back of the crow's neck crested—"any chance to come near to the Al-Aqim will be lost, and mark my words: the battle will never reach them in time."

Atiana stood and moved to the window. The cold morning air drifted in through the gaps. She could not see Baressa—it lay hidden behind the ridge—but she could see two columns of smoke rising to the east. No doubt the battle lay there. She wanted nothing more than to go to her people, to return to a place of safety.

The wind kicked up, rattling the pane momentarily, drawing her attention to the straits. She could see the tall cliffs on the far side and far below the white, churning water. The southern end of the Spar lay hidden by the turn of land, but she could see the northern landing and its elegant, towering arches that defied belief. They looked small from this distance. They seemed less threatening, as if her worries had been born of a dream. It felt—now that the sun was rising—as though her worries would fade, as nightmares do.

But this was no dream. This was no figment of her imagination to be cast aside like childish fears.

This was deadly serious, and she could no more abandon her cause than she could abandon her people.

"I will go to Sariya," she said at last.

Irkadiy rose to his feet. "My Lady—"

"There is no choice," Atiana said. "If I return, our last, best chance will have been lost. I will go, and I hope you will join me." This she said to Sihaş. Irkadiy would go with her, she knew, to the ends of the earth.

Sihaş stood as well. He glanced to the window, and he too seemed to take note of the smoke rising in Baressa.

But then he met Atiana's eyes and nodded. "I will go," he said, "and we will see what can be done."

As the men left to prepare, the crow flapped up to the windowsill. Atiana swung the window wide, and the smell of the sea came to her, strong and vibrant. The crow did not leave, however. It shivered for a moment and performed a strange dance, hopping on one foot, and then the other. Atiana could only assume Ishkyna's control was slipping away now that she was alone with Atiana.

"There's one more thing," the crow said, and cawed several times, low and sad.

"What?"

"Your man is come."

"What? Who?"

"Nik—" It cawed again. "Nischka." Leaning out beyond the sill, the crow dipped its head, pointing westward. "He flies even now."

And then the crow leaned out and winged above the tall snowy grass and out over the straits, cawing all the while.

CHAPTER SEVENTY-SEVEN

It felt strange to return to the streets of Baressa so soon after leaving them, but it was a different day, and it felt like a different time. The battle to the south of the city grew and by the time midday had struck, it had grown until it sounded like it had encompassed a good half of the city. She saw no battles, but she could hear it, cannons and the cries of men. She could smell the gunpowder on the wind.

As transfixed as they were by the battle to the southeast, Atiana often found herself looking westward, toward Nikandr. Part of her wished she had her soulstone, if only to grasp it and to ask the ancients to spare him.

Sihaş set a course toward the Spar. The streets were nearly empty. Only once in a great while did they see old men or women, or sometimes children, peek at them from behind corners or from the insides of their darkened homes. They came eventually to a line of men who were setting up hastily constructed barricades of rough stone, but Sihaş, showing his ring of office, was allowed to pass with little more than a cross look from the Galaheshi soldier who'd stopped them.

Shortly after passing, a whistle alerted them. Another four men on ponies waved to Sihaş. They were dressed in the same uniform as Sihaş, red janissary coats with unadorned black turbans, boar tusk cartridges on their bandoliers and gleaming swords at their sides. They rode with an ease that made it clear these were seasoned men, and from the way they greeted Sihaş and the rest of his men, she knew they were part of the Kamarisi's personal guard. They met and moved further away from the Galaheshi soldiers to speak in peace.

"Where is the Kamarisi?" Sihaş asked.

"He left the kasir early this morning with handpicked janissaries. They rode across the bridge and haven't been seen since."

"Then that is where we go."

The soldier, a man ten years Sihaş's senior, smiled and bowed his head. "As you say, My Lord."

When they reached the Spar, foot soldiers hailed them. "We were told to find you," one of them said. He was a heavyset man with a limp, and he stared at them all as if assessing them, as one might an enemy.

"They know," Atiana whispered to Sihaş.

He heard, for she felt him stiffen, but he did not turn his head away from the soldier standing in their way. "Where are they?" Sihaş called to him.

He pointed to the far side of the straits. The city of Vihrosh, her stone buildings and red-tile roofs, were brightly lit by the noontime sun. "The Kamarisi and the Kaymakam of Galahesh wait for you at the gate to the old city."

Sihaş nodded, spurring his pony on.

The nine of them rode over the bridge, the hooves of their ponies clopping loudly in the relative silence. The smell of the sea grew stronger. The winds blew upward, swirling over the bridge, chilling them as they distanced themselves from the soldiers who eyed their passing with altogether too much interest.

"I don't like this," Atiana said.

"This is the way to Sariya."

"They know we're coming."

"Did you think we could hide from the Al-Aqim forever?"

They reached the center of the bridge, where two squat stone towers sat, one on either side of the road. There, upon the central keystones, was the marking of blood that Atiana had seen only in the dark of the aether. It was dark brown, almost black. She could feel her nostrils flare, feel her gut churn at the memory of watching her father's cold-blooded execution.

Again, as it had so often before, the image of the sword swinging down against his neck came to her. I will avenge you, she said to him, hoping he was near, hoping he could hear her. She could feel the touch of the aether, but could not sense her father. It made her feel as cold as a grave in a long-forgotten cemetery.

She looked to Irkadiy, who rode behind one of the other men. He nodded, granting her some small amount of strength. She wanted to turn back, to find another way that wouldn't allow their enemies to take them as they wanted, but she could think of no other path. She had to get to Sariya. She would simply have to trust Ishkyna once they did. She nodded back to Irkadiy, telling him they would go on. He tried to smile, but he managed only a nervous twitching of his lips that reminded her of a much younger man—a callow youth holding a musket for the first time, a soldier new to the cough of the cannon—but then he swallowed, and the look was gone.

They continued on across the great bridge. Far below, the straits seethed, frothing white. The Spar was wide, but not so wide that Atiana felt safe on a pony with the wind as strong as it was, and so she was glad when at last they reached the other side. As they passed, the janissaries that held this side of the Spar merely touched their fingers to their foreheads and bowed, as if news of their arrival had already been passed to every soldier in Galahesh.

Sihaş guided them through the empty streets of Vihrosh. It was not a large city, however, and they soon came to a gate with tall minarets on either side. The massive iron portcullis was drawn up. Beyond, Atiana could already see dozens, perhaps hundreds of men standing, staring at something Atiana could not yet see from her vantage.

And then Atiana heard a sound that sent chills along her spine. It was like the braying of an animal, or the fearful crying of a child—a child faced with something they could not comprehend, allowing only the most urgent of fears to burst from their lungs.

Sihaş stiffened as another call came, this one louder than the first, and nearer.

"By the ancients," Atiana said, "I've never heard something so tragic."

Sihaş said nothing, but she felt him shiver. His pony slowed instinctually, and when Sihaş kicked its flanks, the beast became skittish and began to tug at the bridle.

As they passed through the gate, the scene beyond the Galaheshi soldiers was revealed. Hundreds of men and women wearing robes of black and gray and umber stood around a hill. These were the Hratha, Atiana knew, the sect of the Maharraht that had overthrown Soroush and his brother, Bersuq. They had been waging a protracted war against her own Duchy, and the Duchies of Bolgravya and Nodhvyansk, for decades.

And yet, it was not their presence that bothered her most.

At the top of the hill were dozens of children.

Nyet, Atiana thought. Not children. She had seen them in the aether, on Ghayavand and Rafsuhan. These were the akhoz, and they were now on Galahesh.

Sariya stood upon the hill's summit near a tall post. She was facing the gate as if she had expected them to walk through at that very moment. Hakan ül Ayeşe, the Kamarisi of Yrstanla stood next to her, his face calm, emotionless, barely registering that a princess of Anuskaya and the kapitan of his personal guard had arrived.

Standing next to them was a tall man wearing robes of ivory over inner robes the color of pearl. His hair and beard were black. This was Muqallad.

And between them was a girl, twelve, perhaps older—it was difficult to tell from this distance.

Muqallad lifted his hand and held it out as if he expected Atiana to take it.

The Hratha turned, and they parted, creating a lane for them to ride along.

Sihaş did not spur their pony forward. He was like a spring, tight and coiled. She could feel it in his arms and shoulders and in the set of his spine.

"We must go," Atiana whispered, and she knew it was so. They could no more turn around than they could summon the sun from the sky.

Sihaş was breathing so rapidly she wondered if he would faint. But as she leaned forward and whispered in his ear, "We must go," he flicked the reins and urged the pony forward.

The beast complied, and slowly they moved forward, she and his soldiers.

She glanced back to Irkadiy. Her countryman. A man who had urged her to abandon these plans.

His look was strong—Irkadiy was nothing if not strong—but it was a thin veneer, for just below the surface was an endless well of terror. He looked as though he could barely breathe, as though he were a drowning man clutching uselessly at the surface of the water.

Her feelings for him, so favorable only moments ago, soured the more she looked. He had tried to turn her away from this path. He had tried to betray her. Betray her! How dare he! For a mere moment, the anger building inside her like a hornet's nest surprised her, but as she looked up to the hill, to Muqallad and Sariya, she knew she'd been a fool to trust Irkadiy. She'd been a fool to trust any of these men.

Somewhere in the distance she heard the call of the gallows crow, but it was drowned out by the braying of the akhoz. There were more of them than Atiana had realized. Dozens of them. They'd moved beyond the Hratha to crawl along the ground as if they wished to leap upon Atiana and the soldiers and their ponies but were prevented from doing so. She looked upon the faces of these creatures, knowing they had once been children, knowing they had once been innocent.

No longer, she thought. Now they were tools of the Al-Aqim.

As it should be...

They reached the hill at last. There were rough stone steps worked into it, allowing them to slip from their saddles and ascend to the top of the hill. Muqallad and Sariya watched closely, but little emotion showed on their faces. The girl, however, was different. She watched Atiana with an intensity that Atiana couldn't understand.

The akhoz closed in behind and followed them up the hill. By the time she and Sihaş and the rest reached the hill's flattened summit, they were completely surrounded.

"Come," Muqallad said over the braying of the akhoz.

Sariya, for some reason, did not speak. She looked pale, as if she could do little more than stand, as if even speaking would prove too much.

In the distance there came again, barely audible, a single, sad caw.

Atiana knew something was wrong, but she could no longer understand what. Muqallad looked at her with a fierceness that made her want to obey. Sariya licked her lips tremulously, as if behind those lips, behind those unsteady eyes, she was holding back a wave of pain she'd never before experienced. Sariya swallowed and shook her head, holding back her misery through sheer force of will.

Atiana wanted to step forward, wanted to take Muqallad's hand. She felt she should, but there was something else she should do. Wasn't there?

But then the girl stepped forward.

And took Atiana's hand.

The moment she does, Atiana knows what she is doing is right.

She walks forward and takes Muqallad's hand, which is warm and welcoming. It nearly masks the renewed cries of the akhoz and the ululating calls of the Hratha behind her.

She turns to find the akhoz ripping Sihaş's men limb from limb. They are a mass of groping hands and writhing legs and gaping maws. The ground before her is little more than screams and flailing and blood.

Even the tall one—Sihaş, she recalls—falls, though he manages to draw his sword and sever the head of an akhoz from its neck. Another he cuts deeply across the waist while fending off a third. But the fourth. The fourth has him. It clamps wiry arms around his neck. It bites with blackened teeth, with lolling tongue.

Sihaş screams, felling yet another of these misshapen children, before he too is brought to the ground and eviscerated by creatures that seem more like teeming insects than children, ruthless and unemotional in their efficiency.

At last it has ended. Only one is left unharmed. Her countryman. What is his name?

No matter. He gave himself over to Muqallad's cause the moment he passed beyond the Spar.

Suddenly she realizes a knife is in her hand, a khanjar, placed there by Muqallad. He motions her forward, toward the soldier of Anuskaya.

The hilt of the knife feels good against her skin. It has tasted the blood of man, and it feels ancient, as if the fates themselves have crafted it from the stuff of stars.

She takes one halting step as the akhoz hold the man in place.

He looks up at her, pleading with her to stop.

His eyes implore her. Wake! Wake from this dream!

But he is wrong. He doesn't understand. She has been sleeping for so many years. Only through the Al-Aqim has she awoken.

She steps forward, angered by his presumption. "Who are you to plead with me?" she says.

And pulls the knife across his throat.

Blood spurts from the cavernous wound, falls warm and slick onto her fingers and the backs of her hands. The akhoz holding him scream in exultation, but she hears little save the furious and heady coursing of her own blood. This feels right. It feels as it must have felt for the earliest of the Matra as they blooded the land before the spires were built. It is just, for his blood now marks this place. This place where a grand ritual is about to commence.

It is the last of the steps needed before...

Before what?

She turns back and sees Muqallad holding two stones. They are a bright blue with veins of copper and silver and gold. They transfix her.

She has held one of them. Hasn't she?

Muqallad brings them together, and they fit perfectly. They are one.

Or soon will be.

The one from Alekeşir, the Kamarisi, Hakan ül Ayeşe, is summoned forth. The akhoz bring him to his knees before Muqallad. They hold his hands out, cupped, as if he is about to accept water into them.

The stone, the Atalayina, is set into them, and it is then that the Kamarisi's face transforms. To now, he has gone willingly, placidly. He has accepted his fate like a lamb led to slaughter. But now it seems as though he has awoken to a reality he never thought possible. How this could be when he is helping to bring the world to its highest plane, she does not know.

She is not saddened by his look of terror as Muqallad forces his hands to close around the Atalayina. The man arches back and screams to the skies as Muqallad holds his hands tight. She feels the power coursing through him from Adhiya.

When Muqallad releases him at last, the akhoz skitter away, and the Lord of the Motherland, the Kamarisi of Yrstanla, falls forward and onto his forearms. He looks as though he's praying to his fathers and his mothers, but she soon realizes her mistake. His hands are now one. They have been fused together, as if they were little more than clay, and within that grotesque mass—still barely visible—is the Atalayina. He now holds the pieces together as if his one fervent wish is to see this ancient stone healed.

Muqallad takes his hands and drags Hakan—immaculate boots kicking and thrashing against the trampled grass, tears streaming down his face—toward the post that stands at the summit of the hill. With a strength that surprises her, Muqallad hefts him up and drives him against the post. The man goes rigid. A large iron spike erupts through his chest, through his opulent clothes of silver silk and golden thread, and blood pours down his front as he eyes Atiana, face shaking, spittle flying from his mouth as he coughs.

He looks down at his hands, and then back to Atiana.

He tries to speak. His expression begs her to fix this. To make it right. To awaken from this nightmare that he and his empire might yet be saved.

But in this he will be disappointed, for he has been fooled like so many others—so many over the course of generations. It is the grand joke, the notion that there is free will, that one can work with a collective toward a greater good, a greater purpose. The truth is that such things can never happen on their own. They must be forced.

And the time is nearly at hand. Can he not sense it?

Her knife still bright with blood, she steps forward and looks up into his dimming eyes. "Fear not. You have done well. Better than could have been hoped."

But he doesn't listen. Blood stains his clothes, drips upon the cold ground. His eyes go distant. And finally his head slumps and his arms go slack.

Atiana feels a hand on her elbow.

It is the girl. She is leading her away.

Atiana follows, moving beyond the akhoz, who form a tight circle around the post. They are warm, Atiana realizes, and becoming warmer by the second. Already, though she stands ten paces back, she can feel them. The girl pulls her further and further away.

Until the first of them bursts into flame.

The akhoz arch back. They release their raucous calls to the cloud-filled sky. Another ignites, and like dry kindling the effect moves from one to another around the circle until all of them are aflame.

Muqallad watches as they twist in pain, their limbs bending at impossible angles. He watches not with satisfaction, but with sadness in his eyes. Perhaps he knows the end is near and does not relish it. Perhaps he wishes the world had arrived at this point by a different path. He turns to Atiana and regards her, as one might regard a flower or a child's bauble. He thinks her inconsequential, and perhaps in the light of these great events he's right.

Sariya merely stares at the burning hill. She seems to remain standing by force of will alone, though this final step seems to have granted her some small amount of strength.

On the hill, the body of the Kamarisi smokes. His skin blackens and then bursts into flame, as does the post he hangs upon. A moment later, the fire licking up from the akhoz pulls into a maelstrom centered on this burning man—centered on the stone he holds in his hands. The fire spins and is drawn upward like yarn from a skein. The thread thickens until a column of flame thrusts into the sky through the layer of clouds high, high above.

It rages on and on, the akhoz shrieking and barking and mewling while the fire rages. The Hratha watch, eyes bright, jaws set grimly. They stare at the sky, faces lit by the roiling column of gold and ivory flame.

Some time later—perhaps minutes, perhaps hours—the akhoz blacken. They still hold their twisted and pained positions, but are now little more than husks. A wind blows across the grounds, lifting the apple-sweet smell from the blackened remains. Some begin to ablate like the ash from a smoldering fire. Their forms collapse into clouds of powder, black and red and white, lifted by the updraft. More and more are consumed thus, their dark remains tainting the wavering column, which now burns amber and rust.

And then, in a sudden lift of wind and ash and gusting fire, the column burns itself out, until at last the sky breathes a sigh of relief.

The hill is utterly silent. Ash rains down on everyone like snow as the sun lowers in the west. Without a word being spoken, the Hratha close in around the site of the ritual.

Muqallad and Sariya and Kaleh stride up toward the hilltop. Atiana is close behind. The ash becomes ankle deep. Atiana wades through it—the ashes are warm, but little more, as if the Atalayina had stolen as much from the akhoz as it could—and she wonders briefly who these children might have been, who their mothers and fathers were, but then they reach the center of the ash, and there they find a mound filled with larger blackened chunks that somehow remained intact.

Muqallad sifts through the remains with his foot, until a glint of blue shines through. Atiana's heart sings at seeing it. But she doesn't yet know if the stone has been made whole.

As she holds her breath, Muqallad reaches down and picks it up. He blows upon it softly. The dust and ash fall away, revealing a stone as bright as any Atiana has ever seen. It does not glow, but it has a way of catching the light from the setting sun. It twists it and reflects it back in unexpected ways. It is powerful and beautiful, both.

Muqallad turns and holds it above his head.

And the Hratha burst into a cheer that is long and stirring and numinous.

Atiana, however—as caught up in these emotions she might be—remains silent.

As she stares at the Atalayina, now whole, she can shed only tears of joy.

For it is the most beautiful thing she has ever beheld.

CHAPTER SEVENTY-EIGHT

With the crow leading the way, the streltsi brought Nasim to a building near the center of the bazaar—the Kirzan, the massive central building and one of the oldest in this section of the city. "Let me down," Nasim said to the strelet, "or I won't be responsible for what they do."

The soldier, who had often sent nervous looks to the akhoz that galloped in a pack behind them, nodded and pulled his pony to a stop, at which point Nasim slipped to the ground and raised his hands to the akhoz. They stopped, their skin twitching, their lungs pumping like bellows, their necks straining as if collared.

"Rest," Nasim said to them, meaning their minds as much as their bodies. Blood lust was upon them, and it would not do to have them remain so among allies. "Rest," he said again, and motioned them to the empty stalls of the bazaar.

They complied, and slowly, their jerky movements began to quell. They settled down into crouches. Some laid upon the ground in groups. Others merely stood, their gaze never veering from Nasim as their lips drew back into sickening grins.

Nasim, as satisfied as he could be, turned and left them.

Near the building stood a gathering of several older men with long gray cherkesskas adorned with dozens of brightly colored medals. One of them had a beard that hung partway down his chest, and in his gray hair was a nasty gash that looked only halfway healed. There was a resemblance—not striking, but unmistakable—to Nikandr. This could be none other than his father, Iaros.

There were many streltsi surrounding these men, and they moved forward with muskets and shashkas at the ready.

"Let him through," Iaros called.

The streltsi parted, watching Nasim pass with mistrustful eyes, while the hoary old men waited with grave looks on their faces. These were hardened and seasoned men; they were not cowed by the presence of the akhoz, but they couldn't help but glance every so often to the stalls where the akhoz waited. None of them knew what he might do with them, or even if he had complete control, but to their credit neither they nor their guard seem overly phased.

As Nasim came near, most of the military men—no doubt polkovniks in the Grand Duchy's staaya—stepped back, allowing Iaros to approach Nasim. Iaros did not hold out his hand, as so many of the Landed seemed to do. Nor did he seem dismissive of Nasim. He merely stared as if Nasim were a curiosity he had long ago given up any hope of finding.

"Do you know who I am?" he asked.

"You are the Duke of Khalakovo," Nasim said, "Iaros, son of Aleksi, son of Vasham."

Iaros raised his eyebrows—not so much, Nasim thought, because he was impressed that Nasim knew of him and his family, but that Nasim knew anything at all. He must have thought Nasim would be little better than the lost child he had heard so many stories about. "I thought we might never meet, you and I."

Nasim didn't know what to say to this—nor did he know why the Matra had brought him here—so he remained silent.

Iaros turned to the men behind him and waved his hand. They all bowed their heads. One of them, however, an old, decrepit man with distrustful eyes and a long white beard, watched longer and more intensely than the others before turning and leaving.

With them gone, Iaros waved his hand toward the immense stone building. "Join me."

Nasim, seeing no reason not to go, fell into step beside the duke.

As they took the steps up, Iaros spoke. "The Matra tells me you've just returned, though we both wonder from where."

"I came from Ghayavand."

They stepped into the building, their footsteps echoing in the harshness of the interior. "And how did you return?"

His final memories of Rabiah were still too close, still too dear, for him to share. "That must remain with me."

Iaros turned his head with a frown—perhaps wondering if he'd erred in his measure of Nasim's character—but then the look was gone, and he motioned to a dark set of stairs leading below ground. "Fair enough," he said as they took the stairs down.

The way was lit by guttering whale oil lanterns. The stairwell continued on and on, deeper than Nasim would have guessed. It felt as though they were drilling into the earth, never to return.

"Where are we going?" Nasim asked.

"I want you to see what we're doing, and I want you to see who's doing it."

"And why do you care if *I* see it?"

"Because we find ourselves at another crossroads, do we not? As we were on Khalakovo?" They took one last turn, and were greeted by a set of heavy iron doors at the base of a long set of stairs. "Except this time Anuskaya is not aligned against you. It's important for you to know this."

"Do you think I would throw in my lot with Muqallad? Or the Kamarisi?"

"I don't know what you would do, but the ancients have seen fit to bring you here, and so I think it's important that you know before you leave."

Nasim laughed. "You seem to know where I'm going. I wish you'd share it with me."

"Are you not here to stop Muqallad?"

"I suppose I am, though I know not where he is."

"He is on the far side of the straits, in Vihrosh, and unless I'm sorely mistaken he will soon move to the Spar."

"How can you be so sure?"

They reached the landing at last. Once there, Iaros stopped before the doors and turned to Nasim. "Because the spire of Kiravashya has fallen. Fallen by our own hands."

"What?" Nasim shook his head. "*You* felled it?"

"*Da.*"

"Forgive me, son of Aleksi, but *why*? You need the spires."

There was a glint in Iaros's eye that made it clear just how fiercely he loved the Grand Duchy. "Their ships were many. Too many. We knew we could not stand against them, so we lured them to the spire, and we brought it down. All of their ships were destroyed in the maelstrom that followed, and in the meanwhile, we had already set sail on seaborne ships toward Galahesh."

Nasim shook his head, lamenting the deaths that had been lost in the trap the men of the Grand Duchy had laid, but there was a part of him that was relieved at this turn of events.

He thought back to the feeling of intent upon the wind. The inhalation. What would happen when the world exhaled, he didn't know, but he knew it would be terrible, and he knew it would be soon.

"The only ones that remain are the two here on Galahesh," Iaros continued. "They stand on opposite ends of this island. On opposite sides of the straits… We came to the island in the hopes of stopping Hakan before the spire could be destroyed, and now it may be too late. But make no mistake"—he reached over and opened both doors, swinging them wide so that Nasim could see the room beyond—"we will try."

Inside the room were dozens of people, nearly all of them women. Most were huddled around a set of eight basins at the center of the room. They were positioned like the points of a compass rose. Many of the women were old—around the age of the Duke of Khalakovo—and Nasim realized that these women were not merely Matri, they were by and large the Duchesses, the women with the most experience in the aether. There were some who were younger, however. One he thought he recognized as Atiana, but he soon realized his mistake. It was one of her sisters, Mileva or Ishkyna.

"So many of them here," Nasim said breathlessly, beginning to understand just how cunning Iaros had been. "They couldn't have crossed the seas after the spire had fallen. The seas would have been too dangerous."

"*Da*. The time for hiding in the palotzas of the islands was over. We knew the place to fight was here, where our enemies are."

"But if they're taken… The islands will be defenseless."

Nasim was interrupted by a flutter of wings. A rook flew from the stairs behind them and landed on the floor near Iaros's feet. "We do not shrink from duty. If we are taken, our daughters will take up our cause."

From the far side of the room, a servant came toward them, wheeling Saphia Khalakovo before him. Nasim realized with a start—the rook… It was Saphia, and yet here she was, outside of the bitterly cold water in one of the drowning basins.

The bird flapped up to land on Saphia's shoulder. Saphia herself was glass-eyed. She did not look to Nasim, nor notice as Iaros took her from the servant and rubbed his hand along her shoulder affectionately.

"We have come to it," the rook said. "We need you, Nasim."

"I—I had not thought to find help."

"And yet here it is. Muqallad has come. The Kamarisi holds the Spar, at least for now. And unless I'm mistaken, he has all the pieces of the Atalayina." The rook turned its head toward the basins and clucked twice. "We move against Sariya, but we need *you* to stop Muqallad."

"I am only one."

A voice came from behind Nasim. "You will have help. Have no fear of that."

Nasim turned and found no other than Ashan stepping into the room. There was an Aramahn man by his side. It was Majeed Bassam al Haffeh, an aide to Fahroz on Mirashadal, the one who oversaw her burial pyre and the ceremony that followed. His outer robes were violet, his inner robes a deep shade of yellow, not unlike the sun when it set behind thin clouds. Unlike Ashan, there was no hint of humor in his eyes. The cut of his short hair, the set of his jaw, the steel in his eyes, and though he was younger than Ashan by a decade at least, there seemed to lie within him a solemn burden that made him seem much older. It marked him as a serious man, a perfect replacement for Fahroz, no doubt hand chosen by the mahtar herself.

Ashan watched Nasim with a hint of a smile and a look of relief. Nasim had seen him on Mirashadal only a little more than a week ago, but as Nasim stood there, looking at this man who had tried to find a way to reach him when he was lost, something within him broke. He stepped forward and embraced Ashan like never before.

Ashan held him tenderly, stroking his hair. "What is this?" he whispered.

"You've done much for me. And what have I done but spurn you in return?"

"You could not have accepted me then. You had to grow, on your own."

"But I caused you so much pain. I've caused pain in so many. They died because of me, Ashan. They died because I refused to learn from you, and then from Fahroz."

Ashan pulled away and looked at him, the familiar smile bringing Nasim back from the edge of despair. "Had you not done what you've done, we might never have come this far. Muqallad may have already gained what he wanted most. You cannot decipher what the fates have in store for you, Nasim."

"The road is bleak."

"Bleak, but not lost." His smiled widened and he shook Nasim gently. "We will find our way."

Majeed had stood several steps behind Ashan, watching this exchange stoically, as if he feared coming too near to Nasim.

"And what of Mirashadal?" Nasim asked. "Will they not help?"

Majeed looked to Iaros. Clearly they had discussed this already. "We will not."

For a moment Nasim felt weightless. "In the name of the fates, why?"

"Forgive me for saying it, Nasim, but a grave mistake was made on Duzol."

Nasim felt the blood drain from his face. "I was *saved* on Duzol."

Majeed nodded. He stood taller, as if these were words for an errant child who had yet to understand the way of things. "The fates should not be trifled with. Things should have been allowed to take their own course, without our interference."

"Many others were saved as well…"

"And how many might die now?" Majeed glanced to Iaros and the rook again. "If the rifts had been allowed to widen then, there might have been many deaths upon Khalakovo, but we might have avoided that which lies before us. Sariya and Muqallad's plans might have been dashed before they'd truly begun."

"It might have happened sooner had the rifts been torn over Khalakovo."

"And it might *never* have happened. This is my point, Nasim. The fates should be allowed to choose the course of the world. Not me. And not you."

"What would Fahroz have done?"

Majeed's eyes became harder. "You know better than anyone that Fahroz is no longer with us."

Fueled by his anger, Nasim stepped forward and stared eye-to-eye with Majeed. "You would rather I lie down and allow Muqallad to do as he will?"

"I would rather Muqallad lie down of his own accord, but if he does not, then that is the path the fates have chosen for us."

"Erahm may *burn*." Nasim was practically shouting.

"Then perhaps Erahm was in need of cleansing."

"Enough," Iaros said. "I've allowed you to stay, Majeed, to observe, but that is all."

"Come," Ashan said to Nasim, guiding him back toward the stairs. "There is much to discuss before night falls and the assault begins."

Nasim was not at all sure the duke would allow him to leave, but Iaros simply nodded.

As Nasim took to the stairs, this time with Ashan, his heart was working furiously. He had known there were many like Majeed among the Aramahn, but to have them stand aside for something so vital... It didn't seem right.

Slowly, his anger cooled, and he realized how strange it felt to walk next to Ashan as an equal. For so long, in those rare moments of lucidity, he had felt as if Ashan were his savior—*neh*, his *creator*—and it had taken years for him to disabuse himself of the notion. It wasn't because Ashan wasn't deserving of honor and praise for stealing him away from the Maharraht; it was that Nasim couldn't allow himself to place Ashan on such a pedestal. He was a man, like any other, and just as susceptible to weakness.

Perhaps Majeed had the right of it, Nasim thought. Perhaps he *should* step aside and allow the fates to play out these next series of moves.

Only... It felt so wrong... It felt as though laying his will aside was not what the fates wanted. Were they not given the ability to reason, the ability to choose, for a purpose? Had not the fates given up some of their power over man when they did this?

And that was the trouble, he thought. No one knew, certainly not him. The fates were inscrutable, leaving him as powerless as a chunk of ice in the floes of spring.

They reached the top of the stairs and stepped outside the squat building and onto the grounds of the bazaar. Ashan looked to the akhoz, who still huddled only a hundred paces away.

Ashan regarded them. Without turning to Nasim, he said, "Much has happened."

"It has," Nasim said, "and one day—"

Nasim didn't finish, for just then a light lit the northern sky. A column of bright, roiling fire shot upward like an arrow to the layer of clouds high above Galahesh. He knew what it was immediately. He'd seen the same thing on the shores of Rafsuhan.

Muqallad was fusing the Atalayina. The stone was now being made whole, and all that stood between Muqallad and his goals was a short journey to the Spar.

"We must hurry," Nasim said.

Ashan smiled sadly, revealing his crooked teeth. "This I know, Nasim. This I know."

CHAPTER SEVENTY-NINE

With the new moon shedding the barest amount of light, Nasim and Ashan and a full sotni of streltsi—a veteran group chosen by Iaros Khalakovo himself—hid in the remains of two buildings ruined by cannon fire.

Only minutes ago, a skirmish with the Kamarisi's forces had died down. The janissaries had retreated further into the city, and Nasim now watched for any glint of light, any shift of shadow, as did the streltsi, who had their muskets resting on the upturned heads of their axes.

A flapping of wings came down the street from a darkened alley.

Two musket shots rang out, echoing among the buildings, and by the flash emitted by the muskets Nasim could see the crouched soldiers pointing their muskets skyward and the rook flapping above them.

Nasim cringed as a dozen shots rang out around him in rapid sequence. The acrid smell of the gunpowder filled the air, irritating his nose.

"Go," the sotnik called, and two dozen men stormed over the broken wall and ran down the street, their muskets at the ready.

As the streltsi stalked forward, a cluster of bright white flashes marked their progress. A handful of shots were returned from the opposite side of the street, more of the enemy lying in wait.

The soldiers of Yrstanla had been wily. Twice the streltsi of Anuskaya had nearly been caught between retreating men and an ambush force that lay in wait. But their enemy hadn't counted on the akhoz, nor the speed at which reinforcements could be called in. The Matri had been deadly efficient up to this point, coordinating the movement of the streltsi and the hussars to the position they were needed, and from a direction that would best exploit the enemy's weaknesses. And so they had made steady progress, marching forward through the city, compressing the forces of the Kamarisi step by step.

But there was no time to waste. Muqallad had fused the Atalayina and would now set his sights on the Spar. Up to this point the Kamarisi's forces had given ground steadily, but Ashan said that these were only delaying tactics. They had given up as much ground as they were going to give. Now the real fighting would begin, and it would be fierce, because they were not so spread out as they once were. There were no longer gaps in their lines, and if one was made by force of arms, they would be able to plug it quickly. Plus, with them so tightly packed, the advantages they'd gained from the Matri would be minimized. Soon, the battle would devolve into a chaotic frenzy waged step by bloody step to reach the Spar.

The unseasonably warm night air grew chaotic from the clatter of reloading muskets. The weather continued to be still—unnaturally still. The last of the spires had been destroyed, and it had left not storms, but a world breathless, as though Erahm were raising its sword before unleashing its fury. Nasim could feel it on his skin—it had started as a tickle, but he had long ago begun to itch, and it was growing as the night progressed.

With muskets reloaded, all became silence. Minutes later, the caw of a rook came high above them. "At the well ahead, a dozen lie in wait." It was Saphia. She had been assigned to them especially, though the Matri had warned them that any of the others might speak through the rooks, in case Saphia was hurt.

For the soldiers, and even Ashan, this meant little—one Matri or another made no difference—but Nasim still was not wholly comfortable having the lone Matra who had tried to assume him so near.

Another flurry of musket fire came, followed by the urgent calls of men as they waged a quick but fierce battle with swords and axes. Soon it was clear the battle was moving further away. The enemy was in retreat.

They would wait, however, until the Matri told them it was safe.

One of the akhoz shuffled closer to Nasim. By the looks of him he had been a young boy when he'd been turned, only eleven or twelve. He would have been promising, indeed, had he been allowed to live.

The boy ducked his head and scrabbled closer. Nasim reached over and touched the taut skin of his head. The moment he did, a memory came unbidden, a memory of this child, scared and frightened, succumbing to the curse of the akhoz hundreds of years before. Nasim did not welcome many memories of Khamal, but this one he embraced; it was painful, but he accepted the pain gladly, if only to honor the sacrifice this boy had made those many years ago.

His name was Cyhir, and he had been one of the first.

His skin burned Nasim's hand, but Nasim had found that such things were welcome conduits to Adhiya. The way to the world beyond had largely been closed to him since his awakening five years ago. Only through others had he been able to reach it. But now, since Rabiah had saved him on the beach below Alayazhar, he'd found the way to Adhiya still difficult, but more open than ever before.

He opened himself to the pain in his fingers, a heat that would blister the skin of normal men. His instinct as the heat rose was to pull away, but he forced it to remain in place, for through the pain he could feel the suurahezhan in Adhiya that would heed his call if needed. Beyond the suurahezhan he could feel spirits of the wind. He could smell them in the subtle shifts of the dead night air. He could feel the vanahezhan in the earth he stood upon and the jalahezhan trapped beneath the city. Dhoshahezhan were near as well, though they were the most distant, the most difficult for him to reach.

Ashan touched his arm. "It is not yet time, and we don't want to warn Muqallad if it can be avoided."

He was right. Nasim lifted his hand from Cyhir reluctantly, savoring the last of the heat as it dissipated.

The rest of the akhoz were far behind him, spread throughout the city. Try as he might, Nasim was unable to keep them from releasing their chilling calls to the night sky. The smell of blood was upon them, and though they obeyed Nasim's command to remain, they did so unwillingly, so rather than keep them in one place, Nasim had decided to spread them out so as to confuse the Kamarisi's forces that had set up a perimeter around the Spar's southern end.

Nasim peered through the darkness. He looked up at the bright sliver moon. The night was already well on its way toward sunrise, the likely time Muqallad would begin the ritual.

"This is taking too long," Nasim said.

"Patience," Ashan said. "There is still time to be patient."

He grit his teeth. They waited, longer and longer. He was nearly ready to stand and begin moving on his own if no one else would follow when at last, calls came from the sotnik for his men to pull back, to allow the enemy to flee so as not to be caught off guard.

He and Ashan moved with the streltsi that had been left to guard them. They treaded down a winding street that led to a large square with a tight cluster of buildings at its center.

The rook fluttered down and landed near the sotnik's feet. "Wait here. It will begin soon," it said before flying off once more.

The Matra meant the diversion. They would be making a large push to the center and the right flanks of the Kamarisi's forces. They hoped that it would draw enough men from the left flank that they could sneak through with little to no resistance.

Deep within Nasim's chest, he felt his bond to the man he'd been connected to since his awakening. Nikandr. He was somewhere ahead, though exactly where he could not guess. Balancing the pull of Nikandr was the taint of Muqallad's spell. By the ritual on the stone, he'd been freed from many of its effects, but he was still held back, and he wondered now whether he would ever be free.

He started at the thundering sound of cannon fire coming from the east. The soft crack of muskets that followed sounded like the sizzle of a pinecone thrown into a fire. It sounded distant and somehow innocent, but he knew that however innocent it might sound, men were dying.

Near him, Cyhir stopped and sniffed the air. Like a feral animal he strained his neck. Had Nasim not placed a hand on his shoulder he surely would have begun to bray. As it was, he stretched his head one way, then the other, then back again, like a mongrel dog straining at a leash.

Nasim peered into the darkness of the streets that led out of the square, wondering if the men of Yrstanla were lying in wait. It felt as though a musket were trained on the crown of his head. He scrunched his brow and the feeling faded, but the longer he stayed there, just waiting, the more pronounced it became. He had just succumbed to rubbing his forehead to clear the feeling away when a rook flapped down and landed near his feet. He hadn't expected one so soon. They had gone no more than three hundred paces from the sight of the short skirmish.

"To your left," the rook said, "move along the second street you come to."

There was something about this rook that seemed different. He knew immediately another Matri had assumed it, though which one it might be he had no idea.

"Where is Saphia?" Nasim asked.

"She's needed elsewhere," the rook said. "Sariya has reached the Spar."

Indeed, even as the rook spoke, the sound of cannons rose until Nasim could feel it on the back of his neck. The tops of the towers at the center of the square were lit by the flashes. Even the clouds high above glowed momentarily bright.

As the rook flapped away, Nasim could practically smell the scent of the Matri. They rode the aether, and he had become more and more sensitive to their passage. He knew few enough of these women, but surely the Matri of Vostroma and Nodhvyansk and Bolgravya were present. Yet he couldn't shake another feeling of strong familiarity.

"Are you well?" Ashan asked.

Nasim wasn't sure how to answer. It was foolish, these thoughts. One Matra or another, what did it matter?

"I'm well," he said.

They headed northwest, going to the place the rook had indicated. As they did, Nasim called upon the akhoz. It was time… Time for them to taste blood.

That was when a meaty thump sounded next to him. As the sharp report of the musket echoed from the far side of the square, Ashan crumpled to the ground, a dark stain welling through his robes.

CHAPTER EIGHTY

Nikandr stood over Grigory, his breath coming in great gasps. Grigory's men, these soldiers and windsmen of Bolgravya, stared at him, some with enmity in their eyes, but many with neutral expressions and some with outright relief.

"Take him below and tend to him," Nikandr said to the nearest of the windsmen, and then he turned to Avayom. All eyes were on the two of them, and Nikandr was not at all sure that he had their loyalty. It felt as though they only hoped to be rid of Grigory, and now that they had, they would take their ship and be done with him.

"Come with me," Nikandr said. He strode to the kapitan's cabin at the rear of the ship. Once the two of them were inside, Nikandr closed the door.

"Why did you suggest *bazh an bazh*?" he asked.

"Forgive me, My Lord Prince, but there seemed to be some question as to the authority we were to follow."

"Go on."

Avayom's grizzled face, his steely eyes, did not waver. "The Lord Prince seemed to have misread the orders from his brother, our Lord Duke of Bolgravya."

He meant the scroll that had been sealed by Konstantin and delivered by Nikandr himself.

"Did Grigory show you those orders?"

Avayom stood straighter, as resolute as he had been on deck. "He did not, My Lord Prince."

"Then how do you know of them?"

"My duty is to my Duke, first and foremost. His brother refused to show them to me, so I made it my business to find the scroll while it lay unattended during a drunken spell."

Nikandr took a deep breath, coming to the most important question. "Will you follow me, Sotnik Kirilov?"

Avayom struck his heels and bowed his head. "We are yours to command, My Lord Prince."

"We go to fight," Nikandr said slowly, "and we fight with the Maharraht."

This time it took longer for Avayom to respond, but he bowed his head once again. "If they fight our enemies, then we will fight with them."

Nikandr took him into an embrace and the two of them kissed each other's cheeks. "The mountain is steep," Nikandr said, giving him half of an old Anuskayan proverb.

Avayom smiled sadly, but his eyes were fierce and grim. "Then we climb."

As the bitter winter wind cut through his coat to numb his skin, Nikandr sat in one of two skiffs just launched from the *Yarost*. They flew away from the hidden bay Soroush had led their ships to. They were tightly packed—nineteen fighting men of Anuskaya in his skiff, another twenty in the other. The men, their breath trailing behind them like white streamers, seemed tense, but not overly so. These were the kind of men that could channel such tension into precise, sometimes furious, action. One of them sitting near the bow of the other skiff, a veteran desyatnik with a scar running down the left side of his face, caught Nikandr's eye and nodded. His men were ready. Nikandr nodded back, proud of them, these soldiers of his homeland.

Soroush and his Maharraht trailed in seven more skiffs. He brought seventy-five in all, bringing their total to a little over a hundred—one sotni of men to stand against all the Hratha and the soldiers of Yrstanla. They had enough munitions for one sustained battle, no more, but hopefully it wouldn't come to that. Hopefully they could surprise Muqallad before it was too late.

And yet, as they flew over the lip of the valley and began heading southeast toward Baressa, Nikandr felt small. They were not enough. They wouldn't make a difference. As the sun began to set in the west, Nikandr could still see the Sea of Khurkhan, dark and deadly in the distance. Ahead, over the tops of the green forest of spruce and pine and white-barked birch, were leagues of flying before they would reach the straits.

"What will we do when we come to a city of two hundred thousand?" Styophan asked Nikandr as the sky was growing dark.

"We do what can be done."

No sooner had Nikandr said these words than he felt a shift among the winds. The weather had been calm, but now it quieted to the point that all was still. The trees below did not sway. The clouds above did not drift. The whole world seemed caught in amber.

Nikandr felt nervous, not only because of the odd quality of the weather, but because he could feel the changes through his hezhan. The spirit felt near—perhaps because of their proximity to the straits—but it also felt drawn, and drawn *away*, as if something momentous were calling it from afar. The havaqiram—including Anahid, who had some skill with the wind—reported something similar. They were forced to draw upon the winds more deeply than they had before.

Despite all this, they made steady progress. Nikandr was watching the horizon for any signs of ships when he felt something different. It was far in the distance, a sense of discomfort in his chest not unlike what he'd felt when Nasim had darkened his soulstone.

Except this…

This felt…

A column of flame shot up into the sky. Off the landward bow, it climbed hungrily and tore into the layer of clouds that hung high above the land. It burned brighter than the dying sun. It eclipsed the stars, a thread of roiling light cutting the sky in two.

No one said a word. Everyone here save the men of Bolgravya knew what this was, and those that didn't were too shocked to say anything.

Nikandr could see wonder in the faces of his men and the Maharraht, both. There was worry as well, and a growing sense of desperation that did not bode well for the coming night.

The third piece of the Atalayina had reached Muqallad, and he had now fused it to the other two. The stone was whole, giving him the power he so desperately sought.

But there was more. Atiana had held one of the pieces. She'd been given it by Nasim. If it now lay in the hands of Muqallad…

He held his soulstone and reached out to her. *Hear me*, he said, staring out beyond the forest, beyond the column of light toward Baressa. *Hear me, Atiana.*

But his pleas went unanswered.

"Be safe," he whispered softly.

Styophan glanced over, but made no mention of his words.

Nearly an hour after the burning column appeared, it burned out. They were closer to the straits now, and Nikandr could tell that the base of the column had been positioned somewhere to the east of Vihrosh, Baressa's sister city.

Soroush's skiff approached theirs, and he called across the gap. "We must go straight for the storehouse."

Nikandr already knew it would be so. They had planned on landing and stealing wagons to bring the barrels of gunpowder to the Spar, but now they had no choice but to transport the gunpowder by skiff. It would seem the quickest way to go about it, but it was dangerous to fly over the straits, especially in the channel where the winds were the most unpredictable.

The winds were low, but something told Nikandr it wouldn't last.

As they neared Vihrosh, the boom of cannons could be heard in the distance. It must be Baressa, Nikandr thought, though who was fighting he couldn't guess.

The building was situated on a rise above the city. With the moon providing only a sliver of light, they landed their skiffs in a snow-swept field near a squat stone building. Beyond the building, limned in silver by the moonlight, was the bulk of Vihrosh, a sizable assortment of old stone buildings and half-timber houses, and beyond Vihrosh was the wide gap of the straits. The cliffs lay dark, making it look like a chasm that would swallow the city whole if given the chance.

A light flashed somewhere in the streets of Baressa far beyond the straits. Moments later a boom came. More flashes followed like lightning in the distance, the thunder beating out a staccato rhythm that made it clear just how desperate the battle was becoming.

As they slipped over the sides of their skiffs and moved silently toward the squat munitions building, Nikandr heard a wailing. It sent shivers down his spine. He'd heard that sound before, on Ghayavand and then again on Rafsuhan. It was the sound of the akhoz.

The sound had come from the northeast, in the rough direction the column of fire had been in.

Soroush stood nearby. He was unmoving, stiff, as if the mere *sound* of the akhoz terrified him.

Another call came—more like the bleating of a goat than the cry of a child. It was higher pitched than the first, and the cry was longer, more desperate. Nikandr could only think that it had been released from the throat of a misshapen creature that had once been someone's daughter.

"Quickly," Nikandr whispered.

They moved. The building was not guarded, a bit of good fortune no doubt granted them by the battle that raged in the streets of Baressa.

They broke in the doors and found the powder room at the back. The place was silent, eerily so, as if Vihrosh had been abandoned centuries ago and they were the first to return.

Two men at a time rolled the barrels out of the building and toward the skiffs. As Nikandr was returning from loading the first barrel with Styophan, he heard the call of another akhoz, much louder now. It was followed by one that was closer yet, a long keening that sent shivers down Nikandr's spine. He could see their dark forms against the white snow at the base of the hill. One of them reared back and cried out to the nighttime sky. The other did the same.

It sounded like a warning. A call that the enemy had been found.

Styophan slung his musket off his shoulder and sighted along the barrel. As the pan flashed, Nikandr looked away so he wouldn't be blinded. When he looked back, slinging his own musket into position, he saw that the nearest of the two had been felled, but it was already up again, and now it was charging toward him, calling in a high-pitched squeal as it came.

Nikandr had been in many battles, but something about the darkness and the sound of the creature staggering toward him made him shake, made the hairs on the back of his neck stand up.

"To me!" Nikandr called.

With the two akhoz coming closer and closer, the men of the Grand Duchy rushed forward.

Nikandr sighted carefully down the length of his musket and pulled the trigger. The musket bucked, and he saw the akhoz go down again.

It rose one last time before three more musket shots felled it.

Some of the Maharraht came forward, including Soroush, but Nikandr waved them away. "Keep loading! We need more powder!"

As more musket shots tore into the other akhoz, calls were taken up by their brothers and sisters, some from afar, but many nearer.

"Go!" Nikandr said.

Soroush did, and the Maharraht moved as quickly as they could with their heavy loads.

More akhoz reached the base of the hill, a dozen at the least.

"Another five minutes," Nikandr shouted. "That's all we need! Hold fire! Be ready, and give them two shots each!"

No sooner had he said this than musket shot zipped over his head.

"Down!" Nikandr called as he dropped to the snow-covered ground.

The first shot was followed by another, and another. The strelet next to him took a meaty shot in the center of his chest before he could lie down. He grunted, long and hard, and fell to the ground.

The rest dropped as more musket shots punched into the earth around them. The akhoz were nearing their line now.

One of the Maharraht behind Nikandr cried out. He dropped the barrel he was carrying and fell heavily to the ground.

"Fire!"

Their muskets rang out, not in quick succession, but staggered so that they could see if an akhoz was down or not. Soon, though, the akhoz were coming too close, and the shots were released in a frenzy.

Nikandr fired. The akhoz he'd sighted fell, but there were two more behind it. He came to a kneel and reloaded—powder, shot, and ramrod—and fired one more time before the first of the akhoz reached the far right of their line.

It crouched and belched flame from its mouth even as it was struck by four musket shots that had been fired in desperation. The akhoz collapsed, but more took its place, breathing gouts of flame. One of his streltsi was caught in the blasts, and then another, both of them screaming as the flames licked their woolen cherkesskas and black kolpak hats.

One dropped to the snow, trying to douse the flames, but the other threw aside his musket and took up his berdische axe. He swung it high over his head, his death cries rising high into the nighttime sky as he brought the axe down on the nearest of the akhoz even as the creature blasted him with another column of bright, searing fire. The akhoz was split from neck to navel. The strelet, amazingly still aware and able to fight, tried to pull the axe free, but then another akhoz leapt on him from the side and bit deeply into his neck.

"Close!" Nikandr called. "Close!"

And then the akhoz were among them.

Nikandr drew his sword and cut one from behind that had just begun to gout flame. It cried out and arched backward. Fire licked Nikandr's sleeve, but he stepped away and batted it out.

The Maharraht were still pulling barrels toward the skiffs, but a dozen had now joined the fray. Several were dropped before they could reach the fight, however—victims of musket fire coming in from the base of the hill.

"Pull back!" Nikandr shouted in Anuskayan. "Pull back!" he shouted again in Mahndi.

They retreated, though many fell before they'd made it halfway to the skiffs.

A shout drew Nikandr's attention. He looked beyond the chaos before him and by the light of the akhoz's flames saw a low form—naked and childlike—gallop like a mongrel dog into the building.

"Run!" Nikandr bellowed. "Run!"

He turned and sprinted for the skiffs. Sensing the danger, his men followed, as did most of the Maharraht. They'd gone only ten strides before an explosion ripped through the night. It tossed him like a rag doll onto the snow.

Groaning with the pain running through his chest, he turned and saw stones flying outward from the rear of the building as a fireball, black and roiling, curled up into the air.

He scrabbled backward as stone blocks and burning wreckage plowed into the ground around him. Some sizzled against the snow. A piece of stone the size of a mastiff fell on top of Jonis, the young boatswain, killing him instantly.

More musket shots rained in as the few soldiers who'd made it to their feet descended on the remaining akhoz. Their mewling cries rose above the sounds of the fire. The acrid smell of their breath mixed with the bitter smell of burnt gunpowder.

"Hurry, My Lord!"

Nikandr turned. It was Styophan, and he was pointing toward the skiffs.

"You're coming with me."

"*Nyet*, My Lord. You're needed on the skiffs"—he pointed to the Hratha coming slowly up the hill—"and I'm needed here."

Nikandr looked to the Hratha. They were many, and if they weren't slowed, they would overrun the skiffs before they had a chance to leave.

"Retreat when you can," Nikandr said. "Lose yourself in the forest, and then meet us at the Spar."

"*Da*," Styophan said as he reloaded his musket, "now go!"

He turned and ran forward, pausing once to fire toward the line of dark-robed men that were now halfway up the hill.

Nikandr moved to the skiffs where Anahid waited. She began calling upon her dhoshahezhan immediately.

Two more skiffs were loaded, each holding fewer men than before. Part of this was out of necessity—each barrel weighed nearly a stone—but part was the sheer number of men that had died in the furious battle.

Nikandr helped Soroush up and into his skiff, and they were off. Musket shots tore into the hull, and Nikandr was worried that one would ignite the gunpowder. He heard two shots puncture the hull and the barrels, and then a third, but the ancients were watching over him, and nothing happened.

Soon they were high enough and far enough that the Hratha gave up firing upon them.

By the moon's pale light, he could see the battle raging, but his men, along with the Maharraht, were already beginning to retreat.

Nikandr put his fingers to his mouth and whistled loudly three times, and soon after, the men turned and ran toward the tree line. He tried to find Styophan but could not. They were too far away, the night too dark.

But then Nikandr recognized something, or some*one*, through his soulstone. He pulled it from his shirt and held it tightly in his hand.

It was Atiana.

And she was near.

She was out there in the night, with the akhoz and the Hratha. But there was something terribly, terribly wrong. He knew this, for he *knew* Atiana, and this was not she.

"What is it?" Soroush asked.

Nikandr did not want to admit it to Soroush, but he saw no reason to withhold it. He pointed toward the base of the hill, at the black shapes of the nearest buildings. "Atiana is out there."

The firefight continued in the distance, but it was softer now, like a memory beginning to fade. Soroush looked to the city of Vihrosh, to the Spar beyond. And then he turned to Nikandr. "Had I not been so blinded with rage, I might have listened to my heart, and Rehada might have been saved."

Nikandr looked to the Spar himself, the shadows of its arches barely visible against the dark gray of the white cliffs. By the ancients who guide, what should he do? But when he gripped his soulstone and felt Atiana, felt the taint upon her, he knew what he must do.

He nodded to Soroush.

Soroush took up a coiled rope and tossed it over the side. "Anahid, lower the skiff."

After only a brief pause, Anahid did.

Nikandr felt like he was abandoning them, but he could no more deny this need than he could the need to breathe.

"I'll find you at the Spar."

Soroush nodded.

And Nikandr slipped over the side.

CHAPTER EIGHTY-ONE

Nikandr padded along snowy ground with the twenty or so men who remained of the battle trailing behind. Styophan moved alongside him with an awkward gait that spoke of the pain he was experiencing. He was wounded. His shoulder had been bound hastily, but he had strength in him yet to fire a musket, and that was all Nikandr could hope for at a time like this.

They had headed deeper into the forest to the north of the city and circled back in the hopes that Atiana would be held at the rear of the train marching steadily toward the Spar.

Among the chill and distant calls of the akhoz, Nikandr's anxiety had grown worse. Normally when he felt Atiana—or anyone else with whom he'd touched stones—he could sense, however faintly, their mood. Whether they were happy or sad or angry, it shone through their shared connection like a scent upon the wind. But in Atiana he could feel nothing—only her presence—and it terrified him. It was as if she were dead, lying in a room so that he could see her, feel her, but could not communicate with her.

As they left the forest and entered the fields surrounding Vihrosh, he could tell that she was close. She might be near the center of the city now, and he was sure that if *she* were there, then so would be Muqallad and Sariya. They pushed, marching at the quick, and came to the edge of the city as the sound of battle on the far side of the straits rose to new heights.

As they entered a square with decorative trees, a bird winged down and landed on the cobbled street. It was the gallows crow. "She has been taken," it said. "You must hurry. You must save her."

The way the bird spoke those words, it reminded Nikandr of someone, but the thought seemed preposterous. "Ishkyna?"

The crow cawed over and over, a low, sad sound. "Speak not her name!"

Nikandr didn't understand, but he knew better than to question her. "How?"

he asked. "How can I save her?"

"I failed her. Sariya's hold on her was stronger than I had guessed—much stronger—and now the Atalayina has her in its grasp. She is lost in its depths." The crow stumbled and fell to the ground, its wings trying ineffectually to help it remain standing. He could see something clutched in one of its talons, which it dropped onto the cobbles. The thing clinked and made a *shink* sound as the crow hopped away. "Take it to her, Nischka. I hope it will return her to herself."

With that the crow shivered along its whole length. It regained its feet and flew off in a rush, as if it had just then awoken to find itself among men in a place it had never been.

Nikandr reached down and found a necklace, a soulstone necklace, and he knew just by touching it that it was Atiana's. How the crow had come by it, and how Atiana had lost it, he didn't know, but he was glad to have it. It gave him hope.

"Hers?" Styophan asked.

"*Da.*"

"What do we do now?"

Nikandr pulled Atiana's soulstone necklace over his head. It felt good to have it resting next to his own. "What is there to do but go on?"

They resumed the chase, faster than before. Light began to fill the eastern sky. Gone were all but the brightest stars on the horizon, the weakest replaced by a swath of indigo that foreshadowed the dawn. They knew when they were coming close from the calls of the akhoz. Few had appeared at the battle at the munitions building, which made sense, for if the ritual was anything like the one on Rafsuhan, most would have been sacrificed to make the Atalayina whole.

They came to a place where six roads met at a large circle with a lawn at its center with a lone, towering larch. This was the heart of Vihrosh. The ponderous stone buildings were old remnants of the power that Vihrosh had once held as the seat of Yrstanla's power here on Galahesh. On the far side of the larch, running down the opposite street toward the circle, was the silhouette of a woman.

"Nikandr!" Atiana called. There was a desperation in her voice that he didn't understand.

Until he saw the creatures bounding after her.

He sprinted toward her, his men close behind. They passed the larch and reached the entrance to the street in little time. The akhoz behind her uttered sickening brays that made Nikandr's skin crawl. They galloped along the cobblestones like dogs. In moments they'd be on her.

"Down, Atiana!" Nikandr called as he skidded to a halt and swung his musket up to his shoulder.

Atiana either didn't listen or hadn't heard, and the first of the akhoz leapt upon her back, driving her to the ground.

It cleared a path for him. He fired at the second akhoz. Styophan, standing to his left, fired as well, as did two Maharraht.

Two akhoz dropped, writhing on the ground as the one that had leapt on Atiana fought with her, snarling and clawing as Atiana screamed.

Nikandr charged forward, pulling his shashka.

Atiana twisted away and kicked at the akhoz. It rolled away momentarily, but it gave Atiana enough leverage to kick again, this time much harder.

The akhoz was much smaller than Atiana, and it was sent reeling backward. It struck the cobblestones while releasing a sound that was half growl, half mewl. It spun over and was back on all fours when Nikandr swept in and brought his sword down hard, aiming for its neck. The creature ducked, receiving a cut across its shoulder blade. It scrabbled away, but Nikandr lunged forward and drove his sword through its gut.

It screamed to the night sky. The sounds echoed among the buildings. It grasped at the sword blade, slicing its fingers open as it clawed for Nikandr's hand. He jerked the sword free, and at last it collapsed to the ground.

"Atiana," Nikandr said as he stepped close to her.

She stood, the whites of her eyes visible in the early morning light. She stared at him as if she didn't know him.

Nyet, he thought, as if she were *afraid* of him.

"Atiana," he said, softer this time. He reached for her hand, but she snatched it away.

It was then that Nikandr realized that all of them—he, Styophan, the Maharraht—all of them were in a narrow stretch of street, one easily defended on both sides.

"Reload!" he shouted, while Atiana stared at him with uncaring eyes.

The men responded, but too slowly. Dark forms slid into the street from an alley ahead. They swept in behind.

One of the Maharraht brought his weapon up.

Three muskets flashes came from the men ahead, and in that brief moment, Nikandr could see that they were Hratha, their black robes merging with the deep shadows.

The Maharraht grunted and fell to the ground. As he wheezed, a gurgling sound coming from a chest wound, the Hratha called in Mahndi, "Lay down your arms."

Nikandr had no intention of obeying. The Hratha could not be trusted, especially now with all their plans so close to fruition.

He drew upon his hezhan, pulling the wind to swirl through the narrow street. Dust and dirt stung him as he grabbed Atiana's wrist and pulled her back toward the edge of the alley.

The Maharraht and the men of Anuskaya took this as his answer, and those that had already reloaded fired.

The Hratha returned fire, and Nikandr saw a glowing stone of jasper upon one man's brow. Another of azurite glowed a deep shade of blue. A cracking sound rent the ground. It shook the street and the nearby buildings.

Nikandr held Atiana close as he called upon the wind to drive the Hratha back. He saw several raise their muskets, but only two shots were released.

Nikandr opened himself wider. He stepped away from Atiana and spread his arms wide. The presence of the hezhan filled him. He felt the flow of the wind through the streets of the city and called upon it to converge here. He called upon it to scour the Hratha from their path.

The wind answered, hungry for the breath of man, but just as it rose to a gale, Nikandr felt a rising fury within him. His mind went wild, memories of walking on the fields below Radiskoye coming to him, of planing curls of wood as he worked on the helm of the *Gorovna*, of those nervous moments before he'd touched stones with Atiana years ago when they were to be married. Those and a thousand more came unbidden. He had no control over them, and soon after he felt his muscles going slack.

He realized in a distant and disconnected way that this was no illness, that this was something being done forcibly *to* him.

He was being assumed, he realized, and he couldn't at first understand who would attack him in such a way.

Stars filled the field of his vision as his knees gave way and he tipped toward the ground. As the ground rose up, he had a sudden moment of crystal clarity. He knew who had done this to him.

He knew without a doubt.

It was Atiana.

He would have felt betrayed if it hadn't been for the stone-hearted indifference radiating from her.

He willed his arms to arrest his fall, but they refused him, and he struck the ground like a tree felled. And then the darkness, held at bay for so long, finally embraced him.

CHAPTER EIGHTY-TWO

Atiana watches as Nikandr falls to the ground.

He goes limp. Beneath him, strangely, are *two* glowing soulstones, not one. She kneels down to inspect them, but the akhoz are hungry. They shuffle toward him until she holds her hand up for them to stop.

Two of the Maharraht charge her, and she's forced to back away.

"My Lady Princess!" This comes from a strelet at the head of a group of soldiers. Atiana has seen him before. This is Styophan. For years he's been Nikandr's steadfast second, a loyal soldier who would protect him above all things.

"Please wake!" Styophan runs toward the Maharraht, dropping his musket and pulling his eagle's-head shashka from its sheath. The sword gleams for a moment in the early morning light. "Call them away!" he pleads, just before the first of the akhoz leaps through the air toward the Maharraht standing before him.

The first of the akhoz loses an arm to a fierce swing of a blade from the first of the Maharraht, a young man with bright eyes and a black beard. The akhoz falls to the ground from the force of the swing, but it is up again moments later, blood pouring from its wound as it ducks beneath another hasty swing by the Maharraht. It is within the young man's guard now, and it is vicious, grabbing the Maharraht's sword arm and snarling forward toward his throat.

"Princess Atiana! You must wake!"

She looks toward Styophan. For a moment, she remembers who she was, remembers that she came to this place for a different purpose. She came to kill, perhaps, but not these men. Not *this* man.

Then something bears down on her and smothers her will. In the time it takes her to flick her wrist toward the akhoz, she has forgotten her allegiance to this soldier of Khalakovo.

The akhoz abandon their attack on the two Maharraht, who have fallen to the cobblestones, moaning in pain, bleeding their lifeblood. The akhoz charge Styophan and the streltsi who stand by him, shashkas at the ready. The first is cleaved through its ribcage where it has no arm to defend itself. Styophan kicks the akhoz free and drives his sword tip-first through the second. This one, a girl who might have been twelve or thirteen when she was changed, is run through, but she reaches out, snatches his jaw, and pulls herself forward until she's able to pierce his right eye with a long, claw-like thumb.

Styophan screams, writhing, trying to shake her away. His comrades step in, and the girl leaps to another man, darting forward until she's high enough to latch her jaws onto his throat.

The last of the battle rises to a bloody frenzy in its closing moments. More and more of the Maharraht and the soldiers of Anuskaya fall, and at last it is ended, and all Atiana can hear is the ragged breathing of the akhoz; all she can feel are the stares of the Hratha as they wait for her.

She ignores them, gazing down upon the soldier, Styophan. Blood pours from his ruined eye, from the jagged cuts along his scalp and face from the akhoz. She watches his chest rise and fall slowly with breath. It won't be long before he passes the veil. She should care that he is about to die, but the truth is she does not. All she feels is a cold satisfaction that the end is finally near. What does it matter if one more is lost before the time has come?

And yet, she's unwilling to order his death, not when he's no longer a threat. Let him lie here in the streets. Let him pray to his ancestors if he wishes. That will be a good enough death for this soldier of Anuskaya.

One of the Hratha approaches, but she turns and points him back toward the Spar, then she beckons the akhoz and motions to Nikandr. "Take him."

The nine that remain obey, lifting Nikandr and bearing him on their backs like food for their burrow. The Hratha in their dark robes and black turbans walk ahead and behind, watching for any signs of the enemy who might be lying in wait. She knows already that the city is all but deserted of military men. All that remain are the huddling inhabitants of this doomed place.

There *is* something that draws her attention, however.

Ishkyna.

She moves through the aether like a moth, barely visible as she flits near the flame. Atiana wants to find her, to rend her as a cat rends meat, but she cannot—not unless Ishkyna falters and comes too close.

For now, Atiana ignores her and heads for the bridge, moving through the old city with its graceless stone buildings. Under the growing light of dawn, they look like things long ago abandoned, the sad remnants of man. She wonders whether the buildings will remain—and the roads and the eyries and the homesteads—or will they be gone? Will they be burned as the akhoz were, forging the world anew as the Atalayina had been?

And what of the world beyond? Will it too burn?

She supposes it will.

The light in the east makes her think of nothing but the kindling of the fires that will soon consume the world. The wind, as if heeding the call of the coming dawn, rushes along the streets. The last of the spires fell upon Kiravashya yesterday, and though the weather has been strangely still since then, it now builds. The wind is strong and getting stronger, and soon it will be a gale the likes of which has never been seen.

The skin between her breasts itches. The tips of her fingers tingle. She can hardly wait.

She comes to the wide thoroughfare that leads to the Spar. She hears the battle beyond the bridge, hears the screams of individual men rising above the calls and cries of war. She sees the brightness of the cannon flashes against Baressa's tallest buildings.

Ahead are those she left earlier to set her trap. Muqallad and Sariya stand near the first stones of the Spar, but they have not yet stepped foot upon it. Why, she does not know. Nearer, the girl, Kaleh, watches. She looks as though she wishes to approach, but Muqallad summons her and she leaves. She cannot hear Muqallad's words, but he points to the Spar, and immediately after Kaleh begins to first walk and then jog across the impossibly long bridge.

As she does, Atiana feels something—a shifting of wind in the dark of the aether—and it comes from the Spar.

She strides forward, steps up onto a wooden stage in the abandoned yard of an auction house, and from here she can see much of the Spar unobstructed. The upper reaches of its white stone are difficult to discern against the white cliffs beyond, but the tall, elegant arches are easy to see.

Atiana closes her eyes, casts herself outward, searching for the source of the disturbance. The sight of the Spar fades and is replaced by the blue-black of the aether. She moves like a marlin through the ocean depths, flitting along the Spar, searching its arches and the supports structures beneath the road deck and the squat towers at the center where the keystones were recently dropped into place. But there is nothing. Nothing.

And yet she knows there must be.

Have you found it?

It is Sariya.

Not yet, she replies. Sariya is weak, but has the strength yet to cast herself into the aether. If she bonds with Atiana, they might find the source together. *Join me,* Atiana says.

The two of them meld their minds with one another. It is not so easy to do, partly because they are unaccustomed to one another, but mostly from the wound Sariya took from Ushai's blade. She is so close to parting the veil it is a wonder she can draw breath much less navigate the currents of the dark. Still, she is Al-Aqim, and she has strength yet. It allows Atiana to search more thoroughly, to sense the subtle shifts in the currents of the dark.

She was wrong earlier. There *is* something on the Spar—she can feel it in her bones, a familiarity that is as much a part of her as her skin or her blood. And yet, save for the blackness of the keystone where her father was murdered, the bridge is pristine. It is empty and untouched. When she breathes the air of the aether, however, she notes the familiar scent of those with whom she once bonded, with those she once shared such intimate thoughts as only sisters in the ways of the dark can share.

The Matri are here. They have moved beyond the chaos of the fallen spire. How, she cannot guess, but she knows it is so, and they are hiding something at the center of the Spar.

She casts outward, hoping to find them, but she does not. Her anger begins to rise. She *must* control it. She can already feel her grip on the aether slipping. It is dangerous, especially here at the straits where the currents of the dark are building and compressing like a wound infected.

As she tries to regain herself, the dark buffets her. It draws her down into the gap of the straits until she is staring upward at the Spar and the midnight blue of the sky above. She feels the currents of the sea swarming. She feels the weight of the cliffs pressing in. She feels the men dying in the streets of Baressa as swords slice through flesh and bite into bone.

She's losing herself. She knows this.

And she also knows the Matri are causing it.

She has lasted this long only through the grounding that Sariya provides her, but Sariya is weak.

The Matri must be found, and there are clues for her to do so. She has long been accustomed to searching for them after taking the dark, and though they try to hide, she can sense them. Their trail is marked like blood upon the forest floor.

She follows their trail back toward Baressa. She passes the raging battle near the center of the massive city. And then she comes to the bazaar. It is large and sprawling, little more than a collection of stalls and carts and tents, but at its center there is a building—an old, massive structure where the rarest of items can be found.

It is there, she realizes. The Matri are in that building, and if she is any judge, they have not yet noticed her.

She is no fool. She cannot hope to approach them directly. With Sariya, she is a match for any one of the Matri, but the twisted cord of individual threads trailing back from the Spar make it clear that there are many working together, perhaps seven or eight of them.

She must be careful.

She allows her mind to diffuse outward. She thins her consciousness so that she encompasses the entirety of the bazaar. She cannot allow herself to go further lest she be drawn back toward the maelstrom in the straits.

She sinks, allowing herself to drop as slowly as a dandelion seed on the wind of summer's waking. She feels the Matri lying in a room deep beneath the building. There are eight. And they are unaware.

She descends upon them, pressing down furiously. Bound as they are, they are all affected, and Kseniya and Polina succumb in those first moments. She feels their fear and their desperation, and then their minds slip from the aether like sand through the fingers of an outstretched hand.

Those who remain, six of them now, fight back, but they are disoriented. Atiana slips in and attacks, pulling back as they turn to meet her. With two of the stronger ones missing, the weakest are especially vulnerable, and Atiana knows just who they are.

She swoops in on Iyana. Iyana has always been a petulant woman, and Atiana baits her. She drifts away from the others, hoping to surprise, but Atiana is ready, and she smothers Iyana the moment she's far enough away to single out.

Rosa and Zanaida are more difficult. They have always been close, and it reflects in the aether. They support one another, and so Atiana is forced to pry them away from the rest. The others return quickly, hoping to bring them back into their circle, but before they can Atiana draws Rosa's mind outward and toward the straits. Zanaida does not wish to follow, but she feels as though she cannot abandon Rosa, and so both are dragged forward. The closer they come to the straits, the more unstable they become, and soon they too are gone.

Only three are now left, and they know their only hope is to stay together. They do not expect Atiana to fight them directly, however. She rushes in, singling out Ekaterina. She expends much of her energy, but she manages to rip Ekaterina away, and from there it is merely a matter of bearing down on her until she retreats.

Saphia and Mileva are the only two who remain. They are the strongest of the Matri. Saphia's mind is still bright, whereas Mileva's is muddled by Atiana's sudden and vicious attack.

Atiana presses down on Saphia before Mileva has a chance to recover. Saphia fights. Atiana's mind is drawn outward like oil upon the water. She is weakened, and she nearly slips from the aether as the Matri did only moments ago, but

534 • BRADLEY P. BEAULIEU

Sariya is still with her. She supports Atiana, and together they turn the tide.

Saphia falls, almost too easily.

There is no time to wonder, however, because Mileva is next. She is nearly as strong as Saphia, and her mind has regained its sharpness. Atiana withdraws, and Mileva comes for her, her anger at having been attacked by her own sister making her overly bold. It is perfect. She overreaches, and Atiana has her.

Something is wrong, though.

Atiana knows Mileva well. Even guarded as she is, Atiana can sense the satisfaction within her.

Satisfaction, Atiana realizes, of a plan that has worked all too well.

This is when Ishkyna strikes.

CHAPTER EIGHTY-THREE

Nasim felt in his chest the battle cry of the Anuskayan streltsi as a rush of janissaries attacked their line. Hundreds of soldiers met with the clash of musket fire and the rattle of weaponry and the full-throated cries of desperate men.

Nasim had known that these streltsi were veterans, but he had no idea just how brutally efficient they could be. The janissaries had formed a well-disciplined line, but when they met the streltsi of Khalakovo, they were divided into small groups. Like this, they were less able to rely on their comrades, and the streltsi, working in concert, would close in on a small group, taking down one or two men, before wheeling to attack another pocket of the enemy. The streltsi had all fired their muskets, but these men were equipped with wheellock pistols as well, and they used them whenever a janissary officer would call to rally his men. One by one, the enemy leaders fell, leaving their line a writhing, chaotic mess.

One of the streltsi assigned specifically to Nasim shouted, "Behind!"

Nasim turned and saw dozens of janissaries approaching from the rear.

The akhoz were close, but still too far away. Cyhir, the akhoz that had accompanied Nasim throughout the night, loped forward, but he was flung through the air and nearly torn in two as the shot from a cannon caught him fully in the gut. A gout of black flesh and blood sprayed from Cyhir's ruined body as some of the shot grazed Nasim's shin and thigh. Nasim crumpled, holding his leg, simultaneously sickened by what had happened to Cyhir and grateful he'd escaped with nothing more than skin-deep leg wounds.

Nearby, Ashan called rain down upon the enemy. Blood still welled from the wound to his shoulder, and his skin was as white as alabaster, but he somehow managed to remain calm through all of this and commune with a jalahezhan. The rain soon turned to sleet, and then hail the size of fists pummeled down on them.

The soldiers slipped and fell and ducked their heads for cover, but the fury of the hail was already beginning to ease.

Nasim, favoring his right leg heavily, stood and used Ashan's link to call upon the spirits of other jalahezhan. He still found himself forced to touch Adhiya through others, but now, since his death and rebirth on Ghayavand—if that's what it truly was—the way was much clearer, and with Adhiya so close, the spirits of water were able to feed upon him much more easily and much more heavily than they otherwise could have done.

Nasim let them.

It felt glorious to bond so closely with these spirits, something he hadn't done since finding himself. So heady was their touch that he nearly lost himself in their hunger to taste of the material world. He knew this was the last thing he could allow to happen, so he rose up and stood against their wishes. He commanded them. He asked that they give of themselves.

And they did. They added their strength to Ashan's. The hail beat down once more, but not as much as Nasim would have guessed. There was someone working against them; a qiram somewhere beyond the line of janissaries was sapping the strength of their hezhan. Nasim thought it might be many of the Hratha's qiram working in concert, but he soon realized it was only one.

Kaleh.

He pressed, more than he ever had since his awakening, giving more and more of himself, if only he could turn the tide against her. But she was strong, nearly as strong as Muqallad himself.

Ashan, favoring his right side, stood and grabbed Nasim's elbow. "Nasim, you're losing yourself!"

He didn't listen. He couldn't. There was so little time. He could feel the power building at the Spar already.

As the wind howled through the streets and a red dawn lit the sky, Nasim felt the hunger of a vanahezhan. It was feeding upon him to such a degree that it may soon consume him.

But this was what he needed. He needed to draw it as close as he could. When tears filled his eyes and stars danced in his vision, when he lost the feeling in his hands, when his mouth began to water so much that it hurt, he opened the way to it and *stepped aside*. The hezhan, feeling the way clear to Erahm, passed beyond this portal and into the material world.

Ahead, the cobbled street split. A massive form lifted, and for a moment it was all falling dirt and gravel and dust. But then its four arms broke away from its body, and its head lifted from a chest as large as a skiff. The clack of toppling rocks accompanied its legs lifting from the earth and bringing the beast to its full height—nearly as tall as a nearby two-story building.

This, Nasim knew, was an elder, a creature that had been in Adhiya for eons, choosing to stay instead of being reborn. It looked down at Nasim, but Nasim could do nothing more than point toward Kaleh and the soldiers of Yrstanla. The other hezhan were continuing to feed upon him, and he was no longer able to control it. He felt his legs weaken, felt his breath go shallow. He coughed as the world began to tilt.

And then at last it became too much, and Adhiya swallowed him whole.

When Nikandr woke, he was lying on the cold ground. His mind was muddied. It took all his will to simply open his eyes, and pushing himself off the ground felt nearly impossible. But he tried and managed to roll over so that he could see the landscape.

His head pounded, pain radiating from the top of his forehead. He could feel the dried blood along the right side of his face, could taste it in his mouth. The sun had not yet risen, but dawn was approaching. Ahead was a wide circle built by Aramahn hands. It was clean and bright, and decorated with traceries that reminded him of the organic curves of a seashell. Five akhoz crouched nearby, but they weren't watching him; they were watching the far side of the circle where Muqallad stood with Sariya and dozens of Hratha. Hunger seemed to fill the akhoz. He could see it in the way they crouched, like wolves sensing weakness in their prey.

Nikandr knew that Atiana was not herself. She was strained. She was under attack, and through his soulstone he knew that Mother and Mileva and Ishkyna were the aggressors.

And suddenly he remembered it all: the landing at the storehouse, the flight from the akhoz, the rush into Vihrosh with Styophan and the remains of his men and the Maharraht. He recalled the battle. He recalled the Hratha. He recalled the sounds of men dying.

And Atiana's betrayal…

Nyet. Not *her* betrayal. She had been taken by Sariya, or Muqallad, or both.

For long moments he struggled with what to do. Should he attack Sariya? Attack Muqallad? He reached down to his soulstone to ask for guidance from the ancients.

And realized he had two soulstones.

By all that was good, Ishkyna had given him the key to helping Atiana…

But he had to hurry.

He struggled and was able to reach his hands and knees. One of the akhoz turned at his movement, a girl with shriveled skin along her flat chest and an eyeless face. She pulled her lips back and heaved out a breath that was half snort, half moan. The others turned now. All five were watching him, their arms and necks twitching as he reached his knees.

He could only assume that Atiana's influence kept them at bay.

But what would happen when he freed her? *If* he freed her…

She stood on a weathered auctioneer's stage not far away. It had wooden ramps going up either side and a set of raised steps where the auctioneer would call to the crowd. She was looking toward the Spar, but she didn't look normal. Her whole body was crooked and tilted, as if she were one of the infirm, nursing pains in her back and hips and knees. And she was shivering—not the shiver of someone who was cold, but the shiver of one with a fever: inconsistent, and occasionally violent.

The sounds of distant battle from the far side of the Spar echoed over Vihrosh. Fire licked up into the sky from among the buildings near the bridge's landing.

The akhoz turned and looked with hungry expressions. They crept away from Nikandr, leaving him unwatched.

Atiana sank to her knees.

And Nikandr was freed, at least enough to stand and run.

He loped toward the platform, making it to the first of the planks before two of the akhoz noticed and loped after him.

The two necklaces swung from his neck. He felt for Atiana's more delicate chain and pulled it over his head. When he reached the top of the platform, the first of the akhoz grabbed at his ankle. He fell and slid along the well-worn planks.

"*Nyet!*" he cried.

Atiana was only paces away.

He scrabbled, knowing he would never make it to his feet. Something heavy fell on him from behind. He felt searing pain as the akhoz bit the flesh of his shoulder. He swung his elbow and caught it across the temple, sending it momentarily sprawling.

The other akhoz had recovered and snatched his leg, sunk its blood-crusted talons into his flesh.

He cried out as he reached Atiana at last and used his hands to pull her toward him as he kicked the akhoz.

He swung her necklace up and over her head. The nearest akhoz snatched for it, but he was too quick. He pulled it down around her neck as the two akhoz fell upon him, shrieking and baring their teeth.

With Atiana's concentration fixed wholly on Mileva, Ishkyna swoops in like an owl in the dead of the night, silent with talons bared.

Atiana feels a deep and sudden pain, deeper than she knew pain could go, but as soon as she tries to find Ishkyna, to take control, her sister vanishes.

Atiana returns her attention to Mileva, forcing her to stumble and nearly slip from the aether. Ishkyna returns just in time, but darts away when Atiana reacts. And so it goes, whenever Atiana bends her will on Mileva, Ishkyna returns and then dissipates like so much smoke upon the wind.

You are Ishkyna! Atiana rages, hoping that by invoking her name, her identity, she will once again become lost. *You are my sister! Daughter of Radia, a Princess of Vostroma!*

I was those things, but I am no longer.

And then, like a slow leak in the hull of a waterborne ship, Atiana realizes how fully Ishkyna has invaded her consciousness. It is nearly complete, but it isn't like what Atiana did to Nikandr. Rather, it is a cleansing. Ishkyna is pulling back the curtains to allow the light in.

It is Sariya's influence, however, that tilts the balance back. She has been weakened, but she also knows the end is near, and this gives her strength. She pushes, harder than she ever has before, and traps Ishkyna before she can escape.

Ishkyna rails against the bonds placed against her. Mileva tries to defend her, but with Sariya and Atiana working together, the tide is turning back.

But then Atiana feels something. Her body in Erahm... There is something near her, something so familiar she begins to weep.

Wet salty tears creep along her skin, and it is this one simple sensation that draws her attention to her soulstone—*her* soulstone. It makes her painfully aware of the connections she'd lost when she'd placed the chain around Ishkyna's neck. It had been in the kasir only two days before.

Ishkyna and Mileva storm over her.

Do not listen, Sariya calls, defending her as well as she's able. *You are mine!*

She *wants* to listen, to obey, but Nikandr is here... He is with her in Vihrosh. He was the one who put the necklace around her, though how he could have come by it she has no idea.

Mileva is thrown from the aether at last as Sariya assaults her.

Ishkyna, however, draws Atiana fully from her trance. She's become a force of nature. Willingly or not, she has given up her mortal shell to roam through the currents of the dark like the goedrun in the unseen depths of the sea, and though she was no master before this transition, she is one now. She is at home. She embraces that which she once feared, and with seeming ease clears from Atiana's mind the final remnants of Sariya's control.

Sariya knows that this battle has been lost, and she flees, but Ishkyna is ready. She snares Sariya before she can fully retreat. As skilled as Ishkyna is, Atiana knows that she cannot do this alone. She joins her sister, and together they press Sariya. They bear down on her soul.

Sariya lashes out, but she cannot hope to hold them off. Soon, she has been taken, and Atiana shifts her attention to controlling *her* instead of the other way around. Unknowingly, Sariya has taught her well, and she uses these skills now to tighten her hold on Sariya's mind.

On the platform in Vihrosh, she pushes herself up to her hands and knees. Nikandr is next to her. Two akhoz are on top of him, biting, clawing, scratching.

"Stop," she commands.

In an instant the akhoz obey. They crouch and bark and then whimper.

Beyond them, Sariya and Muqallad are walking toward the platform. Muqallad's expression is one of confusion as he takes in the scene on the platform. "What's happened?" He stares at Atiana, but the question is directed at Sariya.

At Atiana's bidding, Sariya turns to Muqallad. "As I said, the Matri attacked, but there were more than I'd guessed, and they were nearer."

"Where are they?"

"In the Shattering, but their minds are lost. We won't be bothered again."

Muqallad looks into the depths of Atiana's eyes. She can feel him probing in the aether, trying to determine for himself if all is well, but he is not gifted in the ways of the dark and cannot penetrate her defenses.

Atiana feigns that Sariya's spell still influences her, and Muqallad seems satisfied.

He glances to the east, where the sun's first rays are cresting the horizon. "Come," he says. "It is time."

Nasim woke, jostling back and forth. The sky above him shook. It took him some time, but he realized he was in someone's arms. He looked up and found Ashan grimacing as he carried Nasim away from the battle. Behind them, a dozen akhoz followed, galloping over the ground on all fours like a pack of mongrel dogs. There were no soldiers—no streltsi of Anuskaya, no janissaries of Yrstanla.

Over the tops of the smaller buildings, Nasim saw a gout of fire strike the vanahezhan he'd summoned. The skin of the vanahezhan's chest steamed and cracked like parched earth.

Ashan was nearing the Spar's wide, circular landing.

"Put me down," Nasim said.

Ashan kept running.

"Put me down!"

Ashan stopped, and finally did put Nasim down. His glanced at his own shoulder, shaking, as if he were about to pass out. How he had managed to carry him so far, Nasim couldn't guess.

Ashan smiled as widely as he was able, revealing crooked teeth. "I'll be well."

"Then come. We must hurry."

Together they took to the bridge, both of them moving slowly, Nasim from the wound to his left leg and Ashan from the shot to his shoulder. As they passed beyond the cliff and over the straits, the currents of the wind became chaotic. The wind gusted and howled, pressing against them as they made their way along it. It was so strong it threatened to knock them from their feet if they weren't careful.

They moved lower to the ground, and could see others approaching the center of the bridge from the far side. A cadre of men and women wearing robes of black and gray—the Hratha, led by several Nasim already recognized: Muqallad and Sariya and Atiana.

And Nikandr, from whom he could still sense their shared bond. He was shocked. He thought it had been severed on Ghayavand, but here it still was, a tendril thin as spider's silk.

The wind intensified. It was so loud Nasim could barely think. Two of the akhoz fell and were whisked off of the bridge. They twisted and clawed at empty air, twisting and tumbling until they were lost from sight.

Nasim drew upon a havahezhan to counter these winds—Ashan helped as well—but it was a constant tug o' war, the two of them pulling this way and that in reaction to the chaotic ways of the winds.

They made slow progress, but three more akhoz were lost. The remaining seven Nasim unleashed. They stayed low as they sprinted forward, their calls nearly lost among the thunder of the wind. The Hratha—only two or three dozen were left now—ran forward to meet them. They raised their muskets, but Ashan called down rain to foil their shots. Only two managed to fire, and one of the akhoz dropped. It was up again in a moment, limping after the others.

The akhoz leapt upon the warriors. They belched fire as the Hratha's curved shamshirs arced and spun. Their war calls dimly mixed with the braying of the akhoz.

Nasim and Ashan were now within a hundred paces of the Spar's midpoint, which was marked by two squat towers on either side of the roadway.

From these towers, a score of men emerged—by the fates, they were the Maharraht.

As they ran toward the Hratha and the akhoz, two final forms emerged from the left tower. The first was Soroush, and the second was Ushai, the qiram Nasim had seen those many weeks ago on his flight toward Ghayavand. Her left arm was bandaged heavily, but she otherwise seemed hearty and hale.

How she had come to be here with Soroush, he couldn't guess, but there was no time to wonder.

They both appeared ready to chase after Soroush's men, but when they spotted Nasim they stopped. Soroush glanced at the tower, then down at the roadway, and finally he beckoned to Ushai and began sprinting toward Nasim and Ashan.

They hadn't taken ten long strides when an explosion rocked the Spar. Stone flew into the air, and the center of the bridge became little more than a roiling cloud of black smoke and bright flames.

Nasim was struck by something—he knew not what. It propelled him backward, throwing him down roughly against the roadway. A sound like worlds breaking came immediately after, and for long moments he could only blink his eyes and stare at the stones flying outward and the rubble raining down.

His ears rang.

His fingers were numb.

He pushed himself up so that he could sit and look upon the devastation. The wind had not yet cleared the air fully, but he could see through the dust and smoke the remains of the left tower. It was crumbling before his very eyes. The bulk of it collapsed and fell toward the cold embrace of the churning white waves, leaving only one low portion of wall, as if the destruction of the world had already begun.

At last the wind drew the dust away, and the roadway was revealed. Nearly half of it had been devoured by the explosion, but the rest remained.

It remained...

By the fates, Soroush had failed.

And that meant Muqallad could still complete his plans.

Atiana feels the explosion in her chest. She falls, but the sensations are distant, like a memory from her childhood.

She walks through the currents of the aether more than she does the world of Erahm, and the feeling is heady.

Ahead, the akhoz are the first to recover, but the Maharraht are not far behind. Together they attack what remain of the Hratha, killing many of them before Muqallad reaches his feet. He raises one hand, the one holding the Atalayina, and a bolt of searing white lightning arcs from it to the nearest of the akhoz. It slips through three of them, and one of the Maharraht, felling them in an instant.

Atiana feels the walls of the aether here. They are so close she can almost reach out and touch them. As she did on Oshtoyets years ago, she pushes them away in hopes that Muqallad's summoning will become more difficult, but the pressure is too great. She forces Sariya to help her, and Ishkyna joins as well. The gap does indeed widen, but it does nothing to stop Muqallad from drawing upon a dhoshahezhan again and again until all of the Maharraht lay dead.

Only three akhoz remain, and to these he raises his hand and calls above the wind, "Come... Come, my children."

The akhoz crouch and bare their teeth. They bark and snarl and stretch their necks as if they're suddenly afflicted. One of them turns and looks back to the four souls who approach from the far side of the blackened tower. Nasim is there, as well as Ashan and Soroush and Ushai.

Two of the akhoz mewl and crawl toward Muqallad, but the other sprints toward Nasim. He does not gallop on all fours like the akhoz often do. Instead, he runs, as a child might. In that moment he looks like nothing more than a small, naked boy.

Before he can go more than ten paces another bolt flies from the Atalayina, but it strikes ground short of the akhoz. Another blinding strike is sent forth, but this too is foiled.

Nasim has one hand raised, and he walks ahead of the others. There is something about him that seems different. No longer does Atiana see a boy who cowers from the world, who wonders how he might find his way through it. Instead she sees a young man, confident and strong. Transcendent.

But Muqallad is not weak, and he holds the Atalayina.

Atiana beckons her sisters. *Come.*

Sariya, knowing the time approaches, grows desperate. She rises up, stronger than Atiana would have guessed she could be. She rails against Atiana and her sisters, and she surfaces at last. "Beware, Muqallad! The Matri have come!" With those simple words, she is overcome with pain, and she falls to her knees, clutching her side.

With Ishkyna and Mileva at her side, Atiana advances. The three of them know one another so well that they are able to fend off Muqallad's clumsy attacks. He is not weak, however, and he stands against them.

And then his presence is gone. Simply gone.

Atiana searches desperately, until she realizes the Atalayina is the power behind this. Muqallad has somehow drawn his presence from the aether so that he exists only in the material world.

Muqallad turns, holding the Atalayina high. It is bright and blue. Power emanates from it like the light of the sun.

And then the world slows. The wind stills. A shimmering builds at the edges of her vision, and her mind feels leaden.

With a raised hand, Muqallad calls out to Nikandr. "Come," he says. It is soft, for the wind can no longer be heard beyond a low susurrus at the edge of hearing. The clouds above have not stopped swirling, but they move so slowly that Atiana wonders if they are real. If *this* is real. Perhaps it is all a dream…

And yet she knows it is not. She knows this is the power of the Atalayina.

Nikandr goes to him.

Sariya, however, does not. She has fallen to the ground. She still holds her side, but she is weak and near to death.

Muqallad looks down at her with something akin to sadness or regret, but then he turns, beckoning Nikandr to follow. Together the two of them leave Sariya lying on the ground like a forgotten she-bitch and walk toward the blackened center of the Spar.

Stop! Atiana calls to Nikandr.

But he doesn't look back. Not once.

Please, Nischka! Stop!

She calls to him over and over, but she knows that his mind has been taken. She doesn't understand how at first, but then she sees it, the tendril that connects him to Nasim. The connection that was formed between them years ago. It thinned when Nasim woke in Oshtoyets, but it had never been severed, and here it is now, being used against him.

Nikandr, please wake!

But he does not heed her calls.

Nikandr tried to deny Muqallad, but the command had come not just from him; it had been amplified by the Atalayina. Nikandr could feel it, glowing like a brand against his will, and he could do nothing but shrink from it.

He followed Muqallad to the center of the Spar, where one tower stood proud. The other was ruined, with only crumbling remains.

"I nearly lost him," Muqallad said to Nikandr as he beckoned him to kneel.

Nikandr complied, staring up into Muqallad's dark eyes.

"Had he been taken years ago, all of my plans would have been lost. But you," Muqallad said. "You saved him. You sheltered him."

And then Nikandr understood. He didn't mean Nikandr had saved Nasim in any physical sense. He meant that Nikandr had saved his soul and mind through their bond.

Muqallad held out one hand.

Nikandr stared at it—his right hand. In his left Muqallad held the Atalayina. The stone glowed so brightly it was blinding, even compared to the light of the sun hanging over the horizon. He knew that if he took Muqallad's hand, it would give him what he needed to reach Nasim.

He couldn't do that—not to Nasim.

But neither could he resist.

He put all of himself into defying Muqallad's will, and still his arm lifted. He could hear Atiana's voice, but it was so distant that he heard only disjointed portions of her desperate pleas.

Smiling, Muqallad took Nikandr's hand, and the moment he did, Nikandr felt the connection between him and Nasim grow stronger, more vibrant, like the thread of a web caught with morning dew.

He felt Nasim approach. He was being drawn by this thread, drawn by the will of Muqallad and the power of the Atalayina.

He wanted to call to Nasim, to warn him away. He wanted to wake him from this spell.

But he could not. He was trapped by these events as surely as Nasim.

On the horizon, the sun stood upon the edge of the world. The skies over the Spar were swirling, as if *this* place were the very center of all that ever was and ever would be.

But then something caught Nikandr's attention. Over Muqallad's shoulder, beneath the swirling clouds, was a ship.

And it was hurtling toward the Spar.

It took him a moment to realize it was the *Bhadyar*.

But Soroush was *here*, Nikandr thought. The Maharraht had abandoned their ships at the hidden bay...

With a sudden and shocking clarity, he realized who had come.

Grigory...

Grigory had come with the men who'd been left behind, men too wounded to fight.

Nikandr marveled at the very thought of it.

Nasim watched as Nikandr kneeled on the blackened roadway. He was caught as everyone else was.

Nasim understood now. The Al-Aqim needed to die for this ritual to be complete. Sariya had already fallen, succumbing to the wound inflicted by Ushai. Muqallad had hoped that the ritual on the beach of Alayazhar would free Khamal's link to the Atalayina. Nasim had been saved by Rabiah, but now Muqallad would finish what he'd started, and the only way Nasim could prevent it was by coming to himself once and for all.

To do this, his tie to Nikandr must be severed. Their shared link was why Nikandr had been able to commune with the havahezhan. It was why *Nasim* had been so limited, as well, and even though he was now able to touch Adhiya, it was not as complete as it might be. His bonds to Nikandr and Muqallad saw to that.

Severing his tie was not so easily done, however. He would gladly give of himself, even if it meant he would pass from this world, never to return, but he refused to do so if it delivered the world to Muqallad.

He remembered how it had felt in Oshtoyets, that small keep on the rocky coast of Duzol those many years ago. He had been at the heart of all things. It had felt as though he could reshape the world.

And so it was now

He only needed to embrace it.

He pulled a knife from Soroush's belt and strode forward, wishing there were another way.

To sacrifice himself would be easy.

But this...

He didn't know, even now, if he could do it.

He drew the world around himself like a cloak, like a burial shroud. The other times he'd done this, it had been beneath his consciousness, but now he was fully aware of what he was doing.

Time slowed. Muqallad's movements became a crawl.

Nasim stepped forward and kneeled before Nikandr until they were face-to-face. He looked into Nikandr's handsome face, saw the small scar above his left eyebrow. He knew in that instant that it had been caused by an errant swipe of a fire brand, swung by his brother, Ranos. His eyes were a deep brown with the smallest traces of green, like hidden forest vales in the growth of spring. He'd looked at Nikandr before, but never in such an intimate way. It made Nasim supremely uncomfortable, but he owed Nikandr this for what he was about to do. Nikandr was not his father—he was nothing like Ashan—nor was he his brother. And still, he owed Nikandr much. Certainly he owed him this, an honest look into his soul before he took his life.

Nikandr blinked. There was fear and uncertainty in his eyes, but there was also a resolve that made Nasim proud.

Nikandr swallowed, his gaze dropping to the khanjar before meeting Nasim's eyes once more. And then he nodded.

With one hand Nasim held Nikandr's shoulder, and with the other drove the knife into Nikandr's chest. He drove it until it could go no further.

Nikandr stared, eyes wide and tearing. He looked down. His lips were parted, releasing his final breath. His head quivered, and spittle fell onto the blackened stone.

He met Nasim's eyes one last time.

The look on his face was one of understanding. He tried to smile, but failed to do so. He coughed once, and then leaned to one side, holding himself, barely, against the roadway of this massive work of man.

Nasim lowered him down until he laid face up, staring at the sky, the knife quivering from his chest. His eyes opened and closed. He swallowed once, twice, and then lay perfectly still.

The wind once more began to howl. The clouds once more began to swirl. And Muqallad stared down, his eyes aflame.

He was coming to the realization that he had lost what he had sought, but in his mind there might still be time.

He held the Atalayina high and reached for Nasim.

Nasim rolled away and reached his feet as a bolt of lightning coursed forth from Muqallad's outstretched palm.

Nasim caught it in his own hand and delivered it to the world beyond. It was easy now, and Muqallad knew the tables had turned.

Muqallad stepped forward and grabbed Nasim's robes. He blocked the weak strike of Nasim's fist, twisting his arm until he was forced down to roadway stones. As Muqallad held the Atalayina high, perhaps readying to smash it against Nasim's skull, Nasim saw something large and dark and swift rushing toward the bridge.

Muqallad had no more time than to turn and look before the windship crashed into the Spar.

CHAPTER EIGHTY-FOUR

Nikandr stared at the handle of the knife. It rested over his chest, moving in time to his heartbeat. He should grasp it, he thought. He should try to remove it. He managed to bring one hand to it, but the simple act of touching it brought searing white pain the likes of which he'd never known.

He had time only to look up at a rush of movement at the edge of his vision before the world around him erupted.

Something massive crashed into the Spar at the exact place where the explosion had weakened it.

A ship. It was a ship.

The hull buckled, collapsing like a house of cards as the ship drove down onto the keystones. The masts cracked. The sails were thrown downward. In a mere instant the front half of the ship transformed from a structured and ordered thing into a massive, tangled collection of splintered beams and rope and sail. The bodies of men flew and were dashed against the white stone.

The landward foremast snapped at the hull, throwing the bulk of the mast and her sails sharply forward. Muqallad turned to meet this threat just as the mast's topgallant swung down against the bridge, narrowly missing him. But the topgallant yard caught Muqallad squarely across the head, crushing him and throwing him down against the Spar's roadway in a mass of red.

The rear half of the ship groaned, hanging in the air momentarily before the keystones gave way. The structure beneath the roadway weakened as if it were little more than a pile of stones succumbing to the sea, and then it gave way entirely. It created a gap where the keystones had been, and it widened quickly, moving closer and closer to the section upon which Nikandr lay.

And then roadway fell out from underneath him.

He plummeted, grabbing ineffectually at empty air as the wound in his chest burned white hot. The underside of the Spar receded, faster and faster, until the wind threw him about and sent him twisting and turning and tumbling toward the sea.

The desperate part of him wanted to claw for his havahezhan, but he knew the moment Nasim had driven the knife home that that link was gone. He'd felt it snap—his connection to Nasim, his connection to Adhiya.

Something flashed in the sky above him.

He lost it, found it again a moment later. Something burning brightly.

It came nearer. It was a person, but the wind was whipping him about so fiercely he couldn't tell who.

But then the wind began working on him. He could feel it slowing him down, and suddenly he was hovering in the air not two paces from Nasim.

Nasim tumbled once, but then steadied as he drifted closer. His control was now absolute, and they were close enough that if they reached out to one another, their fingers might just barely be able to touch.

Nasim was holding the Atalayina, and it glowed as brightly in his hand as it had in Muqallad's. He was close enough to embrace. With one hand he held the Atalayina high. And with the other pulled the knife free.

Nikandr screamed. Clutched at his wound.

He blacked out for a moment, and when he woke, Nasim was pressing the Atalayina against his chest as if it were a bolt of cloth meant to staunch his wound.

The Atalayina chilled Nikandr to his core. It was as cold as night, the feeling as wide and limitless as the firmament. The cold filled him, changed him, made him feel whole in ways he could not remember feeling before, and for a moment, the world opened up before him, was laid bare. He saw Erahm and Adhiya and the aether in between. Breath slipped from his lungs at the beauty of it all.

But then the feeling was gone, and the wind began to change. It buffeted them in new and unexpected ways, and Nasim was suddenly and violently pulled away. The Atalayina was pulled away as well, and the moment it was no longer touching his skin, Nikandr felt alone and abandoned and forgotten. It felt as though he'd never been born.

He dropped toward the water, limp, unable to do anything but let the currents of wind take him. Nasim, flailing wildly at the air with a horror-stricken expression, was too far away to do anything.

"*Neh!*" he screamed while trying and failing to come closer to Nikandr.

And then a slight form barreled downward like a cormorant diving for the sea. It was Kaleh, Nikandr realized. She struck Nasim mid-air, and the Atalayina was knocked from his grasp to float free of the twisting, turning forms.

The two of them crashed into the sea.

Mere moments before Nikandr did.

He fell deep, the sound of it raucous in his ears. The air was pressed from his lungs. He flailed in the dark, not understanding which way was up. The salty water of the sea forced its way into his lungs, and he coughed, drawing in more while trying desperately to pull himself up toward the surface.

He kicked. He stroked his arms. All as the salt water burned his throat and mouth and lungs.

Ages seemed to pass, but at last he broke through to the surface. The waves fell down upon him mercilessly, pulling him under. He coughed reflexively, water spilling from his throat.

He tried to stay above the waves, but it was impossible. He was weak. So weak. And the waves threw him about, always tossing him back beneath the surface. He kicked. He pulled, but his strength was beginning to fail.

He grew angry and desperate, kicking at the crest of each wave to look for Nasim. He managed to call to him once, but heard nothing in return. There was detritus from the ship that had crashed into the Spar—some of which was still falling and striking the sea around him—but of Nasim he saw nothing.

And then it became too much. His anger was spent, and the waves once more began to drag him down.

Again and again the water fell upon him. Filling his mouth, slipping down his throat and into his lungs before he could clear the water away. He was beyond desperation. He was despondent, accepting, for he knew the end was near.

Until he heard a crash nearby.

He felt the water roil around him. He felt it push him upward. It lifted him, a column of water above the roiling sea. Not far away was a large piece of the ship's hull, tilting and turning on the sea-tossed waves. On it was a man, and through his wracking coughs he realized it was Ashan.

He could see a wide area of the straits now, and he scanned the water desperately. "Nasim!" he called. "Nasim!"

He tried again and again as the water bore him toward Ashan. He searched, shouting until his throat was raw, but he received no answer, and saw no signs.

The column of water deposited Nikandr down upon the plank. Ashan, his face pinched with concern, moved quickly with strong arms to pull Nikandr to the center of the makeshift raft. In the clouds high above the Spar, a maelstrom spun. Dirt and debris caught by the wind rained down, biting the skin of his scalp and hands as he cowered from it.

Again Ashan called upon the water to bear them swiftly across the channel toward the northern cliff. Massive pieces of the Spar, which was still breaking up, crashed into the sea, sending plumes of water high into the air. On the far side of the straits, a column of stone calved from the cliff face, crumbling as it fell. When it struck the water, a massive wave formed and spread outward, consuming the distance toward the opposite set of cliffs.

Their raft reached a break in the cliffs, a shallow inlet. Ashan lifted them high on the mound of water as the worst of the massive waves crashed below. As they subsided, he set them down on a shelf of stone twenty feet up from the chaos below.

As the wind continued to rage, as the debris rained down, Nikandr looked to the sea for Nasim or for Kaleh, and though he searched and called through the harrowing hours that followed, he never found them.

Nikandr hoped to find Atiana on the northern side of the Spar, so when the storms finally died down, he asked Ashan to take him there. They flew up on currents of wind, and Ashan set them down near the Spar's landing not twenty paces away from the auction house platform where he'd slipped Atiana's soulstone necklace around her neck.

"We should divide our efforts," Ashan said as he waved to Nikandr. "There are those I would search for as well."

Nikandr wandered the streets of Vihrosh, asking questions of those he saw. Few braved the streets early on, but as time passed, more and more came out of their homes and began asking for news and inspecting the damage to their city. He spent hours, asking everyone he could if they'd seen a woman matching Atiana's description, but they all shook their heads.

The storm—so fierce only a few hours before—seemed to have burned itself out entirely, so that by the time Nikandr gave up the search, the clouds cleared and the sun shone down. It was a strange reality to be faced with—a beautiful day after the devastation he'd witnessed.

When he returned to the Spar, Ashan stood at the landing with a young man of fourteen or fifteen. Ashan introduced him as Sukharam, and apparently he'd traveled far with Nasim.

"Do you think him dead then?" Sukharam asked. Clearly Ashan had told him of the final moments on the Spar and the water below.

"I hope not," Nikandr said.

The boy's eyes became more intense, almost angry. "Do you think him dead?"

It was a question he probably deserved an answer to, but Nikandr wouldn't be pushed. Not now.

"I hope not," he said again, and walked past the two of them.

He made his way to the broken end of the Spar and leaned out over the shorn edge to stare at the water below. He still had his soulstone. He had cast outward with it several times on his walk through Vihrosh, hoping to feel Atiana, and now he did so again. As it was before, he could not sense her, but neither could he sense anyone else—not his mother nor father nor any of the Matri. No one. The stone felt deadened, though whether this was due to their deaths or some artifact of the destruction of the Spar and the grand release of energy that followed he wasn't sure.

Ashan stepped up beside him and stared down toward the water as well. His foot shifted a stone, which flew down toward the sea, its arc curving as the wind took it. "Sukharam was brusk, but he had a point."

Nikandr shook his head sadly. "I don't know if he died." Where the knife had cut through his coat and shirt, he could reach through and touch the raw wound that Nasim had healed with the Atalayina. The subtle feeling that he was connected to Nasim was gone. And he was poorer for it. He'd always felt that he would one day find Nasim, that they would help one another close the rifts.

But now...

Now he didn't know if that would ever be possible. Muqallad and Sariya had been stopped, but the world had been left in a terrible state. Who knew what would happen tomorrow?

Movement along the Spar caught Nikandr's attention.

A skiff floated up and away from Baressa, making its way steadily toward the Spar, toward their location. After a wait that seemed like days, it crossed the gap at the center of the Spar and came to a rest nearby. Anahid was in the skiff, guiding it.

And Atiana was there as well.

As she swung over the side of the skiff, Nikandr rushed forward and swept her up in a deep embrace. He held her tight, a rush of emotions soaring inside him.

"I thought you were gone," he whispered.

He heard her sniffling. "I thought the same of you."

When at last they pulled away, she smiled and brushed away his tears. He brushed away hers and drew her in again, kissing her warm, salt-laced lips.

After taking his hand, she led him into the skiff. She beckoned to Ashan and Sukharam as well, and soon all four of them were inside, flying back toward the city.

"Nikandr," Atiana said, taking his hands in hers. She gripped them tightly as she sat on the thwart. "I have grave news." Nikandr felt his insides go weak, but Atiana, with intent emotion, held his gaze, giving him strength. "My father is dead. Sacrificed by the Kamarisi before the first ships crossed the Spar."

Nikandr stared, shocked to hear these words. "It cannot be so."

She shook her head, squeezing his hands so that he would let her finish. "Your father… He came to lead the charge. He commanded brilliantly, but in the end the Galaheshi elite broke through and rushed the commanders huddled behind the lines.

"They retreated, but your father was taken by a musket shot." She paused, steeling herself, giving Nikandr time to absorb this. "He's dead, Nischka. He lasted only minutes after taking the wound."

Nikandr felt himself go cold and distant. The sound of the wind faded in his ears. He felt Atiana's hand on his knee, felt her move to sit on his thwart and hug him, and even though he hugged her back, none of it felt real, especially those words: *He's dead, Nischka.*

Anahid flew them up to Kasir Yalidoz and landed the skiff in the center of the grand patio. Anahid glanced at the kasir but refused to leave the skiff. "You have much to do," she said, "and I would speak with Ashan."

Nikandr nodded numbly, grasping Ashan's offered hand and kissing him on the forehead. "Thank you," he said.

He nodded a kind farewell to Sukharam, but as he passed Anahid, he leaned in and kissed her as well. "And you."

She smiled for him, but in that smile there was only sadness, not joy.

Inside the kasir, dozens of men were gathered, men of the Grand Duchy. The conversation in the room dropped to a whisper as Nikandr and Atiana entered. All eyes were upon them.

Without being given a command, the crowd parted, creating an aisle toward a central table where Konstantin Bolgravya and Leonid Dhalingrad stood. As Atiana and Nikandr walked side by side toward them, the polkovnik, Andreya Antonov, and his aides bowed their heads and left.

Konstantin stepped forward first, kissing Atiana's hand and then taking Nikandr into a tight embrace. As they kissed one another's cheeks, he said, "It's a wonder you're alive."

"It is a wonder even to *me*, My Lord Duke."

Konstantin glanced to Atiana, who nodded soberly. "I'm sorry for your loss, Nischka. Iaros was a great man."

"Thank you," Nikandr replied, though he knew how emotionless his words must sound.

At a clearing of Leonid's throat, Konstantin bowed his head and returned to Leonid's side.

To Nikandr's great surprise, Leonid stepped forward as well. The Leonid *Nikandr* knew would have stood there and waited for Nikandr to approach *him*. The old duke held Nikandr by the shoulders, staring at him with a comforting look. It looked strange on Leonid, this hawk of a man, and it warred with his haggard eyes and long white beard that made him look more like one of the haunting statues that graced the Grand Duchy's mausoleums. They hugged and kissed cheeks, but instead of releasing him, Leonid held him tight and whispered into his ear. "I am sorry for your loss, Nischka. It was your father that saw us through this war. Because of him, we now stand victorious."

As he rubbed Nikandr's shoulders compassionately, a notion came to Nikandr. It was foolish. Preposterous. And yet it was something he couldn't shake, and when Leonid pulled Nikandr back and stared deeply into his eyes, it began to set like clay.

Nikandr knew... Knew his father's death had not been from some act of war. Knew it hadn't been an accident. He knew it had been *planned*, and the one who'd set that plan in motion was staring at him as if he were his own son.

With Zhabyn and Iaros both dead, the mantle of Grand Duke would fall to Leonid. Council would be held, but there was no doubt as to what the outcome would be, especially since Leonid had been the one to finish this battle. He would be the one to reap the rewards.

"I hope you'll bring my regrets back to Khalakovo with you," Leonid said.

"Where is my father?"

At this, Leonid's eyes changed. Though it would be imperceptible to everyone else, Nikandr saw them harden, and his expression of sympathy faded. He released Nikandr and snapped his fingers. A page boy came forward and bowed. "Take what time you need," Leonid said, "but then return. There is much to do before the city is secured."

With those simple words, Nikandr understood that Leonid meant to take Baressa, to take Galahesh as another island in the Grand Duchy. It was a bold move. The Kamarisi was dead, but his eldest son would now take the throne, and he would bend his will against Anuskaya in order to take back what was his.

But really this was the only course of action Leonid could take. He was not one given to diplomacy. He saw things only as property to be won, held, or coveted. Perhaps in time they could have settled this dispute peaceably with Yrstanla. But not now. Not unless another duke was given the mantel.

There was this and much more to consider, but for the time being Nikandr could concentrate on none of it.

He wanted only to look upon his father.

To say farewell.

In a room deep beneath Kasir Yalidoz, Nikandr held Atiana's hand. The two of them stood before the bodies of their fathers, which had been wrapped carefully in white cloth and set upon slabs of bright white marble. Three lanterns hung from nearby posts. Wooden coffins rested beyond the marble slabs, ready to accept the bodies of the dukes for transport back to Vostroma and Khalakovo.

Nikandr shivered from the cold. Atiana, next to him, had not shivered once since they'd been led down into this massive cellar. They had been here a long while already, both of them standing in silence, saying their mute farewells to these strong men. Nikandr's feelings before coming here were a confused jumble, as though he hadn't enough room to grieve for so many, but now that he was here, he was focused not only on his own grief, but Atiana's as well.

"Go well," Atiana said softly. Her words echoed into the darkness.

"Go well," Nikandr said as well.

He took Atiana into an embrace. "I'm sorry, Atiana."

"It wasn't your fault."

"*Nyet*. I'm sorry for what I did to you in Ivosladna. I'm sorry I didn't come when you asked for my help."

She held him tighter, and then released him. By the golden light of the nearby lanterns, he saw her smile sadly.

They walked back toward the stairs and took the long flight up to ground level.

"There is war ahead," Atiana said.

"And perhaps a long one," he replied. "We cannot allow Yrstanla to have either Galahesh or Oramka now. Both must be secured."

They reached the top of the stairs and stepped out through the doors, where an honor guard was set to watch—two Vostroman streltsi and two Khalakovan, each in full regalia. The soldiers bowed deeply and closed the doors behind them with a boom.

Atiana led Nikandr toward the stained-glass doors. They strode through these and out to the grand patio, where a cold wind blew. They walked to the edge, where they could look over the expanse of Baressa and the straits beyond. Nikandr leaned on the balustrade, staring at a column of smoke that rose to the northwest, the remnant of a fire that had stared during the fierce battle. "Where is Soroush?"

"I don't know. I didn't see him after the ship crashed. He must have left with Ushai and the remains of the Maharraht before our streltsi arrived."

Nikandr shook his head, looking north toward the Spar. He could see much of its length and the large gap at its center. His mind was still fresh with the chaos of those final moments. The destruction was incredible, and surely Muqallad was dead, but it still didn't feel like things had been decided.

"No matter what becomes of the war," Nikandr said, "there is still Ghayavand. The rifts will continue to widen."

"And there is the matter of the Atalayina." She meant not only the Atalayina, but Nasim as well. He was their best chance at closing the rifts once and for all. "He's powerful," Atiana continued. "He might have lived."

A flutter of wings in the distance drew their attention. A large black bird flapped slowly toward them, more ponderous in its movements than a rook, but more powerful as well. It winged down to the balustrade nearby and came to a rest. The same old gallows crow that Nikandr had seen on that ship against the cliffs of Yrstanla. It walked along with an awkward gait, releasing a long, sad caw. The white swatch across its breast and the underside of its wings shone bright under the sun.

"I've found her," the crow said.

"Found who?"

"Kaleh," Atiana replied.

Nikandr looked between the two of them.

"She told me of the battle between Kaleh and Nasim," Atiana said, "and she said she would watch for them."

"I saw them fall to the water"—the crow cawed and shook its head vigorously—"but I lost them in the maelstrom. I've been searching for them since. Of Nasim, I've found nothing. I can only assume he is dead. Of Kaleh I felt little, until the faintest of scents came to me. It trailed from here and then far to the west, to the very edge of the Gaji. I traveled there, looking for her, and felt her walking far ahead, but as I neared, her trail disappeared."

"It couldn't have just disappeared," Atiana said.

"It did," the crow replied, "and I suspect it was the Atalayina that allowed her to do so."

"Where is she going?" Nikandr asked.

"With Sariya and Muqallad both dead, she will go to find those who can teach her of the Atalayina. If anyone will know, it will be the tribes who still live in the heart of the Gaji. They've lived there for centuries beyond count, hiding themselves from the outside world, even from the Aramahn."

"Then that is where we must go," Nikandr said.

All three of them remained silent. They knew it would be death to try to invade those lands, but what could they do? They had to find the Atalayina. They had to stop Kaleh from completing what Muqallad and Sariya had begun.

"Go," the crow said as it hopped along the balustrade. "There is time yet to decide. I will watch for her, and for Nasim, though I have little hope for him. In time, we will know the right course."

With that the crow flew off, its wings spread wide as it glided down and over the city.

Atiana turned to Nikandr. "There is Leonid to consider. And the welfare of Khalakovo."

"This is no easy choice I make, Tiana."

"I know," she said.

With that, the two of them embraced, neither one of them feeling the comfort that should have come from the gesture.

"I know we must go," she said again.

ON ELEMENTAL SPIRITS AND THE USE OF STONES

The Aramahn harness the elements by drawing spirits, or hezhan, close to the material world and bonding with them. They do this by way of specific stones, each of which is aligned with one of the elements. The men and women who are able to do this are called qiram. The specific name of the qiram is altered based on the type of spirit they're able to bond with. Thus, a qiram who bonds with spirits of earth, vanahezhan, are called vanaqiram. Those who bond with spirits of fire, suurahezhan, are called suuraqiram.

Earth
 Gem: jasper
 Spirit: vanahezhan

Fire
 Gem: tourmaline
 Spirit: suurahezhan

Life
 Gem: opal
 Spirit: dhoshahezhan

Air
 Gem: alabaster
 Spirit: havahezhan

Water
 Gem: azurite
 Spirit: jalahezhan

The people of the Grand Duchy cannot bond with spirits. However, they do have magic of their own. They use chalcedony, and it can range in use by the peasantry to honor their dead to more formal use by royalty. The Matri use the stones in order to anchor themselves while in the aether. They also use them to find others with whom they've recently "touched stones." Chalcedony grants no direct control over the elements, but the Matri do guide the ley lines that run between the spires in order to create stronger, more predictable currents for the ships to sail along.

ON THE PRIMARY DIRECTIONS OF WINDSHIPS

The windships in the Lays of Anuskaya are in some ways similar to their waterborne brethren. However, they are buoyant, and they never touch the water, docking at great eyries built onto the faces of cliffs instead of docks by the sea. They also have masts not just directly upward from the deck, but in all four of a ship's primary directions.

The list below gives some grounding of the terminology used by the windsmen of the Grand Duchy.

bow: the front end of the ship.
stern: the rearmost portion of the ship.
fore: toward the foremost portion of the ship.
aft: toward the rearmost portion of the ship.

starward: upward from the deck of the ship, toward the sky and stars.
seaward: downward, named so because the windships often fly above water.
landward: to the left while facing the fore of the ship, the side where windships tie up to a perch or a dock.
windward: to the right while facing the fore of the ship, named so because the wind is in this direction when the windship is moored.

mainmast: the central mast in any given direction. Thus, the mainmast that points down toward the sea is called the seaward mainmast, and the one pointing upward is called the starward mainmast.
foremast: the mast nearest the bow. Similar to the mainmast, the foremast can be modified to indicate which direction is being referenced (i.e. the landward foremast).
mizzenmast: the mast aft of the mainmast.

keel: refers to the obsidian cores of the ship's four mainmasts. Another length of obsidian is laid through the ship from stern to bow. The ley lines are captured by these three components of the keel, orienting the ship in a certain direction and allowing it to maintain that position as it sails forward like a waterborne ship through the sea.

rudder: a complex set of obsidian cylinders at the center of the ship, the nexus where the four mainmasts meet the obsidian core that runs lengthwise through the ship. These three sets of cylinders are adjusted by the pilot at the helm.

helm: the helm contains a set of three levers. These levers alter the set of the rudder, allowing the keel to set itself against the ley lines and turn the ship freely along all three axes: roll, pitch, and yaw.

GLOSSARY

Adhiya: the supernatural world of the hezhan; the world beyond the material world.

aether: the realm that separates the physical realm, Erahm, from the spiritual realm, Adhiya.

akhoz: children that have become twisted by the Al-Aqim on the island of Ghayavand. Their eyes have closed over with skin, and they breathe fire, as they're bonded with suurahezhan.

Alif: the akhoz that Khamal chooses to perform his ritual on the beach below Alayazhar.

Ahya Soroush al Rehada: deceased daughter of Rehada and Soroush. Died on the shores of Bolgravya.

Al-Aqim: the three arqesh who created the rift over Galahesh. Sariya, Muqallad, and Khamal.

Alayazhar: the largest city on Ghayavand, now in ruins.

Aleg Ganevov Khazabyirsk: the Duke of Khazabyirsk.

Alekeşir: the capital city of Yrstanla, one of the world's oldest cities.

Alesya Zaveta Bolgravya: wife to the former Grand Duke, Stasa Bolgravya.

Anahid: Nikandr's dhoshaqiram, the cousin of Jahalan.

Andreyo Sergeyov Rhavanki: the Duke of Rhavanki.

arqesh: an Aramahn qiram who has mastered all five disciplines (water, earth, fire, air, and life), and who has also reached a higher level of enlightenment.

Ashan Kida al Ahrumea: one of the arqesh (master of all disciplines) among the Aramahn.

Atalayina: a legendary stone used by the Al-Aqim in their failed attempt to bring about indaraqiram on the island of Ghayavand.

Atiana Radieva Vostroma: daughter of the Duke and Duchess of Vostroma. Nikandr's lover.

Avayom Kirilov: a kapitan of Bolgravya's staaya.

Avil: a strelet of Khalakovo who travels with Nikandr.

Bahett ül Kirdhash: the Kaymakam of Galahesh.

Behnda al Tib: the largest village of the Hratha in the islands to the south of the Grand Duchy.

berdische axe: a tall axe which streltsi use to rest their muskets against for higher accuracy.

Bersuq Wahad al Gatha: Soroush's brother and second in command.

bichaq: slightly curved knife, used primarily in Yrstanla.

Borund Zhabynov Vostroma: eldest child and only son of Zhabyn and Radia Vostroma.

Brunhald: a one-footed rook belonging to the Bolgravya family. Alesya Bolgravya assumed Brunhald shortly before assuming Atiana before the Battle of Uyadensk.

cherkesska: long black coat worn by the streltsi of the Grand Duchy.

Cyhir: one of the akhoz that aids Nasim.

Devrim ül Mert: seneschal to the Kamarisi, Hakan ül Ayeşe.

desyatnik: the lowest rank of officer in the Grand Duchy's staaya, typically responsible for ten streltsi.

dhoshahezhan: a spirit of life.

dhoshaqiram: one who bonds with dhoshahezhan and draws upon their power to wield or alter life in the material world.

dolman: a dress commonly worn by the women of northern Yrstanla, along the coast of the Sea of Tabriz.

dousing rod: a rod with a circle at one end of it, made of iron, used to sap the ability of the Aramahn qiram to bond with the hezhan.

drakhen: large amphibious lizards that sometimes make their home on the rocky beaches of the islands.

Dyanko Kantinov Vostroma: the Boyar of Elykstava and the Posadnik of Skayil.

Ebru: Bahett's second wife, the woman second in power to Meryam.

Erahm: the physical world.

Ekaterina Margeva Rhavanki: the Duchess of Rhavanki.

Evochka: the capital and largest city in the Duchy of Volgorod. Situated near Palotza Galostina on the island of Kiravashya.

eyrie: the place where windships are moored, typically built onto cliff faces with many perches available for windships.

Fahroz Bashar al Lilliah: a mahtar in the village of Iramanshah.

Galostina (Palotza Galostina): the seat of power for the Vostroman family.

ghazi: the local militia in much of the southern and eastern reaches of Yrstanla.

Ghayavand: the island that was once a place of learning for the Aramahn. It became a wasteland when the Al-Aqim attempted a ritual to bring about indaraqiram.

Gaji: a large desert in the southwestern reaches of the Yrstanlan Empire.

Galahesh: a semi-autonomous island that sits between the islands of the Grand Duchy and Yrstanla.

goedrun: large sea creatures with squid-like tentacles that often prevent sea travel.

Gravlos Antinov: a shipwright. Oversaw the design and construction of the *Gorovna*.

Grigory Stasayev Bolgravya: The fourth son of Stasa Bolgravya. Brother to the duke, Konstantin Bolgravya.

Hael: the kingdom of the nomadic Haelish people, which lies to the west of Yrstanla. The Haelish have been locked in a bloody war with Yrstanla for decades.

Hakan ül Ayeşe: the Kamarisi of Yrstanla.

havahezhan: a spirit of wind.

havaqiram: one who bonds with havahezhan and draws upon their power to wield or alter wind in the material world.

helm: the helm contains a set of three levers. These levers alter the set of the rudder, allowing the keel to set itself against the ley lines and turn the ship freely along all three axes: roll, pitch, and yaw.

Heodor Yaroslov Lhudansk: the Duke of Lhudansk.

hezhan: souls or spirits in the world of Adhiya.

Hratha: the southern sect of the Maharraht. They have largely focused on fighting the southern Duchies of Anuskaya.

hussar: the cavalry of the Grand Duchy.

Iaros Aleksov Khalakovo: the Duke of Khalakovo.

ilkadin: the first wife in a harem, which are common among the lords of Yrstanla. The ilkadin sit in a place of power in the household of an Yrstanlan lord.

Inan: Yadhan's mother. The one who instigated the push to cast a spell over the Atalayina and the island of Ghayavand.

indaraqiram: the state that the Aramahn believe the world will one day reach when all its people become enlightened through individual vashaqiram.

Irabahce (Kasir Irabahce): the imperial palace of Yrstanla, home to the Kamarisi.

Iramanshah: an Aramahn village on the island of Uyadensk.

Iriketa Alesyeva Bolgravya: Daughter and youngest child of Stasa and Alesya Bolgravya.

Isaak Ylafslov: the seneschal of Palotza Radiskoye.

Ishkyna Radieva Vostroma: daughter of Zhabyn and Radia Vostroma. One of three triplets, sister to Atiana and Mileva Vostroma.

Iyana Klarieva Dhalingrad: the duchess of Dhalingrad.

Jahalan Atman al Mitra: Nikandr's havaqiram (wind master).

jalahezhan: a spirit of water.

jalaqiram: one who bonds with jalahezhan and draws upon their power to wield or alter water in the material world.

jannisary: a soldier of Yrstanla.

Jonis: a young windsman that joined Nikandr on the *Yarost*. He has sharp eyes and was often asked to keep watch.

Kaleh: a strange Maharraht girl found by Nikandr on the island of Rafsuhan.

Kalhani: an ancient language of the Aramahn. The precursor to Mahndi and many other languages of Yrstanla.

Kamarisi: the supreme lord of Yrstanla. In essence, the Emperor.

kasir: the term for palace in Yrstanla. The kasirs of the Empire tend to be much more ostentatious than the palotzas of the Grand Duchy.

Katerina Vostroma: a Matra of Vostroma; Zhabyn Vostroma's sister.

kaymakam: a major lord under the Kamarisi. Bahett, who is the Lord of Galahesh, is a kaymakam, but there are many others who rule beneath the Kamarisi.

keel: refers to the obsidian cores of the ship's four mainmasts. Another length of obsidian is laid through the ship from stern to bow. The ley lines are captured by these three components of the keel, orienting the ship in a certain direction and allowing it to maintain that position as it sails forward like a waterborne ship through the sea.

Khamal Cyphar al Maladhin: one of the three arqesh who lived on Ghayavand. Along with Muqallad and Sariya, Khamal caused the sundering three hundred years ago.

khanjar: curved daggers used by the Aramahn and Maharraht.

khedive: the lord of a city in the Yrstanlan empire.

kilij: blade with a distinct curve near the middle, used primarily in Yrstanla, especially by the janissaries.

kindjal: the traditional knife of Anuskaya.

Kiravashya: the largest island in the Duchy of Volgorod. Home to the capital city of Evochka and Palotza Galostina.

Kirzan: the large building at the center of Baressa's bazaar, the old seat of power on Galahesh, abandoned after the treaty was signed with Anuskaya after the War of Seven Seas.

Kohor: the birthplace of Sariya, and the village where legend says the Atalayina was first found.

kolpak: a tall rounded hat typically worn by the streltsi.

Konstantin Stasayev Bolgravya: the Duke of Bolgravya. The first son of the former Grand Duke, Stasa Bolgrava.

korobochki: brightly painted blocks.

kozyol: goat, used as a curse, or a derogatory term.

Kseniya Zoyeva Nodhvyansk: the Duchess of Nodhvyansk.

kuadim: an Aramahn teacher.

Landed: a term that originally applied to those who held land in the Grand Duchy of Anuskaya. Over time, it came to mean anyone who hails from the Grand Duchy.

Landless: a term used by the people of the Grand Duchy for the Aramahn. It refers to the way the Aramahn view land, that it is owned by no one, but also the way they move throughout the world, rarely staying in one place for long.

landsman: a general term for the men who work the eyries, lading and unlading windships.

landward: to the left while facing the fore of a ship, where the side windships tie up to a perch or a dock.

Leonid Roaldov Dhalingrad: the Duke of Dhalingrad.

ley lines: lines of power that run between islands. Windships harness the ley lines to orient their ships with their obsidian keels. The Matri use their abilities to groom the ley lines so that travel between the islands becomes easier.

Maharraht: a splinter sect of the Aramahn who have forsaken their peaceful ways in order to drive the Landed from the islands they once had free reign over. Their ultimate goal is to regain control over the islands, but also to prevent the Grand Duchy from abusing and taking advantage of the Aramahn.

Mahndi: the modern language of the Aramahn and Maharraht.

Mahrik: a strelet of Khalakovo who travels with Nikandr.

mahtar: an elder, a leader of the Aramahn villages.

Majeed Bassam al Haffeh: a man close to Fahroz on the floating island of Mirashadal, one of the mahtar of the village.

Matra (plural: Matri): a woman who has the ability to submerge herself in ice-cold water to enter the aether, where she can communicate with other Matri and see ghostly images of the material world.

Meryam: Bahett's current ilkadin, his "first wife."

Mikhalai: a strelet of Khalakovo who travels with Nikandr.

Mileva Radieva Vostroma: daughter of Zhabyn and Radia Vostroma. One of three triplets, sister to Atiana and Ishkyna Vostroma.

Mirashadal: the floating village of the Aramahn. The place Fahroz takes Nasim after he was healed on the island of Duzol.

Mount: the large hill that houses Kasir Yalidoz in the city of Baressa.

Muqallad Bakshazhd al Dananir: one of the three arqesh who lived on Ghayavand. Along with Sariya and Khamal, Muqallad caused the sundering three hundred years ago and has been trapped on the island ever since.

Muwas Umar al Mariyah: a gifted jalaqiram.

Nasim an Ashan: an orphan boy with strange powers.

Nataliya Iyaneva Bolgravya: wife of Borund.

Nikandr Iaroslov Khalakovo: youngest son of the Duke and Duchess of Khalakovo.

palotza: a castle or palace, typically quite large, within the Grand Duchy.

Polina Anayev Mirkotsk: the Duchess of Mirkotsk.

polkovnik: the highest rank of officer in the Grand Duchy's staaya.

polupolkovnik: the second highest rank of officer in the Grand Duchy's staaya, below only the polkovnik in the chain of command.

privyet: Anuskayan for "hello" or "good day."

qiram: an Aramahn with the ability to bond with hezhan, giving them the elemental abilities of the spirit.

Rabiah Wahid al Aahtel: one of Nasim's disciples that he brings with him to Ghayavand.

Radia Anastasiyeva Vostroma: the Duchess of Vostroma.

Radiskoye (Palotza Radiskoye): the seat of power for the Khalakovan family.

Rahid Umar al Gahana: one of the more powerful men from the southern sect of the Maharraht known as the Hratha.

Ramina: the northern city on Galahesh, the one closest to Oramka and Yrstanla.

Ranos Iaroslov Khalakovo: eldest son of Iaros Khalakovo. Also the Boyar of Volgorod.

Rehada Ulan al Shineshka: An Aramahn woman. Nikandr's lover in Volgorod.

Rosa Oriseva Lhudansk: the Duchess of Lhudansk.

rudder: a complex set of obsidian cylinders at the center of the ship, the nexus where the four mainmasts meet the obsidian core that runs lengthwise through the ship. These three sets of cylinders are adjusted by the pilot at the helm.

Saphia Mishkeva Khalakovo: the Duchess of Khalakovo.

Sariya Quljan al Vehayeh: one of the three arqesh who lived on Ghayavand. Along with Muqallad and Khamal, Sariya caused the sundering three hundred years ago and has been trapped on the island ever since.

Sea of Khurkhan: the sea south of Galahesh, northwest of Nodhvyansk, and southeast of Yrstanla.

Sea of Tabriz: the sea between Yrstanla and Anuskaya, bounded by the empire to the west, Khalakovo to the east, and Volgorod to the south.

seaward: downward, named so because the windships often fly above water.

shamshir: a curved sword used primarily by the Maharraht.

shashka: a lightly curved sword used primarily in the islands of the Grand Duchy.

Shirvozeh: the Aramahn village to the east of Alayazhar, on the island of Ghayavand. It became the seat of Muqallad's power when the three Al-Aqim became trapped on the island.

Siafyan: a large village with massive trees and hanging walkways running between them on the island of Rafsuhan.

Sihaş ül Mehmed: an envoy who goes to treat with the Grand Duchy.

siraj: Aramahn glowing stones used for illumination.

Sitalyas: the mountain range to the west of Trevitze.

Soroush Wahad al Gatha: leader of the northern sect of the Maharraht.

sotni: a unit of one hundred soldiers.

sotnik: an officer of the Grand Duchy, responsible for one hundred men.

Spar: the large bridge being built by Yrstanla over the Straits of Galahesh.

spire: a tower of obsidian used by the Grand Duchy to control the ley lines between the islands. The Matri groom the ley lines using the spires and their abilities in the aether.

starward: upward from the deck of a ship, toward the sky and stars.

strelet (plural: streltsi): the military men of the Grand Duchy.

szubka: Hat worn by the women of the Grand Duchy.

staaya: the Ducal (Royal) air fleet of the Grand Duchy.

Stasa Olegov Bolgravya: the former Grand Duke, killed on Khalakovo when a suurahezhan, a fire spirit, attacked his yacht as it docked at the eyrie of Radiskoye.

Styophan Andrashayev: the sotnik of the streltsi who accompany Nikandr.

Sukharam Hadir al Dahanan: one of Nasim's disciples that he brings with him to Ghayavand.

suurahezhan: a spirit of fire.

suuraqiram: one who bonds with suurahezhan and draws upon their power to wield or alter fire in the material world.

Svoya: the southern city on Galahesh, the one closest to the islands.

Syemon: an old gull who serves on the ship, *Strovya*.

taking breath (or, to take breath): the Aramahn act of meditating, where they try to become one with their surroundings, to understand more about themselves or the world.

Thabash Kaspar al Meliyah: the leader of the Hratha.

Trevitze: the city where Nasim finds Sukharam.

Udra Amir al Rasa: Nikandr's dhoshaqiram (master of the stuff of life).

Ushai Kissath al Shahda: one of Fahroz's most trusted servants. She travels the world, hoping to find Nasim and to bring him back to Fahroz.

ushanka: Squat woolen hat.

Uyadensk: the largest island in the Duchy Khalakovo. Home to Palotza Radiskoye and the capital city of Volgorod.

Vaasak Adimov Dhalingrad: the envoy of Zhabyn, sent to Baressa to negotiate for him before his arrival.

vanahezhan: a spirit of earth.

vanaqiram: one who bonds with vanahezhan and draws upon their power to wield or alter earth in the material world.

vashaqiram: a state of pure enlightenment. The state of mind most Aramahn search for.

Victania Saphieva Khalakovo: the only daughter of Saphia and Iaros. The middle child.

Vihrosh: the old name for Baressa, and now the section that lies to the west of the straits.

Vikra: one of the rooks of Vostroma, the one Atiana favors the most.

Vlanek: the acting master of the *Yarost* on Nikandr's journey across the Sea of Khurkhan.

Volgorod: the capital and largest city in the Duchy of Khalakovo. Situated near Palotza Radiskoye on the island of Uyadensk.

Wahad Soroush al Qediah: Soroush's first son, his second child.

windwood: a variety of wood that is specially cured so that it becomes lighter than air. All windships are made of windwood.

windship: one of the ships made of windwood that flies with the help of havaqiram to harness the wind and dhoshaqiram to adjust the heft of the ship's windwood.

windsman: general term for a man who crews windships.

windward: to the right while facing the fore of a ship, named so because the wind is in this direction when the windship is moored.

Yadhan: the first of the children to become akhoz on Ghayavand. She was taken by Khamal.

Yalessa: the handmaid that most often attends to Atiana in the drowning chamber.

Yalidoz (Kasir Yalidoz): the palace in Baressa, on the island of Galahesh, home to Bahett ül Kirdhash.

Yegor Nikolov Nodhvyansk: the Duke of Nodhvyansk.

Yevgeny Krazhnegov Mirkotsk: the Duke of Mirkotsk.

Yrfa: Saphia Khalakovo's favorite rook.

Yrstanla: an Empire situated on a large continent to the west of the islands in the Grand Duchy.

Yvanna Antoneva Khalakovo: Ranos's wife.

Zanaida Lariseva Khazabyirsk: the Duchess of Khazabyirsk.

Zanhalah: the woman who helps Nikandr to heal Soroush's son, Wahad.

Zhabyn Olegov Vostroma: the Duke of Vostroma.

ACKNOWLEDGEMENTS

There are many people to thank for this book.

First, I'd like to thank my wife, Joanne, who allowed me the time to write. This dream I have of writing is only possible with your unflagging support, understanding, and encouragement, and for that I thank you from the bottom of my heart.

To Paul Genesse, for your many thoughtful critiques, endless encouragement, and dear friendship, I thank you. Our many talks over the course of this book helped not only to refine the ms, but also guided me in my development as a writer.

To Ross Lockhart, thank you for the guiding star you provide to this wayward writer. I appreciate your vast knowledge, not merely in the editing of words, but in the tending of my budding career. And to the troops at Night Shade Books, thank you. There are so many things you do that don't get enough praise, and while I know the words of one poor writer won't tip the scales, I hope it evens the balance a bit.

To my agent, Russ Galen, my thanks for your wisdom and your foresight. Even when there are treacherous waters, I know you'll guide me safely through.

To the people of Wellspring (Brenda Cooper, Rob Ziegler, Sarah Kelly [twice], Kelly Swails, Holly McDowell, Greg Wilson, Vincent Jorgensen, Grá Linnaea, Eden Robins, and, last but certainly not least, Bill Shunn), my thanks for the wealth, depth, variety, and accuracy of thoughts on the early parts of this novel. An extra helping of gratitude goes out to Brenda and Rob for reading the full ms at the workshop. You two were the rudder that guided that next, crucial draft.

To Eugene Myers, many thanks for reading the early chapters and then for plowing through the ms after a few drafts had been completed, and to Greg

Wilson, for tackling the ms again after already reading it at Wellspring.

I'd also like to thank a few of my many mentors who've helped me along the way. To Kij Johnson, my thanks for those many classes at GenCon. To the gang at Viable Paradise VII (Patrick and Teresa Nielsen Hayden, Jim Macdonald, Debra Doyle, Laura Mixon, and Steve Gould), thank you for those early lessons in writing. There were many shortcuts and refinements to my craft I might never have found had I not attended that workshop way back in 2003. To K.D. Wentworth and Tim Powers, my thanks for the workshop at Writers of the Future. There are things I still use daily that I learned during that wonderful week in Los Angeles.

To Holliann Russell Kim, I continue to be in your debt for your skill at finding the hordes of tenacious gremlins that hide within manuscripts, especially this one. Your attention to detail has made this a better work.

And finally, to Todd Lockwood. My thanks for taking what was once only in my mind and giving it life in art.

BEAUL   IFICW
Beaulieu, Bradley P.
The Straits of Galahesh /

CENTRAL LIBRARY
10/12

about the author

Bradley P. Beaulieu fell in love with fantasy the moment he started reading *The Hobbit* in third grade. From that point on, though he tried reading many other things, fantasy became his touchstone. He always came back to it, and when he started to dabble in writing, fantasy—epic fantasy especially—was the type of story he most dearly wished to share. In 2006, his story, "In the Eyes of the Empress's Cat", was voted a Million Writers Award notable story, and in 2004, he became a winner in the Writers of the Future 20 contest. Other stories have appeared in *Realms of Fantasy*, *Intergalactic Medicine Show*, *Beneath Ceaseless Skies*, and several DAW anthologies.

Brad lives in Racine, Wisconsin with his wife and two children. By day, Brad is a software engineer, wrangling code into something resembling usefulness. He is also an amateur cook. He loves to cook spicy dishes, particularly Mexican and southwestern. As time goes on, Brad finds that his interests are slowly being whittled down to these two things: family and writing. In that order...

For more, please visit www.quillings.com.